I hope you enj

Evacuation Route

by
Chris Dungey

This is a work of fiction. Names, characters, places, and incidents are the product of the author's imagination or are used fictitiously. Any resemblance to actual persons, living or dead, events, or locals is entirely coincidental.

Copyright © 2025 by Chris Dungey

All rights reserved.

No portion of this book may be reproduced in any form without written permission from the publisher or author, except as permitted by U.S. copyright law.

AI RESTRICTION: The author expressly prohibits any entity from using this publication for purposes of training artificial intelligence (AI) technologies to generate text, including without limitation technologies that are capable of generating works in the same style or genre as this publication. The author reserves all rights to license uses of this work for generative AI training and development of machine learning language models.

Cover Design By: KD Ellis
Author Photo By: Ken Milito

*This novel is dedicated to my wife Sharon
whose love and forbearance survived the
three-and-a-half year process of this novel.
Well, it's actually been longer than that.*

Acknowledgements

The author would like to thank some individuals who helped me through the three-and-a-half year odyssey of writing this novel.

First, my Starbucks research team, which met nearly every morning to open their smart phones to Google facts and info while I kept my pen moving. Ken Milito, Jeff Nedwick, Rob Barton, Jim Hogan, and Bill Slater please accept my undying gratitude.

Tiffanie Shaw did proofreading and formatting for *Evacuation Route.* I will ever value her editing suggestions.

Kady Ellis designed my cover and back-flap while suffering from dental surgery and my fussy, indecisive suggestions over her shoulder. I would recommend her concepts to anyone.

Part I
Homes for the Holiday

Fortune brings in some boats that are not steered. --Shakespeare, "Cymbelline."

Chapter One

*B*ocewicz *and Sons Family Pharmacy*, in northeastern Jacksonville, Florida was finally going to bite the dust. The deepening Great Recession of 2008 probably had little to do with it, but was certainly the *coup de grace*. The demise had been looming for some time.

In consideration of an older, poorer demographic, and to wring out every last dime with an extended ***Going Out of Business Sale***, Warren Bocewicz and his younger brother Walter kept the place open until 10 pm, like the national chain drugstores, pointedly absent from these blocks. Those places had been slowly crushing *Bocewicz and Sons* since the new millennium. The owners of the last *family* drug store hoped to avoid renting a storage unit for leftover inventory. *Everything must go*, if at all possible. The shelves *were* becoming nicely stripped.

Tonight, Walter Bocewicz, who was not, himself, a pharmacist, performed his own personal closing routine before balancing out. He did the legal part for Warren, the actual pharmacist then carefully slipped an emptied brown Vitamin E bottle, now containing a Xanax and a 5 mg Vicodin into his hoody beneath the counter.

It was not a *huge* theft, on the scale of some AA war stories he'd heard. Walter preferred to think of these as a mishandling of inventory, to be expected of one inexperienced in the strict regulations of retail pharma. That's what he'd plead if the pilfering ever came to Warren's attention. Walt experienced only a small twinge of guilt. But he was only stitching together a golden parachute of *brake fluid* (what they called these meds in the jail infirmary, doled out to inmates suffering withdrawal) since Warren first announced that *Bocewicz and Sons* would liquidate. When that happened, Walt intended to subsist in obscure idleness until Social Security kicked in. No more shit jobs if at all possible.

He planned to spend his waning years reading, watching televised sports, and enjoying discretely limited *attitude enhancements.* He would drive soberly to some tranquil locale, there to enjoy low-impact hedonisms in the privacy of a modest dwelling. He must absolutely stay off the roads if he ever again became even mildly impaired. He intended never again to interact with the Florida legal system.

In anticipation of those goals, he looked forward to that day (not too far off, he sensed by the depleted shelves) when a final destruction of remaining Schedule I pharmaceuticals would be required by law. Some must be sealed in bags of kitty litter, he'd learned online. *I can totally assist with that. Clean kitty-litter, though, right?* This was AA *stinkin' thinkin'* writ large, but he was pretty sure Warren would be lining his *own* escape pod. *His* financial instruments were of the more traditional, if now morally suspect, variety.

Walt's brother brought a Wall Street Journal in every morning to follow the evaporating market.

Warren Bocewicz, majority shareholder of the property after repeated loans to Walter for bail and lawyers, was a longtime participant in a Jacksonville theater group. He often referred to Walter's function as *front of the house*. While Walter *had* once managed a B.A. in Accounting, and a minor in English, he'd never actually been employed in either of those fields. But, he retained a strong love for vocabulary, enhancing with ten dollar words every slur at arresting officers.

Numbers could, of course, be used in an infinite variety of configurations to make a job come out even. Those ten dollar words, though, were more satisfying to him. Persons might need to revise first impressions of his slovenly appearance, his need for a shower or haircut.

He put his growing vocabulary to good use during detox and short jail stays: He discovered crossword puzzles. During his last incarceration of three months, he had added a new word each day and often used them.

Walt hung around in Gainesville after earning the BA. He enjoyed the economies of married housing at U of Florida while prolonging a life still low in accountability and expectation. He didn't mind not being accountable, witness his restitution ledger, the child-support warnings. But, the expectations of others made the hairs stand up on the back of his neck.

He failed to complete an MBA, drifting into multiple Incompletes. To his undergrad adventures in alcohol he added the challenge of cocaine on a narrow budget of parental stipends and more student loans. This combo platter was spilled rudely onto his waning scholastic career. *Still don't know how I survived offering my thesis adviser a bump. Nice guy. Took him for a drink at one of the student dives: Assured him I'd make up Incompletes, even take a sincere look at the amendments he suggested to my thesis proposal; welcome additions to a really thin outline. It must have been groping that lady in study group. The poor sport filed a complaint. They needed me to withdraw and vacate married housing immediately. Made another pleading call to Warren within the hour.*

His first wife had already bailed, taking their baby with her after Walt's first post-grad DUI. The charge was augmented with Possession of a Controlled Substance. (Luckily, for a misdemeanor weight.) At least he didn't have to tell her they'd soon be homeless. Nevertheless, he played *that* chip with Warren. The legitimate financial bleedings of #1 soon began, though nothing compared to what wife Number Two would demand. However, with most financial liens satisfied and significant *clean* time, Walt was a suitable candidate for the retail/clerical indenture Warren carved out for him. It beat washing dishes.

For the past month, he'd performed his role at the store with just one additional cast member, Shondra. As he approached the front entrance with keys for the door and security grate, he realized that he'd forgotten to ring up Shondra's gallon of overpriced skim milk. He'd stood at the counter, watched her scrutinize her reflection in the dairy case before lifting out the milk. With his fingers diddling the last prescription envelope, he only hoped she wouldn't turn around.

He decided to let the milk slide tonight and for all the remaining nights. What kind of severance was Warren putting together for her? They ought to let her cart out the remains of the makeup racks. All good stuff, too: *Maybelline, Revlon*. They were trying to avoid an accumulation of perishables so Shondra's dairy needs were doing them a favor.

Anyway, the emptying process was accelerating. When a business such as theirs, in this *depressed* location, announces an intention of Going Out of Business, the gorilla in the room is a Chapter Eleven bankruptcy. Venders require payment up front, preferably in cash. Luckily, their *Coke* distributor continued to honor Warren's personal check for ten mixed crates of 2-liters.

Walt began *his* scheme six months ago, performing med acquisitions at the end of most days: The surplus gallons, the cottage cheese and chip-dip, most with approaching *sell-by* dates, made for clever distractions when he told certain customers to *just take one* near the close of business. These lucky persons, whose prescriptions contained something soothing, selected a free dairy while Walt deftly removed a single tablet then stapled receipt to bag. At first, these petty thefts caused a *minor* crisis of conscience. The karma he'd repaired with the Amends Step, felt briefly threatened. But the acquisitions also showed rare initiative: He was planning for his future. *No, karma. I will never sell this stuff. Personal, discreet use only.*

So far, none of the elderly within their customer-base had poured out their meds to count a discrepancy. If shortages *had* been noted, the aggrieved parties might have recalled the free dairy and so withheld complaint. And, if a pint bottle of milk remained after closing, well, Walt *did* have a cat, the faithful Antoine. His hidden vial, once an attractive fruit salad each day, was now down to a one or two tab rattle. Some relief came with reduced temptations.

Customer-on-the-premises bells sounded as Walt opened the double glass. He stuck his head out and scanned the poorly lighted sidewalk. There was no one sprinting toward the place waving a prescription. This was not a sprinting neighborhood except when domestic disturbances spilled outside or a vehicle was being stolen. Hipster athletes had begun to make tentative probes, anticipating gentrification. They naively jogged through, though seldom after dusk.

Walt didn't feel like kneeling to peek from below the **Going out of Business** banners. So, he poked his head out the doors heedless to robbery, assault or the inconvenience of a late customer. He and Shondra had darkened the red letters twice in the past year and the signs were due to be freshened again. There were once product displays in both windows of their historic place on Perry Street. The building stood twenty geriatric paces from Atlantic Boulevard, which eventually terminated at The Beaches. But, by now, a WalMart, a Target, and a Publix had sprouted within the next half mile. They weren't losing any trade by not decorating the empty display windows.

With the coast clear, Walt rattled the sections of grate from each side and mated them with a padlock. Warren had quit paying ADT for security but made a onetime investment in two realistic dummy closed-circuit cameras. These were mounted front and rear, next to the now impotent genuine ones. The disconnected keypads by the doors were still lighted. *This place needs to sell soon, before we get hit for the last of the opioids.* Walt locked the glass and flipped the warped cardboard sign to *Closed.*

"Hey, Walt! Are we closed yet?"

Warren's call was faint, as though from the farthest remove of his office, behind the bench area where prescriptions were filled. Even so, acoustics in the place gave his voice clarity at the distance. The ceilings in the old building were high though not what one might call vaulted. The old plaster up there had been beautifully sculpted. Warren had invested in cleaning and painting it before putting the building on the market.

This wasn't quite a theater space though that repurposing must have crossed Warren's mind. More practically, the space would be perfect for a grandiose coffee shop or bistro. (Assuming that post-recession gentrification would resume.)

There was room at the back for the *bench* and elevated office enclosure before one reached the staircase to the apartment. The *bench* area, where the apothecary performed his magic, looked down upon the retail floor. Removal of that Olympian perch would have required extensive remodeling. Warren didn't like to be reminded of the old *Seinfeld* bit about imperious druggists. He responded to any mention of the comedian that it was simply more difficult to robbed up there.

"Hey, Walt! Where'd you go?"

Yeah, it was *Walt* who stood to be stabbed or shot while Warren hugged the floor, literally in the bench. The old man, with an immigrant's distrust, had bolted sheet metal to an inside panel under the work surface, a perfect cubby in which to crouch. After folding himself into that space, Warren would frantically try to dig for his phone out of the smock.

From the ground floor of the store, the pharmacist needed to climb four steps up into the bench area and then four more up into his office proper. Eight steps down to the rear took him into a storeroom and then out the back door. Both brothers parked in the alley. Warren tried to think of the spots back there as *sheltered.* But, it *was* pretty foreboding after a late closing time. *No* public lighting survived above the alley. A single civilian bulb shone over their own rear door. But the brothers had saved two of their eight allotted spots out on the street by parking in back. Neighboring enterprises changed through the years as did parking ordinances. But, no remaining businesses (a minority barber, a proof-of-insurance mill) ever needed more than five spots. Most patrons of *Diaspora Cutz and Nails* were walkups from the neighborhood.

"Walt? Are you out there?

"Yeah! I'm here! I just locked up! I've gotta fax the desk audit to DEA and finish balancing out. I might hang around to use the floor buffer."

Let that sink in. See how late I'm working? My recovery work ethic? And, I'm not sulking about losing the apartment. A few more months rent free would have been nice; new carpeting in the bedroom, the fresh paint smell and a crapper that flushes completely. Warren had also installed a new stove and refrigerator to up the ante on furnishings. Walt quickly shrugged off this peevishness. There couldn't have been more favorable surroundings for recovery. He could easily have finished his days living there.

"Right. Okay. But get up here for just a minute. We need to have a quick word before I head out."

Oh, now what? A customer finally complained about being short? His brother had already offered to provision, within reason, whatever non-opioid scripts Walt might need before closing their records. Walt briefly suspected that Warren might be a very discrete *writer,* a term he remembered hearing from detox comrades. Occasional encounters with sweating, jittery customers caused Walt moments of recognition. Who was the prescribing physician and what was the alleged malady? Warren's queries seemed disinterested.

"Just let me clean out the till."

"Hustle. I need to get out of here. I didn't make rehearsal but everyone's meeting at *The Tap Room* after."

On the Monday night of a holiday week? Well, let the man have his passion. It must be nice to have one. But, if their business had only been plunked down over in the area of that theater seventy years ago, they might have survived. Walt didn't think Warren bothered, any longer, to look up the facility or even the prescriber's name as he padded his own nest-egg. Well, maybe that was a common procedure across Jacksonville—laxity in dispensing. *Am I really going to disparage the hand that feeds while accumulating my* own *stash?*

Warren didn't short he or Shondra for decent healthcare. It was also lucky for the neighborhood that civic minded Warren always arrived early up in the bench, ready to dispense, two hours before any of the chain places.

Walt had earlier driven the daily deposit out to their *Sun-Trust* branch. Neither Bocewicz was concerned that their banking routine was on anyone's radar. Nevertheless, Walt became hyper watchful in the alley, the *SunTrust* pouch gripped under his right arm. With three DUIs and possession of a controlled substance on his sheet, Walt could not renew his lapsed Concealed Pistol permit. Barrister Aaron Wineglass, one of Warren's thespian pals, did stellar work getting him that last three month bit. It was a third strike with property damage and he could have gotten as much as a year.

Warren was deeply disappointed to learn that the permit was no longer part of his sibling's resume. The delivery chore fell to Walt, anyway, whose vigilance was quite acute in the absence his old Ruger .38 Special. That little weapon had been pawned fifteen years ago.

There weren't enough daily receipts for an armored pickup. There hadn't been for a few years. Cancellation of *that* service was a nice savings, made at the same time Warren dropped the electronic security. Walt's drive was a legal, work related use of a motor vehicle. The jaunt gave him an opportunity to sit at the helm of his pride-and-joy (not counting his children, of course), a 1978 Cadillac Coupe de Ville, two-tone, two door, 365 cid. The Caddy's vehicle title was currently in Warren's name to keep it out of certain expensively manicured talons. It had come out from under its protective tarp and was a morale boost each time Walt took the wheel. His smile lasted for the entire one mile trip to the *Sun Trust* drive-through.

After banking, Walt resumed his clerk duties. He was taller than Warren; an unexaggerated six foot, one inch and slim--a quirk of metabolism. His loose jointed posture spoke of calm indifference to every reversal. Only the pouches under his green eyes and the slight paunch hinted at a long duration of alcohol abuse. That bulge wasn't liver failure, though it soon would have been if he hadn't quit. Recent blood work, palpations, and an MRI gave him an estimated 80% function, a minor medical anomaly in the opinion of Warren's hematologist.

Walt had relapsed to one fake beer each evening since leaving the apartment, but fear of a jaundiced death made *serious* abstention easy. After a lifetime of intemperance, he couldn't imagine how this moderation was now possible. *Where was this willpower when I needed it? I could have enjoyed a mundane existence with only the rare weekend buzz; I didn't need to wake up a day late for everything, wondering. where's my car?*

Despite this bit of cheating, he had no qualms about accepting the two-year chip from the *meeting* he attended out near the Beaches. Whether the near beer was *stinkin' thinkin'* (one of the less clever AA catch phrases in Walt's opinion) or not, he claimed his chip, proud of having no more hangovers or blackouts. He attended two of these confessionals weekly so that he could present signed affidavits to his probation officer. Working the Steps was coming along and he'd made amends to Warren every day for two years.

Walt shrugged out of his honorary white smock, laid it on the counter of the sole remaining checkout station. He rang the cash drawer open. There were no more than $70 in bills, three heavily vetted personal checks, and $10 in change. He dumped the coins into the empty *Sun Trust* pouch along with the last receipt tape of the day.

"Is the safe open? I'm bringing up our fortune."

"You'll have to do it, Walt," was the plaintive response. "I'm finishing some things at my desk."

Alright, brother man. Alright. No need to be testy. But, there were probably fresh pressures in this economy to cause his brother's abrupt tone. Were hedge funds crashing around *his* portfolio?

"No problem. I've got it."

Perhaps the players were supposed to be *off the book* (one of Warren's favorite theater tropes) and he wasn't yet confident of whatever lines he'd been given. They were attempting *Rent*. Warren vented his worries to Walt a few evenings ago concerning the fear of antigay protests outside the theater. Some Lanford Wilson thing that no one would grasp the point of might have been safer. Walt couldn't name one Wilson play so Warren was probably right.

This was Florida, after all, and the political discourse was becoming chillier while the climate warmed.

There couldn't be more than a few lines for someone Warren's age. The dramatis personae consisted mostly of would-be bohemian twenty-somethings. There *were* two pairs of snooty, limousine liberal parents. Warren might be perfect for one of the fathers. Walt was newly sober when first exposed to the play. He fell asleep partway through the DVD version. Wouldn't Warren have to sing, though? In the chorus? *Yes! That's where that melody's been coming from. It's in my head like a parasite.* Warren droned a few of the tunes around the store. He hummed until he reached the phrase, *la vie boheme.*

Walt climbed to the bench. *Five hundred, sixty-five thousand, three hundred minutes...* That was another one. *Catchy, but is the math right?* He ought to check it sometime. And, he should go to opening night, show some support. Well, if it wasn't on one of his meeting nights, *and*, if Warren comped him a ticket.

He gathered the till then climbed to the office. The exertion left him winded. He really must do something soon about his physical conditioning. Buy a bicycle? Did people still walk laps in malls? Beads of sweat migrated out of his grey burst of hair. Warren's stinginess with the AC had gone unnoticed through the three day cool spell. Thinking about his own hair reminded him of another performance Warren's troupe had put on recently. *That one about the two tramps and the guy who owned a slave. Crazy.* Warren was part of the crew for that one. He ran on stage in the dark before the last act to stick a single leaf onto a bare tree. After tagging along to

EVACUATION ROUTE

the dress rehearsal, some of Warren's friends remarked that Walt's hair reminded them of that very playwright, Sam somebody. Sam Shepherd?

Walt knelt to open the floor safe. The first etchings of arthritis in his knees confirmed the cooler November weather. The safe was set in an ingenious cache, quite undetectable, even after the area rug was rolled back. Whenever he accessed the miniature vault, he was reminded of the finished hardwoods under much of the building's floor coverings. Only in the front room of the apartment did the original floor still gleam. Proprietors of any coffee shop or south Asian bistro weren't likely to remove tile from the store, only to have spills slopped onto the polished wood.

"So what's up? Sounded urgent." Walt twirled the combination. He laid the bank pouch into the safe then rose by increments like an elderly bricklayer. *Early onset skeletal fatigue. No mystery how I managed that.*

Still in his trim tank undershirt, smock neatly returned to a hanger, Warren swiveled on his ergonomic office chair. He broke into a smile. *So, maybe I'm not fired,* Walt thought. Warren brushed his immaculate pill-shuffling hands on look-like-tailored charcoal grey slacks, still holding their crease. Italian *Bonobos*, selected, no doubt by his girlfriend of six years, Charlotte, who kept him sartorially exemplary. But, the man wasn't reluctant to wear any of these things and it must be convenient not to have to shop and make decisions. *Too bad I'm not the same size.*

"Well? Are you ready for your next big adventure? The next chapter in... let's just say, your *eventful* life narrative?"

Oh Lord. What now? Big adventure? "I think I might be adventured out, brother."

Now Warren leaned at the waist and studied the floor for a moment. He lifted his gaze slowly, his down-to-brass-tacks effect, the way he'd do it for an improv workshop.

"Brother, man. It's with great relief, that I can tell you we've been made a very nice offer on this....our relic. Finally. And, I don't believe we'll hear a better one in this real estate market. In fact, I want to close as quickly as possible before the economy gets any worse. The buyer has a five day back-out clause and the clock is ticking. *Pray* that the Dow rallies a little bit and there's no more bad news from Washington *or* City Hall."

"Cool."

Warren rested slowly back onto the head support of the chair. The valence of the office hovered between his celebratory vibe and Walt's placid acceptance. Had Walt said something wrong? Warren rotated 180 to take up three fax printouts from the desk.

"Cool? Is that all you've got for me? It's what we've been waiting for, man. It's our Golden Ticket. We can even give Shondra a nice severance."

Walt shrugged. He hadn't seen any indication that a Chocolate Factory tour was in the offing for *him*. His humble aspirations amounted to that Golden Parachute of *happy capsules* downstairs and a decent used doublewide.

"You hold a 70% share, Warren, after all my loans and bailouts. That's not a complaint. I just figured to get what I get. I'm paid up, right?"

Warren stood up, gathering his *Patek Philippe* watch off the desk-top glass. He slipped it on, flailed the pale violet *Lin Min Pang* around, perfectly sliding an arm into the mulberry silk. *More taste than I'll ever have.*

Warren buttoned the cuff, loose enough to show off the time-piece. *He can't be too worried about how much he'll get from the deal. No wife or kids. Never eviscerated by a divorce. Bonds, IRAs, CDs accruing steadily. Probably not too exposed to this sad-assed market.* His mutual funds, sure, because he never had the time to research his own buys while keeping this scow of a business afloat. *Warren always the ant. I was the fiddling grasshopper, hocking my instrument.* Now I have an old car and a cat.

"I understand that, Walt. But I still value your input. You must remember *some* of your economics. I think you'll be pleasantly surprised at what this move will afford you. As far as any debt to me goes, we've been good for months."

There didn't seem to be a proprietary tone in Warren's voice. Compassion was what Walt still heard after all their years of family drama. *He didn't risk telling me the debts were satisfied. Don't know if I'm hurt or grateful.*

Warren extended the proffer and Walt took it. "Hey, glass-half-empty guy here, I guess. I've functioned much better, lately, with lower enthusiasms. *The Serenity Prayer,* etc? Don't think I'm ungrateful, but I'm not up for grandiose goals. I *have* been mulling a few modest ones."

Part of that was bullshit and Walt knew it. He'd never *had* ex-pectations lofty enough to *meet* with limitation. Throughout high school he'd *never* applied himself. Mother and Papa and guidance councilors cajoled themselves blue in the face. His only serious goal seemed to be good times and getting high. And, then to deal with the consequences.

While a freshman in Gainesville he had gone so far as to tell gathered seniors at his St. Michael's Homecoming, that they, *too*, should focus on fun times while they were still young. *There's time enough to get serious about the GPA once you're in college, just like I've done. And don't worry about that first choice school. A degree from anywhere will be fine.* To this day he wonders why his mic wasn't frantically silenced by the Father/Rector.

Where had his heart been? How did it manage to beat, locked in the amber of his congenital indifference. *They should have sent me for analysis. Girl's? Women? Oh, I liked to look at them, touch them. But, what was that thing called a crush? What was it to be lovesick? I've never longed for anyone.*

His debaucheries had been like water seeking a path of least resistance. What had once been a flood, though, was now sternly channeled. For the past two-and-a-half years (including the last three month bit in Alachua County Correctional), he'd been constricted by a chastity cage of limited mobility and Draconian finances. Who even knew if his libido could still be primed and fired.

"Oh tosh, man. This is your chance to rise from the ashes! Depending on lifestyle and sobriety, of course. Throw in a little frugality. Older guys than you have gone back for their MBAs."

Oh, tosh? But Warren's elocution was outstanding. *Spoken trippingly on the tongue. Probably exercising the pipes in lieu of missing*

EVACUATION ROUTE

rehearsal. Walt folded the pages from the buyer's agent and slid them into a hip pocket. He had yet to collect his pilfered stash and the hoody.

"Not sure the world needs more MBAs."

"Okay, bad example. Anyway, the apartment sealed the deal. It was a beautiful setup for you, I know. I hope you managed some savings."

"Yeah, I didn't do too badly." *Don't know what I can put aside, now.* "It was for the common cause. It's nearly loft size. Should bring near $2K rent to the new owner."

Rent free for two years, Walt *had* managed to save a few bucks. He paid off enough back child support to avoid more jail time. But now he was waking up four times a night in a grubby motel efficiency (cigarette burns in the duvet, basic cable) just to check on the Caddy.

The car sat just outside the protection of his battered door, gleaming under a security lamp. The light might actually *announce* the car's presence, inviting: *Snatch me or scratch me. I can't leave the curtain open and get decent sleep.* He also heard, quite clearly now, every squealing tire, every shout in the night. *The downside of untainted consciousness.*

"Brother, I really need to scoot. Just read that over tonight and we'll talk more in the morning."

Warren tossed on a *North Face* windbreaker. Regular use of his unfortunate 90s- trendy, bomber jacket was still a month away. When would Charlotte intervene to confiscate *it?*

20   CHRIS DUNGEY

Walt went in the opposite direction, back down to the counter to collect his stash and to turn off most of the remaining lights. Only one dim light was to be left on in the bench area, practically advertising the shelves of pills in their wholesale jugs. The opioids went into a safe, but that one wasn't hidden. The other light was a fluorescent fixture hovering over the last active Checkout register.

Curiosity got the best of him after he stretched into his Jaguars hoody, found at a *Goodwill*. He wore it as urban camouflage. A ball cap went with it. Anything related to Jacksonville.

So, what do we have here? Line-item, line-item, provisional rental agreement if not vacated in 90 days; inventory to be excluded from sale, accoutrements of commerce to be included in transaction: To wit: Any and all registers, POS and other business software, mainframe and router, fax. Any functioning CCTV and monitors, all maintenance and janitorial equipment in the basement. All appliances upstairs. Yadda and additional yadda as specified in indecipherable (given my limited interest beyond its sale value) boilerplate. And that critical figure is...drum roll, please.... He leafed over to the final page, tired eyes scrolling to the bottom: *$1.4 million. Holy, jumping Jesus!*

Now that's not very gracious. How about a Praise Jesus!? Even before the inevitable math, *that* was a nice return. His only calculator belonged to the business and was back in his room. The apartment alone would have been worth $400K before the crash, assuming imminent gentrification in an urban renewal neighborhood. *So, was it sold by the vintage apartment (claw-foot tub with white ceramic fixtures, useable fireplace with polished marble hearth, ma-*

hogany wainscoting and crown moldings), or the business potential below? Speculative valuation of the location and building certainly had to be factors in the sale. I grew up here, mostly. Loved falling asleep in that tub. Should have tried building a fire while I had the place. For the memories.

Walt went out front for a moment to take a quart of orange juice. The word *vodka* didn't even occur to him. He made his way through the stockroom in back, small change jingling against his vitamin bottle. He locked the delivery door then locked the interior staircase leading upstairs. Only the steel door was left to be secured from the outside. He began to imagine that he wouldn't miss this. Becoming a productive member of society again had extinguished most of his dumpster fire. Now he was well enough funded to realize some of the minor goals that began, but were not limited to, his modest stash.

The alley was deserted, as usual. Almost quiet enough to dispel the apprehensions that had tainted the business since the advent of free-basing. Walt's biggest fear now was that he wouldn't cleanly find the cylinder of the key lock in the Caddy. His own body blocked the light from the 150 watt bulb above their back door. He set the orange juice down and probed cautiously in the shadows. Remote entry was just a gleam in some engineer's eye when this beauty rolled off the assembly line thirty years ago.

The weather wasn't bad now. It was *never* terrible except for infrequent near misses during hurricane season. But it wasn't yet the month for smudge pots in the citrus groves, either. The morning was quite chilly when he left the motel, but the temperature had moderated. The sun had burned off the overcast by the time Walt drove to the bank. An overnight drizzle had moved out to sea. But for the ambient light of downtown, Walt was fairly certain there would be stars evident tonight; Orion the one constellation he could reliably identify, though not in *this* sky. All that velocity, the running start of millions of years, but then the speed-of-light was too exhausted to penetrate this city's glow.

He was of two minds about attracting appreciative gazes once he rounded the Perry Street block and tip-toed lawfully onto Atlantic Boulevard. What was the purpose of these so-called *classic* cars but for owners to be admired in them? *He* couldn't plead innocent. This thing was not only specious, comfortable, and loaded, but subtly asserted: *Look at ME!*

He squeaked into the bucket seat which still smelled like a new fielder's glove. The ambiguity was that as much as he *wanted* to flaunt it, this time of the night, in this neighborhood, was not ideal for a car show. On certain blocks, the scrutiny he entertained might turn to class resentments. *But people! This baby isn't that audacious! Original paint, not some blasphemous candy metallic! It's an urban classic and we were part of the neighborhood. We hung on here to serve you. Hey, I woulda voted for Obama a few weeks ago, but I had to get to my AA meeting. Keep the PO off my ass.*

Block after block, signal after signal, the Florida scheme allowing citizens of all ages to turn safely was in full effect. Even at this hour, at intersections where no more than two or three cars happened to queue up, the lengthy intervals remained. The wait was the same, rush hour or last call.

Walt's anxiety to get out of the old neighborhood abated. *Don't be* that *white guy.* He clacked the electric door locks back up. While relatively safe within the stockade of *Bocewicz and Sons,* he seldom considered how their role in the location must have changed in his years of absence. Was the business, by now, considered intrusive and colonizing?

When the white (of *course* they were white!) LED stick figures resumed goose stepping across the pedestrian signal opposite, a few local citizens of color crossed passively in front of him. A quick glance to the right showed him a Winn-Dixie, flanked by a strip mall, still open. One old guy with a shopping cart full of Diet Pepsi briefly featured in Walt's headlights. His cargo was full 8-packs, not a homeless bank account of empties. An older woman with a cigarillo strode past with full canvas grocery bags. She paid Walt no heed. Then a slim kid filed past, an Arab kufi atop a single, fat weave of braid thick as a hawser for a frigate. *He* was the one who paused to give Walt a thumbs up of approval for the car. Walt warmed with appreciation.

The fleeting urban scenery along Atlantic Blvd. was broken and buffered by check cashing and payday advance storefronts. Cell phone showrooms maintained their critical presence on nearly every block. Short blocks of single-story bungalows, their tiny yards littered with takeout trash and dried palm-fronds, held their ground between a few transient motels.

Walt knew that the offices for most of these budget shelters were fronted by bulletproof, check-in foyers. He'd gone comparison shopping and learned that the thick glass could not contain the intensity of curry dishes being prepared inside. Most of the places offered door-front parking, which he appreciated. Curbstone blocks kept the angry cars of domestic dispute from intruding upon anyone's brief coupling or wary sleep. Added to the subtropical sleaze of faded pastels and peeling stucco were proliferations of pink, plastic flamingos. These were no longer ubiquitous in the small, private yards nearby (driven out by a blitzkrieg of garden gnomes), but still flocked around the motels' scabbed and empty pools. This bottom rung of tourist commerce held on grimly with pawn shops near at hand. Shabbiness comprised the scenery for the rest of the way out to the Beaches. Surfer, seashell, and sunglasses bodegas took over out there. Judging from a lifetime reliance on such habitats, Walt had chosen the cleanest: The Armada Cove Inn.

The locks of the Caddy were electronic from the inside so Walt didn't need to pry at each with the key to secure them. A car alarm was what he really needed. They made an annoying racket but he could live with that until he relocated. *Need to drop some hints around the store for someone to buy me one for Christmas.* The savings he still managed must be accelerated until he received his share of the sale.

Walt locked then dismounted without eye contact as a procession of residents passed in front of the car. These men were smoking aggressively while possibly summarizing the events of their day in Spanish. They seemed to be headed for the *7-Eleven* which faced Atlantic Boulevard, just off the premises. Their white wife beaters glowed bluish under the security lights. Their beards presented ample *machismo*, while their work boots looked like Hummers for the feet.

Walt nodded, *Buenos noches* then waited until the party had passed before stepping up to the door of his room. Then he recalled the three white pickup trucks with decals of a construction company parked near the back. These were out-of-town roofing-and-siding hombres. Sometimes it took all winter to repair the damage from whatever storms had blown and stomped across the state. *Imagine their day.* There were a couple of functioning payphones in front of that *7-Eleven*. Or, maybe they needed to buy cellular minutes, have a goodnight word with their ninos or a final cold beer. As *he* planned to do. Sort of.

Since ceding back the apartment, Walt had holed up here in Armada Cove, though the ancient Spanish gold convoys would have passed far to the south. There were twenty rooms, only half of which were occupied in midweek, and four efficiencies. Weekly discount rates were available for payment in advance. Walt plunked down for a month. He also paid a pet deposit, the amount more appropriate for the ransom of a child.

There were no programmable entry cards which made possible a larcenous *key* deposit. Walt battled, nightly, with the battered lock in his door. Paint had long since been worn away around the circumference of the knob. He held up his keys to the light, pinching out the appropriate one. He jimmied it in while forcefully arm wrestling the knob, adding his own engravings to the lock. But, then he was inside and it was like Home Sweet Home. If that was to be the case for more than another few weeks, he would have to bring some *WD-40* from the store for the lock.

In halfhearted pursuit of Walt's keys tossed onto the queen-size bed, Antoine leaped heavily off the two-burner stove. One swipe at them was all the ambition he cared to muster. The big tortoise-shell had only just then, apparently, begun to dislodge the foil protecting used olive oil in Walt's one frying-pan.

"Pardon the interruption, but you've had all day to clean that up."

"Puhhr-eoww?" Now Antoine dropped back to the floor. After a quick rub around Walt's pant leg, he repeated a familiar request at the base of the door. "Puhhr-eoww?"

"Sorry old boy, but I just can't let you out. What do you say you ride to the store with me tomorrow?"

Antoine had no front claws for self defense and Atlantic Boulevard appeared to be quite unforgiving to crossing wildlife. The occasional squirrel, feline, and chipmunk carrion by the curbside was a clear harbinger of violent ends for critters. But Antoine could have the run of the apartment all day if he wanted. *Just like old times.* Walt would bring along the litter-box and place it in its familiar spot. The cat returned to the bed. He did his impossibly long stretches on the duvet then tongued a few licks into his wide, soft paws, preparing for sleep.

"Welcome to incarceration, buddy."

Walt left the television on all day at low volume. It was a poor deterrent to property crime, even if he had something valuable to steal. His pill stash and some saved cash were kept in the closet motel safe, to which he'd added a logging chain.

For much of the day, a pit crew of Haitian ladies patrolled the sidewalks of the Inn with their linen carts and toilet brushes, changing out the threadbare sheets and towels. They constituted a Neighborhood Watch of sorts, *possibly* loyal to the Armada Cove residents. As a long term guest, the girls deep-cleaned his little nest every Monday with apparent friendliness and zeal. His sheets would be tight and fresh tonight. As far as the efficiency was concerned, he had no complaints so he tipped as well as he could afford.

When he turned his attention to the screen, the *Orlando Magic* were just then closing out the *Hornets* in New Orleans. *Good. Dinner and a show.* Walt took the pharmacy calculator off the mismatched bureau, found the TV remote and turned up the volume. Just in time for a media timeout. The Orlando station identified itself and then ran two Black Friday car commercials. *0% interest on 2009 Dodge Ram and they probably still can't give them away.* This was a drama, too, being enacted on a national stage. *Is anyone giving the family a luxury crossover for Christmas this year?* And there it was, earlier every Holiday season: A luxury *Ford 2500* in a driveway of artificial snow under a huge ribbon and bow.

Walt placed the calculator on the dinette next to the pages of the real estate proffer. He chose a microwave meal from his tiny freezer. Only college dorm rooms had smaller appliances than this one. He pulled out a *Michelina's* Chicken Alfredo.

Well, hell. Why not two of these? A celebratory feast. But he hadn't brought anything home for dessert. *Home. See there? It doesn't take long to adapt.* Two of those meals made sense for a hungry laborer in any case. The anticipation for his imitation beer had reached its plateau three hours ago and then subsided. A healthy appetite remained.

Walt might plausibly think that *two* O'Doul's Ambers should wash down *two* frozen meals. It was not a rationalization he'd needed to fashion after a shift at any of his previous menial jobs: The ticket booth at a *Deja Vu;* event staff at the *Gator Bowl*. He also successfully closed the safety bars on the Dumbo Ride at The Magic Kingdom for more than three months. It wasn't strenuous but he had to mop up a fair amount of toddler vomit. Then a background check caught up with him.

But he earned his all-time favorite minimum wage by tearing tickets then pointing the patron's way to screens 1-4 (right), or 5-8 (left) at the Regal Cinemas in Gainesville. Easy work, even when they asked him to slide behind the long, glass counter to scoop popcorn. *That* gig soured immediately when someone reviewed more closely, not his rap sheet, but his education resume. They asked him to move up to assistant manager. A dollar-fifty more per hour wasn't sufficient incentive. The responsibility? Walt shuddered. Putting up stock at a Dollar General or herding grocery carts at a Winn-Dixie better matched enthusiasm level.

A review of those dead-end careers no longer soured his moods after two years sober. The images only survived in his mind's Library of Shame because he usually stayed sober long enough to

EVACUATION ROUTE

turn in the application and sit through an interview. He stayed straight for the first few hours of each shift. Then, he'd gravitate toward other staff who were taking hits behind the loading dock. He made *those* friends quickly.

Whoa, wait now. There should be a half-can of fruit cocktail at the back of the 'fridge. Dessert after all. Plenty of desserts and leftovers next week. Warren would drive him for Thanksgiving down to their mother's oversized condo. The place was on A1A south of St. Augustine. Gated, with an ocean view. The great meal was worth listening to her grouse about *her* storm damage (one fallen eaves trough) and *"Why haven't I seen either of my grandchildren since July?"*

Walt sat at his raggedy dinette while the microwave made vacuum cleaner noises, heating his first course. He turned up the TV volume just as Dwight Howard slammed in two points over Mo Pete. Ka-*flush*! Guy was still no replacement for Shaq. Scott Skiles was long gone, too.

The *O'Douls* wasn't nearly as cold as Walt would have liked, but the refrigerator was already dialed to its lowest possible setting. That was *another* motor that grumbled in the dark every fifteen minutes as he tried to sleep. It probably *never* shut off in the height of summer but he should be gone by then. To the *next* place he would call home?

The *O'Doul's* didn't require the old-fashioned church key opener he once needed for his favorite brew, *Red Stripe*. But Walt still had one and why risk a twist-off wound on the stubborn caps? In all the twenty years since acquiring that particular taste, (during a

Bob Marley fascination), the Jamaican brewery resisted twist off technology. Maybe they reused the bottles. He would probably never know. *Hmmm. How much trouble could I have gotten into down there?*

The *O'Douls* cap bent off with a hiss of carbonation. He let it to breathe, testing his self-control while he waited on the entree. At last the timer went off with a single *clank.* The dinger was worn and there was no light inside to observe any boil-overs.

Walt peeled the plastic off and began to eat. Dwight Howard was the hero chosen for the sweaty, postgame interview. *Mmm, cheesy.* The pasta shells were just right even if the chicken chunks were rubbery dark meat. *Needs pepper.* There was a fistful of the tiny, paper pouches from *Mickey D's* piled in the center of the dinette. Walt tore and shook a few onto the meal.

The first taste of *O'Doul's* was a deep, quenching gulp. *Easy, there. Pounding these things like it's a race has always been part of my problem.* He placed the bottle far aside. Having polished off the first course, he set the second *Michelina's* waltzing on the carrousel of the microwave. Only when it was hot did he take the next, modest sip. Then, he traded the bottle for the calculator.

Let's see, 30% of $1.4 million with seven years left before Social Security. Would he need another of the minimum wage jobs he always favored? Any time soon? *Drum roll, please. And the winner is....$420K. Well, alright then!* Walt sat back but wasn't ready to do a Snoopy dance quite yet. Could he manage for seven years on that? There were some legal fees still owed to Wineglass. What about taxes? He thought Warren mentioned that the building had

EVACUATION ROUTE

been included in a living trust or something. Now he wondered about capital gains and inheritance taxes. *I should know this stuff.* There certainly would have been tax exempting measures worked out by Warren and the Old Man during Walt's time of oblivion.

Other amendments must have been made as the Old Man's dreams for both his boys were confounded. Additional codicils had to be inserted each time Warren galloped to Walt's rescue with loans. Full restoration of his driver's license wasn't going to be cheap, either. But, as far as Walt knew, all Child Maintenance payments in arrears, all court costs and restitutions had been made. The microwave's crippled timer sounded again. Walt sipped then retrieved his second helping.

On the bright side, there might be some great housing deals at the bottom of this...whatever the pundits were calling it now. The burst bubble of easy-home mortgages based on derivative funds? *Too long. Dot.com bubble was just right.* How about *hyper-recession*?

And where did Walt *want* to live? The Gulf Coast? The Panhandle? How about the mangrove wetlands of the Nature Coast? Anything but the gatory, wild boar stampedes of the interior. Were those stories exaggerated or downright apocryphal? Aren't the pythons pretty well cordoned off in the Glades? Why wouldn't the wild boars clean out the reptiles? Maybe the big constrictors were too much for the hogs to handle. End-of-day weariness was returning. The second wind of newly realized fortune evaporated like the cheesy vapors of his cooling meal.

Walt stepped into the bathroom and turned on the hot tap for a shower. He could check on the car, lock the locks, clear his dinner mess, and finish his beer before the water would be warm enough to produce a lather from his *Irish Spring*. He dumped the now tepid *O'Doul's* into the bathroom sink. It was going to be fun, he thought, to buy a stack of Sunday papers and study how the housing prices were doing across the state. A refresher course in geography was in the offing.

"Hey, Antoine. I've got people food for you."

The cat's eyes remained closed until the little plastic tray hit the floor.

When he climbed into the shower, the background patter of water smoothed his thoughts. As he relaxed under it, the name of that playwright from the *Godot* rehearsal party came back to him. Just as he was massaging the generic shampoo into his scrub brush of grey hair, he remembered: *Becket, Samuel Becket.* There were two homeless guys, with nothing to eat between them but a fat radish. *Then this loud bastard comes along whipping his slave, interrupting the dialogue. What the hell was that whole thing about?*

Chapter Two

B ella Nguyen-Ruiz was going to be very relieved to turn west, back in the direction of the Gulf. It seemed like an hour since she'd set out hiking from the *Roadway Inn*. Putting a few quiet blocks between herself and the hurtling grit-gale of traffic on US-19 would take some of the jitters out of her clammy hangover. She felt a tiny bead of perspiration trickle down her neck from beneath her *Phillies* baseball cap. She wasn't worried about the sun on her dark skin. It could only help, except if she ever developed some of those cancer moles. She would have to spend a full year up North to even get a look at her true skin tone after being on or near the water for most of her life.

What a beautiful job her cross-pollinating parents had done for her to turn out as she had. Well, appearance wise, anyway. She wore a blend of pigmentations bequeathed by her Cuban Papi and Vietnamese Mama-San. Her genetic tree had literally washed ashore, latter day wretched refuse, or had been dredged from the sea by the *US Navy*. Papi arrived in a leaky boat, the motor of which quit ten miles off their destination in the midsection of the Keys. It was a long row, one amigo bailing while the other two rowed.

They tried to hold position offshore until nightfall, praying not to hear the slap of helicopter blades or to see the white wake of an approaching *Coast Guard* cutter. Then they contended with pretty healthy surf in the dark. Later, taking work as a commercial fisherman, he overcame a strong phobia of sharks. For three days and nights, he and his friends kept constant watch, took turns baling the porous 12-foot boat. Dorsal fins were everywhere.

Mama-San's flashbacks were much worse. These included screaming nightmare images of losing someone, snatched from the surface, drifted too far from the protection of a single .38 revolver and homemade spears. The outboard motor of the makeshift pontoon raft had sputtered dry shortly after reaching international waters. Gone in an instant was her cousin and soon after that, a fleeing schoolteacher, the buoyancy of a life jacket no resistance at all. Each time, those in the water crawled half onto the raft, begging for their turn aboard. They lost four out of the eighteen passengers who shared the swamped craft. Luckily, that shark must have been in a small group. The former ARVN officer with the gun bagged a couple of them, which put confusing blood into the water. No one wanted *him* to take a turn overboard.

Bella never learned to swim, was never out of a lifejacket while aboard their fishing boat. Papi eventually tried some clamming in deserted grounds close inshore to go with his crab venture. But, it wasn't worth the time and risk of running aground. All the best clamming was up north in the Bend waters. Even within wading distance of narrow, deserted beaches, Mama-San would not relax vigilance over her daughter. The single take away from her one traumatic viewing of *Apocalypse Now* was the admonition *you never leave boat.*

How did Bella suppose they were introduced to one another? Certainly they made some kind of small talk and eventually courted, in the Pidgin and Spanglish of the shrimp boats and fish market bodegas. Those were Bella's own first languages, though her parents also forced her, peremptorily, to speak English. She must communicate in the magical words of assimilation. Now she remembered little of her early harbor vocabulary. The ball cap was part of today's disguise though she'd been wearing similar ones for most of her life. The camouflage this morning also included oversize amber shades. But a conical *non la* of the rice paddies would not have been inappropriate. She had the cheekbones for it.

Though she felt exposed, she did not regret skipping a taxi or not calling Merry to pick her up. She was not yet convinced that her roommate's scheme to work the sunset gambling cruises was a viable business model for them. Or, that their previous managing associates would find enough motivating anger to actually get off their lazy butts to come looking for them. Yet, here she was, willingly searching for the little economies that would assure that the *plan* turned a profit.

Whatever was happening with the national economy, it was not helping their transition to self-employed status. The boat she'd chosen was only half full on a Friday night. Fortunately it wasn't exactly a date crowd. The swilling voyagers seemed mostly to be white-collar, office guys having one last fling before cleaning out their desks. Maybe they hoped to score the one big hand or jackpot that would dissuade them from flinging themselves overboard in despair. And, there was one widower salesman (or, so he claimed) drowning his sadness in the insurance money. Bella would total up a full accounting for the previous evening after reaching home and taking a long nap.

Her wadded up cocktail dress with heels to match was in the tote she'd brought with her into the Gulf. Held under her arm, it was the size of that thing artists use for carrying their canvases. *The whata-ya-call-lit. But not the easel.* Anyway, now the strap was starting to rub. What was she supposed to do, lug a backpack on board? That would absolutely ruin the understated glamour she was going for, though she'd seen plenty of them aboard. She couldn't go out looking like a refugee in *this* market anymore than she wished to look like a streetwalker.

They were going to have to iron out some of these evolving concepts. Like, maybe to always leave a vehicle at the dock site? Like, maybe dress a bit more casually. The cruise turned out to be nothing *like* the opening night of the Tampa Symphony as the brochure seemed to portray. She looked like she was on her way to a prom, with everything but a piled-up bouffant and a corsage. Like a high end call girl in other words.

The lights held for a really long time on 19 so that she had to walk past eight to ten idling cars each time the traffic stopped for a red. The grumbling *Harleys* back somewhere behind her posed the biggest worry. Riders and drivers forced to stop had time for a good, long look at her epic tush as she passed. Her face was thoroughly cleansed of makeup after quietly using the guy's shower. She let the decent water pressure batter her features and then the back of her neck. But makeup on her darker skin didn't alter her appearance that much. She was nearly as recognizable without it.

Still, it was always with satisfaction that either she or Merry had the time and liberty to exhaust the john's hospitality (that hot water, especially). Better than having to wait all sticky and smelly for Wood-Chuck or Boog to collect them for the drive back to the one bedroom studio they shared. You might end up sitting in someone else's stank for hours if crazy Boog decided to stop somewhere for a drink. Or, if he needed to attend to other biker business. The girls preferred to wait by the bike on those occasions to avoid an unplanned doubleheader, to exempt themselves from any ugly confrontations Boog might provoke himself into.

Except for *Knuckledick* club functions, she and Merry tried to insist on prompt post-trick ablutions. These pleas were usually heeded by Wood-Chuck but ignored by Boog, who, if he responded at all, would growl a quiet *would ya just shut the fuck up?*

Bella carried a travel size mouthwash in the tote as well as some antibacterial wipes. She swooshed the burning, amber liquid around in her mouth for a long, cootie killing time at every rest pause in the action and didn't much care if the john was offended; or, if he didn't find the alcohol tingle on his cock especially stimulating. They should be grateful. *A mouth is the biggest cootie source in my anatomy.* Nor was she often able to douche immediately. She mistakenly thought that Boog would appreciate a scent of *Sum-*

mer's Eve on the back of the *Harley's* seat. Apparently, though, *any* lingering funk went unnoticed by him.

But last night, a post-coital cleansing was immediately granted by the so-called widower. The guy actually wanted to go down on her...again. *Well, if you insist.* Then the morning shower became a race between running out of hot water and his awakening. Having already used her one application of douche, she went as deep with the little motel soap as she could. Oral cooties. Where had she heard that a person's mouth was host to more bacteria than their genitals? She left the guy with *that* bar and dropped the second, unwrapped one, into her tote.

Now, attempting to obscure her profile, Bella touched her left cheek, mimed the removal of a speck of road grit from her left eye, played with her left ear (though the earrings were already safely in the tote), studied the sidewalk passing below; the cracks that she mustn't step on, the windblown trash, the traffic noise like a surf. It was the only defense she could think of short of wearing one of those Al-Qaida beekeeper veils, whatever they were called.

When the lights turned green, the vehicles leapt forward with a pent-up, impatient roar. Some of the bikes coming up behind her turned out to be *Hondas* and whiny *Kawasaki* ninjas. None seemed to be ridden by what she would define as *bikers.* So far. But who knew those Japanese bikes could be just throaty enough to make the skin on her neck prickle? At least she couldn't be ID'd from the northbound lanes because the highway was too wide. The traffic thinned from a Formula 1 start to a steady parade as she marched onward.

EVACUATION ROUTE

It wasn't just the danger that certain *Knuckledicks* might actively be seeking them here, but that one of them, one of their pimp/manager guys, might pass by at any time. Bella knew that Wood-Chuck had close relatives up north; a family he could reach in about an hour by tooling up US-19. He talked a bit about them. Who knew why? Probably just some innocent, even embarrassed, chit-chat to make him seem harmless or at least less dangerous. He attempted, at times, to come off as warm and fuzzy. Wood sat with her occasionally, in some dark, dive bar, waiting for the prearranged *date* to show up and pay *him* the fee. But he'd also mentioned that he didn't run up to Homosassa very often. *Well, why don't you? You maybe are so not proud to tell your Mami how you make a living?*

Right at the moment, the knowledge of that disinterest was reassuring to Bella, though she wasn't much afraid of Wood, anyway. It was that other *mal hombre*, Boogaloo, that a girl (hell, anyone) did not want to cross. Now she and Merry were crossing them both in a major way. And maybe Merry was right that they could be liable for some kind of biker retribution. She'd had more experience with them.

Finally, Bella turned the corner to head west on Trouble Creek Rd. A light breeze carried a faint scent of the Gulf into her nostrils. Home. The *Sketchers* sandals were comfortable enough but the heat of asphalt and crushed marl macadam was beginning to penetrate the soles. She snorted at this image as she searched up the street for the next shady stretch, of which there would be more in their new neighborhood. *Her soul? Nah.* She'd been penetrated in all kinds of ways, but honestly felt that her soul was still cherry. She would have lost it by now if that was ever going to happen. She successfully *compartmentalized* and proved it by walking away from what some would call a co-dependent relationship: Those dear *Knuckledicks*.

Flex Appeal Deja-Vus. Were they serious? Footwear named after a chain of strip clubs? That was another thing she hoped never to do again. *How in the world had Sketchers come up with that name? Did no one do market research?* Wouldn't earn very much doing lap dances in these things. But they fit nicely into the tote when she was ready to climb down from the high heels. Light blue, soft mesh uppers. Flaming, bunion raising, foam soles. That was another complaint she had for Merry. Heels weren't very stable for that size of boat.

It was always so depressing and dark in those VIP rooms for the short time that she tried working them. Velvet curtains draped to hide plywood partitions that no one ever bothered to paint. There was no honest value for anyone. Do your turn on the pole then talk some poor dumbass into buying you a drink: Hawaiian Punch, $6 per glass. Premium beer, $8. Or. the worst New York champagne ever. It might not even have been real Hawaiian Punch. Probably Cool Aid. Listen, baby. Wouldn't you like to come back with me for a private show? I will make you feel really good. You sure got some legs honey. But you can't to grind on nothin' with both your feet on the floor. And I love that accent.

Then tease the guy with your writhing ass in their faces for five minutes. Or, until they got that wincing, scrunched up look on their faces and you could see they had nutted right through their *Dockers*. Other times, if it was a really hot looking guy, and behaving pleasantly after you led him away by the hand from his office buddies; and if he smelled nice, too, she might end up rubbing her *own* self into lushing up. *That* sure sent the wrong message. *Can I suppose that now and then a customer returns to his vehicle feeling cheered up by this routine; maybe lifted from loneliness he brought in with him?*

It happened to her more often than she cared to admit; getting turned on. The slipups of yielding to her own pleasure might have ended abruptly if she'd ever actually gone out with some of the *VIPs*. She sometimes betrayed herself with a genuine moan, a modest but irresistible squirt. *What the fuck, girl? You're really getting into it, aren't ya? Don't flatter yourself, amigo. I can do this against a steering wheel.* Her eyes never quite rolled back into her head. Her body didn't arrive at any kind of spasm, pushing both chair and john onto the nasty shag carpeting in the lurid, purple light of the VIP room. She tried to explain that, yes, she honestly had been turned on, a little, but would lose her job if caught making outside arrangements. This last discouraging note was actually true.

Not too many years ago, she took to heart the guidance counselors rote advice to every junior: *Love what you do and you'll never work a day in your life.* The Ruiz clan moved around too much; up and down the Keys, as far north as the Panhandle and those Big Bend waters, for her to attend Sunday school or Catechism regularly. Mama-san must have been too exhausted most of the time to go into great detail about available spiritual choices. As Bella entered puberty, Mama-san took time to express in terse utterance her most important moral code: *You make boy wear rubber. We feed no more mouth.* Years of studying the mapping of that lined face warned Bella that continued life on the water would be impossible for her to accept. She scrupulously hid her early career attempts until both parents, worn out and used up long before the mean of their adopted country, were in urns.

The traffic going into the modest neighborhood was slower, less aggressive. There was no congestion, even with a stop or yield sign at every corner. This made the odd motorcycle approaching from behind seem louder, more threatening. They sounded to her like how she imagined a dogfight of very large, vicious dogs. What was it about the *Harley*? They seemed to hammer as if they were low on oil, the broken teeth of their pistons and rods gnashing on themselves. How was that supposed to be macho? It just sounded like poor maintenance to her and she'd heard a lifetime of engines in their death throes among the immigrant crab and shrimp fleet.

The police and municipalities didn't seem to give a damn about noise abatement anymore. Hell, who would even notice with US-19 back there behind them like an all night truck yard. A few hairy, dirty looking guys in their colors occasionally passed through the girls' new neighborhood on their way to small rented homes. They rattled the windows of fellow residents with impunity. God, what those guys in the *Knuckledicks* smelled like after a poker-run on a hot summer day; or, after a gangbang for which some half-wit initiate would have to clean up. Orally. Hell, she *knew* what they smelled like and would probably never be able to forget. Blacks in nice cars, high school kids in their *first* cars were much easier prey to be fucked with by nervous cops. No one wanted to deal with an *actual*, possibly armed, biker.

What were the odds that any of those *Knuckledick* brothers would ever search through *this* neighborhood, *this* particular street? Bella never noticed a shortage of paid pros, or even crazy freelance volunteers willing to entertain bikers. Merry was just having junkie paranoia, imagining Boogaloo on every *Harley* that went by. Some of that fear must have rubbed off on Bella, to be so antsy just walking down the street in her own neighborhood. *She's giving me some kind of contact low.* Bella chuckled at this, hard enough to reawaken her headache. Merry *could* give her some kind of *contact low.* Bella should write some of these gems down in a journal. It was weird, too, because when they first met, two years ago. Merry seemed to fear nothing.

They were a long way from Tampa's mean streets. Bella never really worked 34th Street very much. She was just dipping her toe into *that* depressing scene when Merry diverted her. But now they needed to try the big casinos if this return to freelancing was going to work. *Hard Rock* casino wasn't a biker scene. Their previous handlers were not likely to show up there. Bella had already plied Merry with *this* logic: It was a bachelor party, high school reunion, post wedding rehearsal scene, with mobs of snowbird crones, their little scooters into the mix. The *Knuckledicks* staged their *own* gambling events to satisfy that need. The stakes and jackpots for some of the so called poker runs were *dangerously* high, given the character of the participants.

As it was, the girls slipped up here to New Port Richie during the week of Halloween. This was *way* farther than necessary, Bella began to think. They both got dye jobs to go with new hairdos. They invested in wigs and hats, pooled their savings into a new credit union account. Neither of them used credit cards that could be traced but Merry couldn't get it through her head that the *Knuckledicks*, all together, hadn't the computer savvy to do more than find porn or play video games. There *was* no *Knuckledick* website. Track their credit cards? Not likely. Bella didn't enjoy being a honey blond now, nor the hair-calming chemicals Merry talked her into using. The color actually made her stand out, contrasting unnaturally with her pigmentation.

But, seriously. She still could *not* picture Wood-Chuck missing them enough or caring enough to come tracking them. Boog would be the problem because he was half nuts and might take their desertion personally. They were, possibly, the laziest dudes to ever run girls in Tampa. The percentage they took was way out of proportion to their management services, or the muscle they often failed to provide. The girls were always happier when Wood was in charge and kept Boog from seriously fucking up the few problem johns they encountered. The Cajun/Creole guy was apt to batter a drunken, uncooperative customer sufficiently to draw the attention of authorities. Hospitals would call the police without permission if the patient was brought in unconscious.

Toward the end of their commercial and social arrangements with the *Knuckledicks*, the girls needed desperate side-hustles not to end up homeless. Tips from the bikers they serviced shrank with the economy and their preoccupied handlers didn't work very hard to hustle johns. The relocation just made sense. *But,* all this witness protection dookie was Merry's idea and seemed like more a hinderance to business than crucial security.

On the other hand, Bella *could* picture Wood-Chuck becoming frantic and resentful the next time the *Knuckledicks* wanted to entertain visitors from other clubs. Merry and Bella became the favorites, far-and-wide, of some of the out-of-town degenerates, even though the girls tolerated no rough trade at those occasions. Maybe some verbal abuse if that's what the visiting grease balls needed to arouse themselves. But pretty soon, if he overheard it, Boog got that grim look on his face to signal that he was contemplating an intervention. On more than one occasion, he ruined the goodwill that the girls managed to achieve with their tolerance of slovenly, coarse partners.

The downside to the big parties was, you were absolutely going to get a rash or worse when the gangs got together. The *Jesters,* for instance, brought wads of cash, though no amount of chronic or free beer seemed to mellow the vile tendencies of certain members. However, she and Merry grinned and bore these barbarians, taking home serious money from even the most recent late summer gathering. The *Knuckledicks* were able to finalize a temporary agreement regarding narcotics territories with the neighboring club from the Panhandle area. Never mind the overhead that the girls paid for themselves; for prepping antibiotics which, luckily, were still effective. And, free clinic bloodwork. Everything was dicey these days when out-of-town clubs rode in with their unfamiliar colors to enjoy *Knuckledick* hospitality. They could be carrying unfamiliar strains of gonorrhea native only to Tallahassee and Mobile. With those and other complaints falling on *Harley* deafened ears, the girls finally decided it was time to rethink their career path.

Irene Loop seemed almost sleepy as Bella turned the corner and marched north again. US 19 was now a distant seashell whisper. Was the whole neighborhood as hungover as she was? The homes were mostly bungalows or duplexes. Some of the places looked like mobile homes, and not always doublewides, that she had inhabited as a girl. To distinguish themselves, grandfathered in to satisfy passing fancies of the housing code, the trailers here were cleverly camouflaged with added utility rooms, porches, decks, garages, even second-story additions behind the original dwelling. But Bella's experienced eye was attuned of this fakery. One of the duplexes made her crazy when she thought about it; the place three doors before (make that four doors) their own rental. The porches and front entrances of the building were side-by-side while the one car garages for each were stuck onto either end. The occupants had to share a wall in their front rooms. And, the two bathrooms were probably back-to-back, for the purpose of sharing plumbing and hot water.

Bella was approached on the opposite side of the street by the circus music of an ice-cream cart. The white van crept slowly but there were no kids in pursuit. Christ, shouldn't they have time to

EVACUATION ROUTE

47

digest their *Pop-Tarts* first? Then again, she wasn't really certain of the time, and in this neighborhood one was more likely to see seniors hobbling out to buy treats. Her quiet shower in the motel took awhile, her head resting against the fiberglass until the hot water began to run out. Well hell, the booze was comped to her by *Lucky Seas Excursions*. It was *still* free after she and the sales rep hooked up from adjacent stools at the slots. *Would she care to share a table in the dining room? His treat? Sure, if you don't mind that I'm a working girl. You know, honey, I was hoping you were. You only live once, am I right? What's your name?* She could hear the john's snoring through the closed bathroom door. She slipped out without checking the alarm clock which was flashing 12:00am when they stumbled to the bed. And now, that was one *long* hike she'd just made. It might well be past lunchtime for all she knew.

Bella dug deep into the tote bag for her house key, She found the key ring impaled on one of the stiletto heels. Merry's *GEO Tracker* was parked off their bit of driveway, the hood tucked under the low fronds of a bottle palm. King palms along the property line completed their splotch of shade. Just enough to shelter the geckos which bounded along the walkway toward her, seeking a cooler place to sleep as the sun reached its zenith. She felt a little too jangled to appreciate this migration. She climbed two concrete steps then turned the deadbolt.

The front room was dark except for a small flatscreen television perched on a yard sale lamp table. Anime cartoons flickered, nearly silently. She could never get into them; wouldn't have, ever, unless there was peer pressure. Give her ol' *Scooby-Do*, even with subtitles on the local Spanish station. These served as Ma's English and Spanish lessons together. They laughed along whenever the weather kept them ashore. *Always not real monster! Bad man in costume try scare them. Just wait to see! No, Mama-san. Always a bad man in a costume. Or, uniform.*

Uh-oh. Bella closed the door quietly behind her as she'd been doing all morning. She frizbeed her ballcap toward a far corner. That toluene, nail polish reek had dissipated to a ghostly tang like an aging cardboard deodorizer on a rearview mirror. Not recommended to drive while inhaling *this* scent, however. Merry probably hit it hours ago, but that didn't mean the sun wasn't already coming up when she put flame to pipe. But how much? The AC window unit could have sucked most of it out. Go out and get a taste of *that* condensation; the steady, glycerin meth tears running down their yellow, vinyl siding.

"Merry? Are you in here somewhere? Have you been abusing a substance? What if I had needed a ride?"

Bella's pupils soon dilated enough to make out a junior miss size fetal lump rolled halfway over beneath a black, satin sheet. A frail arm flopped over the edge, skimming the nearest objects on the coffee table. A tall plastic cup spilled. The wand of a butane lighter sailed like a javelin before hitting the floor. Merry narrowly missed sweeping away all of the accessories of her previous evening's diversions.

"Umm--huh."

"Watch out, boo. You'll knock all your works onto the floor."

"Aww, shit. Could ya git me a dishrag or somethin'?" Merry Braniff's halfcup of sangria flooded toward the levee of the table's raised edge. "An' they ain't mah works. Make me sound like Ah'm shootin' up somethin'."

"A pipe is works." Bella scrambled for paper towel from the kitchen then hurried back to stanch the flow. "How messed up did you get this time? You aren't gonna sick up laying there, are you?"

"Ah don't know yet." Merry rolled her feet to the floor and sat up, bringing the sheet with her. She hung her head for a few moments, her spikey, super-black dyed hair flattened in spots where a copious application of product had failed sometime in the night. " Ever'thin's stayin' down, looks like."

"Will you be able to work by tonight? We don't quite have the rent yet. "

"Um-hm. Ah'll be okay. It was just one li'l crumb. Damage yer lookin' at's mostly from the wine. An' hey, Bell? Ah'm already on the run from *one* pimp."

"But you wouldn't mind having a nanny do for you, would you?."

Merry pulled the sheet up around her shoulders. "Mmm. Sounds nice,"

She wore a sports bra to lounge in which was baffling to Bella. Her friend had very little bounce. This could become a dark topic. They both had come to the unsettling conclusion that Merry's junior miss, fourteen-year-old physique was probably attractive to a certain clientele. Pick any hate word: *Cabron* from Papi, or worse, Mama-san's *pe-de.* To Merry's perspective, no john could be totally ruled out from *that* category of deviant behavior. The bar was low, but they both agreed there *was* such a thing.

"Could ya turn down the AC, Bell? Too cold. An' bring me a water? Please?"

"Yes, ma'am. A little parched are we, my little *bui doi?*"

"Talk English, would ya, at least when yer dissin' me? Yeah. Ah'm real dry."

Bella started to unpack her supplies from the tote. That poor, cute, wrinkled dress was just plain overkill unless they decided to branch out and try to do some escorting. *How would we go about getting a 900 number?* She draped it carefully over the back of the only other furnishing in the room, a rattan seat rocker. They needed to acquire an ironing board instead of using the kitchen table. Stand it up behind an interior door; always a nice addition to trailer park décor. She stepped into the kitchen. The water in its crackling, thin plastic appeared to be forming ice crystals. The 'fridge's thermostat must be about to go totally stiff-toe. The *Diet Squirt* she brought out for herself presented the same symptoms when she twisted the cap. She let it fizz out some icy foam over the sink. Then it was not unpleasant going down her dry throat.

"So, how'd ya like it? Did ya do any good out there? It's sure a differ'nt way a doin' business, ain't it? An'why did'n' ya call me?"

Bella handed Merry the water. "You got my predate pic of the guy's driver's license, didn't you? And you couldn't have drove, anyway, it looks like to me. If you had a fender-bender in your lovely vehicle, we would be in a very bad fix. I didn't do... not too bad. To begin with, I always love to be out on the water' That middle-age guy found me in a very good mood. It can't always be that clean and easy, though, I know."

"Ah never claimed it would be, but Ah told ya we wouldn't never starve goin' out on our own. Just lemme sleep a li'l more. Lemme get right 'n' then Ah'll get mahself pretty. You can guard the castle tonight, or we can try'n do a tag-team."

"Oh, no, Baby duck. I'm good. I need to rest my precious assets and have some recovery time. We don't want to get too familiar on that boat, especially together. If we get greedy we will end up arrested. Also, we don't want to go out there any more in prom dresses. I just stuck out, like I was afraid of. We will get the big ridicule in Holding where we *totally* won't make any rent." Bella plopped down heavily at the end of the couch. A splash of the *Squirt* dribbled down her neck.

Merry's eyes were closed and her head was laid back. She said, finally. "Ah wore a mini *mah* first trip 'n' Ah think that's 'bout all Ah got. Some ol' hot-pants, maybe."

"Good reliable hooker wear. But I don't think it's the best idea."

"Yeah, well. You wasn't too proud to wanta find 'em in yer *own* size. Ah have great taste in hooker wear."

"Well, why do you have to be so teeny-tiny that we can't share, jail-bait?"

"Please don't go there, Bell. Ah don't never wanta think about bein' the answer to some ol' pedo's wetdream, let alone gettin' in a vehicle with one of 'em."

"I'm sorry, bebe. I'm too tired to filter out scary things."

Merry didn't appear ready for a trudge to the shower any time soon, even if she could drag herself to her feet and stagger in there. The only reason she awakened at all was Bella's key in the door and calling for her. Bella was already shivering, herself, from the arctic setting of the AC and her crystallizing soft drink. Absent that, the junkie and wine funk which sometimes rose from Mer's skin might have kept her at a distance. Now, the window unit sighed a more moderate purr, a partial answer to the sun's glare on the mossy terracotta roofing tiles. Heat in the attic was building. With eyes powerless to open, Merry swigged her water and sagged deeper into the cushions.

"We're a ways off from earning to our goals and potential," Bella said. "About the rent? Remember about getting a few months ahead?" Bella said. "All in all, I came out with $270, give or take, after the overhead. That's our cost of doing business, right?"

"What is?" Merry whispered.

"Overhead."

"Fuck if Ah know. We'll make it. There was, like, only about fifteen swingin' dicks on *mah* first trip 'n' Ah was pretty pop'lar, 'n' brought home the bacon."

Bella began to drowse, herself, as she tilted toward her friend, roommate; her partner. Partner in crime, she supposed. That word *partner* made them both uncomfortable. These days it meant a step further past what they actually meant to each other. Except for show, when it was requested and well paid for. They brought off the girl-on-girl kisses realistically enough for the *Knuckledick's* entertainment, earning shouts and applause. Luckily, none of those crude boys asked to see anything more. People still said BFFs, though, didn't they? That was an accurate enough term. They were BFFs.

Bella jerked back from the edge of that ceremony where the term *partner* and the peer pressure of strangers would push her if they were...*you know*, in air-quotes. All those candles, effusive homemade vows, strangers in Sunday clothes. *This here's mah first gay marriage Ah ever been to. An unseen voice behind her comments. Mah niece is the bride, would ya believe? Ah think she's the bride, how they worked it out. You expect one of 'em'll wear a tux so we know which one's the husband? Guess they can try to adopt if they wanta have a kid. Ah heard that works out pretty okay. If you been in foster care awhile 'n' don't care what gender Ma 'n' Pop is.*

"Are you awake at all? I think I have my earnings figured right," Bella said softly. "First, I paid for the boat ride which, I am sorry to say, for your business scheme, was not jam packed to the rails. The economy has gone to shit. Everyone was talking about it and you can see good examples on board if you listen. Then, I had to shell out for close to an hour of slots. Which, they must have the worst odds of any casino anywhere. Finally that Dennis guy came over."

With eyes still closed, Merry capped her water lest it slip and spill. She felt herself nodding, drifting further. "Oh, he was a den'ist?" She mumbled.

"Um-hmm. Girl, you are so far out of it. His *name* was Dennis, I said. The sales rep guy? And all white men oughta be so kind as *that* man. I'm certain he was lonely. He travels for ink cartridges, like they put in copiers and printers? Did you know that means to fly all over and sell a product? He *travels* for ink...Ink Cartridge, Inc. Isn't that crazy? Or, *he travels for patio tiles,* like that. It's supposed to be tough because they work for commissions. Except this Dennis is high up in Ink Cartridge, Inc., or whatever, so they give him a salary, too. He writes off his expenses to save on income tax. Except he maybe cannot use *me*, he said. I heard all about it. Giving head in the middle of an accounting lecture. Are you even listening to me, little crack fairy."

"A course. Ah've heard a commissions. Ain't that like when Boogaloo 'n' Wood get their percentage off'n *our* product. Bet your Dennis don't ride a Harley on the job, though." Merry yawned. "Most a mine are, like, named John Smith, and they don't tenda talk much. Unless it's like, Ah'm jus' in town for a optomo...convention, eye doctor, whatever such-like 'n' then... or they don't wanta never shut up braggin' 'bout bein head a this or that department for such 'n' so region. Sounds like you done good, though, for our home office. Now can ya jus' lemme crash for a hour?"

"Yeah, yeah. I might've been just having the beginner's luck, landing a guy like Dennis on my first trip out. A cab home would have cost fifteen. You *know* that much. So being close enough for walking home was a plus, too. But, those slot machines out there? Plus the bad odds, they are *so* rigged. Alright, you have your sweet little junkie dreams."

"Mmmm-hmmph. An' by the way, Ah ain't no crack fairy. Or, much, hardly."

"Yes, you are clean as the new whistle." Bella patted Merry's hip.

They dozed at either end of the couch with their legs entangled, two fauns in a tropical urban jungle, though both would spell it *fawns*. When they began to revive and sit up, the day had been snored away softly to nearly three in the afternoon. Bella rechecked her Basic Math and confirmed that she *was* $270 to the good from the ink cartridge rep. Boo-yah! They were a third of the way toward making the rent in the second week of November. She placed most of the bills in a Zip-Lock and then into an empty carton of Moose Tracks ice-cream, whiskered with frost by the appliance's erratic thermostat. If that thing kept running at this rate, their *Duke Energy* bill would require them to get bedsores earning it. The damn freezer would soon give birth to a...what was it? Some kind of an ice thingy... A glacier! She'd made good grades in Earth Science. And then a glacier could have, like, a calf? When it broke off into the ocean making a big crashing tidal wave? She went down the hallway to her own bedroom thinking of Bart Simpson. *Don't have a calf, man!*

The shower sizzled and dripped behind the closed bathroom door. This, and the closing of the bathroom door was what had finally awakened her, her own hangover nicely gone. She rattled open the bi-fold mirror door of her closet, but closed it again. There was nothing she could offer Merry that would fit. Her nicest blouses, even her tee-shirts hung on the girl like nightshirts.

She went back into the front room and then into the kitchen. The patter of Merry's shower finally ceased with the squeaking of the spigot. There was no girlish shriek of sudden cold water so maybe she'd gotten the knack of regulating the worn handles. In the kitchen, Bella wanted her strawberry *Pop-Tarts*, the ones without frosting. There were none left though the box was neatly reclosed, empty, and replaced on the cereal shelf. Damn that little tweaker! Why doesn't she just throw the damn box away!? Bella took another soda back to her bedroom.

"Hey, Ah think Ah remember Ah might have somethin' that'll work," Merry called from her own room. "Somethin' Ah been draggin' around for a couple a years."

"Yeah? How about you come find me some breakfast, which you ate all of it up?"

"Oh. Yeah. Well now, Bell, ya know, Ah'm still at the mercy a mah dis-ease to an extent, if ya don't mind. Ah ain't turned it over to mah higher power cuz Ah ain't picked out a higher power yet, if ya wanta know the truth of it. Ah been busy. We can grocery shop tomorrow."

Merry appeared in Bella's doorway, wrapped in a towel she could easily have used as a blanket. The spikes had now been completely washed out of her raven hair. She shook the right side of her head into the towel to expel water from an ear.

"Okay, then, where is it? Show me what you have," Bella said. "And let it be classy and not like you are working *Nebraska Ave.*"

"Well, if yacht club fashion is what ya call classy. Ah'm just surprised Ah bothered even to move 'em from place to place. My one sis give it to me for Christmas a couple years ago. Alls Ah gotta do's find it."

Merry turned back into her bedroom. Bella heard the shifting of stacked boxes, the scrape of cardboard flaps being unfolded, which included the hurried ripping of some that were taped. All of this search and destroy was accomplished with slightly less crashing than a city skyline being sorted by Godzilla. *Search, destroy nummuh ten,* probably her Mama-san's first American phrase and Bella was proud to carry it on whenever fitting. *Boogaloo LaVelle nummah ten.* Now. Merry's wardrobe was being fully unpacked after two weeks stacked in a corner of her new bedroom.

After a brief silence building the suspense, she came back out wearing a pair of olive shorts. These looked to Bella to be the length and fit of a skirt. There was a wide belt drawn tight through two rings with that extra length that hip-hop boys allowed to dangle as false advertising. She twirled a slow pirouette.

"These here are called coolits. Somethin' like that."

"I you mean *culottes,* duckling." Bella stooped to take hold of a dangling rectangle of shiny cardboard. "You still have the tag on it."

"Well, don't yank on it. Fetch me some scissors. Ah personally never would a worn this thing. Woulda just took it back 'n' got the money out of it if the damn receipt didn't go 'n' get misplaced."

Bella knelt and snipped the plastic thread with a practiced incisor. "Tag says it's from *Banana Republic.* Nice stuff."

"Carol likes to show off she's got a high payin' job. AhTee is like what, computers 'n' stuff? Wish she'da just stick to *Victoria Secret* for me. Things Ah could use. If she loses her job Ah'll be gettin' somethin' from the *Dollar General,* you can bet. She does that AhTee'n for one a them big banks that been in the news. A branch of it, anyways."

"She might have gotten it from an outlet store but just never let on," Bella said. "My Ma had a few pairs of these; shorts that you can't tell, but they might be a skirt? They were fancy to her. Classy enough, *I* think, for the little social life she ever had off of the boat."

"Now to find me a top. This jungle green's pretty weird. An' shoes. Ah *know* there ain't nothin'll match in *mah* collection."

"But you'll look *so* fly when you are done. I have some gold hoo ps...Never mind. You have them, too. Or, better still, do you know what? Something with, like, emerald? To accent those avocado and olive colors. You could spill guacamole right on yourself and not notice the stain."

"Ah won't be eatin' none a that while Ah'm drinkin'," Merry said. "'Specially out on the water."

"Well then, *chica,* you don't know anything about what is good."

Merry retreated to her bedroom. Bella heard the boxes stirred through again like the bins at a last chance closeout store. When she went back into the kitchen, she found a couple of granola bars to round out her breakfast. The family size box of store brand *Frosted Flakes* like her *Pop Tarts,* was empty. The milk was gone, too. *Where does that little-bit put away all the munchies?*

When Merry came back out, she wore a button-up cotton print of ferns and fronds with, there must have been, all the greens in the *Crayola* box. The big deluxe one that neither of their mothers could afford to put in their back-to-school supplies. Merry did a goofy runway twirl with some exaggerated hip action.

"That looks like the scrubby jungle out on one of the littler Keys."

"Well, Ah believe Ah've worn this before," Merry said. "This's s'pposed to be the tropics, ain't it? Ah've got me a camo tee in there, too, since Ah'm goin' huntin'. Ah don't know *where* it come from."

"What about some sandals to go *with*," Bella said. "Unless you plan to walk home. Don't make that mistake of the wrong footwear, believe me. Take your old black crosstrainers. Or you could wear *them* on the boat, too. Go for the hipster look."

"Oh, Ah *will* be drivin' home, if ya don't mind. An' Ah generally hate hipsters. What time's it gettin' to be? Help me on with some makeup? Shoot, Ah need to get some product up on mah poor head, too."

"You have got time. Just chill. Boat does not sail until 5:00pm so they can show off that sunset like they advertise. Come into my powder room, paleface. I will make you beautiful."

Merry's near pallor required a subtle touch. Bella was skilled at giving her some color without making her bizarrely over painted. Merry sat still on the commode lid, eyes closed, awaiting like a novitiate for the benediction of shadow and liner. She looked as though she might be falling asleep again.

"Hey, open up your peepers. Let me draw out those lashes."

Merry fluttered her eyelids and yawned. "Ah don't like 'em too dark."

"Dang. Don't worry about that, ducks. You'll look a little older and still dominate the *cute* category."

"Thanks. But if yer trollin' for a big tip, you'll have to wait 'til mah ship comes in. In this case, liter'ly."

"Oh, I'm keeping a tab for you sweetie. But I'll settle for you bringing me home some Frosted Flakes."

"Depends how wore out Ah am 'n' how much Ah make. How 'bout if Ah just come home without no dis-ease? Lemme find them *Adidas*, Ah guess. Ah only got about three boxes a Big Lots shoes left to sort through."

When she was ready to go out the door, she borrowed Bella's tote bag.

"It's oversized for you but I don't think anyone will recognize it from me using it. There are maybe fifteen employees on the boat. The hardcore of swinging-dick gambling addicts aren't paying any attention. They're just there for the only blackjack in the state. It's the tourists and party boys drinking and playing slots. They eat the sit-down meal instead of sandwiches and chips. Maybe they're on the boat a couple of times in a year. Oh, why am I telling you. Just reminding you, I suppose. We'll find you your own bag. Let me fit a jacket into there. For me, it got chilly way out."

"Yes'm. Ah still don't know what ya think they'd have against a backpack. Or, mah blue denim shoulder tote. Didn't nobody give it a second glance mah first trip out."

"Well, that denim is frayed at about every seam. As for the back-pack, do you ever look at yourself in a mirror?" Bella turned her toward the one on the coat closet door. "Already you look like maybe a goth type of...you remember that anarchy bomber? He was against all technology and went off exploding mailboxes of scientists? And now, *listen* to me again and hear. Do not get so high that you don't take a picture of the john's ID. After you wear out some dude it might piss him off if you wake him from his bliss. Just stay quiet and call me when you're ready to leave. Leave on your own schedule. You can even call while you're walking away. Do I need to remind you about these things? Our roles have reversed of mentor and beginner."

"No ma'am, but thank ya for yer wisdom. Ya sound like Ah'm already gonna git dumped in the Glades."

"Well...you have been so cautious and jumpy since the move and now it is contagious onto me. You are the one making up a *go-bag,* a thing which I have never heard of. And, even with your little gun in it. You should worry less about those *Knuckledick* perros and more about the gambling locos." Bella gave Merry a quick hug. "I cannot make the rent without you."

Merry went out the door, the tote on her shoulder bumping along against her knee. "Ah love you, too, 'n' Ah hope ya never have to thank me for the gobag idea." The sun was beginning to settle toward its usual sudden, late autumn immersion in the Gulf.

"And bring home some damn *Frosted Flakes*!"

Chapter Three

Darlene Spurgeon held up dinner, waiting on Charlie, her youngest. She wasn't used to all the noise in the place. The rest of the family was getting full, gorging on chips and cheese crackers, even nibbling out of the *Wal-Mart* veggie tray her daughter-in-law brought. There was no grumbling, yet, about delay in enjoying the main course. They were all accustomed to Charlie's tardiness. Her older son, Larry, and her son-in-law, Troy, were foresting the coffee table in the front room with a thicket of beer bottles. They occasionally hollered at the TV. Darlene knew, without looking, that there would be bar-b-q chip crumbs on the carpet, working their way down between the couch cushions, and dusting the slouching beerguts of both those fine specimens of the sub-species, *Buccaneer fan.*

The backs of their heads, including Troy's male pattern baldness, was all that showed above the back of the couch where they lounged at either end. *Special-mens*, she thought, and smiled for maybe the third time since her *Welcome, y'all! Happy Turkey Day!* greeting of two hours ago. That joint, though reluctantly shared, smoothed out her willies at the noisy disruption to her usual weekend routine. *For God's sake woman, them are your own dear children and their sweet offspring.*

The ecstatic, or maybe frantic, cries of a football color analyst reached straight into the kitchen, punctuated by the outraged, or, less frequently, gleeful, commentary of her male guests. She found herself studying her hand on her own hip. *Woah. Maybe better not to hit that shit again too soon.* But, if there was ever a Thanksgiving to beware for her hips and the calories destined to arrive there, then this one might be it.

"Well, fuck *me*!"

"How's that mothafucker get hisself that wide open?!"

"If you can't cover a little white guy no better'n that, then *you* should go onto the waiver wire! And ride the fuckin' bus back home!"

That was the kind of transgression it took to break into Darlene's buzz. "Hey! Hey in there! Watch yer foul language!"

She rolled her eyes, reached slowly, slowly, across the snackbar for her smoldering *don't-get-too-baked* interval of tobacco cigarette. She quit a few years ago but dope, and one other popular trigger always lowered her resistance. She tapped loose the lengthening ash. The glass ashtray was painted with a manatee feeding off a head of lettuce from some humans in a rowboat. *Jesus, but they love their manatees in this town even more'n Crystal River does. An' those folks throw a weeklong summer festival for them big ol' sea cows. Get life without parole, you ever run over the back a one with a outboard motor.* Her daughter Sandy and daughter-in-law Terri (with an *i*, Darlene could never help but think) extended their own smoldering embers at the same moment, colliding like a small industrial spill over the ashtray.

Terry (with an *i*) giggled. "Y'all owe me a Coke."

"That's for something else, I'm pretty sure," Sandy said. "When you say a word or phrase same time as your companion does." She withdrew her damaged butt for one more puff before crushing it out with some emphasis into the earlier disaster. "Sounds like Buccaneers must be getting whipped. I guess *I'll* be driving home," Sandy said. "Those beers'll be getting tears dripped in 'em, before long. Isn't it a shame?"

"You're lucky," Terri (with an i) said. "Larry won't let *nobody* else have the keys unless he's passed out before we're packed up."

"Ah'm gonna have a hard word with that boy. He knows better'n that when them babies're on board." Darlene swirled the ice in her rum-and-Coke. She sighed with relief. At least the daughter-in-law's comment was some indication that they did, in fact, intend to leave. *Don't nobody plan on stayin' over. Ol' mee-maw may have plans for later.* There was supposed to be a euchre tournament at the *Glade* Clubhouse tonight for anyone who'd had their fill of the Holiday. Just bring along your favorite leftover desert. There were two or three old widowers that were likely to show up and she hoped to have a look and maybe kick the tires on one of them.

"Say, one a y'all needs to go chase down them kids. Ah'm new in here and this park's kinda tight-assed about rug rats makin' a racket. Ah don't wanta get off on the wrong foot with some a these Gray Panther types. Act like they never bred, some of 'em."

EVACUATION ROUTE

Not to mention, just the other day someone near saw a small alligator sunning itself in their back yard. That was the kind of gossip she overheard from residents taking their evening walks, around and around the .8 mile horseshoe in small, chatty clusters. She learned of the distance in that same way, eavesdropping through the parted drapes while also listening to local Tampa news on the TV. *They see you leanin' back behind in here, you're gonna be on their creeper watch.* She really needed to start meeting some of her neighbors. *When was the last time Ah had girlfriends to run with? A whole lot less trouble, though. Without 'em. Usually. Oh well, anyways.* The *local* news was from seventy miles south. Easy to ignore. It turned out that the four foot monster in question was way across the street and down at the closed end. A narrow creek there separated the park from the undeveloped (so far) jungle of Florida's Nature Coast. So-called.

But, its ol' daddy's sure to be out there somewheres. Sometimes she heard them bellowing about something, right in the still, dead of night. *Maybe tellin' the screech-owls to shut the fuck up, and thanks for that.* The boisterous reptile proclamations awakened her with a start and a cold sweat in October when she moved in. The AC was off and the bedroom window was open. The jungle vegetation was nearly continuous around them, extending east from ragged inlets and wetlands near the Gulf, interrupted only by the many fabulous homes along Homosassa River. And, planned senior communities like hers. Tangled, reptile-friendly undergrowth resumed across that bordering creek, practically up to the delivery docks behind *Homosassa Publix.*

Darlene wouldn't mind hearing of a big gator strutting down *their* snooty aisles. She only *assumed* snooty because she seemed to get more for her money at the *Winn-Dixie*, even if the deli wasn't nearly as well stocked. The *Super Wal-Mart* south of town was supposed to open before Christmas. Unless it got delayed by the stupid economy falling apart. *But nah, nothin' can slow up your Super Wal-Marts, once they been conceived of and the ground broke.*

"Guess it's my turn to round 'em up, sis."

Sandy swiveled her stool and eased off from it. She took her *Bud Light* longneck along for the kid herding expedition. Show off the Spurgeon sophistication to all of Darlene's new neighbors. *You better start to rein in that ass a your's, too, girlfriend*, Darlene noted. *It ain't a terrible gene to have if you was careful with it. But then, Troy's hardly no Chippendale, neither.*

God, would there even be any pie left, Darlene wondered, *if 'n' when this bunch finally hits the road*. There was French vanilla ice-cream to pile onto the pumpkin one (only way she could enjoy eating it, truth be told*). Ah'll keep that second quart hid in back a the freezer, behind the vodka*. It wasn't that she really *needed* to hook up with another *ol' boy* right away. She ditched Guillermo when the lot rent got raised at her previous place up in *Crystal River*. She took that opportunity to change him out, too, while in the process of finding more reasonably priced living quarters. It was just eight miles to drive back up there to her waitress gig. Bill never came into the *B-Dub's* anyway, and so what if he did? There wasn't any hostility left between them that she knew of.

The split was actually quite amicable on the scale of how those terminations sometimes went for Darlene. Guillermo hadn't brought much emotion to the relationship to begin with. Darlene, herself, was ready for something *new*. Men's different equipment was always a suspense at first, an anticipation to savor. Maybe here in the *Glade*, fresh candidates with unfamiliar ways and means awaited. *Ain't no thing but a chicken wing, as the younger gals at work say 'til it's like fingernails on a slate board. That, 'n' Ah know, right?' until Ah wanta throttle one of 'em. Shoot, didn't they all hear enough about the damn chicken wings?*

Darlene couldn't ever get the damn fumes of the so-called Buffalo sauce out of her nasal passages. And it clung in her hair, down into the follicles, it seemed. She tried everything but to shampoo with tomato juice which was supposed to be a good remedy for skunk spray. A couple times a year it followed her on her vacation tour of casinos and sometimes aboard the ocean liners of singles cruises. *Ah must be keepin' mah ol' booty in some kinda decent shape with all the damn miles a walkin' at work. Ah always have fun on them boats. Never fail to find male company which can be easily walked away from back at the dock. No one ever complained about that B'dub scent. Well, men, right? Maybe why some of 'em wanta bury their faces in it at the critical moment. Aphrodisiac to some of 'em?*

A timer dinged on the oven. Darlene touched a button to light up the inside. Those little popup tabs had burst from the skin of the big bird. It reminded her of that nasty scene from *Alien*. *That ol' boy birthin' that droolin' booger right out a his chest. Who in the hell made me go see that?* She turned the heat down to Warm then slid into her hotmitts. Time to baste again and lay some foil over it. She'd have to keep basting until her crazy Baby-boy rolled his butt in here. Getting lost could not be an excuse for him. It was a straight shot up US 19 from Tampa, just like it was to Crystal River but without the meandering side streets to her old place. Just follow the manatee signs. *Oh, mah goodness, though. This skin's gettin' dark 'n' golden 'n' crispy, 'n' irresistible. Gotta keep it from dryin' out. Gotta keep from takin' off a slice right now.*

Maybe she'd like somebody that was uncut this time. Hispanic guys *were* more passionate, it seemed, but Guillermo could've been a Rabbi. Maybe she'd like a change of pace. Until after, of course, turning immediately toward the television. But, that was pretty much universal. They all wanted a beer and a sandwich. After a cigarette. But, how in hell did that follow directly into her mind from her son being late to the party, as usual? Some more of that crazy Freud bullshit she really didn't believe in anyway? At least what she knew about it. *But no, wait a second. It was the turkey skin Ah was thinkin' about slashin' off, that led mah mind onto the variations in dicks. Pretty twisted either way.* Good weed and the Bacardi was doing *that* to her.

Now why couldn't someone come up with a vibratin' dildo that was uncircumcised? Play with one a those to get a gal used to it. All kinds a realistic ones on the market now. Modern technology. Turn it on, give it a minute to warm up, watch it grow out a itself. Labor savin'. Prob'ly be too expensive to mass market, though.

EVACUATION ROUTE

She lifted the broiler pan out and onto the open oven door, took a last sip of the rum-and-*Coke*, holding it between her mitts, the ice rattling. *Gonna get shitface with Charlie makin' us all wait on dinner.* Now where did she lay down that basting brush. Should she lay off the dope? Or the rum?

"I think I heard him comin', Ma. Clear out on Hall's River Rd," said Terri (with an *i*).

"You have learned the map around here pretty quick. Good on ya."

Sandy led a four child parade up the steps from the Florida room. *Wow. None of 'em're bawlin' nor tattlin' on each other.*

"Y'all can take yourselves on into Nana's den. Y'all got yer own TV in there 'n' we don't wanta hear no violence."

Darlene pushed the bird back into the oven and closed the door. Turkey vapors were making the air close in the small kitchen. Better not be a hot flash starting up on her today to go along with the stove and this full house. Just because she was fifty-three and therefore qualified to move in with these old folks didn't mean it was time to start lubing herself up for every time. She didn't need to. Yet. Nor did she require a *Brazilian* for her upper lip. Yet. *Ah'm still a decent lookin' ol' gal.* No one with normal eyesight could deny it. Walking those waitress miles all of her adult life and lifting those trays kept her toned. *Don't never want a turkey neck nor wings hangin' under mah arms.* She was still lifting and separating without too much sag. *But for how much longer? Before Ah need to reach out 'n' grab a branch from goin' over the cliff into bein' elderly. That branch bein' some ol' boy's...well, let's say hand.*

Sandy prodded the children into the den and closed the door behind them.

"Ma, did you set up the locks and blocks on those certain nasty channels in there? I'm pretty sure you know the ones I mean."

"No, Ah haven't. How old's Junior, now? Eleven?"

"Yup. And he's a sneaky little booger. Knows more about IT than all of us put together. Did you know you could hear Charlie's Hog that far away?"

"He's only been here once but Ah *did* hear him comin' that time cuz Ah was out-a-doors. Louder the better, the way his kinda biker likes it, Ah guess. It's a status thing in that darn club. That's prob'ly the reason there's speed bumps in here that ever'body's gotta ease over. We got some geezers livin' in here that ride, too. And please don't call it a Hog. What Charlie rides on is a Fat Boy 'n' Ah cannot bear to hear another lecture explainin' the difference."

"Speakin' of a fat boy." Terri (with an *i*) put fire to their second joint of the afternoon, toking it to life. "This isn't helpin' the hungries I'm gettin'."

"I still cannot believe a grown-assed man is actually getting paid to be a scooter bum," Sandy said, reclaiming her stool at the snack bar.

"Me neither, but Ah'm just gratified he ain't livin' on mah couch," Darlene said. "The officers and the clubhouse staff *do* pay theirselves pretty good. An' they get to travel a lot, a course. Sturgis, Wisconsin 'n' Daytona. My, but you twist up the bestest joints, Terri. I'm gettin'...pretty well bent, here. Did Larry teach you that?"

"No, ma'am. His ones spill 'n' spark all over everything."

"He always had sorta these sausage fingers. Like a midget might a been his daddy." Darlene giggled. "Hell, Ah don't recall *every* time Ah colored outside the lines when your Daddy was in his frequent absence. Maybe Ah visited the circus one evenin'.'"

"Mama, that's maybe too much information. And, they're called *little people* now. Plus, while we're on the subject, would you *please* wake up and smell the coffee about Charlie? Cuz it's scorched," Sandy continued. "He's Head of *Procurement*? That sounds like horseshit right on the face of it. That boy flunked General Business at the alternative high school. Oh, he's procuring *something*, all right.."

Darlene passed the joint to Sandy. Her cheeks and chin felt numb and she experienced an unexpected wave of love for her boy and whatever type of success he was achieving. To have him living on her couch would be a mother's responsibility up to a point. Downside being that *that* boy would, first thing, be trying to regulate her male company. The concept of being on a parent's couch or in the basement never made any sense. She had a spare room here and never a basement anywhere in Florida. How could she sneak in and out with him on her couch? *Ah'm really down the rabbit-hole here. Now who is it has that joint? No. But, no. Just keep it girls. Ah'm prob'ly good to go. We need a bowl a them chips back in here.*

Terri (with an *i*) rose unsteadily, took her purse from under the snack counter, and wove her way into the front bathroom. When she emerged, a fresh wave of musk scent came along with her, forcing its way through the dope and turkey smells. Guttural shouts burst from the living room.

"*Bucs* must be havin' a rally," Terri (with an *i*) said. "Hey, I only *wisht* Larry made Charlie's kinda money."

Sandy handed the joint back to her sister-in-law. *Jesus*, Darlene thought. *How* long *did she have hold of it? Where did Ah even get that good shit from? Can't even think to remember right now. One a them young girls at work?*

Darlene felt like she might be on the verge of staggering. She maintained a hold on the snack bar while moving around the end of it, then let go and went to the screen door. She peered out through the Florida room. *Now* she could hear Charlie clearly, waking up the gators. Annoyed senior citizens along his route through the park would be cursing, turning down their hearing aids.

"Sandy's just jealous 'cause *she* ain't doin' somethin' interesting," Darlene said over her shoulder. The sibling rivalry between those two had been going strong since Sandy could tattle in complete sentences. "Charlie does mosta the bartendin' for 'em, too, *daughter-a-mine.* That there's a saleable skill and he makes good money at it. Plus, he didn't need to go to no community college 'n' get a certificate. Not his fault *you* decided to get yourself trained in geriatric care. Ah'm not dissin' you, hon. Ah'm proud you went to the effort. But are you really happy, changin' shitty Depends six days a week?"

"It isn't that bad and I don't have to do it that much, Ma. I am a certified dietician plus with the Associate degree." Sandy

EVACUATION ROUTE

could not resist the dope giggles at her own lame bragging. She spent maybe three hours a week planning senior meals. "Those're, those're...what? Damn, Ma. This is some potent...Those're skills I can take *anywheres* in this state. Look on the bright side, Terri, while you're envying Charlie. Larry'll never end up in an orange jumpsuit, picking trash along the highway. Course, he may raise up some melanomas, stripping shingles all day."

"That there is pretty *cold*, girlfriend. Are you *tryin'* to harsh my buzz? Roofin' and sidin' trades makes *outstandin'* money, especially after storm season. He is also a rough-finish carpenter."

"If you don't mind him laying around the house the other six months out a the year," Sandy said. "Anyways, you have *got* to keep nagging him to put on the sunscreen,"

"Yeah, he ain't too dedicated about that. Wish *I* could tan up that good."

Darlene covered her ears as Charlie's Harley pulled into the echo chamber of the empty carport. Her own vehicle and those of the others were parked down at an overflow lot for visitors and boats on trailers. She pushed the screen door open and went down the two steps.

"Well, you sure took yer sweet time!" she hollered. "Happy Turkey Day!"

The bike went abruptly silent. No helmet, of course. Just the pirate bandana holding down the boy's tangled mop of hair. It was part of their uniform. *Charlie assertin' his freedom to get road rash onto his thick skull*, Darlene thought. *Or, to end up half deaf.*

Whoops, nope. Charlie remained in the saddle, digging to remove a pair of orange earplugs. *Well, that's smart.*

"Whaa?"

"Happy *Thanks*-givin'! Ah see you got rid a them nasty dreadlocks! Thank you,

Baby-boy! That a early Christmas present for me?!"

"Geez, Ma. I'm right here."

"Well, Ah don't know how you ain't deaf. Get yer butt up in here! You been makin' all us tokers wait 'n' we're starvin'."

Once Charlie dismounted and entered the Florida room, he gathered Darlene into an engulfing hug. As usual, her son smelled of cigarette smoke, beer, and motor-oil with just a hint of *Irish Spring*. Or, it might have been a fermentation of *WD40*. The other men dragged themselves off the couch and slouched into the kitchen for bro-hugs. It was probably halftime anyway. The girls waited their turn.

"How's it hangin', brother man?"

"Larry, you watch your mouth, now. We got kids in the place."

"Sorry, Ma."

Darlene lifted the bird out of the oven again as the kitchen became a babble of greetings. She poked at the progress of the *Stove Top Stuffing* swelling out of the turkey's open butt end, then stirred the pot of it thickening on a back burner. What a blessing *that* was. As a little girl, it was nearly impossible to pick out all the little bits of gizzard from her mother's *real* stuffing.

"One a you ladies come drain these taters. Larry, Ah ain't carvin' this year. You sober enough to not cut yourself?"

EVACUATION ROUTE

Charlie released his brother and began an intricate *Knuckledick* dap-and-clasp he'd taught Troy, finishing with another bro-hug and a triple back-pat.

"It don't get much time to *hang*. Right, you ol' hound?" Troy grinned."You gotta tell us again how you come to be known as the *Wood*-Chuck".

Darlene aimed a warm dinner roll at her son-in-law, bouncing it hard enough to leave a butter stain on his forehead.

"Hey, Ma! Ouch! What'd ya do that for?"

"Troy, Ah warned y'all once 'bout the language. At *least* once."

"That wasn't *language*. Geez, Louise!" The son-in-law mopped his forehead with a section of paper towel. "They ain't even *in* here."

"Well, they're gonna be around all day. We don't *know* how much they know."

Sandy said: "Prob'ly as much as *some* in this very room."

"That story gets old, anyways, Troy-boy," Charlie said, by way of intervening. He slowly, reluctantly, removed his glittering colors, adorned with enough pins and patches to decorate a Central American dictator. He hung them on the back of a stool vacated by Terri (with an *i*). He chose a piece of broccoli from the large veggie tray that Sandy removed from the refrigerator. He dipped it into the reservoir of Ranch dressing in the middle until only the stalk was showing. "Just take it for wisdom never to sample another person's boner pills when it ain't your prescription."

Everyone in the kitchen laughed except Darlene who reached for another dinner roll. She cocked her arm but didn't fire. "Ah mean you, too, Charlie. Careful a your language with these babies about the place."

"Sorry, ma'am."

They'd all heard, at least once, the embarrassing story behind Charlie's nickname and its moral; the panicked trip to a Tampa Urgent Care, an unrelenting tumescence pointing the way. Larry and Troy would've certainly taken to heart, by now, that Wood's splitting headache the next day was as bad as any hangover.

Sandy stood over the sink, steam from the draining potatoes scalding up into her makeup. "Aw, Ma. Leave poor Charlie alone while he's enjoying his annual green vegetable."

"Well, they got big ears in there and these walls are thin as usual," Darlene reminded her.

Darkness of evening closed in stealthily from a grey sky upon the drowsing family. Silver, 4th quarter reflections ghosted from the lifeless front room. *Wait a minute now. Ah won't call the coroner just yet.* Darlene heard intermittent snoring from someone as she stood halfway into the room, looking at the football score. *Sounds like an outboard motor chokin' on a algae bloom.* One of the boys wasn't *completely* comatose. *Hell, it ain't even the Buccaneers on the screen anymore.*

EVACUATION ROUTE

"Good news. Sounds like *somebody's* still alive in there," she said, returning to her seat. "Who dealt this mess? Looks like the same cards Ah got stuck with *last* hand."

Darlene and her daughters resumed their 500 Rummy game at the snack bar. She arranged her suspect cards then sipped at a warming *Bud Light* which she really didn't have room for. Even the kids were quiet now in the den, except for the faint bleeping sound effects of a *Mario Brothers Galaxy* video. She bartered that popular game out at the great flea market south of town. People seemed to be desperately unloading their toys and spare junk down there as the economy tanked. There appeared to be a jet ski, boat, or dirt bike for sale in half the front yards of *Citrus County*. Was the game a poor bootleg copy? None of the kids were complaining.

"Ma, *you* done it not two minutes ago. Are you still buzzed? You've got to shuffle them more than just the once." Picking from the top of the deck, Sandy immediately laid down a suit of royal hearts. She discarded the deuce of spades she'd just taken. "See? Weren't you playing these same cards in *your* last hand?"

Facing down the short hallway, Darlene watched as Charlie emerged from her spare bedroom. "Ah don't know Baby-girl. Well, look here. The first one to recover from that triplethan."

"I believe it's called tryptophan, Ma."

"You are *so* smart, darlin' and with your help we won't never forget it. But, tomato, potato."

Terri (with an *i*) picked up the deuce and laid down three of them. "I *know* I've seen these cards recently."

Charlie padded into the kitchen, carrying his heavy, black boots.

"Ma, can Ah get me a black coffee for the road?"

"Ya sure can, Baby-boy. An' thanks for not puttin' those shit-kickers up onto the bed. I believe it has started to rain, too, hon," Darlene said. "You sure you don't wanta just stay over the night?" she added reluctantly.

"These here boots are *Abercorns*. Thanks but, no thanks. I got business to do in the mornin'. I'm just glad I thought to put the shield on the bike."

"What does a biker club have planned for Black Friday? Y'all havin' some kinda Door-buster sale?" Darlene dumped the coffee grounds from dinner on top of a crammed garbage bag then knotted the loops.

"Nah, just beer. Cold 'n' cheap for the club brothers. Some of our members've been cooped up with family the whole day and they'll need to get out. Guys with shitty jobs, most of 'em'll have the day off. They'll wanta shoot pool 'n' drink in peace. Plus, I still have to clean the place up from last night and there's a keg delivery comin' early."

Darlene tried to put on a sympathetic expression as she scooped coffee into a fresh filter. She filled the beaker and poured it into the reservoir. "Awww. Sure sounds like a full day for ya, alright. What'm Ah puttin' this into."

Wood-Chuck held up his index finger for a dramatic pause then went out to his bike. He returned to the kitchen with a travel-sipper, orange Harley emblem on the matte black finish.

"Sweet, huh?" He told the women. "It come complimentary with this year's new model. They made it to fit the cupholder."

"Ah'm sure it's pretty clever, Baby-boy," Darlene said. "Sis, how about makin' Charlie up a couple a sandwiches for later. You can keep 'em dry, can't ya, hon?"

"Sure, Ma. That'd be nice."

Sandy rolled her eyes then eased off of the stool.

"White meat, OK, Sis? With plenty a mayo? Yeah, Ma, I got the hard saddlebags. It's this real heavy black plastic but feels almost like leather to touch it."

"*Of* course you did," Sandy said. "Now am I cutting the crusts off a these for you, Peter Fonda?"

"Who's that? I don't get it."

"Oh, Ah loved that *Easy Rider* movie!" Darlene said. "Seen it when it come on TV around the time Ah begun tokin' mah own self."

Sandy snickered as she opened the refrigerator. The foil covered broiler pan took up most of the top shelf. "Those guys Charlie runs with'd be called the *Difficult Riders,* Ma."

"Yeah, I s'ppose I *would* look good as that Captain America character. That would make my assistant, Boogaloo, to be Dennis Hopper," Wood said. "Only, *my* sidekick is a lot crazier. I'd like to have that Stars 'n' Stripes paint job on my gas tank, though, for sure. But listen, Ma. I wanted to ask ya, again. Are you sure everything's goin' okay in here, gettin' settled? I mean, if 'n' when all a your kids finally leave?"

Sandy sailed a slice of bread at her brother. "Watch it there, Captain America. Wouldn't be the first time I spit in some smartass's sandwich. Learned it from Ma."

80 CHRIS DUNGEY

Darlene rinsed out the travel-sipper. "Why wouldn't Ah be just fine? Ah'm a big gal. Ah have changed my residences before, all by mahself, without you ridin' shotgun. Shoot, Ah was all squared away by the *first* time you come up."

"Well you haven't been without *some* kind a man or another hangin' around the place since hardly forever. You know, just to fix shit and move the furniture around. Some good, some shady. You sure you don't need me to have a little word-to-the-wise with that ol' beaner a yours."

"He ain't *mah* beaner anymore, 'n' you got it all wrong. We parted our ways by mutual consent. It ain't none a *your* business, no ways."

Darlene poured coffee and then popped the lid on with a tight snap. It sounded new, alright. She slid the beaker back under the brewer and an acrid stream resumed.

"Don't you never mind about Guillermo. There's some prime bachelors in this park and Ah don't need you runnin' 'em off. Any furniture liftin'll be done by the delivery guys 'cause Ah'm treatin' myself to some new stuff. It sounds like you might be just a li'l bit racist, don't ya think? Ya never use to be. Rest a y'all in that ol' gang same as you?"

"Just a *little* racist?" Sandy said "*Beaner*? Really?"

Wood retrieved his leathers from the stool after Terri (with an *i)* wriggled forward to release it. She continued to shuffle the cards, as she'd been doing for the past few minutes, a blank expression on her face. Wood, without embarrassment, appeared to admire what could be seen of multicolored angel wings which spread across her shoulder blades beneath a sleeveless blouse. Darlene tried to make cautioning eye contact with him. She cleared her throat. She wondered, again, how much the daughter-in-law had shelled out for the entire attention-demanding angel. The top of a halo lay under some gold chain at the nape of her neck. *Wonder what kinda teasin' expression she's got on her face. The angel, Ah mean. Pretty cute all 'n' all.*

"We're just pretty particular is all, Ma."

"Just pretty biased, *you* mean." Sandy insisted.

"No, ma'am. We got a couple a black members now and they're good ol' boys. But, whatever. People're gonna believe what they want. Just remember, we were talkin' about you never havin' to *take* shit no more. Like from my Daddy."

"Do you even hear yourself, Charlie?" Sandy said. "They sure don't wanta hear you call them *boys*. Or, do they just have to swallow it?" She was finished with assembling three sandwiches. She fit them into baggies. Now she pawed around in the pantry closet for a suitable bag. A plastic Ollie's inside of a Winn-Dixie should do the trick.

"This should keep them dry."

"Sis, I *told* you I got those new, hard-shell... saddle-bags. Ah, never mind." Wood accepted the coffee and sandwiches. "Thank you. I will see y'all at Christmas, I guess. you too, *Sandra*."

"Yadda, yadda." Sandy reclaimed her stool. "Thanks for the warning."

Darlene followed her son out through the Florida room and into the carport. She received a sidelong hug from him and a peck on the cheek.

"You slow down on them wet roads, ya hear?"

"And *you* don't take shit from no *man*. Any a these ol' codgers, either. I'm serious. We take care of our own."

"Ah'm not a member a your ol' club an' ah don't want no violence ever committed on mah behalf. Ah cannot fathom from where you get the notion a me as a shrinkin' violet. Your Daddy was the last one used me like a doormat 'n' it's been a good fifteen years since Ah dragged *his* skinny ass out onta the lawn, unconscious."

Wood-Chuck situated the travel-sipper into its holder and dropped the sandwiches into one of the saddle bags. He put on the helmet that had been strapped behind the tank. He hated to do it but the roads *would* be a little slick. "I'm just *sayin'*, Ma,"

"Ah appreciate your concern, darlin'. Just save it for when Ah'm old 'n' feeble."

But then her Baby-boy turned the key, giving thunderous life to his Fat Boy and ending further debate. Darlene covered her ears as he walked the bike backward into the road, the heavy, highly polished footwear already shining with drizzle under the porch light.

Chapter Four

Beauregard LaVelle, was as much Cajun/Creole as anyone from just south of Chauvin, Louisiana, in Terrebonne Parish could possibly be. Aka Boogaloo, aka Beau, aka Beau Valley, aka LaVerne Bogard. *Well, I can't remember all of 'em (let the law's computers keep track).* He roared past valet parking and into the garage entrance of Seminole Hard Rock Casino. There was no admitting gate to give him a ticket that he could cheat out of later. A uniformed guy accepted a $10 bill. "Sorry for the inconvenience," he said, holding out his palm. Boog wrestled his trucker's billfold on a chain from his back pocket. *These boys gettin' theirs up front. I ever hit the lottery (or any kinda major score) there no way in hell any one a these fairy kids back there climbs on this Hog. Hey, though. What about Valet to be also known as, nex' time I need? Might be sweet. Prob'ly go with Beau again for first name. Easy to remember, the name Ol' Pere and Mamere LaVelle give me. Beau Valet? Mebbe no. That sound almost gay.*

The little gate went up and he rumbled up the incline. The Orient garage, it was called. He swung into a spot on the second level so that he could be near the entrance to the casino via the

84 CHRIS DUNGEY

crosswalk. *Still the long hike,* he thought, as he peered down onto Orient Road. Then, on the casino side he rode down an escalator.

His two-room apartment began to close in on him a few hours ago and it didn't have far to close. The *Knuckledicks* clubhouse was shut up dark until Wood got back from his family. Boog had a key but you could only watch so much damn football no matter where you went. The Buccaneers was the only game he really cared about and that was over with and they sucked. He remembered to put in his partial plate, with four front uppers it was one of his most tenderly cared for belongings. Regard for the expensive chompers had also given him brief pause in the past to weigh whether some minor face-offs really *required* maximum violence. Since choosing to do battle usually won out, he became adept at slipping them out. *Wish I scrubbed the rest a them same white.* He put on the *Knuckledicks* bandana; black, with a big fist aiming like a gun, the thumb a phalus. *That all just bullshit that it keeps hair neat under the helmet.* Boog never *wore* a damn helmet anymore but he intended to represent as a *Knuckledick* always.

So, it was time to get out and go for a ride somewhere. He hadn't been in the Seminole *Hard Rock* since the place opened, even though it wasn't a very long ride from either the Clubhouse or his rooms. *Still too fuckin' loud in here with all slots janglin'. Must make that racket whether the place empty or packed; machines clangin' until suckers come back for more. No, wait. Place don't never close. There's always suckers.*

First thing they make ya do is get that stupid card to plug it in machines. Wasn't any more just drop quarters in then arm-wrestle

EVACUATION ROUTE

the fucker. Took only green bills, now. Plug in stupid card to get so-call rewards. Lose enough 'n' they might comp a room. Someday. Card just for somebody to keep eyes on ya, get info. Not any their business, ya ask me. Not givin' my Security number tonight. Gov'ment make 'em do it. Keep score if I win anything. Or, just to learn my habits.

Gov'ment in on this whole scam from the jump. Boog guessed it was to help the Seminoles get some kind of those reparations without pissing off white voters and taxpayers. *Picture ol' Chief Osceola dealin' Texas Hold 'Em. All kind a blacks 'n' boat people, too, workin' in here. Shark bait, droolin' to get their piece a the rock, I think. Freedom? Free stuff, they think it mean. So why did'n' they build this fucker down the Glades, right there on the rez? Answer me that.*

Well, now there they were, already lined up to take a dump on his evening: A black security dude patrolling the first checkpoint, wearing a big handheld antenna communication on his cop belt and a big-ass Glock, too. It gave Boog shivers. Now the guy was eyeing Boog's club colors and his magnificent, braided, (never mind, unwashed) beard. *Yeah, yer lookin' at a real fuckin' Buccaneer, boy. Lemme light some grenade fuses in my beard like ol' Edward Teach. I'm a genu-wine son a my homeboy Jean LaFitte. Watch ya piss right in yer rent-a-cop pants.*

Maybe better check myself. Get off on a wrong foot with these folk 'n' no Wood-Chuck here to put forearm 'roun' my neck: Say c'mon just walk away. Boog get nothin' done this way.

Wood often acted as his emergency brakes. *Fuckin' Wood, though. All fine usin' my temper'ment when it benefits Club 'n' him 'n' it suits the occasion.*

Then a dark-skinned, actual India type of Indian woman from India motioned him forward to the counter to hook him up with the Reward Card and a lanyard to hang it around his neck. *The Player's Club, they call it. Well, I already got a club, fuck-you-very much.* And she was making him *wait*, him the only guy left in line at the moment, while she pretended to do something on her computer. *Don't even have one a those red dots, stuck in her forehead. Mebbe one a the untouchable ones. Like me. Can barely speak English prob'ly. Yeah,...just like me. Cut her the slack, I should.* He wanted so badly to refuse his driver's license and Social Security Number but he gritted his teeth and surrendered both.

So dead in here, like the morgue by Houma when Pere Emile, he pass, was Boog's first reaction to the sparse activity on the broad gaming floor. *Person have to be serious alone or addicted to the bets to be in here tonight. I'm not neither a them things. No way. Maybe the boredom get some a them, too.* But he still had that *Knuckledick* recruiting business to do. So, for a few hours, he would have to be just another one of the dumbasses this place preyed on. *Hard for me, look any way diff'rent, I think. Nothin' I can do 'bout it now.* Was that part of his problem in here? He really didn't appear to be and couldn't *picture* himself as helpless prey.

Even the most shagged out whores would have to be jonesing desperate to work in this scene tonight. It might be a waste of time but he had to get serious about rounding up some bodies. First, he would spend enough to start getting himself comped with drinks; then he'd walk around for awhile. He was carrying enough small bills to make the tribe happy. *Just stick damn card in somewheres 'n' start feedin' the system. Begin with a five until one a these slag waitress pay me some attention. Couldn't even tip with old tokens no more. Cleavage in here like a bunch more slots. No way were some a la tetas real.*

Boog wasn't going to play poker with only the dealer and maybe one other sucker. *Might as well just hand over money an' leave.* He walked past empty tables or tables with only a few other carcasses being bled here and there. Quarter to ten. *It has to pick up in here. Why even stay open on holiday?* He plunked down at a *Laverne & Shirley* machine then plugged in the card. The lanyard immediately tangled through his chin braids like an anchor rope in Cyprus roots. The cash hole was as grabby as a woman, snatching the first fiver away from his fingers. *That leather jacket Squiggy's wearin' is a insult to real bikers.* All of the criss-crossing lines for different ways to score were meaningless to Boog. He pushed the buttons, with no understanding or strategy as he watched out the corner of his eye for the approach of anyone with a tray.

Boogaloo made a few plays at the minimum wager. He managed not to lose too quickly. He took his time, pretending to study and analyze that tangle of lines. But after dropping only three dollars in ten minutes, he began to fume. *Where in hell are comp drinks for moi? Gettin' dry throat in here.* Even the reduced cigarette haze of sparce attendance was worse than any produced in the *Knuckledick* Clubhouse.

From an inside pocket of his leathers, Boog took out his own pack. A cheap gas-station lighter was tucked inside the cellophane. As he lit up, he sensed a human presence at his side. *Finally. Get a mixed drink. Easier make it last. Stay cold longer than beer, so much fuckin' ice with they water down drinks.*

But, no. It was some old flooze who couldn't manage to find, in all that airplane hanger of empty slot chairs, a machine to leave him some elbow room.

"I just love these old sitcom ones, don't you? I like that *Happy Days*, too. How it takes us back to times that *were* happier. And sometimes *Sex in the City*."

Boogaloo grunted, not risking so much as a quick glance. *How long ago was your ass without the wrinkles?* He saw just enough in his peripheral vision, like when he spurred the bike between halted lanes of a traffic jam. *Ol' slag's hair piled up like prom night at Senior Center. Somethin' dyed into it close to Gulf Stream blue. Why no corsage? Some kind a poufy silk scarf cover that wrinkly turkey neck. Why, old mamere, you don't just give up?* He couldn't make out her figure but the noise of a walker being folded and placed out of the way told him that this would not be his first talent interview of the evening. He heard the snap of a lighter and then wisps of menthol smoke invaded his Camel airspace.

"Hey, doll. How are *you* doin' tonight," the woman croaked through her fumes.

Jesus. This one will need the hole in her neck; one a those microphones make her sound like robot. He placed his own heater down on a Seminole *Hard Rock* ashtray. *That's a cool lookin' redskin*

EVACUATION ROUTE

wailin' on guitar. Must boost me one for home. "Don't worry about it, *Grandmere*," he answered. Boog glared straight ahead.

Grandma had no retort except to expel an insulted menthol huff. Still out the corner of his eye, Boogaloo glimpsed a bony claw snatch the Player's Club card back out of its slot. The walker reopened emphatically behind him then the hag (he had enough information to decide *that* much) peg-legged away toward Video Poker.

"What can I bring you?"

Boogaloo swiveled on his seat to peer at the waitress who'd snuck up on him. She looked to be about housewife age. Plus, short and squat, a little roll pooching out just above her change apron. *Still though—her tits, strainin' over one a them boosty-air rigs.* "Where you were hidin', cher?"

Now she cocked her hip and tapped an order pad against it, all annoyed and impatient. *Really? Aren't ya supposed be workin' mostly for my tips?*

"What can I *bring* you?" she repeated.

That attitude and that mouth, though he had done nothing, yet, to deserve it. Maybe he would have to go ahead and *earn* her contempt. *But okay, Boog. Jesus, try'n stay cool 'n' with the cool head. Friendly enough to get along. How you don't know, in this place, who might be usin' their ass for the side hustle. Or, might know other poon. A friend, a relative. All these workin' in here, old 'n' young, flashin' cleavage like that? Does tribe require this, or the girls workin' it for themselves? Little Merry. Small but perfect, hers were. Knuckledick brothers have climb on worse than this here. Or even ol' Grandmere, from before.*

"Jack, straight up." *Can sip that for a hour before all the ice melt.* The waitress turned away. Boog studied her behind until she was gone. *No, you can't rule her out.*

Goddamn that Bella 'n' Merry, leavin' Club to desperate measures. Ungrateful, disloyal, after so long they was treated like family. Nearly. When I catch up with them, an' I will, sometime...Well, there might be some wet work done. Only to decide how hard. A few weeks they be gone, only, but still this grind in my gears like gravel. Disrespect our feelin's. Never for me easy lettin' it go. Never been. They don't know what is comin' from behind over their shoulder. Like gator with jaws into the goat kid, Boog never let go. Pere Emile put it just that way a few time.

Pere was troubled, always, by his son's narrow focus when angered. The little boy set relentless, pointless tasks for himself for getting even. *But ol' Pere, though. He was the one for havin' same ugly streak. Long as he kept sober. He could'n' stay mean after fourth or fifth beer. Sometime I miss ol' Pere Emile every day.*

Like out in front a Pere's fav'rite roadhouse between Lake Boudreaux launch an' home. Called just Cold Beer. I wait outside to ride rest the way with Pere Emile from whole day on the water. Other fishin' kids pull in the parkin' lot. Oh shit, I think. It's Alvin "The Abutment" Malvaux 'n' some the boys from up South Houma High who play football 'n' fuck the cheerleaders like in a teen movie. Their daddies own big trawlers, find fish by the sonar image. Not old school authentic like Emile LaVelle, usin' the local knowledge

EVACUATION ROUTE 91

from many year. "Listen here, Beau-regard," The Abutment say to me. "Glad we find you here. An' your nasty Papa, too. How it is, we have took a collection up, all us 'n' Coach Brusseau, him even, too. We raise enough for you to have a haircut 'n' also for Pere Emile. You go ahead, take it. When we see you Monday, you will look sharp. Yes, boy? Maybe after hot bath, too?" I drop their bills straight onto the ground. They flutter, skitter in white dust like leaves in light breeze off the Gulf, that sound. "Now, don't be that way," The Abutment says. "You gather them gen'rous bills back up or you will eat 'em."

I lunge for that nose-tackle, The Abutment, first. (Do they call him so cuz the nose always broken an' with a Band-Aide?) I'm punchin' for that thick throat in the neck from lifting the weight. I get in one sideways kick at his runnin'-back's nuts, who has charge at me too. I'm screamin' crazy anger of insults like kung-fu Bruce Lee. But second kick he grab it so my damp, bilge-water sneaker come off. Someone fist land from behind. It break open this gush a stars from back of my neck through to my jaw. But, I punch the The Abutment so deep with next uppercut swing my hand stays caught under belt buckle, into fat, but with muscle under his fat 'n' I can't pull my fist back out. Where is it? I am in his belly up to my wrist? More stars pour up from my nose, through snot 'n' blood meetin' the first stars. My fish-scaly hand still trapped in fat of The Abutment. My left hand still loose, maybe come to the rescue, try to find that fat face. No smile now. But, no good power in next punches, mine, throwin' 'em over my head without no leverage. They land soft like girl slaps. Then I sink teeth in his tee-shirt 'n' fat, mebbe deep enough, get into muscle, just above my right hand, caught 'n' yankin' like muskrat leg in the trap. Mebbe I have to chew it off? "Jesus Chris'," he scream. "Rabid motherfucker bit me! I'm gonna... Get him loose a me, somebody!"

I never hear what the nose-tackle intend to do back to me. Anyway, don't just talk about it, I think. Show me, fat cocksucker, I think. But those words don't come out my lips. Tastin' much blood 'n' swallowin'. But whose blood? The stars expand, expand more. They blink out dark, look like picture negatives. Came a punch I never feel, don't remember later, but loosen' four my upper teeth, they hangin' out my gums. From the runnin'-back, he did it? My right hand musta come free, along with a cut from the nose-tackle belt buckle. Bloody threads a torn tee-shirt cloth I still grip, tear it away. Still in my hand when Pere Emile nudge me with a boot, weavin' all around over me. Where you lose yer shoe at? Come on, stan' up, now. We better go for hospital. Hold a hand up on you mout'. Where we have money come from, you t'ink, make you pretty again with dentures? Try hold 'em in place.

Boog waited and waited, playing the stupid game until his five bucks had been fully consumed and digested. He seemed mentally stuck there due to small, carefully timed gains won by Lenny and Shirley, apparently, on his behalf. He always liked the brunette better. Laverne was too much sheeny for his Cajun tastes. *Has that horsey face, too, like that one slut on Sex in City.* He watched only basic cable, shared with three other flats in the dump he currently called home, The *Knuckledicks* watched it a few times in reruns just for laughs. They all would've showed her a Mr. Big, was the easy joke. *Put bag over her head first.* Jesus, his throat was getting dry. Did that skank decide to go on her break? He jerked his Player's Club card out and turned in the seat just as the sullen waitress lowered a tray toward his face.

"Well, *that* was fast." Boog reluctantly dropped a dollar tip onto the tray and took up his drink. He *did* want to continue drinking free-of-charge. The waitress stuffed the tip away without acknowledging his generosity.

Boog stubbed out his cigarette and sipped. Should he move closer to one of the bars, maybe? He surveyed the blinking, chiming horizon; spotted a bank of television screens, most of them showing what must be the same final football game of the holiday evening. *Like trees around waterin' hole to shade gazelles. These gazelles blowin' their mortgage.*

Sitting down where the sparse prey gathered made more sense. If there were any cumdumps working in here tonight, they would gravitate to where the weak ones strayed from the herd. *Most pros too lazy to strut around. Tonight, they feed their own buzz, relax on their moneymakers.* It made sense that they'd let the kill come to them.

Should give a try my own self, with sports above to stare at. Enforce patience on drinkin' 'n' much spendin'. He navigated the labyrinth of game trails to reach the distant oasis then lifted himself onto a stool. He placed his drink on the bar and was quickly offered a cocktail napkin by the reeking bartender. *Euro scent?* The guy looked him over for a moment but then withdrew when Boog did not immediately order. *That's right, Kyle or Chad. I drink free-a-charge right now 'n' will finish this one before I need next. Leave me the fuck alone for now.*

The countertop version of video poker in front of him seemed to wink. *Like any whore; friendly, long as I am generous. No mercy after.* He loaded a five dollar bill into the machine, its mouth as wide as any of the big machines out on the floor. He watched the Eagles and Cardinals for a full minute before pressing the wager button. Old Kurt Warner just got sacked hard and dragged himself back to the huddle, glaring at the Cardinal weak-side tackle who allowed the assault. Boogaloo made a minimum, quarter bet. *Ol' Kurt should get that Bible-whacky wife a his turn her preachy badmouth on them linemen. Sandblasted witch. Look like makeup test dummy. Does ol' Kurt ever picture her decomposing in shallow grave?*

He laughed out loud at what he considered to be pretty sick witticisms, even for *this* bad mood. He reminded himself, again, that he must really *take a pill.* Giving voice to those sort of thoughts had lately caused Wood-Chuck to wince, if he heard them. Shake *his* dreadlocks and say *ouch* or *yikes,* almost fairy words Boog would never use. But Wood's scary hair was gone now, just to please family and enjoy time up the coast. *Serious though. Must do that. Swallow sedation next time in the john. If rest a this Jack does not smooth me.*

There were no acceptable girls lounging, at least on his side of the oval oasis. A single overweight wildebeest and one bartender, both men. He doubted if the opposite side, separated from his surveillance by the neck-kinking HD screens, was more richly populated. He sipped his whiskey again then pressed the button on the machine to deal the cards. With a realistic sound effect of snaps, the cards were shown to him. Two kings. He did not need to know much to touch above the three cards that were no help. The little computer chip inside dealt to him again: *Deuce a hearts, jack a diamond, six a club. Fuck! This rat-bastard rigged six ways from bayou sunset. But hold up now.* The thing rang up some credits in his favor. *Okay. There ya go, see? Game on here playin' now is name Deuces Wild. Read the damn rules first, dumb fuck.* There were six different kinds of poker in the box. *Shit, did I discard a deuce last hand?* This fresh frustration promoted a refueled resentment for his failed seeking for biker friendly whores. *All in vain, this night for Boogaloo. Everythin'. But I have some kinda calmin' opiates in one a these pockets.*

The loser four stools away shouted suddenly as if he had just put together a royal flush. *So why his box in front not go all crazy with bells 'n' whistles?* When Boog turned his attention, the dude was still pumping his fists at the screen above. On instant replay, big Donovan McNabb floated a nice pass into the corner of the end zone to DeSean Jackson. *Now they're all dancin' 'roun' like they do. An', there come floatin' a penalty flag for that bullshit. Good. Nobody wanta that. Guy down the bar must have skin in this game. Hope he didn't bet the under. Fourth quarter. Score already 41-20. Plenty time left for more.*

Time to move aroun' more. Do business before pleasure. Before head become too much hammered. Slow it seem to take in here.

This water hole not attract any interest from predators. Except me. Where are workin' girls, tonight?

Boog cashed out, took his card along with the little grocery slip of $.60 cents winning profits. *No, but how much money you put in, fool?* Peeking around the other side, his belief that it would be just more desolation was confirmed. There wasn't another soul drinking there. He decided that he should find the sports book, though it was probably also a sausagefest of post-holiday loneliness. The drink went with him, now shaded lighter by ice melt. *This level a restraint, though. So far. Slammin' spirits always attract trouble to me. An' for close by civilians. But remember, no such thing as innocent bystander. Where I hear that? Means all did wrong, sometime. Sounds true. Never, was Boog ever innocent.*

Wandering through the maze of slots, Boog saw a distant but much broader display of neon and shifting sports images: More hockey, basketball, and that lone surviving football game, exhausting its two-minute warning with more commercials. *This,* he thought, *"must be headquarters a sports bettin' in Seminole Hard Rock."*

From afar, there appeared to be many more screens than at earlier bar kiosks he'd passed. Now, the postgame talking heads interrogated exhausted athletes, whose bare heads steamed or streamed sweat while they uttered their muted responses. If there was any audio over there, it was swallowed by the constant beep and bleep, the clanging of surrounding slots. He trudged in that direction, now quite disoriented. *Where did I come in from to the gamin' floor? Which way to go back?* But that *had* to be the so-called Sports

EVACUATION ROUTE   97

Book, like they had on big boats moored in Biloxi, along the Gulf Coast where the *Knuckledicks* sometimes rode. There were smaller gambling boats, too, near Tampa. *Sim'lar ones in Mississippi like you see on news, flipped 'n' flung around by Katrina. A mile inland, some of 'em landed.*

Why they call it Sports Book anyways? Scare away redneck boys who don't connect usin' a bookie. Not turned off, myself, now I know what it is. Go in 'n' pick horses awhile. Person could win if he know how. They must still be runnin' races in that Abby-dabby or some such A-rab resort. Still yesterday there. Man made island for rich towelheads. I will pick up a tout sheet 'n' try figure it out. No, but all them workout times 'n' past performance 'n' track condition. Too much to learn in one night. No math for Boog, please. Make as much sense from that as criss-cross lines on the slot screen.

But when he reached the cluster of televisions, there *was* no Sports Book. It was just a bigger bar. No obvious whores there, either. *Three guys. Not even call it a crowd on this night, gettin' neon tan at this oasis.* He swallowed his pride, lit a cigarette then ordered a refill of Jack. After he paid, he asked the bartender for directions.

"Nah, man. There isn't any sports book in here, just like they don't allow craps, blackjack or roulette. The tribe *paid* for a new law pushed through just to have our poker tables. Sorry."

"Not your fault, boss," Boog mumbled. He had *paid* for this drink and now would have to turn back in the direction he'd come from. If he could figure *that* out. He searched two of the zipper pockets then downed two reds with the first fresh, cold sip. "That some strange shit, though, ya know, boss?" He slid off the bar stool, carrying the drink.

Boog now figured that further attendance in the Seminole Hard Rock would only be good money thrown after bad. It was time to cut his losses. As he passed an aisle of nearly unattended poker tables, he saw that even the buffet, a large wing curving away from a distant wall, was closed and dark. The cashier/maitre'd stand was empty. Dark, velvet ropes like at the movies blocked the entrance. *This place startin' to suck without no redemption. Hell, what if it was breakfast I want? Could start callin' it breakfast any time now.* It felt like it must be after midnight though he wore no watch. *Might's well scout for pussy down at 34th Street. Sometime decent lookin' talent found there even on dead Holiday, Might have to contend with rival management. Maybe. But, no fears. Break the boredom. An' there's places to get a slice or a hotdog. Any time in the night. By myself, prob'ly not safe for conflict. That is Wood's whisper to my brain. Outnumber, I get ass beat half the time. Not worth movin' on someone else poon. How would that feel for me? Fuckin' Wood. Almost never think of it to blame my friend. But, if he was here...Damn that fuckin' Bella 'n' Merry. How much I wish to run into either one.*

Back out and past the hotel reception desk. He saw a few out-of-town guests, returning from holiday with relatives, headed for the elevators. Others were already marching the opposite way dragging their luggage. Boogaloo turned left at Reception, past a floodlighted display case of rock-and-roll memorabilia. *Piano from Elton John. Tunes speak to me. Like Crocodile Rock. If you only knew 'gators, sissy boy; would wet in your silly costume. Saturday night, though. All right for fightin'. He sung that true.* But these bits of garage sale after-thoughts on the walls as he stalked out; (Joanie Mitchell's belt from 1968). The rock stars had donated crap. *Signed guitars hangin'. None from Cajun boys. No Michael Ducet, no Buckwheat Zydeco.*

He wadded his jackpot receipt. Turning slightly to avoid littering, he found the domed trash can and, against every inclination, carefully stuffed the little scrap through the hatch. Never know when security might decide to have a problem just because it was *him* and how he looked. Then, over his shoulder, he caught a glimpse of something that quickened a surge of bile into the Jack Daniels, already warming his gut. At the far end of the lobby, just then stepping into an elevator, was a fine looking young ass in a brown leather miniskirt. He felt certain of this recognition. Long brown legs; haunches always strutting. But *this* woman here had nearly blond hair. Maybe cut too short to be who he thought it was at first. *Was she fuckin' serious, cuttin' off all that shiny black hair? I make a mistake, must be. But, no! I know that ass 'n' that mini.* Several middle-aged tourists stepped in between them, all hurrying into the elevator behind the woman.

Hold that, hold that elevator, damn it! Buzzed enough to shout it out loud, but he caught himself. Just enough of the reds were now wandering slowly into his bloodstream to arrest a bull rush through the civilians. Then that ass was gone, into the elevator. He hustled as discreetly as he could, a sissy looking race-walk, double-time toward the alcove of lifts. Too far to catch her. He knew better than to run. There, nearby, stood the black, armed security guard again; a skinny white guy with him, now, but fully capable of a having a bad attitude. *Their trigger fingers even itchier, prob'ly. To show who is boss man.* Boogaloo didn't pass anywhere near the Registration Check-In for the hotel earlier. He carried no luggage. Even these drowsy rent-a-cops were trained to notice such characteristics of arriving guests. And, the irregularities. *But that has to be that meatgrinder, Bella, just as mixed blood like me. She with no luggage, either, just like Bella wouldn't. Well, maybe bring somethin' empty sometime, to steal shit in. Those uniform pricks see me sprintin'. Maybe to assault or harass a legitimate guest? Oh no you don't, biker trash! Hold up there, buddy! Come on back here a minute! Then mebbe vi'lence come out if pills aren't workin' yet.*

There were four elevators, two on each side, when he had quick-stepped over there. He looked back and, *yes siree, one uniform give me stink eye, lookin' me over for any excuse, escort me out. Lookin' down his nose.* But, just as quickly, the guy turned his attention away, eyeing some loud, college aged kids who had just entered. Down the escalator from the crosswalk they'd come; jostling, shoving, poking in the ribs, all with backwards baseball caps. *Oh, maybe this be easier fun then wrestlin' with a grown assed man, that pirate! Oh, please, please, they think: Give us reason to doublecheck for fake ID. Aren't you boys already intoxicated? Just a little hassle fun to liven up their slowass evenin'.*

The girl went up in the righthand bank of elevators. That narrowed it down by half for Boog, but into which half? One of the arrows was still going up while one was coming down. The one

EVACUATION ROUTE 101

going up stopped on 3, but then stopped again on 4. The other one stopped on 2 but then changed its mind, headed back up to 5. It started down again to pause on 4. *Someone fuck up 'n' go too far. Just dumb luck if that was even Bella. Not a sign a that longlegged bitch for a month, then now, outta nowheres, by pure chance, we cross our paths.*

Boog turned and walked slowly back across the lobby. He was reluctant to just leave, to just let it go. That juice for confrontation still coursed in his veins. It would tease for a few more minutes, before relaxing. Maybe come back to him for violence downtown. The noisy young men made it past Barney Fife and his black partner. Now they debated in front of the Player's Club desk whether to bother with Reward Cards. The disappointed Security bulls were split up, one to ride up the short escalator and watch the valet guys get wet. A rain must be falling. Some A-rab in a white jacket mopped up shiny, wet tracks near the front desk entrance. A red sign stood unfolded, warning guests not to slip.

What could he do? Must be *something* he could do? He would love to spring some ruckus upon her ass. Watch those big, brown, sorta gook eyes bug out in surprise. But riding up wasn't going to be a reasonable options. He must realize this and turn sharply on the dime. There. There, the jumpstart flood of adrenalin subsided like indigestion.

Even if I know which floor, what to do then? Run up 'n' down hallway, bang on doors? No john so stupid he open to let me in. En colere 'n' cursin' pirate biker. Or stand aside for public scene a me slappin' cockbreath outta her mouth, or black one a those eyes, draggin' her to elevator. An' then what, suppose I make it down the lobby? An' now I work up myself all over again. That rush. Those reds were bogus? Easy, ami. Think more level. Take two more before goin' in another bar. Or, breakfast somewhere?

She would be in there with the john for most three, four hour. Those two whores thought theirselfs high-end 'n' expected to get paid more than anyone else for just a quickie. Weird, how they enjoyed, with beaucoup fake sincere, addin' more time 'n' extras to the trick. They always try hangin' out, like they was girlfriend to the john. Maybe they wanta sleep in clean sheets, have the long shower, see how big dent they make in mini-bar. They call it the fringe benefit.

Okay, but then they complain why did Wood 'n' me not wanta wait outside for all hours in case payment hassle or for the ride home. They were crazy? Was I 'n' Wood their fluffers? Pissed off cuz of when Wood 'n' me take our cut in advance, then say adios. Don't understand we have important club matters. We leave them to work out their own profit with threats of screams, fake cell phone calls to boyfriends down in a car. They do their mini-bar scam in case, so not to go away ever with hands empty. So then little Merry buys a car. She knew how to drive all that time? Another reason they decide for turning backsides to insult Knuckledick management. Drive their own transportation, now. But what they have got for the safety net? Which always would have been friendship of all Knuckledick brothers.

Back up the escalator then, Boog made the long march through the covered crosswalk to the garage. Back out past the metal detectors *(merci! A-rab cocksuckers! Thanks for that 'n' all close'-circuit cameras now, everywhere) plus two more armed ID checkers. Twice as many security as needed tonight. Union loafers just tryin' stay awake. Even tribal management don't dare send one a them home.* He pushed through the final set of turnstiles, the first and last old school defense against terrorists and underage drinkers.

Boog fired up the Harley after digging goggles out from the bottom of a saddlebag. He couldn't remember where he acquired them. They were just cheap ones for swimmers. Never did he go near a pool or to the beach, but those little bastards worked nicely a couple of times for rain and spray. Astride the Hog, he stretched the headband to get the goggles over the back of his pirate bandana. The damned things snapped, of course. *How could this night go more wrong?* The rush he'd felt of a possible confrontation with Bella now burned lower with a heavy, whiskey sigh. The *fight* adrenalin could only last for so long without being used. He tossed the heat rotted goggles onto the asphalt and then had a brainstorm.

Easing the Hog backward, Boog wheeled around to drive all the way up the garage's incline. He refrained from launching forward with the usual screech of rubber. He wasn't going to escape immediately out of the nearby *Exit* arrow that seemed such a good spot a few hours ago. He decided to bide his time a bit longer. Now, observing the 10 mph rule of the Seminoles and their flunkies, he intended to seek out that shitbox ride of Merry's; have a look all the way up to the last parking slot on the roof. She might even be down the other way toward the rear *Exit,* opposite where he came in. *Can't remember the make, but I will recognize. Green 'n' black, it might be. Had some kinda canvas top over backseat? The cargo part of it? Yes. Yes, 'n' the black part suppose to make it a convertible? Canvas? Prob'ly not. Vinyl. Still shiny, most of it, except cracked, faded from sun along where frame give it shape. Terrific deal, she musta found, just to buy. Would not take one for a gift.*

There were plenty of big Buicks all in one place near the 2nd floor crosswalk, even with the casino so dead. Some gleaming-like-showroom cars in the well lighted facility. *Fuckin' snowbirds start flockin' in. Plenty a Ram pickups, too. Them polished to shine like dealer commercial; oh, please come down! Wax only save repo man the trouble. Fuckin' yuppies, or somethin'. New Age bastards would have to let rides go, try to save the mortgage first. Then comes clean-out-your-desk, severin' pay, unemployment. Beat-up Chevys along here, too; all make 'n' model with doors rust, noisy hinge 'n' quarterpanels prob'ly flap goin' down the road. Confederate flag licenseplate holders ever'where. A few a my people must be in there somewheres, just for fleecing. No way they stay at that hotel.* More than half of the parking spots were empty, so he made good time with his search.

Boog crept up the gentle incline, with just enough momentum to keep the Hog from tipping. He turned right with his boot extended as each level turned upward toward the next. Between the concrete columns, over low retaining walls, he could see the windshields of vehicles parked on the downward slope. *No sign a the little cochon's ride.* He saw it only that one time, parked outside the *Knuckledick's* clubhouse. *Whores came to whine about not enough of work, low tips gave by members. Members in same pinch like everyone. It had to be explain to them. Back in September, with storm curlin' up to the Gulf. Their usual trade mighta been hunkered down already, besides broke. Nailin' up plywood in windows. Was that the last warning they give to us?*

Boog could not remember all the circumstances of the confrontation exactly, except that they nearly needed to draw a picture for them of the logic that he and Wood could not control the weather. They could not control the generosity of Members. They could not control the fact that many of the usual johns may have lost their jobs. *Shoulda ordered girls to give it for free; lesson not to badger me 'n' Wood: From now on, don't come into here unless invited or to service a brother. No more cheap drink. Maybe you are spoiled by our generousness nature. Maybe try screwin' better, 'n' for longer. Nah, never freebies for no one. Only ones in the schedule 'n' lifeless if that man a bad tipper. But we never threaten anything. Me 'n' Wood decide we ain't changin'. Pride. Should be good enough for them.*

Then Boog saw the yellow flashers of a security van idling down on the other side. *Bug zappers. There it come, again. More fight-or-flight juice for moi.* The old caveman adrenaline came pumping into his system, but he almost never heeded the flight part. That vehicle would be headed back up behind him in a few minutes. Boog emerged onto the roof, began to feel the light rain so he picked up speed. At least it was a warm rain, summer tropical and slow. *Merde!* As his lightly braking boot skimmed a shallow puddle. He made a careful loop into the Down exit. Rain upon many old stains of oil made traction like roller-blades on ice had sprawled him onto concrete enough times.

He would easily make it down to the gate ahead of Security if he gave up looking for that whatever-it-was the little *sousoute* was driving. *Merry must share the car with the brown one if she is not here. So where that other workin' at?* He squeezed the clutch and let the Hog roll under its own gravity. *Merry's little shitbox not in here, I think.*

Doubt began then, whether that leather miniskirt had been Bella's in the first place. Then Boog remembered that there were two other parking garages on the property, plus free surface lots nearby that offered shuttle service to the casino. The fresh swelling of adrenaline left him in a few heartbeats, replaced by a cold, uncomfortable sweat.. *In vain, all this plot and scheme going in my head, cryin the wolf.* This happened to be the only parking structure physically attached to the casino. It would make the most sense for Bella to park here if there were open spots. Merry might even have dropped her off in front of Valet guys.

But now there arrived an exhaustion. *Finally, the reds all workin'. Where you've been when I need better control?* There was no use in paying another $10, at each of the other two huge ramps. There was no booth or lift-gate at the bottom to delay departure from this one because they already took his money. Not even enough anger, now, to inspire leaving a long tire stain back out onto Orient Road. Time for more *Jack Daniels* in with the downers. *Go somewheres I know and they know me.*

Chapter Five

Wood-Chuck Spurgeon knew he would have to see Booga-loo LaVelle *sometime* on Black Friday. There was mopping out to do. They skipped the chore Wednesday night so Wood could get a little sleep before traveling. A delivery of beer cases was scheduled to arrive in the afternoon and it was Boog's job to stack them in and to roll out any empty kegs. But Wood wasn't mentally prepared, yet, for Boog's cheery company and the occasional aura of tensions he brought into the space around him. *Please, just gimme a few relaxin' hours.*

He wheeled the *Fat Boy* at idle, through the gate in the high, corrugated junkyard fence of their property, then around to the back of the *Knuckledick's* Clubhouse. He enjoyed his own reserved spot there, a perk of leadership that sometimes came in handy.

Wood had to brake hard when he discovered his sidekick's presence. *Well, shit. What has he done to himself now?* There LaVelle lay, sprawled on the cement slab behind the kitchen door like a cadaver ready to be opened. The porch was just a few inches higher than the concrete curbstones protecting the back wall. Boog's Hog had screened, momentarily, his grim, trafficfatality form from Wood's view. But there he was, greasy dreadlocks and braided beard framing his face like a dirty Rastafarian halo, a forearm shielding his eyes from the early sun. Yep. Wood could see freshly abraded knuckles and a torn flannel shirt under the leather vest. Boog's mouth hung open in rasping, drooling sleep. Bit of a split lip freshly coagulated. *What nightmares has he added to the dogfight already snarling through that brain?*

Dead to the world, Boog didn't flinch as the *Fat Boy*'s front tire skidded to a halt just short of his toe. The tips of his normally immaculate boots looked as though he'd been dragged through abrading gravel. Wood's eyes shifted along the back porch slab to a Styro coffee cup, the plastic stir stick still guarding the sip hole.

Plucking out his earplugs, Spurgeon thought: *Did he lose his key, mebbe? Or just the rest of his reptile mind?*

Boog finally looked up, a forearm flopping away from his eyes. He groaned his way into a sitting position. The grime infused hands now cradled his face for a few moments before he slowly stood. In this effort he resembled nothing so much as a VA patient or assisted living resident. Bike crashes and incidents of violence equal to an *NFL* lineman's Sunday afternoon highlighted *that* health profile. *Looks like my ol' man*, Wood thought, *last time I ever bailed his ass out.* "Lose your key?"

"No, I got it... somewheres." Boog mumbled, patting his thigh pockets. "Just need more of some...need fresh air." He stooped slowly to retrieve his coffee. A sick pallor faded his normally oiled bronze complexion. His features immediately gleamed with flop

EVACUATION ROUTE   109

sweat from the exertion. He hung his head after taking a sip. "Wood?" The voice sounded like a plea for euthanasia.

"Yeah, bro. I'm here. But, fresh air in this neighborhood? Yer sure up awful early. An' ya don't look so hot, I gotta say."

"Thanks for tender thoughts. It's only because of I am awake too late, 'n' jumped by a pimp '*n*' his ho. That's all. Can't even have a word with 'em for free. Way too long after last call. With no Wood that have my back. Real job done tn me, yeah? Some Hondurus youth. I pick wrong chika, askin' was she happy with her management." Now the Cajun man reached inside his leathers again and brought out his partial plate. He held it up to the sun. The metal parts gleamed like a tiara. "Now my head 'n' soul are in the lowest, brother."

No shit, Wood told himself.

"In my gut, too, has gone bad. Mebbe I have got the botuliz poison? I ate late hotdog from Seven-11. Middle a the night. About. Bastards, the A-rabs that run it. They don't change them off rollers, days after days."

Right. Botulism. Why not throw in anthrax while yer shittin' on the Arabs? Prob'ly wasn't even Arabs. Coulda been Pakistani or Indian. Boog wouldn't know the difference. Or Hondurans from any a the other...Latins. That wiener was prob'ly loaded up with onion, Tabasco, 'n' melted cheese. He'd get it down in three bites into the alcohol, pills, energy drink, whatever else, then wonder why it didn't sit right. Who did he think he was foolin'? But, Wood-Chuck seldom had to look at his assistant this early in the day. Or, have cause to picture him rolling around in his grimy sheets (if he used sheets); ill, fresh from the nightmare of a beating and rare defeat. *Mike Tyson, shocked, on his ass to Buster Douglas.* For all Wood knew, Boog's battered condition reprensented a *typical* morning. Either way, he was a frightful, cautionary sight. Wood unlocked then reached in for the light switch. "Well, c'mon in then. Tell ol' Wood where all it hurts at. We'll put ya back together cuz we got chores backin' up on us."

"Bless you, brother." LaVelle followed like a cripple toward Lourdes. He closed the door after tossing the red, plastic stir stick onto the pavement behind him.

Wood was relieved to find clean pots, pans, and the few kitchen utensils stacked on the drainboard and sink in the pantry. He couldn't remember scrubbing them Wednesday night but he'd been pretty buzzed. That night before Thanksgiving was supposed to be the biggest bar night of the year, though the *Knuckledicks* hosted no homecoming college students.

Their simple menu required few culinary tools. The bill of fare was limited by a slim budget for basic groceries which Wood needed Boog to go purchase. There was no deep fat fryer which would have added substantially to the club's insurance premium. There was no grill, either, though Wood often fired up a nice propane one out in back for picnic type meats. From time to time, he also put baking sheets of loaded potato skins or steak fries into the oven. They were the frozen kind, usually bought the day of, a few bags at a time, as the menu was formulated. The freezer above their little refrigerator was too small for more than a few bottles of vodka. Two or three industrial tubs of pasta salad from Gordon's, some lunchmeat and a block of cheese was about all Wood had ever tried to fit into the lower unit..

The members appreciated the modest prices even if these were subsidized out of drug sales and their own dues. All of this was understood. Anyway, what was of most concern to them was to keep the premium craft beers coming at two bucks a bottle. This benefit was also subsidized but where else could *anyone* drink that cheaply?

On his ride in, Spurgeon thought about bean soup for today. If he could get Boog to wash his hands, and then wash them again, he'd have him make up a stack of baloney sandwiches, too. *Orrr,* how about this? Maybe *panfry* the baloney? Send him out to buy a few tomatoes. Now Wood remembered that he'd skipped breakfast. That's where the inspirations were coming from! Extra thick baloney with some tomato slices.

"What time we'll open?" Boog sat on a stool at the end of the bar, his forehead resting on the front padding. The outside coffee was no longer steaming..

"I'm putting up *Noon* on the front door." Wood said. "Lot a guys'll sleep all day if they've got it off from work."

Wood hung his leather vest on a coat hook by the back door. Boog raised up and began, painfully, to shrug out of his leathers.

"Listen, bro. Leave yer gear on. I got an idea for lunch. You well enough to make a ride to the store soon?" At some point, maybe while the guy ran this errand, Wood intended to retrieve an *Axe* spray from his own saddlebags and thoroughly defunk that stool, even if no one but himself would ever notice a disagreeable scent.

"Sure, but listen first, I...part of a reason for me here so early is cuz...still we have the problem to find replacement girls for our brothers. An' for makin' you 'n' me some income on the side."

"Still no luck, huh?" Spurgeon could not shake the notion that this might be a good time to just end that particular perk. There was enough dope money coming in and the guys were more than capable of finding, or rather coercing, their own dates. But what then would be he and Boog's wellpaid function? Okay, he knew what LaVelle's ugly purpose was. But, was providing whores actually a part of the pair's job description? Or, had they taken it on to secure their salaries? To enhance their value.

"Not so much luck for finding. Maybe I spook them away?"

"You?" Wood managed not to laugh. *Ya think*? The question cleared his friend's range of nuance by a safe margin.

Wood drew the curtain back on the pantry cabinet which took up a third of the space along the back wall, after the tiers of spirits behind the bar. The stove and refrigerator were set in a corner at the end of the pantry space, with the office door between. *Yup. Two #10 cans right where I thought. A good start.* He would add to it, of course. That was his chef specialty: jazzing up plain, cheap food. There were two little onions left in a net bag with brown bits of peel molting all over, and two 8-packs of sesame buns. *How old are these, though? Gimme a break here.* He could see two green spots of mold through the bag. *I can pinch them off. Nuke 'em for fifteen seconds, should soften 'em up.*

He'd have to make a quick list for Boog, printing large and as clearly as possible. Add a package of ham lunchmeat that he could dice up for the soup. How much would it cost for a full-size deli baloney they could slice themselves? Slice it thick as a hamburger patty? The *Knuckledicks* should actually be voting him a raise to his grocery allowance. A raise appropriate to his miracle working skills.

"'Cept for *one* thing, Wood. Think I mighta seen one a them."

Wood paused, the can opener just then penetrating the first lid, releasing a bubble of cheesy brown juice. "Say *what*, now? Which one?" He turned back to Boog, leaning the small of his back against the corner of the pantry nook.

"Could not catch up to make sure. It was in the Indian casino. Too much space 'n' with citizen people all around. Security, they watch me like buzzards."

How could they not and still keep their jobs? Wood thought. He watched LaVelle come around to the back of the bar to place his coffee into the microwave. Boog set the timer, pushed the button to send it whirring.

"Yer not s'ppose to nuke them cups like that. Ruins the ozone layer or some damn thing,"

"Where this layer even is at? Fuck 'em." Boog stared into the humming box. The little bulb in there had long been burned out but the Plexiglas would begin to steam up to signal that cooking had progressed. "It was mini-skirt I see. Her ass was just goin' in a elevator. I witness it had to be Bella's. That ass, I mean. Wasn't no way to follow her or I get thrown out. Security watchin' me, like I tell you."

Wood resumed cranking the canopener. He wouldn't need to add any garlic that was for sure "Wow, Bella, ya think? No, but ya know, I can see how that makes sense. Of the two of 'em, she always had the most highest opinion a herself. Always thought she should be a callgirl or a escort instead of hop-in-the-car streetwalker. That's what she was tryin' to do before Merry brought her in, 'n' not very good at it accordin' to Merry. Maybe she could pass for high class, I dunno. But I can't picture li'l Merry, doin' executives. She didn't care 'bout who, what, or where, as long as she could get high while she worked. *Any* work, that one. But if Bella wanted more money, I don't know why they didn't just ask."

"Think they was hintin'. Poutin' most the year. Remember? To me, just noise to my head. Shut it out. Do they want bigger slice from finder fee cuz we won't follow them around? We their fluffers they think, or some goddamn thing? Did they want us stand by at the bed, hand 'em fuckin' towel? Hold bucket for them to spit out? We have got our *other* jobs, too. Lurkin' around by them bad for business, too. Johns get jumpy, take longer."

When the microwave dinged, Boog reached in for his cup. "Oww, *merde*!" Lifting it out with his usual thoughtless grabbing, he'd caught the edge of the door and bobbled the cup. The lid flew loose. The cup landed on the bar floor with a splat. "Jesus H, Christ."

Let's see now, Wood thought. *He left out the Holy Virgin, so far, from all the blasphemin' I'll hear today. Pro'bly had some kind a mixed CajunCatholic. rooster-talon voodoo taught him some time in his swamp cracker youth.* "Soak all that up, will ya, please? We're

EVACUATION ROUTE

overdue for Health Department to come sniffin' in. We needa drag those mats out 'n' hose 'em down sometime this week."

Boogaloo held his hand under a stream of cold water in one of the little bar sinks. There was a gleaming, seldom used one at each end of the long wet-bar. These had no clearly defined purpose for their kitchen things. Beer glasses weren't offered to *Knuckle-dick* drinkers or their guests. As projectiles, they were far too fragile. Quite often, brown bottles did *not* burst into shards, especially if they struck leather clad targets before rattling across the floor. As for dishes, Wood kept paper plates and bowls in bulk behind the bar.

"So what we should do? Stake out that place to watch?" Boog daubed at the rubber matting in the dim shadows at the bottom of the bar.

Stake out? "What? The entire Seminole Hard Rock?"

Boog used a fairly fresh sponge that Wood had just removed from its wrapper on Wednesday night and intended it for a few more days of wiping the fakeslate bar. Maybe for a whole week depending on spills. He stifled a sigh of dismay. If the dude wasn't as loyal as a pitbull and the most conscience-free street fighter in South Florida, Wood'd be interviewing the membership for another assistant. More than once, he and other *Knuckledicks* needed to drag Boog off of some already unconscious enemy to prevent a homicide. *I go to dark, red place sometime thinkin' a the disrespect. I will never lose my face,* he tried to explain to Wood, tapping his forehead. *Keep the face so long of a time until it hurt.* OK, so add some Oriental crap into the caldron of whatever motivated the guy's behavior. Now he pulled a roll of paper towel down off the bar and seemed totally entranced by the process of poking wads of it into the black, rubber grate. Sooner or later, Wood believed, this one is going to flame into an orbit of anger while whaling on some poor bastard and just not come back.

"We can't do?"

"Listen, Boog. Forget about the mat. Like I said, we'll drag the whole thing out tomorrow, early. We needa mop the whole place out with ammonia. An' you gotta forget the skanks, too. I know it's tearin' ya up and that makes *me* nervous. Try to think a little more gentle on it. Like the good times we had with 'em. An' right now, I need to get you goin' on that grocery run so we can fix lunch. Are ya up for it yet?"

Boog poked in a few more clumps of paper as if he was packing a bloody, broken nose. He pulled himself up and brushed the knees of his jeans. "So don't do nothin' about those ungrateful...? I don't know even what to call 'em. Until we find more girls, I try to not use that *one* word they hate. How long you know me, brother? Boog tell's you honest. I *try* to forget them."

"Good idea about eliminatin' *that* particular word. It does seem to set 'em off like wet hornets. But please. For my own peace a mind; ya gotta get past Merry 'n' Bella. It's not worth it. Look at it like this: How much do you figure ya spent in that casino, just for one little peek, and *that* was by accident?"

To Wood-Chuck's amazement, Boog began to rinse out the sponge which was now beyond saving for any sanitary use. He even waited for hot water to reach the bar sink from the heater behind

EVACUATION ROUTE

117

the booze wall; water which, by some miracle of thermal dynamics, could become quite hot. *Watch this fool scald himself again.*

"I get ya. I get ya. $10 bucks every time to park, more for just wander aroun', drink or gamble while lookin'." Boog placed the steaming sponge onto the edge of the sink without attempting to wring it out.

Wow. Good man, Wood thought. "That's the concept I'm talkin' about. It wouldn't be what ya'd call *cost effective*. Lucky it's just whores we're runnin' 'n' not one a them derivative funds, been in the news. We'd both lose our asses like ever'one else."

"Don't know what them are, but...so that's the end on it? Provide 'em good livin' from all the club dates but then they fuck us in our backs?" Now Boog set about pouring coffee into the same big cup from the beaker Wood started; that same scuffed cup that just went top down onto probably the dirtiest place in the Clubhouse. He'd groped around to find the original lid where it rolled under the microwave. He forced it onto his cup, now slightly misshapen by its impact.

"Partner, I'm just gonna keep remindin' you--let 'em go. We'll get more serious about scoutin' around this week and I'll help ya out. Mebbe two or three workin' girls off the street. We get 'em cleaned up by Christmas. That should make ever'one fulla joy."

"Should we mebbe think a black girls? Could put that over, after members used to Bella and Merry? *Knuckledicks* got spoiled. Other reg'lars, too."

"I couldn't say what they might settle for. But a biker club ain't likely to be appealin' to corner girls either." Wood's heart nearly paused a beat when his oily friend said *black* instead of his third most favorite inappropriate word.

"Fuckin' boils my ass 'n' you can see it. You keep on me, to talk down?"

"Yeah, and I hear ya, Boog. But we can be smart about it." Wood almost said *for your own mental health,* a condition which it was probably too late to salvage. "I don't know how you ain't got a bleedin' ulcer already, bein' riled up all the time 'n' then with the junk you eat." Wood found a bit of scrap paper out of the unemptied trash from Wednesday night and began to print a grocery list.

"That can happen? Sometime I need *Tums* very bad. Pissed off make it worse?"

"That's what I heard. Might a been a doctor on TV. It can even cause the cancer inside a you. Now these things here are what I need ya to get," Wood said, handing over the list. *Should I have him read it back to me out loud?* "You better take the knapsack."

Human food should probably not ride in Boog's saddlebags so they kept an Army rucksack of Desert Storm vintage in the office. It had wide shoulder straps for comfortable shopping on a motorcycle.

"Yeah, better do that, ami. Saddlebags, they need the fumigate." Wood tossed the canvas luggage to him and Boog slipped into the straps. He studied the list.

"And listen to me, bro. *If* that was one of 'em you saw, then you're likely to run into her again. At that point, I need ya to don't go nuts."

Boogaloo took a long gulp of the coffee which appeared still to be steaming. "I know 'n' you know that sometime Boog goes too far? The deep end? But brother, I can't never forget *all* the way. But I put in the *back*, up here." He tapped his forehead.

Awww, shit, Wood thought. "An' try to make it back before noon. Go to a *Publix*. Their deli'll sell you a whole baloney so we slice it thick. Go to the one on East Busch."

"Right, right. Ca c'est bon. East Busch. Make groceries then dress up fried baloney. Boog might can eat by then."

Few visitors other their insurance agent and the Health inspector ever drove a civilian car into the fenced clubhouse lot. Well, also the occasional investigating officers, which usually meant three or four vehicles in force. The appearance of a bike, perhaps parked in close proximity to an older, sundried van usually meant that a domestic crisis had forced a member out of the comforts of his home. Wood followed Boog out to his bike and watched him idle around the back corner of the building. The large rucksack looked like an olivedrab child riding piggyback on his leathers. Wood sighed with relief. He just never knew when a misunderstanding of language or meaning might suddenly rub Boog the wrong way, especially while he was in the throes of a hangover. Volatile was not too strong a word.

Wood went back into the kitchen corner, thinking about the man's thick fishing guide accent and the Cajun slang that couldn't always be parsed. As dangerous as Boog might be, as hair-raising as were some of the situations he'd put them both in, it was often entertaining to hear him speak during his days of clarity. Barring those sudden shifts in tone, or until the volume began to rise in an argument with third parties...Well, you just couldn't make up some of his life experiences. Negotiation was not a part of Boog's skill set, nor did he have much of a filter. Provocation rested behind a hair trigger. And, when a dispute went quiet, when he began to stare, unblinking, at the floor...Then Wood might as well look around for a pool cue because they would soon be back-to-back in some sort of screaming, cursing, hairball of conflict. With these thoughts, Wood groaned and smacked his forehead. He forgot to add a bag of onions to further *dress* the day's special. *On-yone*, Boog would have read from his grocery list. Wood still had the two little sprouting ones. Enough to add a little flavor to the soup, maybe.

Now another grumbling engine vibrated through the back wall. When it shut off, the door opened ahead of Archie *The Darkness* Caulkins, the *Knuckledicks* President. Arch held the door open with his prominent buttocks while reaching down with both hands to gather up a 48-pack bale of toilet paper. He inched in backward to get his gut and all of the tissue rolls through the door, still keeping it open with his foot.

"Don't say I never done nothin' for ya, Wood." The boss breathed heavily from those few moments of physical activity.

EVACUATION ROUTE

Beads of sweat down his cheeks found their way to a bandana around his tattooed neck. "Fuckin' pollen's off'n the charts. An' that don't feel like yer normal humidity."

Yes, those allergies and the humidity gave you that lop-over of blubber. Would asthma or the excess flab turn out to be Arch's widowmaker? Wood wondered: *The bending over, the lifting, or the next Winston? My money's on the whole trifecta.* Arch might be only three inches narrower than the door, and had to waddle through like a razorback hog, but Wood knew him to still be as strong as a truck tire. You could hear the metal clank of free weights in his office. *The Darkness* immediately dropped the toilet paper in order to dig an inhaler out of a deep pocket within his leathers. *Damn,* Wood thought. *We need to get a defibrillator in here and some trainin'. Or one a them life coaches for the guy.*

"What is *this* for? I just stocked up last week." Wood closed the door for the Chief. "We don't hardly have room to sit onto the shitter as it is."

"Oh, don't get your panties all into a knot." Arch gasped down two puffs of Ventalin. "Goddamn, that's awful tastin'. They was on sale at the *Winn-Dixie* by me. I had to strap it on behind. The motorin' citizens wasn't kind in their admiration. You 'fraid it'll spoil?"

"Say, maybe we oughta trade jobs." Wood said "If you'd like to take over Procurement you can go bargain huntin' while I try out bein' President awhile,"

"Oh yeah? You wanta armwrestle with Gerard, about crowdin' into our meth territory? The *Jesters've* been makin' noise about payin' us a visit after Bike Week. They'd like to stop in for a friendly parlay on their way home from Daytona. Now how in the hell does that side trip make any sense if they're just goin' back to Tallahassee? I heard they was thinkin' a puttin' in a chapter all the way down to Ocala. That's way outta their stompin' grounds an' too close to ar's. So you gotta figure if they're tryin' to expand then they prob'ly wanta adjust the sellin' regions." Arch squatted as best he could to rummage in the cold locker under the bar. "Gotta rinse my mouth out. We already let him into the I-10 corridor from Mobile all the way to Jacksonville if they want it. Just becuz we're that fuckin' lazy. Mighta been a mistake. But I ain't heard of 'em doin' any business east a Panama Beach yet, so maybe they're just puttin' it out to rattle ar cage. "

Damn, Wood thought. *That rant took every last breath the man had.* But, Caulkins now found two *Copper Tail Unholys* left at the back of the beer cooler that Wood hadn't noticed. *You couldn't say the Knuckledicks don't support their local craft brews.* Now Caulkins swooshed the ale in his mouth like it was Scope.

"We got only one reliable producer 'n' just three members not afraid to get their hands dirty movin' it," *The Darkness* continued, plaintively. "But if you got some solutions so's we can maintain ar standard a livin', then mebbe we *oughta* switch jobs,"

Jesus, sorry I brought it up. Wood held up both hands in surrender. "Just jokin', Boss. I'm good. Yer the man. You find a deal on coffee filters, why, bring 'em on in." *Better tread lightly around our assigned roles in future. Just be happy I'm only hustlin' girls 'stead a product to support the treasury.* Somebody had to do that, sure, and

EVACUATION ROUTE 123

The Darkness was always looking for additional volunteers. The danger pay was higher but whores and this gig right here behind the bar and stove were Wood's niche. No need to rise to his level of mediocrity. He resumed preparations for serving lunch, cranking the opener into the second big can of bean soup.

"While I'm thinkin' about Bike Week, when we gonna get some decent rental poon back in here? I never had to bone ol' Tanya more'n one time in a row since...well, it was early summer, at least. Hopin' you woulda hired somebody by now that I could offer a all-expense paid trip to. I gotta make a run up Savannah 'n' might want some comp'ny."

Wood dumped both cans of soup into the 10-quart stainless pot he took off the drainboard in the kitchen alcove. He turned the biggest burner onto Low. "About that...It's been tough. We were hopin' this rotten economy would add some more unskilled labor to the talent pool. No luck so far. Maybe Bella 'n' Merry raised up the bar too high. Meanwhile, ol' Boogoloo had a suggestion..."

"Oh, Lord. Just *thinkin'* 'bout what he might wanta bring in here'll prob'ly gimme the clap." *The Darkness* took one more toke on his inhaler like a kick-returner that just went 100 yards, followed by another long chug of ale. He put the device back inside his vest.

Savorin' the flavor, Wood thought. "I'll go ahead 'n' ask it anyways. He thinks mebbe we should take a look at some spade chicks? Ya know, it bein' some desperate times 'n' so forth." Wood brought out the little onions and then an oversized buck knife from his front pocket. *Well, there ain't any Health Department in here 'n' this is sharper than anythin' we got in the drawer.* He moved the pot back to the burner.

The Darkness sighed heavily and tipped back the oversized Unholy bottle again. "I s'ppose. These straits *are* pretty dire. I don't have no personal problem with it. 'Good as any,' like they say. That how that ol' rhyme goes? Some truth to it but I'll have to OK it with the Council. Is *that* gonna be the only fuckin' thing on the menu? Yer lucky don't nobody else know how to cook." The biker chief drained his craft beer like it was any other swill then clanked the bottle down on the hard surface of the bar.

Just ignore the stack a cork coasters right in front a ya. Wood gritted his teeth and began mincing the onions on a paper plate "Nah, don't prejudge. Yer gonna like what we got planned," Wood said. "We're gonna fry up some thick, baloney poboys when Boogaloo gets back. An' don't forget, *I'm* on the Council, too."

"Right. So yer hintin' to me it'll prob'ly be just the soup?"

"No, no. He'll be right back. He's comin' off of a epic hangover a unknown origin, an' a solo ass-kickin' from a gang a Latino ninjas. He *says.* Said he was emptied out but would feel like eatin' before long." *Wow, this li'l booger is strong.* Wood lifted a forearm to daub his right eye. "One other thing, then, Arch, on the subject a booty 'n' the clap, etcetera. I been thinkin' it might be a good idea if I had a little more money so we could get any new girls some physicals 'n' blood work. Say, enough to cover three girls? They might be attracted to us if that was, like, for a fringe benefit. We get 'em checked every week or so 'n' build their loyalty with ar heartfelt concern. Prob'ly shoulda done it for Merry 'n' Bella."

EVACUATION ROUTE

Arch came around the bar again and helped himself to a second Unholy. "We can kick that around in Council, too. Guaranteed clean pussy might just push it through. I don't know about how any a the guests'll look at it. Might not be as broadminded as us. The rotten *Jesters*, for a instance, prob'ly see enough a blacks 'n' Mes'cans, both, in their territory. You 'member they was real pleased by them other two last time we parleyed together. Those little gashes didn't know how much they helped keep the *Jesters* to the north a Lake City."

Wood spilled the chopped onion into the soup. "Aren't ya gettin' a little tired a bein' jerked around by the dogass *Jokers*? They talk 'n' talk 'n' float these rumors through the grapevine...It's just silly cuz I don't think they're any more ambitious than us. Gerard's the problem. Shut him up 'n' the rest of 'em just don't care. We could..."

The Darkness raised a finger to his lips. "Don't say it. That nex' thing outta your mouth won't help bring more profits to nobody. Annoyin' as he imight be, we ain't to that point yet. Both clubs together don't exactly amount to a cartel. But it's just enough to maintain our standard a livin'. Prob'ly for them, too, until we see 'em gettin' actu'lly greedy. Now let me repeat the most important highlight a this conversation: What I'm *really* tired of is the same ol' pussy to home." Arch chugged into his second brew. "If I *don't* get some relief from facin' Tonya's big ass twice a week, I'm liable to take ol' Gerard out for some charter fishin' where he ends up as chum." Again, he touched a grubby finger to his lips. "Not the right time. Forget I said that."

They heard another bike behind the building but it was not yet Boogaloo returning with the groceries. Lyle Berkram slouched in and silently shared a *Knuckledick* arm clasp with both of them. Then he walked straight into the office, wriggling a manila business envelope out from under his vest.

"I hope Lyle had a better weekend than ol' crazy Boog." *The Darkness* followed his bag man into the office. "Even if he didn't, we need his vote."

Chapter Six

The Atlantic was nearly flattened under a light offshore breeze, sequined by an unsmudged sunrise. The arrival of spent waves was just audible enough to soothe a Christmas morning in the near tropics. Walt Bocewicz carried a teacup, the dainty handle of which had been left too long in the microwave. It was barely touchable and the coffee smelled boiled as he *"ow, ow, ow, yikes"* carried it back up onto Mom's 2rd floor balcony. What happened to all the coffee mugs? He eased into a deck chair, mopped his brow with the 3/4 sleeve of the pilling guayabera. Jesus, this place was *so* big. *Way* too big. *She rattles around in here with Molly Maid the only other occupants, once each week.* As regarded this piece of real estate, the old man had more money than sense. That, plus he probably anticipated many more grandkids than those that his two boys managed to present him with. Both men were now lapsed Catholics, one a confirmed bachelor and the other incapable of sustaining a job *or* a marriage.

Was his dementia jumping the synapses already when the old man began scouting for a retirement property? Could no one reason with him? Bocewicz senior didn't read the room. His offspring

128 CHRIS DUNGEY

were the definition of hedonism and/or dysfunction. Mom should have been left in a more practical habitat. Now, they prayed for her to get tired of so much echoing space, the four guest bedrooms were almost never occupied. Warren begged her to sell for an enormous profit (beachfront properties, as always, a finite commodity) and move back closer to his care. Now it seemed quite possible that *he* would be moving in with *her*.

The balcony up here, protruding off of his assigned room, was shaded by a dormer. The balcony itself shaded a bedroom exit below. The species of palm trees used in the landscaping weren't quite tall enough yet. Two wings, two floors. The living room was like a cathedral, the foyer its vestibule. My God, Four large bedrooms, three with bathrooms. He patted at a breast pocket of the guayabera for his cheap *Big Lots* sunglasses. *Where the hell? Must have left them in the Caddy last night.*

"And how did *you* sleep, Antoine?" His poor old tomcat had chosen exile out on the deck when Walt opened it in the middle of the night. Mom kept the thermostat at greenhouse level. Hey, she oughta put in a skylight, grow tomatoes in one of the bedrooms up here; practical, humanitarian application.

Walt decided that he must have left his shades in the glovebox of the Caddy when he took Mom to Mass. Everything he owned was in the trunk and backseat of that car but he hadn't worried about it for the 48 hours since he arrived.

Dad set her up in a sweet, gated community called *Sea Colony*. The place featured a uniformed guy in a gatehouse and round-the-clock, armed security. The guy out at the entrance was armed with epaulets, a clipboard and visitor's names must be inscribed there in order to enter. Back and forth, a second fellow drove a Toyota Celica with flashing amber roof lights on the private street. It all seemed unnecessary after the old man removed her to this *safe* distance south of teeming Jacksonville. No racism in *that* plan, but what was wrong with St. Augustine? The security seemed like something put in the brochure to soothe and sell prospective elderly buyers. Probably added a few hundred bucks to the association fees every month.

Well, Bocewicz senior always invested wisely. The pharmacy was not *quite* an exploitative goldmine in that neighborhood for more than four decades. But the profits had gone to work elsewhere. The boys were spared public school, for scholastic reasons (wasted on Walt) but they still managed to rub elbows with plenty of diversity: St. Michael's scholarship kids from the neighborhood, Arabic gentlemen in traditional robes; stumbling black guys weaving in with their a.m. tremors; black UPS drivers dodging around the listless customers with deliveries for *Bocewicz and Sons.* The *Sons* on the sign was an optimistic speculation, which became a delusion. Customers of color were predominant near the end of the old man's tenure: More assertive, plaintive; shortchange artists and angry youths thirsty for Mad Dog 20-20 but lacking ID. They slammed back out through the front doors, vowing to return after hours. Warren and Walt rode the parochial bus out of the increasingly *troubled* neighborhood to St. Michaels's Catholic in Riverside. Quite often, the bus returned with only Warren on board.

"Achhh, geez," Walt snorted. The cat hunched up to do his morning business in the box that Walt also consigned to the balcony. Antoine accomplished the burial process with enough vigor to send clay granules spraying over the edge, maybe onto Mom's ground floor patio vista. There were only a few over-watered foxtail ferns and some perfectly happy succulents down there with some kind of all-weather patio furniture. At least she wasn't paying for a gardener. Lawn mowing and other horticulture were provided, gratis, for the little swatch of lawn and shrubs in front.

Activity on the beach carried on at about the same languorous pace as the previous two mornings: The usual old man left his tracks between zigzagging gulls in the wet margin of sand below the high-tide mark. His pipe smoke drifted straight up, a white djin into the morning. There was one jogger far to the south, a dot growing smaller, and another one, nearer, approaching. The other usual old guy in tall boots who'd been casting bait almost directly in front of the condos, was absent. *Haven't seen him land anything yet and they're probably biting today.* How he could speculate this, Walt had no clue, maybe because it would symbolize another human being's missed chances. He noted all these pastimes with a hand shielding his brow as the sun climbed higher out of the ocean.

"Merry Christmas, Walter." Mrs. Bocewicz emerged through the open slider door behind him. "Ooo, it's chilly out here." Frail and slightly stooped like Walt himself, her silver, old lady bob appeared freshly combed. Or maybe it was just too short to ever become mussed as she slept.

"Merry Christmas to *you*, Mama. Of *course* it's chilly out here when you've come out from eighty degrees inside."

Walt had awakened around three in the morning in a tangle of damp sheet, Antoine tapping his face to go out to the cat box. After the cat piddled and sniffed the saline night air, Walt left the glass open to the soft hiss of an ebbing tide. He closed the guestroom door then removed the damp sheet. He replaced it with a blessedly thin bedspread he'd folded off onto the floor.

"Oh, tosh. It isn't *that* hot. Is it, really?" Becca Bocewicz idly fondled Antoine behind the ears but denied him access to her lap.

Tosh again? That must be where Warren picked it up. Walt would have to flee soon in case the sniffy exclamatory was contagious. "What time did you say Warren would get here?" The teacup was still warm as a fresh biscuit. *Must have been real china. Better not put it in the microwave again.*

"I told him we would open our presents at noon and then have lunch at one because you wanted to get on the road."

"Sure, thanks. Make *me* the Grinch. Won't you be glad to have the place all to yourself again?"

Mrs. Bocewicz clutched her robe at the throat. She placed her own coffee onto a small wrought iron patio table then eased herself into the seashell print cushions of the other lounge chair. "Not at all, Walter. This place is like a fine hotel out of season when I don't have any guests. I've told Warren I might be happier in a condo but I think he wants to inherit *this* place. In any case, it's been a joy to see you in better health. I wish I could talk you into staying for a few more days. I never know *when* I'll see you again."

132 CHRIS DUNGEY

Her voice had gone even more squeaky and feeble as it was apt to do to achieve her will. This tactic had been in use since Pop passed away and was totally unnecessary. Warren, with power of attorney, arranged for her to have most everything she desired. Maybe he *did* want the place. He hadn't yet gone looking for a condo. After the store sold he continued to live with Charlotte. Was he planning to move in, be the caregiver in waiting? With a slightly palsied waggle that probably *couldn't* be faked, Mrs. Bocewicz muscled the mug, twice the size of Walt's, toward her lips. Her head came down to meet the coffee halfway.

"Where did you find that?"

"I'm sorry, dear. I have three beautiful coffee mugs but they were all in the dish-washer. I just haven't run it since you've been here. I'm becoming so *lazy*. I'm not even cooking today. Warren will bring catered things. I've started a fresh pot when you're ready for a warmup. I don't know how you can drink *that* coffee from last night."

"Thanks, but I never waste coffee," Walt said. "Mama, what I've tried to explain is that I've got so many things to do. I'm not even sure, yet, where I'll spend the night or where I'm going to settle down. But, I plan to be somewhere near the Gulf tonight. I've narrowed it down that far. I'll start looking for a place first thing in the morning." He would be accompanied by a fat checkbook and a SunTrust Bank debit card which he planned to use with the same miraculous discretion as his successful fake beer ration.

"I envy your prospects for a brand new life adventure. That's such a long way to drive, though." Mrs. Bocewicz slurped her own coffee slowly, carefully, wisps of steam caressing her nostrils.

"Well, that's where property values are a better fit for my budget. Between three and four hours, straight across. Depending on construction zones and speed traps. I'm thinking of taking only secondary roads. Traffic should be light for a few more hours, before everyone starts driving home."

His Mom must have used up her strength. Now she returned her mug shakily to the little table. "Thank you, again, for taking me to Mass. The late one on Christmas Eve is always so beautiful."

They drove just a few miles north last night, then across the InterCoastal Waterway to St. Elizabeth Ann Seaton in Palm Coast. The place seemed more tropical- modern than he expected, not that he was an aficionado of contemporary Catholic architecture. It seemed to have just the right amount of Spanish modern influence (no adobe mission was ever *that* huge, he didn't think), though the Virgin and the occupant of the crucifix both appeared to have brown complexions. There were wooden pews still, not folding chairs, though the pricey marble dais and wall-filling, impressionistic mural behind the altar were disconcerting. *Diego Rivera wasn't Catholic was he? Nah, nah. A major socialist.*

Walt's mind drifted from the homily. *Okay. I think...that smaller figure has gotta be the Christchild. Gold aura around the head always a good clue. That's a baby's head, right? Is that supposed to be Mary, lower right, other side of the canvas? Then some centurions? A few gawkers? That red splotch in the middle could be His cloak. This isn't a Rivera.* When Mom had said Merry Christmas to the priest they returned to the Caddy. Walt was amazed, for the third sober year in a row, at how quiet the world had become.

Now, he placed his thimble amount of coffee onto the table. It was already cooler than the teacup and in need of a refill. "I was just happy to be available for a change, Mama. And also that I didn't burst into flame. But listen. Your car's running OK, isn't it? If you really needed it?"

"Yes, yes. Of course it is. Warren just took it in for a tune-up and for the front end to be lined up. I *think* that was the work they did. It was, oh...Well, it wasn't *too* long ago. I just don't like to drive at night."

Walt leaned forward, far enough to rest his chin on the white aluminum railing. He thought he could actually see the pier at Flagler Beach in the distance; a low, dark line to the south. You had to pay to walk out onto it. For the maintenance fund, supposedly. Then you could put quarters into the big, mounted binoculars. But, he could look from here, no charge. "Sure, I get that. But you're what? seventy-eight, seventy-nine? Right? We don't need to have the *talk* about taking your keys yet, do we?"

Mrs. Bocewicz sighed. "I am just recently 79, FYI. We all went out to a very nice dinner in August. Those poor young people on the staff had to come out to sing for me. Goodness, Walter. You were *there*. Don't you remember all the silly rhythmic clapping? I may be sharper than *you* are."

"Well, see, there you go. I apologize for my damaged brain cells. I was in the ballpark, though, wasn't I? Warren'll have to take care of

EVACUATION ROUTE

that conversation when the time comes. I'm not passing judgment on *anyone* else's ability to drive."

"I appreciate that, Walter. I hated to ask him to come all the way down just to take me last night since you were already here. He had a Christmas Eve party or something. He has his plays and things but always finds time to come when I need him. I *do* manage to drive myself to the doctor. Sometimes."

When was her most recent trip? She looked like a line drawing even five years ago. Maybe that's why there were 6-packs of Pediasure in the refrigerator. That had to be the pier at Flagler Beach. There were no other such structures on the A1A from Daytona nearly to St. Augustine. He drove the route plenty of times to go partying down in Daytona during his *formative* years. From age sixteen he'd been on one long Spring Break. And now a trawler appeared, far out to the southeast, booms and tackle seeming to stand above the sea on a mirage of glimmer. Oh *sure*, she hated to ask. His old white *butt*, she hated to ask. Warren said there was a call about some little thing nearly every day. *I'd give her your number if you had a decent phone.* But now, after lavishing another $3K on barrister Wineglass, Walt had an unrestricted license restored to him. Last night's brief pilgrimage was the least he could do.

"It was the least I could do, Mama."

Warren must have been having a hearty belly laugh picturing Walt sweating bullets in the Mass. *Well, enjoy it while you can, bro. I and my classic wheels will soon be absent once again.*

"I only wish you could have found your way clear to accept the Host last night. I think you may be ready to open yourself to a little more of His peace."

What a bummer that must be, combing those overfished waters every day, including the ones way out there in front of me. But those catch-of-the-day specials had to to be brought in, he supposed. Some upscale restaurants would surely remain open to serve the non-Christian population left out of all the merriment. Jewish, Hindu, agnostic, atheist; the whole pallet of minority persuasions. But, great holiday pay for servers and busboys? Hopefully. Surely the generosity of the season would be expressed in good tips for the wait staffs.

It was beautiful in the sanctuary last night, I can't deny. They must have fired up plenty of extra candles. A rich, waxy scent and the space inside was very quiet, too, with lovely, flickering shadows. All of the kiddos nestled in their beds. Just a handful of the hard-core elderly, well scattered in the actual hour that it had occurred, the miracle or whatever *it* had been. *You don't have to read very far to learn that the amazing Birth would have occurred sometime in October. But that was before the ancients screwed with the calendars. And then there were crucial compromises with the Druid holidays or some such.* Walt did not share those speculations or express his doubts in front of his mother. He stayed in the pew with arms folded, an *ex* across his chest when she went up for the wafer as the service reached its culmination. He did not want to be mistaken for handicapped, to inconvenience the priest who would try to bring it down the aisle to him.

"I'm just not fit, spiritually, Mama, I keep telling you. I'm still trying to elbow some wiggle room for myself in His *narrow way*," he explained again. "I need to work in a confession beforehand, anyway, don't I? Then I'll think about it. It's been at least twenty years. My sins are the weight of a telephone book. The old fashioned, big city kind." *Will need to consume loaves, absorbent as Brawny.*

Wait, though. Wasn't there some kind of communion in rehab? The very sacrament Mama was pushing? His mind was pretty foggy about it but there must have been plenty of opportunities. He was usually exiled to an RC facility. Each time he went inside those calming baise walls, it was the Old Man's choice and later Warren's, leafing through a file of brochures that Walt's life choices would not allow them to throw out. *The chaplain would have to have been a priest, right? The guy could probably imagine my transgressions without having to hear them from me. Look at my face. Look at my file. But no, I would've had to* say *them out loud. Do some kind of penance.*

What brand of holy man was that one in the Gainesville jail? Another priest? He was drawing a blank again. Public facility though, the ministering angels there would have been more ecumenical. Anyway, Walt was pretty sure that any communion would have occurred at his exhausted, dry mouthed, b.o., assend of a serious withdrawal. *Would the words, under those circumstances, even count?* He didn't hold any resentment against the sky pilots who swooped in on targets of opportunity. It was their calling. They had to strike while the iron was hot, no matter what denomination. Now he was thoroughly mixing his metaphors to include blacksmiths.

"You're doing so much better though, Walter. You *are* aren't you? It took a lot of Rosaries, I can tell you."

"I know, and I'm grateful."

Yeah, divine intervention will get all the credit. My own willpower had nothing to do with it. If he ever told her the truth, it would be that the nightmare of a mangled, fiery roadside death; or, the bloat, incessant bile cough, and jaundiced skin of liver failure had provoked his gasping, bolt-upright, awakening on a sweaty dormitory cot. Fear, like an icicle stabbed through his sternum, was the final the impetus he needed. *My road to Damascus moment? Was there no end to the Biblical analogies? How about likening the whole business to old Scrooge? Something literary: Me puking blood on the floor of my final refrigerator-box hospice. Ghost of Christmas future.*

There were no Sinai voices with his tremens; no golden light struck through a stained-glass window. But he couldn't bring himself to ever deflate her with *the truth*. Nor that he had carefully relapsed to his one fake beer each evening; just enough to satisfy his taste buds; to keep him entertained at the end of the day, yet not enough to extinguish that lifesaving fear. The nightly reward hadn't crossed his mind since arriving at the condo. And he wouldn't permit himself that pleasure until he was securely holed-up in his final destination.

"Do you plan to talk with the children today?" Mrs. Bocewicz brought her coffee mug toward her mouth again with the apparent effort of curling a kettle-bell.

"I'll try, Mama," Walt said. "I'm hoping they'll call *me*. Or if they call you, you can hand me the phone."

"I *do* usually hear from them."

Talking on her landline wouldn't cost Walt any minutes. He bought a cheap Tracfone burner before leaving Jacksonville. This one was supposed to give him double minutes every time he bought a refill card. With great difficulty and many restarts and typos, he texted his new number to anyone who might care to have it: The kids, Warren, Mom, and attorney Wineglass. Walt's jittery fingers keyed the primitive pad; one tap for A, two for B, and etcetera, down to the zero. He would have to learn all those new abbreviations. The girl, Michelle, replied *ok*, in small case. Warren called him back to acknowledge. *There* went one minute, gone from his introductory 120. Mom used up another five minutes, two of them spent with him pleading the limited nature of his plan and her ensuing Q & A. An apology, if his brevity seemed rude to her, took 30 seconds. There was no word from Max, but that was typical.

"Did I tell you that they both called me on Thanksgiving? It was after you and Warren went back to the city." Mrs. Bocewicz slurped again before returning her mug to the patio table; a reverse of the tortuous maneuver by which she'd picked it up. *Just hang onto it.* Walt wanted to reach over and help her ease it down but didn't wish to impinge on what was left of her self-reliance. If she tried to brush his hand away, there might be a spill.

"That was thoughtful of them." Walt heard nothing from either, which down-graded his emotional state, briefly. He might have been despondent if he wasn't convinced, seasons ago, that he deserved their inattention. After a silent ride back to Jacksonville, in November, while Warren and Charlotte traded assessments of Mom's health, he gave in to a *Xanax* in the back seat, then allowed himself *two* fake beers back at the motel. With a final hopeful glance at the *Tracfone* before laying down, he discovered that it had been switched to airplane mode.

"I worry about that boy," Mrs. Bocewicz continued. "Going up north to school is just inviting trouble. How did that woman manage to send him to a private school?"

Jesus, where have you been? Walt wondered. The kid's whole life until recently, had been a chronicle of one scrape or another. At least Max's run-ins with the law were more political than substance related; just the one marijuana bust, and *then* only for possession. Two disorderly and resisting arrest at political actions. Lately, the update bulletins left Warren encouraged and proud. He passed the boys accomplishments along to Walt for morale boosts. "He graduated you know. Don't worry. No one was invited. I think he skipped it and prepared to be a TA for someone." *Isn't Mom in the loop? She seems to have Max stuck in sophomore year.* More concern.

Was any of the adolescent drama hereditary, the apple landing near the trunk of the tree? Well, Walt never cared about *any* social issue enough to demonstrate or protest. "I guess he had good enough grades to make up for my defective genes. And Patrice remarried into money. Anyway, that boy could get into trouble on *any* campus, beginning in prep school. At least he's passionate about some things. *You* must know by now that staying close to Gainesville wouldn't have been a deterrent."

"I suppose that's true. I was so worried about him when he got involved for immigrant rights, driving all the way down to Miami, for heaven's sake. The haters down there mean business, don't you think?" With a forward rocking motion, Mrs. Bocewicz began the exertions required to rise from her chair. Now Walt couldn't resist getting up himself, to steady her under an elbow. She did not fend off his help.

"That's what I hear. The kid's got more social conscience than *I* ever had," Walt said. *Or could ever fake.*

"Just *more* candles for me to light until they both graduate. Between you, them, and Papa when he got sick, I've created quite a glow."

Weren't they both in grad school, now? You're beginning to scare me, Ma. "Warren doesn't get a candle?"

"Warren has already earned his wings. *You* must know that." She drew the slider open with some effort, her empty mug a slow pendulum in her free hand.

"Of course," Walt said. *What was I thinking?*

Walt followed her down the stairs beneath a central skylight above the stairwell and then into the kitchen. He needed to find a more adequate vessel to sample the fresh brew. He would get ahead on the chemistry required for a full, alert day, driving into territory where he had seldom ventured. "Well, you're adding to the season, at least. Light as many candles as you can. That was the best part of that service last night."

"Yes, it was. And you shouldn't be a stranger. You must get to confession so you can partake next time."

"I'll think about it, like I said." Once again they descended into the slow roaster that was his Mom's front room. "I believe I'll work on absolving *myself* first."

In the kitchen, he chose a thick handled mug from the dishwasher. This one was monogrammed with a tarpon rampant. His mother insisted on shakily pouring for him. And lo, the doorbell chimed *Joy to the World*. (A new carol each day of Advent in the condo. Walt had been greeted earlier in the week with *It Came Upon A Midnight Clear*.) Glad tidings were hollared by his brother and Charlotte from the foyer:

"Walt, come help me carry in all this food!" Warren called. "You'll need oven mitts!"

Walt was not allowed to leave without taking several containers of Warren's take-out Christmas feast. These appeared to be brand-new storage dishes that he was not expected to return. He carried them out and put them on the floor of the Caddy in front of the passenger seat. His Christmas presents from Warren included a car alarm with all the attendant wiring (Big Brother had heard his not-so-subtle hints) was wedged into the trunk with all his earthly belongings. He continued to consume more caffeine during and after their exchange of gifts around the silver artificial tree. His *own* hands were shaking by the time they all sat down to dinner.

The theme of the meal was Italian, Mom's favorite. Warren brought enough to feed an army, which they were not. Wedding reception sized roaster pans of mostaccioli, chicken Alfredo, and antipasta salad, covered the countertops of her kitchen. The bounty of leftovers caused Mrs. Bocewicz an hour's consternation about how and to whom these should be distributed. The roving Security personnel and the sentinel in the entry hut topped her list of recipients. Charlotte bore covered plates out to them. Walt hoped that his containers were microwave safe and that there would *be* a microwave in whatever cheap motel he came to lodge in at the end of his trip.

While dinner rode on the front floor-mat, Antoine settled into his travel bed next to his downsized travel litterbox A pretty good passenger usually, he made one yowl of disgust then curled up for a nap. An optimistic house warming gift from Mom clattered a bit behind Walt's seat. "Hope that doesn't make you too nervous, old fella?"

It was a set of oak finished TV trays stacked on the rear seat above Antoine's bed. *Ahh, she knows me so well. I'm not likely to be eating meals at a dinette once I've acquired a front room.* The road was smooth, the asphalt recently repaved. He didn't feel that he

144   CHRIS DUNGEY

needed to pull off, yet, to separate them with clothing items from his garbage bag luggage.

His route began by driving all the way south down the A1A to Ormond Beach before turning west. Once across the Inter-Coastal Waterway, he jumped onto I-95 south for ten miles before finding Florida 40. West again, *burning too much daylight but this's the route I want.* The divided four lane passed through a landscape more rural the further away he traveled from the coast.

Traffic remained sparse at first, just as he'd hoped. He nudged the Caddy up to a satisfying purr, 5 mph over the limit. *Do the cops still give you that or is that grace only granted on expressways?* Pretty soon the highway entered *Ocala National Forest.* He would make it to Ocala's outskirts before the abrupt winter sunset. Then, the truly unknown territory would be encountered after nightfall. *But what am I, eighty years old with cataracts?* God knew, he'd done enough driving through darkness including that in his own booze shuttered brain.

Walt hadn't realized that there were still so many square miles of wilderness scrub in the state. To his caffeine-fueled thinking, there were few favorable places where he'd care to pull off to change a flat along here. The grassy margins might be wide enough but they needed mowing. *Snake in the grass is a derogatory characterization for a reason. Jesus, man, just relax. These tires are like new.*

Walt was accustomed to uninterrupted neon, in the last two years of restricted driving around Jacksonville; *Hooters, Applebees,* and *McDonalds,* etc. and not many dark spots in between. Now he was amazed at the boiled peanut stands in the front yards of sin-

EVACUATION ROUTE

glewide trailers. He saw inactive produce stands and the pumpless relic of a long defunct gas station. In the lot, a sun-bleached van offered, even on Christmas Day, Confederate flags and decorative wall hangings. *The perfect last minute gift?* How had these niches come to be hacked out of the government's wilderness preserve, from the miles of kudzu and Spanish moss drapery? Private holdings of scattered quarter-acre lots must have been grandfathered in when the land was acquired.

Today the produce tables were skeletal, the faded plastic streamers limp in the passive winter warmth of inland Florida. This was the amateur portion of burgeoning Florida commercial congestion he looked forward to finding again as he neared Ocala. *What's the most recent demographic estimate? A thousand new residents per day into this state? That has to be an exaggeration.* Along here, some local *artiste* was making a good living from hand-painted signage in primitive fonts.

When he passed under I-75 on the outskirts of Ocala, he would surely be able to relax. Too much coffee at Mom's all day would have to burn off at some point. *But yeah, I'll probably stop for more. And fuel for this steed.*

Then, with no warning, the strongest provocation to his nerves thus far leaped from the roadside forest. The *Folk Arts Outlet* it was called; an acre of decorative statues cast in concrete, suddenly bushwhacked the unwary from beyond the shoulder: A charging bull and a grizzly bear rising on its hind legs, half hidden by shrubbery, stood ready to leap out at complacent traffic. *Sweet Jesus, happy birthday!* Not quite as Lifesize as the Wall Street bull or an actual bruin out in Montana, *but big enough to maul or gore my Baby*. A cowpoke on bucking bronco, Robert E. Lee (of course), stood to greet customers on the office porch. Shit! Angels, dragons, every conceivable animal, real or mythical, populated the acreage like it was Woodstock. He slowed, strictly obedient to the 35 mph posting.

Silver Springs seemed to have grown from a speed trap into a suburb of Ocala. But a crossroads ambush by a patrol car was still possible, given that the goodwill of the season was due to expire shortly. Walt pulled into a Mobil station that never closed, the expressway gas prices extorted from tourists 24/7, 365. He left the pumps and soon passed beneath I-75, the tank full and a fresh 20oz dark Columbian in the cupholder. At least now he thought he knew where he was, culturally. The landscape reminded him of rural areas outside Gainesville; sideroads where he had too often parked on the shoulder to retch, sleep, or visit with a highway patrolman. Cattle and horses, clinics and golf courses were the essential commerce of Central Florida—enough white fences to rival Lexington, Kentucky. At least those domestic animals cudded the pasture grasses down to the level of pool-table felt where nothing could hide, unlike the bordering ditches. In the dark of early morning, he preferred to urinate on the driver's side if there were no headlights approaching.

Presently the four lane wandered south then west according to the dashboard compass. Walt turned off onto a two lane secondary as dusk closed down, just to make the needle bob more toward south. He switched on the headlights and resumed supplementing his caffeine level, the coffee losing its temperature. *I oughta try some of those Five-Hour Energy shooters. Maybe get some vitamins along with the crank.*

Chapter Seven

I t looked like she was still in the hotel. So she hadn't gone home and neither her clients nor housekeeping had booted her out of the suite. *Nice of 'em after pretty much usin' me up.* She hadn't worked that hard in quite a while, if ever. *An' them ol' boys sure had more imagination than the Knuckledicks,*

Should try 'n' get one eye open for starters. There's mah cell phone, right there on the lamptable where Ah decided not to use it for a ride. Should oughta just reach out 'n' get it now, make a call. Don't want Bell to panic or nothin'. But, maybe not just yet. Maybe Ah need first off to recall mah one meanin'ful purpose back into focus. See if Ah ain't ruined it with this ex-cess.

Merry Braniff almost never dreamed, at least not down into that REM sleep where psychological backwashes of life situations were supposed to wait for a replay. She really couldn't say *what* that kind of nocturnal cleansing would feel like, or what would be revealed to her. Until maybe this doosie she'd just had. *Bella was prob'ly just jokin' around when she said a person could go in-sane if they didn't dream. Maybe that is why you are so crazy, girl. Bella spoke in that odd way, sometimes, like she just learnt English from a dictionary.*

EVACUATION ROUTE

149

When Merry thought about it, never going to bed entirely straight was a good explanation for not enjoying those relieving visions. But, shallowly dozing, bizarre short subjects (Bella came in and woke her if she babbled *too* loudly) often visited and they were all the entertainment she cared to experience. She supposed that *those* brief mysteries could be hints to what was buried in her noggin. But they flashed so rapidly by that could hardly remember them the next morning. Or, they were just quick summaries of whatever waking activity she'd just been involved in, or *had just performed. Mah damn lighter quit on me. Mind holdin' yers under mah glass for just a sec, hon? Yeah, right there. Oh. Oh, Daddy. Right there! Yeah!*

Before opening her eyes again to the New Year of 2009, she must try to retrieve the one comforting, recurring vision that had just evaporated. The first intrusion of consciousness always managed to ruin that one. That Technicolor glimpse was a timely reminder of the formative moment she'd been using as an alibi *(That's mah story 'n' Ahm stickin' to it),* for what had transpired in her life ever since. This morning she really needed it. The physical and monetary rewards she achieved last night ended in a total, exhausted slumber in this fine hotel. *Best sleep in a while, as a matter a fact.* Why couldn't she have clung to that one dream just a bit longer? She was barely past the reassuring part and not quite to the brash *winner* part.

It was a replay of the first time she'd ever taken pleasure unexpectedly and walked away with the last word. Sort of. Some mornings the reminder was a life jacket. So, maybe last night's

150 CHRIS DUNGEY

perversity (*yeah, Ah know that big ol' word*) wasn't more extreme than she could handle.

One a mah boyfriends of not too long ago, a would-be banger named Luis, had just took me, with that rough, macho dominance Ah was well accustomed to. It was in the back seat a his primo, gleamin', lowrider, a course. (Well, he claimed it was his.) We was sittin' right in the crumbly ol' driveway a his family's bungalow. (He said it was their's). Some a his fast talk life story may a been true. He showed me some skill with the hydraulic controls, pissin' off a few pedestrians with the salsa horn after they walked past. The car's insides was a blend a leather (soft 'n' rich), patchouli oil 'n' maybe some carnal stank (Ah know that word, too), includin' mine. There was a played-out cardboard pine tree danglin' from the rearview besides some pink fuzzy dice. He needed a new one with some scent 'n' Ah told him so. He could lose the dice 'n' not replace 'em, too.

Ah sure didn't have any serious feelin's for Luis. Never had serious feelin's for anyone halfway into mah seventeenth year. Ah wasn't waitin', breathless for him to pick me up from mah shift at the Hot 'n' Now. Feelin's for the boy? A little gratitude maybe? He showed himself to not be a total abusin' scumbag up to that point. He was older, like most everyone Ah dated around that time, after droppin' out a Homestead Senior High. That meant he could buy booze and share a joint while chattin' me up. There wasn't no reason, in mah view, to either trust or distrust Luis. Ah always pretty much knew what Ah'd get from any a those boys and what they expected back. Common knowledge. But, before Ah could even slow mah breathin' down or retrieve mah underwear, Luis buttoned his black skin-

nyjeans and tugged the Sunday-white wifebeater over the 5 o'clock shadow a his prison haircut. They, alla them boys looked the same, like cons 'n' for some reason wanted ever'one to know. Wow, that sure sounded white. Just say they looked like they just come out a juvy. Then a-hole Luis hops right out the back door like the car's on fire.

"Listen, babydoll, I almos' forgot. See, I loss this dumb sucker bet on the fuckin' Dolphins to my home boy, Ricardo, 'n' I ain't got the paper for him right now at this moment. I'm sorry down in my heart, spreadin' this onta you, but I got to keep my rep. Know what I'm sayin'?"

Ah didn't have time, neither, to wipe mahself, mop mah sweatin' face with mah abandoned shirt, nor to run a comb through mah dishwaterblond hair which still reeked a French-fry grease. This Ricardo, who Ah couldn't recall ever meetin', tagteamed into the backseat a the car, shorts down 'round his knees 'n' already scrollin' a condom on just when Ah heard Luis's rubber plop in the gutter under the rear window. Luis's homeboy musta been waitin' around back a the house to take Luis's place. He was inside a me swiftlike, relyin' for mah comfort on the lubrication a now this second condom. It wasn't, nor never has been, within mah frame a reference to struggle nor protest, or to react with more'n mild surprise.

This dude was quite a lot heavier then Luis. An' a good deal bigger, though he seemed like still a rookie without no craft at all. Even at mah tender age, Ah could tell. In about two minutes, he came, judgin' by his holler, a load (well, that's what they call it!) which musta been backin' up for a few days. But, even while he's huff'n 'n' snort'n, all the time perspirin' over mah hair and onta mah forehead, mah own first ever orgasm went on rackin' 'n' spasm'n. Ah felt like a bad-tuned engine, spark knockin' for a minute after ya shut it off.

He must a thought Ah was havin' a seizure by the amazement 'n' panic crossin' over his face. "Are you okay? Gee-zus, now girl. I am so sorry. Seriously, I should of give dumbass a few more days, pay up. An' I didn't think to axe was you okay with it. I don't want no hassles. I truly apologize."

"No worries. Thanks for the swell time."

Merry rolled over, burrowed deeper under the sheet then had a flash of panic about the Check-Out time and Housekeeping which must soon come knocking. But this was *so* nice up in here. Alone. Not to mention that she earned it.

As always, she couldn't seem to arrive, in hindsight, at a negative judgment about Luis *or* Ricardo. Ricardo's unapproved violation was an obvious crime, but made pitiful by his unexpected and lame remorse. Did the guy expect, seriously, to be any kind of successful thug after apologizing like that? But it was probably better than a goodbye blackeye. That wasn't the lesson she'd taken from the incident at the time, though.

Mah jaws relaxed and mah screwed-down eyelids fell open to see the red leather upholstery again. That comin' sapped the last bit a energy Ah allotted for that particular date. But it also give me a

EVACUATION ROUTE 153

*brief, zirconium moment a clarity about mah future. It wasn't goin'
to be all that bad, really. It turned out that Ah did have a mar-
ketable skill without no further trainin' nor certification necessary
whatsoever. That damn Guidance Councilor himself reminded me,
tryin' to nag or mebbe trick me inta transferrin' to the Dade Miami
Voc Ed Center: Do what ya love 'n' you'll never work a day in yer life.
Me 'n' Bell comparin' notes, figured they must teach that one to all a
them in the Guidance Councilor classes. He musta said it every time
Ah sat down for ar yearly chat. But, Ah don't believe they taught
mah particular skills out to the Voc Ed. Leastwise not afficially. Well,
Ah might not always love parts a the process, but the end result, as it
was just demonstrated to me again, was reliable 'n' satisfyin'.*

*Right about the moment Ricardo pulled his orange satin basket-
ball trunks back up, Ah had the urge to holler, Next! Only, sarcasti-
clike. The only downside to that li'l afterglow joke woulda been that
neither a them gangsta wannabees had paid me anythin'.*

"Where'd Luis run off to?"

*"Back into la casa," Ricardo got out a the lowrider but then hopped
back inta the front seat. He used the rearview mirror to prong out
his Afro with a pick. He was still perspirin' like rain seepin' through
Spanish moss.*

*"Ya mind goin' 'n' ask is he comin' back out?" Ah found mah
panties on the plush, carpeted floor. The bastard kept his shiny
turquoise ride in all kinda polish and tireblack but didn't have
enough to pay off a bet he owed to his alledged besty? Somethin' didn't
sound right. It occurred to me that Luis might now have a fresh
twenty in them skinnyjeans that Ah would never receive no share of.*

154 CHRIS DUNGEY

"I will if he let me in. That boy act strange sometime, you might of notice. Might think I'm still want more a his bacon; like that after you, I decided he still owe me."

"Now what excuse could he have to owe you more? Is there any way in which you ain't totally satisfied?" Mah flimsy camisole was black satin with a palm tree silkscreened onto it.

"No, no. Baby, now, I didn't mean it that way. We all good. See, how that boy mind work, he always runnin scared. See, if I was him, I'd come back out to axe me for some change, like maybe he overpaid me in trade. You must know it, that you some kinda fine! Worth way more'n twenty bucks he owe me. I never seen a young girl go off like you done."

"Well, ain't you sweet. Just if he does let you in, remind him he was s'posed to take me to Taco Bell an' Ah ain't forgot!"

"Fuckin' A, I will! I let him know you pissed off out here, too. An' I apologize again, yo. He never said you was no young girl. For me, that's like, a personal thing which I don't never do. I hope I did'n' hurt ya."

"Oh, please." Ah give Ricardo what Bella would later describe to me as a shiteatin' grin, which from me prob'ly wasn't so much a grin as a sneer a skepticism.. Oh, it was sort of a smile on the one side, but turned down cynical on the other, like Ah was hidin' a dead tooth or somethin' which Ah wasn't. "Don't take it too hard but yer about as quick as a hiccup."

Mah tennis shoes was no more'n just that. They was faded-out blue seconds from the Big Lots. Ah climbed out 'n' leaned mah tight shorts against the tail fin a the vehicle's quarterpanel. There was a

Minnie Mouse watch, might even a been a collector item, Ah believe, somewheres in mah denim shoulder bag. Ah wasn't in the mood to mine around in there for it just at the moment, cheated out a the deluxe tacos Ah'd been anticipatin' all afternoon. Seems like buyin' mah own always works smoother for just about everythin'.

So, Ah would just count slow to only a hundred 'n' then march back in the direction Luis brought me from. There was a bus stop for the 35A up at 280th street. Catch that back down to 328th street. Jesus, ya'd think the whole system was laid out for New York City. Some genius numbered the streets all the way south from Miami. From that stop it was just a short hike to Lucy St. Or, Ah could walk all the way home if Ah had to. Ah wasn't very sore. Ah reached into the driver's side window to snap off the dice. Silly slimeball. Lightweight slimeball. The car's deodorant come away with the dice but Ah dropped it on the pavement.

Merry was pretty sure that she *would* be sore this time. Her eyes finally opened for good but with apprehension, not quite ready to face the light of the New Year, 2009. Well, she sure *hoped* it was light out by now. *All night* seemed, to the contractor of her services,`a critical requirement of the engagement. Dawn would specify to Merry that her *all night* commitment had been met. Still, she was not quite prepared to peer outside. Hell, it could even be dawn of the *following* day for all she knew.

156   CHRIS DUNGEY

She had worked the casino for the first time though Bella cautioned her that it would probably be mostly a date night. Seminole Hard Rock presented New Year's Eve parties in each of its lounges. Well, so what if it is? Ah'd enjoy to get invited to a party. An' wouldn't there be some guests a the hotel goin' stag or maybe rowdy tables full a recent divorced folks? How about them adventurin' couples lookin' to ring in the New Year with a threeway. Or somethin' else new. Wouldn't there be plenty a booze-fired loss of inhibition spreadin' through all a those young, tan 'n' scanty covered bodies? Sort a the way Ma went downhill after losin' her first breast. Metasize, mastasize? Whatever. It was some creepy cancer word like that just meant spreadin'. Maybe a stupid comparison. Not the same process at all. Ah take it back, Ma. Well, but, think about it. Don't parties get out a control and go crazy? Ah've totally seen it happen. Tonight Ah'l be there to help.

Merry had some skills as a third party. She'd also directed the inexperienced about which parts might fit and where, with gratifying results on minicams and cell phones. She followed Bella's advice, though, to park off at one of the satellite lots. She picked the Lucky Street Garage then rode a casino shuttle. Yeah, Lucky Street. Ha, ha.

She took most of the afternoon to dress for her New Years Eve foray, trying on much of her professional wardrobe. To the nines, she was aiming for, whatever that meant. She finally settled on a little black dress, dark hose, black pearls, dangling black pearls in her earlobes. Bella, who was headed for a party on the boat, fixed Merry's hair as well as it could be fixed after she'd done her own. What else could she do now with those punky cowlicks all over? That was Merry's new fashion for altering her appearance and she found that she liked it.

When all the garnishes had been added, Merry enjoyed a moment of confidence in front of the mirror. She would easily fit in as a paying guest at any of the three lounge parties. But she could also hang back in the slots, random and alone, without the usual slutwear drawing undue attention to her purpose.

She dispensed with the paper trail that she'd leave behind by obtaining a Rewards Club card. Then she began to restrain from parting with her seed money. Her profits always seemed more hard-earned than Bella's. The poker tables were too crowded, anyway, and she really had no sense for it. Like Bella, she'd begun to pick up the basics of blackjack on the boats when it was her turn to cruise out of New Port Richie. Bella added home tutorials (that's what she called them) about systems and strategies to what Merry acquired by watching the regulars and a few of them ended their evening by picking her up. She would never be able to count cards, but she knew enough to keep track of what face cards had been dealt. It wasn't rocket science, which she supposed must be pretty difficult the way folks compared so many jobs.

She ambled past the nickel slots, crowded with dressed-up geriatrics then made her way to the quarter machines. There were fewer walkers and motorized Rascals among the elderly tonight. She wanted nothing to do with social security, Viagra boners. She wanted a New Year's Eve trick should feel something like an actual date. She had just enough time to read the instructions and to feed a five dollar bill into The Caliph's Cash before the first guy sidled up to peer over

158 CHRIS DUNGEY

her shoulder. He was dressed sharp, in the reflection of the screen including what appeared to be a tailored suit. He must have been watching her course through the mob for some minutes because her butt had just hit the faux leather when he placed a second, unsolicited drink before her. He took an adjacent seat.

"Well, good evening, hon. I'm Jack."

She accepted the drink with the merest of sidelong glances, doing her best impression of a disinterest, close to distain. She maintained a fascination with the results of each rapid fire wager. The line and bait waited patiently as she wagered again.

"Well, hullo there,...Jack." She should show some level of gratitude. The free drink hadn't just fallen from the sky and she might want to enjoy another. This was probably just the first installment of her compensation, if her trick radar could be trusted.

She offered another single bill into the maw of the machine where some kind of desert-and-oasis theme was being presented. There were Arab sheiks with camels and swords, leering their wicked smiles at the harem girls. Well, if that ain't...what? Stereotypin'? when ya talk shit about colors a folks's skin an' exageratin' their traits? Can't hardly tell much 'bout the women except they're showin' lotsa curves 'n' skin, lots a cleavage and bell jewelry. Their faces were covered up, too, which Merry knew pissed some folks off.

"How are you doin', tonight, darlin'? What are those, like, old-time terrorists? Why do you suppose they don't have their usual .50 cals mounted up on white Toyotas?"

"Ah ain't got a clue. Are they s'pposed to? Ah think it's some kinda Arabian Nights deal. It sure don't pay out much." Merry resumed

EVACUATION ROUTE 159

making her minimum wagers and tapping the button. The chimes went off now and then but in single chords, not with the prolonged jackpot excitement.

"How are you doin', other than that? Are you havin' any fun, yet? Would you happen to be alone, by some chance?"

"Yup, Ah am."

"Well you're just a little cutie. Anybody ever tell you that? Are you sure you're old enough to be in here?"

Merry snorted. "Ah think you must know Ah am....Jack. They're pretty serious about cardin' ever'body." Now she caught his scent. It was something subtle, which meant classy and probably expensive, she had learned. It was nice to enjoy some pleasant male odors after a couple of years servicing The Knuckledicks. Jack appeared to be a regular GQ sort of dude. As far as his smell, anyways. Like a scratch 'n' sniff sample torn outta that magazine. Versace, was it? She wanted to turn just enough to see if he was wearing cufflinks. Naw, but that woulda been too much to ask. He wasn't no troll but not James Bond, neither.

The music of a live funk band, very brassy, riding above a heart thumping bass, began to blare from the nearest lounge party. It was loud enough to be heard over the constant tambourining of the slots.

"Sure, I sort of knew that," Jack had to raise his voice, now, louder than the confiding purr with which he'd introduced himself. "Silly me. But, my gosh, how tall are you, sweetie?"

"Ah'm 'bout five foot 'n' two inches. Guess mah Mama let me drink too much coffee, huh?"

160 CHRIS DUNGEY

"That's sweet. And you're about cute as a bag a puppies, yourself. But I'll quit blowing warm smoke up ya 'n' just ask you this: Would you happen to be looking for, I guess you'd call 'em dates, tonight?"

Merry finally swiveled around fully. She examined Jack closely. There was no tie with a stick-pin in it, either. "Why, Jack? Are you propositionin' me? You know Ah couldn't come right out 'n' say so, hon, even if Ah was. You might have a badge 'n' handcuffs stuck up under that fine cut a jacket. And if Ah was, Ah would only be takin' one date for tonight. An' not with some ol' boy puts puppies in a bag."

Jack's laughter sounded genuine. "Well, I would hope not."

Now the evening began to narrow it's choices as if she was studying a juke-box selection. Which melody should she cause to drop into the queue? For the occasion and mood, she'd like to hear that old guy that sang about New York. None a Ma's Waylon nor Willie. Jack took a long sip of something tall and clear with a lime drowning in it. Then he wanted to know, just out of curiosity, understand and on the condition that if she actually was a sex worker, how much would she charge for a full night. Merry and Bella had agreed, after Bella's long walk home in the fall, that $700 should be their minimum for bestowing those sort of lengthy attentions. This wasn't Vegas, but they could imagine what a wage scale might be for high-end working girls out there. Their figure was enough to deter junkies yet not put themselves out of reach to well-off citizens. But, then again, they had both considered earlier that this was a holiday. A upward adjustment in their figures should apply.

"All night long, huh? Ah think that'd have to cost ya $800, plus the room and....room privileges, Ah guess you'd call 'em. Ah ain't greedy but that there's mah Holiday goin' rate."

"Oh hon, I can guarantee all those things. I have a suite that's about one level down below bein' a penthouse. Some folks gobbled all those in advance. This one comes with all the amenities."

Merry knew by now what those amenities should included. She was all about the mini-bar and how to exploit it. She was all about the premium free soaps, conditioners and shower gel. If there was a monogrammed robe, she wanted that, too "Ah was kinda hopin' to get mahself asked to one a these bar parties. Would you believe it, Jack, that Ah've never been to one yet on a New Year's Eve? Like, just to have me some holiday fun before business."

Jack chuckled. "That is sad. Well, but sweetie. Here's the thing, an' I hope this won't be a dealbreaker." He swiveled toward her profile which was again facing the slot screen. Merry seemed intent on the palm trees, camels, and flailing scimitars. "I had in mind that you would be the party, or maybe even that I could bring the party to you. You would play the role of what some call the party favor. Do you enjoy role playing? And that's why I'd encourage that you might wanta revisit your first estimate. See, well, what I'm advisin' you, just lettin' you know is, I'm meetin' a few old friends from work to celebrate with me. Us. Some of 'em might soon be without employment. Plus, there's gonna be several of my top employees. So...It's one of those bucket list things for the guys. A pretty heavy scene, I admit. Somethin' they can't really chat about by the watercooler any more."

Merry took the first sip of her free gin-and-tonic. Now this was something new, even if the johns' fantasies were not. The tonic had a tang that made the pine needle notes of the gin palatable to her. Not bad. Besides boxed Sangria, vodka and orange juice was her go-to favorite after hitting the pipe; always conscious of getting her daily minimum of vitamin C. "Oh yeah, Jack. We would for sure have to renegotiate for somethin' like that. Just how many friends would be yer idea of a few?"

"I'd peg it at around five. Plus myself, of course. We're committed to makin' it memorable. It should be epic, as one of the fellas calls it."

"Wow. So, the six a y'all want a experience and none a y'all have a free date that'll help out? Yer friends ain't a bunch a bridge trolls, are they, Jack?" *She used the swizzle stick to poke her own lime to the bottom of the glass.*

"Not at all. I predict that you'll be quite pleased with these gentlemen. I don't believe I even know anyone who isn't at least, let's say, athletic. I can't think of anyone in my acquaintance who's even homely, let alone a troll, as you put it. Now, I'd better learn your name if we're gonna move forward with our transaction."

"Ah'm....it's Merry, spelled like for Merry Christmas, 'cept nothin' like the Virgin Mary."

"Well it's already a pleasure to know you, Merry." *Jack reached out his hand and gently laid it on her forearm.* "So what do you think, in light of the itinerary I've described? What would be fair a compensation, do you suppose?"

Merry let Jack's hand remain. Itinerary, itinerary. She didn't want to sound stupid. Was that, like, some kind of dangerous kink

EVACUATION ROUTE 163

she'd never heard of? Jack began to stroke her arm as he might a baby rabbit. She took up her drink in her left hand, distracted, trying to think whether the caress was warm and sweet or creepy. Part of that itinerary business? "Well, Ah'm thinkin' prob'ly $1500, Jack. Shouldn't be too steep, divided amongst y'all. This'll be like a whole new experience for me, too," she lied. There was no reason to scare the guy off with her biker club resume.

"Easily managed," Jack said.

"An' Ah just got a few other simple li'l ground rules beginnin' with condoms must be used except for any oral or, like, facials. I brung mah own Listerine."

"Absolutely, Merry. Goes without saying." Jack lifted his hand.

"An' just for mah safety, this here's what Ah always do, Ah'll be gettin' a picture a your driver's license onta mah cell phone 'n' sendin' it to mah roommate." She pressed the button on her machine to cash out. A quick peek at the receipt showed that she'd nearly come out even. "Case Ah don't come home, next day."

"That sounds like a wise measure. But, it also opens up all kinds of mischief and jeopardy that you could put me into."

"No more'n Ah might be subjectin' mah own self to, Jack. Ya seem like a nice guy 'n' a gentleman, but Ah don't take no chances. Don't Ah seem like a harmless li'l ol' schoolgirl?"

"Hmmmm. Yes, you sure do." The john made a show of scratching his chin which was shaven baby smooth and tan even in the neon light. "Okay. Well then, Merry. I believe we have a deal. Just so you know...My fellas'll be gettin' their phones out, too. Just to preserve some of the memories, you might say."

Merry turned her seat toward Jack again. Dang, this ol' gin'n'tonic's gonna be mah drink from now on. She wondered if the Knuckledicks even knew what tonic was. She'd never tasted it before. Bitter, but in a nice way. Wood-Chuck didn't actually have a degree in mixology, she didn't think. "Well, then darlin', Jack. Why don't you show me along to this palatial suite yer so proud of. An' Ah'll need to have that cash up in the front."

Jack chuckled. "I just love your turn of phrase, Little Merry. Follow me."

But he didn't so much lead as escort her. Rather like a prisoner in one of those streetcorner roundups she'd witnessed but, fortunately, was never caught up in. One hand held her forearm which was apparently his favorite, but a bit more firmly now. His other hand pressed firmly at the small of her back. Now she could see just how tall he was, nearly stooping beside her to reduce the difference. But gentle, too, in a domineering, Daddy sort of way. From the physical manner of his guidance, she was distracted by his scent. He smelled really good; somewhere between a wood and Luis's leather seats. She didn't like the florals except on herself and her own parts.

Neither that gesture on her thin arm, nor Jack's semi-stern manner gave her any particular foreboding. Submissive, is how she might even advertise herself in the personal hookup section of Creative Loafing, the Tampa alternative newspaper. The goal was to be domi-

nated but also to avoid getting hurt. It was Merry who wondered if Wood-Chuck might look in that publication, browsing to replace them. So, they were avoiding offering their services in its Personals page. Merry clearly understood the basic motives (besides making a living) that she brought to her chosen field. She knew them from those illuminating moments of climax in Luis's car, including with Luis' surprise guests: Pleasure. Release. She included intense pleasure whenever imagining her benefits package.

Though it was difficult for either of the roommates to admit, the most compelling reason driving their careers was the utter absence of any other well paying occupations for which they were qualified. The singlewide trailer in the decrepit park where Merry mostly grew up was not the place to develop a passion for the culinary arts, cosmetology, small engine repair, gardening or any other of the Guidance Counselor's favorite go-to's for kids not on a college track.. (So why wasn't he a short-order cook if it was such a great future?) Why didn't they teach motel bed changing and laundry at the Voc Ed? Changing bed pans. Often enough, the gas had been shut off. Cereal for supper. She grew up on welfare cereal, PB&J, whatever microwave crap her Ma and older sister could find a coupon for. Powdered milk. With any luck they were using it to stretch a gallon of real 2%.

She might've trained for minimum wage elder care. Half the work in Florida was changing bedding in motels or bedding and Depends or both. That wasn't going to happen to her. In an emergency, she sometime, changed her stepdad Frank's oxygen bottles. Like, if Ma was at one of her parttime jobs or snoring off a well deserved hangover. Get the clear rubber tubes arranged correctly into his nostrils before his fingers could climb up under her blouse. Later, she did that for Ma during her chemo. Senior year at Homestead was postponed and then cancelled altogether.

Now, riding a clean, no-graffiti, no piss puddle elevator up to a so-called date, she found herself totally, if naively; comfortable and proudly adept. Anticipation of impending orgasm was so strong at moments like this that her nose sometimes suddenly tickled into a boisterous sneeze. Try psychoanalyzing that. It was as strong an indicator of approaching arousal as involuntarily lubrication a stiff nipple. Those benchmarks were usually achieved shortly after the sneeze.

As Jack put his keycard into the slot, Merry shivered and sneezed. "Bless you. I hope you aren't catching a cold. I'll turn the AC down." He reached in to find the foyer lights.

"Nah, Jack. Ah'm alright. Ah just do that when Ah'm super lookin' forward to this partic'lar activity. Don't know why."

"Well, I'm pleased to hear that. C'mon in."

This was no Red Roof Inn, that was clear. Merry's next thought was that someone ought to close the damn drapes. The entire space was exposed to the glare of Seminole Hard Rock and the other hotel wing opposite.

"I hope you like the pool view," Jack said. "They charge for it like it was fresh, new oceanfront."

Broad glass from floor to ceiling faced the West wing of the casino complex. Three bright blue pools shone in a huge, shared patio garden below. There were two long, sectionals, the usual microwave only it

EVACUATION ROUTE

looked bigger; a desk and a minibar. It wasn't the penthouse, okay, but it had to be almost, as Jack said. Big enough for two kingsized beds, both with night stands and lamps which Jack switched down to low. He stepped to an opposite wall to switch on one of those fake fireplaces. Ain't that festive? Shoulda brought mah stockin' to hang.

Merry did not immediately inspect the bathroom for pocket-ready treasures. She could see the Jacuzzi, the walkin shower, the thick towels, one of which she hoped to add to their collection. She placed her shoulder bag against the room safe in the closet. After taking out her mouthwash and a pocket makeup case, she closed the sliding mirror doors. She placed her toiletries on the nearest nightstand. Then she took up her glass.

"Let's get the business out of the way and get you back to sneezing." Jack grinned. When she was done in the closet, he handed her a manila business envelope. "Fifteen hundred for one full night, as you specified."

Merry flicked through the sheaf of bills with her thumb. "You sure carry 'round a lotta green money." It looked like fifteen one-hundreds. She made sure, another sneeze of anticipation disrupting her count.

"Oh, my. Bless you, sweetie. We better get started. When I party, Merry...," Jack paused. "Well, you'll see. Go ahead and use the safe. I'm sure you know how to put in the combination. You keep the emergency key. Hide it wherever you wish, though I assure you there's honestly no need."

"'Kay. Just lemme take that picture a yer license first." She dipped back into the closet to find her phone in the purse. Jack took a State of Florida Driver's License out of his wallet.

"That's a nice likeness a you, Jack." His picture looked like a model posed for one of those same men's cologne ads she'd just been thinking of. Or, a brochure for a tanning salon. Merry forwarded the pic to Bella. A return text from Bella showed an oldster with a noisemaker in his mouth, posed on the karaoke deck of the gambling boat.

But before Merry could return her phone to the closet along with her cash, Jack suddenly lifted her, his hands under her armpits. She rose off her feet as easily as an American Girl doll, leaving one black spike heel behind and the other dangling. One of Jack's hands easily bridged the space between her shoulder blades while the other gripped her ass to support her. His tongue in her mouth was firm and insistent. He tasted of that gin, the tonic, and the lime he must have chewed and swallowed. But, not a hint of garlic or tobacco products.

Merry gasped when Jack's mouth released her and he had placed her back onto the floor. "Okay, Jack. Ah'm understandin' what ya mean." She sneezed twice..

"Another omen? I do believe you got me started, too. Alright. Put that envelope away while I drain the lizard. Then I'll freshen your drink. Do you want another one of these?" Jack took her tall glass and was already pouring the magic ingredients at the mini bar.

"Sounds like a plan, Jack."

Whatever it was, it must have been added to that next drink. Jack handed it to her and Merry sipped a toast with him. She carried it into the bathroom when he came out. After locking the door, she put the key into a tiny brown box containing a shower cap. She took a few more sips while fine tuning her makeup and a few more while peeing on the commode. After she wiped, it seemed to take forever to reach down and pull up the black, silk panties. The fine band of elastic slipped from between her fingers but she seemed incapable of impatience with it. When that interminable maneuver was accomplished, she examined herself in the brilliant mirror. Well, lookit this here fallen angel. Who would wanta harm...? She faced away toward the towel rack and looked back over her shoulder. There was her cute little urchin neck and the cute little urchin butt. It's often ones like me in the news, though, accordin' to Bell. Searchers fear the worst. Ah'm not even seein' no embarrassin' panty line. If all the guys're wantin' to look at it, why's it supposed to be so embarrassin'?

It took forever to find the slippery, shiny door handle and then to turn the button lock in it. How could the Hard Rock folks afford alla this gold plated hardware 'n' why wasn't they all stole by now? Then she felt like she was skating across the carpet in the direction of one of the enormous beds. Better pick one out before Ah pitch down onta mah li'l urchin face! Oh, girlie! Ya mighta really fucked up this

170 CHRIS DUNGEY

time. These skates don't have no toe-stops on 'em. Must be time for the couples only dance, cuz there's Jack waitin'.

He takes me up'n his arms and leads. Where's his skates? Feels like we're dancin' or doin' some kinda perp-walk, one. Watch yer head, ma'am, like they say. Puttin' ya in the cruiser. Where's them disco lights 'n' that slow spinnin' ball like they had at the Nervana Roller Dome back home? Or that loud, old-timey organ music when the DJ called for All Skate? The showoffs in their spanks 'n' poodle skirts got the rink to theirselves while the kids in rented skates had to sit it out. What a gyp.

Jack helped her onto the bed. "You look kinda tipsy, there, Little Bit," he said. "I think that gin went to your head."

Merry tried to respond, to let him know that she was not a rookie regarding the effects of alcohol and that her drink must have been enhanced. But, somewhere between this cogitation and its utterance, her gears slipped further. The thought went off track and into a ditch. She rolled over with a dumb, silent grin. *Ah don't care for ditches. Come upon a slitherin' surprise, chasin' a Frisbee in there. That pillow's so nice. Whoa, two of 'em.*

"Girlfriend's not accustomed to hard spirits?" A second voice towered above her. She reopened her eyes.

The unbuckling of a belt jangled like the entrance bell of a small store except that an echo came after it. *Just keep that in them loops, now. Ah ain't been paid for no slavegirl role-playin'. An' Ah never been Daddy's naughty girl, goin' home with a buncha welts .*

"Merry, this is Rob."

EVACUATION ROUTE

Ah, what deep, slow voices both ya'll got now, one in each ear plus all 'round me. Not their real voices, neither, but like young boys tryin' for the part a the giant in Jack 'n' the Beanstalk. Not a kid's voice, neither, like them boys in ar 5th Grade program. Jason Parks 'n' Mark somethin', both wanted it bad. Ah couldn't remember all a the mother's lines, nor the sister's lines. Nor the right time to speak 'em. Them dumb boys needed cues in rehearsin' just for the fee, fi, fo, fum. Was Ah with the held-back, at-risk bunch already? They coulda put me in the cow.

She was relegated to painting cardboard scenery. All those vines around Jack's cottage. She didn't panic at all when the narrow waist of her dress caught for a second as it was pulled over her head. Dark inta the light, like bein' born. Little preemie angel child, small from the jump. I'm disoriented mebbe, but no panic. A good sign, though, of bein' a professional...sex worker. Controlin' the situation. Except for gettin' myself roofied. Never been before, that I can remember. Too buzzed for good decisions, yeah but waitin' 'n' waitin' on barstools for the right appraisin' male eye. With money. Never stood on a corner, though.

It musta been some differ'nt kinda drug then that Rohypnotic cuz wouldn't Ah be out cold? Never mind for now, but Ah could still be a prize dumbass, dependin' how this turns out.

Whatever Jack had slipped her, Bella continued, in her twilight state, to caution her: "Mix your own drink and do not let someone else have possession of it." Like when they say at the airport about mindin' yer luggage so no bomb don't end up put in it. Bella must a flown somewheres at one time. Where would Bella ever get to fly to?

172   CHRIS DUNGEY

Ah never flown as of yet. There's plenty a things never happened to me. Well, now Ah can scratch date rape off 'n the list. Mebbe just wait 'n' see about that. Ain't technic'ly accurate term since Ah consented. See, though, still no panic. Ah'am a veteran sex worker.

"*Sweetie, now don't panic. This is just for some fun pictures,*" *another new voice informed her.*

Why would Ah start now? Wait. Did Ah say that out loud?

What she thought might be more trouser belts were unbuckling. Ya can't spank me with more'n one to a time. Ah don't think. But, the buckles cinched back up again, sounded like, so that wasn't it. Something else; soft leather snapping and that crackle of Velcro, snug around her ankles and wrists.

The bedding was gone except for the sheet. The magic carpet ride of that heavy, bedspread was gone, too. Now, she couldn't roll over even if she had the will. Her wrists had been cuffed to her ankles. What'a they got 'n' mind now? Wasn't Ah accessible enough? She wanted to mumble that she wouldn't be able to roll over very quickly for them, but then she felt the first oral intrusion of the evening. The warning words about her loss of mobility were pushed to the back of her mind, replaced by a momentary dismay. Folks in sitcoms joke 'bout women that can breathe through their ears. Well, that sure'd solve some problems. Like, when some fool starts right off want'n deep throat. But, no panic. Ah'm a skilled pr'fessional...

The full penetration actually limited the use of what she considered her skills. Gagging wasn't a problem but her tongue and lips were now compressed to uselessness. Her tongue was numb anyway,

EVACUATION ROUTE

like after one of her visits to the, practice-day at the dental school. Won't earn much with crack teeth. Go a coupla of times each rear.

Oh, yeah, baby! Look at this, Rob! She can take it all! Beautiful, honey! Where did you find this sword swallower, Jack?!

So, her inability to lick wasn't a handicap that mattered to them. Dumb. Just please don't pinch mah nose. Some guys'll like to take a firm grip 'round mah neck, too, just before they nut. This guy don't have much imagination but praise the Lord he ain't jammin' away too hard. Slow, slowly. You'll get there. Back a his hand on mah lips now cuz he has to tug on himself. Why the rush? Ah'm gonna get ever'body off if ya just be patient. Ain't you enjoyin' the use a mah mouth? An' is that a weddin' ring Ah just felt there? Cheatin' bastard. Well, you ain't mah problem.

Between her tongue being immobilized and the guy's yanking, Merry had little to do with causing the splooge which soon erupted. No chance to even taste it, that far back and with yer other, two-timin' hand pullin' the back a mah head. No choice about to swallow or not. Okay, there it is. Guess Ah've tasted worse.

The first guy withdrew and Merry gasped for breath.

"Tommy, you are the man! Smile some a that up here for me, could you sweetie? Nope, all gone."

Tommy? Well, ya could always kiss me 'n' see can ya find some of it. Asshole. But, it don't look like Ah'm gettin' them words out. Jus' as well. Be unprofessional.

The voices were nearly at a normal human pitch now, except for some kinda echo. Autotune, ain't it called? And cellphone cam'ras chirpin' all 'round beside this li'l love nest. Wait, wait. Now who the fuck is Tommy? Never been inter'duced to anyone name a Tommy. So who was the dude all up in mah tonsils? Hope their manners don't break down no further.

"Sean, you're up, guy. I'm feelin' lucky again." This Tommy's voice had gone back down to a fuzz-bass timbre. "Little gal boosted my mojo. I'm going back down 'n' shoot some craps."

Ah havn't been inter'duced to Sean neither.

"Okay. I'll hold your place, keep her occupied," said the one named Sean. "What a sweet little bush. Boss, you look like you're about ready, too. I have got to have a taste of that before I mess it all up."

Taste a what? This guy's a brave one. Most johns won't go nowheres near sloppy seconds with their face. But, right. Ah ain't done nothin' but oral so far. Or, have Ah?

"You're sure wet, sweetie. Jack, can you get some pics then help me tip her over?"

A course Ah'm wet. Did ya come in late? Wooopsy. Ass up. They must want a diff'rent view. Many hand's make light work? Makes no sense or lights in the trailer never woulda been shut off. Stupid sayin'. Are they gonna let a girl breathe? Them big, soft ol' pillows'r gone. Least Ah won't smother in 'em. This Sean, if it's still him, woah...right on in, sudden an' entire.

Just enjoy it. Didn't some Senator say that? Got in trouble. Mebbe it was a TV preacher. Long lastin', this Sean is. Usin' me up while mah mind goes driftin'. Mah very happiest place not far off, now. Comin' can separate mah mind out a long ways from the immediate situation. Gonna need a water break, fellas. Gettin' de-hydrated under here.

EVACUATION ROUTE 175

But then, surfacing abruptly, Merry realized that it was Jack behind her now. Hopeless try'n keep track. He eased into her gently and lifted the side of her head to a better angle for her to breathe. Like that Tommy said, Jack was sure ready. Felt 'im flood out after a few shoves. Yer a reg'lar ol' water balloon, ain't ya? Oooo, it's all escapin'. Come on back here, Tommy. Now's yer chance for a sample.

"Whoo-ee! Merry! Damn!"

Ah didn't really do nothin'. Not gonna tell 'im that.

The one called Sean took much longer on his second turn. He groaned and growled like most of them did. He shivered with his last, leftover strokes. Nerve impulses, Merry believed: Travels down their nervous systems like a floppin' snake ya just took the head off with a shovel. But, she too convulsed again, even as she wondered, casually, why the promise of condoms was not being kept. Prob'ly spoils their pictures. They're gonna buy me a mornin' after pill.

"You came too, didn't you? I don't think you can fake spasms like that." *Sean said.* "You cum like havin' a seizure."

"Mmmmm." *Was all Ah could manage. Ah felt another warm trickle.*

"Does that feel nice, baby? You got a good one outta me." *The dude chuckled, still breathing heavily.*

It's Rob now, Ah think, usin' a warm cloth, swabbin' me almost tender like. Clean-up on Aisle 1. He mus' be next in line. Ah thought Jack was still near me somewheres 'n' Ah see Sean wander by, cleanin' hisself up, too. Ah must be facin' towards the end a the bed. Tommy must be downstairs still, near's Ah can keep track, which leaves Sean 'n' Jack. What do folks say? Ya need a program to tell all a the players? Is that mah reasonin' skills comin' back in focus?

"Merry, are you comfortable?"

Pretty sure that's Jack with another damp cloth for mah face. Might could be a sanitary wipe.

"Let's roll her back over," someone said when she was unable to confirm or deny her comfort level.

You guys 'n' yer pictures. The things Ah used to do for mah Knuckledicks, this woulda been part a the incentive payment structure. Now, this one's gotta be Jack. After the second uppsy-daisey arrives another semi-stiff one inta mah mouth. Tastes used.

The third try at consciousness was the charm. Merry tossed the sheet off with her foot and her eyes opened to stay. She hoped.

Rolling upright, feet over the edge, she found the floor. The only light in the room came from the nightlight in the bathroom. *Don't get ahead a yerself, Daisy Mae. Just a li'l stiff like Ah expected. Go ahead 'n' stand up. Butt's kinda sore but not up inside, it don't feel like. They didn't pay for anythin' like that. Wasn't much Ah coulda done about it, bein' prob'ly sedated. Still stingin' on the outside. Somebody musta thought they was a cowboy. Ah better not be greenin' up with bruises. Or mebbe more'n one cowboy. Thought they was in a rodeo. Ol' Jack musta come back up from the casino 'n' put a stop to it. That was his voice, but kinda muffled. Ah musta managed*

EVACUATION ROUTE 177

some cussin' 'bout the no condoms bein' used, too. An' wasn't that Jack in the room when they was moppin' me up that first time. Likely Ah'll never piece it all t'gether. Have to put some better light onto it, see 'bout them bruises. Must be pretty red still. Sugar shaker, one of 'em called it. Slappin' mah sugar shaker like a cow-pony. Crazy, white collar boys.

She couldn't count how many times Jack or his friends had lifted her over from doggie to missionary before they wised up and just unsnapped her, let her use her hands. *An', tell the truth, Ah lost track a who all joined in unannounced.*

Merry went to the window, weaving off course just a bit with her first step. *Bound to be some lingerin' effects. Head for the li'l sliver a light between them curtains.* Parting them, she exposed herself to the mercilessly bright day. *Worse'n in a cop's flashlight. Pool view from the Gold Suite. There it is, like advertised. Ol' Jack sure had better of paid for it, 'n' not sticked me with it.*

She widened the gap in the drapery. Way down there folks were lounging, gleaming with lotions and tall drinks, even from five floors up. Not a single body in the water, though. *No, wait. Couple a chubby guys in one a the concrete hot-tubs. Shallow end. How can they stand it? 'Course, might be chilly out for all Ah know.*

Turning back to the disheveled room, She felt a mild panic (the sedative must be totally gone from her system). She'd forgotten about the room safe. *Shoulda been the first thing now 'n' there's a receipt papers from the front desk stuck under the door.* She moved to the closet, pulled the bi-fold slider aside with only the slightest unavoidable glimpse at her appearance. Inside, all of her belongings were just as she'd left them. The purse seemed untouched, her cell phonestill placed carefully on top to betray any ransacking. She tapped her birthday, month and year, into the keypad of the room safe. The door popped opened half-an-inch without enthusiasm. *Spring must be wore out.* The manila envelope, still fat with her earnings, was right where it was supposed to be.

Well, y'all was clearly some, sweet gentlemen after all. Sorry for doubt'n. Her ears buzzed and she began to tip into some residual dizziness as she backed out of the closet. *Oh yeah, there's that, too. Bein' drugged was uncalled for. That bein' said, Ah hope some a y'all left yer business cards.*

When Merry switched on some lights there were, in fact, three business cards on the glass top of the TV cabinet. Also, an envelope with a single pill in a pharmacy bottle: "*We took some liberties, but I tried to think of everything. I hope this is your brand,*" read the note. Levongestrel, 1.5 mg tab. *Well, Jack. Ah've never actu'lly needed one before, believe it or not. Am Ah s'posed to eat somethin' with it? It don't say. Ahm gonna put lotsa water with it for sure.*

She found an unopened bottle of water on a lamp table, twisted off the cap and swigged deeply, washing down the pill. There were a few condom foils scattered here so Jack must have straightened his friends out on that topic. *More likely they just didn't wanna get in each other's fluids.* Now, all she had to do was to round them all up and make a count, help her weigh the evening. And, maybe remember some of it. Of course, the cash was always a good measure. She found six scattered wrappers. Litterbugs. She couldn't bring herself to fish any more of them out of the trash

EVACUATION ROUTE

basket. There were a few in there, too, but tangled up with used condoms like some kind of gross pasta in a colander. Merry decided she didn't really need to know the final tally.

Ah still intend to grab a souvenir from them towels or the minibar. Shoot, Ah oughta empty it, startin' with one a those sports drinks. Get back mah 'lectro-lights. Give ol' Jack somethin' to remember me by when he gets his next credit card bill. But nah. That'd just be bad for future bus'ness. Anyways, they all got some pictures. How 'bout a few a them little champagnes for Bell, though. An' Ah can't forget to take all them callin' cards. Seems If Ah was bound to puke this mornin', it would be if Ah took a closer look in that trash basket. Weird Ah got a gag reflex for lookin' at nasty stuff.

It was time to take a shower before a final scavenger hunt. She wished she had stuck an extra strength douche into her bag. *Any a those ol' boys coulda been bacteria compromised, no matter they was dressed up salesman sharp. Like a petey dish, Bella always says, them nasty bugs that mebbe even get on a rubber from their hands. Who knows where them handsa been. If housekeepin' yells in, they'll jus' have to wait a darn minute. Tip 'em good, too, just for that mess in the trash basket.* She snapped the shoulder bag closed with her manila envelope safely inside then took it into the bathroom with her. *Generosity is one thing, but Ah've known too many Housekeepin' folks not to be careful for mah valu'bles.*

Part II
Houses Warming

He that has a house to put's head in Has a good head-piece. - Shakespeare "King Lear"

Chapter Eight

Darlene Spurgeon was happy as a *pig in slops* (more than a worn trope, the phrase was a real thing to she and her mother, for whom she carried on the phrase) that the holidays were over and done, even though it meant a return of the bouquet-de-Buffalo wings in her hair. Her kids had visited at Thanksgiving with all of *their* kids and were back again for Christmas. They stayed over on Christmas night after *that* joyous day. She didn't have the heart to push them to go along home with both Troy and her own dear Larry hammered by halftime of the second NBA game. Excepting for Charlie, of course, her muscle-under-fat biker, bouncer, and baby-boy. He, reliably, ate and ran.

Charlie collected his yearly check and awarded Darlene yet *another* spa'n'makeover gift certificate. She still hadn't redeemed the one from last year and was guessing it might have expired. She'd *never* hear the end of it if he found out she hadn't pampered herself as intended. Darlene mustn't forget it for another year at the bottom of her makeup drawer without testing its validity. Maybe run over to Ocala for an optimistic Brazilian? Or, use it for a cruise around Easter time when the fumes at B'Dub's in Crystal

River could make her woozy. That's when the noisy Spring Break kids crowded in to watch the big basketball tournament. They all seemed to challenge themselves with the most potent sauces. Which then required ridiculously large applications of beer. Well, it couldn't be as riotous as a B-Dub's in Daytona beach or Panama beach must be.

This would be the second year running that she skipped a three day holiday gambling'n'singles voyage to Bimini. Last year she wasted the time on charter fishing in the Gulf with Guillermo; sunburned and nauseous, bobbing around out there way beyond her comfort zone, expecting to see oil platform at any moment. Now she had just used up an entire vacation week of the two she was allotted yearly; added a couple days onto the end of Christmas to play *Grandma* and plus another two *mental health* days trying to initiate a social life in *The Glade*. But, the rug-rats parked themselves in front of their video games and paid little attention to *her*. They couldn't care less that they would all soon be dating and driving and that Grandma would be the last person on their minds. She should have rousted them out for a day at the *Wildlife Center* or the mermaid show down to Wikkiwatchee. *Grandma isn't gettin' no younger. Humor me, sweeties.*

The apparent axis of geriatric merrymaking, the Community Association, was not yet bearing any fruit for her dating life: She attended the dish-to-pass potluck two nights before Christmas Eve; then one truncated New Year's Eve *affair*. She didn't even make it to midnight and the dreaded encounter with unfamiliar dentures. But, she wasn't the only one who ducked out early.

Before bailing, it seemed like every married codger in the park had tried to grab her ass. They box-stepped her around behind the protective cover of the buffet table before making those pathetic advances. Jesus. Couldn't they turn the lights up just a *little*? There were three fake candles at each table plus the still bravely winking fake Christmas tree. Someone occasionally opened the refrigerator in the kitchenette to provide a bit of illumination, or, quickly turned the light on to change the coffee filter. The darkness *must* be a safety liability for those who hadn't yet dealt with their cataracts, but none of the older gentlemen complained.

Most of their wives were either totally clueless or were scheming to let the old boys get themselves fired up for later connubial attempts at home. Neither of the two ruggedly handsome, (or were they just nicely weathered) bachelors she'd encountered at the mailboxes were yet to put in an appearance at any Association function. Crap. Maybe they were together? Partners? Or was it *civil union,* you were supposed to call it now? It *had* to be that in Florida, where gay marriage was never likely to fly. Whatever they were calling it, she gave up anticipation for their arrival.

Driving home from work on the following Wednesday evening, Darlene stopped at a fisherman's dive-bar south of Crystal River. Thursday was her regular day off before taking lucrative evening shifts through the weekend. Since her move down to Homosassa, she'd begun to establish *some* routines and this one had the Community Association beat. So far. These meals, in the noisy tavern, to her pleasant surprise, exceeded the enjoyment of any post-shift rituals she'd observed before the move--except for that

EVACUATION ROUTE

185

matter of headboard abuse, in which category she was *definitely* experiencing a cold streak. It was sufficiently frosty to damage the citrus crop of her libido if it was to continue much longer.

Feeling a spirit of adventure as always after a relocation, she spent more than she otherwise would have on a new bedroom outfit. That exorbitance now seemed like a jinx. Darlene would not, however, under any circumstances she could yet imagine, phone ol' Guillermo to invite him for a booty call. *No mas*, even with the growing anticipation of leisure sleep-in time tomorrow. She wouldn't mind being with *someone*. But it must be someone new, and preferably a heavy sleeper.

These Wednesday nights before a full day off now began with a burger and dollar drafts at *Tall Tales*. Sun-ripened anglers, freshly in off the Gulf or the Crystal River estuary, delayed their home-comings in a neon tanning booth of raucous laughter and country music from the jukebox. The gravel parking-lot seldom failed to be taken up by as many boat trailers as cars. Darlene ordered her *Tall Tale* Burger without onion, probably pointless, she thought, and sipped the first beer from a frosted 16 oz. glass. Her limit was two. The place wasn't heavily populated with a clientele of single, male fishermen, Darlene began to think. She resisted offers of additional free drinks. There were just too many wedding rings flashing in that neon.

Then it was time to drive carefully down the Suncoast Highway (US-19) to Homosassa, pitch her waitress costume and the change-apron into a segregated part of the hamper. She tried to shower off most of the Buffalo-wing funk but then gave her face a rest from renewed makeup. Except for some lipstick. *What ya see is what ya git, ol' timers.* She walked under the dim, yellow streetlights down to the Association Clubhouse.

Bingo nights were catching on with Darlene. They were her first and favorite clubhouse activity after her minimal holiday participation. Show Me the Money took place during her Saturday evening shift, and the euchre tournaments were staged on Mondays. The pool was a bit chilly now which didn't deter some of the New Years Eve fools from accepting its challenge in their underwear.

She brought her tip-cup home on Wednesdays with no shortage of quarters and wrinkled dollar bills to be redistributed for a good cause. (Coffee and baked treats, she supposed.) By her third visit she was playing four or five cards and hadn't yet lost money. Four cards cost her a dollar-per-game. This seemed to meet with some resentment from the crones and their husbands who were all playing two cards. Sportsmanship and the unwritten *spirit of fun* stricture wouldn't hinder Darlene, even if someone took the time to inform her of the unwritten rules. *Explain the ph'losophy to me'stead a sittin' there givin' me dirty looks.* Hadn't these people lived through the Age of Greed in the Eighties? *That sort a old, passive, unassertive thinkin' might explain why we're all of us livin' in a trailer court. Spells it out pretty clear to me. Ooops, pardon me. I meant manufactured home development.*

But, she discovered, she wasn't the only one buying extra chances to win. She'd begun plunking down at the end of a middle table which turned out to seat some sort of rival faction. There

EVACUATION ROUTE

were three of them, relatively younger women she hadn't met before. Or, were they constitute a rival coven? *Hee, hee. Ah know that word 'cause Cher was in Witches of Eastwick, probably mah favoritest ever actress in one of mah all time favoritest flicks.* They all seemed to be an alpha type of female where she now began to sit They spread out their extra cards and goodluck totems in a space meant to accommodate six players. Darlene was the only one who didn't yet have any lucky fetishes but she was on the lookout to find just the right one. Now what small object could she link to any good luck she'd had lately?

There were two disadvantages to sharing a table with these gruff, nicotine voices (excluding little Gracie Goodrich). One, was the burning sensation on all of their ears when they ducked out by the pool for a smoke. They weren't so naïve about the whispers at their backs during coffee break, so they did some dishing of their own:

"Every time I win," Dianne Kaake croaked, twisting a bronzed curl in front of her ear. "I get the evil eye from Sally and Bernard. Bernard actually shook his head like some kinda disappointed preacher. It wasn't much, but I seen it. Like I was a kid that colored on the Sunday School wall or somethin'"

"There's nothin' keepin' those ol' biddys from throwin' down as many cards as they can keep track of," Lucille Loomis said, in the parenthesis of white puffs coursing from her lips now. "I think maybe they ain't *got* the reaction time anymore to keep up."

"Yeah, and any time I yell out a Bingo, I think ol' Bunny Moore is gonna fly out a her seat after me." Diminutive Gracie fanned away smoke with her small hands.

Darlene contributed only a snicker of sympathetic derision and a *tsk*. As the newest resident, it might be too soon to fully commit with any particular faction. Especially since Dianne's husband Curtis, who plucked the balls from the hopper and called the numbers, was maybe the best looking man in the park. She always tried to avoid married men, but sometimes a domestic situation proved, after some study, to be ruined anyway. She could think of only two occasions when that was too much of a temptation to resist, but never for more than a rendezvous or two of using the guy in question.

So, better to cautiously examine the landscape. But, she was probably tarnished already by sitting with these apparent pariahs. Playing from the middle table would also require some careful discretion. Any visual foreplay with Curtis would be too tricky. He had already snuck in a wink last week the moment Diane got up to visit the bathroom. Darlene coyly looked away. Maybe Dianne's friendship would prove to be the better option.

Curtis was a tall man with most of his follicles still pushing out blond hair above a golfer's tan. He seemed to have a nice sense of humor. He was of an age to have acquired modest love-handles and a variety of Viet Nam Veteran's hats though he seemed to bear no sour resentments. Darlene's ex had been an extreme example of those embittered warriors. Post Traumatic Smack and Drag was *his* legacy from the war. Curtis continually cracked everyone up with one-liners related to the game and its participants. These he delivered in a relaxed deadpan and with the timing of a seasoned comic.

EVACUATION ROUTE   189

The first time Darlene attended, Bunny Moore hollered for him to slow down, that she couldn't keep up, even with only two cards. Curtis responded in a heartbeat as if the old harpy had purposely teed it up for him: "Ohhhhhhh sevvvvennnnty-twooooo!

Well, it tickled Darlene whose laugh threshold might, admittedly, be low. The quip left Dianne straight-faced. That sort of hamming from her husband must have gotten old, time out of mind.

The main attraction for Darlene, after his manner and the nice smile, was his imposing build and his resonant subwoofer voice. They'd certainly chosen the right guy for Bingo duty. She'd never heard a lower one, except maybe Bowzer, the front man of the oldies group, *Sha Na Na*. She never missed their TV show. And, she never comparison shopped based on anything but actual length and girth, though she'd often heard about testicle size being relative to a deep voice. Most of her romantic interests were probably tenors if she thought about it. Or, baritones at best. But this guy...this guy must be dragging around a pair of plums, or Grade A jumbos like her kids once colored for Easter. Between games, Darlene tried, surreptitiously, to gauge the distance between the man's thumb and forefinger. But, that might be an old wives conjecture same as the register of a man's voice.

Tonight the *Glade* Association Clubhouse was well attended, this being the first Wednesday of the New Year. Bingo had been on a three week hiatus to accommodate the busy Holidays. The rest of her neighbors, it seemed, were as anxious as she for a return to a less hectic schedule. None of the geezers desired eye-contact with her after their failed gropes of New Year's Eve. Maybe the biddies at the party were more perceptive than she'd first thought. Their men may have gotten asses chewed back at home. And not in a good way.

Then, dang it, there came another wink from big 'ol Curtis. Unless he had something in his eye. Maybe it was a nervous tic. Nope, just the one little blink and the faintest of inquisitive grins while Dianne arranged her four cards and dollar stacks of quarters. *Well, you go ahead 'n' picture it all ya want, big boy. I ain't sure Ah need the aggravation a close quarters adultery at this point. Let me just see how hard up Ah might get.* She made the same arrangements with her own cards and money then took a second peek at Curtis's grip on a can of *Diet Coke. That thumb 'n' forefinger goes all the way around that can.*

"Is everybody ready?"

"We *been* ready!" Bunny Moore scolded.

"All right, Bunny. You anxious to make yer usual donation? You know you can't use those losses on yer income tax. For any a you newcomers, we start with a regular Bingo and eight more to follow. There'll be three Special Bingos thrown in and then our big Cover-All Jack-Pot at the end."

"We know all that! Get on with it! Christmas has broke me again 'n' I'm feelin' lucky!" Eunice Belk hollered. She was nearly drowned out as Curtis threw the switch for the ball tumbler. It growled like a vacuum cleaner with a Leggo in its belt.

Darlene admired the pout Curtis provoked on Bunny's slack mug at the next table. Those ill-fitting dentures would soon morph her lips into a sneer depending on which players, other than herself, had the luck tonight. But it also appeared that she and her friends were beginning to escalate the Bingo arms race. Everyone at the next table was now playing four cards. *Well alright, ladies. Let's throw down.*

"G, fifty-eight!" The popcorn machine halted in deference to the caller's velour resonance..

"Are ya back to yer old grind?" Lucille asked Darlene. "Ah'm ready for spring, That's my next landmark I'm lookin' forward to."

The first half of the evening had culminated in coffee and cookies, their Association fees at work. The women went out onto the pool deck where Lucille and Dianne could smoke.

"Don't forget the green diarrhea for St. Patrick's Day," Gracie Goodrich said in her Shirley Temple voice. Darlene guessed that the little gal was *not* from the south.

"Not for me. That smell a boiled cabbage just...," she shivered, undraping a sweater from over her shoulders. It crackled with static when she pushed her arms into the sleeves. "Yeah, Ah'm back to luggin' beers 'n' chicken wings. Ah need to make back some money 'n' this ain't helpin' so far tonight."

"Christmas always cleans me out, too," Dianne added, smoke blooming. "Santa just picks me up by the ankles and shakes. I been thinkin' a puttin' me in an application out to the Super Wal-Mart. How old do ya gotta be to get one a them greeter jobs?"

Lucille rubbed her arms briskly. "Will it ever warm back up? Bobby Higgs locks his office in there just so's we can't get at the thermostat. Di, I don't think ya wanta do that. I was down before Christmas to the one by Brooksville. Those greeters was checkin' all a folks's receipts on their way out? I heard one ol' granny greeter takin' crap from teenagers about it. Can you imagine?"

Gracie ducked a perfect smoke ring blown by Dianne, who was almost down to the filter. This usually signaled that the coffee break was nearing an end. Darlene looked over her shoulder through the glass slider to see that half of the crowd had returned to their seats. Curtis was ready to return the balls to the bubblegum machine after making certain, again, that every one was in the tray.

"It's a sign a the times," Darlene said, one hand on the door handle. "Business is down so thievin's up. And them minimum wage temps was prob'ly responsible for their own security."

"Well, shoot, then. Ain't no problem for me." Dianne stubbed out the filter in a sand bucket by the door. "If it's one thing I know how to do, it's to take shit 'n' then deal it back out. Them little pricks might get a surprise at what I give 'em back." She held the door for Gracie.

The balance of the evening's event went by amicably. Between games, side topics at the table ranged from the weather again (a cooler winter than usual), to the slipping quality of maintenance in the park.

"I am *not* mowin' my own little bit of a damn lawn," Lucille declared under her breath. "Throw my shoulder out every time I try startin' my ol' piece a junk."

"Remember a-hole Bobby's note last year about cleanin' up our yards or they'd do it at the homeowner's expense?" Laughing, Dianne dumped her markers in a pile and set out her next dollar's worth of quarters. "How dare 'em?!"

"I don't think they can do that about the grass," Gracie squeaked. "Can they?"

"Nah, darlin'," Dianne told her. "Only the junky yard problem is in the Association by-laws. Curtis got it outta the bottom a the desk and read it. Bobby'll whine for awhile and plead poor. Until the owner says he's comin' for an inspection. Then everything'll get done at once, just like always."

"Last time it was warm enough to swim," Lucille said. "I woke up from sunnin' and my Eddie was dippin' bugs with the screen? I said to *put that down, you ol' fool. We pay to have that done.*"

"I ain't even *got* a mower, new *or* junk," Darlene whispered.

"Don't worry about it, hon," Dianne said. "We ain't sp'osed to have to do it 'n' we ain't doin' it. Bobby can fuck hisself."

"Y'all *know* he's tried." Lucille giggled.

The Old Testament voice of Curtis now proclaimed a special Bingo. He moved out from behind the hopper holding up an example of the next game. "This'll be your postage stamp Bingo. You got to cover the four squares in each corner. Can ever'one see?"

Someone at a different table won the postage stamp Bingo. Darlene got no more than two out of the four numbers in any one corner of her cards. The last regular Bingo was won somewhere else as well. The competition was *gaining* on their little coven, now, by playing those extra cards. It put them out of their comfort zones for a few sessions but now they were starting to relax, deftly placing their markers on as many as six cards.

Darlene sensed a note of vindictiveness in the glee at other tables with each win. *Well geez. Is that mah blood, too, in the water, too,?* "Time for the final round, the coverall jackpot." Carl and his ancient assistant, Jeanette Brookins, skimmed a percentage from each of the previous pots to make up an amount at the end that really mattered.

"I'm ashamed a how bad I want this," Dianne whispered.

"Ah *need* it," Darlene said. "Ah might be down a few bucks 'n' Ah don't wanta set a precedence. Not the way Ah wanted to start out the year."

The Cover All was at once more tense *and* frantic than the previous games. It usually took many numbers to find a winner. Most of the available numbers would have to be called. There were

EVACUATION ROUTE

still only four cards in front of Darlene but she kept her left palm full of the tiddley-wink markers. One marker was always pinched and ready between the thumb and forefinger of her right. The tension had much more time to build than in a regular Bingo.

When one of her cards had only two empty numbers remaining, she expected a cry of elation at any moment from one of the other tables. Curtis continued to call the numbers with growing tension in his voice, as if he was narrating a Florida election. After what seemed like another ten minutes, Darlene had only one space left under the I. A second card closed in on completion with one blank spot left beneath the N. Another awaited under the B. *Well, for heaven's sake. Would one a you ol' crones just go ahead 'n' win the damn thing, if it means so much to ya?*

"I, 23." Curtis's tone had begun to betray some frustration.

"That's *mah* Bingo." Darlene spoke quietly in a level voice of entitlement. *Act like ya been there before*, she reminded herself as she snapped down the final button. Oh, and on a lighter note, she told herself: *Suck it, Bunny!* Then, loud enough for all to hear, "Boo-yah!"

Jeanette wheezed over with an envelope containing $32.50. That was the figure written on the outside and Darlene resisted looking inside as she might for a Bdub's bonus. No need to aggravate this management.

"Congratulations, Darlene. Give it up for our newest resident, Darlene Spurgeon!" Curtis voiced this with all the inflections of an NBA starting lineup intro.

Where's mah spotlight? Darlene thought. The round of applause was sparse, except for a few loud *wooo-hooos* and moderate shrieks from her home table. Dianne cut loose with a shrill whistle to rival any referee. Folks who were busy gathering their things jumped in alarm. Darlene and her friends returned their cards, tossing out their Styro coffee cups. They retrieved all the plastic dots, many of which tended to drop under the tables from arthritic fingers in the heat of competition. .

"I'll walk ya home," Dianne said. "You prob'ly ain't learned where all the potholes are, yet."

Darlene shouldered her purse-strap. "Why *are* the streetlights so dim? And the one in front a mah place flickers all night. Glad Ah ain't epileptic."

"It was explained to us that those're s'pposed to look like old-time gaslights. Why they appear yella." Dianne replied "*Why*, you might ask? Anyways, they'd have a soft glow 'n' be just fine if it wasn't for all the cracks and patchin' we gotta stumble over. Seems like the trippin' spots are in the darkest stretches, halfway between lamps. The yella stripes have mostly been wore off the speed bumps, too."

"Yeah, Ah found some of 'em already," Darlene said. "Ah gotta actually obey the 8 mph sign, 'specially in the dark."

The women paused outside for a few moments to say *goodnight* to Lucille and Gracie. The Bingo players disbursed quickly, most of them backing their golf carts out of the lava-rock parking strip between the pool and street. Carts whirred away in both directions of the park's horseshoe.

EVACUATION ROUTE

They hadn't walked fifty feet when bright headlights wheeled into the park and came up behind them, illuminating their route. The low growl of an engine at near idle grew louder so the women moved aside. The thump of an expensive bass speaker approached behind the engine.

"Damn it, I hate that beat noise. Kids think it sounds so great, they gotta share it with everybody. That ain't even music," Dianne grumbled.

As the car moved around them, however, Darlene made out the lyrics. "That's the Rollin' Stones, hon. That one about the devil?"

The tail-lights moved away, speeding up once the car had passed them. The brake lights brightened abruptly as the driver found one of the unpainted speed bumps.

"Ain't they *all* about the devil?" Dianne sighed.

Darlene and Dianne picked up their pace. It looked like some kind of big old luxury gas guzzler. Those vintage car show battleships always gathered on a blocked-off street during Manatee Days in Crystal River. It crept more cautiously after the sharp bump. Again, the brake lights pulsed as the driver came to a complete stop. The women halted as well. A flashlight beam came to life out of the driver's window. It played over the empty carport of an unlighted doublewide until it found the house number.

"They're lookin' for somebody," Darlene said.

"*What's troublin' you is the... nature, of mah game.*"

"They can look all night, hon," Dianne whispered. "That dump is empty. Sticker on the sign, says *Owner Motivated*. Ain't gonna do any good the way property values are plungin'."

"Yeah, ain't *that* the truth. Bobby 'n' mah realtor couldn't talk me into even lookin' inside."

They waited for some silly reason, maybe to see if the driver would get out and peer in the windows. But the vehicle soon rolled away.

"Ooops, sorry. No sale, Bobby." Dianne chuckled.

"Well, anyways, that's *one* lawn he'll wanta keep mowed." Darlene brought out her keys as they rounded the bend at the back of the park. She could see her porch light from there and the faulty streetlight. "Have a nice rest a your evenin', young lady."

"I sure will. I can hear Curtis snorin' from here." Dianne shook her head with resignation. "I should count it as a blessin'. Don't spend that big 'ol jackpot all in one place."

"Well, tomorrow's Thursday. So let's go garage salin'.'"

"Sure." Dianne replied. "Anythin'."

Chapter Nine

Except for dusk coming down so quickly in January, Bella was very much enjoying her return to the sea. The gambling boat was much bigger than Papi's shrimper, and probably a lot more seaworthy. It certainly smelled better, though the odors of fish, seaweed and flotsam of the harbor and the briny deep itself had proved to be a perfume, provoking her memories..

Bella never wanted to return to Seminole *Hard Rock* no matter how nice the accommodations were or the ease of arranging a transaction. That could have been no one other than Boogaloo she spotted in her peripheral vision on Thanksgiving night. No doubt in her mind. She didn't know of anyone else who looked that scary. Or, more out of place. And, what was worse, she was pretty sure that he'd caught a glimpse of *her*. He was in motion toward the elevator just as she stepped in and pressed for the 4th floor. She then took her time with the john, a software salesman (allegedly) from California. Tyler? Tyler must have thought he'd scored a real bargain with the extra time. *Yeah, hon, you are the lucky one hundredth customer.* Now she couldn't find the right argument to impress upon Merry how dangerous it might be to troll there anymore. New Year's Eve had apparently made no impression on her partner in crime. That *was* good money, Bella had to admit. But, not typical.

Would that greasy bastard, Boogaloo, really dare to try recruiting among clean, morally upright cocktail waitresses? Hmmm. Let me examine that thought again. The strange seductive power of biker leathers concealing flabby bodies and skinny souls was familiar to her. Merry argued that it was more likely the case that he'd already found new girls and was just in there scouting for high-end johns. If that was true, the two soliciting bikers must have raised their sights at a new customer base. Then Merry made that big score on New Year's Eve and there was no convincing her to avoid the casino.

Bella made sure to be at the booking office well before evening departure time. The *Narcissus* carried players of all experience levels; hardcore gamblers, casual partiers most interested in a boat ride, and learners like herself. The ones who thought they were card sharks weren't interested in dining. They ordered a grilled-cheese or pre-packaged microwave burger from passing wait staff. There weren't any alcohol drinks being comped so the stewards brought them well drinks and domestic bottled beer on a cash basis. Well soft drinks were free but could be slow to arrive.

She didn't see the same tourists every trip but some of the seasoned gambling veterans became familiar. It was more important that they not see *her* every trip.

Bella made a great show for management and crew that she was a repeat passenger for the purpose of becoming a more skilled gambler. She just needed more practice. Of course, this required the cash investment of early blackjack failures which increased her overhead. Whenever she was successful in securing a *date* before disembarking, she tried to make back her losses by stressing the specialties on *her* menu. Added compensation of an occasional hard spanking or anal usually tilted her balance significantly out of the red.

Her wardrobe became more casual—slacks and a blouse or tank top, cross-trainers on her feet. She went light on the cosmetics; very little, if any, mascara and shadow. She could easily be just another housewife with a husband out of town.

Susan in the dock office took Bella's $10 bill and fastened an admission band around her wrist "Good evening, Marcia. Back for another try? You're getting to be one of our regulars. Diet Coke?"

Bella put on a smile that she hoped wasn't too businesslike and nodded. "Yes, ma'am. I must keep a clear head to do any good."

Susan pushed the complimentary soda across the long table which served as a counter. Behind her, in the shore kitchen, four of the help were completing preparations for the voyage; making sandwiches, sliding hot trays of wings and fries, out of two commercial ovens and into a portable warmer. "Well. I hope you'll have good fortune out there."

"If I don't, at least there is the sea and the sunset."

Bella carried her drink out to a picnic table under the long, pavilion roof of the dockside staging area. A few scattered tourists, mostly older couples, waited with her. There were no single men, yet, but it was early *and* a weeknight. She heard more cars arriving in the gravel lot outside the fence. If no prospective clients showed up tonight, that would be fine with her. The excursion would never be a waste of time. She needed a few trips like this to firmly establish that she was simply an innocent gambling enthusiast, though still a novice. And, she really simply enjoyed a nice evening aboard, even when there was no serious business at the end of it.

Weeks ago, Bella dropped comments to the boat's Captain to the effect that much of her youth had been spent on the water and that she was feeding a strong pull of nostalgia whenever she came aboard. She didn't worry that her frequency of sailing with them must seem to border on some sort of obsessive compulsion. But, hers were dwarfed by the needs of their primary customers

When Bella saw the captain and four white-clad stewards (the earlier kitchen crew wearing fresh uniforms), pushing food carts up the ramp, she reviewed the girls' prohibition against dating *any* of them. *That* was arrived at after long debate. Some loose relationships were beginning to form, anyway, but mention of money for referrals would blow their cover. Now the three blackjack dealers and the roulette and craps guys went aboard. To have even *one* of the blackjack dealers scouting for her would be just such an advantage. The crew's boarding signaled that passengers and players could soon follow.

Bella took up her shoulder bag and slid her chair back under the patio table. She sipped her soda, walking. There wasn't even *one* single guy to be seen so far, but over her shoulder she saw that a short line of passengers were still in the office. More cars were crunching into the gravel lot, but the evening was looking doubtful for making a score. She could call Merry when they got back into port, then just go home. They'd done very well over the Holidays and were ahead on the rent. They could coast for one night.

Wrong! Wrong! Not the way to think at all. No pension plan, no health insurance for our line of work. All they had for that was baggies of leftover antibiotics in the freezer. Their physical assets had an expiration date and needed to be exploited before these sagged or spread.

The *Narcissus* motored slowly down the channel, obeying no-wake rules. Her deeper draft necessitated caution. Day-charter fishing boats and other recreational craft shared the channel, coming home out of the beginning sunset. Marker buoys bobbed, gulls wheeled to their water landings then bobbed, crying their hunger into the wake. The ship would bear off to the northwest (*to starboard*, as Bella hadn't forgotten) once they cleared the three mile prohibition for blackjack.

She stayed on the promenade deck, outside the small dining room which was, so far, unoccupied. She moved slowly aft along the rail as the sun disappeared entirely. *Narcissus* was big enough that Bella barely felt the diesel vibrations through the deck. A pleasant playlist of soft reggae instrumentals was usually piped out onto the narrow walkways of both casino decks. It was currently turned off for the karaoke M.C. who happened to have a decent voice. Well, in her humble opinion.

When Bella reached the forward observation balcony, full darkness hadn't yet descended. A half-moon climbed low behind them.

The nearly submerged shore lights of New Port Richie were still easy to find. In another few minutes, they were gone. The glow of Tampa further south was just beginning to show against the darkening mauve of the sky.

Passing through the dining room on her way aft, Bella dropped her empty soda can into a recycle bin. There were still no passengers eating. Four large, covered buffet pans sat alongside the tables. Tea candles beneath each warmed with steady flames as *Narcissus* plowed the mirror surface of the Gulf. It was too soon to eat. The food was filling but hardly 5-star. Legal blackjack, on the other hand, was her immediate object. The stewards had yet to bring out the stacks of disposable table service and the usual huge bowl of tossed salad. She would sit down when there were some eating companions, hopefully a single male or two.

After going up some side stairs to the blackjack deck, the gambling soon turned into a tough lesson for the third straight trip. Bella won an early hand but then dropped four straight at a table with Jens and Marcia from Fairbourne, Ohio. She won by holding on the first two cards dealt to her; valued nineteen in total. She lost the last two by asking for a card on sixteen, then worse, by hitting on fifteen.

Bella tipped the dealer a dollar then swayed forward and back down the companionway to the slots. Everywhere in this long room, the passengers were playing in connubial pairs. She lost four quarters to an old fashioned one-armed-bandit. But her fifth coin brought her the pulse raising chime music and spasms of neon. *Go. Go,* she whispered, but the cascade trailed off at $8.50, total.

EVACUATION ROUTE

She took the quarters burped out for this minor score and again, walked away. After trading coin for bills, he joined a queue of passengers who'd found their appetites and waited to get into the dining room, forward. Its capacity was only 20 diners but the wait wasn't too long tonight. Her hot streak probably wouldn't resume after the meal but this was the best way to find any singles aboard that she may have missed.

Swedish meatballs, chicken, roast potatoes, whole green-beans in butter sauce. At the end of the buffet, the only single man in the room, a steward, sliced prime-rib under a heat lamp. He was a great looking guy but with a tat of a three-color, garland-draped crucifix up his neck and those black, quarter-sized earlobe spreaders. *Uh-uh. I'm probably not of much interest to him, either.*

"Au jus?"

"Yes please," Bella said. The drippings quickly coursed through her green-beans on the Chinette paper plate. Good thing that she'd put her salad into a separate bowl. The plastic service was the kind that looked like actual silver and she mused about slipping a thoroughly wiped set into her purse. *Bet I'm not the only one.*

She added a roll but no butter (that's how good they were) then went to look for a seat. The five tables-for-four were nearly full. But there was Jens and wife with two empty seats waving her over to join them. Was that even *possible*? That they'd like to kick off their marriage with a little polyamory. Then she recalled their small-talk about their epic blowout wedding and the addition of a gambling cruise to their honeymoon. They were just friendly young people and Bella's speculation vanished.

"Thank you," she said, arranging her food on the table. "Looks like everyone has become hungry at the same time." she observed.

"Or, they wanted a timeout from giving away their money." Jens squeezed Marcia's hand.

"Pass me the salt, will you, baby?" Marcia carved a meatball in half.

They were a pleasant couple but a few years away from being exploitable for bedroom variety. Bella made the usual small talk about the food, the shipboard amenities, and the couple's fleeting luck. Jens and Marcia weren't going to break whatever bank or off-shore account the *Narcissus* subscribed to. (No one was.) They would soon be embracing on the karaoke deck, admiring the moon on the calm water.

Bella wished them *good luck* when she finished. She rose to dump her plate and salad bowl into the trash. In the end, she hated to waste the shiny, ersatz silverware. She cleaned her service as best she could with a clean spot of the napkin then dropped all into her tote. The girls would soon have a complete set at home. She took a couple of the big chocolate-chip cookies that were set out for dessert, slipping them into a baggie for Merry.

Jens and Marcia again joined Phillip's black-jack table when seats became available. Philip had been repeating his beginner's tutorial that Bella heard previously concerning who was showing what but left off when these newbie's abandoned their place. It must be permissible to cost the boat a bit of profit if it led to the players eventually becoming overconfident.

EVACUATION ROUTE 207

Now the dealer showed a deuce. Bella was dealt an ace and an 8. No one else had been dealt an ace so she hit when Phillip gave her a second one, hinting aloud that it was *soft*. The newlyweds went bust as did the dealer. Without giving the boat a chance to get even, she stood up to let someone else sit in. She watched the next few hands and felt the *Narcissus* begin to come about. Time to call it a trip.

She descended again to the dining/slots deck and made her way forward along the promenade. On the bow, below the bridge, was more convenient than the small observation spot above the bridge for watching the glow of the shore rise back into sight. Bella spotted the first channel lights. *"Red, right, returning,"* Poppi taught her, to know which side of the channel they should steer toward. At age twelve, she could take the helm.

A half-moon was still climbing off the port quarter, generously spattering green, broken glass upon the sea. She nudged along the narrow passage forward as *Narcissus* pushed through this mirror of fairy lights. The boat came about, precisely through the narrow first pair of marker buoys. The red, starboard one was briefly screened from her view as the skipper entered the channel. No one else seemed to have joined her though the passageway was safe enough with double railings. It opened up beneath the Captain's overhanging bridge. Two other adventurous passengers joined her from the port side.

"Yeah, you can come to get me, I guess," she spoke to Merry on her cell phone. "I am what Phillip would call *busted*, as far as having a.... you know."

Merry sounded alert enough, not on the nod, which occasionally delayed her from answering. "Ah like that Phillip. He might be kinda swishy though."

"We discussed this, girlfriend. If he *is* gay, it can only help to keep us from trying to exploit the help."

"Mmm-hmm," Merry said. "An' Ah'd fuck him anyways, like Ah said. Lemme grab mah keys 'n' Ah'll be on mah way."

Bella snapped her seatbelt with a sigh. "Take us to somewhere for the *Fourth meal*. It doesn't have to be Taco Bell, either. It will be my treat."

Merry backed out of her spot and slowly crept up the lot's incline. "Ah could do, 'cept somethin' weird just happened on the way in here."

"Weird, how?"

"Well, there was this guy on a fancy bike starin' at me from across the oncomin' direction at a light." Merry idled down the short half-block to Suncoast Ave., US19. "When the green come on, he looks me over kinda suspicious-like, slowin' up as we crossed our paths. Somethin' 'bout him was familiar. Ah couldn't even *say* what. Just was creepy to me."

"Hey, that is your *job* to be appealing to the eye. Aren't you flattered at all?"

"I *know* that. But Ah could a swore he whipped inta *Mickey D's* in mah rearview, tryin' to come back aroun' at me. He must a caught that same light again, so Ah lost him."

"You may have passed up some good trade, too."

"But he couldn't of known mah line a work, Bel. To me, that made him a wannabe stalker. Well, for fuck's sake!" Merry jammed on the brakes, bringing the Tracker to a halt ten yards before the stop sign.

"*What* is the matter with you, crazy girl!?"

Another car with gamblers in it made a panic stop behind them. They laid on the horn then saw that there was plenty of room to get around. Merry just waved then killed the headlights and continued in reverse.

"That's the same guy, right over there at the *Race Trak*. Ah'm positive. Ah had a long look at that pretty bike."

"Mare, that boy is licking on an ice-cream cone. He is riding on a Gold Wing. Are you afraid of someone on a Gold Wing or are you losing your marbles."

"Then tell me what's he still doin' in the neighborhood? Ah ain't *havin'* him follow us home. Ah *know* he never saw me pull in here. So's is this just, like, the hugest sorta co-incidence? Ah don't *think* so, if he's over there watchin' the road, Ah'll let him just finish his li'l treat before we move the hell along. Let's us just ease on back by the dock for a li'l bit."

Bella sighed. "I guess so. You do whatever will relax your mind."

Merry backed along the edge of the *Lucky Seas* drive and lot. She put the headlights on again. Bella didn't bother to suggest that it might not help their carefully woven backstories if the Captain or any of the crew spotted them sitting in a car together. "I suppose we do not get breakfast now? I want a cone now, too."

"What? We neither of us earned nothin' to justify celebratin'. 'Less you managed to blow a few yokels in the bathroom." Merry unfastened her seatbelt then leaned across to dig through the glovebox.

"Please don't be crude. Anyway, it is called the *head* on a ship. And also you should not smoke that shit in a closed-in space with *me* in the car."

"The *head*, huh? Ain't that the perfect word?" Merry slammed the glove-box closed and sat back with a huff. "Ah ain't *that* stupid. Ah was just lookin' for a *Wet Nap*. An' Ah still say, no earnin' should mean no treats."

"That is not so, girlie friend. I will have you to know I am up $6.50 at the slots, and over $8 bucks from blackjack. So what do you think of *that?* I am really getting the hang of that game. My little jackpot from slots came just before dinner. I was hungry so had no time to lose it back. You would have been very proud. The best I have done gambling so far and also the most fun."

Merry rolled the windows up to keep what there was of the rattling AC inside the old vehicle, though the rear canvas was compromised by a few cracks.

"Go back up to the corner now and see what he is doing," Bella said. "I am thirsty and this is starting to feel loco."

Again the car inched toward the highway, dim headlights showing the way. "Sorry, Bell, but Ah just got a sense about some stuff."

EVACUATION ROUTE   211

"Really? Do you have a sense how *you* could have worked tonight?"

"Go ahead 'n' poke fun but you'll thank me *one* day for mah par'noid. Anyways, he appears to be gone. Wish Ah knew whichever way he went to. Was that such a big inconvenience? We can prob'ly still get ya a cone now."

"No, I will find something at home. Take the back streets if you think we should."

Merry signaled a turn south. The traffic on the Suncoast Hwy. was out thinned nicely, midnight to 4am the slowest it would be in any 24 hour period.. Easier now to spot the single headlights of scooter-bums. Or, scooter gentlemen, maybe, in this case. She accelerated.

"Feel better now?" Bella sat up straight instead of her usual relaxed collapse against the door. She studied the side mirror.

"Not total. Ah don' know why one good-citizen lookin' ol' boy freaked me out. Just gave me a bad feelin', the way he was studyin' on me, seemed like."

Bella patted Merry's hand where it rested on the gear shift between them. "Guess I cannot blame you, chica, to follow your instincts. I do not need to eat this late."

"You can unwind in front a the tube. Ah ain't touched yer Frosted Flakes."

"Well, how about the milk?"

Merry altered her route abruptly and swerved into the left turn lane. "Ah guess we're makin' a stop into the *RaceTrack* after all."

Chapter Ten

Since rolling into Crystal River on Christmas night (reaching the Gulf, he could go no further west), Walt had scoured much of the so-called Nature Coast for a final home address. He worked his way through nearly three free real estate catalogues. It had been only five weeks since he unpacked his bags into yet another efficiency unit. This one was marginally nicer than *The Armada* he'd left behind in Jacksonville Beach. The pool had water, at least, and the water looked clean. The towels weren't threadbare or speckled with rust spots. But the *fixer-upper, handyman project* he discovered last night appeared to be the closest, so far, to meeting his criteria. This find came just in time because he felt his patience, his due diligence of the first few weeks of house hunting, wearing thin.

It wasn't too much of a culture shock, given the modest upward mobility he hoped for, that he was once again ensconced in a room with a weekly rate. As at *The Armada,* he shared the motel with work crews from out of the area, and a few elderly tourists. His default parking spot was next to a geriatric Oldsmobile which was nearly the same vintage as his Caddy. His room, off the balcony above, usually had the only light still showing in *any* window if he returned late from his search.

Of course, the best perk (other than cost) of *Manatee Motor Inn* was that he no longer went to his clerk/broom duties. He slept through the night, no longer worried about threats to the Caddy. The new car-alarm was properly installed by an independent repair shop on his first morning in town. But, he maintained an empathy for those asphalt paving, cable stringing, sewer laying guys who fired up their diesel pickup engines at 5:30 a.m. They didn't keep him from rolling peacefully back to sleep. Their evening showers and toilet flushing, which resounded through all of his walls and the floor beneath his stocking feet, weren't nearly so audible as their trucks in the morning. To Walt, this already seemed a more tranquil coast than the one where he'd spent much of his adult life.

He most often left the television off in deference to the laboring class around and below him. He learned on the first night that the hot water for his own shower was of a more generous duration if he took it after midnight. But, how to stay awake until then? Walt had rediscovered, in his recent two years of *clean time,* the reading of literary fiction. Now there was no end of variety after the limited prison and rehab stacks; or waiting for Warren's replenishing visits. On his travels in search of inexpensive real estate, Walt stumbled upon two cluttered used book stores and then a battered *Clockwork Orange* at a garage sale. The efficacy of negative operant conditioning described in the Anthony Burgess classic was one with which he was uncomfortably familiar from his one trial use of Antabuse. Malcolm Lowrey's *Under the Volcano,* bought from *Turning Yellow Book Nook* in Crystal River, was a depressing object lesson he probably didn't need, but hey, it was literature and it was cheap. Maybe he'd resist *Lost Weekend* or *Leaving Las Vegas* if he ever came across them. William Burroughs should probably be avoided, also. Anything by Timothy Leary

Walt wasn't sure what to think of the doublewide he'd stumbled onto in the dark of night except that it would have to be a significant bargain for him to risk purchasing. What a roach trap that place appeared to be. At least the exterior gave that impression. To come back in daylight for a tour would be the prudent course, though he dreaded listening to the property manager push it at him. He could count on hearing that there was an easy, inexpensive repair for every flaw, dent, scrape, or leak. So, how miserly did he intend to be? That was the requisite question forestalling his sleep longer than usual..

Walt found the place out of the third, thick newsprint real estate catalogue he'd pulled from a vending box in Crystal River. This was the last one for him to leaf through, hoping to save himself a realtor's commission. He knew that he couldn't avoid a seller's rep except for the occasional *fisbo* signs he drove past: *for sale by owner*. For those, the title and transfer papers were reputed to be a crap-shoot.

The whole process involved many miles of driving as Walt attempted to match the pictures in the catalogues with signs and properties along the roads. At least he was learning the lay of the land. The catalogue told him only the general area within the nearby towns and villages. Sometimes there were clues; such as that the property was close to this or that school, tourist attraction, boat launch, or downtown. The real-estate agents weren't going to spell out for you *exactly* where these listings were or they'd soon lose work.

There seemed to be quite an active social life as Walt eased the Caddy into the park, called *The Glade*. His first impression was that the road needed work. The clubhouse looked nice enough. He would have to assess the quality of pool maintenance in sunny daylight. The water should be clear enough to see a blue bottom with just a hint of chlorine in the air, though he planned never to immerse himself except on the most humid days. His preference was for the low dosage, pool-side buzz, dark shades hiding a Xanax snooze, the soothing music of a gurgling filter.

He waited patiently while some kind of function in the clubhouse began to disburse. Suddenly, people were exiting the building as Walt decided which of two lanes around the place he should follow. An Australian pursuit race of golf carts ensued. Now, where could he find and purchase a serviceable, used one of *those*? It seemed to be the preferred mode of travel among this demographic that he was belatedly joining. A good bike, too, ought to be acquired, same criteria.

216   CHRIS DUNGEY

When the traffic of carts had cleared somewhat, Walt slowly wove his way through the lagging pedestrians. These folks on foot included, in the polite low beams of the Caddy's headlights, a pair of ladies whose posteriors were neither sagging nor over-wide. Whatever the event was, it had been well attended. The woman illuminated best wore a white sweater draped over her shoulders. Her friend filled out a pair of denim shorts that just *might* look better in summer, on someone younger. This one wore a windbreaker. Walt would have declared it a draw if called upon to judge by some sexist, creeper criteria.

Then, an unmarked speed-bump reclaimed his attention with a jolt, causing him to slow further. The small berm was placed nearly in front of the property pictured in his flyer. He backed up carefully. It sure looked like the same place in the beam of his 6-volt lantern. The light was strong enough to highlight every blemish: Leaves and dried palm fronds were trapped in a back corner of the carport, past the entry steps. A push-broom of time-flattened bristles was blown over in front of the padlocked door of what he supposed was a detached laundry room. A nine in the address hung as a six, a half-step lower than its fellows, of which none were shiny black any longer. The aluminum siding, ostensibly white, would need extended power washing. That picture he'd been chasing must have been a decade old. Raising the angle of his light further revealed a hedge of various windblown seedlings prospering in the eaves troughs.

Those women never caught up to him, though Walt lingered another few minutes, eyeing the oil slick on the carport surface where his Caddy would reside. They must have reached their home, or homes. He *hoped*, for no particular personal reason, that they had gone their separate ways.

Now, drowsing on top of the bedspread (he'd actually begun making his bed every morning at the last rehab), it was not tonight's bedraggled doublewide he envisioned. The view from behind of those two women easily displaced images of *that* dubious structure. It was quite awhile since he'd enjoyed any conjugal company. There appeared to be a *several* ambulatory ladies coming out of that meeting, function, or whatever it was. But half of a Prozac and his one O'Douls neutralized these pleasant images before he could entertain the notion of manual relief. Even *he* required a more complete picture. He struggled to his feet and turned down the bedding.

The cheapest breakfast in Crystal River was from *Denny's*, Walt decided that perhaps he should begin to *support local*; allegiance to place an even newer core value than sobriety. He aimed the Caddy south toward Homosassa again—let's see what that tenement-in-a-box looks like in harsh, broad daylight. It turned out there was a perfectly named eatery not far from *The Glade*. *Annie's Breakfast*, it was called, and it must have been the right place. At 8:30 a.m. there were more cars parked in front of it than at the *Publix* supermarket diagonally across the lot. He had to wait for a table. But, Thursday was a still a workday for some poor minority of the townsfolk so there was a rapid turnover. Walt was completely retired for six weeks and had already lost track of the days of the week.

He waited on line for five minutes in the climbing humidity before a hostess, and not a young one, hustled him in to an open stool at the counter. She handed him a battered, laminated menu and was gone before he swiveled to face the fry cooks. Menu's the size of a movie poster, Walt thought. On the run, one of the short-order guys placed a slopping glass of ice water in front of him. The counter waitress, of the gum-snapping and bouffant hair variety, gave the counter a swift wipe nano-seconds before slapping paper napkin swaddled silverware down in nearly a single motion (well, one motion per hand). "Coffee, hon?"—she called over her shoulder as she darted to the kitchen portal. It was a well-oiled division of labor. A steaming short-stack, not in any way short, next to eggs and a pile of bacon, waited in the window on a platter. *Annie's* seemed not to offer any menu combination that would fit on a standard plate.

"Sure," Walt called, after carefully clearing vestiges of his ancient, remorseful smoker's morning phlegm. His lungs might be growing pink again, but the high-grit sandpaper at waking remained. Why slow up their process? Water was good enough. An offer of orange juice must have been lost in the rush. He could get a bottle when he made the imminent stop to slake the Caddy's thirst.

He ordered a short stack with two eggs over easy, sourdough toast to clean up the yoke with. He declined hash-browns as well as a choice of meats. There just wasn't any more room for take-away leftovers in his room's dollhouse refrigerator.

The pancakes were fluffy, ready to absorb his typical excess of syrup. The eggs were over-easy just enough to retain some runniness in the whites. He forked the bites onto the toast, trying to avoid looking at the floaters.

The Glade was still pretty sleepy when he turned into the entrance. There were a few early walkers. Walt drove in the opposite direction of the predominant pedestrian flow, which was also the opposite route from last night. None of the hikers resembled his female discoveries. Singly, or as a pair, the women who'd captured his imagination might not be early risers. Or, perish the thought, maybe they held jobs. Not a deal-breaker. He gave each slow, arm-pumping hiker a wide berth, moving slowly himself, leery of another jolt from an unmarked speed-bump. But, they were easier to find in daylight. He still dreaded a guided tour inside the derelict doublewide; if the manager was even awake, or on the premises. If the guy would only just hand over the key to Walt, a minor impediment to a sale might be removed.

He took a short leap of faith and drove down to the unit and parked there, halfway under the carport. The trudge back to the office was a continuation of his morning news briefing begun with the babble of worldviews assaulting him in *Annie's Breakfast*. Walt was just current enough on events to distinguish the ideological orientation of the talking heads proselytizing at each breakfast table that he passed. Some of the residents here were having their second cup of coffee in the enclosed Florida rooms attached to most units. There were two or three *good mornings* hailed from out of the darkened, screened-in interiors. Walt's response was a smile and a wave. He did not yet trust his morning voice, to which some phlegm had returned. One thing he could predict with certainty was that he wouldn't be awakening as early as any of *these* folks.

The Association Clubhouse stood unlocked. The *Glade* office was in the rear, next to a nicely appointed kitchenette. A light shone above a desk but no one was home. Or, was *that* the guy, out on the patio dipping debris from the pool? This fellow wore a battered boonie hat with a cord drawn tight under a stubbled chin; homemade wife-beater of raggedly amputated tee-shirt sleeves (Inverness Festival Days); and faded camo cargo shorts. If this was the manager, Walt surmised quickly from the man's wardrobe that a two-year certificate in Hospitality Management had been earned online and then forgotten. Then, Walt heard a toilet flush. A second man, of broad shoulders, medium height, and prominent, front loaded *foopa* emerged from a bathroom door, the sign's silhouettes indicating that men and women must share.

"Good mornin'! I didn't hear anyone come in."

This fellow was wearing cargo shorts, too, but these appeared to be freshly laundered. A clean looking polo shirt was stretched tightly over his girth. He stepped past Walt into the office. "What can I do you for?"

Walt followed the man as far as the door frame of the office. There they were, on a pegboard above the man's desk; a collection of master keys for, it appeared, all of the available units. These were highlighted on a plat diagram of the park next to the keys, hand printed For Sale stickers affixed. *You are here,* a once black *Sharpie* arrow pinned to the office spot, looked much older, faded and permanent.

Walt squinted. "That one, up at the end of the backstretch. Looks like it might be #27, maybe? I'd like to have a look inside that one, I think."

The manager's face lit up and became exponentially more attentive. "Ah, yes. Good ol' #27. Hey, I won't lie to you...are you a handyman?" A smile and a wink, but the guy didn't reach for that key.

"Well, I know a Phillips from a slot screwdriver," Walt said. "I've recently come into a bit of cash. My brother put a number in my phone for this *Angie's List*? Do you know how *that* works? I figure to use people she recommends for anything I *can't* do to get the place fixed up. Even if it *is* Florida, if you know what I mean."

There was still no attempt by the manager to take down the key for #27. Walt wondered how much sales resistance he would have to muster against the empty new models this guy *really* wanted to move.

"You don't have to tell *me*, friend, about the skills and professionalism of the local, nonunion tradesmen you can find on the

Publix bulletin board. It gets frustratin'. But, no, I haven't resorted to *Angie* yet. I have a pretty good list of my own. Of *reliable* folks, that is."

Now the manager extended a beefy, not so tanned hand for Walt to moistly shake. "I'm Bobby Higgs, host and Manager of *The Glade*. I represent the management company *Chalet and Lakes Properties*. They're based out in Colorado. Any future fluctuations in lot rent, you should know, come from them, not me. There's a lot of shoot-the-messenger sentiment goes around in this park that I just have to shrug off." Higgs raised his hand momentarily in the universal gesture of *I submit, don't hurt me.*

"I'm Walter Bocewicz, recently retired." Walt slipped free of Higgs's lingering salesman grip.

"So. Recent wealth and newfound leisure, sir. A combination I envy. Now, are you certain I can't show you one of our beautiful, new model homes? There's six luxuriously appointed, *Specially Priced*, move-in-today units down around the bend of our horseshoe. Save you a lot of bother so you can get on with that *leisure* a little quicker. This week we're thrownin' in free, fresh sod and decorative-block landscapin', gratis. Plus, you get your choice of a big ol' flat-screen or a 'fridge upon closin'.'"

Uh-huh. Take a breath there, Bobby, Walt thought. He had no trouble imagining how nice those places were. But Higgs wouldn't be moving them any time soon without taking a significant haircut. Or ever, if the banking crisis wasn't sorted out soon.

"Nah. I'm gonna have to resist the temptation, Mr. Higgs. I'm good to go for now, see, but I *am* without a pension and six

EVACUATION ROUTE 223

years away 'til Social Security. If I don't want to go back to work full time, and I sure don't, then I'll be living on the interest and probably *Ramen* noodles. I *can* put some money into bringing #27 up to snuff, though, and take her off your hands. How far is she from being habitable, would you figure?"

Higgs emitted a small but unrestrainable snort then finally stretched his wobbling abdomen across the cluttered desk to reach for those keys. "I would say you're prob'ly better off than in a tent or on a park bench. If you could find one an' wrestle it away from one of our local homeless, bless all their hearts. You're gonna want paint and carpet, new floorin', a drywall patch or two. I think it might need a commode, if I recall. And you won't want to ever spend any time in that shower stall in its present condition. I think the previous folks dressed out a deer or somethin' in there. That's prob'ly the minimum of stuff to make it comfortable before you lug in your furniture."

"I've slept on an air mattress before," Walt said. "And I'm currently not burdoned by *any* furniture." He didn't add that he'd also relied on gas station restrooms and *WetNap* hygiene.

"Sure," Higgs said. "The two window ACs they were gettin' by with have been misappropriated out of there, I hate to say. Primitive, but they kept the previous owners from roastin', I guess, 'till they became expendable. Only unit in the park without central air sittin' on a slab out back. Easy for you to replace, I suppose. And, get you a couple of fans, for sure. You don't have to worry about the heat and humidity for a few months."

Walt accepted the keys, breathed a shallow sigh of relief at the manager's apparent reluctance to offer a guided tour. He remembered being sent to the rector's office at St. Michael's for some disorderly or disrespectful behavior only to find that the man was ill and wouldn't be back for a few days. He felt like that "Thank you, Mr. Higgs."

"Call me Bobby. I won't insult your intelligence by lookin' over your shoulder. You'll figure out what you're dealin' with and what it needs." Higgs was just a few degrees less jovial, now. "Actually, that place has gone back into our possession in lieu of back rent 'n' taxes. For what we're askin', just to move it, probably won't even cover *that*. But if you're serious, I'll wave my commission in exchange for you signin' a three year lease on the lot. Guess I'll be happy to get it off of my repo books and back to earnin' some rent again."

Walt jangled the keys which must include those for his attached laundry room, the mailbox, and maybe a shed. He hadn't noticed a shed last night but it might have been hiding in back. "Well then, I'll go look her over."

Higgs didn't sit down to deal with the rent checks, receipts, and correspondence scattered and piled on his desk. There must have been a due-date recently. The checks were paper-clipped and he swept everything into the front drawer then shut off the office light.

"That reminds me. I hope the juice is turned on down there."

Walt flicked a switch inside the door after unlocking. The electricity was on, but not all of the lights functioned. The obligatory Florida ceiling fan with lights had been expropriated, replaced by a single bulb and not even one of the soft-serve configured, ecological ones. This light itself appeared to be on a dimmer but wouldn't get any brighter when he turned the knob to eke out a few more lumens. The fluorescent tube over the sink had expired. The garbage disposal roared, dry, because he tripped two switches at once near the sink. Walt silenced the grinder. He lifted a sheet of cardboard away from the sink window. Those previous tenants had wanted a *lot* of privacy. The water pressure was weak when he maneuvered the faucet handle. The water was rusty. He allowed it to run, hoping to see it run clear before he left.

The dim light in the kitchen didn't do the space any favors. Someone had ignited many cigarettes at one of the gas-stove burners then had apparently smoked them while slouching there. Ashes were flicked and the occasional butt rubbed out in a neighboring burner. It was near to overflowing. Another someone, or perhaps the same culprit, may have hurled a bowl of soup at a small section of wall not taken up by cupboards. A red liquid had streamed down all the way to the floor, just where another person might enter the living room. A near miss?

Or, maybe he shouldn't make any assumptions? With the big lantern ready in his right hand, Walt closely studied the stain to assure himself that it wasn't blood. Not dark enough. Blood would have dried to a darker, scab brown. Anyway, the panel wasn't ripped anywhere by gunshot. So that wasn't grey matter, either. Maggots? He knelt to examine, squinting at the short piece of baseboard running along the bottom of a cabinet to the living room door frame. Between this kitchen trim and a tuck of living room carpet, the tomato based cascade had deposited bits of alphabet pasta. That looked like the top of a B or could easily have been a D, Walt mused. An O or a Q, as well. A lousy cleanup job by somebody had followed. Happily, the white bits weren't moving. How, did Walt suppose, had *these* folks screwed up? That not-such-a-mystery was right in his wheelhouse, though there were no remnants of any cooking apparatus. Were they consumers only? And how was Higgs duped into admitting middle-aged tweakers into the park? Were they relatives or had they, maybe, offered Bobby some kind of inducement before all of their money went up in smoke?

Collateral damage on a kitchen wall and irresponsible smoking were just the first clues to the disposition of the previous tenants. Walt was curious but reminded himself that speculation about the pathologies of *their* disease-of-choice were just slowing him. He must quickly assess the renovation needs of the place and triage the immediate projects that would allow him to move in.

There was no ceiling light in the living room which blueprint-ed a capital L around the front of the kitchen to form a dining room. It was dark in there so he followed his beam to the front windows. The vertical blinds had been left intact. But why would any pawnshop loan against a full set of mobile-home grade blinds? Well, it *was* Florida. When he found the pulley in the corner, the cords were jammed at the top. He tried to use the drawbar but it wouldn't budge. How could that even happen? He took two of the strings, gathered about a dozen of the slats then bound them together. Now there was enough daylight coming in to see that the blinds weren't in such great shape. Walt found the tabs to release one of the sliding windows. He repeated the bundling and opening process at the other end of the window but not much of the tranquil Florida morning came rushing in.

He could see that another light and fan assembly had been *salvaged* by the previous squatters from the living room *and* dining room. No one even bothered to hang light bulbs or to twist-and-cap the wiring in those empty spaces. A small table lamp on the floor next to the outside wall was also revealed. It might belong to Higgs because the *Wal-Mart* price tag was still affixed. The shade was still clad in its plastic wrap. Maybe the manager wanted it to melt and start a fire. But, there was nothing more in the room to dismay or disgust Walt.

There was only one coffee stain next to two footprints of a davenport or loveseat against the back wall. That was *probably* a wine stain near that; again, not dried to brown. He'd have to look closer in better light but the stain seemed not very dark or deeply set. Someone may have struggled out of their stupor to go find a dishtowel. And, he was only guessing that a couch had rested there.

The other pair of leg indentations was lost in the corner on fake wood flooring. Years of nicotine residues left the distinct silhouette of a large picture frame above whatever piece of furniture had once supported its *Cheeze-Its* gnashing users.

Back into the kitchen, Walt shut off the faucet. The water wasn't pristine as a mountain brook but seemed less rusty. Moving down the hall toward the bathroom and bedrooms, he decided that he had seen nothing, yet, to dissuade him from retrieving his coffeemaker and Mom's Tupperware from The Manatee Inn, buying a nice cot, and immediately taking ownership. His checkbook was waiting in the glove compartment of the Caddy.

OK, maybe not so fast. *You better get back to a stronger due diligence.* The overhead light in the main bathroom was the brightest one in the whole place, so far. Bright and probably unforgiving, of himself, if the mirror hadn't already been removed. All of the fixtures were missing. By the looks of it, the sink may have been used to clean sunken ship artifacts. The tub might have been purchased, used, from a failed bait store. There was no shower rod or curtain. Nor, in fact, was there any spray device at the end of the shower's gooseneck. Who *knew* there was a market for all that stuff? *He* should have known, having lived on the edge of that shadow economy for so many years. Every mundane commodity had a buyer somewhere.

It was then that the absence of any taps or spigots in the sink *or* tub registered most heavily in his brain. Is this going to be too much for me? The toilet paper roller must have been part of a set because it, too, was missing from the side of the vanity. He could

EVACUATION ROUTE

see the screw holes. And, sure enough, upon closer inspection, the flush handle had been liberated from the commode.

Walt removed the tank lid, crossed his fingers then lifted the chain. There was a powerful and resounding flush of rusty water into the stained porcelain bowl, with, (hallelujah) no back-up. It seemed to be refilling without leaks between tank and throne, or around the bottom. That may not have always been the case, because the floor covering had been raggedly stripped away from the base of it. Someone had used a Stanley knife, it appeared, to make slashes extending into the remaining lino. It might have even been a steak knife. Walt chuckled as his mental image of the previous tenants was further defined. He couldn't help laughing at the amount of caulk, *Flex Seal*, and *Bare Bond* that has been wedged and wrapped into and around the affected area. An investment in stopgap measures which, taken in sum, might have bought them a cheap new commode. The plywood subfloor, to Walt's eye, was not salvageable. If there was any optimism left about having somewhere to wash his face, a quick survey of the tiny half-bath off the end bedroom revealed a denuded WC fit only for a janitor's closet. In fact, a petrified mop already resided there. Nevertheless, some optimism was restored by another healthy flush of *that* toilet.

The advisory voices in Walt's head, which only a few minutes ago were vacillating between cries of *I'll take it!* and, *Run away!,* had quieted. They were supplanted by a more pragmatic voice sharpened for hard dealing. Whatever *Chalets and Lakes,* whatever Bobby Higgs wanted for this hovel, they weren't getting it from him. He would either pull off a substantial property heist, or just walk away, back to the search. It all depended on Higgs's level of desperation. *Hell, the toilet worked. And I've washed up in kitchen sinks before.* Gas station sinks. He might need plenty of help from the manager's handyman list. And, he was keeping the little lamp.

"Alright, what's your bottom line?" Bocewicz interrupted Bobby Higgs who was entering check numbers and amounts into some brand of accounting software (which Walt couldn't indentify with a gun to his head after years away from that business) into the bulky mainframe computer at a second desk. The manager's back was turned toward the community room so Walt peered over his shoulder. The 1.0, beta keyboard looked like its design wasn't far removed from an old *Selectric Correcting* Walt had once hocked. He knew that the forgiving keyboard had to be special ordered but Bobby was *still* hunting and pecking.

Higgs completed an entry then stamped the check. *That's pretty primitive*, Walt thought. He turned fully around on his squeaking, straining, swivel chair. "Bottom line, it's mission impossible, right? Just let me finish this up and we'll walk down, take a look at those fine models if you'd like. Yeah, seriously, we've been plannin' to drag that hulk out of here pretty soon."

Walt leaned against the office doorframe. "Well, *seriously*, I intend to renovate the place. If you'll point me to the best people."

EVACUATION ROUTE

Higgs shrugged, sucked in and then pursed his lips, his face a map of crashing expectations. He sighed and shook his head. "Well, either way I guess I appreciate your interest. Have to admire your ambition." He looked at the keys in Walt's hand, visibly shattered that Walt wasn't intending to return them.. "Bottom line, bottom line...let me refresh my memory." He wheeled back to the other desk and pulled a three-ring binder from under a stack of new-model brochures, shiny as Christmas cards. Opening the ledger in his lap, he merry-go-rounded back toward Walt.

It appeared to Walt, at the short distance, that there were more homes to unload than just the flashy new models. Higgs moved his very white finger down a list of, perhaps, ten units. It was all for show. The finger stopped on the only line in the list dressed in yellow highlighter. "That little ol' booby prize is listed at $8.8K, Mr. Boce...Boce..."

Walt filled in the man's blank. "Bocewicz. But, Walt's good enough." Now he extended the keys toward the manager, half turning to go.

"Well, now, a course, I do have a *little* wiggle room. Why don't we see what we can work out?"

Walt continued to offer the keys, poised in mid-reach. "$6K," he declared flatly.

Higgs sighed. "Well, sure. That's *one* figure. Yes. But, now suppose I was to come back at you with, say, $7.5K? Does that sound a little more to your liking?"

Walt managed a sympathetic smile. This man had sprouted a row of tiny perspiration beads above his upper lip, some baloney slices under his arms from the same exertions also presented with a nervous tic below his right eye. Or, it was the worst *tell* in the history of barter. "Six thousand, Mr. Higgs. In cash. On your desk today."

"It looks to me like you're a *very* serious man, Mr....Walt. A man who knows what he wants. A man who wants *both* a my poor battered testicles. You have me, sir, at a great disadvantage, currently."

Walt chuckled. "Nothing could be further from the truth. I just know that it's going to strain my budget to sort that place out. But after I do, it'll seem more like home and not some showroom display at a furniture warehouse."

Higgs snuffed and wiped his lip with the back of a hand, a bit of color rising in his neck despite the chill of the AC. "Well, I would have to take some issue, there, Walt. I assure you that our furnishings are of the highest...Ahh, never mind. You know what?" He reached to shake Walt's hand. He did not take possession of the keys. "You know what you wanta do 'n' I'm just arguin' against my own best interests. You're prob'ly gonna save me more work and 'worry just by gettin' into the place." He shook Walt's hand with convincing sincerity. "I'll accept your tender of $6K and welcome you to the *Glade* family."

Oh, no! It's a family? But, maybe I'll do better with this one. They don't know my track record. He released Higgs's hand. "Just let me make a quick run to that *SunTrust* out on the main drag and then we can do the business. How long will it take you to get the paperwork ready?"

EVACUATION ROUTE

Higgs sighed. He used the forgiving chair to half-catapult himself back onto his feet "We'll need to whoa up just a bit there, Walt. I've already got two showings, here, 'round about lunch-time. You'll have to gimme 'til tomorrow to get alla that organized. The title work, for one thing, will have to be faxed from the Home Office. And, I've gotta put in for your background check. That don't take but a week 'n' you'll get your cash back if it don't go through."

Walt must have been broadcasting some kind of his *own* tell; his jaw going slack or his eyes searching the floor for a moment.

"That's not a problem, is it?"

Higgs was a tad crestfallen, as well, when Walt looked up at him. "Well, no, I..." Walt paused for a quick rehearsal of the *next* tap dance he must perform. "Just some driving violations. Nothing major."

"But nothin' involvin' kids, or like that?" Higgs interrupted in a pleading voice.

The man's anxiety came just in time, before Walt mentioned the way, way, too optimistic date he'd put on a large check to a landlord and then couldn't cover. That was just an honest dispute, though, a misunderstanding of terms, which he believed had been resolved. But, was *resolved* the equivalent of *expunged from the records*? "No, no. Nothing like that." Luckily, he hadn't been pinched for so much as *public urination* which was now at the extreme end of the modern sex crime spectrum.

Higgs exhaled long and slowly; sour, acidic coffee, his *TicTaks* not quite up to their job. "Good. OK. That's a relief. Bein' on this or that sorta registry's the only real deal-breaker we couldn't work around. Or murder. Prob'bly. There *was* a vehicular manslaughter fella in here for a few years. Sad old guy. Confined himself to a nice three- wheeler bicycle. But, we make our own bed, right?"

"Don't I know it."

Hmm. Is there a registry for restraining orders? His thinking had been confined to worry over sanctions for drug-and-alcohol offenses. A background check would certainly test attorney Wineglass's recent efforts on Walt's behalf. He was Warren's friend and on a long-time retainer to the family. He must have known to go the extra mile. "I can't think of anything like that," Walt added.

"Super. I'll just need a non-refundable $25 for *that,* up front. And there's a form for you to sign, gives us permission. Privacy acts, yadda, yadda." Higgs pulled out the bottom drawer of his desk and began a shuffling search. "If this doesn't come back clean, well, like I said. Just, I wouldn't make any *huge* home improvements 'til we hear back. I don't think you could hurt the place any if you wanted to squat in there 'til tomorrow. Then we'll do the deal. In the meantime, I'd suggest a call to *Serve Pro.* They'll lay everything bare in there for you."

Walt straightened his posture in the door frame. "Ok. Well I don't know if I wanta shell out for *that.*"

Higgs gave up a half-laugh, half-snort as he handed Walt the release for the record search. "That's how *I'd* start in on 'er, but you look to be in better shape than me."

Walt scrawled his signature on the release and dug out his wallet. The fee nearly cleaned him out, but he was headed to the bank next. "Here you go, Mr. Higgs."

"Walt, I thank you, again, for your business and I'll prob'ly come by in the morning to admire your progress. I must tell you that you'll also have to drive up to Crystal River with the property taxes. We've kept them paid up, but only enough so we don't get fined. The winter assessment is comin' due next week so you might as well get that done. They don't care who walks in and pays 'em. Bring the receipt along back here with you."

His wallet restored to its comfortable place, Walt backed out of the office. "Sounds like it's gonna be a busy day for me, too."

The Caddy rumbled to life but then Walt hopped back out. That dangling 9 of *his* address was comfortably within his reach so he turned it right-side up. It wouldn't stay. Then a close study of the concrete below returned to him the original tiny, black nail. It was not going to stay in the hole, worn too wide by the 9's vibrating through many seasons of Seminole winds. Walt thought chewing gum might work. There was some nicotine gum, probably gone stale in the glove compartment. That never seemed very sticky but he never knew when he might need it. He'd better just put new address numbers on his shopping list—maybe in some kind of fancy calligraphy, and definitely larger. Shiny copper?

The heat and humidity was rising as he backed out of the car-port; a welcome return for the tourists and snowbirds but hope-fully brief as far as permanent residents cared. There were no more walkers and it was likely to be too early for drinks around the pool. Those decent looking female forms in his headlights last night seemed now to have been images in a personal dreamscapes, an optical illusion. He wondered if they were of an age to resent his low-grade objectification even as nocturnal short subjects.

Lunchtime traffic was picking up on Hall's River Road and then was very heavy at the Sun Coast 19 stoplight. Surely, the bank was open by now. Withdraw what he needed and some walk-ing-around cash. Then where next? *WalMart* or that *Habitat for Humanity ReStore* he had spotted up in Crystal River. He'd heard somewhere that that was the place for decent used furniture. Find the tax collector while he was up there. Walking around with a wad like that could never have happened five years ago. *Then I need to find a floor coverings warehouse. Bet the Habitat for Humanity place has remnants. Or...or, find the materials from the Re-Store and then hire whoever the carpet warehouse uses. Do I really want remnants? Do things work that way? Fifty-five years old and stress-ing over first home improvement decisions.*

At the *SunCoast* bank he had to go inside. Though he had an account, he had not yet used the ATM debit card for anything but cash from an ATM. Now, could he use a debit card to pay at the Tax Office or would he need to write a check? Which in-strument did businesses trust more, say, in combination with his haggard driver's license photo? Locking the Caddy, he decided that he shouldn't leave this office without that magic folder of fresh checks.

Chapter Eleven

The *Knuckledick's* Clubhouse usually smelled habitable by Tuesday morning. Wood-Chuck Spurgeon always came in to put up the chairs and do a vigorous mop-out when the place was closed Sunday evening. Even the lightly attended Sunday hangover day with optional poker run could leave a lingering crotch-leather funk. Wood preferred industrial strength *Lysol* in the public spaces, then a concoction of ammonia and the *Lysol*, in a nasal searing blend for the shitters and behind the bar. Vents and the AC left on High setting cleared out most of the toxins by the time he opened the place on Tuesday. They had closed up for MLK Day because many of the deadbeat dads had an extra day with their kids. Some babysat for working wives/moms because schools were closed.

He unlocked and entered, sniffing. Ahh, piney fresh, all smegma notes vanished. When he switched on the light, the grubby, checkered tiles still reflected a dull gleam from his Sunday night efforts. This would be a Tuesday to dread slightly more than usual. *The Darkness* would spend more time in his office totaling up the few collection envelopes from his mules and maybe cursing.

EVACUATION ROUTE

St. Patrick's Day was looming but not yet foremost in Wood's apprehensions.

The teeth grinding he anticipated most would be triggered by many of his *Knuckledick* brothers renewing their Martin Luther King humor. That, and other unpleasant racial opinions will have been bottled up through all of yesterday's national holiday.

That is, except if Mandy (Mandela-Grace), Omar, or Lonnie were present. The two black men had been reluctantly admitted to membership a few years ago to preempt any backdoor civil rights bullshit the Justice Department might come up with to close them down. Mandy, one of the new pros-in-residence, had proven to be a welcome addition to the members. Her four-tricks-per-week on the Club reservations calendar was filled through the end of March. Regarding Mandy, the prevailing prejudice apparently ended where intercourse began.

The Feds had already tried their clever civil rights gambit on another large club out of Tallahassee, the *Knuckledicks* foremost rival, *The Jesters*. There was some brief success until that club admitted a few tokens. There wasn't much love lost for the other gang but the *Knuckledicks* took the hint. So, Omar and Lonnie had been brought in to lukewarm acceptance. Even the most incorrigible racist biker could not dispute the new men's District Court jackets or their intimidating presence at functions beyond home territory.

Boogaloo came in earlier every day now to see who was up and who was on deck in his reservations book. Every *Knuckledick* member was responsible for the transportation of in-house girls, except in cases of suspended driver's licenses or impounded bikes.

When Wood checked the book, kept behind the bar, there was no one on today's schedule who required delivery. Even more important to Boog's position on the corporate org chart was that *The Darkness* had cheerfully authorized him to engage one more girl.

Wood expected to see the girls today when they came in to collect their pay envelopes and clinic vouchers and to look at their schedule. Boogaloo was to verify the documentation of their *Depo* injections. They no longer carried any money and the 90% guarantee of non-contagion was appreciated by all. This *had* led to some arguments about condom use but Boog's will always prevailed.

The new girls were also bi-sexual, or were at least convincing in performance. They were unhurried and competent (according to raucous, easily overheard peer reviews) whenever hired to play with a *Knuckledick* girlfriend, *mama*, or bitch, which tag caused Boog to frown and Wood to cringe. If only he could induce all *those* women of the *Knuckledick* extended family to get regular blood work.

When the girls were expected to report in, Boog would also need to show up with their money and blank paperwork for the clinic. That would give Wood the opportunity to further acclimate himself to the burly man's sudden transformation. Both in appearance and in his formerly brusque manner (or *brus-kay*, as Boog would have pronounced it) the overnight transformation *had* (according to his own rambling explanation) made him a much more effective recruiter of hos: Witness the satisfaction of those using the girls' services and the *Knuckledicks'* requests for additions to their ranks.

Who knew that untainted lady parts would be so warmly received by brutes who never seemed to have given such niceties a second thought before?

And what light-bulb had winked on to give Boog these new Human Resources skills? He swooped around like a helicopter mom to transport the girls to outside tricks on the back of that awful new Japanese bike, relieving them of dangerous accumulations of cash. He carried mouthwash, hair products, poppers, an array of condoms, and even changes of panties; anything Mandy and Luanne might need for completing a day/night doubleheader.

His explanation for the sudden changes, once they'd been wheedled out of him, made *some* sense. He tried to clarify: "I heard of it somewheres, Wood. Mebbe bangin' a hippy chick one time. Had to listen to her in the bar before fun. She yammer about that one commie gook...that Mayo somethin'? So happy, she said, *to be swimmin' in the same sea as the lower classes of people,* like *with the fish in the ocean.* Some bullshit. Do you understand it?"

"Sure, so...maybe it just means, like, you're hidin' in plain sight? Or, like a wolf in sheep's clothin' to blend in? Make sense?"

It was a question for which Wood received, in answer, the dull thousand yard stare of seeming incomprehension, followed by Boog's dangerous, narrowing gaze of frustration at his own bafflement.

"Oh. Okay. Is that is a way of tellin' it easier? But, anyways now I don't look so scary. Boog can swim among the whore fishes without to scare away the jumpy ones. And, with softer vibes off me, too. See?"

Wood exhaled slowly. *Just fucking agree and move past it.* "Yeah, that's what I meant."

Boog blinked, his body language sagging slightly as he put the pin back into the grenade of his nature. "It is hard, brother." He reached across to pat Wood on the forearm. "I shoulda sprung the gangbang onto that hippie. Like, to show what a whole *school* a fishes do for her."

The guy was visibly proud, now, whenever he strolled into the Clubhouse and sat down with his girls. They took their pay envelopes with casual body language, not visibly nervous in the presence of this new iteration of their handler. *Was everyone visibly relaxing around him now? What a perfect scam, this hipster cover Boog has engineered, if he even knows what a hipster is. Is that what he's goin' for? Beware though, people. I sure as hell will. Never misjudge the cover on this book.*

When Mandy and Luanne entered through the back, Spurgeon was glad *The Darkness* hadn't showed up yet. Their unchallenged entrance might be *darkly* frowned upon and then Wood would have the minesweeping detail to remind Boog of the unwritten rules.

"Can I get y'all somethin' to drink? Did Boog give y'all a time he was gonna get in here?"

"He give us a cable-guy time," Mandy said. "A window. Which we are already halfway through it."

"Have you got any coffee hot, Wood," Luanne croaked, lighting a menthol cigarette from the ember of its predecessor.

EVACUATION ROUTE 243

"Fresh is just about ready." Wood eyed the nearly full beaker. He feared that no amount of hot liquid was likely to clear her gravel voice *or* save her, eventually, from one of those throat gizmos making robot voices for her.

"Coffee for me, too, sweet *thang*," Mandy said. "An' maybe a shot a any brandy you got stored back in there."

The girls settled at a table, crossed their legs and seemed not to have much to discuss between them, their lips only moving with occasional whispers of smoke. Mandy had now fired up the thinnest of cigarillos. Wood carried coffee to them and juice glasses of blackberry brandy which may have been on the back shelf since Slick Willy Clinton was ruining dresses behind his desk. When Wood turned back to the bar, Archie *The Darkness* Caulkins entered the Clubhouse, silent as a streetlight going out at 6 am.

"G'morning, Chief."

"You sure about that, Wood? Time'll tell," Archie grumbled. "Lavelle come in yet? I need to hear what yer thinkin' is about what *that* crazy bastard is up to. An' don't tell him I put it that way."

Wood handed the man a coffee. "Right. The new costume? Yeah, I think that's just, like, a new strategy he's tryin' out." He pushed a glass dish of sweetener and sugar packets across the bar. "Seems to be workin'. You like the new girls, don't ya? He was feeling like he needed to start sneakin' up on 'em for recruitin' purposes."

"I can see his reasonin'. Just wish I coulda taken some before 'n' after pics." Caulkins waved a hand tattooed *Thunder* in the direction of Mandy and Luanne. The women waved back, managing indifferent smiles. Mandy touched the cell-phone in front of her long enough to look at the time.

"Yeah, Wood. I like 'em just fine, though I still needa to take the time for a personal sample. But, don't yer boy kinda creep you out? He looks like a damn...one a those amateur...what'm I thinkin' of? A lay-preacher, mebbe? Or a fuckin' narc. It'd make anybody wonder."

"We got those girls partly cuz Boog took to lookin' harmless." Wood-Chuck poured himself a coffee then put a fresh filter-full into the machine. "So what else is new? *Everythin'* about that ol' boy makes *me* nervous. Still. I guess that's why we love the fucker, I guess. It's part a his skill set."

Now *The Darkness* winced, hiking himself onto a stool. Wood knew better than to ask what were the latest disposition of his hemorrhoids. Once Caulkins got unwound, he'd tie the listener up for fifteen minutes describing his increasing difficulties in the saddle. Then maybe a recount of how the condition had affected some hairball he'd fought against a name or names in the biker world that he assumed you'd know. His other favorite theme described bike accidents he'd witnessed, and then examples of how he'd laid his *own* bikes down, scraping the pavement in order to avoid decapitations of one kind or another. All of it had taken a toll. Wood wondered how much of the *Knuckledick's* revenue stream was going up Arch's nose as *pain management.*

"Well, he prob'ly deserves him another girl. The whore money has improved. Recession proof, wouldn't ya call it? I don't understand *what* he was doin' with them other two that they did'n' earn

EVACUATION ROUTE 245

the outside money like they shoulda. They was both cute enough far as skanks go and the members loved 'em. Anyways, you think you could get him to be sure'n park that rice-burner a his out back, Ain't he just a *little* embarrassed?"

Wood sipped. "He wouldn't know what that was, Arch."

The rear door opened again after two Harley motors went silent just outside. Red Bud and Scope, two *Knuckledicks* who almost no one knew the last names of, came in and moved behind the bar toward the office. They were trusted earners and intermediate traffickers for the *Knuckledick's* minor league narcotics enterprise. No one really *wanted* to know their last names because they weren't on Ruling Council. Wood wasn't even certain if Caulkins knew. *But he has to.* It was the general consensus of the membership that those boys kept the lights on and the beer cheap. And no one was turning down the club discount on an occasional white-line bump, either. Red Bud followed *The Darkness* straight into the little back office.

Scope, a wiry dude whose acne scars might have been taken for the mark of the pox in another century, paused to offer Wood a dap of greeting. "Can I get me some a that, Wood?" He said.

"Sure, man. One lump or two?"

"Do whut?" Like Boogaloo, this guy could suffer those in his immediate proximity to experience a rapid loss of warmth.

"Do you want sugar in it?"

"Ah, right. Yeah. Don't think I ever *heard* that one." A weak, close-lipped smile returned to Scope's ravaged mug. "Two packets, boss."

But, maybe to risk a full grin would stretch open that cold sore the biker was hosting. "Go ahead on, Scope. I'll bring it into the office." *So I don't have to look at ya*. He had almost uttered a sarcastic *you're welcome* in the absence of any gratitude for his service. A preliminary *please* would have been nice. Wood was in no way afraid of the guy and took ordering around only from Caulkins. *Ahh, keep things smooth. He's a biker for Chrissake. More than enough nerve wrackin' shit'll go down before the week is done.*

After Wood poured and delivered a steaming cup as far as the doorframe and observed the two stacks of grubby, small denomination bills on *The Darkness's* desk, he turned to find Boogaloo, just then plunking down at his girls' table. *That Gold Wing arrives too quiet for comfort.*

Boog shot Wood an expressionless wink then returned to his consultation with the club prostitutes. Wood lifted another *Styrofoam* cup from the stack. *Why not? I've turned into one of those coffee boys like Mafiosi keep scurryin' around their neighborhood Italian clubs.*

Boog wouldn't want sugar so asking wasn't an issue. Wood carried the fifth of blackberry brandy to give the girls refills. *Oh my God! Is that some kind of briefcase?* Then, peering over the Cajun man's shoulder, he saw that it was more like a leather courier pouch with brass closures. It was the sort of Euro accessory that might have provoked Boog, no more than a month ago, to harass a courier and maybe stomp the spokes out of his bicycle. Now it looked like just the right fit to go hang alongside a saddlebag. Made of black leather, Wood expected to see it stamped with the orange

EVACUATION ROUTE

Harley logo. When Boog removed the physician's affidavit forms and medical payment vouchers from the pouch, he placed it on the floor to create table space. There was some kind of imprimatur of a leather-craft shop on it, too small for Wood to read. The women counted the wads of cash in their pay envelopes, oblivious to the fresh paperwork they would need to complete.

"Much gratitude. Brother." Boog sipped his coffee and put it down. He relieved Wood of the brandy then poured for the girls.

"Listen, bro. Have ya got time to make a grocery run? I'm outta ideas so I'm back to grilled cheese. Maybe with tomato soup?"

An increase of chill not attributable to the AC again descended around the table. "I don't wanta be a a-hole, Wood. But these flowers are keep me hoppin' all from afternoon 'til late. What I am sayin'...I want to say careful words."

Somehow, Wood *could* see it, had thought about it already, enough to have a moment of near sadness that his old sort-of buddy might be pulling away. "I know what yer sayin', Boog. Exceptin' today there's nobody else to go, unless you wanta tend bar and *I'll* go. I won't forget to make the stop myself on the way in tomorrow."

Boogaloo pushed the medical documents further under the noses of the girls. "It will be not possible for me when another girl is with us. Do you believe it, too? I can help today. Or, if these boys 'n' our other friends would limit their screwin'."

There was no point in Boog's argument that Wood could dispute. So what if their friendship, or better word, *alliance*, was not as strong as it once was? If polled, the *Knuckledicks* would always

248   CHRIS DUNGEY

prefer access to talented female flesh than that Wood should have help flipping grilled cheese. Even *with* the side of soup. Even *with* a slice of ham loaf in the sandwich. But, at least Wood's roles as cook, host, bartender and quartermaster no longer included pimping. "You aren't wrong, brother. I'll get my shit rearranged."

Boog screwed the cap back onto the blackberry brandy with finality. "It is a big change, yeah? Some night maybe you ride with *me*, around to guard these."

The women shot furtive glances at Wood but did not roll their eyes. Their expressions sent a silent plea. *Can't you get him to back off a little?* Wood shrugged to indicate his neutrality. *Sorry ladies. No longer my department.* Anyway, *they* were the ones who benefitted from the new system. *Just live with it.*

"If it's ready? Your list? Then Beau can get done quick. These have appointments after lunch time."

So it's Beau now? And talking about himself in that, what? personal tense or something? The Darkness would find that *really* disturbing. But the girls might prefer *Beau* to Daddy or whatever form of address previous pimps had expected. And *Boogaloo* that might be an offensive moniker to Mandy. If she was even offendable. It was probably a cultural misapp...something. Stolen culture? There were better words for *that*, too, he supposed. Didn't everyone attempt to do that *boogaloo* on the dance floor at some point? *Ma's time?* Maybe it wasn't just a black thing.

"We need cheese. A couple blocks of Velveeta. A few packages of ham lunchmeat. Maybe three loaves a Hillbilly Bread." Wood

EVACUATION ROUTE

249

printed the items hastily on the back of an envelope out of his back pocket after removing the utility bill.

"Won't take long. You watch over these? No more shots of the liquor, too, okay?"

"Oh, come on, Beau. Yer puttin' us with some nasty, smelly-assed ones all afternoon," Mandy complained. "I looked in the book."

Wood could see that Boog was trying to soften his death stare. "Hush you, about Club brothers in that way. On that subject I am serious. One more shot, then, for these, okay, Wood? Do girls want it to make yourself be stupid with drink? Tonight's brothers are easy."

Mandy sighed and tapped another cigarette from her pack. "Okay. You're right, Beau, Daddy. Jus' one more li'l shot works for me," she said.

She *had* to be restraining a '*you fuck 'em then, if they're such sweeties,*' And there it was, the *Daddy* Wood had been expecting to hear sooner or later. But maybe that was the *girls'* idea and they were good with it.

"Yeah, alright," Luanne added. "If they're too disgustin' I'll be drownin' the images later."

"Like usual, sister," Mandy said. She leaned her cigarette in the direction of the lighter Boog offered across the table.

Again, Wood wondered, not so aghast as the first time he'd witnessed this courtesy: *Who is this guy?*

Boog stood and scraped his chair back under the table. "This today, too," he said, tapping the forms he'd distributed. "To get done." Then he went out the rear entrance.

"Just after givin' head to some ol' cheese dick, I'm goin' for my exam?" Luanne said. "Is that what you'd call irony?"

"I'm goin' tomorrow, start *my* day off," Mandy said.

After pouring out one more glass for each girl, Wood returned behind the bar. He pulled back the curtain hiding the pantry shelves. There were two institutional gallons of tomato soup left in there. He would start with one because it was likely to be a slow day. But what could he do to fancy *this* up a bit. *Make it cream style?* He wasn't going to dash out after Boog with a late addition to the grocery list and further belabor the dude's razor-thin deference. He wouldn't have thought, as near as a month ago, that he'd have to tiptoe this much around his most loyal comrade. What about these little creamers? The gang members seldom used them while in the throes of hangover. That wasn't actually cream in there, though, was it? Wood pulled the paper top off of one of them. It was a powder. Could he get it to dissolve in the soup?

Chapter Twelve

That old man looked like a hundred miles of dirt road. But, Darlene Spurgeon supposed that his face had some character. All the character of burnt toast. *And* he was a tall one. That would be a nice upgrade from Guillermo. Wow, she was getting *so* ahead of herself. The morning was decently warm. The sun beat full on his stubbly upturned mug. She nudged Dianne Kaake as the women marched near. The man was kicked back on a bag chair, his grey head resting against the hood of that Caddy battleship they'd seen in midweek. A battle scarred tortoiseshell tomcat sunned itself at his feet. Garbage bags were piled on either side of him, more than she could count. Three rolls of carpeting, a heap of Venetian blinds, also waited for collection. He might get a rude disappointment from the fussy waste removal folks who served *The Glade*. Those carpet logs ought to be cut in half if he was to have any chance of saying good riddance to them.

The only response to the women's intrusion came from the tom, who yawned, stretched, and disappeared into the refuse heap. The old boy was either deep asleep or maybe hard of hearing. How

252   CHRIS DUNGEY

could anybody fall that fast asleep in such an awkward position? The women moved along.

On the second pass, Darlene paused to try again. For a moment, she thought that Dianne, leaning in close, was going to snap her finger in the guy's face, but then she straightened, shrugged her shoulders

"Good mornin', neighbor," Darlene spoke louder, glancing at Dianne while sniffing at a strong, not unpleasant scent; the man's natural musk plus some kind of minty disinfectant?

His eyes fluttered open. A mug of coffee, no steam emanating, sat on the concrete next to his left sandal. The footwear wasn't new. It was scuffed into its owner's personal, comfortable shape.

"Wha? Oh, yeah? Am I?" Walt mumbled. "Sorry. I hit the sack late and not for very long. Just catching up. I can't believe all the jungle noises."

"You ain't gotta apologize, hon," Darlene said." It *is* pretty noisy 'til you get used to it."

"I recognized an owl, I think. But, what the hell else? It was like a zoo out there, the other side of that back fence."

Dianne eyed the mound of refuse on either side of the man. "Well, yeah hon. That's exactly what it is. All kinda critters out there eatin' 'n' getting' ate. You might hear a gator bellow, too, now 'n' again. *Them* chill my blood. Looks like you've accomplished quite a bit in there, already"

The fellow sat up and peered down either side of his chair in search of the coffee that must be cold by now. "Yep, it's quite a wreck. I made *some* progress. Anyway, I'm Walter Bocewicz,

the new lord of this...manor. Or, whatever it turns out to be."
He continued to shake off grogginess, straightening his back and
stretching his legs.

"I'm Darlene Spurgeon." She extended her hand. "An' this
here's Dianne Kaake, but not the kind with frostin'. I'm three
places down from her, way the other side."

Walt A to Z, as she was already thinking of him to herself,
dumped cold coffee into the decorative landscaping stone of his
front yard. That stuff needed to be combed out with a rake or,
better yet, dug up and replaced. He turned slowly to look over his
shoulder at his derelict shell of a home. "Can either of you tell me
what the hell happened in there?"

Darlene furtively tried to gauge the man's age. He didn't have
that hair in his ears like they tended to get and his lobes were
still regulation length. There were no turkey- neck wattles, either.
Maybe he wasn't so old after all and her mind flashed for a split
second to those blue boner pills. Well, whatever worked for the
poor ol' guys. Old or not, he looked as though life may have worked
him over pretty thoroughly; plenty of wrong turns and fool mis-
calculations she could identify with. "Actually, Walter. I ain't been
here but four months myself."

"They was just typical stoners to begin with," Dianne put in.
"Guess it got away from 'em into the crystal meth. Don't b'lieve
they was cookin', per se, but their life went down the shitter pretty
fast from there."

"I didn't see any leftover pieces of apparatus," Walt said. "Of
course it could've been sold off like everything else in the place."

'Ain't that a shame, though," Darlene said. "How bad it can all turn out?"

Walt got an odd look on his face, seemed to stare beyond them both. Returning to earth, he sighed. "Yes...How it turns out can be pretty bad."

"Anyways, I'm keepin' a close eye on *this* one," Dianne chuckled. "So her tokin' don't get outta control."

Darlene gave her friend a gentle push on the shoulder. "But who's watchin' *you*?"

"I guess their loss was my gain." Bocewicz smiled weakly and shook his head. "We'll see how *much* of a gain after all the repair folks have come and gone."

Dianne took Darlene by her elbow and made to resume their oval trek. "Listen, now, Walt. We'll let ya get back to yer nap."

"Will we be seein' you down to the Association?" Darlene turned back, reluctant to leave for some reason. Was this guy a prime candidate to provide for *any* of her needs? "There's sometimes a lotta fun down there, with the Bingo and a dinner now 'n' then. Big party comin' up in a few weeks for St. Paddy's Day."

Bocewicz was already trying to resituate himself comfortably in the chair. He reopened his eyes. "That sounds just..."

"Yeah, we know." Darlene halted and watched the man as he groped for a polite word. She braved a wink at him. "But you'll get to sample all our cookin' specialties down there eventually."

"That sounds delicious, if you could see my pantry. Darlene, was it? And, Dianne? Have I got that right? I can always eat." The sun, further above the jungle bordering the park on the east, fell upon his craggy (Darlene wouldn't say *ruined*), features. "Soon as I get this place cleaned out and livable. I'm always looking for free meals and low impact diversions."

"Well said...Walter. I believe you've summed up the local social life pretty accurate." Dianne chuckled. "Low impact. Such a polite man."

"We love a man with an appetite, too," Darlene added. Now it was her turn to titter. "See ya soon. I've gotta catch up on my own house keepin' then put my face on for a Sunday evenin' shift. Thank the Lord for Sunday night hockey 'n' basketball."

"Don't work too hard, now." Walt said, as the women moved away.

"Wrestle ya for him?" Darlene bumped Dianne with her hip as they picked up the pace.

"Shoot," Dianne said. "I bet that ol' rooster would wanta *watch* somethin' like that. I already got one old coot to cook for. He's got some a them heavy-drinker blood vessels on his face look like the canals on Mars."

"Alright then. You forfeit?" *And, in exchange, I'll stay off'n Curtis*, Darlene thought. *Yer welcome.*

Well, then. He believed that was them—the girls from Wednesday night. Walt hadn't much time, excavating his place, to think about them since taking the keys from Higgs. So, they weren't a couple, it didn't seem. Unless on the down-low, which he wouldn't object to at all. Okay, but he should probably focus his attentions on the one who wasn't married. But, now, which was which again? Knowing their names was a start. Wasn't the other newcomer to *The Glade* the single one? Darlene, he thought. Was there a subtle, almost indiscernible vibe there or were the allusions and double entendres only in his head? They were of a type, both of them, the taxonomy of which he could not yet put a name to. But that *type*, to him, would likely be quite compatible: Earthy and maybe a little assertive; in decent shape with nicely maintained bottoms. Pure objectification, but was that his ideal? Those old favorite flavors were coming back to him more and more often.

He opened his eyes, tilted his head to the left without raising it off the Caddy. He watched them reach the vanishing point of the horseshoe's bend and one of the new homes down there. It was time to drag himself up and get ready to greet the plumber, scheduled to arrive first, followed by the bathroom tub folks.

If everyone kept their word, response times to his home improvement searches would be no less than remarkable, given the Florida norm. Carpeting, heating-and-cooling, and an electrician had all been engaged. He hadn't even needed Higgs's black book trove of reliable tradesmen. Not yet. A thin *Yellow Pages* for Citrus County, 2007 edition, still hung from a chain in the laundry shed though the telephone was long departed from its mounting on the wall. Yesterday, after all the arrangements had been contracted, he needed minutes restored on the *Tracfone*. So, another run to

Walmart, where a kid behind the Electronics counter would guide him through adding them.

Walt found that the washer and dryer were missing as well, so that meant a drive back to a Laundromat discovered in Crystal River. It turned out that *Galaxy of Bathrooms* was conveniently near. Dirty clothes churned and foamed in one washer while he picked out a decent reconditioned tub, shower stall, and vanity in the pole-barn of the used appliance outlet down the road. It occurred to him that he might find even his oiled-bronze bathroom accents in there. But, those helpful people also referred him to the plumber with a reassuring endorsement. Of course, there was no warranty attached to any of it.

The clothes were spun out when he was finished at *Galaxy of Bathrooms*. The rest of his wardrobe still rode in two lawn-and-garden sized black bags in the Caddy's trunk. He tossed the bag of damp clothes in with them. Why not save a few coins by using the decrepit, clothesline tree still standing like the *Peanuts* Christmas tree in his backyard? That required only an investment in clothes pins at the *Winn-Dixie* and then he was ready to go home and begin rooting out the place.

That whole process took two long workdays. He ruthlessly gutted the unit of remaining trash and anything else not firmly attached. He placed Higgs's lamp on an empty cardboard box next to the inflatable mattress where he hoped not to trip over it. The blinds in the front room had been dismantled and removed, the stove-burner ashtray lifted out and dumped. *Well, have a good look inside, all you walkers. Drapes will be the last thing on my list.*

With those women gone from view and sleep now elusive, Walt ducked into his Florida room. The big, sliding screen door was still opening freely. Yesterday, when it slid only a few balking inches at a time, he'd soaked the track down liberally with WD-40. It was corroded, possibly bent, as well as encrusted with the scrapings of entering junky shoes. The lubrication helped—good enough for the frequent running in and out that had to be done with the entrance mostly left open. But a more permanent solution would have to found. *Meanin, shopped for.*

He made up the bed, which was just to smooth out the one blanket and center the pillow. This ritual was engrained after several rehabs. (One of the recovery industry schemes for restoring structure to a life.) Then it was time to freshen his privates and armpits with some *Wal-Mart* antibacterial wipes. After that, he dug around frantically for some fresh briefs at the bottom of one of his garbage bags.

The kitchen sink, after an hour's scourging yesterday with gritty cleansers and elbow grease, was ready for limited use. The antibacterial wipes were still more convenient than heating water. Walt discovered, after running the hot for half-an-hour the first night, that the little water heater which once shared the furnace cabinet, was missing. He could only imagine the ingenuity and resolve it must have taken the tweakers to disconnect and remove it. Thankfully, they hadn't taken the shortcut of simply ripping out the wall. If he thought back honestly, his own addiction had likely left him equally as resourceful. A small service panel, pried out of the wall, appeared to have been their only avenue of violation. Did they

EVACUATION ROUTE

not have the right screwdriver for that critical step? To liberate the small gas furnace from its ductwork may have been a bridge too far, so it remained.

In any case, using the freshly scoured sink for a thorough wash-up required the boiling of at least a half-gallon of water on the stove. He didn't want to spare the time in the morning and was too exhausted those first two nights. Was it his low self-esteem or was one of the ladies sniffing. She might have been getting a hint of rot from anything decomposing in his piles of refuse. *Give yourself a break.* But, he stood in front of the sink, anyway, dropped trow then used several medicinally scented wipes. *Sure hope it wasn't me. Take no chances with offensive personal odors.* Also, stay ahead of any rash to be contracted by vigorous work in a filthy metal box in a tropical setting, sans air-conditioning. *Could be a new flesh eating bacteria breeding in here.* He didn't want to wear shorts while wrestling with more of the rusted and rotted interior. He stepped into, quite likely, his last clean pair of briefs. It would soon be time to drive back to that Laundromat or to put underwear at the top of his next shopping list.

After today, or maybe tomorrow, Walt should be able to enjoy a shower. His dirty dishes, all seven of them, could be left in the kitchen sink where they belonged. He brought home all the cleansing agents he could think of plus the necessary sponges and brushes. He also remembered the hot, green analgesic cream to be applied to his elbows. He did this earlier in the morning after activating the indispensable *Mr. Coffee. Hey, either the coffee (Java Time from Big Lots) or the Ben Gay could have puckered those women's nostrils. Too bad, if that was the case. I'm gonna be using plenty of both.*

After using up four of the large-sized wipes, Walt thought he should still heat water for a shave. But, he shut off the stove quickly when he recalled that he didn't know when the first tradesmen might arrive. He must be ready and waiting. And, he really shouldn't get into the habit of *Annie's Breakfast,* as inexpensive an option as that was. His stomach growled through the three cups of coffee already consumed. The used refrigerator wouldn't be delivered until the plumbing was repaired and the plumbers were out of the way. There wasn't anything currently preventing him from bringing home a microwave, adequate enough to boil water for a packet of oatmeal. One more trip to *Wal-Mart,* he supposed. He expected to soon be on a first name basis with some of the cashiers. There were two granola bars on the counter and one last banana beginning to sprout brown freckles. Those things should hold him until lunch.

Walt added another cup of water to the vintage *Mr. Coffee* which spat steam at his face, the element in there still hot and waiting. A roll of contact paper sat on the counter next to the coffee. To resurface the pantry closet shelves was a chore scheduled for the evening, when the plumbers were gone. He wasn't going to do any serious grocery shopping until there was clean storage space. There was a pencil and note pad in the Caddy's glove box and necessities were occurring to him at an accelerating rate. Those women scattered the abbreviated list in his head. Time to write things down.

Walt peeled and munched his available provisions. Shopping bags were filled with his personal trash to save the big, black, expensive ones for serious excavation. Now his wrappers, the used sanitary wipes, and banana peel went into a *Walmart* sack. He might be able to get by with these little bags for a long time, as much business as he was doing out there. He knotted it just as the first truck drew up in front of his landfill heap.

Wow, his deliveries were going to make this street look like a construction zone. *Galaxy of Bathrooms* made way for the *Re-Store* truck. Both were delivering with installation not included.

Not going out for breakfast turned out to be prescient. This order of used furniture, too, was arriving earlier than expected. His theory was coalescing that the Great Recession would make every business employing tradesmen less lethargic. He looked around the kitchen to make sure all loose objects were out of the way, rather like his mother who scurried through the house making it presentable for the cleaning lady.

Then the plumber called to say that they were running behind but would arrive shortly. Those guys weren't likely to need supervision (there was little to steal), so where should he remove himself to keep from under foot? When they arrived in late afternoon, he could have made the next *Walmart* run but now the plumber and his apprentice were blocking in the Caddy. The pricey little water heater he also ordered must be riding in the back of the truck somewhere. Two of the *Re-Store* fellows followed Walt's direction to bring the couch and end-table and recliner around back to the patio. Their parking space was needed almost immediately.

The plumber's truck doors were swung open just as Walt approached with greetings and prepared apologies. "Hello, hello! My angels of hot water."

"You're Walt?" The driver moved to the tailgate and opened it to reveal the water-heater.

"Yep, that's me. You can bring that right in here this way. Sorry about the obstructions." Walt moved out of the way, stepping ahead to hook the back door open.

"Hey, we can work around anything but a gator."

Though he was already asking a lot of everyone, Walt pushed his good fortune with the plumbers. Could he get them to hook up the ice cube dispenser and water stream as well, creature luxuries on the front of the appliance? Asking them to move their vehicle so that he could escape now seemed an unnecessary delay to the work, not to mention impolite. He threw a blue, plastic tarp over the couch. That pending shopping list must be compiled before it grew any longer..

Then he parked himself in the living room where a claw hammer and small crowbar awaited. There were still strips of carpet tacking to be dislodged along the perimeter of walls. When many feet of this were revealed to be rotten and unusable, Walt decided to go with some *Pergo* fake hardwood. No more wine stains, he hoped. After hearing much purposeful activity from the master bedroom, including a *Sawz-All* biting into something (Maybe that bit of wall had to be removed, after all, to replace the missing water heater,) he soon heard water spitting steam into the kitchen sink, Cross *big sanitary wipes* off the shopping list. Add bar soap. He waited to hear ice cubes rattle into one of his *Solo* cups.

Chapter Thirteen

B ella Ruiz did relatively well at the slots in *Hard Rock Casino Tampa*. The odds were simply better than out on the boat. It was just unfortunate that she couldn't sharpen her blackjack skills while playing ashore. It seemed such a shame that the State of Florida chose to take a pass on all that gaming tax money. Out on *Narcissus,* the lousy slot odds made up for the privilege of blackjack.

Cleopatra was fairly simple though she made no effort to understand the play lines. They reminded her of a Tampa bus route map. All Bella had to do was to get three of the reels to match up and then hope for bonus matches when they did. She loved the exotic snake-charmer music and then the pompous Roman Legion marching stuff. The Cleo illustration was actually some famous actress from the movie, same title. It might be fun to give it a look sometime when she *had* time, though the *Blockbuster* a mile from them was down to a very lean inventory. This Great Recession would probably finish *them* off. She and Merry would just have to get a better cable package or run back and forth to the *Red Box* dispenser at *Winn-Dixie*.

EVACUATION ROUTE

The trick to playing these slots was to ignore the flying reels until they all came to rest. She looked about for nearby males showing interest. And, for that other hostile presence who would try to sneak up behind her if he was present. When she returned her attention to the game, the winning matches were a pleasant surprise.

She may have seen Boogaloo the last time she was in here during the Holidays. It shouldn't be hard to see that creeper coming again. She was also getting thirsty. If she had a third eye, it would be dedicated to spotting wait staff to get them started comping her some drinks. All these considerations combined to slow her pace of dispensing money into the machine—that nagging worry about her overhead, again.

A young kid in a white shirt, an empty tray held over his head, finally approached her to take a drink order.

"This is comped, yes?"

"Yes, ma'am. I see you've been at it awhile, so..."

Jesus. She thought a person had to be twenty-one to serve alcohol in the State of Florida. *How could this guy possibly be older than me?* No way. Bella ordered a rum-and-*Coke*, the favored drink of Papi's nation. Well, *viva la revolution.* Except, Papi hated the *revolution* until his rasping, dying breath. The family rarely took a day off for any kind of excursion, but they visited the little *Bay of Pigs Museum* in Miami twice, the exact number of trips the family made across the peninsula. She saw the wonderful *Miami Zoo* on a class field trip. And what *was* the problem with some of these wait staff? If she'd *been at it awhile*, then why did all the waitresses seem to pass her by? She wasn't dressed up in anything especially provocative, she didn't think. Maybe being a young, attractive woman alone signaled something whether she was in a rubber fisherman's apron or a tutu. She could understand their snubs if they thought *that* sort of woman wouldn't tip very well. But, *she* was always generous. Luckily, one of the few *guys* hustling drinks happened to be in her section.

Bella tipped him two bucks when he returned. "Gracias." She'd teach those bitches to ignore her. Who were *they*?

"Gracias back at you, ma'am."

The kid moved swiftly on, two longneck beers and a mixed drink still riding the tray. "Don't forget me!" Bella called after him.

Kinda cute, in a late adolescent, community college sort of way. Tight, toned *culo* hustling away. Mericon? *That isn't nice.* Her gaydar had been unreliable lately. But there she went, no better than the waitresses—judging. That is if they *had* been steering clear of an attractive, solitary, twenty-something female.

She paused between sips of the *Cuba libre* when a brief fanfare of Imperial trumpets proclaimed a small win. The tightly arranged bank of machines where she sat was enclosed at one end, like a cul de sac, with a not-much-better view in the opposite direction. When she looked that way, Bella saw only wait staff flying by or strolling gamblers looking for vacant seats. Boogaloo would have to walk past and actually peer directly inside the alcove of machines to see her. That seemed more and more improbable as the weeks since her Thanksgiving scare went by. Still, she believed that that was absolutely Boog she'd glimpsed as she crossed the lobby toward the elevators. The dude actually turned, looked in her direction with something like surprise on his grubby face. He took a few steps in her direction just as the elevator door slid shut. Her john got some extra attention *that* night because she didn't want to leave.

It still wasn't enough of a fright to prevent her from earning in here. Merry's reluctance, now, certainly had something to do with her New Year's Eve misadventure. The way she explained it, it was super messed-up and Bella didn't buy it. If her little friend sincerely enjoyed the drugged gangbang then why was she reluctant to risk another? *I call bullshit.* Merry had finally put herself into a perilous situation and just wouldn't admit it. It was a matter of dumb luck that the participants in that New Year's Eve fun weren't sadistic psychopaths. Merry's attitudes shifted several times since Bella made her acquaintance—from extreme caution to reckless adventure to paranoia, and now back to extreme caution.

Bella sacrificed three more singles, made one minimum play but then her thoughts drifted. The rum was finding her bloodstream. She ignored the usually negative results on the screen, pausing with the play button under her motionless finger.

They sat at opposite ends of a bar on Nebraska Ave., Merry scratching up and down her thin left arm, dully eyeing Bella. Her drink appeared, in the dim light, to be something clear, in a shot glass which

she knocked back in a single motion. Yes, that's how a shooter is done by the skilled, Bella thought, who sipped everything daintily. After watching the salt be sucked off the girl's wrist, Bella avoided looking in her direction again. Bella had turned exactly three, widely spaced tricks at that point in time, before venturing downtown. Now, she needed to support a one room walkup in an enormous partitioned warehouse a ten-block bus ride away. She had tested various bars in every direction for a week already.

That was a Cuba libre in front of her, of course, which she hoped to sustain for an hour. Then, an enormous black gentleman in a shiny burgundy dinner jacket eased onto a stool next to her. Bella heard the air go out of the seat's cushion. She looked away because the other girl was now obscured by the man's bulk. No more cautionary tales to be observed in that direction. He didn't remove his funny old derby that looked like a New Year's Eve hat only it was made of some finer, real-hat material.

"Honey, I don't b'lieve I've made your acquaintance." The man pointed at a spot on the bar in front of him, two rings on his right index finger reflecting the beer signs behind the bar. Whatever the giant's usual drink happened to be, the longhaired Latino kid placed it gently in front of him with no apparent exchange of money. "You mus' be bran' new...in here to the Fantail Bar."

Bella chanced another quick, sidelong glance. This hombre enorme is a walking eclipse. "I have not before...come into...here." She reverted to the thick accents she'd long grown out of, hoping to thwart further conversation with the man. She swept a hand in a short ark before her to indicate the general confines of the place.

EVACUATION ROUTE

"Well, if you jus' some kinda touris'," The man swiveled to face Bella, more bling around his neck draping over a black, polyester shirt, reflective like everything else on his person. "Then you picked out a bad place for sight seein'."

"Sight?" Now she actually pointed two fingers at her own eyes, so close to breaking into laughter that the corners of her mouth began to twitch. "Sight? To see? Yes, I have."

"My, oh my." The huge man flickered a smile then lifted his own drink. "Do you even got any papers? It sound like you jus' swum ashore. I b'lieve some a my guidance might he'p ya out, though. Jus' to get ya, you know, sorta acclimated?"

"No, no. No paper. Verde? Verde card?" Bella reminded herself again, that whatever cleaned up name, whatever spin she put on this career adventure, she must always remain independent. If she couldn't manage that, she'd just go back to bagging groceries at Winn Dixie, and ride the bus to get there.

"Naw, I bet you sure don't have no vir-day card. Prob'ly don't have no papers a no kind, huh princess? But ya sure are a pretty li'l thing."

Bella stared back at him with what she hoped was a mask of incomprehension. She shrugged, turned away and raised her drink.

"But I tell ya the plain truth, mamma-sita. If you thinkin' a peddlin' that fine ass...culo, I mean. Pardon my French." The man now openly peered down at the seat of Bella's stool. "Ya need some protection 'n' guidance 'round here. These're some a them mean streets ya mighta heard about. I can keep ya safe from the riffraff 'n' gangbangers. I'm Neighbor Jones, what ever'body call me. I'd love to make you's acquaintance." He extended a bling-heavy fist.

270   CHRIS DUNGEY

Bella nearly laughed rum-and-coke out her nose as she timidly raised her own fist for a bump. She turned away again and faked a cough, hoping to sell it that she'd swallowed alcohol down the wrong pipe. There was probably nothing to be gained by disrespecting the man. Her would-be manager took this opportunity to pat her hand with a tentative gentleness that seemed totally unpracticed to him.

"You comprende anythin' 'bout what I'm drivin' at?" Neighbor Jones continued.

Bella gave him another quizzical look. She fluttered her hands near her ears. "No comprende so much. These gang. No, no. No gang," she insisted.

Her prospective pimp shook his head, more amused, so far, than frustrated. "Nah, nah. I know ya don't wanta be part a no gang. What I want is for you not t' be took advantage of by the criminal el'ment 'round here's all, baby girl."

"Nada. Nada crim'nal. Y no nino."

"Ah, man," Neighbor Jones sighed. "How you even manage to live without no better English skills. Listen, now. I'ma go drain mah lizard. Ya'll jus' sit tight, I'll put ya onta ol' Neighbor's tab. si?"

Again, Bella tried to express confusion with a shrug and a shake of her head. The man shifted off his stool. She watched his gigantic figure until it steered, like a docking freighter, into the neon port of the Restrooms. He seemed friendly enough, but as he moved away his posture and body language suggested just one word to her: Manhandle. She considered going out the back door immediately before the silly pantomime of language barrier could no longer br sustained without an eruption of giggles. She would try somewhere else, blocks

EVACUATION ROUTE

away. Or, ride the bus further down to try in classier surroundings. St. Petersburg, maybe.

"Don't you never go nowheres with that man, you hear me?"

Bella jumped. The wraith at the end of the bar moved closer to occupy Neighbor Jones's stool. She used the loud voice that English speakers often hoped would translate their words into another language.

"Sorry 'bout that li'l scare Ah give ya," the girl said, still loud. She patted Bella's arm. "Ah'd be nervous mah own self. See, ever'thin' about ya's screamin' amateur. Just take mah word for it about that pile a...you know. Caca?"

The little...fairy was the only term Bella could think of, held up her shot glass in a wordless appeal to the bartender. "Does it look so obvious?" Would Goth fairy apply?

"Hey, you talk English better'n Ah do!"

Now the girl (Bella couldn't avoid that word either) shoved Neighbor Jones's drink, napkin, cigarettes, and lighter three stools away from them.

"Isn't he going to be very pissed-off?" Bella said.

"Ah hope so. Ah just hope so." The girl raised and eyed her fresh shot which had a yellowish tint in the light of a muted television above the bar. As she swiveled to face Bella, a small derringer pistol showed, tucked into a garter she didn't need under loose fitting white shorts. "What is that accent a your's, girlfriend. Seems like it's between one kind 'n' somethin' else. Ah can't place it."

The bartender came for Bella's empty, rattling glass much more slowly, she thought, in the absence of Daddy Jones's intimidating

272 CHRIS DUNGEY

presence. The guy dispensed a shot of rum and then filled in the balance with cola from the well, all the while glancing over his shoulder at the television.

"Listen, Junior. Ah can tell ya the Rays're up by two runs in the third innin' 'n' they got two runners on. So why don't ya pay attention to what yer doin'. An' not so much damn ice for her nex' time."

"You got it, Merry." The bartender replaced Bella's napkin after swiping it a few times over the surface in front of her.

"Yep, that's mah old-timey name. 'Cept it ain't the same as the Good Lord's mama, nor Mary Magdalene, neither. It's spelled like for Christmas cuz Ahm so fulla joy. Sometimes. Although, Ah do admire that second Mary. She could be mah role model that Ah hope to emulate when Ah walk away from all this here. Ain't Ah ramblin' off'n the subjec' though?"

"What was the subject?" Bella sipped her drink. "It doesn't matter. I'm Bella and my accent is mostly Southeast Asian and Spanish. The Cuban kind. I don't mind talking with you at all. Do you work also, as a...? Are you a...?"

"Yep, Ah'm turnin' some tricks just to get by at this present time," Merry said. "'Cept tonight Ahm just restin'. Ah got me a major date comin' up tomorrow."

Bella turned to look the little sex fairy in the face. My, my. What big pupils you have. "If it was me, I would go to the beach for my day off. I would lay in the sun and then watch a movie at home. I would not come to my workplace."

EVACUATION ROUTE

"Oh, if it was you, huh?" Merry laughed a single ha. "Okay, but Ah like to come on down here 'n' just relax when there ain't no pressure to go out on the corner. It ain't a bad guess if you was to call this here a dive bar; if you was a Yuppie or a hipster, so-called. It ain't a long walk from mah li'l place which, Ah have only the one AC in a window 'n' Ah think it's givin' out on me. Relaxin' in here, Ah can have a hit a smoke, jus' a li'l one out'n the alley or go on home 'n' hit it again for a full night a sleep. That restful kind without no bad dreams? Why can't Ah just shut up, would ya explain that? But Ah ain't like this all the time, understand. Ah am not gonna have a mouthful a rotten teeth. Ha, ha, But Ah'll be runnin' down pretty soon, though, no worries. You still here?"

"Yes. You're teaching me good wisdom." Bella kept eyeing the door of the Men's room where Neighbor Jones finally emerged. The huge man paused at the curved end of the bar. Bella thought he seemed to deflate somehow when he spotted Merry sitting next to her. He moved around them and wedged through between their stools and some bar tables. Merry snickered as they both heard a chair tumble, nudged over by Neighbor's immense, clumsy passage.

"'scuse me young ladies," he said softly before moving down to his new spot at the bar.

"Yer excused," Merry replied, flashing the briefest of smirks in Neighbor Jones's direction. *"For now."* She turned back to Bella and then to her tequila.

"What did you just do? I pictured in my mind that he would pick you up with one hand and put you down again where you were

274 CHRIS DUNGEY

before." Bella took a first sip of her fresh rum-and-Coke. There were only a few ice-cubes in it this time. You must go slower now.

"That ol' lardass?" The little trick-fairy sniffed then held a bar napkin to her nose. Merry tipped her head back then wadded the spot of blood out of sight. She pushed it next to an ash tray. After scratching the graffiti mural decorating her left arm some more, she took another nip of the tequila. "He ain't nothin' unless you let 'im be. Just don't let 'im be. Ah can show ya how to get along without that noise if ya want me to."

Bella held up her glass, peered at its brown depth against the television. "You would do this, even to help out competition?"

Merry laughed, not quite derisively, stared at the tequila briefly as if now reluctant to slam another one. She sipped then quickly snatched up more bar napkins. She tipped her head back again and pressed a few of them to her nostrils. "Well, ain't this embarrasin'?" She said, nasally. "But, competition? No worries, hon. There's room enough for whatever it is you do. Ah don't work around here that much no more, anyways, like Ah said. These hos down here might be competin' for dates but they most times wanta keep each other safe. You go under Neighbor Jones's wing 'n' pretty soon you will have a jones. Know what Ahm sayin'? Prob'ly a black eye now'n' again, too. Ah don't wanta prejudice you but if he's still got more'n three girls, Ah'd be truly stunned. Which means the remainin' ones are all rowin' his sinkin' boat harder'n they oughta have to."

Bella resisted lifting her drink again, with the same rhythm as the first one. "What is your secret that you have no fear of him?"

EVACUATION ROUTE 275

Merry took another quick glimpse at Neighbor Jones and snorted to stifle outright dismissive laughter. She then had to return the napkin to her nose. "Well, it ain't no big secret if ya got the stamina. Ah got me some friend's with who Ah have reg'lar dates 'n' who keep me hooked up. They are friends that truly look out for me 'n' who Neighbor Jones don't want no part of."

"It sounds like you have found the best way for you," Bella said. "But how are those friends not the same as...as Neighbor with his guidance? I wish to be under control of no one."

Merry nibbled at the rim of her shot-glass, hardly drinking at all. The second napkin joined the first by the ashtray. Bella saw that it, too, was spotted with blood. Merry seemed to relax, eyelids narrowing in the television light. She might be past the desire to focus on anything. "Well good luck with that. Ah don't ever see the independent 'terpreneurs work out too good. There's bein' used 'n' esploited, an' then there's bein' respected 'n' havin' real protection. Ah can quit anytime after Ah've earned mah bagful 'n' mah friend's'll just say, "Good luck, li'l Mare. We're gonna miss ya." Now her eyes closed completely. "Buy me a l'll ol' house somewheres away from here. A cottage, like. Ocean view, mebbe. Far off 'n' aways from any city."

"Maybe I could just buy some better wardrobe," Bella said. "Have an interview to be the escort girl. Also, I have danced."

Merry's head drooped for a moment on a collision course with her shot glass. She jerked upright and came back to the conversation. "Ya got enough class to entertain them high-end jerks that want escorts?" Now she did pick up her tequila and pounded it, throwing her head back. This required her, then, to loll her head back and forth slowly as though she was gargling or had hurt herself. "Chrahst, Ahm sorry. Ahm so sorry. What's your name again? That musta sounded pretty insultin'. A course ya got enough class 'n' Ah can see it. Needa go out back for a sec, get right before Ah head on home. Ya wanna hit for yerself?"

"No, no, por favor." Bella had yet to take a second sip of her fresh drink. "And I am Bella, Merry."

"Well, ya like to stick by for a while? Ah'll be right back in. Ah love that accent 'n' yer perfume, too. Ah can tell you all about mah friends 'n' their deal if yer innerested." Merry slipped to the bar floor and ambled a slow zig-zag course toward the rear entrance, even patting Neighbor Jones on the shoulder as she passed.

There were winnings for Bella to collect when she quit daydreaming. She didn't hear the recorded, metallic spilling of coins into the nonexistent winner's trough. Her drink had also arrived unnoticed. Sipping only after a win was a good strategy. She had totally lost focus there, for awhile. *Pay attention to business, chicka. It was* good with Merry's friends, the *Knuckledicks,* for awhile. She spent a little over a year. She didn't keep a diary, but *time flies when you are having fun, yes?* Then the maintenance by Boogaloo and Wood-Chuck became shoddy, while the demands of the *Knuckledicks* became more strenuous.

EVACUATION ROUTE   277

The trick-ferry talked her away from the corners and bars downtown that she'd been steeling herself to attempt when she first entered that little dive bar. For a few weeks before that, the joints along Nebraska Avenue seemed appealing as an option to bagging groceries and the three-days-a-week gig on the Déjà vu stripper pole. That was too much like shift work. And, there was a handsy boss who doled out the hours depending on how *friendly* a girl was to him. Or, how willing to part with a percentage of tips. But technically, she was not yet a street walker. She stepped off the bus from Largo and decided not to go back except to gather up some clothes; take her share of the parental ashes and wish her brothers *gentle seas and full nets*. She had saved enough from the stripping and bagging at *Winn Dixie* for the room and a hotplate. Then she followed her tunnel vision past all street corners straight into any number of bars. *I was a bar walker.*

What was so difficult and dangerous? Going back to her place from trick-trolling, there were even places out of the rain. There was always a bench in the glass-hooded bus shelter. Who tries to pick up someone in a bus stop? Nearly everyone, she discovered. Just sit in there for awhile on some lawyer's face. Okay, so it happened only twice, after a fruitless evening in *Paddy's Pub*. *I turned down a few, give me credit.* Just as the bar-hopping strategy began to seem like a loser, she encountered Neighbor Jones in *The Fantail*. Luckily, Merry's intervention pointed her toward the lucrative year that followed.

The introduction to Wood-Chuck, scary Boogaloo and some king-of-trolls everyone called *The Darkness,* was amiable enough.

They appraised her qualities frankly; her endowments upper and lower. This did not make her uncomfortable with Mare standing nearby. Surprisingly, they didn't manipulate her jaw or inspect her teeth.

She couldn't help notice, before reaching the shelter of a bar, that johns in cars along Nebraska Avenue also stared straight at a girl's cooch, eyelevel in the passenger window. Maybe they'd seen all they needed to of shapes and dimensions as they rolled slow, looking for a spot at the curb. *Crazy they didn't inspect for crack teeth.* Whereas, the dudes in Gentlemen's Clubs gathered around the little round tables *expected* that the flesh twirling on the pole above them would be attractive. They made great show of being jaded *old hands* more interested in their drinks and the camaraderie, knowing that the quality would be there when they were ready to pay attention. *Then they wanted it shoved in their faces.* So, she was creeped out mucho by most men well before Merry led her into the *Knuckledick's* playhouse.

"Is this seat taken?"

Bella's snapshot glimpse showed her a quite handsome man, rather tall, in leisure-Friday slacks and a golf shirt. Too bad that might be her least favorite of all opening lines. It seemed a little too polite for this place. There was no seat holding of adjacent machines allowed. You only had to sit down. That ploy was to be ignored on a busy weekend night. Bella gave a nearly imperceptible nod in the direction of the empty swivel chair. She resumed her attention to *Cleopatra,* letting out a little more line to entertain the first nibble. Her new neighbor slid in smoothly

EVACUATION ROUTE 279

"My name's Jack." The stranger extended a well manicured hand—no wedding band showing. It was some kind of impressive class or fraternity ring.

Now Bella turned halfway around, ignoring the proffered handshake. Jack showed her an innocuous smile but didn't stare or lean any closer. He turned back to feed a twenty into his own machine's money snatcher.

"Uh-huh. So you're *Jack*, are you?" Bella twisted to take a closer look

"Yeah, it's a throwback name but I've been hearin' it given to more kids, lately. We don't need any more Kyles or Zaks, Joshes or Calebs. The Old Testament has been worn out as a source. Haven't you noticed?"

Bella turned slowly back to her own machine and pressed *Play* with another minimum bet. "Listen, uh...*Jack*. Do you remember where you were on New Year's Eve? Did you, maybe, do some very heavy partying in the *Hard Rock*? It has been three months only. You *must* recall."

With big, blue eyes now narrowed, his brow furrowed like some kind of predator, the guy leaned in to study Bella more closely. "I would have to think back. I can tell you that I always enjoy my visits here. I work hard and try to match that effort when I play. Why ever would you ask about that *particular* time frame?"

Bella snuffed. *Cagey, this one is. But you better stand up to him and do not cower back.* "You do not remember her *name*, even?"

Jack relaxed his passive-aggression face, miming a deep search of his memory, going so far as to scratch at the crown of his thinning blond head. "Well, yes, ma'am. I believe I likely *was* here. I was with some old college friends and business associates. You still have me at a disadvantage, though, about details you're suggestin'. Whose name is it that I'm supposed to have forgotten? I know I wouldn't remember *your* name because you haven't paid me the courtesy of givin' it. Let me have a few more clues before I plead guilty to anything."

Bella made a single *tsk* and slowly shook her head. The man was wresting the initiative back, the momentum. She couldn't let him do that, though she was having as much difficulty appearing disgusted as she had in faking a language deficiency for Neighbor Jones. *This* Jack looked pretty good and she began to understand Merry's absence of skepticism and caution. "Just think hard, *Jack.* Did you meet someone very small? Who spoke like a redneck? Do you *prefer* the very *little* girls, *Jack?* Childlike?"

The man drew back and Bella thought that he may have spit out the bait, spooked. "She couldn't have been *that* childlike and still been allowed in here. They're pretty thorough about verifying ages." Jack leaned back and looked toward the cul de sac's entrance. He looked in every direction for the waiter, or maybe for Bella's backup. Her attitude suggested to him a sting of some kind. "Did she maybe spell her name...different, funny? Yeah, yeah, like Merry *ho-ho-ho* not Mother Mary. So what? What about her?"

"So nothing, except she is my roommate. And she will be so *merry* to know that she made such a lasting impression. Did you use the correct spelling in your scrapbook, under her pictures?"

EVACUATION ROUTE 281

Jack relaxed into a leisurely posture then made a lackadaisical play on his machine. "Ah, I see. But now, *that* wasn't my idea. I wanted my friends to have a unique New Year's Eve, that's all. I had your Merry's permission and she was well paid. I don't *need* to collect souvenirs. And I still don't know *your* name."

Now Bella saw her boy waiter hustling toward their chiming cul de sac, one dark mixed drink remaining on his tray.

"I didn't forget you." The kid took her glass, empty of rum but still amply gemmed with ice.

She tipped him again. "My friend, too, please, is thirsty. I can vouch to you that he is a *player*, mucho."

"Vodka and Squirt. Thank you, whatever your..."

"I'm Bella, Jack," She told him. "And if your hand would go near to my drink, I would cut you." Bella flashed the briefest of smiles. It was not a disarming one.

"Understood. And that was also not my idea, the mickey."

"This Mickey is one of your crew who played the bad trick?

Jack looked genuinely confused, eyeing Bella between plays on his machine as if she had just crawled out of a shipping container. "No, no. The sedation, the Rohypnol. To make her...," Jack placed praying hands, palms together, like a pillow next to his cheek. "She becomes sleepy. A little, like...*drogado*? Yes, yes I have to confess. I was talked into it."

Bella sampled her fresh drink and made another simple, minimum wager.

"But, I'm very sorry we did that. It wasn't my idea and I should have known better. My pals thought it would be interesting if she was totally lethargic. Otherwise, maybe she wouldn't be so agreeable to some of their photo shoot ideas. That sounds pretty awful, doesn't it?"

Jack craned his neck, way too early to see the approach of his drink. Bella tried to peer deeper into whatever might speak some truth in his expression. Genuine remorse, or was he just saying anything necessary to close his present transaction? A nervous agitation clouded his earlier appearance of complete command and control. But, she would never, *ever* assume what was under the sheep's clothing.

"You could not know her in the way *I* know her. Your...*mickey* was not necessary." Another small winner made its brief, sound-bite cascade of coins. She felt the casino feeding her more line just as she was doing with *this* guy. It was giving up just enough small money to really sink in the hook. "She was angry at herself for what you got away with because she was careless. Now she's afraid to enjoy her work too much. She is open to extreme experience, because she does not really care. What brings her pleasure is acceptable. Don't you feel low now? All you had to do to make it okay would have been to tell her before."

The man peered at his watch as the waiter arrived. Bella did not see what he offered for a tip. "Again, I'm so sorry. Could you convey that apology to her? When I pay for company, I'm nearly always flying solo. Just like tonight."

Bella sipped almost no liquid from the surface of her drink, a measure of economy and caution she was perfecting on the boats. "This convey is to *pasar*? Is to tell her?" She turned an irresistible

EVACUATION ROUTE 283

smirk away from Jack's view. She was out of practice at performing her immigrant charade and it would quickly become untenable.

"Yes, Bella. When you see her the next time. But not *too* soon, I hope. Can you tell her tomorrow? What I'm sayin' is, are you waiting for someone right now?" Jack leaned forward to take a receipt for his own meager winnings.

High and a bit outside. Don't swing yet. Make him throw it down the middle. Bella realized that she had switched her...what was it when you say that one thing is another thing? Anyway, she had mixed up her...*something*, from fishing to baseball. It was true that Jack and his friends did not cheat Merry. She brought home her biggest payday ever. Bigger than for a *Knuckledicks* swap meet. And, she got to spend New Year's Eve in a very nice...suite, she called it. "I have not made yet, any date. No."

"Well then, can I offer you $5 hundred for the night? That will include a room service dinner. Breakfast is your option."

Bella thought about how comfortable they were at the moment regarding rent, and maybe soon a car for her, too. The future seemed to shine bright green as the amber caution light holding up the deal dimmed. Bella loved the boats for being on the sea, but the casino work brought in *serious* money. She could probably skip spending so much time out on the *Narcissus,* if she and Merry continued to encounter *this* man.

"We will finish our drinks," she said. She doubled her next bet. "I will text your driver card to Merry? You know how we do this?"

"Yeah, I remember the drill. Very smart. *Pa'dentro,* to *you* Bella." Jack eyed her over his first taste of the cloudy, still fizzing drink.

"And my last name is Bancroft. So now I'm completely known to you."

Bella resumed feigning intense concentration on her final wager. She did not lift her glass in the toast. Over her shoulder she said, "*salud y pa'dentro,* Jack Bancroft."

Chapter Fourteen

Wood-Chuck Spurgeon still had no clear idea of where Boog LaVelle was spending his evenings when he wasn't shepherding the *Knuckledick* girls to their dates. Whatever Boog was up to, his absence caused a butterfly effect to ripple through critical levels of the Club flow chart. Well, critical to Wood. Wasn't that how hurricanes were born? A butterfly doin' somethin' way over by West Africa? Seriously?

The addition of Dina, a barely legal Hispanic, to the rainbow cast of biker subsidized sex workers, required yet another delivery that Wood might have to make whenever Boog did whatever he was doing. And, for those hours when Wood was required to step out as a substitute, Ivan Dresbach was paid *something* out of Wood's pocket to move behind the bar. For as much time as that wooly headed (maybe the last Jewfro in the Tampa Bay area) was asked to cover, the compensation of a few free longnecks should have been enough. But, no such luck. Wood and he had agreed on $8 bucks an hour *plus* the beer. Wood didn't want to hear *The Darkness* complain about redundant money coming out of the *Knuckledick* treasury so he covered it himself. He was still hesitant to suggest some level of matching contribution from Boogaloo, so he continued to swallow the deficit.

Under normal circumstances, *Knuckledick* members were expected to pick the girls up and return them in original, working condition. Tonight, however, Bum Crawford up in Oldsmar rated a special delivery. Bum had genuinely injured his back (no, *really* this time) in a legitimate loading dock mishap at his warehouse job. Or, rather, the place where he could be found for eight hours each day. His likely usefulness at that job was a subject of occasional *Knuckledick* mirth. No one could picture him driving a forklift.

This personal hygiene challenged *slacker-who-cried-wolf* had already succeeded in a few Workman's Comp claims from his varied careers, though none for more than a year. Was he accident prone or just a common scammer? But, an insurance company backing the fund was now willing to invest the time and resources to find out. This time, Bum had actually fractured two vertebrae and the checks weren't coming to him yet.

This time, the fresh, new back-brace wasn't a prop. Neither was the unfamiliar sedan with blacked-out glass that began to park near Bum's cheery mobile home. He told Wood to come on ahead with a girl, anyway, he was past desperate. *She could be my licensed physical therapist. They don't know 'n' it's none a their business.*

So, with Boog missing on his mysterious errands, the delivery of the blow-job-on-wheels fell to Wood again. He must accomplish this in an aging Corolla borrowed from that same barkeep apprentice, Ivan. After dolling herself up and applying copious makeup,

EVACUATION ROUTE

Mandy was *not* riding anywhere on the back of a Harley. Wood wondered how Boog got away with it.

"This should be easy money," he told Mandy as they drove in the stop-and-go Friday rush-hour on the 580. "He special requested *you* if that eases your mind."

"Well, it *don't*. Not very much. This Bum, if it who Ah think, he a nasty ol' boy 'n' a lousy tipper. But Ah could tell *that* tale 'bout most a y'all. Meanin' no disrespect. Least, if he really hurt he won't wanta to be thrash'n around too much."

"You 'n' I *both* hope not," Wood said. "I'm goin' back out of his beautiful neighborhood to visit that *Tim Horton* we just passed. Then I'll come right on back and wait as long as it takes."

Mandy lowered the passenger side window then lit one of her brown cigarillos. "You a sweetheart, Wood," Mandy said. "Ah don't wanta be in that shit-box one little minute past when I'm done. Hey, could ya bring me back one a those boxes a donut balls? The assortment one? Ah'm gonna need *somethin'*, clear mah pallet. That ol' boy better have somethin' to drink."

"Ain't you got any mouthwash?" Wood had turned off of the 508 and into the mobile home park soon after.

"Course Ah got mouf wash, silly white boy. Boog always..."

"Okay, Mandy. I'll get 'em for ya. You gotta pay me back, though. Your date is costin' *me* outta pocket to Ivan for what Boog's already bein' paid for."

He had been in here before, for what purpose he couldn't remember. He recognized the bewildering, randomly laid out maze

288   CHRIS DUNGEY

of it. There was no planned system that *he* could see. Maybe that was on purpose for tenants who wished to remain unfound.

"It all good, Wood. Ah feel ya. Where is that crazy boy been to, lately?"

"I ain't got a clue. I was gonna ask you."

"He ain't said nothin' to us,"

China Berry Drive, Mulberry Lane, Locust Lane, Bonzai Drive. *Why'd they leave out any kinda berry ya could eat?* Wood turned in on Tulip Drive. "Could be some kinda special assignment," he told Mandela.

"Good for him. Could ya maybe pull inta somewheres, too, 'n' pick me up a half-pint a *Courvoisier*. Ah'll need somethin' to wash down them pastries."

"Sure. Why not." Wood sighed.

Bum's older-model trailer wasn't even a doublewide and yet it didn't clash starkly with the condition of his neighbor's homes. Siding, roofing, porches and decks sun dulled back to the early 70s. Wood parked behind the biker's gleaming, extended cab Ram truck. *Probably worth three a that trailer.* The Harley, of course, was under a cover and chained to the back porch. The weathered construction of the porch was upgraded not long ago with a wheelchair ramp. The raw, pressure treated lumber was starkly new against the worn, driftwood color of old construction. *Wow. The guy isn't foolin' around with this claim,* Wood thought. Only the dimensions for the front door, the laws of physics, and Bum's miserable physical condition prevented the bike from being wheeled up into the dining room.

EVACUATION ROUTE 289

"I'll get back here quick as I can. Good luck."

Mandy stepped out of the car awkwardly, slowed by the removal of her ample, tightly wrapped booty following her and unfamiliar gravel beneath her 5 inch heels. She opened the rear door to remove her huge tote-bag. She wobbled down the unpaved bit of driveway toward Bum's front door. Even Wood, who should have been accustomed to the view by now, marveled at that magnificent backside now shifting in Ivan's grimy headlights. Her white mini-skirt barely covered it. This, and the matching white halter knotted at the small (a relative term) of her back deserved better illumination. Wood found an empty fast-food bag on the passenger side floor and hopped out to wipe the headlights with it. Mandy was swiftly admitted to Casa de Bum. The guy sure couldn't complain about not getting the full *Knuckledick* treatment, even as an invalid.

Wood backed out slowly, the restored beams this time grazing over a black Buick Regal in front of the neighboring lot. *Shit! And he's facin' the wrong way. He wasn't there a few minutes ago.* If it wasn't for the quick polishing job on the headlamps, Wood might have clipped the guy.

He shifted into Drive and idled, close, around the big vehicle. Tinted glass, the driver's window rolled down. *Well good evenin', fellas.* The driver's eyes remained focused straight ahead, mouth poised unblinking behind a Big Mac held in its wrapper. Wood slid by, miming dull disinterest. That driver and vehicle totally screamed *adjuster, investigator. Or, some such kind of spook. Christ, that thing looks almost like a government pool car.* So much for Bum making himself lost in here, if that was the purpose of these street patterns.

But what was Wood supposed to do? Bum Crawford had every right, as a member in good standing, to put his name on the calendar for the girl of his choice and to have that girl brought, if he was incapacitated, to his residence. If this vice cost him a nice Workman's Comp settlement, well then, that was going to be one expensive hummer. Wood's conscience was clear. Anyway, could the surveillance guy in the Buick possibly see whether Bum was laying in bed like a corpse, getting a therapeutic massage; or, swinging from a pull-up bar with Mandy impaled? *Jesus. Will I be able to drink that picture outta my head?* Did Mandy look anything *like* a licensed homecare nurse?

Wood shrugged. *Just can't be my problem*. He needed a sandwich and some caffeine. Next time either he or Boog did this delivery, whoever the girl was should probably wear some kind of scrubs. And for that, Bum would have to pay.

*Those dirty little...*Boogaloo resisted, in his unusually calm mind, as he was recently able to do, the word he *really* wanted to use. His choice of other words were probably *all* unacceptable; the g word, the t word, the q word. (Quim? Where had he even picked that one up? In one of Pere Emile's raggedy old fuck books?) But, *bitches* was always an option. With all the plotting and stealth he could employ, he was still not able to track those *bitches* to their hidey-hole. It was no help that he couldn't just swing up to New Port Richie every evening. And when he *was* able, there was no guarantee that either of them would go out on the gambling boat.

The random spotting of Merry's *Tracker* seemed more and more like a lucky crossing of paths, similar to the glimpse of Bella in the big casino. By now he could not remember why he'd been riding all the way up here in the first place. *Was that the first week on Gold Wing? Was I just out bondin' with this silly ride? Learnin' her limits?* But the same hoodoo of steady low level brain-rage, even when he believed it was tamed, kept him revisiting the *RaceTrak* gas station.

Boog surmised that the girls didn't want to park the *Tracker* in the wharf lot. The one time he'd run into Merry turning in was on that first night, but then he lost her in the unending *Suncoast* traffic, the signal as long as purgatory. When he saw Bella get off a bus three afternoons later, though, he had riddled out their scheme—turning tricks on the gambling cruises *and* at *Hard Rock Casino.* They were also crazy careful. *But, they could never 'magine how determined was their ol' friend Boog.*

So, how could a determined man not finish flushin' them out, like quail? I am that determined man 'n' none a those shrink words Wood prob'ly thinks about me. Of course Wood still seemed not to suspect how wide Boog's nostrils were still open for this hunt. He didn't know if he should *ever* tell Wood.

If he could just carve out more *time*, find an even closer place to park for his vigil. Beginning this very night, he would try to

292 CHRIS DUNGEY

approach by that parallel back street into the docking area. Sit and sit, he would, if that's what it took, with the same patience he needed for jack-lighting the biggest bull gators; or like Pere Emile, to find the trophy bass for NOLA sport fishermen. *Determination: To clean the catch for them and not laugh in their faces. Determined.* Even his dear old *Pere* could not understand, observing several violent occasions, the *determination;* sometimes lifting the ragged *Saints* ball-cap then to scratch the red, old, liver-spotted scalp and white hair. Pere Emile never would disrespect his teen Beauregard by telling him to *give up.* But he had often reminded the kid to accept the wisdom of *mebbe not today, mebbe not dis time. Why slam yer own head up against cement? (Like an Abutment, mebbe?) Wait for that better day.*

Wood might have a similar outrage, if he knew that his main man was still on the trail of those...*bitches. If he find me out, no more does he take care of my girls. Wood learns of this fuckery and I will be back to my job. Don't wish him to complain to Darkness.*

Boogaloo readied to roll out of the *RaceTrac* station. So large, with the twenty-four pumps and all that inside business: The microwave sandwiches, the ice-cream soft-serve. *More choices than our Tasty Freeze south a Houma. Always a chocolate-dip cone, dyin' ol' Pere Emile must have after fishin' on Bayou Larouche. Soft serve for the bad teeth.*

If he wished, Boog could continue to sit on the *Gold Wing* at the corner entrance to *RaceTrac,* diagonally across from the short street into the marina. No one at the pumps or inside ever paid him notice. But, this overwatch was not bringing im any success. It was

EVACUATION ROUTE

a little too far for a good view except to see when their car entered, and they could easily start to notice him as they made the turn.

It was time to leave when a New Port Richie patrol car turned in, wanting his spot, to lurk like a gull near a scaling table. Boog quickly moved into northbound traffic, the *Gold Wing* stealth-bomber quiet. *Not to alarm the pig in his ear.* Two blocks beyond the side street to the blackjack boat's entrance, he swerved into the left turn lane.

Through a neighborhood of sprawling bar/restaurants and attendant parking lots, he doubled back toward the wharf of the gambling boat. Another marina, the nearest of several, sat on the riverfront which fed past the *Narcissus* toward the Gulf. Mammoth luxury pickup trucks and older rusting ones with rusting quarter panels or missing tailgates took up the back reaches of marinas and bars alike.

Boog idled along the backs of these lots, one after another with US 19 whooshing steadily along on his left. Headlights occasionally veered into the restaurant lots as the dinner hour advanced. There were clientele already waiting outside for tables to become available in *Gator Joe's* and *Hungry Harbor. Marina Grill and Sports* was so apparently popular that it provided a small playground for children waiting to dine with their parents. An old, open trawler with only a small wheel house forward, was rolled onto its side as if blown there by a tropical gale. It seemed to be better attended than swings or slide. All of the tackle had been removed and the hull was braced by thick stanchions. On his next slow circuit, Boog still looked twice at the kiddos trying to climb up into her cuddy cabin. Peres and Mameres nearby slurped their placating drinks, longingly watching their table buzzers. *Better not tip over onta those petite garcons et filles.*

Riding the hard-packed marl trails dissecting rows of parked vehicles, he obeyed a series of stop signs. Then with no warning, the *Gold Wing* rolled into the overflow lot for *Lucky Seas Excursions.* Diners at the bar/restaurants seemed to honor some prohibition to enter there. He couldn't find a prohibiting sign. There were few cars in this space. Boog could see the buildings of the boat's staging area up close now, so maybe he was *too* near. Their first lot, which extended right up to the dock, was about half filled. There was no fence. He could take a long look as he passed then circle back around, taking time. Too bad the ship was still out on the Gulf. Riding past that playground repeatedly at walk speed gave Boog a passing notion of unjustified guilt. *Well, that is how they might think bad of me in these days.* Did he have time to slip into one of those bars, legitimize his presence?

It was easy enough for *him* to find a parking spot. Boog chose *Gator Joe's* which, remarkably, offered parking for bikes near the broad entrance porch. There was one spot left with a thick, steel eyebolt in the concrete for his cable. He lifted it out of the saddlebag. He removed his courier bag and tucked it into a saddlebag. If he heard it called a purse, his old identity might emerge with bad consequences.

All of the benches and tables on the porch were crowded. *Must be best food around. Or, cheapest beer.* Waiting diners sat with preliminary drinks, as they'd been encouraged to do by hostesses in

EVACUATION ROUTE

295

the foyer. They sat with their *table is ready* devices, awaiting the signal that service and food were imminent.

"Will you be dining with us? We have an approximate 45 minute wait." One of the two hostesses prepared to offer a menu for him to peruse.

"Just into the bar," Boog said.

The hostess pointed to her left. "Right in there. You may have to stand."

Yes, I can stand. Drinkers were two and three deep behind occupied stools. To Boog, there didn't appear to be any recession in here at all. The established etiquette was to call an order to one of the bartenders, wait to take ones drink, and then make room for someone behind you to step forward. He caught an elbow in the arm of his denim jacket. The guy on the stool apologized with all the sincerity of *have a nice day. Must be patient, Boog. Polite, with this many citizens close.*

"Sir! What can I get you?!" The bartender had to shout.

The kid wore a flannel shirt with the sleeves rolled up and now Boog noticed that *none* of the wait staff wore uniforms. *They make it to feel like down home, they think.* But he'd bet there was no one allowed barefoot in the place. "*Bring the pitcher!*" There was no *Jax* on the bill-of-fare for beers. Nor was his favorite craft brew, *Copper Tail Unholy,* available. "*Budweisser,* I think!"

"Just plain *Budweisser*? How many glasses, sir?!"

"One!"

To his credit, the kid's expression didn't falter. He soon returned with the foaming half-gallon of draft in a glass pitcher that looked pre-frosted. "That'll be $12.50 or I can put it on a tab with your meal!"

Boog handed him a ten dollar bill. The trucker's wallet was halfway down the back of his *relaxed fit* khakis but he dug in and drew it out again. He handed the kid a five then waited for his change, his face as stoic as a guard at Buckingham Palace. With money back in hand, he went against his usual inclinations and left a one on the bar.

An' now what, coujon? Stand in the crowd pourin' for myself this half-gallon a beer? He did just that after moving back from the crowd at the bar. His first glass was half-gone at a swallow when a couple on his left *whoo-hooed* with joy, their device lighting up like a merry-go-round. Boog quickly slid into one of their vacated chair, between a college kid, maybe, and a taller, darkly tanned fellow in a fishing cap. Dark from the bright Gulf waters; ripened by *Jack Daniels. Just say something, I will practice to be a citizen.* The quick maneuver gave the sissy at his right shoulder no time to conjure lies about a friend gone to the toilet. There were four flat screens above the tiered liquor. Both of his new companions seemed more interested in the Ray's baseball game than in disputing with a stranger over possession of the seat..

Boog had no idea what time it was when he emerged from *Gator Joes*, heavier, after all, by an enormous burger and steak fries. There

EVACUATION ROUTE

were still plenty of cars parked in the lot for *Lucky Seas Excursions*, now. He saw that the ship had come in to tower above its port facilities. He crept closer, through their overflow lot right up to the curbing of a side street, It was a good enough vantage and he dared go no closer. After only a few moments (*just in nick a time*), exiting passengers appeared beneath the security lights, streaming out from under a *Welcome and Reception* sign. The voyage had ended: First, two small groups of men wearing the shorts with many pockets. *For all their cargo.* Then men with women in pairs followed by a few more men alone, maybe the most fleeced. *Merde.* Was there no one else to come ashore? Was this trip and his time wasted again? But then, *sweet mamere,* there went the little one, right before his eyes.

A gambler led her, under his gambler's hipster hat like Boog won at Opelousas County fair one time. This one was without the long, stupid feather. The john's arm was draped over her shoulder.

They swayed against each other, at least one of them weaving drunk. But Boog *knew,* had seen all of Merry's games played for johns from distances farther away than this. *Let down his guard, this man will.* But those whores wouldn't be so stupid as to steal, not if they wanted to keep sailing. Bella was always careful or she claimed to be. When Boog didn't pick them up on time, she went whining to Wood. *Mare not stupid as you'd think by the way she talk, and paranoid careful until she light the crack. Just keep going, cher. Don't look up here. An' don't let this guy kill you in a car crash, before we have our parles.*

He thought Mare had *made* him a few weeks ago, at that same *RaceTrac* intersection. Her expression melted, twenty-five yards away from him.

Now, how can follow this john with my little skank? Roar down there and have the reunion scuffle right in front of him and any others? This sad bike did not roar so much. It was perfect for following quietly, though, if he wanted to. *What if the guy is carryin'? He looks like a guy to have equalizer in one of cargo pockets.*

The happy pair moved quickly out of his view and into *his* car, must be. Merry never left her car in the lot, Boog believed. He'd seen her pick Bella up that one lucky night. *Add up the math. They no more work in pairs? Bella drives to get her?* Perplexing him still was the hindrance that he couldn't spy here every night.

Boog leaned against the *Gold Wing*, which was not yet fully his friend, to watch the last of the passengers leave the dock. In his brain, he tried to douse the ember that wanted to flare. Up in his head or on his shoulder somewhere, the fluttering sissy angel spoke *Wood's* advice. *Let it go.* Still simmering, the rage he must resist; but also the *impotence* he felt along with that. Where was his red-ass angel to debate this whimpering one? The only voice speaking for him was his own, ridiculing him: *Limp dick.*

Some of the vehicles leaving *Lucky Seas Excursions* swept him with their headlights as they turned into the back street access to the bars. The Merry *he* knew wouldn't waste the time for dinner. But a free meal and more drinks with the john? Maybe their financial situation had changed their approach. He walked

EVACUATION ROUTE

the bike backward to get out of range. But no more gamblers used that exit.

It was just him then, on his own behalf, to somehow remain the big dog, whose jaws cannot release, even when clubbed senseless. All he *has* in his tool bag of skills is to be relentless and to have a reputation. Not as big, or as smart as the others in this *Knuckledick* pack. But *determined*. Slowly, the brain fire licked lower, back down into the glowing coals. How long had he stood there like *le mort vivant*?

Idling at walk speed back out to *Suncoast Highway*, Boog resisted a frustrated burnout though there was more power in this *rice burner* than he ever would have given it credit for. The traffic had thinned out considerably. *That cop has gone to stop and harass somewhere else.*

It was in the very moment of motoring calmly, without the wait for streams of cars to clear, that Boog had his first hopeful thought of the evening. Well, except for confirming his theory about those whores' new system, proven out when little Merry was led from the boat. This humiliating disguise was better treachery than theirs. And, he now had a shortcut to an eventual reckoning. No more of only watching for them. He needed only two, three more nights of deceiving Wood. Just park the *Gold Wing* in that reserve lot then go on the ocean with the *fonchock* gambling suckers. Those, those...(alright, *whores* was the only description needed), wouldn't miss more than a few trips between voyages to ply their trade. *Then, what a surprise for them. Boo! Remember me?*

More warning than I give The Abutment. Took all the way into basketball season to catch so called nose-tackle alone. Not so many posse of friends leaving the locker room together from basketball practice. And, more dark in December; one light pole where players park junky cars and pickups behind the gym. Rain, but still warm late November, still fall for the school and south Houma. Worth six months I serve in Juvey for assault with intent to do great bodily harm, less than murder. Not usual two-and-half years. Court investigated provoking incident; the hospital documents of injuries; all my four broken teeth, x-ray of crack ribs. Mitigating circumstance.

I moved quick from behind tailgate of Alvin Malvaux's pickup, catch him when driver's door was unlock 'n' open. Sent round-house slap at The Abutment right ear, stun him perfect. Easy then, drop him with kick to back of a knee. The Abutment's head hit the ground with more impact than I plan. Oh, well. Too heavy to set him down easy. The parking-lot just pea gravel. More yield than asphalt. But, we went to maybe poorest school district in Louisiana.

"I owe you a haircut but can't afford," I yell aloud in his ear. "Holiday coming. You grew hair since football. For Senior picture? A good look for you, but just need the quick trim."

I took hold a lot of hair in one hand, him groaning with curses. You might have concussion. Don't go to sleep, now. Take aspirins at home.

I hurry away, still snappin' Mamere sewing shears. Malvaux struggle to his knees, hair all around him like shed pine-needles. I hope some prickly ones go down his neck. "You are ready for family Christmas card," I call to him from darkness.

Such a shame that Bella cut and dyed *her* beautiful hair. Her *Knuckledick* johns once loved to hold the mop of it from behind like the reins of a pony. Her short bob now eliminated *that* as an act of retribution. And he must be on time at the *Knuckledick's* Clubhouse tomorrow. *Put in the few productive days for Wood to clear time I will need.*

Chapter Fifteen

That woman was signaling her availability, Walt thought, at every single chance encounter between them. From the beginning, she didn't try to avert eye contact. With that came a wink. But some people winked at others all the time to convey: *You and I are in on the same joke.* Or; *Let's humor this situation or circumstance together.*

But, what made this a *vibe* to him? *If* that was the thing she was communicating. Walt had little recent experience at recognizing these subtleties. Was there some pulse of pheromones crossing the noisy room like too much body spray? Walking into the St. Patrick's Day dinner/dance suddenly felt like a trap springing. Their eyes locked before the door of the Association Room had closed behind him.

After nearly a month of a microwave menu, Walt was ready for a decent meal. A signup sheet highlighted prominently with green tinsel on a bulletin board caught his attention when he went into *The Glade* office to pay the March lot rent. It wasn't that he didn't trust the gas range or his mastery of the control knob not to cause an explosion. But he'd never used a gas oven before.

EVACUATION ROUTE 303

He made no errors, so far, in lighting his one favorite burner, the one that once doubled as an ashtray for the previous owners. The igniter no longer worked so he had to strike a kitchen match. The next problem, or excuse, was that he hadn't accumulated more than one saucepan, one frying pan and a teakettle. A boiled dinner; corned beef and cabbage with spring spuds was to be provided out of Association money. The signup sheet was for desserts. So, was anyone bringing pie? Without his reading glasses, Walt leaned close to study the list on the bulletin board. Alright, anyone not bringing fruit cocktail in lime *Jell-O was* bringing pie. Oh well, then. He guessed he'd be one more. He picked up the *Sharpie* dangling on a string and committed to the gathering.

Walt spent the afternoon of the party working in the large, end bedroom he had claimed for himself. He was able to shower under a leisurely amount of hot water. He could then step out onto a clean new bathroom floor. This particular floor constituted his first unnecessary personal indulgence. He'd picked out glazed black slate. The structure of joists beneath the rotten bathroom floor was shored up to manage the stress. The floor guys carried the supplies to do this, telling him it was a common procedure. Just keep the white grout nice with an old toothbrush.

Walt spent time in the afternoon sweeping up the last dust and trimmings left in his bedroom by those same floor guys. The workers were happy to be gluing down more contemporary materials in there after the challenge of the bathroom. He inaugurated this already shiny surface with a baptismal coat of *Mop 'n' Glow*. When it dried, he rolled out a new oval hooked rug from the *Beall's* Outlet clearance in Crystal River. He partially assembled a secondhand twin bed which came with a two-tier bookshelf at the head. *Leave the library for tomorrow.* He screwed down three new outlet covers and one new cover for a switch. Something easy to round out the day. Yeah, they looked like pricey, beaten pewter but they were out of an odd-lot bin at the flea market. The smaller bed was intended to give him more space in the room; for yet another bookshelf and a chest-of-drawers. No more clothes in garbage bags.

What a wonder was the sprawling *Citrus County Flea Market*, two miles out of town. It was just the place to invest those savings he'd just earned at the *Super Wal-Mart* another mile south. The bed frame was from there; heavily polished hardwood, not warped after a week beneath a tarp in the carport. Any and all furniture acquisitions could be protected with tarps from his blue and brown stack until all of the room floors were ready. Walt paid for delivery of the bed components and the whole rig fit perfectly within the oval perimeter of the area rug.

"Walter! Walter! Over here, sweetie!" That was Dianne Kaake hailing him. Her husband next to her, stared at Walt, dead-pan. Curtis, wasn't it? Darlene made a little wave but didn't call out. So what *were* these social dynamics, playing out here for him to decode? Was Dianne simply ahead on her drink consumption while the husband was simply a sullen dick.

At the end of a buffet table that appeared to consist only of desserts, Walt placed his high-end Publix peach pie. It was Bobby Higgs, of all people, who at that moment called for a quick moment of blessing. He got the necessary quiet except for a modest volume of Dolores O'Riordan bemoaning, in the background, some lover's finger around which she was still wrapped. Who in the world snuck *that* in? Someone researching Irish bands on the internet, he supposed. The only reason he even knew of the band was by having Gainesville U. of Florida public radio still cued up on one of the FM buttons in the Caddy. Well, no chance *that* was going to last. The Troubles were not a preamble to any of this demographics' concepts of St. Paddy's Day.

It made him feel like a spring chicken to imagine himself the sole representative of geopolitical cognoscenti (on an amateur level) in the building. Unless the owner of the *Everyone Else is Doing It* CD *hadn't* chosen it at random. Further, Darlene's table looked as though it might be the locus of potential nonconforming high-jinx to confound the tottering, older adults. *Snap judgment*, he told himself. *Keep an open mind.*

Walt was trying to make his way toward Dianne's exuberant invitation just as many of the honorary starving Irish drinkers bolted to load up on the main course. It was easier just to turn and go with the current, so he found himself carrying a steaming plate of the traditional fare toward what he supposed was the equivalent of the *kid's table*. Where had they found soda bread if that's what it really was? Home baked by a traditionalist or someone recently emigrated?

"So you're the salvage guy." Dianne's husband extended a darkly hirsute hand. That voice was like a foghorn drowning in silt. "I'm Curtis. Dianne mighta mentioned me. Or, mighta not. I'm her husband. You also likely seen Lucille 'n' Gracie struttin' around the loop to keep their figures. They was just now in the stampede. You plannin' to flip that place when yer done?"

Let me address that last part first, Walt thought. *Let me sit down and I'll say I don't blame them for staying fit. Secondly, hiking seems to be working, especially for your wife.* Walt sat down behind his plate which he observed to be more like a platter. He spilled the table service out of its napkin wrapping. "I intend to stay and I *have* been introduced to all of them. We've spoken a few times. They're dedicated walkers, that's for sure. Tell you the truth, I can't yet tell all of them apart. I think I can distinguish Darlene from Dianne."

Curtis eyed the shortening line of diners. "They're mostly birds of a feather, you'll find. None of 'em believe they're really old enough to be livin' in here. You prob'ly won't need to tell 'em apart all that close. Dianne and Dar're about joined at the hip most a the time. That's how I'd like to approach it."

His little chuckle with half a sneer at the end of this declaration did not give Walt a clear idea of what the hell he was talking about. But it left an intriguing idea to be examined later. The women were shooting glances amongst themselves to communicate a revision in the seating arrangement, Walt supposed. He ended up face to face with Darlene while Curtis sat within easy, under-the-table kicking distance from Dianne. Lucille and Gracie claimed the prized outside seats, easy to abandon for the bathroom or dance floor.

"What were y'all gossipin' about?" Dianne spoke up emphatically now above the raucous, fork clattering dinner noise.

Someone had yanked the *Cranberries* off the laser CD machine in favor of *Irish Rovers*. Nothing said *up the rebels* like *a long*

EVACUATION ROUTE

time ago, when the Earth was green, Walt thought with a grimace. *Cranberries' music never had an Ulsterman's chance in the Vatican.*

"Your husband was just giving me advice how to tell the difference in plumbing fixtures between *Home Depot Moen* parts made to lower factory standards than *Moen* stuff from a plumbing supply."

Dianne sniffed. "I'm just wonderin' where he would a come by *that* wisdom. Our shower head has dripped hot water since…well, I can't even recall, exactly."

Snip. Snip. Walt nearly cringed at the thought of the emasculation being performed on Curtis right in front of them all. *Curtis? Been there, my friend. Been there. But I invited it, like you probably have.* "I went with the *Home Depot* stuff," Walt said. "I'm on a tight budget."

"Eh, well, you might get lucky." Curtis said.

Dianne's foot found Walt's knee beneath the table with a gentle nudge. "Well, then ya better eat up. We'll see you get some leftovers to go home, too."

"You need to keep up yer strength, Walter, for all that work yer doin'," Darlene told him, again trying to lock onto him with some eye contact. "How are you comin' along?"

More signals to decode. He'd already given the women a quick progress report that morning, pushing the twin mattress partway back into the Caddy's trunk to turn around and be polite. Was this just small talk? Should he make some encrypted responses of his own? "Throwing that trash out was easy. Putting the right things back in is more complicated."

Then he focused on his plate. The corned beef was sliced thin. It was very lean and probably from the *Publix* deli. The cooks only had to dump ten pounds of it in with the cabbage for twenty minutes. No one had to carve off any fat.

"I'm not much of an interior decorator, I guess. After what I walked into, the bare, minimalist look will be fine for awhile." There was only butter to put on the cabbage and he wished for a cruet of vinegar.

"Gracie over there'd be the one to consult 'bout your color schemes 'n' whatnot," Darleen said. "When yer ready, Ah mean."

"Ain't nothin' wrong with a woman's touch, make the place just a *little* more welcomin'." Dianne tittered. "Any of us can do the *bare* look." When Darlene swatted her arm she added: "What?! Or, the *cluttered* look, whatever. I'm just sayin'."

Gracie and Lucille had apparently taken their dinner time gab into a cone of silence. Neither of them responded to the other women's decorating referral.

Walt leaned in to politely thank the gals for their offers of assistance. He saw Curtis roll his eyes. Darlene stared resolutely at her plate with what might have been embarrassment, Walt thought. She might have too dark a tan (he *didn't* think leathery) to *ever* blush. Then she shot Dianne a quick *desist* glance to go with the gentle slap.

Darlene put a napkin to her mouth and finished chewing. "It ought to look just like however you want it, Walter,"

"Yeah, pardner. All *you* need's one a those HD big screens," Curtis said. "You'll make all kinda friends in *this* neighborhood."

The big man scraped his chair back as far as the chair behind him would allow.

Let me make a mental note: *Find an old analog floor model that needs to warm up and put some rabbit-ears on the roof. Discourage social interaction with all the fishing and golfing residents.* Well, but wait. Then he'd miss watching his Orlando *Magic* and his newly adopted *Devil Rays.*

"Line's gone down short enough for ya, big boy?" Dianne spoke to her husband's back as he wriggled through a gauntlet of chair backs. "Bring me back some more a that soda bread."

"It *is* pretty good," Walt said.

Darlene took her next bite out of a buttered slice. "You're gonna stay 'n' dance with us pretty gals, ain't you."

Walt looked up from his cabbage but there was no additional eye bait being dangled from across the table. "Maybe. Maybe," he drawled. "Let me try some of these desserts first. Which one is yours?"

Darlene finished chewing, found her napkin and replied behind it. "Ah gotta ad-mit. Ah didn't have no time after work. Ah asked Di to double up on her Jello creations. Like one a them with the little marshmallows. An' then I managed to bring out a double chocolate cake from the *BDubs* where Ah work. Used my employee discount."

"Well, those'll both be a nice change of pace from all those pies," Walt said. "I'll look for them. But tell me this: How much actual dancing gets done? There's not much space that I can see. How many of these folks make it past nightfall?"

Darlene smiled across the table and blinked another wink, if that's what it was meant to be. "You have hit on our little secret for havin' some fun out a these deals. We'll have twenty or so a the younger residents left for dancin'. After a few pitchers a that nasty beer, the old folks turn in, the chairs 'n' tables get folded out the way."

Now a first tentative sip of the already dark brew tinted with green dye was hazarded to Walt's lips. In his rationalizing way, however rusty, he factored the risk of its foreign potency compounded by the fatigue of a reasonable day's labor and sated appetite. Shouldn't be too much danger from an ounce or two. But, he decided on a mouthful. "I might stay for one if they start out with a slow one. Would it be impolite, this one time, if I don't get around to everyone?"

"Why, it sure *would* be, mister!" Dianne reached diagonally across the table to pat Walt on his nondrinking forearm. "Nah, I'm just funnin' ya!"

"You can leave *me* off'n your card." Curtis returned, wriggling past the back of Gracie's chair.

"Goes without sayin' but I got plans for you later. Don't you go nowheres," Dianne told him.

"I ain't dancin' like a idiot," Curtis said.

"Now that Valentine's event was mostly *all* slow ones, wasn't they?" Darlene said.

"Lotta *Vi-agra* got ate *that* night," Dianne said. "But listen, y'all." She announced abruptly, standing up. "Green beer's startin' to work through."

EVACUATION ROUTE

"Too much information all the way around, baby," Curtis told her.

The way out from the crowded table was easing as some of the seniors groaned their way toward the door. Most carried their desserts in pie shaped plastic. One squat old leprechaun took a green stein full of *Guiness* in one hand while dragging his oxygen tank in the other. He turned awkwardly, trying not to become entangled then saluted the room with about his fifth loud *slainte* of the evening. Walt didn't keep close count but the man's *Erin go braless!* was something new. *Well, leave 'em laughing,* Walt supposed.

His attention returned to his own table and his apparent dinner partner. Darlene was just returning from a trip to the dessert buffet. Looking up, he noticed behind her that Dianne was no longer in the ladies bathroom. She was over in the corner with the boom box shuffling through the stack of CDs contributed to the festivities. *Well, you scheming little...*

"This here's goin' right onta my hips and that's no lie," Darlene said.

How do you answer *that* politely, Walt thought. *Think of something, quick. Start with a smile, at least. Shake your head.* "Maybe you can dance it off."

"Yeah me'n Di. We both prob'ly should do that."

"Listen, sister." Dianne plunked back down with a variety of narrow pie slices. "I'm comfortable in *my* own skin. Who'm I s'posed to be trimmin' down for?"

312   CHRIS DUNGEY

Curtis didn't even dignify the comment with a cross look. Walt heard the clatter of folding chairs. It sounded as though the moment of truth was imminent. What romantic gush had friend Dianne slipped into the music queue?

"I wish I could help you out, ladies, but I'm fading fast. Also, I don't wanta sprain an ankle. It's been a *long time*." How was their radar for double entendre? "You two'll get a workout if you can recruit ol' Bobby. There's a man who should burn off some calories."

"Oh, don't we know it. That ol' boy'll come callin', no worries," Dianne said.

"We know what you been up against from *that* one, hon." Darlene forced a shiver of distaste in the muggy room. She patted Walt's forearm again across the table. "You're off the hook for dancin' tonight."

Wasn't That A Party came to an end for about the third time. Then Karen Carpenter surprised what remained of the banquet into near silence. *Close To You*. Hell's bells, Dianne. Thank you *so* much. Walt heard, from all directions, chair legs scraping and one tipping over as the celebrants lurched up to head for the cleared dance floor. This charge was nearly as frantic as their attack on the buffet. Slower, ambulatory oldsters settled for whatever empty gaps remained along the perimeter of the space.

"Looks like there's no good excuse," Walt said as he eased to his feet. "Ma'am?" He gestured toward the tight little mob already dancing.

"Well, sure, Walt. I'd be pleased."

EVACUATION ROUTE 313

"Go polish them belt buckles, y'all!" Dianne stood up, too, and Walt feared, for a moment, that she intended to join them. "Get yer ass up, Curtis, or I swear; I'll fuck the pool guy."

The big man rose slowly, with no change in expression. "Alright. But only 'cuz I *like* the pool guy."

The woman was moist. That's what Walt thought but tried to think of another word. No, moist worked. She was perspiring in the AC which could not have been turned up very high. Walt felt pretty damp himself so she might be sticking to him in places. Way too warm in here—boiled dinner still hanging on the air, alcohol. Fortunately, *Guinness* wasn't a beer he'd been tempted to guzzle. Ever. He'd taken the one sips. All of these remaining party animals were gripping each other on the dance floor like horny adolescents. What hormones were left to make a resurgence in here? Walt's right hand was clammy on the material at Darlene's waist. That might be where he would stick to her. Time would tell. He held her right hand aloft in his left, old school. But...clammy there, too. *Hope we don't make fart noises with this particular grip.* He tried to establish some Middle School distance as a long reclusive erection presented. Neither fatigue nor age nor an ounce of *Guinness* could prevent it.

"Thanks for hangin' out, Walter. Yer holdin' off Curtis 'n' Bobby 'n' God knows who else by waitin' awhile."

"My pleasure," Walt said. *Is this the box step? These people are all just leaning back and forth against each other.* "I've been under a rock for awhile but I'll be better rested next time. Waking up at 6 am for my own purposes is new to me."

314 CHRIS DUNGEY

"You'll get use to it. That ol' place'll let ya have some leisure time before long. In clean, new surroundin's"

The Karen Carpenter tune ended but Dianne had stuck in some Anne Murray which followed quickly. Walt and Darlene were the only ones to leave the floor. His hand came free of the green satin without a hitch but he must have left a damp handprint of some kind.

"Ah'm gonna hold ya to that." Darlene didn't try to keep ahold of him as they found their way through tables, chairs, dancers, and a few innocent bystanders by the entrance. "Listen, Ah'm gonna get mah money's worth so that Ah'll be here when they divvy up the leftovers. Ya want me to bring ya some?"

Hmmm. How will that work? Maybe don't read too much into it. "I hope to be sound asleep by then, but I'll leave the door unlocked. Sorry I haven't wired up a new fan light but the 'fridge isn't hard to find. That little light bulb inside took a dump shortly after I found it on *Craigslist.* There's plenty of streetlamp that shines in."

"Ah'll figure out somethin'," Darlene said. "I got me a li'l penlight on my keychain."

"There isn't much in the 'fridge. Plenty of room."

The evening wasn't fully dark yet, the temperature turning seasonally cool after a beautiful 78 degree day. *They ought to just open some damn doors.* Before Walt could aim himself down the street, Darlene planted a peck on his cheek. "Ah'll come in quiet like."

"Thanks," Walt said. Wow. Female lips other than Mom's. How long had it actually been? Two, three years? How was he to decipher it? But, the erection was still fully awake.

Walt had a notion (how could he not?) that he might not have seen the last of Darlene Spurgeon for *that* night. But, he *was* tired. That was no exaggeration. The shopping excursion to *Publix* half-a-mile away had taken the place of a justly deserved nap. He chose to save the tight little joint of *Purple Urple,* one of several a thespian buddy of Warren's gifted him with upon the brothers' shared retirement. He began to speculate which of his standard boilerplate commitment disclaimers would best serve when his head hit the pillow. New pillow. Nah, he shouldn't need any sleep aids tonight. If Darlene actually showed up now, they would *both* be covered by the alcohol clause. Or, in Walt's case, the *I don't even remember waking up* provision.

No dreams of anything alarming or even memorable had visited since that last rehab stint and four months in jail after that. Those were some visions he wished never to experience again. Unburdening himself of them in counseling and then in group seemed to disarm them. He was a month back into the world, living above the pharmacy, before he realized that the twisted marathons of nightmare were missing from his sleep. Why complain? Only the introduction of legitimate scripts for anti-depressants, honored by Warren with stern provisos, returned him to *some* nocturnal entertainment.

316   CHRIS DUNGEY

"I was having bizarre nightmares." He told Warren at the time. "Better than going insane, right?"

"I believe that's an apocryphal concept. But, your waking sublimations and other junk in your subconscious, has to play out somewhere."

"Like, I could burn them out with exercise? Take up jogging or maybe keep a journal?"

"Listen to me, brother. Have you *ever* been able to heal yourself? What you need to do is to stay with your group. Telling your war stories in AA helps because they're supposed to be merciless when they hear bullshit. And, you also need to share whatever is going on *now*. Get it *out*."

So, he knew he wasn't dreaming the sound of a closing refrigerator, to be followed shortly by someone stumbling over an obstacle in the dark and muttering *shoot*. Then those were probably high heels being abandoned, clattering across the new kitchen *Pergo*. It couldn't have been that earlier bit of alcohol, surely, or the half a *Xanax* causing him these auditory cues. Soon the scent of *Breath Savers* arrived with the leaf flutter of a dress, maybe, tossed through the cooling air of his bedroom. That he heard *anything* above the laboring AC unit in the bedroom window was remarkable.

Her hands were cold—the one on his shoulder and the one reaching under the light blanket to cup his package. She pushed herself against him; a deluxe spoon with the added feature of the firm thrust of a triangular patch of plush fur, steady against his buttocks. Smaller than he had pictured. He supposed though, thoughts still drifting out of shallow sleep, that the Brazilian process was available everywhere.

"Oh, my goodness, hon." Darlene's breath was warm and still more beer yeasty than peppermint on Walt's back. "Ah appear to've wandered inta the wrong dang trailer."

"Please. Mobile home," Walt grunted. Was that a descendent of the erection he'd come home from the party with? Didn't seem likely, as quickly as he'd zonked out.

"Ah knew that. But see how drunk Ah am? Ah thought Ah was *home*."

"Nah, you didn't. Weren't those the promised leftovers just now going into my 'fridge?"

Walt rolled over onto his back, nearly going off the twin mattress. He shifted his weight back to a more stable position.

"You wasn't asleep? Ah don't feel so guilty now. So're you gonna wake up now 'n' humor an ol' gal?" Darlene had lost her grip on his scrotum and could only stay aboard the bed by climbing halfway onto him.

"I sleep pretty light. Probably that's the least I can do for now. But you might *need* a sense of humor. Sure you're not gonna regret this?"

"Regret what?"

Darlene was already rearranging herself athwart Walt to begin what he supposed to be some very competent oral (though he was hardly an experienced judge). He hoped that the long estrangement from this pleasure wouldn't be the cause of a too-abrupt finish. Unable to quite reach the buried nub he hoped to massage,

318   CHRIS DUNGEY

he used what arm strength he had to drag and lift her hips up onto his chest. There. Was *that* the little trigger he was looking for? It seemed already to be awash.

Emitting a guttural sigh of approval, Darlene pushed back against his face with some force, her knees gripping his waist. Hey, he'd found the thing right where he'd left it quite some while back. *Anatomy's pretty consistent that way.*

What he believed to be most women's favorite preliminary went on for a long time, it felt like. *Accurate time, too, because I didn't touch that joint.* His mind wandered, as if toward sleep. Back to those old selfish disclaimers he hoped wouldn't have to be uttered. Was he experiencing oxygen deprivation? Shouldn't be. He remembered the *Zanax.* Should he bring an end to what might already be, for her; a futile effort? postpone a full production until he could buy some condoms? But, now wait. Darlene had to be fifty-three. And no more than fifty-five. What *was* the absolute expiration date on fertility and how does one discretely ask? What about disease? He could easily rationalize a clean bill of health for her though he knew he should get himself tested. He had reassured himself and procrastinated, hardly able to imagine this sort of lucky occurrence. He had never resorted to the needle; had never partaken in any of the makeshift same-sex couplings available in jail. And when was the last time that he'd ever had any flu-like symptoms? Other than hangover discomforts. No sores or rashes. No searing urinations.

But hey, what about her? He would never have the nerve to ask her about Hep C or anything else. Then came a whisper from the

EVACUATION ROUTE 319

past which hadn't crossed his mind for a long time. He was never able to fully dismiss the young adult resolution that he just didn't care and wouldn't. Here it was, renascent as acid reflux after tacos, but now he found the concept disagreeable. *Christ though, man. You must care about AIDs and herpes. I might as well have kept drinking if that was my mindset. I cared about my sobriety, right? I care about not harming others. Well, now. Like a doctor. Physically harming, I should specify. Maybe that's the new boundary, the new resolution.*

At some point in his reverie, Darlene came with bucking intensity. The battering of his upper lip returned him to awareness. Darlene was sitting up now, the small of her back pressed against his rib-cage. Her feet were over the side, planted on the hooked rug. "Darlin, you need a bigger bed."

Walt refrained from telling her, in the moment, that *not yet* did he need a bigger bed. This little thing made the room spacious, he thought. "We made it fit, didn't we," he said.

"Yep, we sure did." Darlene chuckled, "Usin' extraordinary measures, in a manner a speakin'." She gathered a corner of the sheet and swabbed it across Walt's mouth and jaw. "Ah might a made a dang little mess. You was sawin' some z's but you went right on tendin' to business. Couldn't a made ya quit even if Ah was inclined."

"Dreamt I was in a watermelon eating contest and they were perfectly ripe."

Darlene slapped his arm. "You are one naughty ol' boy, ain't you? If that's what you was dreamin' then you musta won the prize. An' you sure found the main seed. It was nice. You, on the other hand denied me a nice protein reward."

Walt sat up. Darlene lifted up and slid down the bed to get out of his way. "Now you owe me more'n a dance. *Well*, I worked dang hard! A gal deserves to make that happy endin' for a fella that done such a good job. You kinda went absent at the end, there."

Walt got to his feet and stretched. If that was the case, then it explained why he was still pushing around this full mast. *Maybe you just quit on me too early.* "No excuse for it, ma'am, though I *was* pretty tuckered out. You can absolutely hold me to a rain check for that, too."

Darlene flopped heavily down onto Walt's pillow. "Now, don't panic, darlin', but Ah just need to close mah eyes a minute. Ah ain't one to wanta stay over'n' cuddle."

Oh, shit. Here come the ground rules and boundaries. Even if that's a pretty good one. "Not a problem, Darlene. Guess I'll jump into my shower then make us some coffee. You slumber just as long as you like."

"Mmmmm. Thanks, but don't let me sleep *too* long. Ah've got a early shift to pull mahself together for."

"Oh, I promise," Walt said. *No worries.*

He might as well test the limits of the new water heater. You couldn't find *those* used. The spray was dialed into a tight, fierce

EVACUATION ROUTE

pattern. He turned his face into it until he was gasping for air. He stepped back to bring the shower's aim lower, found his new bar of *Irish Spring* in the plastic dish. *Hey, how about that? Just right for the day.* The 8-bar supply was from the *Big Lots* in Crystal River and it was a bargain.

Then the nearly matching Plexiglass door rattled open behind him. The fit wasn't perfect after he'd mated it to a track from the *Habitat for Humanity Re-Store* over by Inverness. "Mind if Ah join ya, Walt?" Darlene was halfway in before nearly teetering back out. Walt reached for an elbow to steady her. "B'lieve Ah may be still just the slightest bit buzzed."

"Well, climb on in here, sweetie," Walt said. "You didn't sleep very long."

"Mah motor must be still hummin' so Ah might's well get on home. Now Ah won't be all sticky when Ah've gotta roll out, 'bout four hours from now."

"Well don't slip. And I can't guarantee how much longer this hot water'll last."

"I'll lean on ya."

"Lemme just get some shampoo on my head then we can switch places."

He was already propping her up, those two softened, first points of contact brushing his shoulder blades.

"Ah sure am glad Ah cleared out from that dang music," Darlene said. "That nasty beer's prob'ly gonna ruin mah whole shift."

As he scrubbed the dab of shampoo into a lather, Walt felt a terry washcloth slowly lavishing over his shoulders and back, then a surge of soap foam running slick down to the cleft of his buttocks. He leaned forward, hands on the fiberglass shell, taking the pulse of water on his scalp now. Then he moved her around to the front, his hands on her hips. "Steady now."

"Mmmmm, that feels nice. You got it set to pore cleanin' strength."

Walt resisted a brief urge to assist with the lathering of Darleen's breasts. "I'm amazed we still have hot water. And I'm also amazed at those codgers swilling down that *Guinness*. They must've chilled it overnight in a meat locker somewhere. I had something a bit less dangerous waiting for me at home, already twisted up."

"Did ya save me a li'l toke?"

"Well, I wasn't sure you were really going to stop by. I actually never did hit it. I haven't needed it for some decent sleep, lately. Maybe just save it."

Now that little thatch, less coarse than the terry-cloth, pressed against his upper thigh.

"Ah just had the sudden inspiration Ah wanted to take ya for a test drive. Had good enough of a buzz to spur me in motion. That Curtis brought in a fifth a Jameson's for ever'one that was still dancin'. You don't see it yet like Ah do, Walt, but most a these single gals in the park, plus prob'ly Dianne too, wanta do the same thing. Ah decided just to get in ahead of 'em."

Ah, there it was: the *alcohol clause* and Darlene used it before he had the chance to. To shut off the shower tap, Walt reached awkwardly around her. He didn't want to risk any gesture, like an embrace, signaling a desire to renew the night's amusements.

That pesky erection was still not totally deflated. The flow of spray squeaked to a stop. "You don't mean I'm likely to get more visits, *tonight*, do you?"

"Well, ya can't rule nothin' out with some a these crazy ol' gals in this place." Darlene rattled the sliding Plexiglass aside. "Ah don't wanta drip on yer nice new floor, Walt. It looks like it might be slipp'ry."

"Yeah, that slate's got a glaze on it. I love how it looks but I haven't stood on it with any kind of a buzz going. I do need to get a bathmat in here. Let me climb out first and put down a towel." He slid around her carefully, his hands again on those slick, firm hips.

"Okee-dokey. You do me'n Al'll do you?" Darlene laughed.

There were three clean towels in the cupboard (*Big Lots*, Jacksonville). "Well. sure. It's worked *mostly* fine, so far." Face to face, he wrapped the thicker one around her after putting another on the floor. *Just dry her off. Pat dry, don't caress.*

"I think I'll lock up behind you. No more test rides for me tonight." Walt hung Darlene's towel on the new, oiled brass bar, screwed into the, as yet, unpainted wall.

Part III
Doggie Days

... the star they call Orion's dog - brightest of all But a fatal sign emblazoned on the heavens, it brings such killing fever down on wretched men. -- Homer, The Illiad

Chapter Sixteen

Regarding his supposed right-hand man, Boogaloo, Wood-Chuck Spurgeon began to relax by the early part of May. Except for the frat brother appearance, Lavelle had resumed some of his normal functions around the *Knuckledick* clubhouse. He seemed nearly back to his old self, demeanor-wise.

The Cajun man invested more time in an almost parental care of the girls and their health needs than he ever had for Merry and Bella. Had he learned something? He managed their calendar without serious conflicts and found time to do occasional stints behind the bar. He made grocery runs for Wood but still said little concerning his recent mysterious absences. Right around the time Wood became accustomed to the revised division of labor, Boog mumbled a balking amends for the winter's disruptions. If that wasn't surprise enough, he followed the apology with emphatic assurances to Wood of resumed dedication to his normal role.

"I guess it wasn't all that bad, brother," Wood answered. "Took me back to the good ol' days a last year, before those two little angels split. I'm relieved for you lettin' go a *that* bone."

EVACUATION ROUTE

Boog made no response but continued sipping his coffee while Wood finished writing out a grocery list for him. "Felt a little less like bein' a pimp this time," he went on. "I mean the way we're runnin' it now, them women seem to be totally on board. Feels more like it's our service to the community. While I'm thinkin' of it about the girls, Caulkins tells me we'll be hostin' the *Jesters* for some kinda Memorial Day ride up to Brooksville 'n' back. Then a pig roast back here."

"For why we joining with them?"

"Well, there was some kinda bike festival up there in March. The *Jesters'* boss told *The Darkness* it was pretty cool. Said they had a shit-ton a bikes and we need to match them for patriotism or some bullshit."

A grunt of skepticism was another sign of Boog's return to form. "We can do this pig?"

"I'm thinkin' we'll hire out for that. Find a professional crew'll do it. They're all over the place—unemployed crackers that think their sauce's the best." Wood said. "We'll get it catered, like."

"Just that I will need some few days off after it's done. Ride home to see my old Mamere. First get ready the girls for *Jesters'*. Hang around, make sure all them strangers play nice."

This was a new twist. Wood didn't realize that the Lavelle matron was even still living. He'd heard only once, related in cryptic fragments, the awful story of Lavelle Pere's decline and, finally, death from frequent intrusions of melanoma. The years of sun reflecting off fishing waters of the bayous, with never an application of sunscreen, finally claimed their victim.

CHRIS DUNGEY

"Yeah, for sure," Wood said. "Just gimme a few days notice so I can line up Ivan or somebody to help. And, I'm gonna try convincin' Caulkins to add a couple more girls to our welcomin' committee."

"For this ol' Boog would wish you many thanks. Not so hard on regular three."

Something had been nagging at the back of Wood's mind and now talk of homecoming pushed it to the fore. He *really* needed to run up to Homosassa for a visit and maybe more than the usual brief *howdy*. Might even make it like an actual vacation, a few personal days for his own *mental health*. Stay up there 'til Ma was sick of him. This notion usually reminded him that no one would call it a real vacation day who knew how much he preferred the Club routine in Tampa. Compared to any other employment he could think of, what *he* did for a living wouldn't be called a *job*. "I might need to take a few days for my own self this summer. I ain't been up to see *my* Ma since Christmas."

"Then you will be the better good son then ol' Boog. Two years, I have been gone."

Wood tried to picture Boogaloo choosing a Christmas or Mother's Day card in *Wal-Mart*. But, a tipsy Valentine's Day phone call and then an Easter phone call was the only contact he'd made with Ma Spurgeon since the Holidays. She always seemed in good, or maybe it was *high*, spirits as though *her* single life was also one long party. Especially at Valentine's Day, when she answered his call while apparently out of breath.

"Some kinda big doin's in God's waitin' room tonight?" Wood asked. Good to hear an actual civilian party of wholesome fun, though during some phone calls ambulance sirens passed in the background. Would he, himself, ever be satisfied with such entertainment? To live a low thrill existence every day?

"Oh now, you shush. Ah just had to come out'n get me some air."

Wood was no fan of traditional Country music, but those were certainly strains of Patsy Cline swelling and waning as a door slapped open and shut behind Ma. "So what's been goin' on, up your neck a the woods? You behavin'? You need any furniture or appliances shifted around? Any codgers to set straight?"

Now Darlene came within kissing distance of her cell phone and, in fact, that's what Wood heard next; a sharp smacker that she couldn't have foreseen the amplified strength of. "Your ol' Ma's just out wishin' love 'n' kisses to ever'body and now to my very favoritest Valentine. Darlin' Ah got everythin' handled up to this end, 'n' if Ah don't there's plenty a local assistance to be had."

"You know that's what I worry about," Wood said. "Plenty of ol' geezers up there willin' to help you out because maybe they'd enjoy havin' a live-in maid with a job."

"Oh, Charlie, now please." Darlene sighed, again loudly into her phone. "Don't you know me no better'n that? Wow, my ol' ticker is still just a thumpin'. Ah been out on the dance floor with Dianne for almost a hour, Baby-boy. There's also a couple ol' boys in there might just meet your standards, not that it's any a your bee's wax. Wow, it's got kinda chilly out here."

"Yeah, I know you always think I'm pryin'. It's just I can't stand the idea of you bein' took advantage of."

"An' I'll just have to go on remindin' you a my status as an adult that can take care a herself," Darlene said, though still in a lighthearted, party voice.

More oldsters brought their drawling conversations within range of his mother's phone. He pictured her standing just outside the main entrance though he knew there was also a pool and patio out a side door. Two different persons seemed to be coughing over each of her shoulders. Ah, right. The cigarette breaks were taken outside as now required by law. The Knuckledicks were in major noncompliance with that one.

"Brrr," she hinted now. "An' look here. Ah'm out here durin' a slow one. That make ya feel any better?"

"Yeah, I can hear it. Patsy Cline, right," Wood said. "And yeah, it does make me feel better. Anyways, you better get back in. Did you bring a jacket or a sweater?"

"Oh, for heaven's sake. Ah'll be fine. At least Ah'm dryin' mahself out, here. So when am Ah gonna see your smilin' face in the flesh?"

Wood hedged his reply with some generalities of chronological measurement, wished her a happy Valentine's Day then said good-bye.

"I think we'll make up a big pot a mac'n'cheese today, Boog. Get about ten boxes of *Kraft*, not the store brand." Wood put the eraser end of the pencil into his hair, rubbing it down to the scalp. "And whata ya think of some chili-mac?"

The Cajun man could only shrug. "Make up them separate, what I would do. Let men choose if they mix. I don't care so much, just pour on sauce."

Of course, Wood thought. Whatever it is, just dump on the ol' cayenne. "Well, I guess get about three large bottles a that, then. You ain't the only one'll wanta ruin perfectly good food."

Boog stood and draped his leather vest of pins and club colors onto his shoulders, the distinctive fist-with-middle finger penis on the background of a chrome and black wheel. Wood handed him the barracks bag for grocery hauling, eyeing again the Euro courier bag. The temperature outside must be starting to bear down upon the metal roof of the Clubhouse and to creep indoors. Boog downed the rest of his coffee. Luanne LaSherry came in panting, a surge of heat entering with her.

Boog gave LuAnne (LaSherry possibly *not* her real last name; possibly a stage-name from pole-dancing days) a gentle hug as they passed each other in the front door. "Sweet Lu, my very toppest girl. Hang out for awhile in the AC. I come back soon 'n' we must have the important charrue with every girl."

Two idle *Knuckledicks* at the pool table looked her over with something like reverence as she strutted in to take a bar stool. The door whooshed shut just as Wood dialed up the AC.

"What the hell does that mean, again?" LuAnne placed her oversized, stripper gym bag onto a neighboring stool.

"It's a Cajun phrase. He wants to have an extra special important conversation with y'all, startin' with you."

"All that ol' boy wants to do is chew our ears off with pointers how to make the client more happy at the finish. Wood, I swear. He talks shit like he mighta once had a pussy a his own." Luanne hauled the backpack over to her lap. She took cigarettes and lighter from a side pocket. "I mean, I *know* what I'm doin'. Most a the time."

"Sure, I understand. But, I used to not be able to get a understandable sentence outta the guy."

Back behind the bar, Wood was treated to a strong whiff from the large cotton candy perfume aerosol he knew she carried, as if it may have been dislodged and somehow fired off a few spritzes in her purse. "Geez, that's pretty strong, Lu."

"You don't like it? Well, I *need* it to create my own, what-d'ya-call-it. Aura? Just so I can stand to get next to some a y'all. Not you, a course, but then I've never had the pleasure."

"It's maybe not *enough* spray, then. You don't care for randy funk? I, personally smell like WD-40." Wood reached under the bar where he kept the cognac near at hand.

"WD-40, I can take. Gamey is what I can't handle. How's about a little splash a that in some black coffee?"

"Well, this here I just brewed is a eye-opener all by itself. But yeah, any way you like it."

Wood poured coffee and then mixed the liquor in an actual coffee mug with paint wearing away from the kissing lips of a *Lipstick's Show Bar* logo. Each of the girls had brought in a personal mug after Luanne's example and Wood needed to acquire some sort of peg-rack to hang them on. While he thought about

EVACUATION ROUTE

finding an appropriate one for himself, he hoped that the concept wouldn't catch on with upwards of 150 members and their girl-friends. Or significant-others-of-the-moment.

Wood placed the spiked coffee in front of Luanne as *The Darkness* entered through the back door. "G'mornin', Chief. How're they hangin'?"

"Wood, Ma'am'zel, g'mornin'. Hey, I been in *there* many a time," Caulkins gestured toward Luanne's mug. "They're hangin' warm and sweaty, Wood. Warm 'n' sweaty. Gettin' to be like summer out there. Your sidekick been around yet?"

"Come 'n' gone on an errand." Wood poured a Styro cup of coffee with two packets of sweetener and two of creamer. The personalized mug idea had not yet stirred the *Knuckledick* prez's imagination. It seemed, from Wood's perspective, that Luanne's pole-worthy tits, not her coffee, had attracted his focus.

"Did you remind him about our upcomin' festivities?"

"Yeah, I sure did. He's aware. I was just gonna map out the pro-gram to Lu, first, when you came in." Wood placed *The Darkness's* cup in front of him where he sat, a respectful two seats away from Luanne.

"What're these festivities you gotta map out for me, Baby-boy?" She slurped her eye-opener. "Well, *good* morning, LuAnne," she told herself.

"That's pretty good, ain't it?" Caulkins turned on his stool and offered a toast with his own coffee.

Luanne winced a less than genuine, flash of smile in the direction of her ultimate boss. "Peachy," she replied again, still facing front.

Wood slid along behind the bar to disarm any potential friction, mopping the surface with a fairly fresh rag as he moved. If anyone in the table of organization was more attuned to notes of disrespect than the girls, it would be *The Darkness.* "Lu, we're gonna to be hostin' a bunch a riders from another club over Memorial holiday. Y'all'll be in even more demand than normal. There'll be some great tips in it, though."

Caulkins chuckled, apparently untroubled, yet, by Luanne's minor display of attitude. "Honey, I got some pictures back home of our 4ᵗʰ a July with that same *Jesters* outfit as last year if ya want a little preview. It was at their crummy place up to Panama Beach."

Wood reached across the bar to gently pat Lu's hand. If *The Darkness* would look away for just a damn second, he'd try to subtly shake his head. *No, baby. Be sweet.*

"It was a lotta fun for a lotta them boys. One a the best times *ever*. You remember that one, don'tcha Wood?"

"Sure do, Chief. Our girls rode up with us 'n' made a bagful. Didn't realize when they had it so good."

Now Caulkins courteously tugged out a red snot-rag, from the pocket not strained by a trucker-sized document wallet on a chain. As he honked his acne scarred beak into the linen, Wood made the eye contact to caution Luanne.

"Yep, 'n' they was just two of 'em, too, at that particular time," *The Darkness* continued. "I'll bring them pictures in. There's one

EVACUATION ROUTE   335

of 'em I *really* like with li'l Merry 'n' Bella next to each other in the ol' *doggie* position. I took it at the angle so ya can see a few a the fellas linin' up behind. We got 'em to kiss, too"

Luanne shrugged with disinterest but managed to give Caulkins a broader smile of a longer duration. "Who? The ones waitin'?"

Wood again paused his breathing. So much of his role in the club felt like a term he'd heard on the TV or somewhere; *conflict resolution*, in this case between some pretty volatile personalities. He tried to fall on the grenade: "While we're on the subject, Chief. Wouldn't you figure one or two more girls'd be really impressin' to the *Jesters*?"

Caulkins swirled the dregs of his coffee in the bottom of the Styro. He straightened his back, trying to release his beer gut from under the bar where it had momentarily become wedged.

"I mean," Wood added. "Can you think a any other bunch than us that runs girls better? An' think a what a sweet pic that'd be, your doggie line with four, five girls."

Apparently distracted from Luanne and having achieved his most presentable posture for mixed company, *The Darkness* tipped back a last swallow. He presented the empty cup to Wood. "Gimme some a what Sweetness, there, is havin'," he said. "Ya know, Wood?" He continued. "You have painted a mental image that's tough to ignore. But, I'm wonderin' if showin' off to the *Jesters* all we got goin' down here is the right tactic. I don't know. We like to brag on it but mebbe shouldn't get their mouths wa-terin' too much. Remember that showdown we discussed awhile back? We might do better not provokin' 'em at all. Just say fuck 'em. Tell me honestly, do they really look like any kinda threat to us."

Wood reached beneath the bar for the dwindling flask of *Curvoisier*. "Depends if they been costin' us any proceeds."

"It ain't that significant. Surprised *me* when I looked at Scope's latest tally. Meantime, lemme speak with the Rulin' Council about more fundin' for the event. I will poll 'em today. Now...Let me see about *this*." Caulkins accepted and sipped carefully the steaming, spiked coffee.

Oh my God. Scope does our drug books? "Ain't I on that? So that's two votes oughta five idn' it?"

"Mmmm. Uhhmm-hmmm."

Ruling Council meetings were not regularly scheduled. The most recent, full scale, in-person, Ruling Council meeting was the one to approve additional whore money and to sanitize any new ones. Whether any of those new ones should be black was also debated and approved. Now, it appeared to Wood that he was also going to need more hard liquor money if brandy in their coffee caught on with other members. Well, whatever kept everyone happy. Caulkins smacked his lips.

"Like that, do ya Chief? Keep a good thought towards my cognac budget."

"I like ever'thin' *in* here at the moment," Caulkins said as he cast a sidelong glance at Luanne. "Sweet thing, what's your dance card lookin' like for the rest a the week?"

Wood thought he saw the woman stifle a cringe. *Prob'ly wonders if The Darkness bothers to wash those parts he can't possibly see.*

"You'll have to check with that ol' Cajun boy," Luanne said. "He's holdin' the keys to my little bit a paradise at this time."

Caulkins sipped again. "I'll do it. You get done listenin' to his little pep talk an' then I'll sound him out."

"Another one for me, Wood?" Luanne sighed with resignation.

Yes, the quality booze for the girls was a good investment if it smoothed out their more unpleasant hookups. "When you're pollin' the others, tell 'em we need to boost the liquor budget."

Caulkins drank again, relaxed the abdominal muscles briefly tensed while speaking to Luanne. "Wood, my brother. *We* are on the same page."

His ruck crammed tight with groceries, Boog *gunned* the *Honda* (He would never have used that word before, but the *Gold Wing* had surprising acceleration) through the thickening noon traffic. Florida 61 presented to him nearly every conceivable retail outlet and franchise eating place incorporated in the US of A. That's where he had to go; to Brandon, out on the edge of the grubbiest section of Tampa wherein the Clubhouse was located. There he could find a *Winn Dixie* or *Publix*. They carried everything pleasing to the *Knuckledicks* indiscriminate pallets, and cheaper than *Tampa Grocery* (Liquor, Lotto, EBT honored), only a few hundred yards away on Broadway Ave. When he made these trips for supplies, he never gave a thought to the inconvenience of the

338 CHRIS DUNGEY

retail dead zone in which the *Knuckledicks* and their few neighbors resided.

Broadway stuck out into Hillborough County like the fat index finger of an amateur prostate exam. The *Knuckdick's* compound was set back one rutted city block from the strip of auto salvage, car parts, and used tire emporiums which comprised much of the commerce along *Broadway*. Three places to sell your scrap metal within half-a-mile; small engine repair, used appliances, independent hitch-and-trailer rental (repainted, obsolete U Haul discards), and the shacks and sheds of other oil-stained enterprises extended back into the city. You *could* pick up the tributary of Orient Rd. a ways further west on Broadway and follow it north to the oasis of *Hard Rock Casino*.

This would not be the scenic route preferred by the, what do they call theirselfs? Business Chamber? Somethin'.

That much Boog believed after Pere's photo shoot taken by the chapter down in Houma, Louisiana. Their publicist looked Pere Emile up. They were refreshing their tourist brochure. The Chamber loved the angles of his face, the Creole blood exposed there; the boat and the big bass landed and relanded into his net for additional takes; the dark, scarred hands, immune by now to the sting of dorsal spines. *No, no, Mr. Lavelle. You can leave your cap on. Maybe tilt it back just a bit. We'll capture you as the serious, knows-his-business, veteran guide. Maybe you're studying the shadows among the reeds, the edges of the cord grass.* Scars on the back of his head, they did not want to show; and another mole to be razored off in two weeks after the current one healed. His full smile

EVACUATION ROUTE

of the wide dental gaps might also send an unproductive image of people down there. Even his rural neighbors didn't want to be reminded of their poor oral maintenance.

Arranging to get aboard the gambling boats at the same time as one of those ungrateful deserters shouldn't take more than one or two more trips to New Port Richie. If Boog had their scheme figured out correctly, the girls would not want to miss more than a few sailings each week. *Must be rollin' in their own money now without Wood 'n' me. Just like they roll aroun' in their own stank. Independent now, they prob'ly think.*

What he planned to do was to arrive early at his vantage point up that side street he had scouted, then wait until he saw one of them go through the gate. He'd idle into the back of the lot, lock the bike and hustle up the gang-plank. He would need to be the very last passenger aboard and hoped not to be recognized, if whichever one of them came near. He had great shades and a hipster, newsboy cap. Passing a hair-and-nail salon on the way up (*must be for the blacks 'n' chicas of this road*), he had a twinge of missing his own dreads and braided beard, visible signifiers of his potential mayhem,

Into the *Knuckledick* compound with lunch supplies Boog rolled. He saw that the vehicles of his other girls, Mandella and the new Hispanic flavor, Dina, were parked next to Luanne's, just far enough from the daily row of bikes to avoid a reprimand. He, too, avoided that space. He stood the *Gold Wing* up in some shade cast over the sheet metal fence (a live oak tree in the back lot of *The Axel Doctor*) then entered by the front door. The girls sat up straight at

340   CHRIS DUNGEY

their accustomed table, nearly causing a blush of pride to rise on his tawny face.

Boog waved at that table then carried the ruck behind the bar. He plunked it down in front of the pantry space. "There is no *Darkness*?" He lifted a fresh cup off the stack and poured the last of Wood's coffee.

"He's in the shitter," Wood said. "Ya know, that there has been on the burner for almost three hours. You sure you don't want me to draw you a beer?"

Boog allowed his second best smile to form, a curl of his lip on one side. "Need the clear head for a *charrue* with these." He nodded toward the trio of house prostitutes. "They never play yet, all together at a *fais do-do*. Mebbe I must explain to all to them and convince, gentle like."

"Well, if it helps, I've started in on Caulkins about bringin' in a couple more girls, at least for this shindig."

Now Boog's smile broadened to a second curled lip. "Only for just the pig roast, yes? Maybe I can't keep up special attentions for more fulltime girls. I should not too much spread their money."

Wood turned to start a fresh beaker of coffee for Boog's briefing. When Boog heard the toilet flush in the Gent's, he moved quickly to join his charges. At least he could start with the welcome news of help on the way. They wouldn't resent, he hoped, the reinforcements just for a few days. *Depend how greedy are they?*

"This will be somethin' you have not done for Club yet," he began, scraping a fourth chair from under the table. "A *fais do-do*. Big party we throw for a guest club. This one we plan for the

EVACUATION ROUTE   341

Memorial weekend. I have strong confidence for all you that you can earn a lot. Even if the Chief add for us two more girls, they are only temporary."

Mandy, now well fortified on her third coffee'n'cognac, snorted. "I knew we'd get around to some kind a twisted shit, sooner or later."

"About our tips." Luanne said. "Define your term, *a lot.*"

"It will be more than in your biggest imagine," Boog replied. "And mostly the plain boom-boom with them already drunk. *To make sleep*, is what *fais do-do*, it means."

Dina, who was warming to the nonsexual social fellowship of the club declared: "I don't never be pissed on."

"Uh-uh, honey! Aww, hell no!" Mandy affirmed.

Luanne hesitated. "Well, not by no big group, anyways."

"Boogaloo don't allow," he assured them. "This the unnatural thing we never do. And never with beasts."

"You speaking of the *perros?*" Dina's chair made a small screech on the floor as if she might bolt from the building.

"Boog? Ya tellin' me anal is natural?"

"So, now mebbe you oughta define *beasts*, too, honey." Luanne laughed. "The hairy long-tongue kind that their thing can get stuck in ya, or the kind that sometimes can't get it up *in* ya."

Boog scratched his head. The word *define* raised the uncomfortable image of a fat, school dictionary in his mind. The one with small print on its own little pulpit in the high school library. Little drawings of what a thing looked like. *Water moccasin.* "It will be only humans. I think men. Mostly. In the ass is not natural?"

Chapter Seventeen

Darlene was doing her level best to keep her relationship (even *she* cringed at that word) with Walter Bocewicz informal, and, to the extent possible, on the down low. *How 'bout callin' it an arrangement? Yup, that might be the best word for it.* She discovered that in a community comprised mostly of folks in their late sixties to seventies, there might always be wakeful eyes to observe either of them traipsing home late at night on the horseshoe street. They get up to pee. Or, insomnia. Just up and around for their latest dose of *Fox News* before the crack-of-dawn.

Dianne was privileged to know about the pairing. By extension, her damned, nosy husband, Curtis, most likely suspected it. Darlene couldn't help but notice that her friend seemed envious. She had, so far, ignored or laughed off Dianne's suggestion that she should somehow be included.

"C'mon, hon. Curtis's dumb as a bag a hammers. I'm startin' to think *longlastin'* is overrated when he keeps talkin' shit through the whole act 'n' wants *me* to contribute somethin'. Would you b'lieve I'm lousy at talkin' dirty? How 'bout sometime while he's out on the boat fishin'? Allegedly."

EVACUATION ROUTE 343

Darlene chuckled. "Aww, darlin'. It ain't that spectacular. Besides, Ah don't know if you're exactly my type."

"Well thank *you* very much. We could prob'ly take care a that ol' boy and not make any serious contact with each other. C'mon. There ain't no serious side play left in the park that ain't hooked up already. You'd likely be helpin' to prop up a marriage."

Darlene could only smile and shake her head. "Ah likely couldn't sell it to him 'less we promised a glimpse a us playin' 'n' Ah'm just not inta that. You 'n' Curtis ain't goin' anywheres from each other, anyways."

Dianne momentarily hung her head. "An' that's the problem, Dar. Well, how 'bout just, your standard ol' swap?"

"I don't know, sweetie," Darlene smiled. "Did'n' you just inform me Curtis was dumb as a bag a hammers? Ah ain't a very hot *dirty talker* either, 'less the guy probes in the wrong openin'."

Dianne sighed. "That's not part a Curtis's attraction, darlin'. It ain't his intellect I'm bringin' to the table, if ya know what I mean. You are just plain selfish."

Making the hike to each other's residence unnoticed was sometimes problematic. It required more innovation than did sneaking home, especially as the evening daylight hours lengthened. For that purpose, Dianne grudgingly provided some cover. The social threesome, which sometimes added Curtis, often sat outdoors as darkness crept out of the jungle or down from their bit of clear sky at the north end. Discretion was even more difficult on weekends, when throughout the *Glade,* smoke and laughter drifted from behind many of the units.

The Kaake's rear patio included a permanent brick fire-pit and blazing Tiki-torches at its corners. Curtis was proud to employ it year 'round. Sometimes there were other guests, toking (non-420 friendly residents were never invited), drinking, elaborating variations on the same bullshit opinions that most had already heard at the Association Hall. Darlene nervously eyed Walt, quiet and reflective as he sipped his one fake beer. She sensed that he might be close to biting his tongue at some of the uglier politics unveiled by the other men and sometimes their wives. Feigning a stretch-and-yawn before calling it a night, he excused himself. Darlene made sure not to express parting words to him with any more sincerity than the others. Her eyes resolutely did not follow his departure. Darlene waited to exit at a discrete interval as with other *Glade* functions they both attended. Sometimes she held out with Dianne, even after Curtis turned in and the embers died.

"Well, have fun, sweetie," her friend said. "I mean that, but don't ya think ya could at least bring me a descriptive account? Anything?"

"*You* are incorrigible. Lemme think on it," Darlene said.

"That's what *I* wanta do. Pictures or a video'd help."

Less often, Walt offered to host the evening round-table, where he, nevertheless, remained the least voluble. He purchased a cast iron fire bowl that stood on its own legs in the middle of his small patio.

EVACUATION ROUTE

The cleanup was easier and the bowl left no permanent hole in the ground. His landscaping tiles still needed to be scrubbed with a powerful, as yet unpurchased agent but he felt he should take a turn with the gatherings. He bought gas station bundles of camper firewood. He even ventured onto the ground bordering the jungle to pick up windfalls. Thicker twigs, dried palm fronds from neighboring trees jumped the chain link fence for his convenient gathering.

As at the Kaake gatherings, he and Darlene played their waiting game; like parents whose child has already performed in the talent show, patiently enduring countless other acts before they could politely leave. Walt nursed his one *O'Douls Amber,* usually combined with a half of something from the stash of pills to enhance his musing quiet. His preferred persona was best assured by this formula. He came to realize that, politically, his views weren't much shared in *The Glade,* if not despised outright should he reveal them. Darlene either had no strong political convictions, or she, likewise, preferred to keep them to herself. She *did* make known a strong bias for organized labor (the lack of which at *Bdubs,* she had publicly bemoaned), and brief displays of irate feminist sentiment: *No ol' crust of a im-potent Senator's gonna tell me Ah can't take mah pill, even if them days are behind me.* In support of their reluctance to be found out as a couple, she sometimes returned early to her own place, leaving Walt to poke the embers and restrain his liberal sentiments until all of the guests had departed.

So, is this here gonna be our end game after six weeks? Right where we're at? If Darlene began to imagine any evolution of the *arrangement*, it never went beyond a desire for more openness. She might like to skip the inconvenience of sneaking around. What difference did it make and who cared? *Why did we even set out that way? It don't make sense.* The idea of actually moving in together never crossed her mind, or, hadn't *yet* without a flinch of reluctance. That was just one step down the slippery staircase to boredom. She understood this, finally, after fifteen years as a single woman. She saw one couple after another make that transition in her previous park. The jury of nosy peers was still out when she moved. She hadn't seen anyone married to anyone, yet.

That particular couple, she recalled, had turned the guy's unused unit into an income property. If the relationship fell apart, it would still be available to him, depending his tenant's lease. So now there remained only the question, to Darlene, of *exclusivity*. *Ah'm still too young to come down with no second or third hand STD. Or, too damn old,* if she thought about it.

"Walt, I have got to ask ya somethin' kinda important." *Now how would I react to an opening like that?*

"What's on your mind, Dar?"

"Well, you don't really think you can survive in here with them two li'l ol' window units, do ya?"

"You're too hot?"

"You 'n' sometimes me're gonna dehydrate when it gets to be high summer. But, nah, Ah'm just hedgin'. That ain't actu'lly

EVACUATION ROUTE
347

what Ah wanted to discuss but it's a uncomfortable thing to bring up."

A baseball game glowed on them from Walt's small HD screen perched on one of his milk crate shelves. She didn't know the difference between the Tampa and Miami baseball teams and wasn't ready, yet, to care. She just hoped he liked football, too. They sat on his new couch. *Yep, new. Somethin' not from the Goodwill that Ah don't have to worry about sittin' on in mah underwear. Or without.* Walt's two window units, one at each end of the place, were almost equal to cooling them back down as the May humidity grew daily outside. Walt politely muted the game.

"Yes? Well, what's on your mind?"

It wasn't quite trepidation (a new word she'd picked up from him) that she thought she heard in his voice. Still just curiosity. *So keep goin'.*

"Ah just been wonderin' have ya ever been tested for any a them nasty sexual transmitted bugs?" *Talk about an' ol' nag of a horse gettin' outa the barn before closin' the gate. But that's the directest way Ah know how to put it.* She felt a small squish in her panties as she twisted toward him. There it was right there, the very first biochemical weapon in history. "Ah have to admit that Ah ain't done it in a while."

"Don't you think we would have noticed some symptoms or discomforts by now?" Walt rearranged his arm from around her shoulder to under her armpit. He gently supported a breast, its post-coital sheen not yet evaporated into the struggling AC. "All I can tell you is that I haven't had any blisters, sores, chancres, lesions, ooze, critters or flu-like symptoms in longer than I can remember." Two fingers found the relevant nipple, loosely, without apparent renewed intent. "I was celibate in jail. Just no interest."

"Ah've avoided jail but Ah guess Ah can testify to about the same history," Darlene agreed. "Got tested maybe five years ago. Snuck it in with a pre-employee physical. Ah got a bill for it from insurance but nobody from *Bdubs* musta looked at that part. They never said nothin'. There's been just the two diffrent roommates since that time. You s'pose we both oughta? Or, just ride the luck."

"Well yeah, maybe."

Walt did not visibly react to a base-clearing double and now Darlene could see it was the *Devil Rays. Big ol' hairball of opinions that ol' nickname caused among some Bible thumpers.* She overheard that from a booth full of clergy in a tavern she was working for at the time, Well, it was noon and the place had a good hamburger.

"See, here's the thing about me, Dar." He released the nipple, then the breast, then withdrew his arm. He flexed his arm and hand above their heads. "Went to sleep on me. See, I don't much care, for myself. I don't know why and have never talked to anyone professional about it. But for the longest time, make that most of my life, I've just wanted to skate along and make myself happy. Find a way to always have a good time, first and foremost. That's been me. Hasn't worked out in a lotta cases and the philosophy, if you'd call it that, has got me in lots of trouble. I haven't been terribly disappointed in myself because I never invested in any particular *dream* to begin with. It's a paradox but I now try to keep

EVACUATION ROUTE

349

my mind clear enough to *enjoy* the ways in which I'm altering it. Yeah, that doesn't make much sense, does it? But I also try to clear my mind of *all* thought now'n'then. It's a Zen Buddhist thing. And if I'm still burdened by dark thoughts, like maybe about the people I've hurt along the way, I try to alter those with just the minimum amount of modern chemistry. After some of the shit I've done to my life and survived, I feel like I'm playing with house money. Have you ever heard of the Samurai concept of *already dead*?"

"Can't say as Ah have, but wow," Darlene said. "Your still waters are sure runnin' deep. But, Ah love listenin' to ya tryin' to push somethin' through mah thick skull. Wait now, ain't that those kung-fu guys, dress all in black? They swing them long swords all around?" Darlene drew her hand up Walt's exposed thigh to fondle the damp bulge in his boxers that he wore for pajamas. "You don't appear anywheres *near* already dead to me."

Walt stretched his arm back around to its previously friendly position. "You're thinking of ninjas. I must be doing it right, then. When you've heard more of my war stories, and I mean *war stories* the way they tell them in AA, then you'll understand about *already dead*. I'll get the blood-work if you want me to. I'm indifferent whether you do or not. Except for *your* own health, I should say,"

"Nah, I ain't worried about *that* so much as I am about what you might acquire goin' forward into the future,"

Walt resumed fondling that left breast, no longer slick from their previous exertions. Forward into the future? Getting onto Social

Security and Medicare were worth looking forward to. Or, maybe a miracle visit from one or both of his kids? The next *D-Rays* game, possibly? Whether or not he should switch allegiance from his *Jaguars* to the *Buccaneers*? Those things were fair game for consideration as he pondered the future. One thing he'd taken from AA was to not worry about anything but the current day in progress.

On the screen, the Devil Rays' closer, who finished his warm-up throws in the bullpen, strolled from the dugout to face the Orioles' last-chance batters. Darlene slipped her hand fully under the elastic band of Walt's shorts. Her light touch inside the cloth had an immediate effect. "Ah'm interested in *stayin'* disease free, Walt. If you wanta play somewhere's else, just please use a condom? But, Ah think we can talk about your future activities at a later time."

Like a punter attempting a last ditch tackle, the leadoff homer by an Oriole pinch hitter could not thwart Walt's personal rally. Darlene now had something to grip. She began to gently tug.

'Looks like this is going into extra innings." Walt reached for the remote. The rectangle of green grass and uniformed figures gathered on the brown, dirt mound again, went dark before the old guy in a windbreaker could take the ball from the failed, departing closer.

"An' we oughta push this one inta extra innin's." Reaching down for her purse, she withdrew a tightly rolled joint and a lighter.

"Make it slow and dreamlike," Walt said.

Walt and Darlene dozed in the closeness of the bedroom after the nightcap game of their own doubleheader. Darlene was scheduled for a lunch shift so had no reason to leave immediately. No one in the park, that she knew of, was up and moving before the dawn hour. Even little Gracie Goodrich who swallowed her nervousness about teen shoplifters and took a job at the *Super Wal-Mart* during January clearance didn't leave her home before seven.

Was Walt going to wake up and roll out for their shower together, an activity that had quickly become a ritual?

"Walter, you 'wake?"

"Mmm-hmm."

"I'm gonna get a shower 'n' mosey on home. You comin' with?" Darlene put her feet on the floor, stepping onto the clasp hook of her bra. "Ouch! You little booger!"

Walt drawled, "Sleepy. Too much of that herb a yours. What'd you do?"

"It's nothin'. I just stepped on a li'l piece a the metal that helps hold up mah ol' titties. Right into mah heel." She kicked the bra further aside and rubbed her foot. "Ya give any thought about what I begun to speak of in the front room?"

Walt rolled onto his side and propped himself on an elbow. "You mean while I was trying to keep that cowgirl from bucking off of me in slow motion?"

Darlene smiled in the dark. "*Before* that. But I sure grinded down a long time in the saddle for that one, didn't I. Didn't break anythin' did I?"

"No. No old men were harmed in the making of your happy ending."

"So, but I'm still wonderin' about are we gonna limit ourselves to bein' exclusive. Just for safety sake?"

Was someone actually asking him to care about them? Other than from Warren and his mother, who were the most recent, he thought he'd never hear that sort of plea again, however modest. Walt sat up when Darlene stood on the floor. *Fake it 'till you make it,* that worn AA trope, came immediately to mind. He hadn't planned on *any* kind of committed *caring*, but only to test whether he had anything to give it. Was he even capable? Fearing that he had paused too long in thought, he reached out to softly stroke Darlene's hip.

Walt said: "I'm going to go ahead and say yes. You deserve that much. I phrase it that way, not to sound tentative or lukewarm, but because that level of caring hasn't been asked of me in a long time. With the wives it sort of went without saying. In the vows, I guess. But who's thinking in that moment that *this will be all there is.* Before that, as an undergrad, I enjoyed a long series of alcohol fueled one-offs. Nothing ever serious. While I was occupied getting sober, I never thought whether I'd ever *have* sex again...until just recently. You arrived as a genuine surprise."

Darlene gathered her scattered garments. "Hope you're thinkin' of it as a *pleasant* surprise. I like you a lot, Walter. You ain't exactly the life a the party 'till we get back here alone. Most a the folks in this park, 'cept for certain cougars I could name, think you been damaged somehow, by somethin'. Not my job to illuminate 'em as to your past. But when I hear ol' Curtis brayin' like a jackass out in polite company, I appreciate ya even more. You just tell me if 'n' when you feel like samplin' elsewheres and I'll figure it out then. Meantime, I *will* enjoy the peace a mind."

Walt sighed as he, also, got to his feet. He did not yet feel the need to retrieve his boxers which would require a walk into the front room. There was no light since they'd left the curtains tightly closed. He would have to grope around for the switch to Bobby Higgs's little lamp sitting on a garage sale end-table. The poor thing had already been bumped to the floor during a previous search.

"You shouldn't walk around danglin' that thing." Darlene reached out to touch him in the glow of the bedroom nightlight while she waited for the hot water. "Sure you ain't gonna shower with me?"

"Nah, but I'll sit on the toilet lid and listen to you scrub," Walt said. He followed her then toward the bathroom light. "Maybe I'll help out with the toweling off."

"Aww, well, oh-kay. Ah really do need some decent sleep in mah own bed. An' we need to see about gettin' you a real AC before Ah seriously dehydrate myself."

"I'll grab you a bottle of water," Walt said. "What? You don't *enjoy* the gentle breezes of my two hardworking window guys?"

"Yer window guys'r *overworked?* Ah hope *these* two guys ain't bein' overworked." Darlene reached to grasp Walt's scrotum as he left the bathroom.

Walt laughed. "I'm hoping for all of my attendant parts to make it through the summer."

When he stood in front of the refrigerator, a water for himself seemed like a wise idea.

Chapter Eighteen

As Wood-Chuck Spurgeon gazed out over the *Knuckledicks'* compound from the front door, he experienced a fleeting moment of sadness. He *called* it sadness. The Memorial Day, which began with an impressive, if not exactly solemn, parade of bikes and flags in Brooksville then degenerated into a drunken, roaring carnival back at the Clubhouse.

As it turned out, by a show of hands (*The Darkness* queried their own riders, just to satisfy his curiosity and maybe gain some bragging rights) of the sixty or so *Knuckledicks* who gathered earlier, that seven were veterans. *That* was not a question ever posed during membership interviews or during the probation period. The topic during *that* time was usually probation of another sort, the kind which would typically preclude military service. Unless the presiding judge recalled the difficulties of his own boot camp. The *Knuckledicks* didn't want to invite any ankle monitors onto club premises so *those* applicants were put on hold until the applying member shed his legal entailments. *Come back without the surveillance attached.* They were also leery of anyone who might have been flipped by harsh the alternatives of the judicial system into confidentially informing.

Wood strolled out, closing the door quickly behind them to contain the AC. *Damn,* it was too hot in the compound already. Was the heat of that big broiler out back, being trapped, reflected by the Club's stockade-like barriers, making it worse? What was 4th of July going to be like if this was still Spring? He wore no shirt beneath his leathers. Perspiration made his armholes gummy, releasing various intensities of perspiration and deodorant scents. There were plenty of similar compromises being made. Black tee-shirts were draped over bike saddles to dry. Wood suspected that the collective, what, vortex of funk? might be trapped in the compound along with the heat of the roaster. *Greenhouse effect, I think they call it.*

Wood-Chuck watched Boogaloo for a few moments as the Cajun man scrambled from vantage to vantage, keeping an eye on his girls like a sniper on *over-watch.* The Ruling Council rounded up three small camping trailers volunteered by members. These private nests helped to show off *Knuckledick* wealth and class to eager *Jester* fornicators.

Why'n hell are we doin' this? Wood wondered, again. *Just advertisin' what we've got goin' down here and how good we're doin'. Like sayin' 'so why don't y'all come on down, try'n get some.' Of course makin' it look like we're dyin' might motivate 'em even stronger.*

The worrisome *Jesters* brought only twenty-five riders back down for the party in Tampa. Caulkins was offering an enhanced *Knuckledick* hospitality that Wood still didn't understand, but he didn't believe the Chief was stupid. He would never allow them to be outnumbered on their own turf. *The Darkness* started Gerard Grampian, his opposite number, off with a few lines of blow in the office. Wood resisted the coke and remained behind the bar. He heard *The Darkness* give Grampian first choice of the five prostitutes, including two temps, now on the *Knuckledick* payroll. Then he was directed to the one trailer Boog needed to rent. Boog and Wood were both further instructed not to put anyone else in there while Girard was getting his jollies.

'Don't time him out, either, LaVelle. *Now* we have to honor this bastard's service, too, on top a the hospitality. Don't ya think, Wood? Can you imagine sharin' a rack with that fucker on a Marine assault vessel?"

Everyone in the *Knuckledick* leadership was amazed when Gerard rendered a crisp veteran's salute during the tinny National Anthem. A few of the '*Dicks* saluted as well. Who knew? Hundreds of bikes were gathered for an opening ceremony on the steps of *Brooksville* Town Hall. Some of the few riders who still bothered to wear helmets removed them. Then the parade route and other instructions were given over a loudspeaker, followed by a deafening ignition of all those engines, nearly at once.

Let's get this stupid swapmeet over with. Wood aimed his Fat Boy in the opposite direction of the parade route with the purpose of racing ahead of all the '*Dicks* and their guests back to the Clubhouse. An easy forty-minute ride at most, if he didn't run into more processions of *VFW* color guards, high-school bands and Boy Scouts.

358   CHRIS DUNGEY

Now, he stepped out the back door to see how the *Pullin' Your Pork* team was progressing with their hog roast. One of the three guys, all of whom wore matching tee-shirts, lifted the door of their huge smoker on wheels for basting. Wood saw the deeply darkened skin and whiffed the tang of sauce which was slathered over its flanks with a paint brush. *"It won't be long now,"* he was told. He hoped that the girls could take a lengthy break while the two clubs gorged themselves.

He met Boog in the door coming to find him. "That Gerard? He slows up taking turns for all."

"Who's he with?" Wood moved quickly to resume drawing premium beer into the red cups of a short line that formed. The *Jesters* wouldn't taste the difference between the kegs of *Heineken* and *Pabst Blue Ribbon* in cans. But the *Dicks* would.

"He has that little Dina. More than half-hour and I can't go in to check. She will not be ready to it, I think."

"I don't know what to tell ya, brother. It's Caulkins's orders. Their top guy is not to be disturbed. She's a big girl. Maybe she'll give that greedy fucker a heart attack."

Lavelle took one of the *Solo* cups of draft that Wood was lining up as fast as they were taken. "Thanks for all of his service? How much of it in the ship's jail?"

"They call it the *brig*. I was just as surprised as you." Spurgeon thought Boog nearly smiled as he went to resume his watchdog duties.

"Maybe we go soon to *his* service, yeah?"

EVACUATION ROUTE 359

Caught up with serving those in line, Wood yelled for Ivan Dresbach to come behind the bar so that he could go back out to mingle. His earlier twinge of patriotism was gone. Bar-b-q smoke and fumes drifting over the Clubhouse into the compound proper eased his disgust for all this irreverence. The few neighbors, mostly people of color, must be salivating plenty if they weren't out grilling something themselves. Or, they were pissed off and muttering (not loud enough for any passing *Knuckledick* to hear) about all the cars parked in the narrow street. Wives and girlfriends of the bikers were arriving late and there was no room for their vehicles inside the corrugated fences. Distributing leftovers to the needy on the block might be a cool move. But that carcass was prob'bly gonna to be stripped clean by these piranhas.

A volunteer disc jockey in *Knuckledick* leathers played golden oldie CDs from a huge boombox. A *Jester* peered over this guy's shoulder like a teacher inspecting a student's cursive. But, Wood thought they might also be speaking in polite terms, unlike their leader in the VIP trailer. A line for requests formed in front of the DJ's card table. He heard a *Jester* request more *Metallica*. It didn't *matter* which tune.

Rented picnic tables had been brought in. The three owned by the '*Dicks* would never be enough. A driver and his assistant who delivered them unloaded quickly without being asked. Two long rows of gleaming machinery took up a good share of the space inside the compound. Spurgeon made a quick count of bikes along the fence; maybe forty of the *Dick's* steeds behind and the twenty-five *Jester* rides parked in front of them. Just in case they needed an early exit, Wood thought, even after all the cautious pleasantries. Maybe not an angry exit, though, he hoped. Never-the-less, after any kind ot departure, he and the Leadership Council, could relax and enjoy the rest of their holiday.

"Ever'thing looks pretty sweet in here, Wood." *The Darkness* waddled up, a *Solo* cup in each hand. "Kinda tame, but nice."

This is tame? But, damn, was the guy at least taking one of those to a guest? Wood held his own cup upside down, clearly empty. There was no response to the hint. "So far, so good. Those tables were worth gettin'," Wood said. "You been into one a the campers yet?"

Caulkins sipped one of his half-empty cups. If the other one was meant for someone else, he wasn't in any hurry to deliver it. "Not yet, brother. The wife's here and maybe not hammered enough to give her blessin'. That's usu'lly what it takes to get her involved in...well, some a the club's *activities,* let's just say"

"You thinkin' of includin' her in one a your *doggie* line up? You ain't mentioned that lately." *Nope. Not gonna offer me the extra beer.*

"Oh, I ain't *forgot* it. But that might not turn ol' Tonya on, tonight. I ain't decided, yet, if I even wanta be in the same picture with..." Caulkins took a quick glance over both shoulders. "Him who's name don't need to be named. Anyway, little Tanya might wanta turn with one a them gals. Mebbe that new little Mex'can."

"I didn't know *that* was gonna be part a the program. That fool Gerard is wearin' himself out in there on Dina right now. He's been at it near an hour. Him outta sight and unheard from boosts ever'body's spirits, but Boog's gettin' irritated." Wood smiled.

EVACUATION ROUTE   361

"Oh, man. I'm countin' on you to keep the lid on that boy," *The Darkness* said. "Anyways, I better get this to the ol' lady. She might gonna be disappointed that little firecracker's busy. We about to eat any time soon?"

"It won't be much longer," Spurgeon said. "I'm gonna get the slaw and potato salad out on the tables in about ten minutes.

The refrigerator back in the kitchen corner was too small for the additional food—three gallon tubs, each, of bulk store sides and a gallon of dill slices, lots of catsup and mustards, hot-sauce. Wood had scrounged up three large coolers from members to put all of these containers on ice. Now he dragged them out from around the counter. Outside, the plastic wheels trailing behind him made a racket to attract hungry attention. Some of the loud folks outside would have to give up a picnic table if they wanted to eat.

"Comin' through!" He chose a table near the disc jockey, "Clear it off if y'all wanta eat."

One of the *Pullin' Your Pork* personnel was just then arriving with the first platter of meat. Four bikers and two women hopped up quickly as Wood hoped. He lifted the tubs out of melting ice and told the pork guy: 'Leave the foil on 'n' stand guard for a little bit, would ya? I've gotta bring out the forks, buns 'n' paper plates."

The kid set the pan down and didn't look pleased that he might have to persuade *this* crowd not to begin sampling with their bare fingers.

Wood raised his arm, waved and yelled: "Listen up, y'all! Get yourselves a fresh drink 'n' give us three more minutes! Don't put yer oily mitts into this fine feast just yet!"

362 CHRIS DUNGEY

The bar-b-q employee relaxed but Wood knew he'd better hurry. "Boog! Where are ya?!"

Wood found his sidekick emerging from the Men's bathroom, his citizen's haircut freshly combed. *My God, is that aftershave comin' off him?*

"Still here. Porta Potti is...Some don't use the piss trough. They don't lift the seat. I put paper towel in so ladies wipe it first. No respect."

"Is everything goin' smooth for our...*your* girls? Help me for a minute. Could ya bring that box a plastic forks 'n' some a the buns?" Wood held a stack of *Chinette* plates under one arm and two cafeteria size bags of sandwich buns in the other hand.

Boogaloo managed two boxes of table service, including knives, plus two more bags of buns. "They make the good tips, what I can see. Like we hoped. I'll bring them sandwiches, lock the camper one hour to give a break. No one fucking them while they have bar-b-q in one hand."

Pushing the door with his back, Wood emerged from the Clubhouse with Lavelle following. "Is everyone behavin'? Any bitchin' from *Jesters* about condoms?"

The cluster of bikers not yet seated at tables made way for the food to pass.

"Some guests, they don't like it, cuz our own men can bareback." Boog laid his items onto the food table which had quickly emptied. "*We don't know you*, I say. *Use the rubber or settle for hand-job*. Don't complain more, I say, or then they get kicked ass

EVACUATION ROUTE

out the trailer 'n' also campers. Some become crude when they finish. Girls have to put used rubbers in trash themselves."

Boog disappeared quickly, back into the profanely roaring crowd. Wood was reluctant to remind him, too loudly, not to *literally* kick any *Jester* asses out of the little brothels. Beneath the altered appearance, the *old* Lavelle's animosity in the presence of a rival gang must surely still simmering, like some kind of crazy bayou volcano. The evening's revelry was not an ideal setting in which he should erupt. '*Keep the lid on,*' spoken softly within earshot of the *Jesters,* in the racket outdoors, was not adequate warning to convey *The Darkness's* concern. Wood guessed tt would have to do.

He opened a bag of buns. The *Pullin' Your Pork* kid lifted the heavy foil from the first platter of meat then quickly stood aside. The queue of hungry bikers surged forward, now hindered only by Wood, standing firm like the steel pipe guarding a gas pump..

"Okay, here y'all go!" Wood stuck one of the little forks into each of the tubs of sides then made an exaggerated leap out of the way. "That pork won't last very long," he told the caterer. The kid hustled away, careful to avoid collisions in the intimidating crowd, many of whom now balanced heaping plates of food.

Returning to the dim lighting and AC of the Clubhouse, Wood caught up with Boog making sandwiches. The growing stack of them suggested that they were not for himself but for the girls. A *Chinette* plate of bar-b-q sat on the kitchenette counter, its dissipating steam reflecting neon from behind the bar. He added slaw to some of the sandwiches from a small container that Wood could not recall buying.

"They cut special for me out back," Boog admired the pork. He allowed his lips to turn up in the semblance of a smile. "Right away, no problem, they say. Good kids."

So, despite the alterations to face and hair, Boog somehow retained the menacing presence that the *Knuckledicks* appreciated. When needed. The warning seriousness, his subtle tone of threat somehow breathed within the softened, level voice.

"That's great, man." Wood congratulated his assistant for his mysteriously acquired caring. "But listen. Ya wouldn't really, you know, physically kick someone out a the campers, would ya?"

Boog cocked his head quizzically. "This would cause upsetting?"

"Well, yeah, buddy. We're tryin' to make nice with these people for some fucked-up reason. Not the time yet to throw down, I guess. *Darkness* says we'll wait 'n' see. And now, today he sounds uninterested in *any* kinda hassle, ever."

"Wood, Wood, mon frer. You see how weak it is?" Lavellle chuckled. "But, I only make a joke. I'm not so stupid. But, it's only important that *I* know this."

Geez-us. Wow. The guy corrected me without staring at the floor 'n' ballin' up his fists. "Cool. We'll keep the evenin' runnin' smooth, try'n have some fun yourself. In honor a all the fallen heroes, of course."

Fun for his friend now amounted, apparently, to making sandwiches for the Club prostitutes. If he had only bothered to regularly retrieve Merry and Bella from *their* dates...If he had only taken *them* the occasional sandwich, poured cognac into *their* coffee... Spurgeon shook his head in wonder as he'd been doing for six weeks into this transformation. But, he was coming to believe in it. Boog's unbridled violence was only a nagging memory having not been unleashed for quite awhile. *Maybe I gotta start picturin' this butterfly as fully crawled outta the caterpillar.*

Now came the more disagreeable duties for which Wood-Chuck earned his nice salary from *The Knuckledicks*. That he had not had to perform these chores since last summer was some consolation. *It's just the night before Thanksgivin' times five,* he told himself. Then, if he considered Boog's part in the cleanup, his annoyance lightened further. Many of the biker guests, '*Dicks* included, did not trouble themselves to clear their tables or the stained pavement beneath them.

Boogaloo Lavelle was already vigorously addressing, with a mixture of ammonia and *Mister Clean*, a concoction of his own devising (with no mask on, of course), the bio-hazardous floors and other surfaces in the rented trailer. The *Knuckledicks* were liable for forfeiture of the deposit reserving *that* orgy space if it was not returned in pristine condition. It might even be owed to Boog personally, based on the Cajun man's emphatic mopping. Spurgeon watched as his assistant occasionally staggered from the trailer gasping for fresh air. *No rubber gloves, either, dummy. Well, all I can do is suggest.* Ordering Boog directly, to do anything, was always to be avoided, no matter his freshly civilized disposition.

Wood wriggled into rubber gloves before snapping open the first black garbage bag. Construction grade. *Dollar General* kitchen bags were no match for *this* job. As he worked his way to the table where the girls were decompressing, they paused in their post coital reflections to rattle his chain:

"Where you goin' to in them stretchy gloves, Wood-row? You gonna give Boog a prostate exam?" Luanne hooted. "Or a fistin'!"

"Nah, what *that* boy need is a enema!" Mandy laughed.

"That is the only gross thing boss of *Jesters* did'n ast me to do for him," little Dina said. She turned away from the table and spat with contempt. "That was a mos' nasty of all cheese-dick gringo. Dolour es perro. I know for sure, too."

"But did y'all do alright? Did they take care a you okay? Keep eyes on the prize, ain't that what they say? Yer bottom line?" Wood spied what appeared to be the freshly broken seal on a fifth of cognac. "Looks like Boog's takin' care a y'all, too. Like a fine stable of thoroughbred fillies."

"Oh yeah, Baby-boy. You ain't *never* lyin'. He know what make us whinny." Mandy poured two fingers of brandy into a *Solo* cup that Wood hoped, if it wasn't clean, had at least been emptied of beer. "He right on top a ever' li'l thing."

To Wood, the laughter at this observation sounded less than genuine. "He still might could need a enema," said one of the added temp kids, called Honey. *The name describes her skin perfect,* Wood thought.

EVACUATION ROUTE

Now, the laughter was hearty and general. "Aww, Baby-girl," Mandy cried. "Most a your time in the life you ain't had no better top guy then Boog!"

"Just don't relax ya'll's manners around him though. I'm a livin' witness that ol' Boogaloo can give you attentions of a whole other kind." The table did not respond except with the quiet puffing of smokes and mannered sipping. "I hardly know *this* here new Boogaloo myself," he added.

"We get it, Wood," Mandy spoke at last. "It ain't no thing. We *do* love that ol' boy. Hard to 'magine him as ugly like you sayin'.'"

With that, Wood decided to take a break. The girls made way for him to sit. "So anyways, how'd ya'll do for money? That's what I meant to ask."

Now all began to chatter at once, with figures that seemed quite impressive to Spurgeon, maybe even remarkable:

"We done way fine," Mandy said'

'Well, *you* was not with perro-face," Dina said. "Two hour he take his turn, an' he could not finish. His breath was...like the buzzard who eat on roadkill. He tip to me twenty dollar."

Exclamations of outrage erupted from her four associates. Wood felt it prudent to add his own scorn though he didn't know, yet, whether the Latina was particularly skilled. Given the new parental relationships, Wood wasn't certain whether he could rely on Boog for an unbiased assessment. "The guy's a pig, sweety," he offered. "But listen, ya might not wanta let Boog hear about that, least of all from any of y'all. We're in the delicate position a keepin'' peace with the *Jesters*. Boog's liable to lose it."

"Yup, hon," Luanne agreed, patting Dina's shoulder "We don't wanta provoke no unnecessary homicides." She poured another dash of cognac into the Latina's cup.

"Si. Yes?" Dina sighed. "Later on, see how you think, when I tell *you* the delicate position I perform for this *Jester*."

"Nah, I'm good, sweetie," Luanne told her. "I prob'ly heard or seen it already."

Wood rose and returned to his work, eventually filling three of the big bags. He dragged them to a dumpster around the rear of the clubhouse then muscled them into it. He checked on the safety of leftover sides in the small refrigerator where he'd earlier wedged them in gallon size Zip-Loc bags. These remained sealed, intact, conforming themselves nicely to available space without nudging the door open. Bean soup again? Burritos? (the flatbreads, one-at-a-time into the microwave?). A soup or chili using *this* pork would damn sure be better than some of his recent creations. Wood filled a pitcher with the dregs of the final keg until the little nozzle spat air and foam.

Outside, the girls disbursed from their table, which Wood could now clear of the last party trash. He emptied the *Courvoisier* bottle into a clean *Solo* cup. *Two fingers left. Were they fit to drive?* They were advised a few days ago to carpool and were now gone, unescorted by Boogaloo. Wood heard his sidekick hollering directions at poor Bum Crawford, whose mammoth pickup truck came creeping in reverse, nearly into the necessary alignment beneath the trailer's hitch. *Hey, a nightcap 'n' a show. I deserve this.* Wood sighed.

EVACUATION ROUTE

"Five inches more, Bum. Nudge to right. No! No! To the right, *my* right! Very close! Just the light touch!"

Wood thought that Bum probably didn't want to actually *attend* the *Knuckldick's* holiday pig roast. Were those shadow investigators out there on the street somewhere, waiting for him to emerge? Wood, Boog, and, finally, *The Darkness* prevailed upon his club loyalty for the loan of the truck to drag the orgy trailer back and forth. The now legitimately handicapped Bum was likely to resume whining about the burden of club dues while contributing the use of his powerful vehicle. Wood could envision Boog's enticements to assure Bum's attendance; above all, complimentary oral sex from Mandy, bar-b-q and free chauffeuring from Boog until the Cajun man drove him home after the festivities.

Earlier in the afternoon, Bum eased himself down and out of the truck's cab. He tottered to a cushioned Adirondack chair back near the *Pullin' Your Pork* crew. He needed to stay out of the view of any persisting insurance spooks with their telephoto lenses (he insisted) and parabolic listening dishes. No final judgment had been arrived at yet by a majority of *Knuckledicks* as to the legitimacy of Bum's pain. Boog, for one, was convinced. He reparked the truck out back that morning after positioning the trailer. Now he needed Bum behind the wheel. "Yes! No! Too far, Bum! Put in neutral. Maybe let truck settle back!"

The immediate plan was for the two of them to bunk overnight then return the trailer to the RV rental place when it opened in the morning. Boog intended to drive.

Wood found his eyelids growing heavy. The day's tensions and responsibilities lifted from him. *Has my jaw been clenched since morning?* It was time to lock up the place and go home. There were no specific personal rewards he planned for his completion of the job. By most accounts, the day had been a great success. Have one of the girls? Too late. They fled and he didn't think he could have mustered the brutality to impose one more penetration on them. He might should just crash in one of the popup campers. The *Courvoisier* pressed softly at his temples. It made the most sense to stay. Consultation with his *Harley-Davidson* wrist watch showed the hour to be nearly 3 am. *Someone's got to be onsite first thing in the mornin', anyways. Flatbed from the sanitation company due to take back their Porta Potties. That deposit's mine.* Wood opened his eyes when Boog seated himself and lifted the tilting *Solo* cup from his grasp.

"Got 'er all done, eh? Ya didn't punch no holes in Bum's tailgate?"

Boogaloo poured a cup of beer for himself from the last pitcher. He poured for Bum, too, who sat down with a wince at the table. "We are good for going early," he declared. "Also to visit Mamere, now party day is finish. You remember? We take back the trailer. I come back for the bike."

"Yeah I remember," Wood said. "An' many thanks for puttin' that off."

"This job is mine to do." Boog said. "But now I shouldn't wait longer. She is failing, I think. I hear in her voice from the phone."

EVACUATION ROUTE

"You have to go. No worries. Take all the time ya need." Spurgeon emptied the pitcher into his own cup after Boog returned it to the table. It didn't sound like he'd drained the *Courvoisier*, yet. Liquid met liquid. "When you get back, I'm gonna take *my* turn. I promised Ma I would take a whole week a vacation this summer. That'll be some real boredom up there."

"For the mother you just do it." Boog sipped almost daintily. Wood tried to rewind through the whole day. Had Boog taken even a single drink? Could this really be his first one of the party? *Even now he ain't chuggin' it down like he's bein' waterboarded. This guy is a constant mystery. Least he didn't perform any ass kickin's on the Jesters.* "Grim business for them, the getting old."

Spurgeon tilted his head but kept the puzzlement out of his face. *If ya comment on it, he'll describe all the recent, personal examples suffered by Pere Emile.*

"It sure seems to be, pardner. Lucky my Ma's prob'ly healthier then me. She'll outlive both of us."

Now Lavelle drained his cup at a gulp like it was something to be gotten over with. He stood up as easily as he had arrived. "I will have to make up the funeral when it comes. Hope not, but with closest brother so lazy...Laurence only one there most times. On the phone he keeps me into the loop. Until it is a noose, yeah? Need to buy the suit, though. Be ready."

Rental is prob'ly the cleanest trailer. Boog scrubbed that one out better'n when they towed it in here. But if I stay over in it, I'll have to listen to all their night sounds; Bum whimperin' every time he rolls over. Don't wanna find out if Boog screams in his sleep. Might be fumes lingerin', too. "Well, I hope you find she's doin' better 'n' you can just spend the time."

Wood reached up to share a *Knuckledick* handclasp. Boogaloo leaned down for the hug and triple back-patting. *That's the same Axe spray like Larry 'n' Troy use up home. He musta added another layer every hour since the parade.* "I don't envy you to go through all that. It is grim for sure." *Now, which camper? I'm usin' that bedding for sure.* Sleep in my clothes.

Chapter Nineteen

The South Florida humidity became a palpable weight on their mood and prohibitive to the fashions the girls preferred. Bella and Merry could no longer remain totally nocturnal in their enterprise, so the weather heating up had an effect. These days they might have to spend as many as four hours in stifling daylight out on the boats. The gambling craft *Narcissus* depended on the ventilation of small fans and the caprice of Gulf breezes for passenger comfort. Alternating, the pair took turns shivering in the gooseflesh chill of *Seminole Hard Rock Casino-Tampa*.

A shopping trip for an upgrade in their work wardrobe was thus proposed, discussed, and approved. The state of their business and savings suggested that a mini-vacation for that purpose was within their budget. They sat at the dinette as Bella separated one roll of bills from the ice-cream carton for rent and utilities and a smaller wad for fashion and a couple of days of relaxation.

Merry renewed bemoaning their inability to claim tax benefits from wardrobe purchases until Bella reminded her that they seldom ever filed a return of *any* kind. *But, ain't we entertainers? Ducks, but then we would have to withhold every three months and pay into Social Security. This I know. Papi, they said, was an independent contractor. Well, we aren't anything if we are not that.* This conversation always led down a rabbit hole to speculation about their ultimate goals, their retirement plans and the dangers of a 401K paper trail. The danger of continuing to keep large amounts of cash in an ice-cream carton, from which Bella withdrew the wads for money orders to rent and utilities, was a nagging worry. And don't forget handy bail-bond money.

"Tell me, Bell. What do you consider as a va-cation? Ah don't feel like drinkin' and dancin' nor to meet any men, even legitimate. So what's left if we ain't gonna try'n work?"

"Sweetie, no we will *not*. But we could just enjoy dancing without motive. We could lay on the beach to see how red you will get. Shopping is better than museum tour. Or whatever people do."

They decided that a jaunt across Alligator Alley to Miami and the Beach might make for enjoyable outfitting. Money spent on filmy dresses and outfits of minimal coverage were investments with measurable returns. Okay, and a couple of high-end sweaters for inside the casino.

They packed overnight bags and locked up the bungalow. Merry pushed the *Geo Tracker* along at a vibrating 65 mph. "Ah need a alignment or some damn thing in the front end. Tie rods, is what it feels overdue for."

"Well, just slow down. Our purpose is to relax."

"An' you insist we ain't takin' *no* tricks at all? Are ya sure? What if it was a sweet ol' billionaire 'n' we was invited to go onto a yacht?"

"I am not holding my breath for that. I will sleep in late and see my face without makeup. Going onto a yacht is too much like work and we end up as white slaves."

Merry was as stunned as she was capable of being when Bella told her that her family only ever made two trips across to the Atlantic side. "Wasn't you even curious for that part a yer hair'tage?"

"Why? We were fishing people of the Gulf side. Papi became the fan of *Devil Rays* for his baseball. The best cigars were near. He took Mama-san a few times to visit his shirt-tail Cuban cousins. I stayed home most times to keep Enrique and Kwan from destroying our home. And maybe the boat, too."

"Girl friend, Ah will show you the sights an' other places 'sides the Zoo. Places Ah ain't actu'lly been into, a course, but that I know where they are 'n' they looked classy from just drivin' by."

"Do I get to meet any Braniff family? I can try to diagnose what might have gone wrong with you?" Bella laughed.

"We won't be goin' anywhere near to Homestead nor any a mah fam'ly." Merry eased the accelerator down to 62 mph where the ride and handling smoothed.

"Don't you want to see your sister?" Bella knew from sporadic mention, that Merry's mother and her most recent stepdad had both passed away. No one, especially the sister, wanted to inherit the single-wide family estate.

"Carol has bailed out from the area all together. She's up by Orlando. Reminds me. Ah need to give her a call, see'f it's still her ol' number. Don't wanta hear the third degree about mah current career but it might be nice to know where she's at. Lucas's doin' time for a minor grift somewheres. He wasn't done stealin' after they fired him off'n a cruise ship. Jonah's prob'ly still in the Navy, if he ain't been kicked out. He was the smartest one outta all us but never the best with obeyin' author'ty."

They passed a *National Preserve* parking-lot near the 42 Mile Mark, east of Naples. They passed a stretch of boat launches where sports fishermen and their guides could access navigable portions of the Everglades. Bella placed a foot up against the roof post of the open passenger window, curled her toes to slice the hot breeze. They passed *Big Cypress Emergency Pull-Off*. A sign read that there was a museum for the work of some famous alligator photographer.

"I wish I could see a live alligator for just one time." Bella said. "I don't mean just alive in a pen. But in the open, like. In the wild."

"Ain't ya seen one, never?" The *Tracker* shuddered in the wind of a passing diesel semi, its fumes blasting into the partially opened windows.

"Just in parks," Bella said.

"There's places we can stop 'n' walk a nature trail if yer serious," Merry said. "But Ah don't think you wanta be up *too* awful close, like when one of 'em brings ya to a screechin' stop on a dark road."

"This has happened to you?"

"Some guy Ah was datin' who had him a car. Wasn't no trick nor anythin' like that, back when. Ah was still dumb 'n' innocent. Ah mighta been pushin' fifteen. Hope so, anyways." Merry pointed at an unopened bottle of water, the nearest out of a 24-count case on the floor in front of Bella. "Get me out one a those 'n' opened for me, would ya, sweetie?" Merry watched out the corner of her eye over Bella's legs at the righthand verge of the road. There was most often a big-rig or some other high-aspect vehicle blocking her view out the north side. *Shoot, motorhomes. Oh, the business we could do, in far, flung-out places if we had us one a them.* "Ain't it flat swamp, though? How's anybody make a livin' out here?"

Bella handed Merry the water. "They did not go to a job. Living and making a living were the same thing to them. Always hunt, always fish. I believe indigenous people grew rice, too. *This one big paddy,* Mama-san said, both times we traveled this way. But it is all drying up, too, I saw on the news."

"Ah don't recall much a mah Flor'da history. They required it in eighth grade. Ah musta passed it, though. Ah'm drawin' a blank on those, what'd ya call 'em? Indigestion folks in it. What *was* they?"

"Oh-kayy, then." Bella laughed. "It was and *still* is, the Seminole people! Like the name of the casino they own? But what they should be called is Indigenous People. So, what about the gator you came upon in the road?"

Merry finished her first long chug of water. "He was a big 'un but he quick scooted out the way. They're usu'lly shy a headlights. Not like them ya see on the news, takin' their sweet time in the middle of a golf course. Did'n' matter to me. Ah told that young boy Ah wasn't parkin' with him anywheres 'cept back to town."

"You were a very careful girl from the beginning. Yes?"

"Ah slip up now 'n' again, as you know." Merry snickered. Bella would not have forgotten New Year's Eve. "But Ah ain't been ate by a gator, 'n' Ah ain't got no stretched marks."

378 CHRIS DUNGEY

Into the city, Fort Lauderdale, where I-75 terminated and then quickly south on I-95, as fast as they could manage, ducking between semis down to the Dixie Highway exit. Bella gazed up into the shade of office towers which seemed to her more massive, numerous and packed closer together than those of Tampa.

"Ah think we'll find mosta what we wanta look at down to Coral Gables. You heard a the Miracle Mile?"

Her head still on a swivel for both sides of South Dixie, Bella said: "But I wanted to see the South Beach. I want to eat a plantain sandwich for breakfast and drink a decent Americano. This I owe to Papi."

"But we can stay cheaper on the mainland where all the shops're in a bunch for our convenience. Do ya realize what well needa spend for even a long distance glimpse a sand 'n' cabana boys?"

"I don't know what those are. Well, *sand* I do. But I told you already, no dates," Bella said. "They have got these smaller, old time glitzy hotels built like some kind of art-work. Maybe across the street from the highrisers? I sure don't need an ocean view. But, come on. We need to just relax."

"Ah s'ppose. Ah've heard about them cabana boys that we prob'ly wouldn't earn much from most of 'em. Don't know where you heard about the lit'ler hotels."

Bella shrugged. "Hey, I read. Or, I used to."

"Okay. You must mean them little dumps the big developer boy's'd like to scrape off and then put up more a them beach skyscrapers. That used to be all in the news along with other graft.

One a my Daddies use to get all riled when he seen investigatin' reports on TV. Ah'd have to quick fetch him his in-haler."

Now Bella was enthralled with the variety of eateries and fashions behind broad expanses of plate glass. They inched along in traffic through a stretch of wedding shops. Rich, Cuban princess fantasy dreamscapes. But they didn't have *her* cheekbones.

"We also got to be careful a where we park at. Anywheres in this city. It's a whole rigged bus'ness a towin' folks 'n' writin' tickets. We can look this here over'n' then run on out to the Beach."

They were able to find a spot on the street because it was early afternoon and past lunch hour. Bella dropped more than enough coins in the meter for them to take a short stroll.

"Ah'm tellin' ya, though. Ah don't wanta be outta sight of her. All they need is to get 'er onto the hook 'n' then even if Ah sprint back an' catch 'em, it costs for a *drop fee*. So-called. Pay that an' they let 'er back down."

Bella didn't think she had ever seen Merry use air quotes before but didn't need, at the moment, a long origin story. *Something new about a person keeps the world fresh, yes?*

The women walked up one long block and then back on the other side, still just window shopping. Merry insisted on remaining outside to keep an eye on the distant *Tracker*. "Ya don't understand the shit ya gotta go through for payin' the fine 'n' gettin' yerself a ride way the hell out to the impound lot."

"But, duckling. We are here to shop, no? How will I get your expert opinion if you are out on the sidewalk?" Bella opened door of *Essence Boutique* halfway.

"My expert opinion? Huh! Just have 'em escort ya up to the window an' Ah'll give it a thumb's *up*. We *cannot* lose mah ve-hicle."

After ten minutes, Bella reappeared in the glass, a saleslady miming critical approval behind her. She modeled a finely textured white cardigan, took it off and pressed the tag against the glass for Merry to read: *Chiro's $99*. Merry shrugged but then nodded her own approval.

Merry waited, occasionally glancing at the *Mickey Mouse* watch now riding her thin wrist on a new band. Bella emerged after another ten minutes.

"I bought you something. I took a chance that I know enough what you like."

Merry was already walking quickly east. "Thank you so much but Ah b'lieve we're down to about ten minutes on the meter. That'll be inta what the bastards'd' call the margin-a-error or some made-up shit."

Bella kept close behind with her longer strides. "Okay, okay, Little Bit. Anyway, it is by the same designer, those *Chiro's* people. It is crochet so fine and light that you will not believe your eyes. A kimono sweater made of cotton. White like mine, with three-quarter sleeves. It will be long on you but just right in the casino. I would accent it with a white belt."

"Ya got the extra small didn't ya?"

"Yes, yes, the most petite without going down to a child's size. And, you are welcome, by the way. Will you please not run?"

Merry sighed when they were safely back in her car. She waited for traffic to clear then pulled out and looked for a righthand turn

EVACUATION ROUTE

to double back and go east. Bella removed the purchases she'd made for her partner-in-crime. "This should keep you cozy in the most chilly of AC."

Merry examined the sweater while they waited at a light. "Yup, if Ah ain't swimmin' for mah life in it."

Bella folded and returned the sweater to the *Essence* bag. "Why do you put it that dark way? Most would say only *swimming in it*."

"That'd be wrong anyways. It ain't *for* the boat." Merry accelerated the *Tracker* toward the next light. "Ah'm sorry, Bell. Ah don't know where that come from. Just the dark side a mah nature. Ah wasn't thinkin' about yer Mama-san 'n' her horror raft."

"Maybe I must keep you *and* the sweater away from the ocean."

Out on the Beach to *Collins Avenue*, then closer on *Ocean Drive*, they continued to cruise, changeling dodos among peacocks. They passed huge luxury hotels with names of vague, local familiarity to Merry and of television legend to Bella.

"Hey, the *Clevelander!* But nothing over five stories for us, please."

"That how they decide if it's Art Deco? All a of 'em just look old-timey to me." Merry crept along close to the parking lane, more and more doubtful that there would be any spaces before they reached the big parking ramp structure on their city map..

"That is their charm, plus the luxury inside. According to pictures."

"Well, that 'n'....Hey, there's one with a bo-teak on the bottom floor. Try to remember that one. Called *The Webster*. Wonder if they even got one single room left."

"C'mon, Mare. Quick. Circle back around. I've heard of that one."

"Well, geez. Lemme just find a street that's goin' the right way."

Her maneuvers took them in front of the *Miami Beach Municipal Parking Garage* which had vacancies. Merry made an impulse decision to pull in and take a ticket. They found a space on the fifth level. As they ascended, occasionally fooled by motorcycles centered in some of the slots, Merry expressed the hope that *The Webster* might prove to make for one-stop shopping. "Can't help but to think we coulda done this back home."

"Yes, if your paranoia would let you enter Tampa in daylight," Bella said. "Let's just hurry back there and then we will relax. You'll see."

"Ah'm relaxed enough, Bell. Ah think," Merry said. "Feels like Ah oughta be workin' with all these hotels left 'n' right. Looks like it'd be easy pickin's findin' rich ol' white men 'n' rich ol' Cubans. Ah might never a had to pack up 'n' *move* clear across the state to pursue mah livelihood if Ah'd explored this layout more thorough."

Bella said: "You hurt my feelings. We would never be friends, then."

They each hoisted a backpack and a tote from the cargo space of the old *Tracker*. Bella hung the feather-light sack from *Essence* on her pinky with the tote. Merry touched the sun-cracked vinyl

EVACUATION ROUTE 383

material that enclosed the rear space. "Least we ain't leavin' nothin' nobody'd wanta steal."

"Your spare tire looks like it is not too old. So tempting to the car thief." Bella chuckled again. Merry closed the back of the *Geo* then they moved away toward the elevator. They admired the *Mercedes, Accuras, Corvettes, Beamers,* and *Porsches* surrounding Merry's old ride. "What is wrong with this picture?"

"Bet mine's the only one with no fancy alarm system," Merry said.

"Would you *please* relax. No one wants your old beater."

"'Cept them tow-away bastards."

They wandered, infallibly, following Merry's urban intuition, the block-and-a-half back to *Collins Ave.* They paused only to study window dressings in several shops.

'I can smell the ocean, Little Bit," Bella said.

"Ah can't get the piss smell a that parkin' place outta mah nostrils." Merry resumed strolling, leading them away from each enticing storefront.

"Slow your little butt down." Once they turned onto *Collins Ave.,* Bella paused at every window treatment. "You know nothing about how to shop."

"Let's just find ya a hotel to suit yer artistic taste so we can dump off our stuff. Just go pick one."

"*The Webster* should be just a little ways more. I thought I saw a cool place next to it."

384 CHRIS DUNGEY

They checked in at a lovely building very near *The Webster*, where they could resume shopping in the morning. The summer rates at *The Marlin Hotel* were a pleasant surprise.

"We could stay two days for less than $400." Bella said. "I thought it would be much more."

"An' it's under yer five floors limit, too," Merry said, bringing up the rear as a bellboy lugged their bags up two flights. "'Cept them big ones are blockin' out our ocean view."

"Could you even *stand* the luxury for one extra day, Dumpling?"

"Ah guess so, if you 'llow me to lift one a them thick 'ol beach towels they're temptin' me with."

The porter turned his head, smiling, as they reached the third floor. "I can hear you, little chicka. They are very cheap in the Gift Shop," he told Merry. "But we expect many to go missing. Spring Break rates recover our costs." He led them to one of the ten rooms on the top floor, placed the backpacks and totes on the dark red carpeting, then inserted their key-card.

"I will keep a sharp eye on this one," Bella told him. "She has, already, a large collection."

"So, you're seasoned travelers?"

"Something like that." Bella tipped the kid, hoping the fiver was commensurate with seasoned travel.

"Gracias, senora."

"I will take my shower first," Bella said. They tossed their luggage onto an immense king-sized bed.

EVACUATION ROUTE

"Why? You ain't done nothin'." Merry followed her backpack with a dive onto the mattress which did not bounce at all. "Ah'm a take me a l'Il snooze 'fore anything."

"*Oh no*, you do not! You will *not* crash out on me. I walked just as far as you everywhere. You do not want to be all stinky to try on more things."

Merry's eyes were already closed. She lay on folded arms, the landslide of decorative pillows still far from her, arrayed against the headboard. "Ain't mah fault. Mattress suckin' me in. Takin' care a the relax part yer so concerned about."

"You will get a cold glass of water on you to awaken up," Bella warned. "And I will inspect into your pupils also."

"Aww, girlfriend. Ah keep tellin' ya Ah ain't *that* stupid."

It turned out that Merry had no fatigue problem, yet, as regarded their mission. She rolled immediately off the bed when Bella returned from the bathroom drying herself. She dug a fresh pair of panties out of her backpack and pushed the used pair into a separate space. Nearly nude, she unfolded and smoothed a sundress from her tote.

"I guess I will write underwear onto our list, in case for an extra day," Bella said. "Do not forget to take off your anklets."

Merry weaved groggily into the steamy bathroom. "Lookit all a these Eur'pean conditioners 'n' shit. You try any of 'em? Ain't you ever just turned yer drawers inside out? Have you changed yer mind about mebbe takin' a few dates?"

"No, I have not. We are not doing that. All of the complimentary things on the vanity, you are welcome to have if you want to act like a homeless."

Merry's only response was the shower's hiss of sharp spray and the clear, sliding door clanking shut.

There was only an hour of shopping left by the time the women came back down onto the street. They lightened the travel items from their totes to make room for new acquisitions. Both bought (in different shades) *baggy harem* kaftan tops by *Miss Selfridge*. Merry showed unusual enthusiasm for hers, rendered in a salmon-rose shade.

"This here's the smallest one," she said, emerging from the dressing room. "Ah ain't *quite* lost in it."

"You look like a sushi roll."

"Long's Ah don't smell like one," Merry said. "Don't think Ah ever wore nothin' this light."

In the next shop, both floor walkers hinted that the place was about to close. The girls had just enough time to admire and reject a dress by *Akris Punto* ($695). "I am happy we did not bring all our monies from the freezer," Bella said. "I would have spent it just now."

Dressed for the lingering heat of early evening, they moved north looking for just the right outdoor eatery. Between the store glass and their tinted shades, the light broke into colors in their eyes as if through a prism.

"Why's there so many 'I-talian places. Ah wanted to show ya some a the genuine food of yer people," Merry complained. "But

EVACUATION ROUTE 387

there ain't that much a the fashion, really, out here on the Beach. Ah think we wanta go back over to *Little Havana* at some time."

"Don't worry about me. I get enough empanadas near home and enough Cuban culture, too. Just find us where to eat for not too much," Bella said. "I am growling in my tummy."

They spied a place just a short way up 14th Street with a long snack bar and stools under a cabana.

"*La Sandwicherie*," Merry said. "We might's well found us a *Subway* if that's where we're headed. Ah can get a Cuban san'wich at any dang *RaceTrak* gas station."

"Take a closer look at the menu, sweets."

There was, in fact, a Cuban sandwich listed on the sidewalk chalkboard. Merry thought that it was *probably* genuine, so they went in to order. Bella settled for the *Tropical,* a mixture of mango, pineapple, cucumber, and cheeses on a hogie roll. (Add turkey, $2.95). Merry said it looked pretty good, so changed her mind about the Cuban sandwich. She wanted that salad, too. They carried these creations back outside and found two empty stools. The sun was brilliant, blinding, off all of the west facing glass of the beachfront towers. Meanwhile, the shade beneath the cabanas of *La Sandwicherie* was elongating into the street.

This was the time of day that tugged at the muscle memory of both women. The heat daily slowed their final hours before commerce, their faces in mirrors not so bright as the light from highrise glass, but more critical. And now there rose that anxiety to be dismissed, that their opportunities could be fleeting.

"Nothin' that can't be made up," Merry said out loud.

"What?"

"Ah just...Ah was thinkin' out loud. It's awright."

"Okay, but listen, bunny rabbit. Tomorrow morning, we will find you your fried plantains for breakfast," Bella said, spilling tropical fruits from her huge sandwich.

"That's why they give us the forks, Bell." Merry lifted a bite of freshcut pineapple off her plastic plate.

Not yet totally stuffed, the women walked north toward 10th Street, passing up several *rooftop* bars which promised views of the ocean.

"I'm sorry. I don't see how those claims can be true." Bella said. She had been peering east but saw only slivers of the Atlantic. "I think this will be as good of place as any." She halted in front of a club called *High Bar at the Dream*, South Beach, craning her neck at the very edge of the sidewalk trying to see just how *high* it might be. Neon in the windows lured passersby to a Happy Hour.

"Them drink specials'll be a outrage," Merry said. "Ah just wanta watch the tourists walk by."

"That sounds too much like waiting on a barstool in the *Hard Rock*," Bella said. "And plus, you know some of them will wanta watch us back."

"They're gonna up there, too. So, Ah guess it don't matter. If you say we ain't workin' t'night, then Ah stand informed."

"We will go up to have a look, then." Bella took Merry by the elbow. "Don't you hear music?" A beatbox or maybe a real bass thumped far above them, echoing of the tall buildings opposite and into the street.

EVACUATION ROUTE

"Not sure what it is anymore; a band or a car comin' from down the block. An' Ah'm not dancin', neither." Merry was escorted by Bella into the lobby.

"Hey, *Ladies, No Cover!*" Bella read a sign in front of the elevators.

"They gotta supply their ol' meat market," Merry said.

The place looked like fun though the ocean might be only a mirage. It showed only a bit more of its deepening blue from eight stories up. But wait, there was a cruise ship just heading out. Well, *that* had to be on the ocean.

They found seats at one of the round tables, but could not get close to the best view. Though the *High Bar* might have been only half full, they were limited to pool side where a jungle-like live garden restricted their range of vision. No one was swimming. One couple danced to some kind of Latin-techno fusion that neither of the girls would be able to identify.

"Maybe the moon will rise above the pool!" Bella shouted against the bass which thudded steadily, beating deep, like the heart of a gigantic baby pressed to her bosom. She pointed at the near perfect lunar ball emerging from the Atlantic.

Merry probably didn't hear her. "Ain't any waiters that *Ah* can see!" She shouted back.

Now Bella spotted a bar set up near the DJ. Several young men in cargo shorts and tropical shirts were queued up for refills. She cupped her hands and leaned closer to her friend. "That must be the Happy Hour deal! You must serve yourself. What do you want? I will go!"

"Mojito, a course! An Ah'm comin' with. Hope they make 'em good's at the *Seminole.*"

They both stood and walked to the two bartenders in white tunics and shorts. Bella waited her turn behind Merry, struck by a sudden urge for a tall glass of *Blue Moon*, orange slice and all. Well, not so sudden, really, as the taste for that beer was acquired in *Hardrock*. It must be the power of suggestion with that orange, tide-tugging sphere out there, briefly accented by the lavender negligee of a passing cloud. She felt her body begin to move, the pulse of rhythm; primal, irresistible without concentration. The little space for dancing was, as yet, unattended. Two more of the waitstaff, chicas, resumed table service to get the drink line out of the way for dancing.

They stayed for almost three hours according to Merry's heirloom watch. And they *did* dance, but only with each other. Some other women got up together, also, scorning the moldy introductory lines, solicitous small talk of heavily scented young Columbians and five-o'clock-shadowed junior sheiks. These guys actually cared little for dancing, as Bella was aware. The girls took a break and watched the lethargic motions of women who had succumbed to male invitations.

They walked quickly and with (they hoped) purposeful, alpha strides back in the general direction of *The Webster*, The sidewalks were still reassuringly peopled. No one approached them with prurient or larcenous intent in the few blocks they needed to travel.

"This'll get scary in another coupla hours," Merry said sagely as they hustled along. "Gets kinda wild 'n' then everythin' smells like piss in the morning. Mebbe we oughta stay out so you can have a *genuine* South Beach exsperience."

"No ma'am. I am good to go," Bella answered, though she might easily have been talked into one more *Blue Moon* somewhere else. Her thoughts buzzed pleasantly. The drinks were tall and not too outrageously priced. She wondered if, by some stroke of luck, there was a bar in the hotel that had escaped their notice.

In the morning, both women awoke with mild headaches and loss of enthusiasm for staying a second day. They took their showers and then their turns in front of the mirror, but for minimal makeup. They fit yesterday's clothing purchases into the packs, empty now of the one change each had brought. Merry stripped the bathroom vanity of all complimentary toiletries.

"Ah think Ah won't bother pilfferin' a wet towel," she said. They'd used two sets between showers for end-of-trip road funk and the morning-after dance funk.

"You have some mysteries you have not yet shown to me," Bella said. "But I am proud of you."

"Yer mah guildin' star," Merry said.

They followed *Collins Ave.* all the way to its south end. Bella spotted an *Armani* shop before taking the old *A1A* across the causeway into *Little Havana*. She quickly whipped into a parking spot. Traffic and pedestrians on the sidewalk must be slow, for the hungover start to the Saturday.

"We'll just go in for a quick look and to drool," Bella said while Merry tried to figure out a more modern parking meter than yesterday's model.

"Ah need a damn credit card."

"Oh? When are we going to get one? We will have to take a license plate picture to have the bank account. Then we give our mail address to receive the bill. We will be back on the grid. Have we quit looking over our shoulders? Have you forgotten our last employers?"

Merry snorted. "Get a checkin' account, too?"

"Next thing, we will have to pay into the Social Security," Bella said.

"We'll just say we got a cleanin' service set up. Or mebbe we can just keep payin' with money orders?"

"Any time we mess up on the highway, a picture could be taken of your plate," Bella countered. "Just like if you use a card in the meter."

"They will be sendin' it to the wrong address, then, based on the deal Ah made with the previous *so-called* owner. Let's hurry up anyways."

What they discovered on their way out of the city was a store called *Armani Exchange*, which apparently functioned as a sales outlet. Both women were quickly stunned at the discounted prices.

"We have hit the mother lode," Bella said.

"That sounds kinda nasty. But, there's sure plenty a bargains."

"That is just a deep spot in a mine where the gold begins." Bella laughed. "Please take your mind off of work."

"Well, Ah hope they ain't all factory seconds."

To her Friday purchases, Bella added a green linen romper and a fluid viscose dress in white. The two $100 tags exhausted what she considered her share of the cash they'd brought.

"Ah like yer style, girlie." Merry admired the romper as Bella did a runway sashay out of the dressing room. "Always wisht we coulda shared stuff."

Merry's purchases were less expensive; another viscose dress printed with abstract blossoms on white and a white cotton shirt dress with three-quarter sleeves for comfort in the casino refrigeration.

They moved on through *Little Havana*, looking for a likely diner to find Merry's fried plantains with, hopefully, another easy place to park. Pretty soon, though, Merry had to turn northwest, following her dead reckoning instincts to find I-75 again.

"We've got lotsa time, Mare." Bella tapped her lightly on the arm. "Why don't you circle back around."

"Nah, never mind it. Lemme just find us a *RaceTrak* station. We can gas up 'n' Ah'll get me one a *their* Cubans. Been thinkin' about it since Ah first thought about it."

When these prerequisites were accomplished, Bella took over at the wheel with a banana and a granola bar next to her on the console, a tall, Caribbean dark roast in the cupholder. Merry continued to offer navigational instructions until they were back onto *Alligator Alley*. Bella left behind no affinity for the first city of her father, even *Little Havana*. And she sensed none in Merry.

"I never did get to see more than a horizon of the Atlantic," Bella said.

"We seen a couple a cruise ships didn't we?" Merry said. "It ain't no diff'rent water than the same salty, stinky, stuff we ride on every week 'n' sometimes twice. You can ride out onto it tonight, if ya miss it."

With the sun straight above them now, Bella brought her sunglasses down from the top of her head. "You are trully *not* a romantic person. But you are likely right. I will be taking one more night of relaxing, thank you. We can cut the tags off these dick-bait things tomorrow."

"Exactly mah feelin' about it," Merry said. "You get to see plenty enough a water."

Chapter Twenty

Walt and Darlene arrived at *The Glade* Clubhouse separately, though the pretext that they weren't trending toward couple status was wearing thin. Or, *in a relationship* as Dianne would try not to term it for her small circle of Facebook friends. Walt Bocewicz and Darlene Spurgeon sat together at every *Glade* game night though their discretion regarding sleepovers was not yet relaxed. Dianne Kaake, of course, believed that she was being told *all* by her friend. Nevertheless, she continued to tease and pry for stastitics; weights, measures, volumes, and durations. Her husband, Curtis, was no longer merely curious. Reflecting his own personality, he merely *assumed* that the new guy and Darlene were humping like middle-aged rabbits at every opportunity.

Walt and Darlene climbed into the airport-shuttle size party bus and moved all the way to the back. Dianne and Curtis entered close behind them with Dianne lugging a portable bar-case the size of an accordion. Curtis hung back as if he might veer off to choose a seat by himself somewhere. But, he was tall enough to appreciate the chance for extra legroom in the rear. Dianne knew that his social estrangement from their company would also be tempered

396   CHRIS DUNGEY

by the presence of a toilet booth in the space across from Walt and Darlene. The man's growing prostrate discomforts trumped all other considerations and Dianne's bar sat in a seat next to her, one space up from Darlene.

"Now, tell me again why we're doin' this?' Curtis asked. "Didn't we just go up to a whole festival for the damn things a while back?"

"Cuz Bobby Higgs got us a nice group deal an' if we don't take advantage of it he'll quit tryin'," Darlene explained. "Or, unless Gracie Goodrich finds herself a reg'lar boyfriend 'n' Bobby quits arrangin' near proximity to her."

This did not fully satisfy Curtis: "Then tell me why it is, again, that we can't all just meet at the boat?"

"Okay, let me repeat," Dianne addressed her husband who hadn't yet placed his long legs into the aisle across the empty seat next to him. "Would you like to write this down? This is so's everybody'll have the same designated *driver*. Did you not recall specifyin' the damn *Southern Comfort Fireball* into the travel bar? And probably cuz Bobby's afraid to ask Gracie to ride up to *Crystal* in his car 'n' get rejected."

Snip, snip, Walt stifled a smirk as he did each time he heard the Kaakes boring into each other like ship-worms..

"I don't think you're s'pposed to be drinkin' if you're actu'lly gonna swim with the fuckin' manatees."

"Have you got *your* bathin' suit on?"

Curtis shook his head *no.* He now fully took up two seats opposite Dianne with legs protruding.

EVACUATION ROUTE

"Well then what're ya worried about?" Dianne rose onto her knees to address Walt and Darlene over the back of her seat. "Are ya'll plannin' on swimmin'?"

With a slightly incredulous expression, Walt replied, "I think Darlene might. But as with drinking, Dianne, I believe I'll remain an observer."

"Awww," Darlene groaned. "Y'all're gonna be a party pooper, too? You guys, I got my ol' suit on underneath."

"Good for you, hon," Dianne said. "These ol' boys're a couple a fuds."

"Is that a two-piece under there, Dar?" Curtis leered mischievously.

"I will yet set *fire* to you in your sleep, darlin'." Diane glared at her husband.

"Actually, no one should want to *see* me in a bathing suit," Walt chuckled. "I'm doing everyone a favor."

Curtis stood to make his first venture into the toilet enclosure as other outing participants buckled into their seats. "You gals won't be in the water very long. Them big ol' sea cows'll scare ya'll right back up the ladder."

"Hey, that's hurtful. I'm really quite harmless." Bobby Higgs called from the front of the shuttle. He glanced at a clipboard and then up and down the aisle. "I think ever'body's here," he spoke to the driver.

"Can we have a dang cocktail, yet," Dianne pleaded.

"Darlin' it's eleven o'clock in the mornin'," Higgs called. "A course you should have a cocktail!." He placed his hand on the driver's shoulder as he took the last step up. The door wheezed shut behind him. "I know I said this here would be a party bus but you got to use a little discretion. Keep them drinks down. We don't want Syd, here, to lose his chauffer's license."

"What chauffer's license?" The driver said, loud enough for everyone to have a laugh.

"Alright, I guess. We're all here," Higgs said, taking a seat near the front and opposite the object of his current affection, Gracie Goodrich. "Away we go!"

Dianne Kaake was already pouring an orange mixture from a fancy insulated thermos into a small plastic cup. "I ain't wearin' my seat belt, either." She passed the cup back to Darlene.

"Screwdriver?"

"Not just yet, hon," Dianne said. "This is my first try at mixin' up some mimosas. Ain't that s'pposed to be a mornin' drink ya don't have to feel ashamed of?"

"Ah'll never judge you," Darlene assured her. "Pour me a sip."

"It's s'posed to go good with your after-church brunch buffet," Curtis said, ducking to emerge from the cramped WC. "Or a weddin' breakfast."

The bus purred gently away from *The Glade* clubhouse. Walt made no effort to take one of his brews out of the ice-packs in his cooler bag. His self-confidence concerning the one beer per day discipline had grown to the risk of two the Non-Alcohol brews he'd brought along. *Just for this special event. Yep, that's your stinkin' thinkin', writ large.* So he didn't want to challenge it with drinking before noon. That didn't even sound good to *him* by now.

The ride up to *Crystal River* took not quite twenty minutes through stoplights and single lane construction zones. The Friday morning traffic of working stiffs became shopping tourists and snowbirds. When Dianne appeared to be distracted by a conversation with someone in the seat in front of her, Darlene was able to get in a few private words with Walt. "I got some news we need to speak of later on, in more *detail*."

"Oh great. Now how am I supposed to enjoy myself with private business hanging over me?" Walt said.

Darlene sipped carefully from the mimosa. 'Alright, but it ain't nothin' critical. It's just my boy Charlie's comin' for a visit this summer, and he's promised to stay longer'n usual. Like maybe even a week instead of two hours. Ah never get to see him."

"That's the biker one?"

"Yup. It ain't a big deal, hon, except he's kinda funny 'bout my male friends. We can sort it all out later."

"So, funny *ha-ha* or funny *peculiar*, like could I get beat to death with a timing-chain?"

Darlene placed her hand fearlessly on Walt's bare knee. She had talked him into wearing shorts more often though she had yet to coax him beyond khaki. "It ain't nothin' like that. He's a lot more nicer 'bout mah friends then he use to be, especially when he ain't met 'em. It might come as a shock to you learn'n Ah've had a few asshole boy friends in mah past."

Walt patted her hand, the shuttle bus swaying and grinding over the rumble strips of a construction traffic shift. "Well, I'll be anxious to hear how I might stay on his good side. Maybe I'll just absent myself."

Darlene kept her drink gyroscope-steady in front of her. "We'll figure it out. Ya might not even have to meet 'im if you don't wanta. You might even like a break to yourself."

"Long as you understand, I'm not looking for one," Walt said.

"What's the topic a discussion, now?" Dianne asked, returning her attention rearward again over the back of her seat.

"Charlie's comin' for a visit later this summer. I'm just givin' Walter a heads-up."

"Oh." Dianne lost her jovial aspect for a moment. "Oh. I get it. Awkward? From the way you describe 'im, maybe I should keep ol' Walt, here, busy for a few days."

"Oh, *would* you?" Darlene scowled. "I don't think that'll be necessary."

"Do what, now?" Curtis caught some small bit of the women's exchange between opening chugs from his first *Bud Light*. The man was apt to go forward in life with only random portions of talk, advice, news, information, instruction. He reached his cowboy boot way across the aisle to poke Dianne's hip with his toe. "Why don't you stay on outta these folks's bus'ness, honeybunch 'n' tend to yer homework to home."

EVACUATION ROUTE

"Never mind it," Dianne answered him sharply. "That don't sound like no more fun than usual. Really, Dar. It ain't no inconvenience to *me*."

Darlene gave Walt's knee a reassuring squeeze. "We'll be fine, ya'll, includin' any nosy ears within the sound a my voice. It ain't no big deal. Charlie ain't as crazy as he once was.." She lowered her voice, the highway noise of gathering speed and the growing chatter in the bus an aid to privacy, "We'll talk about it later."

"Not fair!" Dianne laughed, but diverted her attention away from the friends behind her.

On the outskirts of *Crystal River*. The driver, Syd, made a careful left onto *Fort Island Road*.

"This here's the way out to the wildlife refuge on the river," Darlene said. "If you follow it all the way on out, there's a pretty decent beach. You can actually see the *Gulf* from there, finally."

"Yeah, I've been out there," Walt told her, recalling his wonder that anyone could find an address in the winding maze of cul-de-sacs carved out of the jungle and wetlands. "A couple of times, looking at real estate. For most of it I just didn't want to shell out that much cash."

"Well, *I'm* glad you didn't find anythin'," Darlene said.

The party bus turned onto another winding asphalt road and soon parked in a paved riverside lot. Syd was already kicking back in the driver's seat with an open paperback as the *Glade* passengers stood and gathered their things. "Have fun, kids. Careful a the gators," he laughed.

"He's joking, right?" Walt said. "About the gators?"

CHRIS DUNGEY

"Most a the time." Curtis grinned.

There was no tour office but the skipper walked ashore from a public dock to greet them. "If y'all are from *The Glade* park, I'm your Captain. Captain Fred. Those a y'all that plan to swim can pick a wetsuit outta the van, if you want. Water's colder due to some springs and with the tide in. Snorkel and mask gear in there, too." The man directed them to the open rear gate of a white *Mercedes* van. "Everything's been sanitized. There's mostly your larger sizes in there."

"Is he hintin' what I think he's hintin'?" Dianne frowned.

"Well, if the wetsuit don't fit...," Curtis said.

"I think I'll jus' risk it, then," Dianne declared. "Show off these big ol' nipples at ever'body."

"When did you ever need an excuse?" Curtis snorted.

"Hey, play nice, y'all," Darlene scolded.

Once aboard, Captain Fred outlined the rules for interacting with the manatees: "This ain't the peak season, understand, when you'd see hundreds of 'em in here. The water warms up and most of 'em head out closer to the Gulf. But we have a resident population of around forty that hang out close to those cold, feeder springs I mentioned. You *will* see manatee today."

"Or we get our money back?" Curtis crowed.

"Uh, no. And don't chase, poke at, dive on, or otherwise harass 'em." Captain Fred forced a laugh in Curtis's direction. "Or you'll swim home."

EVACUATION ROUTE

Walt only half listened, stowing his insulated bag under one of the cushioned bench seats. He had no plan to enter the water for *any* purpose other than if the boat sank.

The nine other *Glade* guests filled out the seating capacity of the pontoon craft. Half of them had picked out wet suits which they struggled into as Captain Fred slowly motored away from the dock. Leaving very little wake, the boat moved at almost drift speed, westward toward the Gulf. When they veered into a likely looking lagoon, Walt lifted a non-alcohol beer from his cooler. Today's brand was a pretty decent effort at imitation *by Becks*. He twisted the cap while the anchor was gently let go by the Captain. The ultra quiet *Evinrude ETEC* motor propelling them ceased it's nearly inaudible purr. The craft eased to a halt. Walt could see in the distance where this part of the estuary broadened into more open water.

Captain Fred pushed two padded gates open on either side amidship and secured them. "Alright. Swim ladders are open. Don't push, don't crowd. And you won't see many a these animals if you go cannonballin' in."

"You sure ya don't want in on the fun? No one'll mind if ya get in with yer ol' boxers," Darlene told Walt.

"Now yer talkin'!" Dianne giggled. "An' how do *you* know what he's wearin'?"

"I seen 'em dryin' on his clothes tree." Darlene stuck out her tongue at her friend. She slipped out of her cut-off jeans and top to reveal a plain, black one piece suit. "Left over from my days on the Olympic divin' team."

404   CHRIS DUNGEY

"Looks pretty good on you still," Walt said. "I think I'm fine just watching all of you. There could be some severe shrinkage I wouldn't be proud to show off. Try to get one of 'em to surface for a breath near the boat." A quick Google search about the creatures on a newly acquired pawnshop laptop had given Walt *some* insights.

"We don't mind a li'l shrinkage, hon!" Dianne laughed, halfway down the starboard swim ladder. "We'll take it into account. Curtis, if you splash me ya won't need to worry 'bout yer *own* shrinkage never again." With a boot tugged off her husband was inching down the rail to hang his leg over, hoping to reach the water with his foot.

The passengers in wetsuits were already treading water comfortably off the port side. Super helpful Bobby came back to the ladder to adjust the snorkel band behind Gracie's head. Bunnie Moore and her wizened little husband Griff drifted closer to shore. A small inner-tube, with handles and cargo netting stretched across the donut hole, bobbed between them. Griff never removed his rictus grip from the two handles that Walt could see. There were several sealed drink containers riding in the netting.

"Slow movements. Don't thrash your flippers," Captain Fred called. "And don't make any ass-up surface dives. Just let yourself sink gently."

So what was she going to tell me, if anything, and why? Walt sipped thoughtfully at the first *Beck's NA*, wishing to consume enjoy it while it was still cold. Now it was Darlene's turn to enter the water. She stood on the top rung, hanging onto the padded rail, waiting for Dianne to complete her squealing immersion. *Am I supposed to be a free agent for that week? Shouldn't the word* love *be mentioned by this point, by at least one of us. Not sure I oughta go there. But I could. Might not be true just yet. Or fair. It's coming close, though. And, commitment by the default of aging. Doesn't seem to be on her mind. And what's the deal with that boy of her's? Do I feel just a bit...? I don't know what. Of secondary importance to Dar? Stupid question. Of course I am. But should I feel threatened? Is she protecting me or covering up an embarrassment? But, wow, that bathing suit. That is a good looking middle-aged woman. I like admiring her even more in the light of day..*

"Oh! My! Freakin'! Lord!" Dianne shrilled as she pushed herself away from the boat, the spring water surging up between her breasts and up to her chin.

"Yer gonna scare all them boogers away!" Curtis lifted his leg back over the railing and moved closer to the ladder opening as Darlene resumed her descent. *The man apparently never gets enough of peering down cleavage,* Walt thought. *Kinda creepy, actually.*

"Push him in, Walter!" Dianne called, vigorously treading water away from the port side pontoon.

Walt sipped slowly. "Not *me.*"

Curtis looked over his shoulder at Walt, his usual shit-stirring grin vanished for the moment. *You better believe, 'not you,'* his eyes spoke.

406   CHRIS DUNGEY

Walt recognized Darlene's little yelp as she at last steeled herself to drop away from the swim ladder. "Throw us another tube would ya, darlin'" she gasped.

"Hey, somethin' just touched my feet over here," Gracie Goodrich cried from the opposite side of the boat.

"We've got one!. She's comin' up close 'n' personal!" Bobby Higgs's mask surfaced just astern of Gracie.

"I see her," Captain Fred said. "Go on down and have another look, ma'am. She's trustin' you and there's a calf with her, looks like."

Now Darlene and Dianne dog-paddled their way around the front of the pontoons, trailing the inner tube that Walt dropped to them. The Moores moved in a similar manner, away from shore toward the mother and baby.

"Easy now. Don't thrash," Captain Fred reminded them.

Walt stood up and carried his beer to the opposite rail. Curtis Kaake opened a second *Bud Light* but sat back down, apparently satiated. Or, all of the visible cleavage had moved out of range.

"Pretty cool," Walt said. The large and smaller shadows were visible from his angle where he stood at the rail.

"It really is," Darlene put the mouth piece of her snorkel back in. Her mask tilted and submerged again for a few moments. "That little'n's almost cute," she gasped. "But Mama's homely as a road apple."

And why is that, Walt thought. *Unattractive creatures often the most docile and gentle. Maybe that's my problem. Always been passive, but am I homely, too? Or is that a false premise? The manatee*

EVACUATION ROUTE

407

example might be anecdotal. Then it's my own self-effacement that makes me unattractive? Rather be that than a braying ass-hat that could pose for a firemen's calendar.

It's all in my worn out brain. Should be focused on Darlene's deal right now. Wasn't she the one worried early on about me branching out? Needing space? Well, her needing a week for this Charlie's exclusive attention maybe isn't so unreasonable. But, screw that. When did I start caring about whether a woman's signals were mixed or not. Hey, bovines are pretty homely but gentle. Chimps aren't so great to look at and they can be assholes. This Charlie must be a piece of work if she has to hide me. Judgmental. Maybe he looks like Brad Pitt. Did I take a speeder but forgot about it?

"Hey, gimme a hand, would ya, sport?" Captain Fred addressed Walt. "Up front there. Would ya pull the anchor up a few feet. There's a pod of manatee lying further in to shore." He eyed the waters on all quarters of the craft to make certain of where his tour charges were swimming.

Walt heard the quiet ignition of the smaller of two outboards on the stern. He brought a yard or so of anchor chain up, dripping between a gap in the railing cushions and into its locker. The craft eased past the cluster of *Glade* swimmers hovering over the mother manatee and her offspring. Walt spotted the cluster of hulking shadows in the shade of some bordering mangroves,

"Hey, don't leave us!" Dianne hollered.

"Okay, let go the anchor." The Captain told Walt.

Walt released the chain, still in his hand. It rattled out again. He felt the gentle but virtiginous sensation of the outboard's reverse thrust.

"Wait up for us!" Gracie Goodrich led the school of pursuing snorkels, leaving Higgs and the Moores to tow the alcohol life-ring. Darlene and Diane now swam with decent freestyle strokes, pushing their inner tube ahead of them.

"Easy, out there! There's no need to churn up the river!" Captain Fred reminded them. "Anyway, it's illegal for me to leave without ya! A pretty hefty fine!"

The tour culminated in a wider bay inlet back near *Crystal River*. Captain Fred brought the *Glade* folks to shore at a large dock facility owned by a combination restaurant/hotel/fishing camp. *Captain Mike's Waterfront Social* read the large sign above the longest pier. A young man wearing a *Manatee Experience* teeshirt matching the Captain's, caught the line tossed to him. He fended off with an expensive cross-trainer as the pontoon nudged into dock bumpers. *Spending the dough from the summer job,* Walt thought. *I owe myself some better kicks.*

"Thank you, Nathan! All ashore that's goin' ashore," Captain Fred spoke jovially. "Gather your coolers and your other belonging's, put 'em in your van. It's waitin' out front. We'll get all the swim gear stowed 'n' then we'll eat. Is everybody starvin'?"

"I could sure eat," Darlene nudged Walt who was lost in thought, staring across the breadth of the dock area.

"Sure. Fresh sea air's supposed to do that," he replied, wondering if anyone ever bought cruisers and runabouts any more. There were *so* many pontoons in adjacent piers and docks. Well, that was preposterous. Of course they did; anyone who was more serious about fishing than in having family picnics on the water would be drooling for a *Boston Whaler.*

He put the two empty *Beck's* bottles into his insulated bag. And what about those two genuine looking old wharf pilings with the fat hawser stretched between them. It was a good ten yards from the water with three benches behind it awaiting the sunset aficionados when they were finished dining inside. How did the *Mike's Waterfront Social* people get those two very clean and apparently well fed gulls to perch just there, picture perfect. *Duh. Birds are probably too fat to fly from eating boaters' leftovers.*

He and Darlene were the last ones off the pontoon boat except for the kid, Nathan, who gathered the flippers and snorkel rigs. The hurriedly stripped wetsuits would have to be turned right-side-out and disinfected of all the customer sweat before being worn by the next bunch. A lot of work, but at least Nate wasn't home loafing in front of the insidious video games.

The main restaurant offered a cavernous dining room inside with a bar at a far end but not separate. The *Glade* party opted for the flagstone patio with tables beneath beach umbrellas and a view of that rapidly approaching sunset. The gulls rested and preened with all the time in the world to be offered the odd French fry.

CHRIS DUNGEY

"They've got the best portions here, Walter," Dianne said. "Ya won't need to cook tomorrow."

Walt grinned. "What makes you think I cook at *any* time?"

There was no way to have an intimate conversation without rudely whispering and betraying more evidence for their relationship. *Hell, maybe there's someone that still doesn't suspect.* Several tables had been drawn together so that the manatee explorers could all eat in one spot. *That's all we seem to do. This outing's a little different but here we are, all chowing down together. It really begins to feel like the family Higgs welcomed me to.*

Luckily, the table arrangement could have seated twenty and they were only fourteen, including the Captain and the late arriving Nate. There *were* a few gaps. Walt sat, backed up against a sizeable palm which thrust up between of the flagstones making several of them look like continental plates rubbing. Darlene sat near him and Dianne gave them an unexpected two chair buffer. Curtis plunked down to his wife's right, his outdoor voice and increasing alcohol content exaggerated his proximity. Too close for Walt's comfort. A young waitress arrived at Captain Fred's end of the table, the sunset end, to distribute laminated menus and take their drink orders.

"So, when is Charlie due to arrive?" Walt spoke in what he hoped was his lowest audible register. Dianne appeared to continue a consultation with Curtis over the entrée choice; a brief respite for the pair from all who might be curious about their business.

"Don't really know, darlin'. Sometime in the comin' month," Darlene said. "He tends to just roar in on his own schedule. I just

EVACUATION ROUTE   411

know it's s'pposed to be more of a relaxed stay this time. Now, are you interested in sharin' one a the appetizer samplers?" She leaned into Walt to point at the colorful representation on the menu.

"Maybe with you, Dar. *"But wouldn't we need to order something like that for the whole table?* Walt thought. "I can't afford to feed all these...uh, I've seen them eat." He eyed Curtis in particular. And there was Bobby Higgs to consider. A bottomless maw there.

"Yer prob'ly right. Ah can't afford three platters, either." Darlene said. "Shoot. Ah was thinkin' we could make a whole meal for ourselves oughta one a those." She turned a page in the menu. "Share a plate a tacos, maybe?"

"Sure, but I'm not a fan of the fish ones." Walt found the page of pizzas and tacos. He followed Darlene's gaze, sure that she was still studying the large variety platter. "Let's go ahead and get that. Just have it brought out as our order and not for the table."

"Well, ain't *you* the problem solver." Darlene said, closing her menu and stacking them together. Glad we live a little inland if that's how the sea air affects mah appetite. I'd weigh 200 pounds."

Walt said: "Nah, I can't picture that. You get more than enough walking between your job and around the park. I need to find a bike or something."

"You mean to claim you been keepin' slim by yer own metabolism?" Darlene sipped the diet cola that was placed before her. "Am Ah helpin' out with that at all? Don't know if Ah want you wastin' energy on a bike."

Walt stole a glance at Dianne who was still locked in an intensifying debate over food choices (he assumed) with Curtis. "That might well be the case, lady. I'll probably put two pounds back on every day until Charlie goes home."

Darlene forced a pouty face in which Walt found little sympathy. Then she said, her voice growing louder. "Yer a big boy, Walt. Ah think you'll survive. How'd you manage before you stumbled inta *my* life?"

"Not stellar."

Now she raised her voice loud enough to be heard by all, including Captain Fred at the head of the table. She stared past Dianne, straight at Curtis, a *Bud Light* longneck protruding from under his mustache. "But, until Ah hear Charlie's Fat Boy roll in," she proclaimed. " An' right after he's gone, Ah'm gonna screw yer dang socks off."

Well, alright then. Walt sipped from the heavy mug of black coffee he'd been served. He resisted the urge to read the table for dropped jaws, Curtis's in particular. *That's cool enough with me. I won't worry about anything else.*

Chapter Twenty-One

Wood-Chuck Spurgeon made an executive decision to part with the last of the potato salad from the *Knuckledicks'* Memorial Day revelry. It still passed the sniff test as far as *he* was concerned, but he'd been poleaxed before by leftover potato salad that gave no warning. Was it the mayo in it that eventually went rogue, or the chunks of hardboiled egg? *But mayo is eggs, ain't it?* Anyway, he couldn't trust it after three days in their small refrigerator.

The last of the pulled pork should be good enough to go into chili. Friday is a good day for chili, but in this heat? What the hell, he could boost the AC for lunch hour. Wood lifted the jammed-in *Zip-Lock* bag in which the potato salad had become the consistency of guacamole. He carried it out the back door, The green dumpster lid banged down behind him just as he heard a phone ring through the rear wall, approximately where Archie, *The Darkness,* Caulkins would have his huge ass parked behind his desk.

"Why in thee hell does some swamp-jockey in Lou'siana have our office number?" Archie waddled out of his managerial space, a new personalized coffee mug in hand, to plug Wood's passage back to the refrigerator.

"That likely woulda been some a Boogaloo's people," Wood said. "Back there, over there, down there. He's got a burner phone that most be turned off, muted, or outta minutes."

The Darkness handed Wood a tiny *Sticky Note* with a phone number written on it. "Sure, but some ol' boy conveyed to me it was urgent: *Bo-regard call this number, soon's possible*. Apparently, Boog's number has been lost ever'body down there that ever knew 'im," Archie laughed like a bowl full of liver. "That tell ya somethin'? He comin' in anytime soon?"

Wood had not talked to his assistant since Boog gave the club prostitutes two days off to recover from their pig-roast marathon. "He was in 'n' out yesterday just to collect his harem's pay envelopes 'n' take a look at the screwin' schedule. They all been on the fly since then. Did the caller say what it was about?"

Archie poured what must have been his fourth coffee of the morning, emptying the beaker. "Jus' said it was urgent family bid'ness."

"Oh-kay, then." Wood said. "I bet I know what it's about. Can ya shut that off, Chief, so the stain don't get baked in?"

The Darkness pressed the toggle down on the coffee maker. "I sure don't need no more. Is it gonna mean another absence for that ol' boy? You gonna be back to runnin' the girls around for him?"

EVACUATION ROUTE

Wood reached the beaker and ran water into it at the little bar sink. "I think it might. We already discussed it, to take turns for a few weeks off, each of us. So I guess it ain't unexpected to me. His mother's been in teeterin' health."

The Darkness said: "I sympathize, but remember...you hire yer assistant outta *your* budget."

I'm well aware ya tight bastard. The extra girls brought in for the pig roast had been let go. Wood decided to go ahead and start more coffee for the remaining pros, should they and their handler come in for a break. Archie reverse duck-walked out of Wood's way. Wood dumped the grounds. "I'll get Ivan Dresbach in here again. He's gettin' the hang a bartenderin' just fine 'n' he likes the money."

"Ol' Ivan the Terrible? Terrible haircut?" Archie called from his office door. "We was any other place, he'd have to wear a hairnet over that mess when he's around the food."

Boogaloo LaVelle arrived before any of the girls. Apparently in a rush, he nodded a greeting and went straight to open the girls' Reservation Log. When Wood handed him the *Sticky Note* message, he asked *The Darkness* for use of the office landline. "I need to buy the minutes, I'm out of."

"Sure, bubba." Caulkins winked at Wood.

Boog closed the office door behind him. The number on the *Sticky Note* was unfamiliar. The answering voice was not. It was Laurence. "You not in that jail now?" Boog asked.

"Nah, Beau. Fresh got out 'n' I been tryin' to track ya down. It's some bad news, I got." Laurence LaVelle's voice was mumbled-up with, probably, a dip of *Kodiac* under his lower lip.

One bad habit I never touch, by luck. Boog said: "I been afraid for this call awhile, if what I think it is." He heard his brother spit. *Wow. Sounded like into a cup. Even if he's out on the porch?*

'Yes, it's Mamere. She has gone over."

Boog swallowed around a sudden lump in his throat. Then he thought for a moment about how Laurence had expressed his message. "Ya mean she pass?"

Another spit. Boog was sure now that Laurence was being unusually civilized with his chew. He heard juice hit other collected juice and shuddered at what it always looked like.

"Yes, Beau. She has passed over to Glory, I think's how they say it. Strong believers. Makes me think of *glory hole.* That would be disrespect. Anyway, I been just in time home from *Terrebonne Work Program*. Last three months of an eight-month bit, cleanin' roadside almost by home. I'm at the funeral place south a Houma, at this very moment."

EVACUATION ROUTE 417

That explained his younger brother's politeness with the spitting. "The *Dropeau Family* place, yeah?." Boog said. "We ought at lease bury her instead out in her garden that she love."

"Well, that is outside the law of what you can do legal no more, Beau. I think of that first already and Bropeau warn me. 'Sides that, I am on probation. I ain't gonna make it through for one year if I fuck up. Whata *you* think, Beau?"

Boog looked at the shitty old clock radio on *The Darkness's* desk. If it was correct, he'd been on the phone only a few minutes. *That tub a lard can just wait. This the darkest time for any fam'ly, even in Knuckledicks. Bust a cap in his fat ass, he interrupt.*

"Nah. Who could go back a year? What you was in for?"

"The 'mediate cause was for drivin' off with a lawn mower. Some fool left it by the roadside with key still in. One a them ones with the zero-turn, too—get up close 'round a bush or, like the tires onna boat trailer? It was used, so not grand larceny. Maurice Roulin took my pickup 'n' was s'possed to meet me with his flatbed out on that one back road, goes out to the *big* lake. You know the one. That soggy two-track Pere Emile use sometime, when he's avoidin' *Fish 'n' Game*. It was one thing goin' wrong after another from then on. An' they inpound my truck. I never see it again, so far."

Always the same with you, Laurence. Unlucky 'n' half fon-chock. But Boog didn't want to interrupt.

"The flatbed wouldn't start for him, and no phone with me for Maurice to warn. So he haul ass back in his ol' *Jeep* just in time meet with *Highway Patrol* arrivin' to the crime scene. We get to

CHRIS DUNGEY

jail 'n' Maurice had older movin' violations like you would guess. We spend couple hour in the same cell while they dig up my back child support. It was late by a year across in *Mobile*. Fuckin' Lori. That's in another state, would'n' *you* think?"

"They can find you easy," Boog said."Everythin' you done all in a computer."

"Well, that's what they done, I guess. Me 'n' Maurice under some black cloud a juju, you bet"

Boog heard more mouth sounds; Laurence putting in more *Kodiak*, getting it situated for maximum effect under his lower lip. "So tell me how this trouble apply to our Mamere's ceremony."

Another spit. "It don't, really. I was just wanderin' off a the track with news from home. Truth is, I found a old joint in hidey hole behind Mamere's washer machine. An' how it applies to me is havin' enough onto my plate already 'n' I need ya to come 'n' clear up her last bills 'n' such. I needa just go ahead an' skip outta here before I gotta do the work-search 'n' start kiss *l'ane* a that PO . Also we need sell the place an' all the stuff. I won't have time for it, whether I stay or go."

Boog said, "I needa think on it. Ya'd leave without your share? An' what about...? What do ya hear from Frank? Or, Marielle?"

"Frank's very sad but out somewhere in a desert. He said to sell the place 'cause he'll be a lifer Marine 'n' he look us up when he retire." Laurence coughed. "He has the pension plus three hots an' a cot, how *he* say it. Marielle sad too but can't afford to fly from North Dakota. She shacked up with a oil guy."

Boog wished his brother would switch to speaker on his cell phone. His *Kodiak* noices were what the girls sometimes said—too much information.

Laurence must have swallowed some joice. His voice returned in a hoarse croak. "Why the Marines in that desert, can you tell me this?"

"I don't know, brother. But when will be the service?"

Laurence spoke to someone away from his phone. Boog couldn't hear the jist of it until Laurence resumed. "That was this undertaker. I must go sign papers for the casket. Lucky for Mamere she take all money from out the bank or I couldn't get at it."

"So when? *When*, Laurence?" Boog repeated.

"We think for Monday will be good. I must talk to the priest more. He's new 'n' I'll make it for sure he is not one a the *le folle* kind. They made me to sleep with one eye open in *Terrebonne*. For the meal, I haven't arranged it, but..."

"I will head out, then." Boog abruptly hung up the *Knuckledick* phone. He didn't want to hog it any longer from *The Darkness*. There were things to do before he could ride back home to Louisiana.

Even Caulkins hung around, taking a seat after Boog related his news. "It's tough, brother. Sorry for your loss. Ya know, you're

420   CHRIS DUNGEY

in-title to a few brothers to ride along. Excludin' yer partner, here. For security 'n' to help ya out. *Knuckledick's* always show respect."

"Don't worry about nothin'," Wood-Chuck said, presuming to pat Boogaloo on the shoulder.

The Cajun man didn't flinch at the rare encroachment upon his physical person. Boog had forgotten about the color-guard escort of a few select *Knuckledick's* whose presence would seem most prominent at the funeral *meal*. He had to wriggle out fast if he wanted a few days on the trip home to take care of that *other* private business. "Much gratitude, but them boys can stay home. Boog will need to remain longer than what Wood 'n' me already speak of. Family, they want Boog to finish alla Mamere business. Sell the ol' house, share out money for brothers an'sister."

"Not a big deal," Wood said.. *My* Ma's used to waitin' on me."

"No one fuck with Boog down there, I think, Chief. Related to most peoples around, far as findin' pall bears."

"Okay by me, guy. I was just remindin'."

Making coffee was part of his job description behind the bar but Wood felt sometimes that it was becoming his *primary* function. He began to do it again. *Well, Ma didn't sound that over-anxious for a visit the last time we talked*. That lukewarm reception was quite different from their chat in the winter. It promoted the thought that maybe he'd better get up to *Homosassa* soon, to see just what was going on. How long could it take Boog to wrap up his mother's affairs and sell that old homestead? Even in this market, Wood thought. *Could't be more'n a fixer-up or starter home.*

"I will stay 'n' tell the girls. If you have plan for a meal, I make a quick run to the store."

Wood had chili in mind to be made with the remains of the pulled pork bar-b-q. "I've got alla what I need, I guess. Who's in the reservation book for today?"

Boogaloo eased off his bar stool and came around the end. He kept the book tucked under that end of the bar nearest to the back door. He returned to his seat and opened the spiral-bound notebook. "It isn't the heavy work load today for them. One date for each, an' it's tonight." He returned the schedule to its place.

"That'll give me time to work somethin' out with Ivan." Wood offered Boog his hand across the bar.

"I will be back to see ya when I see ya." He clasped Wood's hand and dapped with less enthusiasm than usual.

"You do what ya gotta do, brother," Wood said. "An' you know I'm really sorry for your loss."

Two pair of jeans, four black tee-shirts, a black *Born to Ride* hoody missing its draw-string. Boog LaVelle had room in his saddlebags for the *Axe* spray Wood gave him for some reason, his toothbrush and shaving kit; items he seldom found it necessary to pack. Just enough room left for the Euro courier bag. *Don't let Laurence see it.*

Heading north on US 19 in late morning, he realized that he *must* think, at some point, about stopping at a motel. Did this mean that he was no longer very young? Calculations of time and distance crept, muddled, through the grief in his thoughts. Two eventful years had gone by since he last made this trip, so it was sure to show him just how old he was becoming.

Boog felt ashamed for thinking about the ungrateful whores after hanging up on Laurence. *It has been always with me somewhere an' I can't shake loose. This I might get relief from to be busy at old home.* Now, for a few weeks, he must give all care and attention to the memory of *Mamere* and the possible windfall from her possessions and the family property. With growing interest, he recalled that the mortgage for the old home and acre of land were miraculously paid off in total. But were there any recent liens? *I cross these fingers for no.*

Mentally restful delays in his reckoning with them not withstanding, he slowed while passing through *New Port Richie*. He kept his eyes peeled while filling the Gold Wing's tank at his favorite surveillance spot, the *RaceTrac* station. Outside of town, he gave his full focus to the road, his speed, and the likelihood of lurking Highway Patrol.

If he was going to stop for the night, anyway, he might as well take time to stop somewhere and have some breakfast-for-lunch. He found a likely truck stop diner where *US 19/27* ran into the east-west artery of *Interstate 10.*

The scenery along that major thoroughfare of the Gulf Coast was depressing to him about the same time that sprinkles, then

EVACUATION ROUTE

light rain, began to spot his leathers.. There were long miles of forested areas on both sides of I-10 that had been flattened or tilted by one of the named storms since his last visit home. When? What name? This was not information he would have retained unless the winds carried away his bike or flattened the *Knuckledick* Clubhouse. *Laying down like broke broom straws, all in one direction.*

When *was* Katrina? A while ago. A long enough time for him to have been home and found the place still standing. When was that last trip for *Pere Emile's* funeral? *2007, but don't take Boog's word. That* storm left their own small patch of woods down home at a serious angle with a few root systems pried completely out of the mucky ground. *Not this bad though.*

The rain gathered intensity out of a sullen afternoon sky from which Boog could no longer estimate the time. He spotted an overpass where he could take shelter and dig his new pair of swim goggles out of the saddlebags. Sad thoughts descended harder upon him as well; destructions and death. Not of the violent sort this damage, so worse. Boog suspected more to follow. He understood this. Bayou life. And his biker life was spawned out of that. *What I need is the shot and beer. Jack. Or, some a that blackberry brandy.* The girls, who he thought of as *his*, but loyal now, were onto something there. *Maybe stop for the night, eat in a tavern. Drink just one, for the sleep.*

The rain eased, but still spilled in reddish-brown mud-water down the landscaped incline. It puddled in the ditches running under the overpass. He fired up the Gold Wing and made a long, fierce acceleration up the wide shoulder, looking for a spot to ease into traffic. With rearview mirror fogged and beaded he chanced it into the far lane, but not far enough away from the tractor-trailers jetting spray from their aerodynamic skirts. Motor homes tried to pass the trucks, forcing him to go dangerously faster, ducking and weaving, a Russian roulette slalom.

The swim goggles worked fine. Halfway to Tallahassee, Boog got off the *Interstate* and ate a heat lamp cheeseburger from another *RaceTrak* station. He gassed up. Emerging from the bright store, he felt worn, finally, by all of the day's news and the stress of road conditions. He wasn't going to make it much farther than *Mobile*. A cheap motel near a tavern sounded better by the mile to his fatigued brain.

"Beauregard, *you* have changed," Laurence said. He came out onto the small stoop in bare feet. "Didn't know who was it was in the driveway. What kind a sissy-ass Jap bike you up on there?"

I would reco'nize you, brother, ten year past or ten year later. Our family coujon. Unless that's s'pposed to be me. Prob'ly the toss-up. "Yeah, brother. Now I'm tryin' out wolf-in-sheep-clothes. Part a the job." *Don't feel like to repeat 'n' break down the parable a that ol' Commie Mayo what's-'is-name, swimmin' among the peasant fishes.* "The bike deceives. Makes me look weak. I have underestimated riceburners all of these past years. They have some muscle you wouldn't b'lieve."

EVACUATION ROUTE

Laurence held open the skillfully patched screen door. "Don't sound as good, though. Hardly hear ya roll in. Come on 'n' take the load off. I have claim on, already, the couch for sleepin' tonight. Couldn't find no easy rest in the bed of *Mamere* 'n' *Pere Emile.*"

"Did you feel chill a the *fantome*?" Boog asked. "I will dare the bed 'n' be ready to run. I don't pay them boogers no mind. So, tell me why there's no For Sale sign stickin' in front."

"No there ain't as a yet, brother. I been too busy with that undertaker. Settin' the day 'n' time 'n' how we want all a it to go. An' that priest bein' new like I mention. He didn't know *Mamere* so good. I hadda harp on 'im to do thngs ar way to make ever'thin' go more quick."

There was no division of labor between front room and kitchen. Laurence brought two *Jax* beers from the refrigerator which still maintained the rounded contours of the 60s. "I *do* have a lady to make her pitch to ya on Tuesday, after funeral. There's a list a others on the kitchen table, if ya don't like her. The vault is paid off, but the undertaker cut comes outta any estate. An' the realtor cut."

Jax, of course was the beer brand that was passed down from the father to his sons. Boog began to map the frustrating days ahead of him to be dealt with. Was he supposed to abandon the last of his revenge anger, already dulling? Maybe to be the coujon was for Laurence's advantage. Take *nothin'* personal or to the heart But, this beer was so cold. How could parts still be found for that old refrigerator?

"What about the ones who decide the price?" Boog asked.

426   CHRIS DUNGEY

Laurence plunked down in a recliner of *Duct Tape* patches. It pitched way back with a clunk against the wall. *Knicknacks* rattled on a shelf. "The lady will give a idea to you. But the bank appraisal happens from the buyer. Maybe bank won't loan 'em what ya want. I leave to you how much you can get. I will be in…Arkansas maybe. Wherever the desperado from child support can breathe easy."

Mamere must have chewed on brother Laurence, his skinny ass, plenty, before he did his latest jail bit. She expected nothin' about nothin' else from us but said, always, responsibility for bebes must be met. "You will want your share, though, yeah?"

Laurence closed his eyes. The wall behind him opened on his right into the parental bedroom. In lieu of a door, a curtain hung, pulled back on a dowel fastened into the frame. An old sport coat hung there as well. He tipped the beer back and sighed. "We must trade the cell phone numbers if ya have one. You take extra from the sale for all troubles but I need to be away. Then I call you sometime with address to send money."

"I will buy a new burner," Boog said. "What crack thugs call 'em in Florida. My other one run out a minutes. Left it home."

Laurence said, "I came to here straight out the gate 'n' except to stop at *Wal-Mart* by *Houma*. It took half a my walk away money for a phone 'n' minutes. I thumb down here 'n' that ol' *F10* a *Pere* Emile, she starts right up, so."

"Does that *Pere* Emile dress up jacket fit on you?" Boog drained his first *Jax* and carried it to place it in the old, chipped sink. There

EVACUATION ROUTE 427

were no dirty dishes but a garbage bag stood on its own by the backdoor, full to overflowing with takeout trash.

"Almost. The sleeves'r long. Some. But I found no ties or white shirt. *Mamere* ran a yard sale for much a his stuff last year."

"We can ride back to the *WalMart*? For me to get a phone?" Boog asked. "I have no shirt with collar."

There was only silence from the recliner until Boog thought his brother must have fallen asleep. He opened another *Jax*. It *was* cold inside the old fridge even though the motor labored noisily when it ran.

"Ain't we the pair a...you know," Laurence spoke softly. "As for offspring we wasn't very..." Boog settled back into the creaking couch. "We was pretty...shabby, yeah?"

"Ya think *Mamere* care about that? What do ever'body say now for almost anything?" Boog scratched his stubbly chin and hoped there were some old razors left in the bathroom cabinet. "'It is what it is,' they say.'"

"It is what it is," Laurence mumbled. "An' then they say 'It is all good.' Have ya ever found any truth in that?"

Boog carried the beer out onto the porch. He picked up a hoe, inexplicably leaning against the 2x4 railing, except for maybe this very purpose: Time for him to inspect his inheritance. Maybe Laurence had already carried it while looking around. That grass needed to be mowed, for safety sake from copperheads. And for the real estate lady. *Well. It all is good.*

The shed was unlocked. There was an aluminum skiff on a trailer, a cement block under the tongue. Registration number on the bow was four years out of date, but the craft appeared seaworthy and saleable. Three outboard motors of varying horsepower stood clamped to homemade stands. Two trolling motors shared another rack. Boog found a small push mower but no gas can. There was a two-pump place back up the road called *Party Store and Bait*. When Laurence woke up, the chore would have to be done.

Laurence swam in the suit jacket and the trousers were impossibly long. *Pere* Emile had been a beanpole while his youngest boy was wiry and slight as a cattail reed. Or a piece of rebar, when he took his shirt off. The jacket proved to be misshapen as well, Boog reminded Laurence of another infirmity Pere had suffered along with the melanoma. *"Empha-zema done that, I bet. He always walk with shoulders hunch over.*

Laurence and he, both, invested in white, collared shirts at the *Wal-Mart*. Neither of them knew or remembered how to knot a necktie so *that* was a savings. They put their jeans into the old washer and it still worked. There was no detergent to be found so they squirted in of dish soap from under the sink. When it came time to dry them, the dryer motor ran, crabbily, but the drum wouldn't tumble.

"Okay. There's a close-line outside," Laurence said. "I'll try'n' find her steam iron for our jeans."

"We shouldn't worry," Boog said. "There won't likely be nobody more'n the priest."

Luckily, humidity was low throughout Sunday afternoon. Their jeans moved lazily on the stained line which the brothers expected to part at any moment. They changed underwear and tee-shirts. They loaded these grubby items and ran the washer again while pounding a few more *Jax* brought home from Party Store and Bait. Out on the front porch in *Pere* Emile's old robe that fit him like a sleeping bag, Laurence commented that the sun seemed to shine directly on their trousers.

Boogaloo sat next to him, peeled down to his boxers. Sporadic pickup trucks passing the homestead, most towing boat trailers, paid them no mind. "I wouldn't read no mir'cle into it," he told Laurence.

On Monday, then, in clear weather, the LaVelle brothers interred their *Mamere*. The women and some old men who showed up in *Chauvin* were rural neighbors or parish members—a Venn diagram of the area with a broad, overlapping center. These were way more mourners than they would ever have expected and almost all of them carried casserole dishes into a Fellowship wing of the sanctuary. *Father Mike* had made himself way too involved; probably assisted by *Thibadeaux* behind the counter at Party Store and Bait just two miles down the road from home. Those were the only two

430   CHRIS DUNGEY

community figures with whom Laurence had spoken. So, there would be an unexpected hot meal.

A strong revulsion to the noise and the scurrying rat humanity at that *Wal-Mart* up past *Houma* lead to several visits to the versatile wayside stop for bread and beer. The country store was as much a clearing house for communications as was the parish office. This was where *Pere* Emile took most of his trade on the way out to the surviving wetlands or *Lake Boudreaux*. It was sufficient to his modest needs and a taste of bayou life for his fishing clients: Ice cold Jax, red worms, cigarette makings, and gator jerky. Thibideaux was a reliable link in the verbal grapevine and one of the boys *may* have let slip the day and time for *Mamere's* proceedings. Or, Father Mike stopped in for bourbon.

The cleric was a weak link and the word had surely spread in every direction from him. No one who might be interested knew the LaVelle boys' cell numbers, but they knew to call the priest when they heard about *Mamere*. With the church and parsonage just five miles north in *Chauvin, His Eminence* was well positioned to influence events. Even the graveyard nearby lent to convenience for assembling a fair number of locals. The Father gave in to the Lavelle's requests concerning the *Rosary* without much argument. Who knew it was supposed to be performed the night before? It didn't matter to *them* if there was no viewing at the funeral parlor, which would have been the normal venue for a *Rosary*. *Father Mike* reminded them of this, to no avail. *Padre, let's just do everythin' together at the same time 'n' we'll get outta yer life.* After

EVACUATION ROUTE

431

a few brief sit-downs (the Father sat) that sounded like a good idea to him.

Laurence was unable to find a picture other than a few snapshots taken by Murielle. *These prob'ly ten year old. When was those one-time-use throw away cam'ras pop'lar?* No appropriately large portraits were available to place on the lid so they left the casket open. The brothers were, perhaps, ashamed to see the old woman they had visited so infrequenly in the last five years. But *Father Mike's* will prevailed on this, explaining that there had been no visitation; neighbors and friends deserved to bid farewell up close and personal.

He instructed that the casket be parked in the narthex when *Dropeux Family Mortuary Parlor* arrived to deliver it from *Houma*. When the doors were opened, old women and a few codgers crowded around it. The first to arrive got ringside views while some bought and lighted votive candles. Laurence and Boog took a peek when they arrived. The mortician hadn't added much. *Mamere* had probably last worn makeup during the Reagan years.

"She would like it," Boog said, his voice thickening for the first time since leaving Tampa. "All this big deal."

Laurence said, "*Mamere* look like herself, very much." His last stop for a quick visit was eight months ago before doing his time at *Terrebonne*.

Boog, who calculated that he had been absent for two years, agreed. "I came for *Pere* Emile last days." Was he really going to choke up? "Never even thought a borrowin' some morphine."

432   CHRIS DUNGEY

"I asked *Mamere* for dollars to deposit in the commissary. She had $14 to spare."

He dipped his fingers into the Holy Water touched a watering eye with that finger. Entering the sanctuary, he did a split second kneel in the center aisle then genuflected. Boog crossed himself for the first time in those two years, distracting his emotions long enough to avoid weeping like la folle. He followed his brother to an uncomfortable front pew. Uncomfortable, because Boog never liked to have strangers behind him in *any* social setting. The viewing and ad hoc visitation wasn't just for a last look at *Mamere,* he suspected. *These old folk want a good look at LaVelle prodigal who has returned. Take picture, then, to have it last.*

To Boog, the *Rosary*, however abridged by agreement with *Father Mike*, still seemed to drag. After the first few lines the sequence came back to him sufficiently that he could lip sync through the *Our Fathers*. Laurence and he, both, envisioned only the one famous *Psalm*, to be spoken just before the actual interment. This truncated *Rosary* felt interminable, even with the collar of his new shirt unbuttoned. *Ceremony is spun outta control by Father Mike.*

The *Drapeau Family* sons closed then trundled the casket back out into the narthex. There, it became evident that *Father Mike* had, once again, been steering the course of events. Six vaguely familiar faces took positions around the casket and lifted it off the gurney. Across the parking lot and through a wrought iron gate they bore it. The LaVelle boys and an assortment of shirt-tail relatives walked behind.

EVACUATION ROUTE 433

Lawrence put his hand out to rest it on the lid of the casket. He spoke softly to the last bearer on his side. "Are you that Patrice Rolan, use to hunt duck with Pere Emile?" "Oui, Laurence. I have aged since he pass. This my boy Eugene, you fish with some times. Both when y'all was runts." The older man gestured at the adolescent opposite him.

"Merci. Merci, to both," Laurence said

When he saw Laurence's gesture, Boog did likewise. "Merci, Rolans. I remember."

The cargo arrived at its final destination and the men lowered it back onto the gurney with which the *Dropeaux* men had rattled ahead. This was cranked down a few notches. The casket was rolled back into an opened vault, plunk on top of *Pere* Emile. Then the padre made the whole business official with the familiar *Psalm*, the only tradition the Lavelle brothers needed. *There we go. Finally, the fearing a no evil 'n' the valley a that shadow. I like always to hear this part.*

Some spicy dishes were whafting fumes out the open door of the Fellowship wing. These lured the mourners back, conversing in low voices across the parking lot. *A good seafood jambalaya?* Boog wondered: *Maybe crawfish etouffee? Are the grievin' brothers in-title for leftovers? Do I gotta speak? I aint speakin' except aroun' the room.*

Laurence did not even wait overnight before heading out in Pere Emile's old pickup truck. He loaded items of value into the bed; a chainsaw, a circular saw, the two trolling motors, and the biggest outboard, a fairly recent model Mercury. He dragged a small, four-gallon shop vacuum from the shed. "Just minus these from my share, if any," he called. "Did ya ever know *Pere* Emile 'r' *Mamere* to clean out the truck cab?"

"It don't sound like 'em."

"This he use for dryin' out the boat, I think." Laurence concluded. "Clean as the gator tooth. No rust in it." In a few minutes he carried a small trash bag from the truck. "Ya sure ya don't mind me to take objects a…a mebbe some value?"

"No, brother. Best profit share of the house is enough for me. Why don't hitch up the boat an' take?"

Laurence scratched his head. He knotted the bag and dropped it at the road, by the mailbox. "I already think on it. But there is no license on the back 'n' I am loaded heavy enough, too."

"Ya should go through closets one more time, anyway." Boog made a sandwich from the funeral cold cuts that were offered, in the end, to the grieving brothers. "An' I'll make a best try to find alla you with some money."

EVACUATION ROUTE 435

"All these things," Laurence nodded toward the driveway. "that I need to raise more funds 'long the way. I have got cash for mebbe two tank of gas. For coffee 'n' cigarettes, mebbe a day."

Laurence took a last scavenge through the parental bedroom. There wasn't much there.. *Mamere* owned nothing other than junk jewelry. He lifted what appeared to be some very fancy *Rosary* beads from the box. *For the Lord she could get all adorn up, but for no one else. Wait, now. She must have them plain ones wrap 'round her hands forever into the eternal, mebbe? But this box.... Looks old 'n' ornate. Cajun craftsmen. Hell, you don't ever know. Find someone to check it out on that eBay.*

He must add *owns laptop* to his checklist for the next female companion. *No regeton, either.* Into the bottom of a brown paper bag with handles, Laurence placed the box; zirconium, faux pearls and all. He took the family Bible from the bottom drawer of a nightstand. *All our births 'n' death. Someone should keep. Someday young ones wish to know. Mebbe deliver it to Marielle, our most steadiest. Track her down, livin' up on that cold prair-ee.*

He made a last pass through the kitchen. "The microwave. You need it?" It was very old but clean. The timer was a knob you turned to the required cook time. It had two power levels.

"Ya want I have to eat cold, leftover gumbo?" Boog thought for a moment and then relented. "I can do. You take it. We haven't use it even once, I can think of."

"Merci, Beau-regard."

Laurence took a turn at the dinette, making sandwiches for the road until the *Hillbilly Bread* was gone. He stacked them into the empty bread bag and put that into a second shopping bag, this one plastic. He dropped *that* into three more layers of bag along with a handful of cookies in a *Ziplock*. "Yer outta bread 'n' meat, now, brother. Sorry. We both have each other cell number, yeah?"

Boog stood up, still chewing the last of *his* three meat, two cheese sandwich. He couldn't speak with his mouth full but moved to embrace Laurence, who'd piled his final treasures by the door. "Listen. I will see ya when I see ya." He broke loose from hugging and handed his brother a couple of wadded twenties from his jeans. "Hope this help. Come by to Tampa 'n' ask for the *Knuckledicks*. Ya'd be welcome always unless yer bein' chased."

"Merci, again, brother. You will 'member Marielle when the sale is made?" Laurence patted his brother's damp back.

"A course. An' I hope ya don't have to beg at no gas pumps. But ya see it alla time so I guess there ain't any shame left in it."

They walked out to the old truck together. *Motor in this thing, he'll be tradin' that junk for gas today, later.*

"Well then, *pote ou bien*." Laurence clunked the door shut.

"*Pote ou bien, ami*," Boog said. "Better oil that hinge."

Laurence backed out onto 56 and headed slowly north. Boog wasn't near to shedding a tear but his eyes followed his brother to the first kink in the road. "*Pote ou* bien," he whispered. *Any glimpse of a loved one might be the last*, he was thinking. Not because of the manner in which his siblings chose to live, but for the darkness he and they carried away from this place years ago. That tavern parking-lot beating and the high school lot, later? The reptile whisper of the *feu follet* that crept at dusk from the deepest glades and wetlands, its juju lights seen even from churchyards?

But then it was time to shake off the *fantome*, to saddle up and go in the opposite direction. *Only* as far as *Party Store and Bait* for now; buy some bread, more beer, and wait for the meemaw real estate lady tomorrow.

Oh, but b'fore that...What tricks have Voduon dropped on most unlucky Boogaloo now? Two Louisiana patrol cars and one from *Terrebonne Parish* were parked in the LaVelle driveway and on the lawn when he came back from the supply run. He was daydreaming about hoops yet to jump through before returning to Tampa and the bosom of *Knuckledick* brotherhood. He was halfway turned off the road, too late to pinwheel out of there. One of the State bulls, a black man, stepped up quickly to grab hold of one handlebar. The guy knew what he was doing and reached to push the ignition button, killing the engine. Behind the black one came sauntering a coonass Smokey Bear. "You are Beauregard Lavelle?"

Outnumbered but still belligerent enough for verbal brawling, Boog slowly removed his sunglasses. "Are you sayin' this to me or askin'? Yer accent I cannot hear through it. Who want to know this and do they have the warrant?"

The *Smokey Bear* flashed a grin and a wink at the *Mountie* easing in behind Boog. "He don't look much like his sheet. He look like young genius at *Best Buy*. "You, Beau-regard, have got a outstandin' warrant that you never comply with, *ami*. Along with, now, a *Failure to Appear*," the Mountie said. "You was the very disgraceful son, warrant says. You trash *Li'l Caillou Bar* where they was kind enough throw yer *Pere* Emile the wake. Then you skip before payin' damage. You lookin' at prob'ly three weeks with interest. You still owe the rest'tution, too, *coujon*."

Boog stared at the ground, but not with his usual gathering of affront, readying to explode. *Why they didn't see the truck a Laurence, loaded up like he just rob a flea market? But they wouldn't have no beef with him 'till he miss first probation visit.* "Alla that slip my mind, *ami*," he growled. "I had heavy grief then."

"Whut's that, baw?" Now Smokey Bear leaned in to close-talk his mint *Copenhagen* breath at Boog's face.

There were too many of them, even for Boog. Maybe even for himself, Wood, 'n' *The Darkness* altogether. *Thank to God or Ja too I leave the Glock in the shed under potting soil bag 'n' more praise if they don't take everythin' apart for evidence.* "I just forget, with my heart heavy, so." Boog began to slowly dismount from the *Gold Wing*. The officers backed away so as not to leave themselves at too close quarters. "Just lemme lock up the place? Mebbe put in the bike?"

Again the bear and *Mountie* exchanged telepathic eye contact. "I think that be fine, Hoss. We pat you down first," Smokie said.

Boog lifted his arms. *Be cool. They gonna touch their hand's on. Easy, Boog*

EVACUATION ROUTE   439

"You got anythin' on your person gonna poke or cut me?" The black one said, who *had* to be a *Louisiana State* patrolman. (There were *no* black officers to be found south of *Houma*) He began a vigorous inspection up and down, out and back, of Boog's extremities.

"Nah. Nothin'. He clean," the other cops were informed. "You can put this ride away now. You want it inna house, yeah?"

Boog did not reply but began to walk the heavy machine toward the front steps.

"Be safest there," he said, finally. "Can y'all gimme the helpin' hand?"

"Hell, why not? He didn't bring us riot like my dispatcher said might be." *Smokie Bear* came up from behind to push on the other side.

"An' you think can I take my change a underwear? An' The cell for my call?"

The *Mountie* arrived to help push the *Gold Wing* up the steps. " You ain't shy a takin' advantage, are ya boy? The phone, you just gonna turn it in to properties, anyways. We wait, you put on three pair. Go ahead 'n' get a tee shirt, too I think you prob'ly have quick appearance tomorrow."

"Does your skivs go with orange?" The black cop laughed.

The other two joined in. "Good one, Cletus."

When the bike was safely on its kickstand in the front room, *these pigs not so bad,* Boog thought. He figured now that they might *not* work him over in the back seat. *Ahh, for reason bein' there's only one in each car.* Boog mumbled his *thanks.* "Only one more thing?

I can call *Thibideaux* at *Party Store 'n' Bait*? Get 'im keep eye on this place?"

"You can call the Gov'nor 'n' the 'ttorney General, you want to, till we drive through the gate."

Then Boog layered on his underwear while all the cops watched. They helped themselves to Boog's cold Jax they brought in with the bike. "Won't go to waste. Should I give 'im one?" One of the *Mounties* asked *Smokie.*

"I 'spect it's okay. Put the rest inna fridge for *Thibideaux.* He a good ol' boy."

Chapter Twenty-Two

Their security was becoming lax and Bella felt some relief. She was afraid to explore, too deeply, Merry's fading paranoia. She would leave *that* sweet, sleeping puppy lie until it could explain the whys and wherefores of this change in attitude. They even ventured out in the *Narcissus* on the same night once, though they boarded separately and then avoided each other.

When they made this joint expedition, just before the 4th of July, Bella brought up her own concern about leaving the Tracker in the parking-lot for five hours:

"I dunno Bell," Merry said. "Ah don't see no alternative if we wanta go out together now 'n' again. Ah just felt that damn, wad-da-ya-call-it? A kinda nasty ol' presence, like we're bein' watched."

"So, in other words, your mystery biker," Bella said. "You saw him just a couple of times and we have been cringing ever since. He probably live in this neighborhood."

Bella opened the passenger-side door, ready to walk to the ticket gate. They would arrive at the entrance separately then wait, apart,

442 CHRIS DUNGEY

with their complimentary pre-boarding drinks. "Even so, it is best we don't do this too often."

"Ah have felt better about it, but we did make eye contact, Bell, that ol' biker 'n' me," Merry said. "It felt plenty weird for a couple weeks. Yer prob'ly right, though. Ah don't think it's the same worry as *you* had from the casino. We can mebbe do us a girl-on-girl in there for guys sometimes. They don't pay us no special mind in there, Ah don't think. But on the boat we gotta not know each other."

Bella closed the door and pulled her tortoise-shell shades down from the crown of her head. *You're wearing those ironically, right?* She'd been asked. *That is a good thing to remember, to repeat.* Her hair was beginning to take on its usual brownish highlights as it always did in summer. It was growing longer, natural curling like many angel hair springs coveting to touch her forehead and shoulders "We have not done that show in a long time," she said. "We must think what it should earn by now."

"Just a idea but it oughta earn very good, the way them *Knuckledicks* was always droolin'. An' Ah didn't totally hate it, Ah mighta told ya." Merry tipped the visor down to use the yellowing makeup mirror. It was her time of year to apply large quantities of sunscreen. "Anyways, Ah'll see ya back at dockin' time. If ya don't score, just sit back in the car 'n' Ah'll be right along, either, or Ah'll wave ya to go on home."

"Bon voyage, duckling," Bella said "Be safe."

"Back atcha, Bell. Ah'll be along."

Not so far away, Wood-Chuck Spurgeon idled his Fat Boy into a cul-de-sac of modest seven-figure dwellings out on *Clearwater Beach*. *Latana Avenue*. He continued to be amazed at how little a million bucks bucks bought a person on the Gulf side of the causeway. He tucked his ride in behind a silver *Lexus* that probably didn't fit into the dinky garage here.

He would have been wandering around out here until nightfall, even on this, his second trip, if not for an investment in a *Garmin GPS* unit. Why had he come so late to this technology? Of course Boog knew every alley and byway of Tampa proper. No neighborhood, it seemed, was without its horn dog or whore monger. *The rich,* Wood snorted. Boog was still riding a thin mattress in some 3rd World jail in Louisiana, spiking up litter and pitch forking road kill just to get some fresh air. Likely a lot a thin grits 'n' baloney for dinner. His predicament gave Archie *The Darkness* Caulkins a chuckle every time the subject came up with Wood, the *Knuckledicks'* so-called *Head of Procurrment*. Wood discretely reminded the Chief that Boog was a brother in custody. The same situation also gave Ivan "The Terrible" Dresbach a second income as bartender. Out of Wood's pocket, of course.

"I know, I know, Wood. Yer absolutely right 'n' I needa check myself. But tell the truth, ain't it more relaxin' around here."

Wood looked Caulkins in the eye. A grin tried to shape his closed lips. "Mmmm hmmm. But I ain't sayin' it out loud,"

There was some glimmer of light back in that distant bayou for both Wood and his incarcerated sidekick. A daily land-line phone call related that Boog was just four days from finishing his stint. At each cigarette/water break of the *Terrebone* trustee's roadside crew, he was maintaining communication with his real estate person, greasing a guard's palm for a few minutes on the man's cell. This lady (Boog spoke of her as promoting *fuck me* with the throatiness of her voice) found a buyer at an agreeable price for the old homestead. The closing required only Boog's discharge from the orange jumpsuits, his presentation of the deed, and his signature. He promised that he would cash the check, mount his *Gold Wing* and be back on the road. He intended to ride straight home this time and leave all bayou and familial *fantome* behind. *For good 'n' all, I will not be drag down myself further,* he'd told Wood.

Wood shut off the Fat Boy and studied the bungalow that a million and change could buy a person. Did the gentleman inside dream of recouping even 700K in this market if he wished to change residences? Despite all market calamities, the fellow remained a quite bullish tipper according to Dina Sanchez who was currently plying her trade in there. She'd been at it for five hours.

The client was referred by Caulkins on the basis of having participated in some long-ago misdemeanors together as high school students. *I wonder which one of 'em graduated.* Now Wood enjoyed a chuckle of his own.

The date must be going well into overtime which was normally fine with Wood. When she came out, Dina would turn over the basic fee to him to be parted out back to her on payday. This arrangement was meant to keep the girls coming in for Boog's peptalks and to maintain their hygiene regimen. The incentive was probably unnecessary by now since they were all thinking of themselves as *Knuckledick* girls. Dina would give Wood a tip but keep whatever *extra*s Harvey had paid for. The usually generous gratuity made it worth the trip and Wood's time. But, he would have to remind her that Luanne and Mandy were waiting back at the Clubhouse for their own home delivery. He didn't mind making up time with the fresh, *shadow economy* cash in both their pockets. The girls tended to hang onto him extra tightly when he was gunning the bike to get back on schedule. It was a bonus; a pleasant treat when they'd had time to shower after their exertions.

Chapter Twenty-Three

In high summer, the horseshoe street of *The Glade* was often deserted from 10 am until the short, tropical gloaming. The most dedicated walkers did their work early. The rest waited for near darkness. When Walt Bocewicz finally abandoned the ship of his renovated mobile home, his window unit ACs were no longer keeping him comfortable. He preferred not to sequester himself in the master bedroom with door closed and curtains tightly drawn, more evidence of his reclusive reputation. *Might as well take my chances with dehydration outdoors.*

Walt's quest for shade began in the Florida room, which, with a metal roof above, became stifling and untennable by 10 am. A new bag chair (too cheap at $6 bucks to resist from *Wal-Mart*, though it had no drink holder) was carried outside. He grasped a two-liter bottle of water ($1 from Ollie's) in the other with a battered hardcover of Norman Mailer's *"Tough Guy's Don't Dance"* tucked under his armpit. (From *Turning Yellow Book Nook* in Crystal

River, $1.) He wouldn't be trading it back now after leaving a perspiration stain on the cover.

Walt followed the shadow cast by his home all the way around to the still quite dark patio in back. He soon drowsed in from a meditative view of the thriving jungle beyond the chain link border of *The Glade*. The AC stuck in a rear window of the master bedroom exhaled a steady drip pattering onto the patio blocks. *Might be my morning rainforest if I close my eyes.* He closed his eyes. Provincetown in winter sounded like a quaint but dangerous place. The preoccupation with alcohol and drugs of the locals in winter constituted the danger aspect. Were there that many murders and beheadings or were they in Mailer's imagination? Insular communities, cabin fever (or cottage) could go sour. *Too expensive for my budget. Even a no-plumbing shack in the dunes.*

His mobile home, on the other hand, was transformed into a marvel to all of *The Glade* residents and a source of buried chagrin to Bobby Higgs who'd been too lazy to perceive that diamond in the rough. Expenditures for, admittedly, cut-rate powerwashing and semiprofessional (The Publix bulletin board) excavation of maturing vegetation in his eavestroughs, did wonders for his home's appearance.

The economy was creating a vast pool of unskilled laborers, some of whom actually showed up on the agreed day and time. Nevertheless, Walt performed some tasks himself. A generous wash of muriatic acid, applied to the oil spills in his carport, was followed by his own vigorous scrubbing. All of these brightened results were now on display to the walking public. But only Dar-

448   CHRIS DUNGEY

lene, so far, could bear witness to Walt's notion of restored interior design.

All of the walls were painted after vigorous scrubbing. Walt took no chances that the meth/dope/tobacco would someday, in this pervasive humidity, resurface. He worked quickly through to the end of June, priming every surface, ceilings especially, with Kilz. Then he chose the faintest blue tint in an eggshell white, his concept of a distant horizon, where sky meets sea. He did not skimp on quality, the paint pouring like a thick gel into the pan. Darlene helped when she could but Walt hated to impinge on the sleep she needed between her shifts at *B-dub's*. (With seniority, she chose the most lucrative ones, rather than a fixed schedule). And, he had to admit that he was still a bit hesitant to allow her *too* much stake in the place. Probably silly since she showed little inclination toward cohabiting. Yet. But how could he balk? *You'd better not rule that out. You'd be stepping on your own dick once again.*

With practice, his drips and runs became fewer and further between. When they *did* work together, their rest breaks were taken languorously in the bedroom, or sprawled on the speckled drop cloth, admiring the ceilings. Was the painting of former meth trailers a possible career path for him, if the worst should occur and he must earn additional income?

He did not attempt to install the blond wood Pergo on his own but he *did* pick it out to compliment his tropical theme. *Sunbaked Sand. Pricey, but perfect. Maybe I'll just stick to honing my painting talents.* Skilled flooring tradesmen with an Angie's List endorsement were retained for this operation. They laid it

EVACUATION ROUTE

throughout, except in the kitchen where stains could be expected and in bathrooms where he enjoyed the slate. .

Walt and Darlene made two short road trips to flea markets and antique barns (of the *pole* variety) in search of the right tropical furniture. Even the connubial couch might soon be reupholstered if Walt could spur his flagging summer ambition to call around for estimates. As his first acquired piece, he was reluctant to part with it. Was it accruing sentimental value? He and Dar had left no traces so far.

Around noon, the sky above *The Glade* clouded over to signal the first five- minute rain shower of the day. Walt roused himself from the home improvement reverie, stood, and guzzled a major portion of his water. Heedless of a soaking, he rebagged the chair and carried his other loafing accessories back around to the front. From the Florida room, he resumed his vigil of rain pounding straight down onto the street. The timpani of the carport roof was too loud for dozing.

The deluge ceased as abruptly as it began. Steam poured up from the hot asphalt of the street. *Rinse and repeat,* Walt mused. Darlene should be awake by now after her *Bdub*'s night shift. They planned to meet at the pool. He found his flipflops and a rag to wipe down his favorite lounge chair. He brought a second water and his book.

The smallest of geckos bounced, refreshed, leaping in the postage-stamp front yards; over, under and out of everyone's landscape masonry as Walt made his way toward the *Association Clubhouse*. If the Great Jehovah himself had cast these tiny creatures earthward amidst the downpour to castigate him for past and current transgressions, Walt could not have proven otherwise. They were suddenly everywhere, traversing the pocked road surface from one puddle to the next. He moved slowly, zig-zagging to avoid stepping on any. *Do we have a truce with the geckos?* He smiled at another *Seinfeld* reference his brain had just given him, unbidden. It surfaced from buried memories from any of several smoky rehab Common Room. Who, or how had the tinny audio of the television programming been wrested away from early evening game shows?

He entered *The Glade* Clubhouse, waved at Bobby Higgs's flushed, perspiring head, just visible through the office window. Intent on his computer screen, the park manager did not see him. Walt went out the slider door onto the pool deck, apparently the first visitor of the day. He circled to a far corner, to the reclining lounge chair he always chose. More of the property defining chain link guarded his back from the dripping jungle, while birds renewed their pre-rain discourse. The table umbrellas had yet to open *their* blooms so he cranked up the one nearest his seat. He wiped down the lounger and placed his water jug next to it before making himself comfortable.

"Hey, g'morning!" Higgs entered the patio and quickly unfurling the other four umbrellas. "Shoulda left 'em up. Never got the wind we was s'pposed to get last night."

"Can't be too careful," Walt said. "I suppose these can take off like hang gliders."

Higgs pushed water off the first table with his forearm. "Oh, I know it. I've had to fetch 'em back outta the jungle at great risk to

EVACUATION ROUTE

myself. An' from the other end a the park. Fortunate they didn't smash somebody's lanai."

Walt watched as an ellipsis of cigarette smoke approached on the other side of the redwood fence. Then Gracie Goodrich, a prospective new boyfriend sniffing up behind, entered the patio. Higgs glanced tracer rounds for a split second at the fellow, another new resident bachelor. Bobby probably wouldn't maintain the hostility for too long since Max Widener purchased one of the laggard new models without much haggling.

Gracie was coming out of her shell, it occurred to everyone. But, this guy was clinging to dehydrated hippy roots, his hair in a very long, yellowing-white ponytail. In what universe was he Gracie's type? He was a smoker and also cultivated one of those awful Civil War beards that were beginning to appear; some sort of manhood celebration akin to drum circles. Bobby must be assuming that Gracie'd be back in general play before too long. *Max is older than me, for Chrissake,* Walt thought. *That abrasive personality can't be hid for long. Just bide your time with grace, Bobby. Ooops. Or, for Gracie. Heh, heh.*

"Good morning, Bobby. Walter," Gracie greeted them, her voice its usual flute solo.

'Good morning," Walt said, folding the corner of his page in the Mailer as a bookmark.

"Yeah, it is," Bobby managed. "Mostly."

"Hotter'n a two dollar pistol," Max grumbled. "Mebbe I can bake out some a my rheumatism."

452   CHRIS DUNGEY

The fellow was taller, even, than Walt, and already more stoop shouldered. *Played a little basketball, did you? Wide receiver at some junior college in Texas? How's that feel now? And why in the world am I feeling protective of Higgs?* "That's why we're here, friend," Walt said. "Bake out the follies of youth."

But, before he could double back to kinder thoughts for the newcomer, Darlene came out of the Association room through the sliding door. "Mornin' ever'one!"

Higgs shook his head in poorly masked disgust and made his escape around Darlene. He closed the door behind him.

"Better lookit yer watch, sweetie." Max instructed. "You oversleep?"

Forget about kinder thoughts from me, a-hole. Oh, my! Higgs gave the finger to Widener's back through the glass. *I hope Gracie saw that.*

"Hey, I'm still on *Bdub*'s time 'n' it don't have much definition a mornin'," Darlene said. She came around the pool clockwise, avoiding the table where Gracie and her ass-hat admirer were unloading their sunbathing paraphernalia. Higgs reemerged with a coffee travel-sipper in hand. He followed Darlene. Widener could put up his own umbrella.

"Hey, babe," Walt said.

Darlene gave him a quick peck on the cheek as she plunked down her own beach tote. "Hey to you 'n' y'all," she said. "Ain't it hot, though? Between the AC at work 'n' this sauna we're livin' in here, I'm 'bout to have me a big 'ol plugged up head cold."

EVACUATION ROUTE

"I've got a neti pot ya can borrow, sweetie pie." Max called across the languid blue water. The last of the steam reaction from the rain ghosted off the surface, chlorine in its vapors.

"Ah ain't turnin' 'round," Darlene whispered. Her back to the pool, she leaned forward and spoke toward Walt's chest.

"I'm trying to be nice, *sweetie-pie.* Any reaction will just encourage him."

"Ah can't picture ya bein' anythin' but nice." Darlene pulled a padded chair from under the patio table and dragged it near to Walt's lounge.

"My memory is shoddy, but I've never been very intimidating. Coulda been a real bad boy during a blackout. We'll never know. An edge might be a new benchmark to strive for."

Darlene brushed water off the synthetic cushion cover before sitting. "Is it too early for a stiff drink?"

"Not if you're on *Bdub* time." Walt marked the book again with his thumb. He reached over to pet Darlene's knee. "I'm barely resisting to initiate my own futile hostilities. I might have to go back to the trailer for a *Xanax* unless that old boy drowns pretty soon."

"Don't ya dare leave me alone out here," Darlene said. She patted Walt's hand. She removed a *Diet Coke* in a foam Koozey from her beach tote.

"What's the latest update from your boy?" Walt asked. "Is his fact finding visit still on hold?"

"Same ol', same ol', near's Ah can figure. Haven't heard anythin' new. Guess he's still pinned down b'cuz of his hair-brained assistant bein' in the klink. An' Ah also wanta speak up for 'im wantin' to see his Ma." Darlene popped the tab on her cola. "It *ain't* totally just for checkin' you out that he's comin'. He owes me a long visit 'n' himself a vacation. He must be busier 'n' all get-out."

"Well, why don't they just hire somebody?" Walt posed the rhetorical question only to further polite conversation. He surmised that there was some gang format involved, and frankly, he didn't care if Charlie *ever* showed up. The idea that he must pass some kind of inspection by the hood offspring of his girlfriend was beginning to feel a little degrading.

"Ya'd think. But Ah guess that ain't how it works. In the less civilized kinda club, anyways." Darlene sipped and coughed. "*That* is some powerful carbonation. Nah see, their seniority system's tighter 'n'...Ah don't know what. The *Post Office*? They're pretty tight, right? An' it's for sure tighter 'n' any wait staff Ah ever worked on. Plus, this ol' boy that Charlie's holdin' a place for is a definition of a sociopath for vi'lance 'n' mayhem."

"Hard to get fired from the PO I understand," Walt agreed. "It'll be fine, whenever he comes along. I'm easy to get along with."

"Ah know it, baby. Ah keep hopin' the boy'll grow outta some a his petty attitudes. Ah'm forever remindin' him Ah ain't no dormat, like mebbe Ah was when he was a youngun. He mighta witnessed some pretty warpin' scenes before Ah acquired my present assertiveness."

"I cannot picture you without your present assertiveness," Walt smiled, recalling some of those moments when Darlene put herself forward.

EVACUATION ROUTE

Then a shudder ran up his back. The high-def audio was still with him, ready to play; perfectly cued up, preserved with marvelous clarity: *That screeching exchange of f-bombs beneath a porch light. He'd returned to a former residence after a doubleshift at the cinemas. Wife Number Two batted a large bucket of popcorn (with butter and cheese flavoring), into the shrubbery. He brought it over for kid number two, the boy, without the mandatory phone call for permission. Did he wake her from her beauty sleep? He didn't care if she had company.*

Then there was that day of tremens and crawling skin as he led both children by their cotton candy hands through the Happiest Place on Earth. Might as well use his employee discount. This benefit was achieved by a rare stay on the same job for more than ninety days. He had, predictably, celebrated the night before. He didn't forget his kids, though. He had no idea how that day trip was miraculously coordinated. (Mom? Warren?) He'd actually been allowed to transport both of his children in a motor vehicle. Did wife #2 assume that Warren would accompany them? Someone must have used whatever remained in escrow of family charm and persuasion to arrange the joint visitation with both kids. Any such future excursions were lost, however, when he left them waiting alone in the endless line for the Teacups. He needed to sprint far enough out of their sight to hurl into a trash barrel. They weren't old enough or cruel enough, then, to disavow him by looking in another direction. But they had not yet inherited his guile, either. Daddy trusted us on our own for just a few minutes. He had to barf.

A sudden explosion of water at the other end of the pool announced Max's immersion via cannonball. The farthest ring of collateral splash reached the back of Darlene's neck and Walt's leg. A few drops appeared on the yellowing pages of the Mailer.

"Ain't ya s'pposed to yell *cannonball*?" Darlene spoke to Walt without turning to dignify Gus with any attention.

"It's the polite thing," Walt said.

"Hey, you lovebirds! C'mon in! Feels like the rain cooled off this bathwater." Max hung onto the lip of the pool, halfway to the deep end, shaking water out of his hair and beard like an aging golden retriever.

Darlene still did not deign to turn and face the annoying presence.

Then, a vestige of his depleted testosterone taking him by surprise, Walt said: "There's no diving in the fucking pool, friend." Behind his sunglasses, he watched Max's life-of-the-party countenance falter.

Max's head tilted and his eyes narrowed in reappraisal. "My bad, sir, sweetie pie," he called. "Please accept my humble apology."

Facetious, okay. But it looks like I won't get my ass kicked, Walt thought. *Bobby, for God's sake. Get your big butt out here and put up some resistance. Give poor Gracie a viable alternative.*

Now Darlene gaped at Walt. "Who *are* you," she whispered. " Ah guess Ah'm gonna peel down to my bathin' suit right now 'n' not worry about this yah-hoo. What were we discussin'?"

EVACUATION ROUTE

"We were on Charlie. What's your plan? Are you going to introduce me or something? Go out for a nice family meal?" Walt tipped another swig of his drink. *Doesn't stay cold for long.*

Darlene passed the soda from hand to hand in its Koozey. She stared at the redwood planks beneath her feet. When she next looked up at Walt, she said, "I dunno, hon. Are we there yet?"

Walt poured the rest of his water out and it seeped quickly through the cracks beneath him. *These are about due for some stain and waterproofing, Bobby.* "I guess we should define what *there* means. That sounds like Slick Willy Clinton. Any other relationship *I've* been in, which isn't many, the fifth or sixth months begin to pose questions about an endgame. But, I guess I ought to pass muster with Charlie, whether we're *there* or not."

Darlene's smile seemed a resigned one. "That sounds reasonable. Ah'd say that Ah could use you up for a long time into the future. But, mebbe that ol' line about 'takin' it to the next level,' so to speak, just ain't in my vocabulary anymore. Is that okay? That's to your advantage, more 'r less? Does there need to be a endgame?"

Walt shrugged. To his relief, the quiet, broken only by the filter motor, did not become loaded with any kind of suspense. Even Widener treaded water almost silently. *I guess I should start to think of it that way. It's just a concept I've never confronted before. My former wives sharpened their fillet knives with no concept of laissez faire.* Walt stood up and stretched. "You think that vending machine water is halfway cold."

"You can give Bobby a good boot in his keister if it ain't." Darlene began to unbutton her shirt, eyed Gus Widener and paused.

With a sneer in his direction, she resumed uncovering the black one-piece. "I don't believe in kicking a man when he's down." Walt rolled his feet off the lounge and stood up, patting for his wallet. "Of course, I might change my mind if that machine steals from me."

After Gus Widener hoisted himself out of the pool, Walt left his wallet and the fresh drink (cold enough, so far) to follow Darlene down the ladder. He intended to swim in his cutoffs. Bobby never said anything though these were supposed to be prohibited. Unraveling blue threads could clog the filter, read one of the rules on the gate and on the glass slider into the Association room. Whatever cooling the rain had performed on the surface margin of pool water was going away as the couple stood at chest depth.

Walt faced the parking lot side while Darlene looked into the jungle beyond the chain-link. "Is he eyein' at me?"

"Nope," Walt told her softly. "He has decided to be a gentleman. All his attentions have returned to Gracie."

"Lucky her. He must be a small tits guy."

"Hey, don't be arrogant. I used to be." Walt recovered his smile. "I've only recently discovered the pleasant nature of bounty."

Darlene gave him a quick kiss on the mouth. "You always know just the right thing to say, keep yerself outta trouble."

"Actually, I can hardly *ever* do that."

Then Darlene, the pool having emptied of annoyance, began to swim short laps. Walt dragged himself back onto the redwood planks. He eased out and moved, dripping, to his lounge. His guyaberra didn't seem any drier for being partially draped in the sun. But there was no way he'd be walking home without it covering his slack, pale flesh. It might be time for some regular lifting of objects other than furniture.

They walked back to Walt's place, Darlene in her shorts with a towel for a shawl. They didn't hold hands but strolled very close together, bumping hips. In broad daylight, Walt slid the screen door of the Florida room, metal scraping, aside for Darlene to enter. Then he applied fresh WD-40 to the track.

In the kitchen, she turned to him for an embrace. "Ah just wanta nap type of a nap." She said. "Can ya take one with me, just a nap."

"Sure," Walt smiled. "I'm *all* tuckered out after my strenuous morning."

Darlene dropped her towel and scuffed off her flipflops. "Ah need to make sure Ah ain't hurt your feelin's. Leastwise not too much,"

"I believe I'm comfortable with the status quo. In fact, I've been thinking that I probably owe *my* mom a few days." Walt placed his own bottle in the sink then went to the 'fridge to trade out the one from the vending machine. There was always a bottle waiting. The *Glade* tapwater was quite potable if sufficiently chilled "I didn't mention, yet, that my brother and his girlfriend have moved in with her. The place is big enough for *three* families. I just hope they aren't hiding some health issues from me. I don't know why they would, but I should try to be a little more involved."Darlene took his hand now and moved toward the hallway. "Gimme sip." She took Walt's fresh drink in her other hand. "C'mon. Lemme show you what Ah value most 'bout this *relationship.*"

"Oh, Lordy." Walt laughed. "Here comes the kinky stuff. I thought you just wanted a nap."

"Yep, Ah do." Darlene handed the water back and sat down on the bed. "With you. Close. An' only when Ah don't wanna be alone. Is that more selfish or more weird?"

Chapter
Twenty-Four

I t seemed to Boog that he had been on some of these same roads not long ago. He was on a different side of it now, legally and not for cleanup purposes. He walked on the shoulder with the flow of traffic coming at him, half-turning every ten feet or so to stick out his thumb. After Houma Municipal Corrections loaned him out to Terrabonne Trustee Camp, the maintenance guards insisted that the crews always work facing oncoming traffic. It was the correct way for pedestrians, yes, but Boog would never be convinced that it wasn't part of the punishment. Every passing motorist was awarded a long look at all the guilty, beat-with-an-ugly-stick faces. Wretched, meth and alcohol singed faces, mostly unshaven. And his.

For weeks he faced the ground, stabbing paper trash, *Mountain Dew* bottles darkly filled with a sickening saliva stew or chewing tobacco and cigarette butts. Or, he found himself suddenly slamming the tool repeated down on the head of a terrified snake. *Wrong place, wrong time.* The surprise they gave him made him angry, his long-untapped reservoir of adrenalin coursed into his blood. He would pause, then, to viciously boot the carcass far into the deeper roadside thickets. "Ya really got some issues there, ami." A guard once laughed. They wore only a Taser and pepper spray and were generally uninterested in anything but full garbage bags. And, probably a full homebound roster at the end of the day. "Yup," Boog answered, forcing a smile. *Ya don't even know half about it.* Now he kept his head up and did his best to look harmless, his personal effects in a clear hospital bag closed with a drawstring.

With one ride, he reached Hwy. 56 in an hour. Rain had just begun to fall out of a grumpy, humidity infused sky. This guy was the very model of a good ol' boy driving his pretty new pickup truck; camouflage ballcap, half his face bulging with chew. Boog noted the usual NRA sticker and Tulane decal on the already dented bumper. *Ah, then. College dropout boy, fell into Daddy's construction business.* Boog couldn't help chuckling as he loped to catch up to the vehicle on the shoulder. *One brakelight you have out, ami.*

Boog thought he might have to ride back in the bed as the guy eyed his things wadded into the clear hospital bag, his unshaven face and windblown hair growing back in. His clean-cut appearance had begun to erode in the trustee camp and he forgot to shave in the rush to clear out of there.

The driver rolled down the passenger-side window. "Been in detox or somethin', ami?" He brushed a Burger King wrapper and bag onto the floor. Boog climbed in.

EVACUATION ROUTE 463

There was no point in confiding the drunken mayhem that led him to an enforced vacation. "Somethin' like that. They find my potager petite. Seven plant only they find on bogus visit to serve a warrant for my brother. I see them chop it all down but not to burn. They take for evidence. Get what I mean?"

His chauffer accelerated ahead of a hail of gravel, the truck leaping back onto the road. "That sucks big time. Ya coulda sold *me* some. Hey, I been there, b'lieve it or not."

I don't know if I do, young boy, Boog thought. *An' I don't know you to sell to you.* He would not sell his fictitious crop to anyone but *Knuckledicks* and family. And maybe not even family. He would have liked to just close his eyes. "Wasn't enough crop to charge felony distribute. Illegal possession they decide. Terrebonne Trustee Camp. *Why I bother build a story for this.*

When the guy let Boog out to continue south on 56, the rain was still light. "Much thanks, ami," he said. He closed the cab door and gave it a light slap.

Just a few hundred yards down the road and with no luck yet, the burner phone that was returned to him rang from an inside pocket of his vest. The properties officer at Terrebonne Camp allowed him to give it a quick charge while they awaited lagging paperwork for his release. There were still some minutes remaining on it after communicating with Wood and the real estate lady as he rode into captivity.

"Yuh?" Boog halted and placed the bag of his belongings on the ground between his feet.

"This is Patrece Moutain, Moutain Realty. This is Mr. Lavelle?"

"It *is* me speakin'."

The woman sighed at her end. "Wonderful. I thought I had the day correct. And you are no longer....indisposed?"

Boog pushed a free hand through his hair. It was not holding the rain any longer and dripped down his forehead and temples. A haircut must be arranged somewhere along his way home to Tampa. *You should say whatever is comfortable.* "I am speakin' with you, so yeah. I am rehabilitated, complete. Makin' my way back down to Chauvin at this very time."

"That is wonderful news, Mr. Lavelle," the lady said. "Your friend Mr. Thibadeaux was kind enough to let me into the house. I needed to find the deed 'n' title, the mortgage discharge. Under these circumstances, I...."

Boog lifted his bag of tee-shirts and underwear, prison laundry fresh, and resumed walking. "It's no big deal. He was authorize. I left them on my Mamere dressin' table like I told Thibadeaux."

"Yes, I found 'em, no troubles. Can you come into the office, tomorrow at opening? 9am? We will close with the buyer first thing. I have the check drafted for you, all ready to go."

Boog made a quick turnabout and extended the thumb of his phone hand. Still no luck. "I don't have much to pack. Just to make sure my bike, she'll start up good." He walked faster. Much of the traffic was turning on their headlights.

"This sounds like a plan, Mr. Lavelle. Just call if you have any more delay. An' please lock all the doors against vandals? Bring in all the keys with you, too."

"Je vais 'n' bon soir, lady." Boog tucked the phone back under his leathers.

One more night for Boog to spend in the ol' place. Now without Laurence the fantome may visit. Fen follet come out the swamp. Maybe I don't sleep in that bed again. Laurence never see anything of fright on the couch.

Well, damn it. Ma must be gettin' way tired a my excuses. This has gotta be the last one. The news from Louisiana was discouraging but not the end of the world. Or, so that's how he would have to relate it to her.

"I am out from slam," Boog informed him;

Was it good to hear that Cajun voice again after a month--part molasses, part the worm in the bottom of a shot glass?

"The title, they screw it up at Terrebonne Parish Clerk. Three days they say to me still, before I close sale," Boog continued.

Has Boogaloo ever lied to me before? That old Thibadeaux person from Boog's neighborhood liquor store called to say it was all set up for Boog to sign and go, soon as he was released. Boog's voice sounded odd. But that could have been his cheap cellphone, bad internet. Or, maybe fatigue and the crummy food of a trustee camp. *Should I picture a chain gang? "Takin' it off, here, boss!" Wires're bound to get crossed up comin' outta that place. Hell, they all sound like manure salesmen with their mouth fulla samples.*

"Just wait, Wood. I got the stories to tell, ami'," Boog had assured him. "Just a few more days 'n' ol' Boog'll come roarin' back home."

You ain't roarin' at no time on that riceburner, my crazy friend. I guess if he says three or four more days, I might as well just take him at his word. What'm I gonna do? Fire 'im?

Wood locked his apartment door and went down the wide, furniture-friendly staircase. His bike was parked in the nearest slot of the long carport, intricately chained to one of the curbstones that kept residents from lurching through the shelter and onto the sidewalk.

Managing this trio of girls was not such a difficult chore except having to pay Ivan for his rudimentary bartending. The *Knuckledicks* had lucked out again in finding generally friendly ladies with some sense of humor (comfortably aimed at themselves, not the members). They seemed to enjoy their work just as Merry and Bella once had. Wood could begin to understand Boog's dedication to this part of the job. When he was here to do it.

Wood unchained the Fat Boy and then rolled out of the sprawling complex in low gear. With a minimum of aggression. Responsibly. Christ, but there were so many children in these starter, one and two bedroom places. Section 8 single moms or with entry level careers. *Yeah, but also baristas and low-seniority casino staff; short order egg chefs at Waffle House.* It *was* summer vacation. *Shouldn't all these rugrats be indoor playin' video games?* Maybe when the day is hotter in their crummy playground. Or, maybe the parents (well, *parent,* mostly) couldn't afford the best game systems. The place must have infected him. *All I got is basic cable, too. So, what's that make me?* He rented here for the same reason as all the others; affordability

Single moms gravitated into here, sure, but a good many older make vehicles seemed to head out in the early shift hours. He wasn't often up at this hour but he heard the groggy engines go past outside. Sometimes if he rolled out to pee, he'd watch the parade out his bedroom window. Dents, and bashes in some of the vehicles like a demolition derby. Plastic bag door glass. After another hour or so of light sleep, some internal alarm clock coaxed him out of bed to begin his own less-formal workday. Little kids on porches went with the territory. They skipped rope, little black girls, little Hispanic girls, the occasional white one. He heard their rhymes until he revved up the Fat Boy to clear its throat. The elementary school artists kept the sidewalk colorfully chalked. *Too young for spray paint 'n' entry level taggin' vandalism.*

Wood bought a few groceries on his way up from Riverview. The market he stopped at was well within the radius of jacked-up city prices which steepened the closer he got to Broadway Ave. A vague notion of spaghetti and garlic toast was forming. A couple of bags of little frozen meatballs was out of the question at this store's prices and he didn't feel like shooting out to the big food stores on Brandon Ave. Now, *there* was a good reason to resent Boog's absence. Wood hated shopping and consistently forgot to bring the big seabag home with him for hauling groceries. How about cut up hot-dogs? This seldom failed him as an addition to any biker dish. By now his poor saddlebags had nearly lost that new saddlebag smell but they offered *some* empty space.

Wood made an uneventful ride. He liked to catch the short lull between 9am office shifts and 10am clerical workers. His mind drifted to the phone call he must make to Ma in Homosassa. *Don't give up on me. I'm feelin' like I actu'lly need a vacation.*

Chapter Twenty-Five

In the last week of July, Merry and Bella, too, were ready for a summer break. They enjoyed a very lucrative month and the ice cream carton repository was again packed tight with cash. The main feature of the month was an extreme tag-team event at the Casino with their old friend Jack Bancroft for his friends and business associates. (*Who has that many friends, Bell? Maybe they were all in the same fraternity. Well, Ah don't know whut that is, so...*). Both girls thought that the possibility of such an engagement must have been festering in the mens' minds for awhile. By mid-July, whatever their relationship to Jack was, they began to call for individual dates. A cluster reunion was inevitable.

"Ah wonder why it took that ol' boy so long for it to occur to him," Merry speculated after the marathon event.

"Suspect they talked Jack into it. He would hold it off for a special event."

There were a few additional *friends of Jack* and then a *lot* more money. This time they were in a full Seminole Hard Rock suite, a little higher above the glittering pools than her last time, Merry thought. The inevitable request by the partiers to watch the girls playing together resulted in a $500 tip, on the spot. Soon after their little show was over, Jack's guests found a revived intensity of lust to carry them through to the wee hours of morning. Another excellent tip was added when Bella discovered the sleeping head-count to be more heads than they had agreed to.

"You came, Mer. You cannot deny it," Bella claimed later.

"Nah, Ah didn't neither."

"You don't think I can tell the difference?"

"Ah'm sure ya prob'ly *can*," Merry snickered.

"Now what is that supposed to mean, jail-bait?"

"Ah don't mean nothin' by it except you wasn't exactly dry yer own self, Bell. An' so what if Ah did? So yuh've got irresistible skills. Ah was prob'ly ready to go off b'fore hand. It was a dang orgy, for Crahst sakes."

"There's no *shame* in it either way. I only wanted to remind you that *I* am not that way. Or, not very strongly. In real life, I mean."

"Course not. Ah ain't either, Ah don't s'ppose. Dependin' on what ya wanta call *real life.* Ah ain't been to my ther'pist lately. Why're ya botherin' me 'bout it now?"

The notion of a summer break resurfaced as Bella dozed, just before rolling out and emerging from her bedroom. She turned the television volume down on a Sandals Resort commercial. Was that some kind of omen for them? She shook Merry's shoulder gently. "Why are you out here?"

Merry opened her eyes. "Didja change channels on me? Ah waked up 'n' come out here to watch mah cartoons."

"It's the same channel. I didn't touch it. But, I don't understand why Sandals is on Nickelodeon. And I woke up wondering if you have given more thought to a vacation?"

Merry sighed. "Ah ain't in favor a more sun'n'water, Ah can tell ya *that* much."

Bella stepped into the kitchen. Left-over coffee would have to be nuked in the microwave until some ambition was rekindled in one of them. She found a French vanilla creamer (restaurant plunder) in the refrigerator door. "And *I'm* not in favor of being blown out to sea off of a cruise ship in a hurricane. August'll soon bring it's usual dicey situations."

Merry closed her eyes though the childrens' program had resumed. "Them boats clear far aways from danger a *any* kind. One a my brothers worked a few years bussin' tables, 'til Ah think he stole somethin'. That coffee smells good. Where's mine?

Bella poured the thimble of creamer into her mug and passed it to Merry. "Don't hog it, Mare. Why didn't you start some fresh before floppin' in front of Dora, or whoever this is?"

Merry could only shrug and hand the mug back. "Ah just wanted to get a smile without much thought behind it. Ah ain't very responsible, am Ah?"

Bella slurped. "There is maybe a cupful left but I'm not getting right back up. Listen, though. Have you ever visited Disney World?"

472 CHRIS DUNGEY

"That'd be a *nope, ma'am*. Never had no desire. Ain't it a lotta blubberin' rug-rats 'n' sunburn?"

"Mare, *you* are watching Saturday stories for children," Bella said. "Well then, have you ever been to St. Augustine? It is the very oldest place in the whole country. There's a Spanish fort and the first village ever on the continent. Well, it's been reconstructed."

"Nope, ma'am. Never been north a Daytona that Ah can recall. If they was writin' a book a my life, it'd be pretty borin'. Both them places sound like where we wouldn't be tempted to work, at least."

"That is the idea of a vacation, girlie," Bella said, offering her coffee back to Merry. She giggled. "I could let my Brazilian go for a week."

"An' Ah got my sister 'n Orlando, if Ah can find her address. We can meet Mickey 'n' ol' Goofy. Princesses 'n' like that. You can shave yer legs though, can't ya? Not to scare no kiddos."

"Will not be a problem, Little Bit. We'll wait long as we have to for the Flume Ride just to get splashed."

Merry's brow furrowed for a moment. "Yeah, Ah forgot Ah heard they got them long lines."

"Can you believe there is a ticket you can buy, lets you cut to the front of the line? There is a ride that goes inside of a mountain, too," Bella said. "And you can look at it this way; that we would be waiting on a line instead of a line waiting on us."

Merry took a half-empty bottle of water from the coffee table. "It wasn't *that* bad. Ol' Jack just invited a couple more than he remembered. There was a nice bonus added on, wasn't there? An' thank the Good Lord, no ropes nor whips."

EVACUATION ROUTE

473

"Sure, sure. I wasn't complaining," Bella said. "I'll have a look on the laptop to see about St. Augustine. So, we'll have to sit in a Starbucks later on for some free WiFi. I think there are carriage rides to take us around to the sights in St. Augustine."

"Mmm-hmm. Ah'm gonna be a princess ever'where Ah might go this summer, seems like."

After Dora had outwitted some kind of dishonest fox character, Bella lifted herself off the couch again. Going for coffee and free internet would require a shower, but makeup today seemed like pure drudgery. In her bedroom, she dug deep into the bottom of the chest-of-drawers, looking for her most casual shorts and top, young mom Saturday stuff. Going out in her around-the-house gym shorts and mesh tank top would not do. She soon discovered that she owned *no* plain underwear. *That's not such a terrible standard to maintain. And I never wanta feel like the young mom. To change diapers on hatch cover. Baby dookie blotting out crab, fish gut stink. Snotnose bambinos in double carriage. Mama-san's high decibel farmer's market, fish market, bodega bartering. Bringing Anglo scorn. How many babies you intenda have Char-leen? GI bring you home for a Green Card?* Bella carried the seldom used garments into the bathroom.

Then, beneath the spray, the soapy cloth paused for a moment on the back of her neck: "Shit!" She cried out, into the shower's echo. "Shit! Shit!"

"Whatcher problem in there, girlie?" Merry must have followed her in to use the mirror.

"I have one more promised date that I forgot," Bella told Merry's shadow through the shower curtain. "Do you remember that printer-ink salesman that was so generous to me last fall? He lost his wife?"

"Just like it was yeste'day." Merry mumbled. She spit tooth paste and snorted, "C'mon, Bell, Ah remember ol' Jack 'cause a the money an' cuz he 'n' all them was a re-peat. Other'n that, it's all just one long document'ry a strainin' red faces 'n' me dehydratin' myself."

"Well, it was my first time out on the water. He was very nice and generous. He called my cell and I just *can't* be a no-show for him." She rinsed her hair, hung up the cloth then twisted the knobs to off as tight as she could. There was always a drip. *We'll go have the expensive coffee and scone, anyway. I'll search out St. Augustine. We have no reservation to lose by waiting one day.* "Hand me a towel, would you, Mare?"

Boog could give it only two nights and one of those had already been used. Then he would *really* have to let it go, about those ingrate whores. He promised Wood that he'd be back on the job by Friday afternoon and he was missing his girls; the new, *loyal* ones. Should he have paid the same attention to Merry and Bella? *But I took a lesson, yeah? We done the favor, too, takin' 'em in. These new ones savin' us. Make us most special club of any.* He even missed

EVACUATION ROUTE 475

Wood. *Knuckledicks not feared so much any more but still most like fam'ly.* He didn't miss his own blood kin in the more than two years absence before Mamere's passing. *This why we call each a brother.*

There were moments, while stabbing cardboard shrimp-n-fries takeout trays or Mickey D wrappers up into the government issue garbage bags, when he realized that he was blanking to picture their faces. *Is that Bella still havin' the hair short like she looked at the Casino? Why she do that crazy thing? Eight month ago. How could that long time even be true? Mebbe time go by quick with resentment pushin' forward a person.* And Merry he saw only a couple of times.

Now he tried to remember when was the last time his gut burned with that sustaining anger, and not just cayenne sauce. What was all of the plotting *for? Mebbe just clap her on back then tell the bitch what I think. Give her the li'l cuff on the mouth? Just to have her stare in my face 'n' reco'nise who is without old beard 'n' all cleaned up. Look a shock 'n' fear on either them faces might be enough. Close the book. Might even be li'l Merry the first one I catch on that boat.*

The Gulf Breeze Motel. He had it for one more night. *What the fuck kinda name that is? Only breeze is traffic from out on 19.* Boog peered out through a parted curtain then let it close. The Gold Wing was cabled to the curb just outside his window The sun on the parking-lot had begun that particular slant to suggest that most of an afternoon had slipped away. *One more try only. Then? Have to just say, fuck 'em.*

In the bathroom, the mirror was a little too well lighted. *But you want truth about yer mug, yeah ami?* This shaving every day would soon come to an end; the expensive haircuts, his latest from a so-called *style* shop just off the first Tallahassee exit coming home, was going to be the *last* one. It took awhile for the hot water to arrive. He squirted Wal-Mart shave cream into his palm from a travel aerosol. *Office guy, Boog looks like. Clean 'n' smooth like Wal-Mart manager. Need pocket protector.* He waited for the rest of the day to pass like an elderly funeral procession.

Tonight, Boog decided that he would park the Gold Wing closer, right in the *Lucky Seas Excursions* lot. He was pressing his luck if one of them remembered the Honda. Little Merry might, the really cautious one. He didn't know about Bella. But, there was a chain-link fence in there that he could thread the bike cable through and around one of its posts. It would soon be in the shade, too.

The fruitless trip of the previous evening showed him the routines and procedures of the boat—where he could sit to best remain anonymous before boarding. He studied the nooks and crannies aboard, where he would have to play slots with his back turned uncomfortably to everyone, but his face buried in the neon and chimes. There was no special Club rewards card on a lanyard to plug into those old school machines. Just bring cash money, including lots of nickels and quarters. And that's what the win returned to the player, spilling for real into a traditional metal tray. Not a recording—the sound was one you expected from treasure. Or a machine-tool spitting nuts and bolts.

EVACUATION ROUTE

Boog had purchased two polo shirts and one pair of cargo shorts for these voyages. The first shirt was seen last night. He sweated liberally on his way to the boat. Then, air-conditioning out on the water amounted to sea breeze and several small fans churning at the tops of the bulkheads. Boog counted three on each side, six total in the first deck slot area. He looked for security cameras. There were none until he found two on the second deck dedicated to blackjack. These were camouflaged next to the humming fans. *That skipper, he watch for card counters. Prob'bly a screen up on the bridge.*

Dressing for the final attempt on the boat, he nearly tossed the shirt from last night into the metal trash can. When would he ever wear it again? *The color of a lime. But comfor'ble. The fans dry it quick. Never know when I will be secret agent again.* There was plenty of empty space in his one closet back at the apartment. He owned mostly leather vests and black tees. He folded and rolled the garment then put it back into a Wal-Mart bag.

The second shirt was a baise polyester/cotton blend with a small sailboat monogram over the right breast. It almost matched his cargo-shorts. *If I wear these ev'ry day, bottom pockets would look like two elephant nuts hangin' with all keys 'n' junk.* He fit his trucker's billfold into a hip pocket and brought the chain around to a belt loop to snap in front.

The afternoon wore away, with some tension building. Boog left the refrigerated room. He locked his door and freed the bike. As usual, the door of the motel room was too narrow to admit the Gold Wing. And yet he heard someone's pet barking in a room

478   CHRIS DUNGEY

above. He'd cabled it to a ring provided in the retaining curbstone. That was a courtesy you didn't see everywhere. *Here and at Gator Joe's, thinkin' a bikers. I will remember.*

Boog intended, again, to roll into that RaceTrak station near the Lucky Seas to make sure of having enough fives and singles. He bought a small coffee and one of the small chocolate soft serve ice cream cones he'd discovered a strong taste for. He broke a fifty into a wad of small denomination slot offerings. After finishing the cone, he placed the coffee securely in a cupholder and rolled out, heading north on US 19. He circled back toward the Lucky Seas parking lots on the back street. How long had it been since he discovered this industrial park of taverns. It seemed like half a year, not two months. Mamere. Laurence. He would soon have time to think of them unhurriedly. Jail time never stuck long in his thoughts. He would clear his head and his life of civilian worries for good. The Gold Wing idled past the little playground provided by one of the bars. That old trawler was still propped securely on its side.

A few other passengers had arrived before Boog, who hoped to be first aboard for this evening's junket. This did not trouble him. It really didn't matter when he arrived. More important was where you sat before boarding was signaled by the Captain. He found a sliver of shade along that fence in the main parking area. The Gold Wing might be totally unnoticed there by vehicles entering the other short street from US 19, the intersection of the gas station. He took a newsboy's skimmer hat out of the a saddlebag. He lifted out his courier bag, another prop. *Am I now top of hipster fashion?*

EVACUATION ROUTE 479

Or, yuppie fashion? He had never kept track. There were entire generations, probably, since the yuppies, to which he paid zero attention. *They all are at the end a the alphabet. I wouldn't know of hipsters if I haven't spend four month in this camouglage, among citizens.* He was no longer disgusted with himself as he caught a glimpse in the bike's mirror. The hat might be a keeper to go with his new shirts. Maybe not to the Clubhouse.

Boog's security cable barely reached the chain-link fence separating Lucky Seas Excursions from a bordering lot. There were two well-constructed outbuildings on the other side of the fence. *It look like mebbe storage for that Gator Joe's.* He had to practically lay the bike against the fence in order to thread the cable around a post and back through two spokes. *This shit gotta come to end tonight. I'm startin' to worry 'bout scratches.* There was no mistaking that the bike *had* grown on him. There was a nice cargo box besides the hard saddlebags. *Wish just to park in the shade, closer by that office. No more trips after this.*

Boog's shades were as essential to him as boots, especially for creeping activities like this and with the sunset glare out on the water. At one time in his life he had worn pairs from Big Lots. When they broke, he simply spent another five bucks. Now these were twelve dollar ones marked down (the vendor said) from a swap meet. He chose dark ones over some cooler, amber aviators because they covered more of his face below his eyes. And those boots? What was more like hipsters than sandles? Dark leather, of course.

No doubt about it, Merry hated this weather. It seemed to her that every venture out of doors in the past three days had left her wrung out and lethargic. Hell, where were they going to vacation that would be any different than this sauna? She told Bella to just go ahead and take the Tracker, even though the prearranged *date* with the ink guy was a *known variable* and the ride home with him would have been assured.

"Are you sure you won't change your mind and get out of the house?" Bella said. "What if you decide you want to work?" She stepped into the bathroom.

Merry stood with spread arms in front of a floor fan they had acquired. It moved their feeble AC along from their bedrooms toward the front room. The kitchen was written off and any activity in front of the stove. Standing with the refrigerator door open was also not practical for their finances.

"Ah told ya, Bell," Merry said. "Ah'll resume mah life's callin' when the damn eve'nin' temper'ture dips to upper seventies. You go ahead on."

Bella emerged after a final examination of her teeth and make-up. She, too, stood in front of the tall fan.

"Hey, yer hoggin' it," Merry groaned. "Yer gonna be enjoyin' them sea breezes in a hour or so."

"Sure, sure." Bella hugged her from behind.

EVACUATION ROUTE
481

"That's just the kind a close bod'ly contact that's becomin' oppressin' to me."

"I *see*. But the Weather Channel says for a low of 76 degrees by midnight. Don't you think you could make it from the Tracker into the casino without melting?"

Merry shrugged. "Mah mind is made up. Humidity has wrung all a the horny that Ah rely on right outta me."

"Poor baby," Bella said. "Well then, it is time for me to make my carriage ride. I just need to grab a water to last me to the docks."

Bella took a bottle out of the refrigerator. She wore a Devil Rays ballcap to augment her oversize shades. All of the windows were rolled down for her less than two mile drive to *Lucky Seas Excursions*. The AC was just as worthless as it had always been, its squealing not worth the annoyance. *What part of the compressor can sound like a bluejay in a cat's mouth.* She watched her makeup in the visor mirror for the first gleam of perspiration to break through.

We could fix it with that gas they sell. That freon. I could do it even if the rest of this thing falls into pieces under us. Too hot to go for vacation in this. Another AC for the front room might be a better investment?

At a stoplight, Bella consulted the visor mirror again. Her make-up might last just long enough for a breeze to save it out on the water. *I will go into the Auto Zone to find the price for freon. They loan tools, I think. A long time since handing tools to Papi at work on the diesel.* She signaled her left turn onto the short street that ended at the boats. *That blinker flashes like crazy. Bet it has quit working*. She moved her face as close to the window and the flow of air there as she dared. There was nothing to straighten in her wild, regrown hair. Bella waited for the bit of dust she raised to pass over and around the Tracker then opened the door. The hinge groaned. *Mare, she has had a good run but I think the writing is up on the wall.*

Boog admired his look again in the mirror. *What do I order when I wear this hat? The skinny double latte, no foam?* He must have picked that up on the handful of occasions when he had no choice but to enter a Starbucks or Digby's. *That noisy place go quiet when I stand into the line. Just your tall cup black coffee, cher.* Calling that cup they gave him *tall* was a joke. The real *tall* one had some kind of Italian name.

This would be the same level of chance and risk as yesterday. An evening booking on *Narcissus* was best for whatever kind of confrontation he hoped to achieve with one of those traitors. It seemed to him that most of the passengers last night were more interested in partying and drinking than in the gambling. *Those are ones the girls want. That's where I will find one of 'em, where bachelor parties sing drunk karaoke or ask to dance with 'em. Hardcore blackjack player, he don't care for pussy until he hit big.* He entered the shade of the booking office, signed the manifest and

EVACUATION ROUTE

paid. He hadn't yet cut his paper bracelet off from last night. The lady wrapped on a second one.

Under the broad pavilion roof of the waiting area, it appeared to Boog that some of the partying was off to a head start. The loudest was a group of six twenty-somethings. *Yup. The bachelor party.* At the far end of the sheltered area, two picnic tables were pushed together with balloons floating from one end. He saw a cake and mixed drinks. *That look like a good combination.*

He went back into the booking office to purchase a screwdriver. *Better remember who was my name I signed.*

Something new. Merde. Was Perdue it? Perdeaux. Yeah, Paul Perdeaux. Somethin' diff'rent from my driver license. What if I must show it? Even in a grocery they card me sometime. But it wasn't an issue last night. One of the kitchen/bar staff poured his vodka and orange juice without comment. *No worries.* Boog shook his head. *A piss ant. How they could remember all passenger names?*

He carried the drink in a clear plastic cup to a picnic table at the back of the waiting area. Boog supposed there was *some* vodka in it. *Now, that Wood. Say what you want for bikers, he mix the most generous drink. Make members slobber-knocker after just a few. Tomorrow, late afternoon, I have one while I sit with my girls. Home again.*

Like finding the last matching symbol on a lottery scratch-off, there suddenly emerged Bella from the ticket office. Lightweight fabrics and pale colors, letting her darker skin of summer work for her. She was looking around for a seat. *You are the prize conass to sit at a empty table.*

But Bella must not be looking for somewhere to sit. She seemed to be looking for *someone*. Someone she was expecting to meet? Then she sat at the end of a bench where two couples already sipped their weak drinks. *She looks for the play that bring more money. The ménage, mebbe? An' to throw in her extra specials that she can do.*

Boog went up the gang-plank at the head of the line. He knew where he wished to position himself. He didn't pause at the bar, placed just where passengers entered the lowest deck so that their drinking might continue uninterrupted. The other side of the bar was open to a starboard side dining room. One of the staff was spreading round, checkered tablecloths, which, by their sharp, remaining creases must be paper. *Make sense for the spills at sea of land people.*

Past the narrow stairs going up to the blackjack deck then straight to the aft end of the slot machines, Boog sought the ideal seats he had scouted the previous evening. Here were four slots that allowed players to turn their backs on the rest of the deck. He could watch from between the machines the wake churning out behind *Narcissus*, crazy gulls swooping down at some food source stunned by the props. *Look like how they do over landfill. Hear 'em soundin' off. Found somethin'. This is mine!* Screen panels at the top of the viewing glass were opened for ventilation. He could turn slightly between plays to see who was near. He peered surreptitiously up at a fisheye mirror above him to observe who was entering the slots. He would save the karaoke deck for after sunset.

EVACUATION ROUTE 485

Boog felt the movement of the ship begin, imperceptible but for the wharf facilities receding. He was going to have this view of leaving for awhile as *Narcissus* made her slow way into the channel, observing wake speed rules. *These homes by the river have docks big as Lucky Seas's. How many boats they own? For each home? Each condo with boat, a yacht to have parties way out. Some might fish.* Rock music drifted to them across the water, a bar somewhere nearby, on the streets of condos.

That Bella might wish to sit near a male passenger playing solo, was another oversight in his surveillance scheme. But, there she was, primly seating herself in his peripheral view; not *right* next to him but one seat removed. The last machine on the starboard side remained unattended but passengers were still entering the deck, balancing their drinks. *This the hugest brain fart yet. Myself all disguised I don't trust so much, in close-up.* But who was she still looking for? Boog watched Bella in the fisheye mirror. She hadn't played a single coin yet, but swiveled her stool around 180 degrees twice to watch who was coming into the slot deck.

Boog cashed out of the machine as quickly, keeping his face turned to the portside bulkhead. He dipped his winnings out of the tray and into a small plastic bucket. 'See Purser for Change or Cash-Out' read a sign above a booth in the center of the deck. An older woman sat in there making piles of quarters and nickels. *A cashier at the Hard Rock is called purser out at sea,* Boog considered. *I don't got a purse. I got a courier bag at the bike. I put winnings in the pocket for exchange later.*

486   CHRIS DUNGEY

He swayed forward then hopped into the last empty slot chair not being used on the entire deck. He quickly discovered why it was empty. The machine was vacant because passengers were lining up and squeezing through at the player's left elbow space in a steady stream to enter that dining room on the starboard side. A porter stood in front of the door to count heads. A sign above him warned: Capacity, 20 Guests. When this number was reached, the kid tried to divert people back around to the portside bar where they had all boarded. Like many another popular eatery, guests were encouraged to keep drinking until vacated tables could be cleared.

Bella headed forward soon after him. He glanced up just long enough to reinforce his opinion that she was looking for someone specific. Boog leaned into his machine, his face turned toward the dining room. In another of the mirrors above him, he watched her go out to climb the steel steps to the blackjack deck. She seemed already to have made a date but was having trouble finding the guy. *Whatever I wanta do, she have to be alone.*

Boog lost a few more dollars then abandoned this crowded slot as well. When Bella was ready to eat, she would have to push right past him or wait in line at his shoulder. There would be ample time to examine him more closely. *Hey, a lineup lookin' at one suspect.* Out the same door Bella exited, he found the stairs to the blackjack deck. It led up from the narrow portside walkway. In the brief glare of late afternoon sun, he realized that he was still wearing his shades. That might draw attention except on the exposed karaoke deck. He hung them from the neck of his shirt.

EVACUATION ROUTE 487

He didn't stop at the second deck but continued climbing, emerging at the top of the steps into loud, flat, karaoke singing: *Tie a yellow ribbon 'round the old oak tree,* a heavyset blond was nearly monotoning. *Tie a yellow ribbon round yer wore-out voice box,* Boog wanted to sing. *That sound would be mebbe worse.*

He noticed immediately that passengers up here were also eating. A beefy guy in a shiny, burgundy, lounge-lizard suit must to be the karaoke MC taking his lunch break. The guy was backed up against his big speaker and a half open cabinet that appeared to store microphones, bits of electronics and many cassettes. A steward delivered two baskets of fries and probably chicken strips to a couple sharing the singer's table. There was another beer on the tray for him. *That the man who earn it. He talk them into a song and then have to listen. That meal look like perfect for me.* He motioned to the kid in the white smock.

"What kinds beers you've got?"

"Bud, Bud Light, Miller Lite." The steward stood by but rested his tray of empties on the unoccupied side of Boog's table.

None of these choices appealed to Boog, who had thirsty yearnings for the Coppertail Unholies back at the *Knuckledicks* Clubhouse. He'd sipped rum-and-coke last night so told the kid to bring that. "An' chicken come with fries like that?" He nodded toward the MC's table.

"Comes with the chicken tenders, yes. But it's real chicken like The Colonel's. It's $7.95 and $3.00 for the well drink."

"Sound good," Boog said and began to extract the Fort Knox capacity trucker's billfold. But the kid was already gone, out and back down the stairs. *That kitchen. Where they have room? Down by the engine room, must be?*

He watched the companionway door. A few more passengers entered, who'd chosen against the dining room. When he thought about it, this was the biggest boat he'd probably ever been on, but it was feeling smaller all the time. How was he supposed to manipulate a few private moments for ambush with all of these citizens crowded in everywhere? *This might need the lucky break. Keep cool, ami, for waiting.*

Last night he munched only a bag each of chips and pretzels with a few soft drinks after the rum-and-coke. *Keep easy stomach until I have the sea legs.* There wasn't much motion to the boat then and just a light chop now. How was a full meal going to ride in this slight roll. But he was on the karaoke deck which was ¾ open to the sky. *Just go to rail 'n' look toward horizon. No good, wait all this time 'n' then yack up all my guts over rail just when time to pounce.* Where *was* the horizon in the dark?

So alright, Wood-Chuck Spurgeon thought. *The boy had some personal business to take care of includin' a month on a Cool Hand Luke chain gang to hear him tell it. Mebbe even spent a few days a actual grievin'. An' he took his sweet time with all of it. But now it's finally gonna be my turn.* He just had to make the assumption of a few lies from the guy and move on.

Boogaloo had given him a date certain: The last Friday of July. *The one comin' up 'n' today's Wednesday. Eeeee-hah.* Oh yeah, though. He remembered how he had pledged to spend his time off.

"Ivan, don't forget to stir that goulash." Wood did not put his phone away. He decided to make his next call in privacy, outside and behind the building.

"Yep." Ivan Dresbach watched *The Price is Right* on a small flatscreen that was recently mounted in the middle of the tiered liquor bottles. His back was turned to the stove.

"How is that crap even *on* in the morning?" Wood asked.

"It's a rerun. This is the Game-Show Network. There's a network for everything."

Wood never would have imagined Ivan staring at such nonsense, totally slack jawed. He'd previously believed that the man was one of the smarter *Knuckledicks.* He also wondered how the club could get this programming with their basic cable package. Did *The Darkness* make the executive decision for an upgrade?

Nevertheless, Wood was simply not going to turn any sort of kitchen duties totally over to Boog while taking his own vacation. So, Ivan, intelligent or an idiot, was his best hope to keep the lunches running smoothly. Should he hint at the idea of a hairnet to keep confetti of that Jew-fro out of their food? *Christ, there's a hair pick sticking right out of it. He's gotta know that's there.* "Beer coolers all restocked?"

490   CHRIS DUNGEY

"Yep." Ivan turned the reflections in the lenses of his aviator specs back to the stove. He gave the contents of the 10-quart stainless pot a slow stir.

"If it starts bubblin' up, vigorous like, turn it down to simmer." Whatever misgivings Wood might have about Ivan's culinary skills, he had only to imagine Boog forgetting about a pot on the stove. Maybe everyone would just have to get by on sandwiches for a week. He was pretty sure the pair of them could smear butter on bread. But such an idea was an affront to the pride he took in his meals. "I'm gonna make up a simple menu and get all the shoppin' done ahead. No worries."

"I'm cool," Dresbach replied, once again gaping at the Drew Carey rerun.

Damn. If *anyone* in the *Knuckledicks* paid attention to local new or even a news network, Spurgeon would have put his money on Ivan. "I need to make another call. I'll be out back," he said.

"Yep. Gotcha covered."

Well, that's comfortin' to know at $7.00 an hour outta my own pocket. "Just keep it stirred'."

Outside, the air was loading up with moisture. Wood found five feet of shade still clinging to the far corner of the back wall. He carried his cellphone there. *Rain in another half hour. Ten minute waterfall then the sun sucks it back up.*

Now, would he catch Ma at home? Was Wednesday still her day off from the Bdubs? It had been awhile since he heard her mention that. Her phone rang four times and Wood began to compose what he would tell her voice mail. Then she picked up.

EVACUATION ROUTE

"How's mah Baby-boy doin'?"

"Were ya busy with somethin'? What'd I interrupt?" *Be cool for a change, dummy. Try 'n' don't piss her off from the jump.*

"Ah was danglin' mah poor, tired feet into the pool, Mr. Nosy-pants," she lied.

"I wasn't suggestin' nothin', Ma. You mighta been in the shower or on another call."

"Nope, Baby-boy. Just tryin' to relax 'n' stay cool on a day off. They ain't regular anymore cuz Ah pick the best shifts. It hot down there, too?"

"It's Florida." Wood said. "Anyways, are ya finally ready to host some company?"

"Well now, don't go teasin' me. Absolutely, I want ya to come on up soon. Ah've had four vacation days on hold."

"I don't know what you got planned for me, but I feel like I could sleep for half a them days." The Homosassa end of the call went silent for ten seconds. Wood heard the snap of a lighter close to the phone. *Now she's tryin' to come up with some entertainments.* "You still there?"

"Ah'm just thinkin' about where all Ah can drag ya to," Darlene said at last. "And rememberin' not too long ago tellin' somebody that at least you wasn't livin' on mah couch."

Wood heard her exhale so long and loud it might have been a respiration test. He could picture the plume of smoke and picture a beach robe. "Were you apologizin' to somebody for my job again?"

492 CHRIS DUNGEY

"No. More like just explainin' all about yer duties for that club 'n' yer bartendin' skills. It was to a friend I've made in here. Ah take it that yer assistant has returned?"

Now to whom would she need to describe his job responsibilities? *Girlfriend? They do tend to jabber, any bunch Ma's ever socializin' with. She does have my back when Carol starts in with her views a my chosen lifestyle. Bet she'd describe me in them terms to a new boyfriend, too.*

"Yep. Ol' Boogaloo has returned from his fam'ly business." He knew batter than to touch on Boog's jail stay. "An', for the record, you always have the best sleepin' couches."

"Ah like some comfort, too, Baby-boy," Darlene said. "So, tell me when, so Ah can lay in some groceries."

Wood retreated another step toward the far corner of the Clubhouse. The sweaty end of the morning was chewing into his shade. The time must be nearing noon. "I'll be up Saturday. Might have to sleep in a bit cuz we don't close up the place 'til 3am."

"Yer hedgin' but Ah'm holdin' ya to it. Ah'll start mah off days from B'dubs Saturday mornin'."

"You won't be disappointed no more by *me*. Kisses," Wood ended the call just as *The Darkness* roared up to his backdoor parking space.

"Lunch ready?" Caulkins yelled, the Hog probably still ringing in his ears. The *Knuckledicks* leader never wore a helmet, and earplugs only for longer rides than his daily commute.

"Such as it is." Wood slipped the phone into the new holster he'd bought for his belt. He walked quickly under the merciless sun toward the back door.

The Darkness held the door for him while managing not to block it. "Such as it is is usually pretty...alright. There, I got to get a compliment in to our chef now 'n' again."

Darlene Spurgeon flopped her arm over the edge of the narrow mattress to stub out her cigarette. The ashtray was on Walt Bocewicz's floor. This seemed like such a waste after only three puffs. Her consumption of nicotine had greatly curtailed since entering this *relationship*. She was still uncomfortable using that term. With her friends in the park, she used the phrase *since Ah took up with Walt* or, for the girls at work: *Ah've taken up with a fella in my park.* She supposed that her toothbrush standing in Walt's bathroom glass made it *some* kind of *relationship*. Why did that make it sound like she could end up on *Dr. Phil*. She had one at home, too. *Ah guess Ah brought that big ol' ashtray over here, too. Kinda my responsibility.*

After having sex with Walt, Darlene still enjoyed a cigarette. Just one, to slow her heart back down and in deference to the fresh paint that now brightened every room in his salvage project. She still needed one with morning coffee at work and one in the break room, later. *What'm Ah down to, three 'r four most days?* Oh, and

494   CHRIS DUNGEY

she still joined Dianne Kaake for a few drags during coffee and desert break at Bingo every Wednesday evening. But that was more talking and eating than puffing. Were the occasions the *real* habit?

Ah never finish that one, either. Gossip savin' mah lungs. Three'n'a half then, call it, lottsa days. That's a big improvement. But what is it, 'bout sex 'n' caffeine seems to call for a side a nicotine? One's a stimulant and one's a...a, can't be a depressant, can it? Mebbe. If the guy don't get the job done.

She couldn't say she was ever depressed by halfway decent sex. Relaxed, sure. *Is relaxed on the way to bein' depressed? Nah, but Ah shoulda paid more attention in biology class.*

"Well, what's the word from Charlie?" Walt sighed and rolled back toward her from his final resting position at the edge of the twin bed.

Ah have got to talk this ol' boy inta at least a reg'lar size bed. It wouldn't take up that much more room from his library 'n' his little set a drawers. He's collectin' more books then underwears. Ah gotta get him some better skivvies, too. Them all look like they was washed in a slow stream somewheres.

A new ceiling fan slapped, mesmerizing, above them. The AC window unit labored audibly to make the bedroom somewhat comfortable. "Am I gonna be stuck using my hand for awhile?" He laid his hand on Darlene's hip.

She, too, rolled back toward the wet spot in the middle. *Well, really, ever'thin' in this li'l ol' bed is damp by now.* "Darlin', you can manage your ol' natural urges any way you see fit. I do. We discussed this, Ah thought."

EVACUATION ROUTE

Walt said, "I know, but then it's been off and on for a month. I guess I forgot where we left it. Is it supposed to be like, what-do-they-call-it? A hall pass?"

Darlene rolled over a bit more to lay her arm over Walt's matted, grey chest, also damp. "Well, if that's how you want it 'n' how we left it. Ah can only tell ya Ah hope not. Ah mahself don't have plans for nothin' 'cept some time with mah youngest who has just announced his need to catch up on his sleep."

Walt eased his arm out from under Darlene's neck. "Does that mean I can sneak down there when his snoring is just right? Or, vice versus?" He sat up on his side of the bed, where he wouldn't kick over the ashtray. It was really a heavy piece of dark, amber glassware with rounded notches meant for fat cigars. He only needed to find it once in the night to give it a wide berth ever after. "But you'll find activities to keep him awake and attentive. Take him to the gator preserve."

"Funny you should mention it." Darlene laughed. "Ah already been told to take that one off a mah list. There's a comedy club opened up in Crystal River 'n' then Cicis Senior night in Brooksville."

Walt could not keep an image of a burly biker wrestling an alligator from crossing his mind. And then he pictured Charlie gorging at the popular eating event. "I'm gonna miss overstuffing myself. Why don't we coordinate separate visits? Anyway, we can let our naughty bits cool awhile. I'll be notifying my *own* mother of *my*, pending visit. It'll be very difficult to....you know, while I'm there. Hey, you've heard of the butterfly effect haven't you??"

Now Darlene sat up as well. She eyed the still viable cigarette smoldering near her feet. She had allowed herself *one*, after all, so that *one* was still in play. "Ain't that some kinda oral technique? An' Ah can't imagine what you're talkin' about not doin' at Mom's. You got to describe both them things to me. In detail."

Walt laughed. "I'm sure it's probably a technique somewhere, but this is different. It's based on the idea that the smallest variables in nature can cause major occurrences elsewhere. The most commonly cited example is of a butterfly batting its wings off the coast of West Africa. That little twitch and the infinitesimal alteration in air pressure beneath the wings triggers a series of events which eventually cause a tropical depression. The end result, three weeks later, is that we're in a traffic jam somewhere inland because our little tin houses might blow away."

Darlene sighed and retrieved her cigarette for one last, long drag on it. She savored this and then exhaled fully. "You know *so* much stuff, Walter Bocewicz. Why wasn't you ever a professor? Wish Ah could force mahself to do more readin'." She stubbed out the smoke. *Ah helped paint these walls.* "But now tell me whatever in the world that has got to do with you callin' yer Ma?"

Walt rolled back onto the bed. He dipped his head to kiss the small of Darlene's back where she sat. "It's about the chain reaction. Charlie's friend overcomes whatever difficulties took him away from that club; *he* calls Charlie; *Charlie* calls you; and now I'm about to call *my* mother and go across the state for a visit. What results from that likely won't be as serious as a *named* storm."

EVACUATION ROUTE

"Darlene wriggled away from Walt's mouth. "Don't get me started again, Professor. Ah got to do some cleanin' 'n' shoppin'." She stood up. "This one ain't gonna be a *hot* shower. Just assure me how there ain't gonna be no catastrophes at the end a *our* chain a cause 'n' effect."

Walt rolled out on his side of the bed again. A fresh change of undershorts was near at hand in his small, factory outlet dresser-drawers. "I wouldn't want to predict, Dar. Probably nothing. My analogy only goes as far as that phonecall I have to make. Hell, I don't know but what Mom has other plans." He knew that was quite unlikely but now that Warren had time on his hands he might be hauling her all over the country.

Walt followed Darlene into the bathroom. He stroked his cheeks in the mirror as the shower began to hiss behind him. *Probably shoulda had a shave, first. Didn't hear any complaints.* "How's the water pressure this afternoon?"

"Just fine, Walter. Ain't you gettin' in?"

Walt opened the new medicine cabinet (same factory outlet as his dresser) and took out the Gillette Foamy. "Not if you don't wanta get started up again. You know I'm gonna want to help with the soap."

Darlene sighed. "Well, now...Ah guess Ah could be of a divided mind about it. Just seems like Ah'm wastin' all kinda warm water in here."

Walt placed the shaving crème back in its place. It didn't make sense to pull fresh underwear on over old funk. He rattled the shower door open far enough to step in.

"Careful. It's all slippery in here."

"I love your slippery," Walt said.

Part IV
Residents are Strongly Advised

"It's almost like God asked Nature where She wants to go for dinner."

"Hurricanes are like women: When they come, they're wet and wild; but when they leave they take your house and car."

Chapter Twenty-Six

"Nao e'bon [no good]," Fillo said. "How does this happen?"

This was the second dip in the glass in four days. They still called it the glass though the trajectory and fall of millibars of atmospheric pressure showed on a monitor near the helm. There must be a glass somewhere. In a satellite? *We fish in the cradle of hurricanes.* He hoped that cousins and uncles in New England would not eventually suffer the brunt of these *two* butterfly kisses when they arrived at their final destinations. For the rest of America do Norte he could not give two shits.

"Captain, the boat is sluggish wallowing. Calha [troughs] starting and I see another squall line. Three kilometers east." First Mate Sandoval did not have to speak on an intercom. Captain Abrahan Fillo had taken, the last few days, to napping in a small cubby just aft of the bridge. They were chasing water temperatures and optimum soundings for the last four days, up and down sea-mounts off most of the Azore's slopes. It was the usual contest of attrition

EVACUATION ROUTE

501

between a decent haul of fish and diesel fuel low in the tanks. "Captain?"

"I am awake, Fermin." The Captain sniffed and cleared his throat. The chains and springs of his rack groaned above *his* groans as he rolled out of it. "Sondogen [soundings]?"

Sandoval did not like the characteristics of this helm with the sea kicking up. He waited, expecting its slack to make a sudden shift under his light grip. He leaned over to consult a depth monitor. "At 38' 2" north and 29'5" west. We have gone off soundings again."

"Porro! Well, get us back on! Add five no' [knots]. Hold steady while we bring nets in. Then come about slowly. East. I will work out a new course."

Captain Fillo placed a communications rig on his head as he emerged from his cubby. "Bring them up," he spoke into the microphone bud near the corner of his mouth. "From here we fish our way back to Herta," he told Sandoval, studying the current compass heading over the kid's shoulder. "I will take the helm after some café`." Now he spoke to the galley: "Martim, wake up. Martim! Bring café to the bridge. Duas!"

Sandoval dialed up more RPMs from the engine. He felt the 120 tons of *Candido* respond, no longer seeming to wallow quite so sluggishly as the swells continued to build. He heard winch motors firing up and watched as the six crew members scrambled to keep dripping lines and cables from tangling.

"Hold steady," Captain Fillo said. Then he addressed his boatswain down on the deck. "What more do we have to take home, Luis?" Moving up to observe through the forward window, he knew what the deck boss would say:

"Pitiful, Abrahan! Scrap! Chum!" The bridge intercom buzzed with the words as well as into the captain's ears.

"Well, don't throw them back! They are cat food!"

"A few bream, some porgy," Luis crackled back. "One tuna. We trolled so deep as the lines would go."

Fillo sighed. "Put them on ice then stow hose the nets for shore. We will fish shallows for two days. Artisan fishermen, eh? Break out all hand lines and downriggers. We will cut the bait when we are closer to home."

With both huge nets wrapped on their drums and rivulets wrung out onto the deck, *Candido* slowly eased to starboard. Fermin Sandoval now turned his attention to the sonar. "Give us a bottom," he prayed, to no deity in particular. "And fishes living there."

She wasn't totally devastated, being stood up by the printer-ink john. Bella didn't even bother to make her usual calculation of lost income for a no-show. *Most definitely it is time for the vacation.*

None of these folks aboard *Narcissus* appeared likely to step up and fill the void if she could even manage the enthusiasm to improvise an approach. *I don't have to approach.* There were, perhaps, three single guys on the entire passenger manifest and she returned

EVACUATION ROUTE

to the thought: *Why not give that Phillip a free taste? Why not even Karaoke Sid? Are they altar boys?* She could just ease into it with either of them. Or, any of the crew for that matter. But only one. Invest the freebee, before risking someone's discretion to give her referrals.

Two of the dudes Bella profiled as singles turned out to be hardcore donators on the blackjack deck. She saw them at separate tables. They were in there both times as she made her way up from the slot deck to Karaoke. *Why am I wandering around, tonight? If blackjack is my main chance to hook up, I must go sit down with one of them.*

That third probable single was a mystery, even a bit suspicious. It seemed to Bella that he wouldn't stay on one deck long enough for her to, at minimum, make some subtle eye-contact. Almost, at the aft end of the slots deck as *Narcissus* eased down the channel, but he quickly stood up and moved. *The guy may not know the first thing about stalking'. But, pretty good as just a plain ol' creeper.*

He reminded her of a carny; super tanned, oily complextion above the crisply ironed shirt. *That shirt has just been unwrapped.* He walked like a cowboy or something. *Have I ever seen a cowboy walk? In movies? I have seen bikers walk like that.* It didn't seem to her that this person's waddling stride went with someone who'd wear a bowling shirt and that hipster cap. Bullies walked like that, in her experience. *Doesn't matter so much. It is your loss you don't want to sit by me.* Maybe he wasn't having any luck at the machines with the distraction of wealthy scenery sliding away behind them. His jump up away from her near proximity was so abrupt.

Bella next encountered the guy as he tried to play a slot with the dining room line crowding past and around him. She stood with *that* bunch long enough to become bored of studying the sweat splotches on her mystery man's clinging shirt. *What is it about hipsters and their tattoos? This one wears more ink than a biker.* Much of the art seemed as meaningless as graffiti tags flying by on freight cars.

It didn't appear that the abnormally muscled hipster was going to turn around for her to have a better look at his face. *That is just rude.* Did he spot her moving just after *he* moved? Then she saw the fisheye mirror above his slot. *This becomes more irritating than puzzling. Well, I don't care for these little kid games. Maybe I am up for some cards after all. I am not so hungry, yet.*

Up on the blackjack deck, Bella took a seat at a table with a berry-brown married couple. They were old enough to be snowbirds, but this was nearly the end of July. Maybe they *were* vacationers at one time and had been suckered into the leather-skin lifestyle. Alonzo was their dealer while, two tables away, Phillip entertained the other two that Bella had tabbed as single men, playing against each other now.

Brenda and Scott complained about the heat. They loathed the traffic like longtime Florida residents. Then it was revealed that they were grateful to be out on the water and could not wait to get back to Wisconsin after flying down for a nephew's wedding. *So...never assume, chica.* Bella saw the odd hipster climb the companionway stairs toward the karaoke deck. His quick glance down the line of blackjack tables was skillfully unfocussed.

EVACUATION ROUTE

Scott from Wisconsin had some experience. He took a few hands from dealer Alonzo and herself while describing the couple's hometown tribal gaming place near Kenosha. In fact, Brenda knew what she was doing, too. When Bella had played six unsuccessful hands she gave up her seat. "Time to eat something, I guess. You good people have brought all of the luck down here with you."

She followed others up to the karaoke deck. The word had spread among the uninitiated that the dining, topside, was less formal. If one didn't mind more of a fast food type menu. And there was that brownish fellow *again,* his back to the portside bulkhead, near the stair entrance. There was just barely enough room to slide through sidewise between his table and the singer's spot. *My ass in your face for you to regret.* A steward had just placed a beer and food in front of the man. Bella found a seat at a table near the stern end with two older ladies who hadn't been waited on yet.

"Join us," offered the first. "It's filling up. I'm Muriel and this is Laney."

"Many thanks," Bella said, placing her shoulder-tote beneath the table.

Muriel's friend, brilliant auburn hair styled as if for prom night or maybe a wedding weekend, lowered her laminated menu and eyed Bella. "I didn't drag my new hip up here just to eat. We wanta sing some duets. When does the crooner get off his ass again?"

"Laney, shush. He'll hear you."

"That's why I'm here. To be heard."

"He had one chicken strip left when I slid behind him," Bella offered.

"Mmmm. Those sound good. *That's* what I smell."

"And maybe we can get some beers up here to go with?" the bronze haired one said.

Boog watched Bella enter, just ahead of the steward returning with a tray of drinks and steaming food. He stared at the tabletop after laying some bills in the kid's hand. "You keep it, the change."

She ain't notice me. Relax. Don't be all crazy. These not too bad. Fries always gotta be hot. That voice I ain't heard for long time. Yackin' with old floozies. Uh-oh. Now this dude wanta sing while I'm try'n' eat.

The karaoke MC wasn't really so bad but Boog was just sitting too close and the tunes meant little to him. Okay, *Blue Bayou*, he liked. He couldn't move his food and beer away from proximity of the big speaker without showing Bella an excellent profile view and probably getting closer..

He emptied the oil-stained plastic basket and tipped back the last of his drink. If the ship's stated capacity was 100 passengers and crew, how could the slot/dining room deck and this open top deck be so crowded? *Overbook against regulation? Like little closet for payphone at Terrebonne.* Maybe he could find some elbow room below now that so many seemed ready to eat and sing up here.

The singer's dinner companion began dancing by herself on the far side of the guy's music locker. Her eyes were closed. *Her motions for the tune so sensual, she think. Alcohol.* Then a man with a protruding beer gut and golf tan made florid by the same beer, took over the mic to do a low-pitched, nearly monotone rendition of *Twist and Shout*.

He reading it is all. That ain't singin'. The two grandmas twisted and shouted, anyway, in Boog's peripheral vision. *Alcohol. Those the same hens Bella clucking with.* Yup, and now Bella danced with them. It was time to remove himself. No opportunity for private confrontation was going to present itself up here, at least not in any of the ways Boog had rehearsed it.

Merry poured another glass of wine. Rather, she had tapped a glass of wine from the clever spigot protruding from the box. It was wine in volume but she wasn't likely to abuse it, given its third-place standing in the table of her anesthesia choices. Their basic cable ran out of programs to interest her. *Sponge Bob* was kinda funny. She *got* most of it, but then Nick-at-Night *wasn't* really very funny generally. *To my weird sense a humor.* Sipping, she drowsed through a *Charles in Charge* episode then raised herself to switch channels. A summer rerun about some high school football team in Texas was not funny ar *all*. Back to Nick-at-Night, but they were now off the air for *satellite maintenance. Well, WTF. Is this a*

*reg'lar thing? Ah never noticed it. My time a the night to be sleepin'
under the influence or workin'.* It was new to her and she watched
TV all hours of the day and early morning, at least semiconscious
when not on a date.

Merry switched back to the local network station. She traded
the remote for her phone off the coffee table. Her *glass dick* pipe
rested there, too, in a metal ashtray. She ignored it. For now. There
was still no word from Bella, yet. Not even a text. *Ah can prob'ly go
sleep in mah own bed.* But, sending no driver's license pic was just
sloppy, even if Bell *did* know the printer-ink guy. *Thinks she knows
a guy? That right there's usu'lly a mistake.*

Well, that does it, thank ya very much. Now Merry was wide
awake. She sat up. Maybe she should rouse her little butt off the
couch and get dressed, make the walk over to the dock to eyeball
the situation up close. Another peek at her cellphone showed that
the time was already nearing 1 a.m. The *Lucky Seas Excursions*
boat should have docked an hour ago. What was she going to do?
Stand there and watch everyone leave? Bella with the printer guy or
some other date, and her, gawking stupid in the headlights? There
was *nothing* to be done but keep texting, though neither of them
wanted the chime to disrupt, possibly, an intimate moment. She
tapped in *Are you on scedgle? You never sent license pic.*

Merry eyed the pipe again. *Wrong time, Mare. Wrong time.* She
darkened the TV screen with the remote and laid back. On the
other hand, she really needed to relax. She groped for her wine
glass by the light of her cellphone, which remained silent.

Chapter Twenty-Seven

Bella drank, danced and laughed with her dinner companions. *Is this the normal life?* She forgot about the strange guy who might have been the last viable single male aboard. Well, she couldn't help him if he wouldn't meet her halfway. Now, where had he even gone? But, she was enjoying her evening now and so why ruin it with worrying about missed work. To her new friends, she was Donna, a hostess at a bistro in Tampa.

"I think we're heading in," Muriel said.

"Darn it," Laney said. "Good times seem mostly fleeting."

The karaoke space emptied quickly and was nearly abandoned except for the MC, his girlfriend, and one other older couple, those folks from Wisconsin. Those two called for the singer to do something slow.

"I felt us turning while that one skinny blond sang *Hit Me With Your Best Shot*," Bella said.

"Gawd. I hope that wasn't *her* best shot." Laney giggled

"Don't be mean, hon," her friend said. "She sure didn't wait around. What do they call it? *Dropping the mic?* It looks like all the rats are abandoning ship."

"Must be they want to lose more money downstairs first," Laney said.

"Oh, I saw some of them going forward," Bella added. "There isn't much room up there but it's a good place to watch us go in. I guess I'll go down and give a few more dollars to the slots."

At that moment, an explosion and its echo met the boat from somewhere ashore.

"What the hell?" Laney moved forward toward the opening, ten feet away, in a permanent canvas divider, backdrop to the karaoke station. "Hey! There's fireworks!"

"Okay, then. Oooooo. Ahhhhh." Muriel sighed. "Another New Port Richie festival-for-whatever. Maybe they forgot 4th of July."

They stood at the divider, Muriel holding an open, zippered flap aside for Laney.

Laney turned. "Nice to've met you, Donna."

"Yes. Maybe I will see you again. I try to go on the sea every week. My addiction is to the peace I feel out there. More than gambling."

"You're further ahead with the peace, for sure, hon," Muriel told her.

Two more bombs went off in close succession, their echoes nearer, bouncing off both shores and overlapping. The boat eased down the channel close enough that they could now hear the falling sizzle of a horsetail round. "You stay well," Laney called.

EVACUATION ROUTE

Bella entered the companionway stair and descended, first through the blackjack deck and then to the starboard walkway. This ran along the outside of the decks from the stern forward. Lighted docks and front rooms of beautiful dockside houses and condos ashore seemed near enough for shouted conversation. She could see many of the other passengers gathered in the dining room to watch the fireworks and have one last drink. She took one step forward to join them when someone's hand fell on her left shoulder, halted and drew her backward.

A second hand slipped up Bella's right arm to flop over that shoulder, lifting her tote bag as it moved. Was she being robbed? Right here? But then her neck was pinched by the inside of someone's muscular elbow and bicep.

"What are you do...?" She could not turn her head. There were dim lights shining from the narrow overhang of the second deck. She saw that dense maze of tattoos from earlier in the evening on the back of her assailant's forearm. *That timid hipster guy? No way!* It was that arm which held her neck like a vice but she could plainly make out the *Knuckledick* logo in three colors on the wrist.

"You don't remember old friends? Why you don't never stop in polite to say hello?"

That accent could not be mistaken. But what had Boog done to himself? He began rocking her head from side to side in the crook of his elbow. "You leave us hangin' without... notice of two weeks for respect. Now you owe *me* to explain."

"Let me loose," Bella croaked. Boog brought his left forearm up and across her throat as well. He abruptly jerked her around so that she was facing aft. From the dining room this might be mistaken for a couple in an embrace. Or, two tipsy gamblers who'd decided, at the last opportunity, to hook up? But who hugs with both arms around a person's the neck?

"You want to be loose, yes?" Boog hissed. "No one is more loose than you."

Bella lifted her foot then and stomped. The heels she'd worn were modest enough but the shoes on either side of her right foot were not biker's boots. But what? There was no resistance. Boog wearing sandals? She didn't noticed the strange guy's feet before, but felt the satisfying crunch of penetration. Some kind of fireworks round from the shore screeched down with more of the sizzle. Part of that shriek must be Boog because now he lifted her with all his kinetic violence, at least one undamaged foot climbing onto the bottom rail for leverage. He brought his full weight down on her pelvis, folding her over the top rail.

We don't look like lovers now. Unless someone has a sick imagination. Can someone please be curious? More bombs detonated above the harbor. *Won't anyone please turn around!* her mind screamed. *Look back here! He is trying to...*Boog had ahold of the heel of her left shoe so he must have let go of her throat. He was trying to lift her but something was caught. She felt him trying to wriggle away from her, untangle himself from her right shoulder. It was his weight that now kept her from drawing breath enough to yell. But, both her arms were now partially freed. She was able to reach back just far enough to find his ears. *His head hanging past mine and over.* Bella awkwardly clapped at his ears but couldn't generate

EVACUATION ROUTE

enough force. *Grab and twist?* Their balance was tilting to the overboard side and then she felt him slip. *I hope it is your sandal that is covered with blood.* The railing was crushing her abdomen. The blood was going to her head. He had lunged too far.

Bella recovered her left arm on the way down. Her right arm was still hung-up on something. *We are falling and coins fall on us.* Heaven's pennies? Then the hipster cap. Maybe Boog failed to grab the rail because *his* right arm was still jerking, trying to pull free of an entanglement with her's, elbow to elbow

There were stars, still, and other lights on the surface, even in the washboard wake of *Narcissus*. They belly smacked into the color bursting sky, reflected now on the petroleum rainbows of the water, coins reflecting, briefly, while there was light, as if the pair now struggled in a wishing fountain. More bombs burst, in harmony of their slap-in-the-face splash. She screamed just as twin bursts of water shot up her nostrils. Was that the big, orchestrated finale going off above them?

His weight drove her under and *he* went well under on top of her, streaming quarters from an inverted pocket. Could he not swim either? He wasn't going to swim very far, tangled up with her. She could only separate partway from beneath him. In trying to get away further, she found his right leg between her thighs. He wasn't kicking. She kept trying to kick, either him or the water, but couldn't. *What is wrong with you? I broke your fall. You cannot be out cold.*

Boog's left hands began to thrash, trying to claw them to the surface. But he succeeded only in delivering a blow to her forehead.

Where is your other hand? Someone must swim for us. They broke the surface for a split second, long enough for Bella to glimpse the stern of *Narcissus* moving away. The hipster cap still afloat.

"My arm." Boog coughed. They went under again.

He couldn't hold them up with only one leg barely kicking and one hand. Bella understood the problem now as Boog tried to yank away from her. The same arm that had first squeezed her neck had slid up through the straps of her tote-bag. *Fool. How did you fuck up so bad?*

She tried to help him by shrugging her shoulder out of the tangle. *We could make it with working together.* But, they were going down. She couldn't find the strap now. Then his elbow...no, his free hand, thrashing in total panic, struck the side of her head.

The blow opened her mouth and parted her from reason. She clawed at that arm now, the one trying to take her bag, and it would not shake free. *This will look so stupid.* She had no air left to laugh out the foul harbor water.

Mama-san was there now, standing on her raft, all the way from the South China Sea, reaching for her. My hand is bound, Mama. Take this one. No, no. not go close to edge. You reach hand to me, I take. Never leave boat, I teach you. Again, again. Hard lesson. The sea have teeth.

Papi, please. Can you reach? Kneel closer. I won't pull you in.

That is surely Papi, standing on the edge of the precarious raft, unstable as a paddle board. Why does he have the .38 revolver now. What became of the fleeing ARVN officer, hero of Mama-sans tale?

EVACUATION ROUTE 515

What if a shark come, Bell? I shoot so you swim away. Yes, Papi, shoot. Please shoot this one who pulls me down. Where is you life preserver? You keep tread in the water. Only one bullet left. Why you not snap onto lifeline on deck? I tell you this always, no joke. Pinch you nose. Kick. Kick like frogman

The bursting star display was finished. Or, too far above for her to see. Boog kicked more slowly, now; he tried to stroke a few more times, weakly with his free hand. But he was turned around in the opposite direction and only drew them deeper, now out of coins. Not enough air left to even scream *cunt*, at which point his last breath would be replaced with the gagging water.

Jamming her right hand into a pocket, Bella made certain he wouldn't get away from her. Like, come back here with me you sick fuck. But when her last popping neurons drifted back to find the fading Mama-san, she was pleased to find Merry on the raft.

Chapter Twenty-Eight

"Good morning Tampa and St. Pete's! Let's get your weekend started! I'm Shawna Landry along with my co-anchor, Kyle Vasquez who is on assignment up in New Port Richie. We'll hear breaking news from Kyle about a gambling cruise that may have returned without two of its passengers. Then we'll catch you up on all you need to know to start off a well informed Saturday: Miguel Bianchi will tell us about the *Rays* win last night. He'll be reporting again from out at *Buccaneer's* training camp where preparations have wrapped up for the preseason opener tonight. Mikala Trumbo has our beautiful weather picture which, unfortunately, includes report from NOAA of a *pair* that's right, *two* tropical disturbances we can start worrying about soon. Good morning, Mikala! It looks like our guys have cleared out early."

"It appears so, Shawna. They've left us girls to hold the fort."

"Well, it's what we do, sister. We'll have that weather picture in just a little bit, but first I believe Kyle is ready with that remote

EVACUATION ROUTE

from New Port Richie. What's the story up there, Kyle? Two passengers from a gambling boat really didn't come back?"

"Right, Shawna. Behind me you see three teams of officers, divers and their boats getting ready to launch for a search of the channel out into the Gulf. There are *definitely* two gamblers missing according to passenger manifests and eye witness reports. Ken, can you pan over to that fence behind the *Lucky Seas Excursions* Booking and Welcome? More to the right. There. That vehicle in the picture, Shawna, is an older model Chevy Geo Tracker. It and the Honda motorcycle about twenty feet away... there it is, were left here when all other passenger vehicles had departed. Police are already attempting to learn the identities of the owners. Shawna, this is Susan Tillman, an Associate Manager for *Lucky Seas*. Susan, tell us how you first learned that a tragedy may have taken place."

Said what, now? What about *Lucky Seas?* Did she just dream that? Work related images were often likely to surface when Merry was about to awaken. Older, family related issues and traumas, when she dreamed those and could remember the dreams, dominated deeper slumber and were difficult to climb out of. *Why have Ah left it on the dang news, anyhow. An' droolin' like a li'l tittybaby, stickin' all over to mahself. Oh, right. Finally smoked that iddy-bitty crumb a crystal 'n' looked for a rerun to go with. That one show about the playboy guy who his brother 'n' nephew move in with him. Ah seen some a that one before. That one ol' boy's a piece a work on ET.*

Now here was the morning news, which she would never watch on purpose. How early in the morning it actually was, she had

518   CHRIS DUNGEY

yet to determine. The blinds were closed over both living room windows.

Oh, mah lord. Merry reached to the coffee table, scrabbling about for the TV remote. She back-handed the winebox of merlot she'd been drawing from all through the previous evening. It tipped over easily though she heard a slosh inside. So, she hadn't killed it, *that* was encouraging. *Aww, fuck. Wine hangover comin', too. Fuzzy 'round the edges from somethin' Ah guess Ah musta smoked.*

"Shawna, police say they will be contacting passengers for interviews and statements this morning, including two ladies who waited for a third to emerge from the boat. So, they know that one of the missing is a female. Here's more from Susan Tillman: "So, these two women I mentioned were waiting for a young lady named Donna they'd met to give her their contact information. They did not remember her last name. When she didn't leave the boat, they came to me. We immediately began a bow to stern search of *Narcissus*. I'm afraid there was no Donna signed onto our manifest. "

See there? Someone name a Donna, Relax. Merry turned up the volume of the talking heads on the screen anyway. Now a guy was droning baseball scores, and the weather was coming next. *Decent lookin' guy. Shirt sleeves 'n' no tie. Must be a casu'l Saturday. Okay, okay. Rays won. What about Narcissus?*

Another commercial. Don't fuckin' doze off, now. Bell has used made-up names before. She closed her eyes on the headache image of Bell playing a few last hands while the boat emptied and then the parking lot. She'd be playing against Phillip, maybe even just for fun, happy not to be earning from the printer-ink guy or a new stranger. *Yer still gonna get a earful 'bout not textin' back to me, either way. Ah'm gonna pay it some attention, so this better not be 'bout you.*

"Thank you, Mikala. We'll all enjoy a picture perfect Florida weekend while we stock up on water and batteries. I guess I need to locate where I stored the plywood sheets from last year. We'll get back up to Kyle Vasquez in New Port Richie for any new details about those gambling cruise disappearances after this word from your Bay Area Chrysler Jeep dealers."

Someone disappeared off the *Narcissus*. Even in her present brainstate, she could put *those* clues together. *Them new models a Jeep Wrangler ain't exactly flyin' offa the lot, it don't look like. Hey, that'n with the canvas hoody over the back end looks like a ripoff a mah Tracker. It's even green, for chrissake.*

"Welcome back. You're looking live at a vehicle thought to belong to one of the missing persons."

Confused for only a split second, Merry was up on one elbow again. Her right hand flew to her mouth as her feet wrestled out from under a robe she'd flung over her legs. A gasp became something like a sob as her feet hit the floor. She didn't scream, yet, but her groaning went on-and-on, growing in volume from a low, sad, song into a loud keening. *Bell, no! Bella, no. no, no, no, no!* She turned up the volume. *Bell? Bella, please no?* When the camera

520 CHRIS DUNGEY

shifted from the Tracker to the motorcycle, and she recognized it, then she screamed like the loud yelp of a large dog. *Who the fuck..? Who are you? What in the...fuck? What'd ya do you...ya crazy bastard?* Some tears, unfamiliar to her now bloodshot eyes and pale cheeks, began to stream.

Remote still in hand, she surfed down a few stations. Maybe another report would straighten it all out, wipe it all away. A later...what? An update. A correction. *Denial.*

She stopped on an NBC affiliate. What she wanted to see had to wait for the end of a Chevy commercial, a jovial manager trying to fake a genuine smile, shouting his bargains in front of a full lot of new vehicles. *Just get yer fat ass off'n there! Y'all're goin' under!* Then Merry saw Susan, a different microphone poked in her face. It was the same story though, and the camera returned to the reporter's face:

"That's all the information we have for now, Toby. Police say there will be another briefing at 10am. Meanwhile, they'll be scouring their database for those registrations. The rescue slash recovery mission continues.

The broadcast returned to the news desk. That Toby's kinda pretty. Merry paced down the short hallway in a pair of satin boxers, leaving her robe on the floor. On her next lap back to the front window, she turned up the AC. She wiped another tear with the inside of a wrist. *Omigod, Bella. They're gonna come knockin'. What'm Ah gonna do, Bell? Ah did cream pretty hard that one time. Ah mighta been a li'l that way. Don't know why Ah couldn't admit to it 'n' Ah'm so, so sorry. Mighta been lez with you, if anybody. But wait a minute now, wasn't there some problem Ah had with that registration. Ah ain't had the Tracker long enough to show the papers 'n' get plates. That ol' boy Ah bought it from. Can't remember what the deal was with him, but somethin' funny about it.*

She sobbed at an image in her mind, the softness of a makeup brush, light on her forehead. *Don't let me leave this house shinin'.* Bella's other hand would have gripped firmly between shoulder and neck to keep her still. There was always the perfect hint of blush, too. *Ah know Ah got the title in mah handbag 'n' not in the glovebox. That was parta him sweetenin' the deal... that them plate tags had almost of a year left on 'em. No registration because the VIN number got jimmied somehow but we had plenty a time to figure out somethin'. Bell? You remember how that went?*

Merry sat back down on the couch. *Now girl, you gotta get yerself right and quick, too. Find out who that fucker was 'n' go from there. How could thata been you, Bell?* Would there be any identifying papers in her bag, other than a driver's license she had to get. What did she use for an address? *No way, Bell. Was you try'n to decide about playin' with somebody ya shouldn't of? Do Ah hang loose, just sit tight 'til Ah know for sure? Ain't they the same thing though? Fuck. Ah don't know.*

For the first time since she awakened to the story, the idea of Boogaloo and Wood-Chuck maybe still watching for them crossed her mind. *But, that foreign bike, the one Ah seen? How could Boog sit on anythin' but a Harley? They called them bikes rice burners because they was Jap built. Rest a the 'Dicks woulda not thought it*

522   CHRIS DUNGEY

was very funny. Boog crazy enough not to worry what any of 'em thought.

Refocusing on pulling herself together, *getting herself right,* Merry went into the bathroom and started the shower running. She swallowed two aspirin then crossed to her bedroom for fresh underwear, some shorts and a top. When she opened the bifold closet door to flick through her tops, she nearly kicked into her old *go-bag* project. *Bell, ya was always teasin' me about it. Ah hate it that what ya said was just my paranoia has come out true. We shoulda both paid more attention.* She dragged the duffel out and lifted it onto the end of her bed. This wasn't going to serve if she had to go on foot.

Leaving the bathroom after a final burst of cold water (*Geez-us! Don't give yer li'l ticker a infraction, or whatever*). She wrapped a towel around her shoulders and went to stand behind the couch. Still showing the Tampa NBC affiliate, the anchorman once again referred his viewers back to a New Port Richie remote feed:

Toby, police are now saying that the motorcycle left here last night, probably by one of the missing passengers, is registered to a Beauregard LaVelle of Tampa. They are puzzled that the name does not show up on the manifest of the *Lucky Seas* craft, *Narcissus.* By process of elimination, it appears that Mr. Lavelle had used an alias for some reason when boarding. Compounding the identification mystery is that the other vehicle left in the lot, the Chevy Tracker, was believed stolen in Ft. Meyers two years ago. The VIN number beneath the windshield appears to have been

EVACUATION ROUTE 523

altered. Police will, sadly, have to await recovery of bodies to determine the ID of the other victim.

Merry had to sit down. Again, she began a long groan as if never to stop, as if for a pain just short of requiring her to scream. She groaned until she was out of breath. She *had* screamed for her real Daddy—the one who cracked up his car when she was ten. Then she grieved awhile. Not as long as Ma, but probably because she had a child's concerns for approaching puberty to distract her. Step-daddy was accorded little grieving after his wracking lung cancer. She had to help clean up after his ruined digestives system for three years, ducked and dodged his semiconscious groping. Ma gravitated toward a particular type and Merry sorrowed for her. But, that passing was mostly a relief.

She had nothing, particularly, left unsaid to any of *those* ghosts. But already she was thinking of things she'd have to pray into the void for Bella. *Like, Ah loved you. Sister love mostly. It wasn't nothin' 'bout when Ah mighta cummed because it was you 'n' we was wrapped up swapends for the Knuckledicks or Jack's pals 'n' Ah mighta forgot for awhile they was even in the room. Shoulda said somethin' like "love ya, sister" with 'sister' not bein' just some slang.*

An' all that time, ever since Ah first seen that fucker 'n' his bike at the light on 19, it was crazy Boogaloo. What'd even possess his sick soul to wait on us 'n' stalk us like that? It don't make normal sense. What'm Ah gonna do, Bell? Should Ah take off to somewheres?

Did she even have time to hang around and *learn* all the details? Could the cops find her through that bogus VIN number? It wouldn't lead to *this* address. She had not even bothered to transfer the registration because the plates were good until late fall. What would the police want from her anyway? There was no probable cause to enter the bungalow, no reason for them to probe the girls' source of income. Did she or her *partner* know this LaVelle character? *What happens if Ah get caught in a lie? They're bound to go callin' on the Knuckledicks. Better just sit tight 'n' see what happens? Might be too late by then. No. Hang loose, dummy. You ain't even for certain if anybody's dead yet. An' if Boog drowned, do ya think ol' Wood-Chuck has the ambition to keep after us?*

Her whimpering finally ceased as groping for strategies reclaimed her thinking process. She decided to remain in front of the TV reports until all the critical information was known to her. *An' Ah gotta stay awake now. Shake off these adverse effects 'n' not invite no more. No one goes onto the nod at them candlelight vigils if a vigil is what Ah'm keepin'.* But Merry's mind *did* drift to the go-bag now resting on her bed.

'"Wood, are you seeing this here?" Ivan Dresbach asked Wood-Chuck Spurgeon. He was sitting at the bar, watching the television while Spurgeon reviewed the appointment book for the Club girls. A policeman on the screen stood before several microphones in front of what appeared to be the hull of a big boat. With every other line, the officer looked back at his notes.

EVACUATION ROUTE

"Good morning. Ah'm Captain Barth, New Port Richie Police Department. This is the 10am briefing as promised regarding gamblers reported missing off the motorcraft, *Narcissus*. Uhhm...which you see behind me."

The camera jerked away to show the first catwalk/promenade and then the two upper decks. The shot returned as abruptly to Captain Barth. "Nice production values," Ivan said. "Hey! Holy shit! *Now* has it got your attention?" On screen, the officer had been replaced by a Louisiana mug shot of Beauregard "Boogaloo" Lavelle.

"The owner of the Honda Gold Wing motorcycle left in the passenger parking lot last night is this man, Beauregard LaVelle, whose arrest record we have located in Houma, Louisiana. This individual also has a record down here; a number of complaints for violent incidents, assaults, and disturbing the peace in Tampa. The other victim we've recovered carried a Driver's License identifying her as Isabella Nguyen-Ruiz of Gulf City, Florida. No known current address. No papers in her possession link her to the other vehicle left in the lot of the *Lucky Seas Excursions* dock facility. Due to the disposition of the bodies recovered by divers from the Pasco County Sheriff's Marine Division, we are suspecting some manner of foul play or misadventure on the part of one or both of the deceased. We'll provide another statement this evening, pending coroner's report and positive IDs of the victims. This has to be done since the male body does not much resemble Mr. LaVelle's police photograph, though height and build are consistent. We

526 CHRIS DUNGEY

continue, also, to interview other persons listed on last night's manifest.

"Wood?"

Wood-Chuck Spurgeon sat his usual comfortable position two stools away from Archie Caulkins. He could only shake his head, hoping that would signify a stunned disbelief. *Had me fooled. Shoulda had a sense. I knew he really wouldn't let go 'n' I ignored it. What could I a done? That poor...*

The guy had always been such a stressful pain-in-the-ass to manage, to keep control of, but they'd somehow worked together for a long time. *Who else in this bunch do I know as well as that whack-job? Now I'm gonna have to do somethin'. Step up 'n' set an example a heartbreak. Would rather shed a few tears for poor Bella. Just gonna have to get those hard things done. First off, how'm I sup'osed to contact his people? An' I gotta have a uncomfortable chat now with my own people. Ma. She's gonna be as near to pissed off as she ever gets. Tired a bein' a disappointment to her. An' you know the cops're gonna come for a visit, sure as shit.*

"Chief, if we're holdin' any product on the premises at the moment, ya think we better move it out? Quick, like?"

"Way ahead a ya, Wood," Caulkins agreed. "Well, it prob'ly occurred to me about the time you said it, but...I don't think there's any distribution weight in the place. Just for my personal use 'n' it's flushable. How 'bout you, Ivan?"

"I wish," the substitute bartender said. He held the TV remote, flipping through for more news of Boogaloo.

EVACUATION ROUTE

"Hey, Wood?" *The Darkness* said. "What ties him to us, anyways? It don't sound like he was wearin' his colors. They'da been here already."

"That's a fine, not wearin' 'em in public," Ivan said. He paused the TV on an infomercial for copper infused stockings.

Wood shot him a sour glance and *The Darkness* said, "Geez, that's kinda cold, don't ya think?"

"Too soon?"

"Yeah. But you might not be far off," *The Darkness* said. "He mighta had some Club cash on him for errands and we'll never see it again."

Wood left his seat to go behind the bar. "He was taking a couple more personal days. I *thought*. There was a couple of assault beefs that was Club related, I believe. They was both pled down to Disturbin' the Peace; maybe Malicious Mischief or some such because the victims was just other bikers. But the cops'll figure out who to come visit."

The Darkness waddled around the end of the bar for a refill of coffee. "Ivan, would ya get out the brandy for me?" He, like all the girls, Ivan himself, and a few other members, had acquired distinctive or personalized mugs. "Ain't that just the way of it, though, Wood? It's prejudice. Maybe we should do a toy drive at Christmas like some Clubs do."

Really? Our standin' in the community is what yer worried about? "Won't help. Always been that way, Chief." *Why don't you think about how we're gonna honor ol' Boog who was nuts long*

528 CHRIS DUNGEY

before we knew him. Somethin' scary drove him to have this stupid reckonin' with them poor girls.

"Listen, Chief." Wood called after *The Darkness* who now headed into his office with sudden purpose. *Anxious about his stash.* "When alla this settles out, we gotta have the ceremony. Put his ashes in some special place around here if we can get ahold of 'em. I'll try'n reach his next-a-kin."

"Wouldn't we be doing *all* those folks a favor, taking over the remains?" Ivan Dresbach's search had landed on CNN. "Hey, I forgot that we get this in the Basic Package. It looks like they've picked up the story. They love weird violence. Especially in Florida."

"So now we're weird?" *The Darkness* passed behind the bar again from the office and into the bathroom. This time he carried two whithered, snack size Zip-Lock bags, one with muddy green shreds gathered in a bottom corner, the other dusted white inside. "There's never no justice for bikers."

"Nah, Chief. *We're* not the weird ones until Boog's life story leaks out. Right now they wanta make the gamblin' boat folks look stupid 'n' us just violent." Wood said. "But, I guess it all lumps inta their category a Florida people."

"This ain't enough weight for anythin' but Possession. I just don't need the hassle. I been meanin' to quit anyhow." He laughed out loud and didn't bother to close the crapper door. Everyone within earshot laughed.

Wood and Ivan heard *The Darkness* sniffing deeply and then a prolonged, choking flush. He reemerged still snuffling and wiping

EVACUATION ROUTE

his mustache. "We gotta get a plumber in here. Glad it wasn't a pound 'r somethin'."

"I'm pretty sure we got plumbin' guys or an apprentice mebbe on the rolls." Wood said. "I'll check."

"Whew! Okay, Wood! Whatever!" Caulkins shook himself like a wet dog. "Whew! My, my! That there's still a good way to start a shitty day!"

Chapter Twenty-Nine

It was Maxwell Bocewicz who answered Walt's mother's door on the fourth gong. Walt was puzzled for a beat by the presence of the unfamiliar, squared away looking young man standing in his mother's stained glass doorway. "Oh, my gosh!" This exclamations took most of his breath as the realization smacked him at the top step of three. "Max?"

Max reached to offer a steadying handshake. "Careful there, old-timer. Yes, it's me in the flesh. Hey, good looking ride."

Walt returned the firm grip, glancing over his shoulder, *Oh yeah, the Caddy.*

It could be no one else as Walt looked his boy in the eye. The kid's face had filled in to adulthood. Raggedy jeans were replaced by flawless skinny ones. His hair was cut much shorter than the last time Walt saw him.

"You've never seen her, have you?" Walt's voice was constricting with emotion.

EVACUATION ROUTE

"Dad," Max maintained the handshake, drawing Walt into the surprisingly cool front foyer. "I haven't seen *you* in about three years. I think I saw it under a cover at Uncle Warren's place."

"He had protective custody, yeah. But, well, what...?" Walt didn't want to say *what are you doing here.* "What's going on with you?"

"I had a few days free of academia," Max said. He stepped back to close the door. "Better close this quick-like. It was all we could do to get Grams to turn up the AC. It's so damn humid down here."

We? Walt wondered. "Big storm coming, I hear. Probably. So who else is here?" The sky above the last hour of his drive had turned a deep grey. It had a poised look and seemed to be holding its breath, as if sentient and trying to impress upon him that it was serious. There was no movement of air as Walt stretched then went up to the front door.

Max led him through the living room, dining room, and kitchen with several pauses to turn and enlighten. "You knew Uncle Warren and Charlotte moved in here, right?"

"I thought they would. Kinda hoped they would. I've been so busy. You wouldn't believe the wreckage of the little dump mobile home I've been renovating. Well, I hired and supervised a lot of it."

"Yeah, Grams has been telling me. As much as she knows. You haven't sent any pictures is her big complaint."

"Not sure it's photo ready yet. I'll try to do better but my phone is pretty low tech." Walt said. "They didn't put a camera in it.

The place was pretty appalling. I called her on Mother's Day and a couple other times. Is everyone doubtful of my carpentry skills?"

"Oh, yeah. So, anyway...do you want something to drink?" Max pulled open the refrigerator half of the buffed, stainless side-by-side. "Michelle is supposed to roll in, too, before she does a couple of semesters in the UK. Uncle Warren wants us to do some kind of intervention with Grams."

Walt shuddered. "*There's* a term I hoped never to hear again."

"Sorry. That might be too strong for what he wants to do. We're supposed to convince her to clear out of here until these storms have passed or taken a different route. I think Uncle Warren is the one who wants to go and he can't just leave her here."

"Well, that's a relief." Walt sighed. "You had me going there. I thought she might be mainlining again." *God, I'm gonna turn to salt. Why don't I keep my mouth shut?*

Max laughed. "I can only imagine what that *is*, Dad. He'd like to take her to Europe and do some kind of EuroRail grand tour thing. Three weeks long is the one he showed me. Cool brochure. But the main thing is to get her out of here and moving around until storm season is done."

"And Michelle is going to study in England. I'm floored. Oxford or Cambridge?"

"Well, nothing like that." Max lifted drinks from the refrigerator. "London School of Economics."

Does that count as an apple not falling far from the tree? A distant cousin to accounting? Walt chose a bottle of water from one of his son's hands. The other hand carried a Diet Coke and a Squirt

EVACUATION ROUTE

533

between his fingers. "You guys and Gram really ought to put out a Christmas letter. I'm getting behind on everything again." He tipped the water back while eyeing the coffee machine and its beaker on the counter. It *looked* hot. *But aren't I getting enough stimulation?*

"Come on out on the patio," Max said. "They're all mesmerized by the sea. It's a game of chicken, seeing who will start packing first."

Geez, I just got here, people. He followed his son through the living room. "So, do you think they've convinced her?" *Wow. I'm having a conversation with my son who seems to have become an adult.*

"I think they can get her to take a road trip. Uncle Warren was talking about some chloroform left over from the store. I *think* he was joking. He wants to get a few days north before the motels along I-95 or 75 fill up. I don't know how the Europe idea is going over." Max pulled the large slider aside for them to go onto the patio.

"Hey, look who's here!" Loud welcomes from Warren and Charlotte at the Plexiglass patio table greeted him like a surprise talk show walk-on. His mother turned slowly, found him over her shoulder: "Join us, Walter." The umbrella remained furled, a padded flagstaff pointing into the morose sky. Warren and Charlotte rose to approach with hugs while his mother turned slowly back to what was most likely a mimosa.

"Am I in time to help nail up the plywood," Walt asked. "This place will need a *lot* of plywood."

"Nah." Warren pulled an uncomfortable looking chair out for his brother. "It's starting to track more south, the usual route across Cuba. It'll be a few more days. They haven't started modeling the second one yet."

"Well this weather seemed incredible already," Max said. "I feel like a tourist at this point because I don't remember it being so...equatorial, I suppose."

"Isn't that extraordinary? Two on the map at the same time?" Mrs. Bocewicz squeaked.

"Mom, are you getting laryngitis?" Walt said.

"Global warming, Grams," Max said, still grasping the back of a chair. "We don't have any climate change deniers in the house, do we?"

"It's only like this in the morning," Mrs. Bocewicz said. "Until I irrigate my throat."

"Actually, we've had it scanned," Warren said. "She has some tiny tracheal nodes. We were told that they didn't warrant a biopsy. They're keeping an eye on them." He made air quotes.

"I haven't looked very deeply into climate change, Max." Walt saw the beading pitcher of mimosas on the table. "I've been oblivious, followed by very busy. Maybe you can bring me up to speed."

The boy must have been following his father's gaze. "Oh. Yeah. Let me go get you some coffee or something first." He turned back toward the house before ever sitting. "Black?"

"That'd be nice." Walt watched his son reenter the house. *A grown man's build. Wonder what his recreation of choice is.*

EVACUATION ROUTE

"As a practical matter," Warren resumed. "Global warming or not, we want to get Mom away from here before the rush. She'd like to visit an old sorority sister up in Savannah, as it turns out." He replenished his own glass from the pitcher.

"It was only a thought, after your badgering. I still have to call her, Warren," Mrs. Bocewicz cautioned. "Make sure Margot has no other plans."

"Right, right. In which case, or if this storm heads that way, we'll look up someone else."

"Good heavens, I'm not afraid of another silly *weather event*. That's all it is. So some daredevil can stand in the surf with a microphone in his hand." Mrs. Bocewicz reached for the pitcher and Warren helped her pour.

"Warren *has* been rather an alarmist." Charlotte looked up with a disarming smile. "If he wasn't so ecology conscious, he'd probably would have left the car running and ready for this one."

"*This one* is called Danielle, sweetheart, and she has a kid brother trailing along behind. With the ocean water so warm, you can't take them lightly. No more hurricane parties."

"So I'm just in time to head back home?"

"No, no Walt. We're going to hang on for a few more days until Danielle decides for sure where she's going," Warren said. "I am *not* the alarmist that Mom and Charlotte are suggesting. Mom will make a list of friends and I'll coordinate reservations near them. Right, Mother?"

"Oh, tosh. I suppose so."

Was she the perpetrator of 'oh, tosh?'

536   CHRIS DUNGEY

Now Max placed a steaming mug in front of Walt. "Well, whatever else, I'm heading back to NYC where I won't have to change my shirt three times a day. Yeah, Dad. Like Uncle Warren said, our immediate jeopardy is all about rising ocean temperatures. You don't want to hear about the *tipping point*, the thawing tundra, or the collapse of the Gulf Stream."

"So you can run, but you can't hide, Max?" Charlotte laughed.

"No he cannot," Warren said. "They used to peter out in Georgia but now they cross back into the Atlantic, catch their second wind and head for New Jersey."

"Second wind. Good one, Uncle Warren. "I hope it goes straight up Wall Street. Wash away all the hedge fund corpses."

Well, easy to see why he isn't going into Economics, Walt thought. *Mom should go anywhere she wants. Or just stay here and watch the surge rise. But it looks like I'd be the one keeping her company.* What he really wanted to do was catch up on his son's life.

"Can we at least settle on going out for some brunch?" Warren drained his glass. Walt, have you ever in your life been asked to be a designated driver?"

"No, that would be a first."

"If there's a brunch where we're going," Mom Bocewicz said. She likewise finished her drink, though more slowly and with both hands trembling around the tall glass. "I haven't totally committed to any road trip or whatever and I don't want to end up chloroformed in Walter's trunk."

"Hey, we didn't think of *that,*" Charlotte said. "Mom, I don't know what you have against a tour of sorority sisters and Civil War

EVACUATION ROUTE

battlefields. We can start at Look-Out Mountain. Chattanooga has a wonderful aquarium, too, I hear."

"Remind me to bring something to read."

"Say, Warren, my trunk is clean and quite roomy if you wanta go with the chloroform," Walt said, earning a laugh.

When Warren stood up and slid his chair back under, grating the patio stones, the change of venues was signaled. "Walt and Max, we should lug all of these things inside when we get back. This table is pretty heavy."

"Sure. This'd make an easy projectile." Walt dug the Caddy's keys out of his pocket.

"Let me use the bathroom first," Mrs. Bocewicz rose from her seat with some assistance from Charlotte who then took her arm to cross the patio stones.

Well, she seems in a steeper downward trend than at Christmas. I should have been over here every month. Warren must not have wanted to bother me about it. Nodes on her larynx? I'm thinking that deserves a second opinion. Walt waited for them to totter into the house then closed the slider. *All of them clearing out of here is probably the smart thing.* He hoped to have Max sit up front with him for this brunch outing.

"It's *still* lookin' like another nice day in paradise," Dianne Kaake said as the women hiked along the horseshoe layout of *The Glade*. "A little sweatier than usual, maybe."

"When ain't it sweaty," Darlene Spurgeon said. "Yeah, hon. Them ol' storms are a ways out. If one of 'em even heads this way. Don't it ever seem to you when folks start to get excited that they kinda *want* it to come?" *And why'm Ah up so damn early when Ah ain't got a shift? Oh, right. Better look in on Antoine.* She held the key to Walt Bocewicz's place in her sweat-slippery hand.

"Sure, I've thought that," Dianne said. "I remind Curtis all the time, them hurricane watch parties'r overrated. Get us all down to the Clubhouse 'cause of its got concrete walls. Prob'ly ain't much safer. Say, you gonna let me come in 'n' see where the magic happens?"

"Goes without sayin'. An' you can help me dust 'n' make the bed if he left it. Ah'm gonna do up any dishes 'n' get the garbage out, too."

"Hell's bells, girlfriend," Dianne said. "If I'da known this was a work detail…well, I already got a man, so-called, 'n' I don't do no more for him than necessary for basic hygiene."

"Okay, then. How're you at cleanin' cat boxes?" Darlene turned in under Walt's carport. She moved the screen door slider aside with a warped screech of metal and stepped into the Florida room.

EVACUATION ROUTE

539

"WD 40 ain't gonna fix that no matter how much he uses." She unlocked and Dianne followed her up two steps into the kitchen.

"Wow. He has really done a good job," Dianne said. "This here's gettin' to be almost livable."

"He's gettin' there. Antoine! Antoine! Dinner time!" Darlene found a serving-size can of cat food in the pantry closet. "You ever taste this stuff?" She held the can for Dianne to read. Roast Turkey Bits in Gravy.

"Hell, no. I ain't ever been *that* hungry."

"It's pretty much tasteless," Darlene said. "Ah just had some a the gravy on mah fingertip. Antoine! Bring yer big ol' butt out here 'n' say hello! Ah think it's 'cause he don't know you."

Darlene's cell phone chimed from the hip-pocket of her cut-offs. *Honkey-Tonk Bedonkadonk.*

"How'd you get that on there? I love Trace Adkins!"

"This is mah theme song," Darlene replied. She opened the flip-phone and pressed the green telephone icon to accept. "Well, good mornin', Baby-boy! When are you gonna get on the road?" *It's Charlie,* she lip-synced to Dianne. "Hold on for a second. Ah'll put'ch y'on speaker if Ah can find it. Say hullo to mah besty, Dianne."

"Hey, Dianne," spoke a metal-shadowed voice. Don't know if we met. What're y'all up to? Have ya happened to look at the news this mornin'?"

Darlene held the phone away from her face so that she could aim her voice at the tiny mic holes. "Naw, we're just on our second cup

540 CHRIS DUNGEY

a coffee after ar mornin' walk. Ah'm at Darlene's place." She held up a constraining finger for Dianne not to betray the fib.

"Well, ya'll need to check the news. Some weird shit went down last night up to New Port Richie. That friend a mine, my assistant at the Club, went and got himself killed."

Darlene's free hand went reflexively to her chest. "Just tell me yer all right, Baby-boy. What the hell've they got you into down there?" Maybe Sandy was steering her true when she warned that there was something fishy about Charlie's job.

"I'm uh, totally...well, you know...a little blue, now, but I'm fine, Ma," Charley said. An unusual quaver had crept in to stumble his words. "We don't even think...yet, we don't know if it was anythin' to do...with the Club. It's a mystery to us. The cops'll have to sort it all out. Just check it out when the news bulletins rolls around. Ever' station in Tampa's makin' a big deal out of it. But, the long 'n' the short of it is that..."

Oh, yeah. This is gonna somehow bite mah heart in the butt, Darlene thought. *Ah know when that voice ain't very confident if it's truthin' or not.*

"Anyway, I'm gonna be held up."

Now Darlene's reaction shifted into an aggravation she couldn't filter from her voice. *He's heard it before. Ever' report card. Well, it shouldn't surprise him.* "Now you ain't gonna show up! After scarin' the beJesus outta me with more a that gang stuff? What's this boy got to do with you takin' vacation time?"

Darlene could hear a television in Wood's background noise, the arguing and loud opinions of rough voices. Whiskey and cigarette

EVACUATION ROUTE 541

voices she'd heard all her life. She motioned Dianne toward Walt's TV in the living room and mimed a remote in her hand.

"Nothin', except we're shorthanded at the moment, is all. We gotta put together some kinda ceremony 'n' I've gotta line up some bartenders. Then there's this storm comin', that I'll have to help close up the Club."

"Oh, blah, blah, blah."

"No, listen. If we have to evacuate, or even if it's just close up, I'll be on my way to y'all."

"Ah'll believe *that* when Ah see it. You keep goin' on playin' with yer poor ol' Ma's feelin's. Ah've gone 'n' bought all yer favorite food, too. Yer Honey Nut Cheerios. Ah was gonna fix ribs one night. Have a party 'n' show you off to mah friends,"

Darlene was gratified to hear, she believed, some real anguish creeping into her son's voice: "Ma, come on. Won't it keep a few more days? *Please,* don't bust my nads about this? I feel bad enough already. It won't be more'n two more days. Three tops."

"What channel?" Dianne called from the living room.

"Tell her 28. That's ABC for Tampa."

"Wow. You could hear that?"

"Yeah, Ma. Ya don't have to put yer mouth right on the microphone hole. You've got a decent phone if it's the same one I seen at Christmas."

"Yer tryin' to deflect me. It just irks me to think it was that long since Ah seen ya. BTW, is *nads* any way to speak to yer Mama? Is that standard for bikers talkin' to their Mamas?"

"Sorry," Wood said. "But I feel guilty enough without no help. The guy was sort of a close friend, I guess. An' besides, it always seems like whenever I'm up there, yer anxious to get the place back to yerself."

Darlene shifted into the living room to see the television but stepped back through the kitchen arch as the cell coverage wavered. "Hold on one sec, Baby-boy. Ah think Dianne found that story." She tried one step into the living room again, leaning far enough to see Walt's small screen. "Ah'll admit that yer accusation is sometimes true. Ah do love mah private, not-that-old-yet Grandma time. But, it's never been *you* Ah had to shoo outta here, Charlie. Oh, mah Good Lord. Is *that* your friend?" A stark, black-and-white Louisiana mug shot of Boogaloo LaVelle had appeared.

"What are ya watchin'?"

"What station is that, Di?"

"It's CNN, darlin'. Wow, this here's a big story if *they* picked it up."

Wood's voice had begun to break up a bit. "Yeah, they picked up the story 'cause Boog 'n' this young woman didn't come back with the rest of a gamblin' trip out in the Gulf. They was somehow left out to sea or in the harbor somewheres."

Darlene's brief glimpse of Boog had been enough. She retreated to the clearer reception in the kitchen. "That boy, there, looks like the wrath a God. It sure don't make me feel more easy about yer job, 'n' the folks you 'ssociate with."

EVACUATION ROUTE

Wood said: "It's an old picture, Ma. He recently cleaned himself up. Another mystery to us. Us 'n' the cops both are tryin' to figure out what he had to do with the other victim cuz it looked real suspicious."

"Like how, Charlie?"

Dianne called loudly from the neighboring room: "They was all tangled up! An' not in a friendly way! It looks like they mighta drownd each other."

"That is plain awful, Baby-boy," Darlene groaned. "Ah hope none a that blows back on you nor yer Club."

"Well, listen, Ma. I need to get off from talkin' to y'all I so can keep up with the story 'n' get things done here. They're coverin' that storm already and it only just come past Cuba. Guess it's a big'un."

Darlene felt a tear beginning in one eye. She sniffed. "Ah ain't worried about that, yet. Ah been clearin' mah calendar for you. Now Ah gotta worry about this thing, too. Just get your butt on up here, okay?"

"A few more days, Ma. Cross my heart 'n' hope to...Well, anyway. I love ya 'n' I'll see ya soon."

Wood ended the call before Darlene could return the sentiment.

"Ain't that somethin', though? Charlie might get to be on the TV if the cops go to interview them bikers."

Darlene returned the flip-phone to her hip pocket. "Ah'll be just as happy if he *don't* get his fifteen minutes a fame or however many. Now Ah'm gonna go dip a few turds out the cat box. Antoine! Then we can go watch it unfold at mah place.

544 CHRIS DUNGEY

Dianne turned off Walt's television and returned to the kitchen. "Don't ya wanta go through his drawers 'n' see if he's kept any x-rated pitchures a y'all?"

Darlene carried a bag of kibble down to the master bedroom where the cat's dishes were placed. She carried the water dish back to the kitchen, rinsed and filled it. "We ain't got around to anythin' like that, yet, but you give me an idea."

"Oh, boy. Why don't ya'll make a video. I need *somethin'*." Dianne followed her back down the hall.

"It ain't anythin' like that. Ah'm thinkin' a emptyin' out this collection a woreout tighty-whities 'n'replacin' back some colored briefs."

"My, oh my, girlfriend. Y'all try 'n' make sweet love on that l'il ol' twin bed? Does Walt feel like he's still in high school?"

"Well, Ah think he's been in various rehabs 'n' so-forth where he's use to a cot," Darlene said. "Anyways, it just about guarantees cuddlin' afterwards. You wanta make an underwear run with me out to Wal-Mart?"

"I guess that's about as much fun as I can expect today. I got no idea where Curtis went off to. Prob'ly gone off somewhere buy'n up ammunition. He's always hopin' for looters. So, Walt was in rehab, huh? Must be why he sips on them *O'Douls* like they was a nectar a the Gods."

"They been a lifesaver to him." Darlene spilled dry kibble into Antoine's dish to overflowing, in case she got very busy tomorrow. "Ah know yer under there," she addressed the bed. "Ah'm tellin' Walt you was unsociable to Dianne."

Darlene gave the place a quick inspection. Walt's bathroom sink had a slow drip that he hadn't gotten around to fixing but everything else was squared away. Dianne followed her out. They locked up. Darlene gave the slider screen frame a heavy dose of WD-40 that had been left conveniently, companion to a flyswatter, on the lanai table. "What're you doin' raidin' Walter's refrigerator?" She noticed the quart of 2% milk Dianne carried.

"Don't want it to turn on 'im, do ya." Dianne tipped it back. "Ya know, Wal-Mart'll be jammed today. Mebbe we should get batteries 'n' bottled water, too, if there's some left."

"These snowbird residents panic about ten days early, Ah've noticed. Ah want them colorful skivvies 'n' a tub a sweet coleslaw. Figure mebbe Ah'll go ahead 'n' do them ribs. Throw a hurricane party."

"Darlin' don't get ahead a the weatherman like a Yankee or somethin'. Jim Cantore ain't even took his fancy raincoat out the closet yet.

Her decision to stay in the bungalow, to hold on for the time being, was a compromise that Merry was proud to have reasoned through. *Pretty good for me under the circumstances. Ah might have that grace-under-pressure thing.* She took a break from the news and the Weather Station to make coffee. She cried for a few moments into the steam of the first cup. Then it was time to do some more serious and sustained figuring.

She mustn't flee until she absolutely had to. Or, before she could determine the best place to go. For now, try to make the place look uninhabited, abandoned, *like, nobody home*. But, how to do that and still have the TV glowing. She went out into the front yard. There wasn't a glimmer, actually. *Right, them curtains've got some kinda insulatin' layer*, keeps *the AC in*.

Better put the go-bag by the back door 'n' keep mah shoes on, ready to book outta here. Mah fancy trainers that Ah never run a step in to date. First, she went out the back door to look for a Merry-size gap in the unkempt juniper hedge separating them from the backyard of someplace on the next street. *Might get a few scratches. One a them tenants next door has a yappin' nuisance dog, too. But Ah'll be high flyin'*.

The neighbors beyond their shared wall were an unknown quantity to the girls. A few glimpses, some laughter and arguments from the backyard. They looked like stoners and sometimes hosted parties of other stoners who carried Doritos and Little Debbie boxes from vehicles parked out front. They weren't likely to evacuate until it became mandatory. If then.

The duffel bag she'd chosen as a go-bag would have been fine for throwing into the back of the Tracker. But now Merry hefted it from the closet onto her bed. *Gonna be awkward as hell, bumpin' along against mah hip, takin' up one hand*. She decided to switch everything into a backpack.

EVACUATION ROUTE 547

It was an old thing her brother had brought home from the Navy. *Ah thought they had them seabags which Ah know Ah couldn't lug down the road.* It came in handy for moving from one apartment to another but probably bigger than she needed. *Pack as much as Ah can carry cuz it's lookin' like a new life somewheres else.* She wondered what she was going to look like as a hitchhiker.

The first item in the pack must be her bankroll, to be covered with essential clothes. More clothes would depend on how heavy the thing became. Merry brought the ice cream carton from the freezer. She sorted by denomination and then tallied $2,432. Well, there wasn't going to be any more rent due. She had yet to pay any car insurance, She paid for her phone minutes by buying a card every few weeks. *Guess it's all mahn, free 'n' clear. Don't put this all in one place.* She put a couple of twenties in each front pocket of the cut-offs. *Where else? Mah trainers?*

Merry found two Zip Lock baggies in the kitchen. The $100 bill in each shoe didn't feel too uncomfortable. Now the essential wardrobe went in on top of the cash. She began to put in her provisions; granola bars, some juice pouches, a few Slim Jims. Bella giggled each time she saw Merry making these preparations. *Duckling, are you taking 2nd grade snacks to eat before naptime?*

Merry sat down on the bed for another brief breakdown. *Awww, Bell. Awww, baby how'm Ah gonna deal? When Ah met ya Ah was already tired a workin' solo. Now Ah gotta do this next craziness on mah own again. It ain't right 'n' yer gonna miss a big ol' adventure. Prob'ly.* She sniffed and wiped her eyes on a handful of sheet. *Ah ain't makin' this bed, y'all. Leavin' ya all this stuff.* Then she remembered her little pistol between the mattresses. That had to go in along with her six bullets, also in a baggie.

Merry tried on the backpack, took it off to tighten the shoulder straps and sternum band as small as they would go. She hoisted it onto her back again and looked herself over in the closet door mirror. *Well, for a hitchhiker you won't look too threatenin'. Shoot, you could be headin' to Girl Scout's camp. Cops out on 19 ain't gonna bother ya if they're makin' ever'one evacuate.*

The backpack was placed just outside the back door for a panicked exit. She returned to the television.

Chapter Thirty

Wood-Chuck Spurgeon spoke with his mother less than an hour ago when the combined reconnaissance of three law enforcement entities *rolled up* on the *Knuckledicks;* silent as usual, flashers only. That was some kind of *gangsta* slang, Wood thought. And the manner of the squad cars' sudden intrusion illustrated the expression. *Well, hell. Guess we are mostly white gangstas at that.*

While shuffling a few bikers from table to table, he mopped the floors. He had just ventured out to see how hot and humid the day on the eastern outskirts of Tampa was becoming. *Guess they wasn't exaggeratin'.* Toward the west a dun shaded sky seemed to thicken. *Loadin' up for somethin'.* Each of several early arrivals for a bit of Saturday fellowship (having, in all likelihood, no other welcoming place to go) remarked on the sauna-like qualities of their city and neighborhood.

The cops streamed in; six cars, probably at an unsafe speed: One Pasco County, one City of New Port Richie, three from Tampa Police Department, (the hosts), and one State Highway Patrol car. It was a new record, topping the four vehicles of three years ago when the '*Dicks* attempted the community outreach of hosting a

Halloween Party. That one could he blamed on the neighborhood, few of whom brought children, but sensed free alcohol.

A Tampa car wheeled around to the back (also a gambit familiar to the Club). The Florida Highway Patrol angled themselves across the entrance. *Good plan. Good plan. In case we call for reinforcements. Now, are they gonna jump out with weapons drawn?*

The New Port Richie officer climbed out first, wearing a sport shirt and tie. His partner followed, donning and straightening his cap.

"Good mornin'" Wood offered. "How'r y'all this fine Saturday?"

"Hot. Too damn hot," the driver said.

"How can we help ya?"

"How can we help you providin' you brought a warrant." *The Darkness* wedged himself out the front door around Wood. "Been expectin' y'all. We seen some disturbin' news on the TV couple hours ago."

The fellow was already loosening his tie. "I'm Lt. Morris, New Port Richie PD." He pulled an official letterhead note pad from one of his belt pouches. The one between the pepper spray and the *tactical* flashlight. "This's Sgt. Benitez. No, no warrant. We aren't here but to have a little chat, ask some questions about one a y'all's members. Well, former member, as you know. Who do we speak to as your Club leader."

Wood looked at Caulkins who nodded consent. "Yer lookin' at 'im," *The Darkness* said.

EVACUATION ROUTE 551

"And you are...?" The Lieutenant poised pen (tactical?) above notebook.

"Archie Caulkins, cap'n. Current club President. This here's Charles Spurgeon, one a our Board a Gov'ners. Not sure'f there's any other Board members here."

Now Lt. Morris began writing. *There they go,* Wood thought. *He's addin' to my permanent record that somebody begun in seventh grade. "This's goin' in your permanent record, Spurgeon." Can't remember, even, what that was for.*

"Mr. Caulkins, we just have a few questions concerning your *former* member Beauregard LaVelle; AKA Beau Valley, Laverne Beaugard, and a new one, Paul Perdeaux. Is there someplace we can go to talk where both of us don't leave puddles?"

"Well, sure, officer. Come on in." *The Darkness* reached back to open and hold the door for them.

"I don't know about *that*, Mr. Caulkins," Lt. Morris said. "Don't know if I'd be comfortable with that. How 'bout if the two a y'all climb in the back seat a the cruiser, there. You can leave the doors open and one foot on the pavement if ya don't trust us."

The Darkness and Wood exchanged glances. "I'm just a little hurt you fellas don't trust *us* any more'n that," Caulkins declared. "Have we *ever* been less then hospitable when y'all come for a visit?"

Wood shook his head like a disappointed gym teacher on the first day of calisthenics. "An' how exactly do ya intend to keep yer car cool with the doors open?"

552   CHRIS DUNGEY

The Lieutenant brushed his notepad with the end of the loose tie where drops of perspiration had speckled his scribbling. He sighed. "You make good points, though I can't say I ever been in here previously. But, look here fellas. I don't wanta inconvenience y'all with a unnecessary ride all the way up to New Port Richie just for a coupla statements." He held the notebook further out in front of his beading face.

"Okay, here's what we'll do for a compromise," Caulkins offered. "There ain't no more'n eight, nine members in the place. Why don't y'all come on in with, mebbe, three other officers 'n' we'll give ya all we know about poor Boogaloo. Them other boys a ours might have some helpful observations, too."

The Lieutenant turned back to his partner who shrugged a neutral opinion. "Boogaloo, huh? Well...I'm dyin' out here. Sgt. Benitez, would you invite one a the states and a couple a the Tampas to come join us? Just remind 'em, if you need to, that New Port has the lead on this. For now."

Sgt. Benitez went back toward the other cars in the middle of the compound. He removed his cap to mop his brow with the back of his hand. He motioned two of the cars to lower their driver-side windows.

"Well alright, then," Lt. Morris said. "We'll proceed along the lines a your suggestion. Beforehand though, I have to ask you if there might happen to be any illegal weapons on the premises."

Wood stifled a laugh. "Here we go, Chief." *As if we'd tell ya.*

"That's okay, now, Wood. Easy does it," *The Darkness* cautioned. "I can't speak for us all. I have a registered Sig Sauer 9mm locked in my safe. "I will poll the members to put 'em aside if anyone is carryin'. Just remember, though. You ain't here for that. You don't have no probable cause checkin' on any of 'em."

Morris sighed. "I don't think that's exactly how the law jargon reads, but hell. Okay. See no evil. Let's just get inside to your AC."

Benitez approached from the parked cruisers with three other cops behind him.

"Well, come on in, then. Don't be skittish." *The Darkness* opened and held the door. Wood and a retinue of the peace officers entered.

The gathering was not totally collegial, even before the police committed a major *faux pas* at its conclusion. But, the *Knuckledicks* managed to satisfy all the angles of the inquiry. Yes, Beauregard was a member in good standing. Yes, everyone present could attest to his volatile character, prone to violent interactions which all agreed were *mostly* kept in check at *Knuckledicks* functions.

"Now what y'all need to understand is that Boog...uh, Beauregard, recently cleaned himself up. His *demeanor*...Is that a word y'all'd use? His *demeanor* was almost that of a upstandin' citizen. For a few months. We, none a us, could figure him out. It was puzzlin'"

"It was a baffling, counter-intuitive transformation," said Ivan Dressbach. "None of us was brave enough to pry too deeply."

"I wasn't scared a Boog," Wood said. *Counterintuitive? Mebbe he is the smartest of us all.* "But he was just tired a scarin' other folks." *Prostitutes.*

Lt. Morris was seated at a neighboring table to the *Knuckledicks'* brass. The other officers were satisfied to spread out; one at the front entrance and one in the rear. A fourth sat at a table behind Lt. Morris. Sgt. Benitez perched on a strategic barstool, not quite an *overwatch* position, with Dresbach leaning on an elbow, inside the bar, behind him.

"I guess that explains how your boy looked so diff'r'nt from that Louisiana mugshot," Morris said. "So, nobody has a notion about why he'd kill this girl? Nobody knows if there was some kinda relationship? 'Cause that's what it looks like happened. Some kinda lovers' wrestling match."

Somebody say somethin' 'n' don't hesitate makin' up a good lie. Wood himself was combing through his mind like for ticks on a dog. "Now, there's nothin' proved yet. Don't you boys get ahead a yerselves," he said, an edge sharpening in his voice. "He *never* brought lady friends around. Far's I know he didn't have no regular. B'lieve he may've resorted to prostitutes now 'n' again."

"Yeah, I think he resorted to that pretty reg'lar," *The Darkness* said.

"So maybe this woman was a prostitute?" Lt. Morris continued to scribble. He startled a bit when one of the members broke for *eight-ball* at the pool table behind them. "And no one here ever saw her before? Maybe a transaction gone bad?"

EVACUATION ROUTE

"I don't think I'd wanta speculate," Wood said. *These boys're doin' a good job a ignorin' cops in our very midst. Or, they got bored real quick.*

"We'll look inta her closer, of course. We've got a line on her family, at least. A couple of her brothers musta seen the news 'n' called New Port Richie about the body. We're going to visit them next. See if they knew what she's been up to."

It appeared that Wood would have to be the one to ask. Other concerns must have been running through Caulkins's mind. Maybe about his gun in the safe. Was it, in fact, registered? Would Scope and "Red Bud" Berkram freak out at finding a cruiser blocking the entrance? Was *The Darkness* expecting them with a deposit? Whatever meth money they had to turn in wouldn't take them very far. Nah they were stand-up members. "Sir. I believe that Beauregard has a coupla brothers 'n' a sister. Ya might try the Marine Corp."

"Way ahead a ya, boss," the Lieutenant said. "Private, formerly Lance Corporal Franklin Delano Lavelle...ain't that a good one ?...is currently residing in the brig at Camp Pendleton for some Marine Corp infraction or other. They're doin' the paperwork to *get* him Compassionate Leave. Brother Laurence, no middle name, is currently a skip bail from Houma, Louisiana."

None of the members, seated or at the pool table found the youngest Lavelle's middle name to be remarkably funny.

"I b'lieve he also has a sister, somewhere," Wood said.

The lieutenant scraped his chair back as if preparing to leave but wasn't quite done yet. "She has not shown up in any law enforcement database which is all we have to start with. But, thanks anyway. We weren't aware of her. It doesn't matter much. None a them can claim the remains until the investigation is closed."

"So, what about the body after that?" *The Darkness* asked. "When can we plan a memorial a some kind?"

Now the Lieutenant stood. "Geez, I'm almost reluctant to leave y'all. It's quite pleasant in here. As far as all that goes, you can have your ceremony today if ya want. We'll have to wait 'n' see what the Marines and Pasco County Prosecutor wanta do." Morris stifled a smirk. "What would you fellas wanta do? Prop him up 'n' parade him around in a sidecar?"

Wood and *The Darkness* both silently gripped the tabletop in front of them as their own chairs screeched back. Both began to rise at once. The pool shooters must have been listening after all. Both tossed their sticks clattering to floor and the table felt. They came around the table glaring at the Lieutenant. The other cops stepped forward from their positions at the entrances, hands locating holsters. Morris's closest ally scraped out of *his* chair. When Ivan came out from behind the bar, Sgt. Benitez slipped from his stool to face him.

"Hey, now fellas," Morris's right hand quickly found the strap of *his* holster. "Easy, now. That there was a dumb, insensitive thing to say and I'm admitin' to it. Alright? I apologize, I truly do. You been nothin' but hospitable 'n' I...*we* all appreciate it. Let's not ruin anything. We'll just back on outta here leavin' our gratitude behind."

EVACUATION ROUTE

"I think that'd be a good idea," Wood-Chuck Spurgeon declared, in a voice that could not be mistaken for anything but warning finality. The officer who'd posted himself at the rear door did, literally, back toward the front like he'd walked up on a wild boar rooting in a hiking trail.

"Thank y'all so much for yer service." *The Darkness* waddled out behind Sgt. Benitez. "We'll be watchin' the news for ya to solve this crime!" None of the police bid him farewell.

When the cruisers retreated from the compound after a volley of closing car doors, the task-force drove with much more deliberation than upon their arrival.

"First responders." Wood waved *go away*, resisting the display of his middle finger. He couldn't believe how penetrating and heavy the heat had become. The fish crows and blackbirds that normally gathered in branches of a gnarled live oak tree hanging over the metal stockade from the Axel Doctor, were curiously quiet. Upon narrowing his view, Wood saw that they were absent. *Signs 'n' portents, Boog would have said. What fireside juju could he have picked that up at? Well, RIP, Boog. Mebbe those flyin' rats just decided to shit on someone else's lot.*

"Get on in here, Wood! Yer lettin' in the day," Caulkins yelled.

Chapter Thirty-One

The Bocewicz clan was disappointed to learn that Walt's daughter Michele would not be joining their reunion at his Mom's place on the Atlantic. Her arrival in London was time sensitive and she could not risk air travel delays in and out of Florida. This only slightly dampened Walt's delight at spending time with his son Max. The kid had TA duties at his grad school up north so he, too, could not be trapped by approaching weather.

"Fall term is coming fast and I'm working for the laziest prof at Columbia," the young man told Walt. "I've got to edit his syllabus, make sure all his required readings have arrived in the bookstore. And besides all that, I never thought I'd need to get back to NYC so I could breathe. It get's hotter every time I come down here. This has been stifling. I'm bailing out tomorrow."

Walt rolled over in one of the twin beds Warren installed in the second floor room where he'd bunked during the Holidays. *Nice trick of social engineering, brother man. What if the kid had decided to hate my guts?*

EVACUATION ROUTE

His son was still sitting up beneath a headboard reading lamp on his side of the room, some weighty tome of sociohistorical speculations in his lap.

"Who's running you to the airport?"

"Uncle Warren. I didn't want you to have to drive your...fossil fuel guzzler and I didn't know what your schedule was for heading out."

"Well, I'm ready any time. I coulda gone right *through* Orlando. I'd really love for you and Michele to come by some time and check out my DIY skills."

"You'll have to tell me what that is," Max said. "It's not out of the question"

They sat in the recreation room, earler, the murmur and hiss of an ebb tide against a building sea was muted when they closed the slider. There would be rips developing out there, Walt had mused. The rest of the family watched a big screen TV, engrossed by the models for Hurricane Danielle as she wheeled out of the Florida Straits, with most models inclining toward bad news for the Gulf Coast. A couple of minority trajectories pointed at Tallahassee or Mobile. But the worst news was that the Gulf could strengthen Danielle past Category 3. No one was even talking, yet, about the second storm except that it was certainly a phenomenon of global warming. And, oh by the way, it had been named Eduardo.

When Max finished his reading, he sighed, "Well, alright then. That's one way of looking at it." He switched off the reading lamp. "What I really need to know is how Professor Young looks at it. Pop, I'll see you at breakfast."

CHRIS DUNGEY

"Mmm-hmm. Listen. Max?" Walt stared at the slowly slapping ceiling fan which moved the cool air. *He,* would have liked to leave the balcony slider open. Warren must have taken charge of the thermostat. *It's not too bad in here, actually. Sheets cool, not damp. Better go ahead and say your piece before the boy falls asleep.*

"What? I'm listening."

"Do you...? Do you think you can forgive me?" Walt said softly.

The boy rolled over toward Walt again, sighing noices of disrupted relaxation, as though he had already been dozing. "I never think about the past, Pop. So, I guess I forgive you. If we're talking about the same thing."

"Not being there for you?"

Now it was Max's turn to ruminate. *If* he wasn't *now* falling asleep. Walt remained alert, waiting for him to speak.

"Okay. Early on I was resentful because I missed you, even though you weren't home much even before that. Then I waited for you to show up every other week, listening to Mom complain. Then, for years, we only got reports of your deterioration. Pretty one sided from *my* Mom, pitying from Michele's. Resigned and sad from Gram and Gramps.

"Any rime I was with them, I had to go to Mass and pray for you. I don't know about Michele. Her Mom wasn't Catholic. Then, pretty soon, I was just too busy. They didn't give me time to sulk. Stepdad sent me to any and every camp I wanted; any dance, karate, band, guitar lesson, or sport my whims might briefly find of interest. It was a strategy, I think. They didn't see my activism coming. That worried and pissed *everyone* off, probably as much as they were disappointed in you."

Walt had to clear a thickening from his voice. "You're really letting me off the hook pretty easy. Absolution, I guess I should call it. I'm supposed to be Catholic, too, according to my High School Diploma. Not too many years after my First Communion, they began to consider an exorcism.

"So Catholic is what I ended up being. Nominally, I suppose. Thanks for *that,* by the way. Well, my mother pushed it along, too. But the only time I go to Mass now is when I happen to be here. Did you ever get the sense that I was out there somewhere, with Grams helping me light candles for you?"

"No," Walt admitted. "Much of the time, Max, I didn't think clearly about much of anything. I was an empty vessel for varied sensations provided by substances. I have no inkling why *that* seemed to become my life's work. When I got sober, all of the normal, sane emotions arrived, piling onto me, getting even. Well, except for overpowering career ambitions." He tried to lighten that with a chuckle but it failed against the lump in his throat.

The silence in their room, except for the soft breath of the central air and clicking of the fan, lengthened until Walt believed his son had taken the pause as permission to sleep. Or, maybe he'd been reminded that he should be more pissed off.

"Max?"

The kid snuffled. "Early flight, Pop. Want me to wake you up?"

"Yes, absolutely."

Sometime later, awake and musing whether he could care enough about Darlene who had fallen into his life along with all the other unexpected new concerns, Walt tossed aside the sheet and stepped to the balcony slider. He gently allowed the muggy sea air to enter. It should be just about balanced out by the AC. That surf was pounding harder, though Hurricane Danielle had chosen another route. *An enormous area could be affected by that disturbance. Go to sleep. Darlene deserves your full attention.*

She knew it was selfish but after four days, Darlene was definitely missing her man. The cellphone was in her hand a couple of times. She thought about just giving Walt an informational call, something neutral and of minimal heat. Just tell him *how're ya doin' over there 'n' oh-by-the-way...the coast is clear. Charlie won't be up for a few more days. Selfish.*

And then *one* of those times, the equivocation was interrupted. The phone startled her, went off in her hand like one of those devices they sometimes needed at Bdubs: *Your table is ready.* It was Charlie. The bikers were ready to close up their building and possibly evacuate. They had satisfied the cops about his friend Boogaloo and he'd be up tomorrow afternoon.

"This damn storm still ain't decided exactly where it's goin'," he told Darlene. "But it's gonna come close. We're just gonna lock up tomorrow 'n' then I'll be up."

EVACUATION ROUTE

563

"Ah'll just see ya when ya get here." She put the phone in her hip pocket and went for a walk to see what Dianne Kaake was up to.

It seemed to her a bleak inevitability that she would run into Curtis first. He was carrying patio chairs around to the front from the Kaake firepit. The door to their utility/laundry room was propped open and she could see a teetering stack of chairs.

"You know somethin' Ah don't?" Darlene said in passing. She intended to go straight to the back door.

"Oh, we're gonna get it, alright. You better start payin' attention. Why ain't your ol' lover man here to take care a ya? Ya need any help boardin' up?"

The chairs were of white wrought iron and didn't stack very well. Darlene never sat on one. They just *looked* uncomfortable. She always brought her own bag chair to gatherings.

"You don't know me very well if ya think Ah can't handle mah own business," she told Curtis. "Walter has family 'n' stuff to worry about. Ah'll have Charlie up to help me by tomorrow. Charlie might wanta meet *you*, as a matter a fact. He's kinda peculiar about mah male friends 'n' companions. That ease yer mind any? Now've you got a new storm prediction Ah mighta missed?"

"Just try'n to help you out," Curtis raised both hands in surrender. "Anyways, most a the guesses have it makin' landfall real close to us. Somewheres between us 'n' Crystal River. Now it's the timeline they ain't sure of cuz it's crawlin' slow. That ain't a *good* thing is the majority opinion."

Darlene entered the Kaake unit without knocking. She followed the voice of an invigorated weatherman to the front room. She found Darlene watching with an expression of concern. "They are gonna expect us to drive inland to some crowded-assed, stinky high school gym 'n' I ain't sure I wanta go."

"Where is this now?"

"Well, it's called the Lecanto High School," Darlene said. "I shouldn't put it down. It's that big complex you go past on the way to Inverness. Nearly big as a college campus. We was there a few years ago. I can't remember the storm but they had plenty a FEMA cots. Don't think we was even there a full day 'n' night."

"Yeah, Ah been past there," Darlene said: "That's only about five miles further inland. What's the point?"

"Gets us beyond the tidal surge. The creek on the north end a this park will rise about five inches. That's for a normal storm."

"Have ya got any coffee left?" Darlene hadn't sat down yet so Dianne stood.

"If Curtis ain't drank it all." She led the way back to the kitchen. "We'll plan where we're gonna hunker down. Then I guess I'll pack a bug-out bag. Not sayin' I'll go anywhere, though."

"An' *you* gotta talk me outta callin' Walter."

"Why would I do that, hon? More the merrier at a hurricane party. He'd raise the level of adult conversation, I'm pretty sure."

Chapter Thirty-Two

S he'd been holed up for four days. The television (basic cable) was not a cheery companion. There was no *good* news, even when the case of the drowned gamblers began to lose its fascination for the local media. No one came to the door, cops, bikers, or Girl Scouts selling cookies. So, Bella must not have carried any sort of paper trail in her purse. Merry retrieved the go-bag from the back door. Was the coast clear enough for her to take a walk for some TP and sodas? Mebbe a few frozen burritos, a can of soup? Dollar store staples. Finally, she had no choice.

In the back of her mind, through all those first days as a fugitive (or, so she imagined), was the idea of simply calling a cab and driving to reclaim the Tracker from County Impound. But the vehicle was likely sitting right there like a big ol' piece of rusting green cheese with the cops waiting to see what rat would show up to claim it. The hidden prize for *her* might be a Receiving Stolen Property charge. Then there were going to be loaded questions about her and Bella's relationship to the *Knuckledicks. You don't seem to have any visible means of income Ms. Braniff. Can you explain to us how you happen to be carryin' such a large amount a cash? Don't you think that might be a bit unwise, economic conditions bein' as they are?* It was a relief to have crazy Boogaloo dead, but she didn't want to piss the *Knuckledicks* off all over again by ratting their business to police.

She hoofed it to the nearest dollar store wearing shades and the lightest hoody she owned. The weather wasn't threatening, exactly. Just weird. She'd never seen it so hot with the sun only a bright spot in the overcast. *Yeah, the callin' card a that storm out there.* She'd been more interested in the drowning case of her friend, but word that Danielle had entered the Gulf also also stuck in her mind.

Good Lord, lookit the lineup in the Marathon. Ever'body fillin' them gas cans for their generators. She walked south on US-19 instead of north to the *RaceTrak* station. There were none of the frosting-free strawberry *Pop Tarts* in the *Dollar General* next door to the *Marathon* traffic jam. *Some kinda no-name or weird named stuff from Mexico 'r Canada. A li'l extra sugar for emergency energy.* She bought a two pack of TP, the *family size* rolls. *That oughta do for me 'till Ah decide to clear out. If Ah lay off the cheap wine. In fact, that's how Ah'll make mah decision. When Ah'm outta asswipe, it's time to go.*

The place was running low on canned goods already but she scraped quite a few peanut-butter cheese crackers and one can of Chunky Chicken soup into her basket.

EVACUATION ROUTE

By Friday morning she still had plenty of TP and the cardboardy so-called *toaster pastries* left. She'd eaten can of Chunky soup with half a box of salad croutons. But by noon, the weather guy on the news was ramping up the ominous tone in his voice:

From KFTS 28 Weather desk, this is the latest NOAA statement concerning Hurricane Danielle. The storm remains as a Category 3 but could strengthen due to its slow movement. FEMA and Florida State Disaster Management officials strongly advise that residents of Pasco and Citrus counties make preparations to evacuate. This is not a mandatory evacuation yet, but stay tuned. If you have friends or relatives inland, it may be time to make arrangements for a visit. A quick survey of accommodations in Central Florida by the Florida Tourist Board shows that unreserved vacancies are disappearing quickly. KFTS will continue to scroll public emergency shelters across the bottom of your screen.

Then the guy at the map backtracked to repeat that the storm was moving unusually slowly, enhancing its power. *Well. whata you expect me to do, prettyboy? The damn thing needs to shit 'r get off the pot.* Merry laughed out loud at her own impotent expectation then realized that she hadn't heard her own laughter in a quite a while. *Danielle can do that now if she wants to. Ah got plenty a TP to spare.*

The weatherman repeated the entire NOAA/FEMA statement then turned the news over to the lunchhour talking heads. Merry didn't care to figure out what they were saying about the congress vs the banks so she studied the list of public accommodations crawling along the bottom of the screen. *Ah ain't gonna be man-*

ditoried inta anythin'. They oughta know that by now. Still, the necessity for her to flee was approaching fast. *FEMA advice's good as any, Ah 'magine. Let's see what the Weather Channel's sayin'.*

Some arbor vitae on the west side of the bungalow was intermittently flogging the girls' bedroom windows and the aluminum siding but she wasn't sleeping in there anymore. Still, it woke her on the couch. Should she be able to hear it that loud? *Sounds like they wanta come indoors.* She'd been sleeping in her clothes for the last two nights, ready to move. The occasional claps of thunder and heavy rain pounding the roof kept her slumbers light. She was out of wine. Her pipe lay cold on the coffee table. She was down to a few crumbs of white girl and something called root beer crystal. *Ah don't think Ah need any little sharts. Hazard a wine 'n' crack together. Underwears clean enough for one more day. Ah better get a few more z's. Might not get no sleep on the road.*

Outer bands. Danielle inchin' towards me. Somewheres near. Then she dozed and listened to Bella relating the details of a date with some dope client of the *Knuckledicks* for which Wood-Chuck had shown up an hour late to retrieve her. The girls were lying at opposite ends of the couch playing accidental footsies. *Didn't ya care for the overtime? Ar moneymakers do git weary, though.* Merry giggled and pushed Bella in the butt with her stockinged feet. But there were only throw pillows.

Outer bands, the guy from Weather Channel was repeating it now. He was shooting a remote, outside, in his fancy rainsuit. *A course, the surf's gonna be white in the dark. Weeki Watchee he said it was? Bet them mermaids're long gone. It don't look that bad yet.*

EVACUATION ROUTE

His suit was wet and the wind was slapping his hood. *Why don't ya zip yerself up a l'il tighter.* He looked uncomfortable but hardly fearing, yet, for his safety.

Her own knowledge and experience of hurricanes suggested that she should move in the direction of where Danielle had already passed—inland and tending south. *Lakeland? That'd be fine. Ooops, though. Forgot about that other one out there sneekin' and lurkin' like a total creeper.* It was official now that they give it that dumb name. *Eduardo? Man, woman, man, woman. Ah get that. An' now they wanta keep all a the ethnic groups happy. When're they gonna name one Billy Bob or Joleen?*

Right around 24 hours, give 'r take. That's good enough for me. Mebbe wait for daylight. Couple more hours. She went into the kitchen and set the microwave timer for two hours.

With a jolt Merry rolled her feet to the floor, just as the beeping ended in the kitchen. With no further deliberation, she was up and evacuating. She put makeup items, her toothbrush and paste, a first change of underwear and a shirt on top of everything else in the backpack. The last roll of TP went in (*cuz ya just never know*) some cheese crackers and two packets of those foreign *toaster pastries. Why waste 'em. Ah figure they'll sustain life. Wear them same two hoodies again. Good for hidin' under.*

She hoisted the backpack up and behind, snapped herself in. *Okay, it ain't that bad heavy, long's Ah don't have to run too far.* She intended to lock up and put the keys in the mail-box. *Got mah shades. Turn the TV off? Yeah, why stick 'em with a big ol' 'lectric bill. Don't s'ppose Ah'll be comin' back for ar deposit.*

Merry was just opening the front door when she noticed that old baseball cap of Bella's on the lamp table by the entrance. *Right where Ah left it.* A flower print compact umbrella rested under it. She'd been reluctant to have it wrecked on her previous walk. *Well, shoot. See how long this'll last. Wonder who give her that hat. Wore it for camouflage alla time when we thought we oughta be hidin' out. We shoulda done a better job a that, Bell. Ah can't plead to ya enough.* She put the sunglasses on. No one would want to pick up a hitchhiker who appeared to be weeping.

Was that a week's worth of black tees and underwear? He put the newer looking Harley ones in, wondering how many new dealerships there were in the southeast that he hadn't collected a shirt from. *Mebbe I should just take off pretty soon 'n' find out.* There were two pair of his best looking jeans in there. One black, one blue; his favorite the faded blue. It would all have to be enough because Wood-Chuck Spurgeon had discovered the downside of his hardshell saddlebags. When they were full, that was it. You couldn't bulge them out, overpacking like the old canvas ones,

EVACUATION ROUTE

till they looked like oversized rugby balls. Ma's washer would still churn, he assumed.

Wood locked up the little apartment then aimed the Harley north for the clubhouse. He seemed to be tugged and released by the crosswind but the big bike didn't move much. It was just trying to move him on the seat. There were some driven sprinkles appearing on his leathers but he had put the windscreen on last night. *Might have to put the helmet on later.* Was this the *outer bands* the Weather Channel kept yammering about?

The announced cleanup and closeup session was poorly attended. Wood counted four bikes, a sun-bleached *Pontiac G6*, and a really sweet, newer Dodge Ram pickup truck, rain-gleaming, ready to star in a commercial. *The Darkness. Hope he ain't dippin' inta our little bit a meth funds.* There were a couple of *Knuckledicks* stacking the three club picnic tables between the side of the Clubhouse and the west fence, where they might not have enough room to take off airborne. Now Wood remembered Caulkins's sidehustle. *I believe he said he's been doin' taxes in the spring? Sit down in a Liberty Tax storefront 'n' yer preparer comes out the restroom rubbin' powder off his moustache. Enjoy yer truck, Chief.*

"Yeah, there. I see you got a li'l sample a Danielle. She must be a squirter." Archie Caulkins was actually pitching in, pushing a mop and bucket around. Someone had put the chairs up on the tables. "You ain't *got* a vehicle, do ya?

"It's a *bike* club, ain't it?"

"We're just catching an outer band, so far. What they call it," said Ivan Dresbach from behind the bar. "Thing's still 20 hours or so from landfall, but it's so massive..." Boogaloo's heir apparant as Wood's assistant was putting liquor bottles from the mirror shelf into cases. He turned his attention, with nervous frequency, to the television.

"I b'lieve you can relax," *The Darkness* told him, squeezing out the mop. "It's gonna hit up north."

"I figured that, Chief." Dresbach said. "But a depression this big'll be throwing off all kinda tornadoes 'n' shit. There wouldn't be a whole lotta difference between 70 mph winds and 100 mph winds as far as the outcome for *this* building goes."

The Darkness flopped his mop with a splat onto another section of grubby floor tile and began shoving it back and forth like a heavy shuffleboard cue. "It's goin' north, my bookwise friend. Count up yer blessin's." As if to offer a rebuttal, rain suddenly thundered upon the metal roof. Caulkins paused to eye the ceiling. "Ain't a lotta wind at least."

"Sustained, maybe," Ivan cautioned.

The men who'd been working outside scrambled indoors. They were promised the opportunity to finish off a keg.

"*Don't* drip on my damn floors!" *The Darkness* warned.

"Hey, Chief." Wood wiped his own rain speckled face with a bar towel. "Does this barn have any hurricane anchors at *all*?"

"Ya know, I b'lieve it does, for what it's worth," Caulkins told him. "Ever'thin' built in the last twenty years. You seen them cables runnin' up in the corners? They tuck outside to some big ol' eye-bolts in the foundation. Might hold 'er in place up to a point."

EVACUATION ROUTE

"Well hell, fellas." Dresbach laughed. "Why haven't we volunteered the place for an emergency shelter? Get some cots in here 'n' earn us some community goodwill."

Caulkins rested the mop handle against his shoulder. This chore might have involved more exertion than he was prepared for. "You can go right on ahead, Ivan. I, myself, am gettin' the hell outta Dodge. *In* my Dodge."

"Me too," Wood said. "Though I'm prob'ly headed in the wrong direction."

"Well, what about it, Ivan? Want us to leave ya the keys?" *The Darkness* wrung his mop out again with somewhat less vigor.

Dresbach had taken a longer pause to change channels. There were new graphics and now a graph of falling barometrics. The storm was taking a wide sweep out of the Florida Straits as if readying a roundhouse punch at the central Gulf Coast. "Ya know, men. I think I'm probably good about clearin' out."

"Okay then. Let's turn out the lights 'n' shut 'er down." Wood opened the front door where everyone present had parked. He stood with his back holding the door while the few members who'd showed up to help filed out.

"Well, shit the bed," one declared, pausing under the overhang. He had no helmet. The rain had eased to a drizzle in volume but that was being thrown along slantwise by the stiffening breeze.

"Keep the rubber side down," Wood called to the member. Then he took his own a step out under the minimal overhang above the entrance slab. He tried to look in the direction of the wind. *That is one ugly sky, I don't care how outer that band is.*

574   CHRIS DUNGEY

The first biker and two others darted past him to their machines. Their Harleys rounded out of the main gate, still louder than the wind. Wood stepped back in and closed the door partway.

The Darkness put the mop bucket away in the Women's bathroom and emerged from his office. He carried a grocery sack of Club funds and probably the balance of their crystal inventory in old-fashioned dime bags. His other hand held an automatic pistol wrapped in a bar towel with the butt protruding. "Looters'll be violated on sight," he announced. "But, I know damn well we'll be right back in here day after next with mebbe a few branches blown around the property."

Ivan Dresbach dapped and hugged Wood and Caulkins at the door then sprinted to the old Pontiac G6 he'd been prescient enough to use that morning.

"I admire yer optimism, Chief," Wood said. "But I b'lieve you've forgotten about ol' Eduardo yet to come."

"Well, fuck me!" *The Darkness* shouted into the closed door. "Hold these for me, Wood?" He handed off the drugs and the weapon. They shared the bit of shelter on the entrance slab while the Chief fumbled to lift a key chain from a pouch in his leathers.

"On the bright side, it ain't likely both a them storms'll track exactly the same path." *The Darkness* shot the deadbolt and then tested the door. "Is that yer one ray a sunshine? Hell, man. Ya mean if this Danielle misses then the other one gets to take a shot?"

Wood handed back Caulkins's packages. *All a that's gonna get soaked. I just can't picture him in that vehicle. At least the dope's in baggies.* "Guess I didn't think it through." He turned and readied to run for the bike. "First order a business, we get back'll be to honor Boog, right?" Wood raised his voice as the rain lashed harder.

"Yep. Right now, we the could end up drowned, too. I'll try back here tomorrow, see'f ever'things okay between times. Hey, pull up outside an' help me wheel the gate across."

"Meet ya there!" Now Wood had to shout.

The Darkness stepped into the gale. He waddled faster toward the truck than Wood had ever seen him go, even at a biker dust-up. *Protectin' the dope. Take a Category 2, minimum, to pry that outta his hands.* He pulled his own keys out, found the little one for the helmet lock then legged out.

Around the corner to Trouble Creek Road, then a couple of blocks to the Suncoast Blvd., US 19, gusts heartily clapped and rippled across Merry's back. Once on the big highway and walking north, the wind tried to peel off the windbreaker's rainhood and the satiny casino hoody beneath. There was little traffic going north. Merry began to doubt, already, her choice of direction and wondered if she would be able to make Brooksville before heading inland. Trying to hitch directly through Tampa didn't seem promising, though. *Ah'll end up walkin' most a the way if this don't pick up.* There was a good map sitting in the glove compartment of her poor, orphaned Tracker.

Bayonet Point, now. Ain't that just up the road? Ah can cross over to Dade City from there. Don't recall the road number but it's sure to be a two-lane secondary. Might not be a solitary soul on it or might be a traffic jam. Ah been to Brooksville. That'n's Cortez Avenue. Ya can't miss it.

It came as a surprise to her that some businesses were still open. She crossed to the east side of 19, pausing in the turn lane for only two cars to go by. Her favorite *RaceTrak* station was still open and pumping gas. *Limit Five Gallons,* read the big red marquee by the entrance. There were no red cans now. *These folks're just gettin' out. Mebbe got no generators. Ah better go on in 'n' pee. Ah'll have to shed alla this dang thing, though.*

And, what did she want to drink for the road? As she pushed in through the glass door she read the sign: *No Bottled Water. Well, so that's out. Mebbe a Mountain Dew, just for a good kick in mah butt. Just a little one so Ah don't needa do this again for awhile.* She also had a craving for a big cookie. *One a them big ol' ones wrapped individual like somebody's grandma just baked 'em. Ah'll be supplied up like a hikin' pro. Differ'nt kinda pro.* Again, she enjoyed a little laugh of her own. The cashiers turned and watched her go into the Ladies Room.

Wood-Chuck Spurgeon had just topped off the Harley for gas. $5 bucks a gallon didn't mean anything to him. He obeyed the speed limit through New Port Richie, feeling the wind's push and a slight hydroplaning of the bike over rain that gathered in the traffic depressions of the left lane. He moved over toward the curb, surprised at the sparse traffic. *People must be waitin' for the cops to kick 'em out.* He pulled off the highway once more to call his mother, but there was no service. *She better be there. Nah, but mebbe she cleared out, too. Authorities'r differ'nt ever'wheres. They mighta rousted folks outta that park already. Them buildings got a bad rep 'n' I told her so. They attract tornadoes. I'll find 'er.*

Back underway, Wood gave the Fat Boy as much throttle as he dared. A half mile up the road, he spied a figure dangerously near to the curb. *Yer s'pposed to walk against traffic, dumbass. Yer about to get wet.* As he rumbled past the figure, he moved toward the left lane again so as not to splash the person too much. *Wearin' light colored clothin' at least. Whoa! Holy shit!*

At the last moment, the hiker had turned to put out a thumb. It was a female and Wood thought he recognized her profile, the minimum of profile that stuck out from a hoody drawn tight. He applied the brakes and checked his mirrors before executing a u-turn.

The hitchhiker had turned on a dime and headed it in the opposite direction; walking as fast as she could. *That's Merry. Gotta be, Merry. Where the hell's she think she's goin'? That's too much she's tryin' to carry.* Again, Wood moved carefully into the turn lane to creep the bike but still keep it upright. He made another u-turn.

Wood lifted his helmet visor. "Hey, Merry! Hey! Merry, that you? C'mon, hold up a minute, would ya?!"

The person turned abruptly into the parking lot of a drive-through bank, double timing past the first dark teller window. She disappeared around the back in the exit lane. Wood followed, slower, now walking his boots along on the wet asphalt. *C'mon now. Crazy boy's dead.* "I don't mean ya no harm. Yer hitchin' 'n' I'm goin' the same way *you* was."

When he'd rounded the back corner, he stopped short of her and planted his feet on the ground. Merry was turned to face him. She had dropped the backpack and was frantically digging around in it. Her hand came out holding an oversized derringer pistol. "You still carryin' that peashooter?" He took off his helmet.

"You just stay back, Wood. Ah'll put a hole 'n you and then yer gastank."

"With that li'l ol' thing? A .22 ain't it? It might go through my leathers if ya can even hit me. What're ya, 20 feet away?" Wood turned the key to shut down the Fat Boy.

"Naw, 'n' it never was no ,22. Lookit the size a the chamber, dummy. A .410 slug." Merry raised the weapon in both hands.

She'd holdin' it steady, I'll giver 'er that. "Aw, now, okay. That's a *formidable* piece. But ya don't need it 'n' a cop car's gonna roll through here any minute. They love sittin' out front to watch traffic when these places're closed."

"Why'd ya let him do it, Wood? Set that crazy fucker onta us? We never did nothin' to you boys that deserved killin' us! Mah best friend ever." Her voice wavered, broke. With renewed emphasis, she held the gun higher.

EVACUATION ROUTE

"It wasn't *like* that. We all told 'im to let it go." Wood held his helmet like a shield in front of his midsection. "Didn't none a us know what he was up to on his own. One day he come in with a shave 'n' haircut ridin' that Jap bike; then begun takin' time off 'n' bein' away from Club. Ya musta heard the cops couldn't figure how he didn't look like none a his mugshots."

Merry took a step back. She bent to drag the backpack after her. The wind, which had been blowing a spray of rainwater off the bank roof onto them, relaxed for its now predictable interval."Ai n't you headed in the wrong direction?"

"Well then, so're you," Wood answered. "What're ya thinkin'? Safest is to go south." *If it wasn't for ma. But this girl has no reason.*

"Mebbe for you. Ah'm bein' extra careful a all you *Knuckledicks* now, runnin' all over in the Tampa Bay. Can ya blame me? Anyways, there's a second one s'pposed to clobber us, if ya ain't heard." Merry lowered the derringer slightly but kept her eyes on Wood as she scrabbled around for the backpack with her left hand.

"Yeah, I'm aware 'n' I can't say as I blame ya."

Merry found the backpack and lifted the strap onto her shoulder. "Ah'm gonna turn inland up the road a ways. Mebbe out towards Brooksville."

Wood did not want to spook her so stayed on the bike. He leaned back and relaxed into as passive a posture as he could manage. The wind and rain resumed. He had to raise his voice. "Outer band," he called.

"Damn, Ah sure hope that's all."

"I'd like to head inland too, same as you but I gotta go rescue my Ma first up to Homosassa. I b'lieve there's still time to get clear if ya want a lift. You ain't got no better offers."

Merry tucked the pistol into a pocket of the windbreaker.

"That thing's stickin' out like a turtle head 'n' yer gonna spill it on the ground."

"Only turtles you ever seen ya p'robly *run* over."

"C'mon now, Li'l Bit. Yer just bein' kinda hurtful. You 'n' Bella had *some* good times with us 'n' I *never* meant you any harm. Why don't ya bury that piece back hid in yer tote 'n' climb up aboard?"

Merry slowly eased the backpack from the pavement once more. She buried the derringer deep into her clothes, all the while keeping Wood under frowning scrutiny. "Where you plannin' on haulin' yer Ma to? Am Ah losin' mah seat at that point?"

"Not sure *where* I'm takin' her, but we can find out in less'n a hour. See where the thing is 'n' where it's goin' 'n' plan from there. She might even a pulled out to a shelter already."

Merry lowered he eyes just long enough to zip, snap, and buckle up her load. "An' then whut? Ah'll tell ya this much, Ah'm not holin' up with three hundred strangers in some highschool cafeteria. Ah'll chain mahself to a telephone pole first if Ah have to."

They stared at each other as rivulets blew over them like sea spume. "We're burnin' daylight. C'mon," Wood said, as he settled the helmet back onto his drenched hair. Merry approached the bike tentatively until Wood fired the engine. Then she deftly swung a leg over the slightly elevated passenger hump. "Sorry I ain't brought a extra helmet," he yelled over his shoulder.

To hear any reply would have been futile, Wood knew. There was plenty of room so Merry wouldn't have to hug onto him if she didn't want to. And, as he wheeled back out onto US 19, she apparently did not. But, he could feel that she had secure handfuls of his leathers. The warmth of Dina or Mandy always stirred him pleasantly as he delivered one or the other to a client, though he had never put his name in the date register. *I might should a for this l'il bit sometime. Wonder where them other girls'r hidin'.. Safer stayin' down here for a few more days, if it wasn't for Ma.* He wasn't likely to get much body contact from *this* passenger. *It's gonna take a sizeable amount a remorse 'n' restitution to get me past what that dumbass done.*

The Kaakes were enroute to bugging out. In front of Darlene Spurgeon's doublewide, Dianne hopped out of their big Buick retiree car. She moved around the front of the car but paused for a quick look at the weird sky. The overcast was smudged in hues somewhere on the narrow spectrum between algae and verdigris. She heard the window whirring down on the driver's side.

"Hurry the fuck up, Di." Curtis's voice was its usual *too loud* in the eerie stillness.

"I heard ya the first time. What're ya gonna do? Drive off without me?" At that moment, they both heard the tornado siren at Homosassa Fire and Rescue go off. "Oh, my God," Dianne whispered as her heartbeat stepped up its pace.

"Well, get goin'." Curtis added.

Dianne went into the Spurgeon Florida room. She stepped up to the kitchen entrance and rapped sharply, twice, before entering.

"Ah'm in here," Darlene called. The big-screen of her television decorated with the red and yellow mandala of Hurricane Danielle. The scythes of the storm's outer bands already reached out over Wikki Wachee and Homosassa. With counterclockwise wheeling, she dragged herself forward like a crab, those blades whitening then dissipating.

"Have ya got yer stuff together? We're clearin' out. Sirens 'r' goin' off," Dianne announced. "I seen enough a that booger on TV. Less'n ten hours out and she's gonna scrape somebody nearby off the map. You oughta just follow or come with."

Darlene left the couch wringing her hands. She reached down to slay the approaching banshee with the remote. "Ah don't think Ah should. Charlie's s'pposed to be on his way."

Diane reached to touch Darlene's arm. "Sweetie, c'mon now. When did ya last hear from 'im. There's already some cell towers could be out between here 'n' Tampa."

"Ah know, Ah know. Ah can't reach *him* 'n' he ain't gettin' through to me." Darlene stood at the sink from which she could see no sky, only the ceiling of the Florida room and Curtis's headlights trying to reflect off the pitted *Glade* asphalt.

Now the horn of the Buick blurted twice, long and annoyed.

EVACUATION ROUTE

"Fool!" Dianne shouted. She raised a middle finger in Curtis's general direction. "Go ahead 'n' leave without us. I will hunt you down!"

"Ah don't know what to do, lady. Ah need to check on Walt's cat again 'n' Ah promised to keep an eye on his place."

Dianne put an arm around Darlene's shoulder. "Screw that ol' trailer. He wouldn't expect ya to watch it blow away, would he? Y'all were gonna have to get out to the high school anyways. Why don't ya just leave a note to both of 'em where ya've gone?"

Again, Curtis leaned on the horn. "I will brain that fucker with the nearest blunt object. I hope he attracts some flyin' sheet metal. You g'won 'n' throw some things t'gether while I shut *him* up."

"Ah just don't know? Shoot! Okay. Prob'ly crazy stayin' in here. Gimme a minute 'n' Ah'll find paper 'n' a Sharpee. Won't it just blow away?"

"Don't worry 'bout it. You got masking tape? Put it on this kitchen door 'n' hurry."

As Darlene rummaged in a kitchen drawer for the ingredients of a sign, she saw Dianne gesticulating angrily in the driver's side window. The rain came down in earnest once again, the wind rippling and tugging at her friend's windbreaker.

Dianne rushed back into the doublewide, drawing the string to her hood tighter and tying it under her chin. She followed Darlene into the first bedroom. "He's been notified to go ahead on. We'll feed Antoine 'n' leave a note for Walt, too Yer car's runnin' ain't it?" she said. "Now what're we doin' with this here?"

"That's the only bag Ah got," Darlene said, pointing to an old, shiny green one with more than a few popped seam stitches.

"Get a few tops, an extra pair a jeans." Dianne yanked open a few dresser drawers until she found underwear. "You are one naughty ol' lady," she said, holding up a black thong.

"Ah guess Ah want *all* of 'em if the place is headed for Oz."

Chapter Thirty-Three

H e was being incorrigible again. No, no. Nothing like the *old* incorrigible. But, he just wasn't hearing their logic. Why would he deliberately put himself into certain harm's way? Would he *please* just wait another day to see where the storm was actually going. But *Warren* wasn't waiting. Mom's and Charlotte's luggage had proliferated in the vestibule, ready for him to fit all of it into the rear of the Ford Expedition.

"Stay until they *both* go away if you want," Warren told Walt. "I'll leave the keys and you can lock up."

Walt had carried his own duffle bag and overnight toiletries kit out to the Cadillac. "By that same wisdom, you oughtta sit tight as well," he said. "I think you're gonna catch part of Danielle, anyway, if you head north."

"Not if we leave now. I'm going to take I-90 and start Mom's grand tour in Savannah," Warren answered. "We can be there by mid-afternoon. If the storm reaches that far, it should be pretty well spent."

The weather on the Atlantic side had turned deceptively benign. There was some relief from the humidity and scattered patches of blue sky. The strong breezes had clocked around and now blew offshore. *Danielle, you bitch. You and your minions are circling like hyenas.* Walt brought his travel mug in to pour coffee for the road. His mother was working a crossword puzzle from the Jacksonville paper.

"Listen, Walter. Will you at least stay in touch," she said hoarsely. She slurped from her own coffee.

Geez. It's like she smoked her whole life. Walt snapped the lid securely on his own mug, held it up to eyeball it. *Don't want it on the upholstery or down my crotch.* "I miss my little place, Mom. I've put a lot into it." He knelt next to her chair for a hug, hoping she wouldn't try to get up.

"I don't know why we can't all just stay here," Mrs. Bocewicz nearly whispered.

"Mother, you need to replace that with water. I'm really pleased at your dedication to *something*, Walt." Warren came in, ready to herd his own charges toward their departure. "But there isn't a single thing you can do when it's a mobile home versus 100 mph winds. Well, other than get yourself killed."

"Hey. Maybe there's someone you aren't telling us about?" Charlotte came into the kitchen, made up and stylishly outfitted for the road. "Now *that* is a dedication *I* could understand."

"Maybe," Walt said. "I've made a few new friends. It's all pretty casual in the park, though. I prefer casual."

EVACUATION ROUTE

"Sure, sure." Warren winked and grinned. "I've heard about some of these 50 and older *retirement villages.* But I've also heard that they're just a minor league feeder system for horny assisted living places."

"So why didn't you warn me, brother man?"

"Warren. Let your brother have some happiness," their mother said. She began a Herculean effort to rise from the kitchen table.

"Mom, you don't need to...well, okay." Walt stood up next to her. She lingered in his parting hug. "Everyone can relax. My friendship, friendships that is, plural, aren't ultra serious. What happens to my home *is* pretty serious. I've never accomplished anything like this renovation but the replacement value will still only be about $6 grand. Except if it's swept away by flood. I didn't have much to do with my kids' successes." He helped his mother ease back into the dinette seat.

Warren moved in to hug his brother. "Look. Don't try to keep driving if it get's too bad. Pull off the road and get behind something massive. And Mom had the right idea. You'll be scouting ahead so call us."

"I'm your canary-in-a-coal-mine," Walt pulled out of the hug to extend a handshake.

:"Essentially." Warren chuckled. He walked with Walt, out through the cathedral living room to hold the door. "I shouldn't have made that remark about assisted living places. As a staunch Catholic, Mom'll *never* want to go."

"Hey, *you're* supposed to be the assisted living," Walt reminded him before climbing behind the wheel.

Warren had followed him out and closed the driver's side door behind him. "Yes, and I don't mind. Look at the benefits." He nodded over his shoulder at the house. "I just wish I was a doctor, too."

"You're doing a fine job if I'm any judge. I'll see you when I see you, Warren."

"I hope so. This thing should be heavy enough to stay on the ground."

"Yeah. A pilot's license is another thing I never got." Walt buckled up then craned his neck to look over his shoulder. He backed into the cul-de-sac.

His previous route across the state began by taking I-95 down to Daytona then turning east on Florida 40. This trip, Walt decided to go further by a few miles to New Smyrna Beach then try Florida 44. The most recent reports, graphics and projections indicated, by *his* interpretation, that he must approach Homosassa from the south, if possible. He might still squeeze in ahead the main event. *But then what? Take a chance on riding all my dearly bought work into the jungle?* Hurricane parties and diehard evacuation holdouts didn't often fare too well. Partiers ended up on the roof waving their arms at a helicopter. Maybe he would just see how and where traffic and weather conditions applied before taking his final course of action. He topped off on fuel upon exiting I-95.

EVACUATION ROUTE

It didn't take long to drive out of the temperate, placidity of the Atlantic coast. Walt encountered heavy rain just beyond Deland about 35 miles west; then a driving, slapping, wind driven rain on the road into Eustis. By the time he reached Leesburg, the lashing of his windshield had completely subsided. *What the hell?* The Leesburg interchange for I-75 offered three different truckyards, all of which appeared to be filled with idling diesel big rigs. Well, if the weather wasn't going to stop him, he determined that he would carry on.

He went into the crowded Pilot station/store for more coffee and to use the restroom. When he came out, the queue for each pump was an impatient gridlock. Walt stuck the nose of the Caddy into one line and waited. He needed to top off if he was going to make it home with enough fuel left for further evasive action. Only when he finally drew up to a pump did he notice the 5 gallon limit per purchase. He left the car and dashed back in to pay. *I'll bet they're not limiting diesel.*

Turning left out of Pilot, he waited at a bobbing stoplight and then passed under I-75. An opportunity to do the prudent thing was afforded him at a second set of lights. There was the left turn for the on-ramp to Tampa-St. Petersburgh and at least temporary safety. (*I haven't forgotten you, dear Glade. And everything that's entailed.*) The red didn't last long enough for him to *see reason*, as Warren had urged. He drove straight through at the green light.

He needn't have bothered about slowing his battleship or driving with a light touch on the accelerator. Forces of nature were about to 86 the Caddy's thirst. Approaching the crossroads of

590   CHRIS DUNGEY

Wildwood the wind smacked him again with a nearly horizontal rain and zero visibility. He slowed and moved blindly toward what he hoped was the shoulder. Was that really the front-end skidding to the right that he felt? He'd heard the country-western tune *Jesus Take the Wheel* on Darlene's kitchen radio. *Classic Country, she called it. Talking about Jesus with me buck naked looking for a snack for us from the 'fridge.* This was newly laid pavement he'd observed, with little friction in its gleaming, onyx surface. *I've never had to drive on ice. This must be part of the big one. I've gotta get off of here on my own volition or get rearended.* Walt guided his chariot a few more feet to the right then turned off the engine.

Something glanced off the windshield. *There. That was absolutely my car moving. Am I gonna get pushed into the ditch? Is there even a ditch?* Another object impacted the front glass more directly, leaving the beginning of a crack. A clap of thunder, seemingly overhead, caused Walt to jump in his seat. It was followed by a broad sheet of bluish lightning in the overcast. *Was that a garbage can? Flash of green. Lucky it was plastic.* It was long gone over and behind him, seeking other targets of opportunity.

Bocewicz set the parking break. There really wasn't much else he could do to protect himself from debris acting like shrapnel. He wasn't getting out of the vehicle to climb into the backseat. *I'll just lay down, turn my eyes away from the glass. Best I can do.* Thunder and the varying pitches of the wind's alto sax kept his mind from drifting back to the *Glade,* to how Darlene and her hoodlum kid might be faring.

EVACUATION ROUTE 591

The fit was a bit awkward but Walt was nearly comfortable when he dangled his feet into the driver's side floor well. Rolling onto his right side, he chose to watch the rain jetting over the passenger side window above his head.

He felt the Caddy give up another inch to the right, as if it was the prize in some howling tug-of-war. *Driver where you takin' us? Is this the right time to be channeling Jim Morrison? You've got to take this seriously.* He heard a sharp crack against the windshield above his head.

Then the rain ceased. Maybe that blast of water was not yet *it*. But there was no time to marvel at its sudden pause. He scrambled back into position behind the wheel. The Caddy hadn't moved too far. It wasn't even fully on the shoulder but only a couple of feet over the white line on the passenger side. There were taillights, beacons in the gloom fifty yards ahead and headlights behind him just beginning to move forward. He fired the engine. Why did it give him reassurance that others were sharing in this adventure. *Maybe we can't all die, right? Don't assume. But, so what the hell was that? One of those so-called outer bands? A more powerful inner band?* If these were part of Danielle, which supposedly hadn't made landfall yet and was still in the Gulf, then she must be a monster. He wasn't sure which category was what strength. *See what happens when you don't pay attention most of your life? Seems like a five would be the worst.*

Now there was a slalom course of branches, lawn décor, lawn chairs, even a small bar-b-q grill for him to guide the Caddy through. Spanish moss, brown-grey, sodden as Kleenex flowers

592   CHRIS DUNGEY

blown off a high school float, like flattened loofas on the asphalt;
sprigs of cudzu, some still ambulatory, helixed across his path like
crepe ribbon until they caught on other flotsam.

The guy behind Walt must have been in a more nimble vehicle.
It soon closed the distance between them to lay its headlights on his
trunk. Conversely, the one ahead of them zigged and zagged with
extreme caution. It must be much slower and Walt soon found
himself behind a Schwann's truck. *Hey, we've got us a convoy. You
go ahead and cut the wind for us. If anything happens to you, we're
all having ice-cream.* The car behind him seemed to approve of the
concept. It fell back a few lengths to have a better look at whatever
it was about to run over.

They moved by halts and starts beneath a sky that had brightened to mottled, with hues not consistently charcoal grey, but with
a lighter grey break far ahead. The dark portion they drove beneath
now showed a serration of teeth against the backdrop of the frog
belly horizon. One of those canines or chipped molars could drop
and begin to form a funnel at any moment. The tandem carried on,
making four or five more halting miles. Walt tried to study the road
while stealing glances at that distant, threatening sky. At worst,
it would move from left to right in its classic counterclockwise
wheeling, like a scythe being swung into tall grass.

Then, between glimpses at hazards, the engine temp light came
on. *Not now, baby.* He slowed and moved onto the shoulder. `He
knew enough about engines to not go any further without looking
under the hood.

EVACUATION ROUTE 593

The wind was buffeting and gusting again when he climbed out, slinging the rain like rubber bullets. The caravan, which now included two other vehicles, both SUVs moving at a wary speed, passed him by. Luckily, after futilely searching for the hood latch, Walt discovered what he believed to be the trouble. Driven leaves were plastered over the radiator like a grave blanket with various twigs and fractured stalks hanging out of the grill. Now he *had* to excavate that hood latch.

With the radiator and grill cleared (he remembered seeing release levers for the gas hatch and the hood under the left side of the instrument panel), he cautiously resumed the road trip. The trouble light went out in a few hundred yards. He crept forward, dodging major debris but now heedless of running over smaller branches and the shag carpet of palm fronds. The temp gauge dropped to 210. He sighed with premature relief and sipped at the Pilot coffee, now tepid. *Mom would probably love it if I crossed myself. Let's see how this plays out, first.*

Walt found his way into a seemingly deserted Inverness. EMS vans and police cars were everywhere, parked in what he supposed were watchful, strategic positions. At a traffic light careering like a carnival pirate ride, he made a tricky right turn to stay on 44. Once clear of the quite wooded downtown, the sky ahead was visible again.

However, his heart skipped a cold beat for one of those dark teeth had, in fact, dropped in the distant southwest, stretching and extending by slow undulations, was forming a distinct funnel. Where was it headed? Left to right, with brief, opposite hesitations. He was going to have a problem. He pulled off into a strip mall on the outskirts with no clear plan coalescing, yet. He decided to get behind the incongruously spliced businesses but not close enough for the nail salon or the Buy Your Gold; Best Prices to collapse on him. He backed the Caddy up against a low retaining wall that separated commerce from the wooded grade leading up into a neighborhood. Spying a pair of industrial sized green dumpsters, he went forward again to reposition. With that same wall behind him, the steel bins might buttress the car from moving. *Unless everything gets spun up and flung somewhere else.*

When Walt stepped out of the car to assure that the radiator could breathe, the wind had completely stilled. The sky directly above the strip mall was the shade of a grass stain on khaki. *Awww, shit. This can't be good.* He climbed back into his protective shell and drained the cold coffee. Now to find that just-right, comfortable fetal position on the front seat again. But first, he remembered an emergency aide in the glovebox. Just to keep him on his toes. He had sequestered a few two-tone green amphetamine capsules in a worn baggie. *Hell, these are four years old. Not gonna beat myself up over it. Any truckdriver can find these in Pilot.*

Wood-Chuck Spurgeon spurred the Fat Boy on as fast as he dared. The water was now sheeting across US 19 and there were wind-blown objects to beware of. *Damn. Am I gonna make it in time to*

EVACUATION ROUTE 595

do anythin'. I mean we. The wall of wind and occasional swerve of the bike coaxed his reluctant passenger into closer proximity. On his left, a mile or so distant, he supposed the Gulf was preparing an epic storm surge. He rolled into Homosassa which looked the same except for scattered vegetation everywhere and an absence of traffic. A police car sat in the Publix parking-lot at the intersection of US 19 and Halls River Rd. Wood made a careful left without stopping at the darkened, hang-gliding signal. *Don't even think about followin' me. I ain't a looter.* Had there been a mandatory evacuation? Those warnings *never* convinced everyone, even when the cops drove through neighborhoods, their metallic *Roger-that* voices strongly advising residents to flee. *Don't know what I'd tell 'em. My Ma's in the Glade's all I can tell 'em.*

The patrol car did not tail them. Though many of the residents had probably evacuated, the full, actual hurricane hadn't struck yet. *All the thunder 'n' lightnin', twisters 'n' gale gusts a wind was just warmup acts; prelim'nary bouts at the bottom a the card.* Was this the time when looting occurred, when homeowners and shopkeepers might still be in residence? With weapons? Or did scavenging for free stuff follow after places were totally ripped open. *Guess I never been in the exact bullseye a one a these. But now this Danielle is like a blindfolded kid swingin' at a piñata with a crowbar.*

Wood made their way another quarter mile around an even more dense clutter of misplaced vegetation. He didn't have to tell Merry to lean this way or that way for her weight was negligible.

The jungle continued uninterrupted on both sides of the road, insensate to any loss or breakage suffered so far.

The two-lane entrance to *The Glade,* between two massive palms and two artfully rusted steel sculptures of (what else?) manatees, was completely blocked by a flood.

"Lift yer feet," Wood shouted over his shoulder. Merry's soaked cross-trainers immediately appeared in his rearview. He inched at just above idle speed through the overflow of ditches on both side of Halls River Road. The pond was a foot deep, Wood guessed.

He'd had some doubts about the upkeep of the park after his first visit last Thanksgiving. This road or drive still needed to be repaved. *Isn't there some sort of Association to put up a beef? Guess they none of 'em want their lot rent jacked up.* He splashed from one pothole to another; difficult to distinguish where they were. The storm water immersed the entire width of the road. Where were the cars? *Looks like they all bailed out.* No lights were showing anywhere in *The Glade.* Wood wheeled into his mother's empty carport.

He hopped off the Fat Boy, made sure it was sitting level on its kickstand, then entered the Florida room. Merry climbed off and followed. Wind direction was from southwest to northeast so that the mobile home next door provided little protection. *They built the carports on the wrong damn side.* Wind around the support posts swirled in the space blocked on two sides.

Wood could see it testing, probing the siding. The roof of the structure hummed and shuddered above them. Merry followed Wood into the lanai.

EVACUATION ROUTE

"She's already gone to some shelter! Shit!" Wood loudly informed her. "Come on in, The crazy woman left the place unlocked for me!" He peeled and pulled Darlene's note off the kitchen door then entered. "Double fucking masking tape."

Merry hesitated.

"Damned it!" Wood yelled. "I got enough worries without takin' stupid revenge on yer ass. I didn't care at the time y'all left 'n' I don't care now! Get over yer damn self!"

Merry jumped at his loud voice but then followed into the kitchen. The wind slammed the door behind her. She shivered. "What's yer plan now?" The double windbreakers were plastered to her tee and appeared not to have kept the rain out.

"Sorry. It's colder in here than outside," Wood observed. He opened the refrigerator. There was no light. "Wonder how long the power's been out. Not long if it ain't already cookin' in here."

"What's yer plan, Ah asked ya?" Merry repeated.

"Lemme think a minute." Wood opened the refrigerator again. "There's water. Want one?"

Merry pulled the bow knot loose at her neck and stripped off the first thin hoody. Her hair was wet. "Do Ah look like Ah'm thirsty?" But she took the bottle.

Wood opened and drank the off-brand water. "She left coffee but I can't nuke it."

"Alright. Ah got water. But've ya got a *plan* yet?" Merry said. Above them, the steady groan and thrum of the wind's course over the low pitch of roof suddenly stilled. "Somethin' happenin'. We better have a look," she added.

"Yes ma'am." Wood swigged from his water again and went back out through the Florida room. Merry followed, out onto a sheen of rainwater in the street.

They both studied the strange colors of the sky. The horseshoe arrangement of homes in the *Glade,* set in dense tropical forest, allowed no view of any horizon. Dark udders of cloud still raced over them. *'Bout five hundred feet up 'n' calm down here. That don't make no sense.*

"I think we gotta move," Wood said. "Ma left directions out to this Lecanto High School. It's 'bout five miles inland. She drew a map. It's gotta be a solid structure or FEMA wouldn't approve it. They prob'ly got generators."

"Uh-uh. Ah told you. Ah ain't gonna be trapped with a crowd a folks Ah don't know 'n' their squallin' kids. Ah can smell it already."

"Well whata ya think yer gonna do? You ever seen one a these things after a twister. They turn into a meatgrinder 'n' then they blow apart." Wood held up a finger in the dense quiet then walked to the other side of the street. There was nothing to see. "You hear that?"

"Ah don't hear nothin' except Bell in the dead a night 'n' she'd be tellin' me *don't go no further with Wood.* Just lemme stay here. You ever known me to be a thief? Ah'll take mah chances."

Wood's finger went up again. "Fuck if that ain't that freight train sound survivors claim." Wood walked back under the carport and straddled the motorcycle. "C'mon. Mount up."

"Ah told you, *no*!" Merry insisted. "You don't know what that is nor where it's comin' from."

"It's in the southwest. We got no chance if it's comin' this way! Even if it don't there's gonna be a Category 4 storm surge comin' later 'n' it can reach to here!" Wood turned the ignition key.

Merry stepped closer and had to shout. "Ah don't know what that even is! It'll hit here or it won't 'n' Ah don't think Ah care!"

"Jesus! Yer just actin' crazy!" Wood shook his head. "I gotta see to my Ma!. I ain't gonna force ya!" He pulled his helmet back on and the visor down. He walked the Fat Boy backward into the street.

"Say hi to 'er for me! Thanks for the ride!"

Wood was still shaking his head as he started off, weaving the bike around torn limbs and sundry items blown out of carports.

Darlene and the Kaakes found cots together; she on one side, Diane in the middle for quiet conversation. Curtis was relegated to the far side of Dianne. Darlene had left their light luggage out in her car. Dianne peered into a tote bag of treats as soon as she was seated on her cot. Darlene thought to bring a sixpack stringer of water. A full case was left in her car in case Charlie showed up. The bag of apples was borrowed from Walt.

"This's one a them Tac Lights as shown on TV." Curtis showed off the rugged looking black flashlight. "The Tac is short for *tactical* like the Navy Seals use. This here'll blind ya." He grinned and lifted his North Face foul weather coat. "Look here what else." There were two pints of Johnny Walker Black tucked under his belt. "How d'ya like me now, ladies?"

"Well, no less," Dianne snorted. She turned halfway around to look Darlene in the eye, hoping to convey the joke.

There were probably 200 refugees in the enormous, vaulted Lecanto High School fieldhouse. The FEMA and local Red Cross had run out of cots shortly after the *Glade* refugees arrived. Wrestling mats and rolled-up, foam yoga mats were being dragged out or passed around. Darlene got up to go in search of other neighbors. She was near the main entrance when Charlie arrived. "Oh my! Thank you, Lord! Mah Baby-boy." She embraced his sodden leathers and didn't let go, even as the lights went out.

"What've ya got me into here, Ma?"

Darlene took him by the elbow. Flashlights and battery lanterns came into immediate use all across the gym floor. "Lemme lead ya back to our spot. See that lighthouse beacon over there? That's mah girlfriend's fool husband showin' off his Tac Light." She and Wood both shielded their eyes. "Please just take Curtis's hot air with a grain a salt. Dianne's mah very besty."

"I'll try, Ma. But he already ruined my night vision. I got a small one out in my saddlebags somewhere. I'll go for it in few. When're their generators gonna kick in?"

"Ah couldn't say, Charlie. They s'pposed to have generators?"

Wood followed his mother, both taking short, tentative steps around cots and sleeping bags on the floor. They halted when some heavy object bounced twice, banging along the roof. Lighter

EVACUATION ROUTE 601

pieces clattered behind it. A dust settled, as from a haymow. All conversations in the gym were stilled by the sobering racket of ricocheting junk above.

"Somethin's come knockin'," Darlene whispered. And yet, she could not say that she was frightened. *I never been right in the path a any kinda storm, but that there sounds serious.* "And it's got a shrill voice." She didn't know how they could hear the wind indoors or what it was fluting around to make it scream so.

"I knew I shoulda pushed the bike inta the lobby," Wood said. They resumed their slow progress back to the Kaakes and the cots.

Chapter
Thirty-Four

A twister had bullied through Inverness. Of that, Walt was confident. It sounded like a tornado, anyway, for he'd left all the windows down an inch to keep them clear of condensation. It didn't last very long, but must have passed within a block of his improvised hiding place. He knew that hurricanes spawned them, tossing them ahead like Frisbees. He'd covered his ears after they popped the first time. *Danielle previews. How are tornados classified? Is it magnitude?* He couldn't recall and swear by it if he ever knew. *I'll go with magnitude. Wow. So much for doubting the shelf life of the Christmas- tree uppers. Dorm mates would be calling me Chatty Cathy back in the day.*

It missed him, was the grateful conclusion to be drawn; and moved on, by whatever malignant forces determined their routes. He wasn't a storm chaser. But, what would you call a person who drove directly toward a dangerous meteorological event? *Probably a storm chaser.* Or, *just a plain idiot except that I'm not following*

EVACUATION ROUTE

that one. Which begs the question: Which storm are we talking about?

He felt the Caddy rocking but did not sit up from behind his narrow shield of padded dashboard. He'd witnessed enough of the wind's power already that day. Now its long freight train rumble had faded to the east. The car had less than a foot to move and had done so. Now, Walt couldn't open the door more than an inch before meeting the steel of the garbage bin. *Waste Management. You folks are about to get very busy. You and ServPro.*

When he climbed out to stretch and remove whatever was collected in the radiator, he found the styro Slurpee Cup that was forcefully wedged between driver's rearview and doorframe. A fair-sized evergreen branch had shot over the hood, leaving a snail-trail of resin before submarining the passenger side wiper. Walt pulled it gently out to toss it aside. The wiper looked undamaged. *Wait until I have to use it. These are probably just the first of Danielle's experiments with installation art.*

Shallow scrapes and other pockmarks from airborne debris were defacing his baby but he knew that the assault was just beginning. *Between the flying junk and my dumpster retaining wall, I'm gonna owe you a couple of weeks in the shop. Hope they can match this paint. You'll need some glass, too.*

Walt again relieved the radiator of leaves and twigs. There was nothing sharp or heavy enough to get through the cowcatcher grill and penetrate the radiator. He relieved himself then climbed back behind the wheel and turned the ignition, *Aah, that purring GM iron. Can you get him home, darlin'? Why had he thought that last bit in Darlene's voice; from her point-of-view.*

Calling him? He'd never given any validity to such supernatural occurrences; the unexplained streak of light in photographs from a wake; the apparition in the curtain shadows that wakes you and then you learn at breakfast that a grandparent has died. *The whispers of an abused substance, perhaps?* He needed to find her first before dismissing that little voice out of hand. Recumbent on the Caddy's leather, trash abrading the windshield, there were no missed calls on his phone.

The backlot of the strip mall was carpeted in small, torn limbs and palm trimmings of many taxonomies. Fronds lay jumbled all the way around the corner of the last business and up a short incline to the exit. *It's a total sacrilege, but is this in reverence for my safe and triumphant exit? Well, loud hosannas, then!* Walt chuckled out loud. *Just keep in mind what came after that little pony ride.*

Six miles to Lecanto, another four into Crystal River. The road sign appeared to be leaning forward. He'd learned the back roads into Homosassa while house hunting and later on his used furniture scavenger hunt. He'd found some great bargain pieces, but...*Hope I won't have to do that again.* Florida 44 became a four-lane upon leaving Inverness. It now felt like four bowling lanes and any vehicles struggling forward being dashed like the pins. He only needed to reach Lecanto before taking the one short-cut he knew of.

EVACUATION ROUTE

Walt's fuel gauge indicated just over ¾ full. All of the slow driving had helped curtail the Caddy's thirst, he thought. But the constant debris field had also forced some stop-and-go driving.

Fewer forests now crowded near to Florida 44. Still, Walt could see that the dim cattle grazed surface of the acreage on the south side had been littered heavily with relocated objects from the west. Much detritus of all sorts then hopped the ditch to skid over the pavement. He was *more* than fully alert as a premature dusk descended. *Couldn't be more alert. I just said that.*

He turned on the radio. Were there any of the five pushbuttons still programmed ? *Hey, there's Gainsville. But coming in like a drive-in movie speaker.* There wasn't too much static, but it was an evangelist. *No help and I already get it that none may know the hour. This is an act of God, right? How about if He gives us the hour of landfall, at least. Landfall, as if Danielle were a starving navigator with a royal commission to baptize natives and bring home their gold. She probably wouldn't do nearly as much harm, even at 16th Century exchange rates.* He touched the button to switch reception to FM then began a reverse of his search *Lecanto, three miles. Woo-hoo!*

Walt saw no other cars coming or going until an EMS siren wailed up behind him. He cranked the wheel, moved over toward the shoulder. The white vehicle was uninhibited by the collage of palm and evergreen grafting carpeting the road. Just as the Caddy picked up speed, another EMS truck flew past him, followed by a keening fire-and-rescue with every available light flashing. *Am I going to see something horrific up ahead? Just after a quick palpita-*

606   CHRIS DUNGEY

tion of hope? He decided to come to a full halt to finish his radio search.

The wind was now seriously trying to get under his baby's skirts. He felt the hood vibrating. *Trying to lift it off. There, that's clear as a bell. Hey, my dear old Alma Mater! I'll be damned! My God! WUFT! Could this be some kinda flashback? They must have added 20K of wattage.* The clear, young voice of a University of Florida communications major was just finishing the 7 pm campus news before turning the airwaves over to NPR:

One more time, here is the latest NOAA weather bulletin regarding Hurricane Danielle: The storm is currently estimated to be a Category 3, which may bring sustained winds of 120 mph or more. Expect widespread power outages, significant or devastating storm damage, and a storm surge of 10-15 feet over an already high tide. They add, and I'm paraphrasing: Persons in Citrus County who have not already done so, are stongly advised to clear out now, if at all possible. The landfall of Danielle is expected in less than four hours, somewhere between Homosassa and Crystal River. They go on to speculate that the longer the storm spends in the Gulf, the better the chances that it will move up one Category. Yikes! Okay, that wasn't very professional, but...sounds like Danielle don't play.

Just to repeat a notice from earlier in the broadcast: All summer session classes and student activities at University of Florida are cancelled thru Monday. All summer residents are advised to be aware that a *shelter in place* order may become necessary. I'm Kenny Church and I'll be broadcasting that notice since I'll be

EVACUATION ROUTE

here until the transmitter blows down. I brought a flashlight and a doorstopper of a novel. William T. Vollman's award winning *Europe Central.* Find a copy when you go out to buy batteries.

A Prairie Home Companion will re-air a broadcast from last season after these endowment acknowledgements.

It's still Saturday night. All right, Garrison! Kid has a wry sense of humor, too. I should write that book down. I used to have a dry sense of humor? Same thing? That kid is having the time of his life. Walt turned the radio off and the headlights on. Almost dark at 8 pm. Before he reached Lecanto, he had to slow the Caddy even further through a particularly trashed stretch of highway. It looked like a garbage truck had been t-boned by a flatbed of potted palms. What he could see of a wide swath of wooded development off to his left had been returned to nature but with many of the trees knocked down or uprooted. *I have been in the near proximity of something truly malevolent. Nah. You have to quit anthropomorphizing these things. There may have been one tornado or five but they don't come back around for structures they missed. They aren't conspiring.*

Then a lengthy acreage of splintered white fence meant to keep horses out of the road had come to threaten the road itself. Walt tiptoed over the fresh kindling but immediately had to cut over into the oncoming lane to avoid an inverted shed. It looked like it had been a nice one, too. *Could put your golf cart in there; all your lawn chairs. Hide all manner of junk.* He'd been wanting to buy a decent sized one that he'd admired at Home Depot to add behind his doublewide. This one was upside-down. Its peaked roof had been scraped off like a gum eraser during one of several long bounces. *Bet there isn't so much as a trowel or a garden hose left in there.*

A leisurely walk through that field in the next few days should be quite illuminating. See what all of our high achievement prizes become in five minutes of a twister? Is this a variety of that AA stinkin' thinkin'? Just hope I'm not further illuminated when I get to the Glade. Wonder if that was the same one I ducked in Inverness. These cyclonic systems don't behave like a tag-team, damn it! We just discussed that.

He arrived at the intersection of County Road 491. The party store on the left was dark, its bulletin style sign out front smacked over into the ditch. The Marathon gas station on the right was free of its per-gallon price signs, blown out of their tall, steel framework. The roof over the island of pumps had shifted nearly off its steel pillars. *Design flaw or construction shortcut?* Walt made a careful turn under the nonfunctioning stoplights which tried to point horizontally east on the steroid gale. *Don't break loose until I get clear. Wonder what those things weigh.* He had to get moving but the crosswind from the west was now a serious driving hazard, *Three hours left and this bitch is already trying to push my baby over the center stripe.*

There were more chattering sirens and lights coming at Walt and another far behind in the rearview. *Something has happened.* He decided to get off the road again to let all of the first responders go by. The road wasn't wide enough with everyone being bounced

EVACUATION ROUTE

around. *How do those high silhouette vehicles not get blown over? And they're gonna meet.*

When he had the road to himself again, Walt got back underway. In a few minutes he arrived at an intersection with County Road 490. This was roadblocked by a Highway Patrol Car. An officer in the passenger seat rolled down his window and made the universal gesture for Walt to do likewise. *How long will that cranking motion be understood by motorists who've always had power windows? But, okay. I'll just assume that neither of us is gonna climb out. Just don't shine any light on these pupils.*

"Where're ya headed?" The passenger cop was going to get soaked. He'd taken his Smokey Bear hat off. "Where'd ya come from?"

"There are valuables I need from my place in Homosassa." Walt yelled. "I just turned off 44." The Caddy was more favorably angled to the wind, but Walt felt his words being pulled from his mouth. Would they even reach the cruiser?

"I strongly advise you against that! Tell me *where* in Homosassa!"

"The *Glade* mobile home park on Halls River Rd.! I've got nearly a three hour window by the latest bulletin! You wanta see some ID?"

The officer at the window conferred with the driver. "Not unless you wanta walk it over here! I guess it's your neck, sir! You'll have to go in on 491 'n' we won't be comin' to rescue ya! We got one mess goin' already!"

610   CHRIS DUNGEY

"What happened?!" Walt waited for an answer until two more ambulances had entered and departed on a paved road going east. His eyes followed the EMS headlights and he saw the brick encased Welcome sign for Lecanto High School. It too was without power.

"Twister!" the cop paused the raising of his window to resume hollering. "A big F3, they're callin' it! Surprised you missed it."

"I don't think I did! Had to get off the road at Inverness for half an hour!"

"Mighta been the same one! A fuckin' brute! Knocked down a wall of Lecanto Field House! FEMA approved it as a shelter. Now we gotta get ever'body pulled outta there before that landfall!"

"That's terrible! I'll get out of your way!" Walt could already see more flashers growing in his review.

"I'm tellin' ya, sir! Get in 'n' get out!"

Walt powered the window back up tight and moved around the rear of the cruiser to make a righthand turn. Now he couldn't go south a few more miles to take Grover Cleveland Boulevard (Pretty optimistic to call a two-lane country road a boulevard,) which was a straight shot into Halls River Rd. The CR 491 route he'd been directed to was pretty twisty and heavily wooded where it entered Homosassa. CR 491 was designed for *Florida man*, who was no kind of *man* without a four-wheel drive truck made behemoth on lift-kits and oversized tires. *Useful once or twice a year unless he poaches gators for his side hustle. Let's show 'em what we've got baby.*

But oh, man. Oh, shit! Was that the shelter Darlene and her son would've used? It couldn't be the only one in the area, could it? Might've been their closest. He slowed the car which was already straining into the wind. *Think, think.* There would be shelters in Crystal River, too. Should he go back and volunteer? It would be time lost if they then told him to *just stay out of the way.* There was nothing practical to be done. *Better just carry on and make sure I still have a home. There's a little cash in the place. ATMs won't be functioning and I'll need gas and a room somewhere. Okay, Mom I guess this can't hurt: Holy Merry, Mother of God, blessed is the fruit of thy womb...But geez. I'm not gonna think about the hour of my death just yet. I'll save the Our Father until the last critical moment.*

She was one of the first to be pulled out of the rubble. A cement block landing across her knees should not have caused her to pass out. It could have been caused by her instinctive roll, away from the pain, off the cot and onto the floor. *Ah bet Ah'm concussed 'n' mah leg's still up there.* Why did she think that crawling under the olive-drab government canvas would protect her? The block that hurt her was still attached to several others which had crushed the end of her cot. The x frame legs at the end were folded the wrong way, not quite flattened *Ah seen basketball players bounce their heads on the hardwood. What'd they call that one play? Ah ain't finishin' mah thoughts.* "Hey! Hey, somebody!" Darlene cried out to a flashlight. *"It's takin' the charge! Darlene stood in 'n' took the charge.* No, that light's on the guy's head. "Ah don't think Ah can walk!"

612 CHRIS DUNGEY

"We don't want ya to walk, ma'am," the guy behind the miner's lamp called. His beam shone on her face through a whirl of dust motes, some moth sized. Wind was getting in, stirring it. "I got that masonry off ya and went for some help. Don't move no more."

"But...what about mah Baby-boy? He went to use the bathroom." Now shock and concussion brought a cry of despair and then tears from Darlene.

"Is your Baby-boy a child ma'am, The only toilets are in both locker-rooms."

"Nah, he ain't a child. Christ, it hurts!"

Another hardhat arrived to throw an exposure blanket over Darlene. He aimed a smaller penlight into each of her eyes. "Hey! Hey!" The second fireman yelled hoarsely back into the dust and crosshatch of laser-fighting beams. "Right now, Godamn it! A gurney or a spine board, one. I've got a compound fracture here; possible head trauma, and prob'ly shock!"

"Hang on, man," someone shouted back. "We gotta get folks off of 'em first."

"He's got a Harley out front. Wanted his flashlight. Was goin' to the toilet first," Darlene slurred. "Rode from Tampa."

"Ma'am, ma'am? I'm gonna stick you with some morphine," the first headlamp said. "If your boy was in the locker-room, he should be okay. The gym wall didn't fall on that, but it's blocked. We're gonna get them out through the hallway entrance."

Darlene didn't feel the first syringe. Or the second. *Family's ever'thin'. Both mah boys. Sandy. Ah feel bad for Walt, been cut off from his. He invites 'em. They're sure more busier'n mah crew. Hope*

EVACUATION ROUTE

they drop in on 'im soon. Lucky be over there. Other side from alla this mess.

"Good Christ," the hardhat said. He had lifted away the exposure blanket then parted Darlene's pantleg with the heavy scissors for cutting casts. "Okay, ma'am. Stay with me, now! What's your name, dear?"

"Ah'm Darlene Sturgeon 'n' my boy's Charlie."

"Alright, Darlene. When that takes hold I've gotta put a ton a gauze around your...injury 'n' then use an air splint."

"Mmm-hmm. Mah baby, Charlie woulda carried me out," Darlene drowsed. "Can Ah take me a li'l nap now?'

"No! You mustn't do that, Darlene," said the fireman above her. He clapped latex sheathed hands close to her face.

"Mmm-hmm. Ah'm sorry. Mah mouth's so dry. Tastin' lotta dust some sort."

One of the firemen took a bottle of water from a deep, yellow pouch in his jacket. He touched it to her lips. She took just a sip as two before more miners arrived with a stretcher board. Someone took the water as she suddenly soared above the cots. *Nope. Now Ah stopped short. Thought a second Ah was bein' called.* "Charlie! Charlie?" She groaned.

The wind tried to strip the foil blanket from her when she was brought outside. It lifted it at the edges and wherever the straps didn't hold it tight to her.

Someone laid a clear piece of plastic over her face then tried to hold it in place. She heard the rain on it. "Ma! I'm right here!" Wood-Chuck had just emerged from another exit.

CHRIS DUNGEY

"Keep that loose, there. Don't suffocate her!" The lead medic said as he backed his way up into the ambulance. "Ramon! Lift! Hey, are you Baby-boy?"

"Prob'ly!"

"Grab on with Ramon! This thing is like a sail!"

"Where ya takin 'er?!" Wood shouted when Darlene was safely loaded and secured.

"What?" The medic leaned next to Darlene, search-lighting her pupils again. Rain swept over the ambulance like a carwash.

"Where do I go!" Wood competed with the wind, more thunder, and the ear-splitting ferocity of several rescue saws biting metal and concrete inside the standing remains of the field house.

"Brooksville!" The EMS operator tucked his penlight away and stood. "Takin' 'em below the storm! We think!" Now he had to cup his hands to his mouth with Wood about two feet away. He shouted: "Go back to 491. Take it south to Florida 98! You can follow this vehicle if ya want! She'll be on her way in a minute!"

Wood leaned into the back of the ambulance where the riding medtech was hanging a bag of saline for Darlene. "Love ya, Ma. I'll see ya at the hospital!"

Darlene's eyelids lifted droopily. "Please call Sandy 'n' Larry, let 'em know Ah'm okay. My boy, Charlie, too. Say Ah'm okay. Tell Dianne..."

At that moment the stretcher medic firmly pressed Wood to move aside. He slammed the rear door.

"Tell 'er I'll see 'er in Brooksville," Wood yelled.

"Roger that!" The first responder shouted back, rain like a sandstorm in the beam of his flashlight. But then he turned and loped back into the fieldhouse.

That freight train of Wood-Chuck's came and went in just a few minutes. Merry climbed out the vacuel of Darlene Sturgeon's bathtub. She couldn't remember where or when she'd heard to do that but there were none of the preferred interior rooms in the place. From across the hall, where she supposed there was a small children's bedroom, she'd heard a grinding crunch and snapping of thin studs and ceiling panels. As she emerged from the bathroom, it appeared that a portion of the roof had been heavily impacted by something and that the bedroom window had been popped out, it's frame severely mishapened. Parts of their window lay on a small spare bed, while the new aperture admitted a warm but civil breeze. *Afraid that prob'ly the last a the teasin'.* She closed that door after borrowing a pillow. She closed two other doors off the hallway, including the one for the larger end bedroom, reasoning that these might add some structural integrity.

Well, it looks like Ah'm alive. Now Ah could find my way around blind if this was the narrow one like Ah grew up in. Layed out mostly the same. Merry wasted a precious moment of pity for the woman whose entire life had earned this modest dwelling. *And a son that's a professional scooterbum. Now that ain't fair. Maybe a pity, but Ah don't know how her other kids turned out. An' Wood sure gives her back some dedication. Might be his only savin' grace.*

Pity. Now there's a co-mmodity Ah should ought add to the world's supply of. She'd likely been granted *some* small amount in her own life. *It was two elderly neighbor ladies fannin' theirselves at Ma's graveside. Ol' Fred Smalley from across the street was there, too, trailin' a oxygen tank. Helped drink stepdad to death 'n' Ah had to tell 'im there wasn't no meal bein' provided. He stayed anyways. All their hugs carried genuine pity, Ah believe. Then Ah dropped the first clod. So sandy the way it burst. Wouldn't be hard to rise up through. Maybe Ah can express the pity in person some time, Mrs...Ah feel like an idiot, Ah can't think a yer last name.*

Did Bella's brothers ever contribute pity, love of any kind, or had they written her off with scorn long ago? *It don't matter. Between Bell 'n' me was plenty an' Ah'm wastin' daylight.*

Out the kitchen window, night was drawing down fast. Wind now filled in the void that the twister (if that's what it was) had punched as it traveled inland. She carried her go-bag into the bathroom. The sink coughed some water and air, but then failed.

How many hours ago did she leave the bungalow? The ride with Wood didn't last very long. The tornado seemed to take hours but couldn't have been more than a few minutes. *Prayin' in a old lady's bathtub. Where mah life's taken me. Well, Ah don't know for certain sure she's a old lady. Offered up a prayer, anyways. Who wouldn't? Tacked on Wood 'n' his Ma at the end. Bella, too, a course. A prayer don't take but a minute or so if you ain't askin' for much.*

EVACUATION ROUTE

617

Nah, that ol' SuperDaddy was pro'bly out there, up there, but he ain't getting' no more promises then Ah can keep.

When Merry tried to venture into the Florida room, she discovered through the door's window what had crunched the little bedroom. The part of the roof that extended over the laundry room was out there, folded over onto the main structure. Looking in the opposite direction, she saw that the carport roof had done likewise, but in its entirety.

She tried to open the back door but some object restricted the door's travel. Even she could not squeeze through the narrow space. She could see one edge of the round, white plastic patio table out there that had been flipped over against the door. Still she should have been able to move it back. She pushed with all her strength but the table would not yield. *WTF? Have Ah got that weak, layin' low for a few days? It's like the thing's been jammed under the doorknob. Pretty clever, Danielle. Ya seem to be somethin' of a cunt. Never mind though. This thing's got a front door 'n' steps somewheres.*

Merry found it in a second enclosed porch built off the opposite side from the Florida room. She entered through the livingroom. *Pretty dang classy. Glass all 'round. Sleepin couch's prob'ly a foldin' out mattress. Lamp 'n' table. Little chest-a-drawers. These doublewides that get additions built onto 'em are the mansions a the mobile dump lifestyle alternative.*

The park street looked nearly impassable with junk. Merry opened the inner door easily but when she tried to open the storm door, wind snatched it from her right hand. The door smacked

618   CHRIS DUNGEY

against the screen on the outside of the first window. *So dang dark now. Shoulda been lookin' for a flashlight 'stead a fiddley fuckin' around. Ah'll have to grope 'round in the pitch-dark now. See'f Ah can get this one closed at least.* Then she heard the hoarse pleading of a cat.

"Meeep-neeeow. Meeep."

"Kitty? Kitty, kitty! Ya gotta come to *me*! Where are ya?"

This here's crazy. But Ah'll hear that poor thing in mah dreams. Ah know Ah will. Mah eyes're adjustin' but not enough to see objects flyin' at Mah face.

Merry stepped out anyway. She only had to get to the backside of the sleeping porch, as she'd labeled it. The wind tried, but failed to carry her past her destination. She grabbed and swung herself around the corner of the building. *Ah'm no more'n a dainty feather, still.* She stumbled into the pocket of relative shelter between Mrs. Wood-Chuck's mom's unit and her neighbor.

Now to 'void gettin' mahself crushed between 'em. Merry inched slowly forward, her right hand guiding her along the screens. The home on her left now began some sort of degenerative process from its roof. She couldn't see what was happening but there was a flutter above as if oversized playing cards were being shuffled. Then, a backwash of some particulate matter began to descend onto her head and shoulders. She blew fibers off her lips and spat. Now she kept her lips tightly closed. *What is this shit? Ah ain't swallowin' any. She squatted and lowered her head between her knees.*

"Purrr-eoww? Mee-eeprow?"

EVACUATION ROUTE

The cat stepped under her, trying to dry its head by rubbing against her wet jeans. It rubbed its whiskers forcefully against Merry's dangling hand and then her calf as it circled. *Whata ya wanta do? Take me for a human shield?* She began to pet the animal but was soon brushing fibers from its coat. "Whata ya got all over ya? We gotta get shed a *this* whatever it is. Ah don't think we can stay here much longer." *If this dang animal can really see in the dark, it oughta be leadin' me.* "Wanta throw in with me?" Merry gathered the cat into her arms and then struggled to stand. "Yer a tubby one ain'tcha? Mebbe between us, we won't blow on down the street."

She turned her back to the blast as she rounded the front corner of the sleeping porch again. Walking backward was a slow, tentative process as she deliberated each step. But, the strategy protected her face and the new companion. Mrs. Wood-Chuck's mom had put in a flowerbed of small decorative stones extending from the front corner of the structure all the way to the front steps. "Ah think yer keepin' me on the ground, puss. Why would somebody go 'n' leave ya behind?"

The cat made no attempt to escape Merry's embrace as she reached back to find the doorhandle. The storm door had not returned to it's original position and function. The wind wouldn't let it, even if the hinges and hydraulic bar at the top hadn't been sprung. *Yer a load, Mister 'r Miss.* When she let it down she heard the galloping paws leave the sleeping porch and cross to the kitchen floor.

Merry forced the inner door closed. "We gotta find us some light!" *Oh right. You can see in the dark.* She felt her way through the living room and to the kitchen and found some drawers. Storm tossed debris struck the dining room wall in front with the velocity of a pitching machine. *Gonna cut mahself, ah go grabbin' out the wrong drawer. Alright, this is junk right here. Ah don't even wanta get in that knife drawer.* She sifted carefully and soon touched an object that *might* be a slim flashlight.

It don't feel like...plastic nor metal, either. Feels like... Merry held it to her nose. *Smells like pine, feels like wax. Damn if ain't a candle!* "Hey, cat! We're in luck" She put her hand in again, combing with he fingers until she found what was likely a butane lighter. There were a few of them. *An' just one candle. Are you a smoker, Mrs. Wood's Mom? Don't be gone dry, now.* She gave the thing a braille examination then squeezed down. *Fire!* "We're in business, cat!" She lit the candle then tucked the lighter into her front pocket.

Merry took a cursory look into each of the three shallow kitchen drawers. *Don't think Ah need silverware. Why aint there a flashlight anywheres. Coupla C batteries. C'mon lady. Mebbe took it with her. Better have a look in the 'fridge.* The candle dripped some splotches onto the kitchen floor.

There were yogurt cups and string cheese in the dairy bin. *Mebbe Ah'll need me a spoon after all.* In the meat keeper, she found a half-used package of hotdogs. *Ah gotta find a bag.* A couple more drops of wax fell on the top of the freezer drawer.

Above Merry, the ceiling was vibrating steadily louder. She looked up to see if it was beginning to part ways with the shell of the house. The carport roof, now resting above the kitchen and dining room, made its own frightening racket, bitch slapping the roof beneath. *Time to get back in the tub. Just forget the bag 'n' make two trips.* She carried the hotdogs and yogurt in one hand and the candle in the other. She held a teaspoon in her teeth.

"Cat! Kitty, kitty! C'mon now. Ah'm closin' the bathroom door 'till this blows by. Ah got meat! An' dairy! Ah still got a Slim Jim!"

Merry had just closed the door when the cat scratched on it. "Yer cuttin' it close, buddy. *If* yer a buddy." She reclosed the door and stepped into the tub. The cat curled up on a bathmat. "Don't wanta snuggle? See if Ah care. An' if ya gotta poop, keep it over'n the corner.

She huffed out the candle, now half its original length, then laid it in a soap dish. She pulled down a thick towel from the bar above her head. *Won't be the first time Ah used one for a blanket. 'Cept if Ah roll it up for a pillow. Whatever this fiber shit is, Ah hope it don't start to itch.*

Passage on CR 490 was not the ordeal that Walt had envisioned. It wasn't totally blocked by uprooted trees. *Thing mighta crossed the road out of a field back a ways. Pretty open the first few miles.* He *did* have a close encounter with a fallen and smoldering transformer near the shoulder that still raised an occasional flame to scorch the rain. The smell of molten wiring made its way through the vent system. Walt held a hand to his nose. The transformer had shed its lines across the road. There were no sparks sizzling so Walt drove over them without much thought. *Still some pretty strong amphetamine invincibility in this old circulatory system. Don't want it to get me in trouble.*

All was darkness in the village, which really consisted of a wide spot in US 19 where big box stores and a few fast-food places had set up commerce. Now, there were no lights of any kind to be seen except a few security lamps here and there using up their solar storage.

Walt warily crossed 19, straight into the north end of the Publix. The supermarket commanded the prime position on a large plot facing both US 19 and Halls River Road. This acreage was shared with several other businesses: His favorite, *Annie's Breakfast*; a *Hallmark store*, *Dynasty Wok Buffet* and *Rent-a-Center*.

Walt circled the lot slowly, compensating for the puissant sideswipe of the wind. Back out in the direction of US 19, a dump truck, bulldozer, and backhoe were left by Florida Highway Dept. to fend for themselves. *That* interminable project to narrow the medians and add turn lanes all the way to Crystal River was not going to be completed next week. He curved past the Hardee's parking-lot then steered back toward the Publix, into the fist of the wind. *Alright. No more time to dick around. Better see if I can get into The Glade.*

He had to brake for a threesome of shopping carts, still conjoined but on their sides moving at the speed of a curling stone. He gave them the right-of-way but they stopped short. In another fifty feet, he made his left turn into the exit for Halls River Rd.

EVACUATION ROUTE

623

Any partially conceived plans had to be immediately revised. At least two large trees had blown down just west of the exit. *If that's how our local jungle is holding up...I don't think I'll make that walk at this time. So now what? Been trying to anticipate, solve problems since the time I left Leesburg. Now gotta keep thinking.*

Walt reversed out of the exit and swung the battleship around. It felt to him that the wind wanted to move the front end further. He arrested the maneuver and put the car into the lee of Publix a second time. He moved into the left lane to get closer to the building. The drive extended from a small insurance office on the grocery's left to a hard right angle turn in front of *Dynasty Wok*. Walt paused halfway, by the north exit door of the Publix. Water was spilling in a steady torrent from a roof edge that had dropped its eaves and downspout. The water looked as if it was probelled by a hottub jet. It launched from the roof far enough to reach his door glass if he proceeded. *If I was at the carwash, that would be Deluxe level. No blue and pink wax tonight.*

As he equivocated how to proceed further, sheet metal, vents, and associated flashing sailed into his path. He sat for a moment, fatigued enough to be easily transfixed against his better judgment. The object of his amazement was the interior of a fresh-air impeller which landed in his path, upright with it's turbine still spinning like a child's windmill on a stick. Then it was blown over and began to crawl toward the curbstones between drive and parking. *You cannot stay to see if it hops over that.*

Now strips of tar roofing flew over, grazing the Caddy. *This building is delaminating. Gotta move.* He started to back up to find a lane into the lot. Before he could turn in, a satellite dish with plenty of cable bounced off the roof, chased along the ground by the remains of a vent turbine.

Walt navigated back to the strip-mall side, turning right again at Rent-a-Center. *Probably everything you need in there to cut into a mobile home.* With Danielle now at his back, he encountered no more airborne objects. Except for continued assault of bangs and *crumps* off the trunk lid. *Annie's Breakfast. Always a wait, but worth it. Will I ever share a waffle in there with Darlene again? She wanted blueberries. I wanted the apple pie filling. Annie worked it out for us. I'm staying in this town, whatever else.*

With the next right turn, Walt began another lap of the property. There were those earthmovers again. *Heavy equipment operators. Where do they learn those skills? Army? Bet they wish they could take 'em home. Heavy is the key word.*

He tried to get behind the bulldozer first. There wasn't enough room between the dozer and a curb that marked the terminus of parking. Could he ask his baby to make the climb on the passenger side? Those roofing strips were catching up to him, slapping harder, seventy yards from the Publix roof. More shopping carts were approaching, singly and in tandem, intent on leaving the premises. Walt put the shifter into reverse to go around and try the other side. That dump truck wasn't going to budge, either.

Two shopping carts grazed the Caddy before Walt could get behind the truck barricade. *Didn't anyone think to chain those bastards up?* One was stiff-armed by the front bumper. The second scored a bullseye on the rear passenger door.

The dump truck had not drawn up even with the bulldozer so he was able to squeeze tightly in front of it. Now his only escape would be out the passenger side. *This is my place to be. For cover and in the broader sense. Collect some insurance. I did buy some. Won't cover flood if the surge reaches that far. Start over somewhere nearby. Darlene won't go far. Hope she wasn't in that damn high school. I love the Publix when I get tired of toasted cheese sandwiches. Chicken potpies. Their deli. Soup of the day. These speeders can let go of me anytime now. Thank you for your assistance. Can't make a habit of it. Getting too old.*

The amphetamines were not going to let Walt sleep and simply ride out the storm, oblivious to the tumult. He replicated his former positions on the front seat and made an attempt to close his eyes. Could enough wind pass under the truck to get under him, too? He couldn't keep his eyes closed. He was exhausted, yes, but the nervous energy continued, unrelenting. The wind, a dog whistle shriek by then, was modulated to a sustained ghostly moan over the dump truck.

"You been tri-aged into a surgery," Wood-Chuck told his mother. "In a coupla hours. Just be a temporary patch job for now, they said. Coupla screws 'n' see how it goes."

"All good, Charlie. Jus' can ya make sure this morphine keeps pumpin'." Darlene looked up at the IV drip. "Mah poor varicose

CHRIS DUNGEY

legs. Ya think Ah'll ever waitress again?" The beginning crowsfeet crinkled out from her eyes as though she was trying to smile.

"I counted twenty litters still waitin' out'n the hall so this stuff is prob'ly what you'll get for a while. Be happy they're holdin' a bed for ya. In a room."

"Ah know. But, Charlie..." Her eyes closed again. "My friends. Can you...? Find out anythin'"?

"Ma, ever'thing's a mess up there. I can't go from cot to cot interrogatin' hurt folks. An' the responders don't know. They're only interested in gettin' bodies out 'n' on their way."

"Dianne 'n' Curtis?"

"Can't I just stay here 'n' worry about you?"

Darlene groaned. She reopened her yes, eyed the drip, then closed them tighter. "Get 'em to turn it up? Am Ah gonna lose mah dang leg? An' mah friends? Charlie?"

"Nah, Ma." Wood stepped closer. He fiddled with the drip flow, trying to appear merely curious as to how it worked. "Listen. Mebbe I'll ask if they got a list yet up to the front desk." He watched his mother, hoping that her eyes would remain closed. But, nope.

"Somethin' else, too," she whispered. Another silence followed.

"Yeah? C'mon, c'mon. Get it out 'n' then ya need to sleep."

"Well. There's this guy."

A course there is. Aww, now. Shit. But, try'n be cool. This ain't the time. Grow up about it.

EVACUATION ROUTE

"It's Walt. His name is. Good ol' guy. Been through a lot 'n' it burned 'im down. You can get...the nurse? About more morphine?"

"Yeah, Mama." *Yeah, lemme get clear. Hear no evil, ain't it?*

"It should be in mah phone, Charlie. Jus' so he'll know somethin'. Damn, this is startin' to really hurt."

Charlie eyed the saline bag. How do they even get the good stuff in? "If it was in yer purse, Ma, they didn't bring out no personal belongin's."

"Walt won't..."

"You'll be talkin' to 'im soon, Ma. I'm gonna find ya that nurse, now. If there's any around." Wood moved out and down the corridor quickly; a dodging course of groaning, supine exposure blankets.

Chapter Thirty-Five

S he felt the mobile home move to a soundtrack of rending vinyl siding and thin, popping studs. It came to a quick and sharp halt and now she lay tilted toward the wall side of the tub. *Don't you move another inch.* There was no sleeping porch to block the back end of the trailer from moving. *So where've Ah come to rest. Nex' doors? These stupid things'll mash together like a row a dominos.*

The wind had not abated. The angle of the tub now allowed Merry to see the window in the shower wall. The night looked even darker. She couldn't see the rain except for splashes falling past the little slider window. Above, the flow was horizontal, slowed only a little by the neighbor's wreckage as it blew from roof to roof.

"Pree-owww? Pree-owww?"

"Aw, so now ya want in." The shower door was significantly heavier for her to move now, gravity pressing its weight downward in the frame, The cat practically fell into the protective space.

EVACUATION ROUTE 629

"Well, hullo. Not sure ya've found a better deal, taggin' along with me. Time to have us somethin' to eat."

Her go-bag now lay face down but she knew there was a water bottle in the top layer of her belongings. The package of hotdogs had fallen off the slider edge of the tub to land on the calf of her jeans. *These drawers ain't gonna dry out in this sweatbox, no ways.*

She removed two paperclips holding the plastic wrapper shut. She withdrew one weiner. *It's all we got, so...* The cat pushed its muzzle against her hand. "Just a dang minute." Merry took a bite then pinched off a bit from the ragged end. "Try it, at least. Might seem kinda salty to ya."

Her half of the house continued to shudder. Stray wind was getting in from somewhere to rattle the bathroom door like a barfly with a full bladder.

"Nobody to home, ay kitty?"

The cat resumed pushing on Merry's hand until she offered more meat. "Are ya interested in a second course? Lemme find ya some a that cheese."

The two individually wrapped sticks of mozzarella had also been jarred off the rim of the tub. One of them lay under her right thigh. *Ah wondered what that was. Didn't recall bringin' in a carrot. Hope this ain't crushed.*

It wasn't in great shape and she had to savage the wrapper with her teeth. There was no finding that little tab in the dark to pull the plastic open. Once freed, she pinched and stripped off a narrow strand. She held it aloft and could sense the cat stretching up to give the cheese a sniff, its paws braced on her hip. "Just eat it 'n' get offa me. Yer a heavy booger, alright." *Now it's gonna want a drink. How'm Ah gonna manage that?* She poured a few drops into the palm of her hand, felt whiskers and sensed sniffing. It wasn't thirsty enough yet, apparently.

Merry was either exhausted or the constant roar of wind and rain had become a lulling white noise. The cat added contented purring as it groomed itself. Merry didn't pull the towel over her in the humid, coffin-like space. Now she repositioned it, rolled under her neck. She closed her eyes, The cat worked its way behind her on the higher side of the tub. "Ah don't ever find no comfort in spoonin' you should know." She sighed, then yawned. "But, you must be a tom, Ah bet."

Danielle didn't leave sun and blue skies in her wake. But, Walt figured the storm had passed. What a time to crash and what an appropriate term. He would pay for last night's stimulation with a headache. He sat up on the passenger side of the Caddy. Rain continued to fall. The trees still waved their branches, but somewhat lazily. There was no more roofing material sailing by as he peered north, in the direction of Annie's Breakfast. Most of the view was still blocked by that bulldozer.

Walt climbed out the passenger side wearing the haggard face and body language of a rescued miner. It probably wasn't a wise plan to back straight out of the narrow hidey-hole without clearing

EVACUATION ROUTE 631

the path behind the Caddy. A grassy verge and sidewalk separated the Publix Plaza from US 19. His footing in the saturated grass was unsupportively soggy. *Yeah, that could've been 20-30 inches and it's still coming down.* Was this now a trailing band?

There were two pieces of HVAC sheet metal behind him, one lying flat but the other propped on the curb, perfectly lined up to vivisect the passenger side rear tire. Lucky so far, but he'd only driven over branches and small limbs, mostly. This morning's obstacle course would look more like a scrapyard. *Do I even have a spare tire? Is it inflated? I've had almost three years to check on that.* He flung both pieces of sheet metal onto the grass.

After backing out of his dump truck fortress, inches at a time, Walt took another slow, zigzag course in a generally diagonal direction toward the blocked Halls River Rd. exit. There, he left the car again and walked out into the road to reconnoiter. A full view of the way to *The Glade* entrance looked like twenty cans of green pick-up-sticks spilled into a pile of dirt, green macrame. *Afraid of that. Gonna have to wade through that.* With lucky foresight, he'd put on a pair of jeans yesterday by the Atlantic. *Why didn't I borrow some boots? A machete? Maybe Warren had some stage swords in the back of a closet. There are likely to be reptiles everywhere I step.*

Armed only with a length of window frame from the insurance office (well, it was laying in front of there), Walt set out for *The Glade.* He tried to hop from trunk to trunk of the thicker felled trees hopint to clear any waiting fangs. When the distance was farther than his sad, late-middle-aged broad jump capability,

632   CHRIS DUNGEY

he examined the crushed tapestry of vegetation below long and carefully before stepping down. There was water below the green refuse, as well, he soon discovered. Maybe three inches in depth. The creek that ran along the north side of *The Glade* must have overflowed. Or, it was a stream unknown to him, leaving its course to race across the forest floor from the other side of the rosd.

"Hey! Hey, buddy?! Where ya think yer goin'?!"

Walt turned to see that two trucks, a bulldozer and maybe seven men in Carhartt overalls, orange vests and hardhats were unloading behind him. The vests stood out brightly in the morning gloom.

"I need to rescue my cat and some cash from my place in *The Glade.*"

Someone handed the boss a loudhailer that managed to win out over wind and tree noise. "Sir, can ya show me some ID?!"

Walt cupped his hands to his mouth. "Yes, sir! I could!"

The metallic voice reached him again, calmed by the humid air. "How 'bout if you walk it back here, then?! It's gettin' to be primetime for looters!"

Fatigue pressed down on Walt. He had already refrained from another helping of trucker amphetamines. "Sir?" He shouted. He tapped the white length of metal into the next brush in his path.

"What?"

"Look here! How many televisions and DVD players do you think I could carry, Aren't you here to clear the road?"

EVACUATION ROUTE

"Yes, sir! We got EMS calls waitin' out toward the Gulf 'n' I ain't got time for this. We can have 'er cleared in 40 minutes. You had oughta wait."

"Can't do it. Look! I'll just get in there, do my business then wait for you by the entrance! You can pat me down!"

Three chainsaw erupted in sequence to split the air. The crew boss waved him away. "Have a nice day!" He lowered the bullhorn.

Walt was already turning to probe cautiously forward. All he heard from the crew leader was a garbled crackle of feedback. *Don't wanta chase me in all that gear, make me more important than those folks out in the surge.*

Curtis and Dianne Kaake were both deeper into the Lecanto Fieldhouse than Darlene, further under when the heavy, flyswatter blow of the wall came down. Wood didn't tell Darlene when the list of fatalities became available from first-responders. These exhausted men and women continued to come and go in the lobby of Tampa General North, Brooksville. Nor did he tell her that her purse had yet to be recovered out of the partially collapsed gymnasium. There were higher priorities, he was informed, including that two remaining walls of the gymnasium must be braced up before any fine sifting could be done in there. And, there were still some people missing who must be quarried out soon before they ripened in the hot weather. Someone, who seemed to have *some*

authority over *some* aspect of the rescue and cleanup, assured him that great care would be taken in excavating the gym floor. Darlene Spurgeon's purse was hardly the only one missing.

"Ma. Ma. How're ya doin'? I didn't wanna wake ya, except I gotta run some errands then come back."

Darlene's eyes fluttered partway open. "No purse?" She whispered.

"Still lookin'. Don't give up hope, now. They gotta be so careful combin' through that mess. It ain't safe 'n' there's still bodies, they think. How's the leg feelin'?"

As if to supplement her answer, something in the bed began to buzz. Darlene's blanket rose from over her leg. "They got it wrapped in somethin' to stimulate blood flow. Goes off ever' minute or so. Hard to sleep."

"Yeah, Ma. That there's a pneumatic compression cuff they told me. Think I got that right. Are ya still in a lotta pain?"

"Aww, no. They been bringin' Demerol." A blissful smile crossed her lips. "They was sayin' a while ago they was worried about a fever. They said anythin' to you about goin' back in to clean it out better. Cement dust." Now a tear slipped from her eye and streaked quickly to her chin. "Mah friends, Dianne 'n' Curtis?"

"Yeah, Ma?"

"They was on cots a li'l further in from me. It mighta been bad. Has any...?"

"I'll ask around, but these people only seem to know what's happenin' right in front of 'em," Wood said. "They told me downstairs that a lot a y'all was taken to Inverness. Yah know, that ol' boy Curtis had just offered me a slug a Jack as I was headin' for the bathroom. I told 'im mebbe later. Ma?"

Darlene's eyes remained closed. A few more tears leaked. "Ah think they was prob'ly right under it," she groaned.

"I'll keep askin', Ma."

Darlene groaned as the circulation cuff grew to squeeze her wound. She broke into an involuntary dope laugh. "An' keep a eye open for Walter? He's kinda tall 'n' a little stoop-shouldered. Got a nice bushy head a grey hair, standin' up like…"

Wood brought her hand up, patted and then kissed it. "Sounds like a People Magazine Most Sexy. I'll be back this evenin' with fries 'n' a shake."

"Mmm. From *Steak 'n' Shake*?" Darlene murmured as her hand returned to the blanket.

"Sure, if I can find one open."

Her first adventure of the morning was to find their way out a mobile home with a reimagined floorplan. Merry lifted and pushed the sliding shower door aside. She stepped up from the tub's bottom to plant her right foot on the slider frame then stepped carefully down to the tilted floor. "C'mon cat. Ah ain't liftin' yer big carcass outta there. Yer sure a pretty one. A male a the species, too, or ya was. Must be why yer so fat. C'mon. Leap on up here."

Antoine put its front paws on the slider frame. Finding no purchase for his back claws, he half jumped and half pulled himself up to perch on the frame. From there he watched Merry cautiously open the bathroom door, The little, spare bedroom remained where it was supposed to be. But, the hallway no longer lead into the kitchen. *That* was six or seven feet back and a pretty long leap to get there. Looking down, she could see about three inches of water with breakfast cereal, paper plates, hotpads, and a pair of overripe bananas still clinging to each other. *How're we gettin' over there? Ah'll bet neither one a us can make that leap.*

Merry slid down the bathroom floor. She leaned into the shower enclosure to lift out the backpack. Her second cheese stick had rolled out of her reach as had the candle stub. She shouldered the backpack and fastened the strap across her chest. "Ah think we're gonna have to drop 'n' then duckwalk our excape out to where Ah found ya. Ah can see daylight between the trailers."

"Purr-yeeoww?"

"Don't want a hear you can't even take a short fall."

Merry splashed down without losing her balance. The distance was no more than four feet. *Now dear Lord don't let nothin' shift down onto us. Ah remain yer fallen angel chile, in need a some Grace, Lord.* The cat was, finally, too reluctant to leap into a few inches of rainwater. "Now Ah know dang well ya already survived a worse drenchin' last night than this here. So, c'mon." Antoine hesitated but finally stepped down into Merry's reaching grasp. "Damn, but you are a load. Someone's been spoilin' *you.*"

EVACUATION ROUTE

637

She hugged the feline to her chest, crouched and waddled out of the disjointed shell of Wood's Mom's ruined home. The gap between the ladies doublewide and its neighbor had been reduced by three-quarters but broadened when she reached the sleeping porch in front. The two structures had not made contact in the domino effect Merry imagined. When she came around to park the cat down on the porch steps, she saw that that scenario *had* played out across the street. Five homes had been shoved together like a folded Japanese fan. Now chainsaws whined and barked through the trees back out toward that main road. "They're comin' to ar rescue, big boy." She stroked the tom's head and scratched behind his ears. "Oh, happy day, huh? unless yer a property owner."

Merry stepped out into the street to look both ways at the destruction. Braving the three inches of water, she stepped cautiously around to the roofless carport. The neighbor on that side had been pushed over, crushing some shrubbery and overturning Wood's Mom's golf cart. Merry walked as far as the detached laundry room and tried the door. *Looks like Ah could find me a chair to sit on 'n' mebbe a warm Coke. Shoot. It's diet. Ah need some sugar.* She eyed all the corners and shelves from the doorway then found several bag chairs leaning in a corner. She hung one on her shoulder, the Coke in her right hand. *How long'm Ah gonna be wadin' in this? Don't want no case a toe jam. But when'm Ah likely to work again, anyways?* The chair was unfolded next to the front porch and then she sat, elevating her feet to the second step. A light rain fell again. The trees were reminded of brisk wind. She pulled both hoods over her head again and resisted the urge to remove her shoes. Still there, the cat weighed exploration of the disaster against an additional soaking. The presence of Merry's feet decided its next course.

"You ain't findin' no warmth in *them* feet," she told the tom as it circled to get comfortable, finally draping over her lower calves and ankles.

Merry wriggled out of the backpack and lifted it around to her lap. She removed her cellphone and charging wire from one of several pouches. *A course it's dead. Prob'ly ain't no coverage anyhow.* She took out a Slim Jim and a packet of cheese crackers.

"Well, hello there." A deep, yet hoarse voice spoke behind her.

"Jesus Chrahst!" Spooked, she jumped, spilling the go-bag and dislodging the cat, who resoaked his paws but dashed in front of her to wind around the stranger's legs.

"So, who are you and what're you doing on my girlfriend's porch? And how'd you happen to meet my cat?"

Part V
Old Habits

"You almost can change the stamp of nature." --William Shakespeare

Chapter Thirty-Six

"Ah've had me one hellatious night, mister. An' Ah 'bout wet mah pants just now. That'd been the cherry on the top."

"Okay, but tell me about it walking. I have to get back to my car and outta these shoes."

"Yer headin' the wrong way for the entrance."

"It's fine. I've gotta say goodbye. I'm Walt, by-the-way."

"Sure. Walt. But Ah don't think there's another livin' bein' in this whole place."

"Nope. But I mean where my place was."

They cut across on a curve of pavement that dissected the horseshoe layout of the park. One tall Florida Royal palm had been dropped in their path by another home pushed off what was supposed to pass for a foundation. It looked like they'd used three-block stacks. Merry saw a couple of these cheap-assed block pilings tipped over under Wood's Mom's place.

"Walt. Ah been puzzlin' over somethin' since Wood 'n' Ah parted ways. Ah think it was yesterday?"

EVACUATION ROUTE 641

The man swung himself over the palm trunk like it was a pommel horse. The cat peered over the man's shoulder, eyeing Merry with sleepy disinterest. Walt kept going a few more steps but then came back to help her. "Wood, huh? I thought his name was Charlie. What did you wanta know?"

They listened to the chainsaws, the growl and clank of the bulldozer as it dropped its shovel, nearing *The Glade* entrance.

"Charlie, huh? Well, now Ah'm totally blankin' on his last name. So Ah guess it's her's, too. Ain't that disgraceful?"

"It's Spurgeon. And his given name is Charles. Charlie."

They walked on with wet feet, Walt not volunteering to trade the cat for the backpack though that might have improved the pace."

"Mah Lord, so Wood-Chuck is Charlie."

"Wood-Chuck, huh? How did he...? Never mind. I don't need to know. Are you a biker Mama, or whatever their lady friends are called?"

"Nah, Walt. Ah ain't, as such. Ah was a employee, a contract employee for various Club functions."

"So, like security? Catering or waitstaff?"

"Yeah. I did some waitin'."

The pair stopped then, at a junction with the other long drive of the horseshoe. Across the street and for a hundred yards toward the entrance, there was little to suggest that this scene had once been of mobile homes in an orderly row with well kept yards and garden sheds. The jungle beyond the chain-link fence had been churned, blown over, around and through the trailers, each now a bus-bomb of unidentifiable pieces and shards. That chain-link and

642   CHRIS DUNGEY

its metal posts were woven through the wreckage like a drawing of the nervous system

"Ah can't find no words."

"I've been trying not to use the ones I found," Walt said. "This along here was done by a tornado. My place was over there." He waved in the general direction. "Somewhere."

"Yeah. Ah was here for that. Ah heard it, anyways."

"I believe I may have seen the same one twice." The man's voice caught. He coughed to clear it. "But why on earth did that numbskull leave you behind?"

"Simple. Cuz Ah wouldn't go with him. Ah can't tolerate crowds in a confine space. An' Ah got a little bone to pick with Wood...Charlie. Call it a *big* bone."

"Well, you might've caught a break, not going in there. What's your name, kiddo?"

"Ah'm Merry."

"That's a nice old fashioned name. You hardly hear it anymore." Walt turned in the direction of the entrance. He waved at the first-responders who'd reached *The Glade* and now stood smoking in front of where the pool and Community Center should have been.

"Thank ya for the kind words, but it's the Christian one 'n' not the Virgin. Aww, hell. Ah get tired a explainin'. Ah don't know what Ma musta been thinkin'. Say, ain't you gonna walk on down 'n' see if ther's any valuables left?"

"Merry, it can't me more than a few hundred bucks and its likely scattered. I'm not poking my hands around in that mess."

EVACUATION ROUTE

They strolled south, the flood deeper than their shoes in places. "Now you didn't take anything that wasn't yours did you? I promised these guys up here that I wasn't a looter and they might search us."

"Antoine, huh? Alright, Well Ah confess to me'n Antoine shared a couple a Mrs. Spurgeon's hotdogs 'n' one cheese stick," Merry answered as they moved ahead more

"Merry?" Walt jumped back and stuck out his arm to restrain the girl. "God *damn*, I hate those things. Fucking water moccasin. Going to curl up in the junk. Antoine? What the hell? He never even growled. What good are you?"

"Oh, an Ah got a little derringer pistol in mah go-bag."

"Aww, Jesus. Would you mind just tossing it aside in the next twenty yards?"

"Nah, Ah would not, Walter. Those ol' boys won't object to a personal snake killer. Ah thought you was *from* Florida."

Walt sighed and lifted the cat up so he could stretch his arms. "Maybe you better take it out then and you take the lead."

"Ah'll do it, Walt. But you might be the better shot."

"Somehow I doubt that."

The road clearing crew didn't bother them. They had taken a smoke break. Two of the men had wandered a short distance taking

pictures. One had taken an old Polaroid from a knapsack. Walt heard the whirr of the film drive.

"Where d'ay even get film for that piece a junk?" the boss hardhat asked.

"Amazon, old man," the photographer said. "Ahm makin' up a DVD of this whole storm," he asked.

"I see you ain't carryin' a big screen HD." Now the supervisor turned his attention to Walt and Mary. "You find what ya needed? Who's this?"

"This is Antoine, a skilled survivor. He's still here but nothing else."

"Ah meant this young lady," the crew chief said. Everyone else had moved ahead up the road, one truck following. "Looks like they ready to head on without me."

"Ah'm a survivor, too," Merry said "Y'all do any rescuin' later, always look in the bathtubs."

"Alright, Ah will young lady," the hardhat said. He climbed onto the step of the last truck for the short ride west, toward the Gulf. The chainsaws erupted into action again fifty yards up the road.

Walt and Merry waited for the bulldozer to clank past them then two EMS vehicles. They waded the pond in *The Glade* entrance, which now must certainly contain water from the absent pool.

When they had reached Publix, Walt did a walk around inspection of the Caddy and its grill. When he had climbed in and started the car, he turned on the heater.

EVACUATION ROUTE

Merry unlaced her shoes. "Ya oughta try it, Walt. Yer gonna get water blisters 'n' Lord knows whatever fungus."

"First things first. Do you have a cellphone? Any service?"

"Naw, it was dead. Service Ah don't know about." She began undoing some of the zippers and snaps to her backpack. "Want a Pop Tart?"

"I haven't got a cigarette lighter adapter to charge either one of them. So...Yeah, I could eat." Walt accepted a bottle of water and a two-pack of the frosted Pop Tarts that Merry handed him out of her gear. "Now then. Do you have any *money*? I had some in the trailer but it was probably reduced to lint. All I need is to find an ATM that's working."

Merry lifted her feet into the flow of warm air. "Oh, mah goodness that's nice. Ah ain't gettin' toe jam from outta that mess. An' yeah. Ah got a little money. You know you got a crack spreadin' over here."

"Thank you." The crack looked like a chart of the recent Dow' angling downward toward the defroster vents. "Where are you planning to go?"

"Well, for now, wherever yer goin'."

"I think we head south. I'll find an ATM and we'll check out the hospital in Brooksville. See if there are any motel vacancies opened up."

"Why the hospital?"

"Oh. I guess you'd have no way of knowing," Walt told her. He hesitated before continuing. "That high school where your friend Wood-Chuck went to join his Mom? The gymnasium they were using partially collapsed. I came by it on my way home from my mother's place. The tornado had just blown through. That's why I wondered if it might have been the same one. The road down to Brooksville was blocked off for all but emergency vehicles. I met ambulances headed to Inverness, too."

Merry breathed a spot of vapor onto the passenger window where rain still dotted the glass Walt wondered if some cooler air was moving in behind the hurricane. "See? Ah made the right choice. It was just business with Wood...I mean Charlie. We wasn't what ya'd call close." She sniffed and pressed her forehead to the glass. She daubed her eyes with the nylon sleeve of the outer hoody. "Ah'm just tired, is all. An this summer has sucked."

"So...Brooksville?"

"Walter, right now Ah ain't got a fuck left to give. Would ya mind if Ah climbed in the backseat?"

"No, of course not." He waited for two pickup trucks with yellow flashers to sort their way through the debris in the US-19 intersection, which now included the signal lights that had fallen but not slid far enough out of the way. "You'll have to share it with my lummox cat. Let me pull over. Be careful of the cat box."

Merry climbed out onto the shoulder, seeming to stagger a bit before climbing back into the Caddy. She slumped immediately. "This Antoine 'n' me. We fit each other purty good, Ah think. But Ah know it's just all about body heat."

Danielle's impact became somewhat less severe as Walt drove south at the minimum speed allowed. US-19 wasn't anywhere near free of storm trash. *Maybe not so many big chunks.* He encountered no more patio furniture or grills, but now the car was passing through a thinly populated pine barrens of sorts. Bear Area. Next 10 Miles. *Hmmm. Not in daylight, please.* Arriving in Wikki-Wachee, Walt used the left turn lane under one out of four functioning traffic lights, onto West Cortez Blvd. "I've got to top off the gas," he told the backseat. There was no reply except for a soft nasal snoring.

Well, how far will I have to go? After a few fruitless miles he found a RaceTrak that appeared to be open. Into the plaza, he found that all of the pump nozzles wore yellow bags. Looking closer, he read the Sharpee message on cardboard signs stuck onto the pump faces. These informed drivers that premium octane could still be purchased for *$6 Dollars per Gallon; Limit 5 Gallons. Cash Only. Pay Inside. Well, hell better than nothing. Where'll that take me? Maybe eighty miles?* Walt did not want to awaken his passenger. He thought there were fifty bucks still in a wallet that was beginning to chafe his left buttocks. He parked at a pump. There were cars at a few of the others but most pumps were free.

Inside, the *RaceTrak* had become a diner, though the rollers were running low on hotdogs and Roller Bites (Buffalo chicken cheese). There remained a bounty of Tornados; various fillers in-

648   CHRIS DUNGEY

side rolled tortilla shells, perpetually rolling under a heat lamp. *Maybe not. Too soon.* There were still a few hot breakfast sandwiches in a clear warming cabinet. *But, were they from this morning? Had the power gone out at any time?* A few pizza slices circled listlessly on a carrousel in a neighboring case. All of the Crispy Crème items were gone.

Customers bought large coffees but then loitered near the front registers, trading storm stories. Had they, too, been living in cars?

Walt joined a line of two other refugees at an ATM. "Jes-us Chrahst," the man at the machine exclaimed. "A $3.75 fee? What'm Ah s'pposed to do? That's just fuckin' gougin'," His pleading eyes darted about the room searching for sympathetic witnesses. "Sorry, 'bout mah French."

How about you just pay it? Oh, and don't run it out of money, Walt thought.

"Nah, man," said the fellow next in line. "They was rippin' folks off *before* the storm."

The first man turned away with a sheaf of bills and his receipt. "Ah'd like to pay back a visit with mah forklift." He marched swiftly to the coffee bar.

Walt withdrew $200 when it was his turn. *Now what is she going to wanta eat?* He carried two pepperoni pizza slices on one plate and two large coffees to the front counter. "And give me $30 premium on pump..." He had to step through a dense coffee klatch in front of the entrance doors to see his car. "Pump eleven," he called out to the cashier. He went back to pay and take the change. "Say,"

EVACUATION ROUTE 649

Walt told the kid behind the counter. "I need directions to the hospitals in Brooksville." He moved aside for the next customer.

"Ya passed one a couple miles back. But the biggest is just up a ways on the right. Mebbe two miles. Ya can't miss the signs."

A customer three spaces behind took hold of Walt's elbow as he headed out: "You from Citrus County," the man said.

"Homosassa."

"Oh boy. Well, so am I. Wasn't that a mess out at that high school? My sister was in there. Never shoulda been. I'm going to see her. Now I don't need directions."

"I'm sorry to hear that about your sister," Walt said. "I'm hoping to find my girlfriend there. My cellphone's been dead awhile. You take care, now. Maybe I'll run into you."

With his hands full, he took a brief detour down the automotive fluids aisle. There were plenty of USB plugs, but the spindle for in-car chargers was empty.

Walt added the five gallons. *Like peeing in the ocean for this tank.* "Merry, wake up. Want something to eat?"

The young woman sat up and rubbed her eyes. Walt retrieved the coffees and the plate of pizza from the hood of the Caddy. "That was plain blissful," she said as Walt passed the pizza over the seat. "Yer car rides nice. Are we there yet?"

"The hospital is close by. Let's go have a look." He steered out of the station's Cortez Blvd. exit. The way to Tampa General North, Brooksville, was a long commercial tentacle extending east toward old Brooksville. There were few single-family homes interspersed with the big box stores, eating places, and clinics for every conceivable medical specialty. Walt noted the cleanup efforts going on in parking-lots of business's all along the route.

There was little or no parking at the hospital. He circled through the first lot and the second, twice, with no new spots opening. Then he spied a dubious plot of uncurbed grass where other visitors had improvised spaces. He could see by the tracks of *those* explorers that the ground was saturated and yielding. All of the other trespassers left distinctive footprints upon exiting their vehicles. Even then he had to go to the end of the row which gently sloped toward Cortez Blvd.

"Merry, I don't like this." They climbed out and Walt studied the tracks his baby had left. *Just try to remember, she brought you through a tornado.* "Crack the windows for Antoine, would you please?"

"Ya locked it."

"Right. I'm losing my bearings. I'm gonna need a snooze, too. Sooner than later." He reentered, put the key in and turned it to *Accessories.* Peering over the driver's headrest, he saw Antoine crouched and tensed-up in his litterbox. He put the rear windows down a few inches. "Just in time. We'll need to stay out of the car for an hour, minimum."

Before they reached the hospital entrance, they had to walk past several motorcycles, variously chained and cabled to a bicycle rack. "Walt, Ah *know* that'n." The *Knuckledick* logo had been stenciled in red at the bottom of both hardshell saddlebags.

Walt came back to study the emblem. "Clever," he said. "And just a little unsettling. A fist, with a penis for the thumb."

"Purty cool, huh?"

"That's...one description you could use." Walt resumed walking toward the multidoor entrance, choosing one that didn't revolve.

"Ah don't know who come up with it back in early times a the club. But it tells me Wood-Chuck...Charlie must be in here somewheres."

In fact, Charlie was in the lobby. Merry spotted him, just then turning away from the front desk. She ran up and leaped to put a hug on him, nearly knocking some paperwork from his grasp. He held them aside. No one in the lobby looked askance, these reunions were likely the norm throughout the afternoon.

"Didn't think I'd see *you* again. At least in one piece," the biker spoke softly. "Who's this?"

Merry let herself down to the grubby floor. "This here's Walter who ya must know from yer Ma. He found me at her place."

It appeared that Wood's face might be unable to smile *or* scowl at his mother's boyfriend. "Right. Yer the famous Walt."

"I thought you were angry with him." Walt spoke to Merry while extending a handshake that Merry feared would be ignored.

"It's a familiar face. Ah don't *hate* 'im."

But then Wood let go of her waist and passed the hospital forms to his other hand. He shook Walt's hand with two shallow pumps.

652   CHRIS DUNGEY

"Okay. My Ma speaks real highly and she's been desperate to make contact with ya."

"I'm looking for her, too, but my phone is dead."

"She just got her purse back 'n' her's is dead."

"Can I go up to see her?"

"Nope. Sorry. She's been transported down to the main branch in Tampa. She got a sepsis in her leg that was already pretty mangled. Compound fracture." Wood hung his head for a moment. "What about y'all's places?"

Walt could only shake his head. "I think *my* plan'll be to find a vacancy and drop Merry or..."

"No worries. Ah've still got mah li'l cottage in New Port Richie," Merry said.

"Good enough. I'll leave her off then find that hospital. I don't have anywhere else to go. I'm not driving back and forth every day from Tampa to Flagler Beach. There's not much gasoline anywhere and I need a lot."

"Fuck. Reminds me. I ain't even had time to follow that other storm." Wood spoke with the hoarse voice of sleeplessness that they were all beginning to recognize. His eyes were red and a nervous twitch flickered in his right cheek.

"That's right," Walt said. "We're not done surviving."

"Ah know ya got a lot on yer mind, but..." Merry followed Wood as he trudged slowly toward the entrance. Walt followed Merry. "Ah'd like to talk about returnin' to work, if there's an openin'."

EVACUATION ROUTE

653

Wood brightened a bit and chuckled thinly, still following the progress of his scuffed boots with downcast eyes. "Bet ya musta heard we had some staffin' problems a while back."

"Aw, no. Who wouldn't wanta work for the *Knuckledicks?*"

Wood put the hospital boilerplate into one of the saddlebags. "We'll see 'bout it. I'm gonna be busy with Ma the next months or however long."

"Beautiful bike." Walt said.

"Yeah, thanks. I like her. Can ya give my Ma a call soon's ya get yer phone up 'n' runnin'. I'll take anythin' lifts her spirits."

"Sure I will, Charlie," Walt replied, before fully parsing the backhanded compliment in his worn-out brain. "And I'll get down there first thing. Sleep in the car if I have to."

As they walked gingerly on the sodden turf, Wood-Chuck roared past out on the street. "Whew! Antoine. Dude!"

Merry walked around the trunk to open the passenger door. "Ah've got to be up'n front now."

"What'd you feed my cat?"

"He got the same's Ah did."

"Well then, give me a little warning so I can crack the window."

"'Less Ah'm asleep."

Walt backed out of his spot very slowly, trying not to break traction and start spinning in the soft ground. *I owe you, baby. I'm throwing in a detailing and a hand wax. It'll be like a spa weekend.*

Chapter Thirty-Seven

H e took Merry to her home and it was only another half hour down US-19 in light traffic. No Vacancy signs were ubiquitous, parking areas at the motels packed tightly with the cars of relatives sharing rooms.

"What day is it, Walter?"

"You're gonna be shocked. It's Sunday. I left my mother's condo yesterday at about 11 a.m."

Merry turned and studied him with weary puzzlement. "That ain't even possible. Feels like a week." She began to enumerate recent highlights of her life, one finger at a time. "Ah left mah place. Ah hitched awhile. Wood spotted me 'n' picked me up 'n' we stared each other down cuz Ah had reason not to trust 'im. We came up to his Ma's place 'n' she was already gone to that high school. Ah wasn't goin' there so we parted our company. Sirens was blarin' 'n' the tornado come along right after. Ah'm outta fingers. So then Ah went outside to find where Antoine was pleadin' from 'n' then brought 'im in. We waited out that Danielle an' Wood's

EVACUATION ROUTE

Mom's trailer broke in two. Did Ah leave anythin' out? Over on the right's the famous *Lucky Seas* gamblin' boat that let Wood's friend kill..." Merry turned her face to the window, sniffing again. She spoke into the glass. "Yer gonna turn right at Trouble Creek Drive."

"Did you know that girl?" Walt felt an odd premonition that was growing in clarity like an LED lightbulb. He began to glance at each passing street signs. "Are you crying?" He thought he'd heard a single hiccupped sob.

Merry did not reply.

Two long blocks down Trouble Creek Drive, Merry directed the Caddy into a side street. Irene Loop necessitated further slowing.

"Turn in this li'l place right here," she spoke again. "You can pull up next that li'l bottle palm on the right. Don't worry 'bout ar yard."

Our? Walt shut off the engine.

Merry did not hop out of the car with great energy but went ahead to unlock with her go-bag over one shoulder. "Ah'll come back for Antoine but then Ah call dibs on the shower first."

Walt opened and probed his trunk for a change of clothes and shoes. Luckily, he'd brought some loafers to his mother's place.

Inside the bungalow, Merry had already turned on a big floor fan and a ceiling fan in the kitchenette. Walt put the cat box down in a far corner of the front room. Merry came back in, lugging the cat. "There ya go, big boy." She plopped Antoine onto the couch. "Ah've got to get shed a these clothes. Feels like they're crawlin' with cooties or somethin' an' them pink fibers down mah

CHRIS DUNGEY

neck. Darlene's neighbor's roof come apart while Ah was findin' Antoine Ah don't have no recollection of what's in the 'fridge, 'cept water. Make yerself to home. Ah hope ya can run me to the Dollar General before ya move on."

"Of course." Walt closed the front door. "That's some kind of old insulation. You gotta get that off of you."

Merry closed the bathroom door. Walt chose a bedroom wherein the bed was neatly made up, assuming that the disheveled one across the hall was Merry's. This had to be a guest room unless, or, as he was beginning to suspect, there was a missing roommate. He took his cellphone from a jacket pocket. After plugging the charger into an outlet behind a lamp table, he then switched on the dim, little lamp. He sat down on the bed.

To Walt's relief, the phone came immediately to life with some kind of wakeup chime. He'd never had to use it while it was on life support. There weren't many numbers in his Contacts cache. He touched Darlene's.

Her phone rang enough times that Walt was ready to end the call. Then a tired, male voice answered. "Yeah?"

"Charlie?"

"It's me. You Walt?"

"Yes it is. How's yer Mom doing?"

An uncomfortable silence metastasized, raising Walt's anxiety. "Are you still there, Charlie?"

"Sorry, Walt. Almost nodded off. I'm in a padded chair with my feet up on one a Ma's safety rails. Watchin' the lines on the screen. The li'l blips."

EVACUATION ROUTE

"Hey, I here ya," Walt said. "I might need a nap before I come find the hospital." The seeming absence of jealous menace in the guy's voice eased Walt's nerves.

"Where you at, Walt.?"

Without hesitation, Walt told him: "I found a Roadway Inn a couple miles from Merry's little place. I just took a chance, sat in the car until someone packed out."

"You was as favored as Merry was gettin' outta Ma's place."

"It sure seems so," Walt said. *I don't think I even swallowed hard with that little ad lib. Haven't had to pull an untruth outta my butt in some years. Must still have the art. Artifice.* "Can your Mom talk for a little bit? I won't keep her."

"Yeah, she's pretty fragile right now. She lost a good friend in that fuckin' buildin'."

"Oh, no. I haven't seen a list of fatalities. No, that's too much."

"Ma? Are ya still with us? Somebody wants to talk at ya."

"Walter?" Darlene's voice was barely audible through a Chia-garden of phlegm. She cleared her throat. "Sorry Ah'm in such a bad way."

"I'm just grateful you're alive. What's the prognosis, hon? Are you in a lot of pain?"

"Naw, they got me purty doped up. Bad thing is..."

Walt waited patiently, fearing that he, too, might drift off.

"They're sayin' Ah might lose mah leg. This infection from the dirt 'n' dust in the wound is a nasty thing 'n' they don't wanta risk that necro...necro somethin', flesh eatin' bacteria 'n'...whatever. Breathed in a good few lungfulls of it, too."

658   CHRIS DUNGEY

Walt sighed. "It just doesn't matter as far as you and I go. Been my mantra all my life except that now you're included with me. But, you staying alive is the first thing."

"B'low the knee, if 'n' when," Darlene's voice rasped into a whisper that needed water.

Walt heard her sipping through a straw. "Thank you, Charlie." The glass came to rest somewhere near her head. "That's better. Ah guess it could be worse."

"That's usually true," Walt said. "And then it *does* get worse. When you get recovered, we both gotta find a place to live. I know my way around this time."

"Yeah?"

"You'll have to be somewhere near. Do you still like Homosassa?"

Now Darlene began to weep loudly. "Yup... Ah like it... fine. Not the town's fault. 'Cept now I need...Ah got to find me some new friends. Charlie told ya 'bout Dianne, huh?"

"Yeah, in so many words." Now Walt let her cry it out and then catch her breath.

"Guess Ah'm lucky. Ah never made but one close friend in that park, so far."

"Hey, we're even, hon," Walt said. "I've only made one myself. But listen, I told Charlie I wouldn't keep you too long. I need a nap and then to find your hospital."

Darlene sniffled. "If Ah was to say Ah love ya, you can just 'tribute it to the Demerol or mah fever. Anyways, Ah love ya Walter."

"I think I'll take it seriously, Dar. I love you, too. To the extent I'm capable, anyway. I'll find you in a few hours." He ended the call.

Walt didn't think it would signal or threaten anything to drop trow at the edge of the bed. He left his damp, swamp stained jeans on the floor like two collapsed tree trunks in a puddle of denim. He flung away his jacket, one of the arms pulling inside out. He made a headfirst dive onto the bedspread then reached over to switch off the lamp. The pillowcase onto which he lay his head gave off a subtle memory of perfume.

Darkness covered the Gulf Coast when Merry entered the guest bedroom. She placed an ashtray and her little pipe on the lamp table with a tiny chirp of ceramic on wood. She laid down naked on Walt's back. He awakened, though she was barely heavy enough for him to notice. That patch of down and its little ridges on his buttocks would have brought him around at some point.

"What're you doing, Merry?"

660 CHRIS DUNGEY

She raised her arms far enough to work her hands under his armpits. She pressed her small rigid-tipped breasts into his back. Then she turned her head away and sneezed.

"You're probably catching a cold from exposure."

"Oh no, Walt. That ain't it. Just means Ah'm 'bout to express gratitude the way Ah do. Ah like ya, an' it's all about body heat anyways. Ask ol' Antonie."

Then Walt made the mistake of rolling her off of him. When he turned on his back, her hand went straight under the elastic of his tighty whities. "Can Ah taste of ya for a little while, Walter?" She deftly tugged his shorts down to his thighs.

"Why? I'm probably... I need a shower and...oh. Oh, damn."

Merry lifted her mouth away from him. "Ah don't mind the musk of a man. Ah think that's what they call it. Or biker *funk*, is what Ah'm used to. Ah like it, truth to be told. Don't pay me no mind if Ah'm a little outta practice"

"Merry? Merry, now...hold up a second. What, exactly *was* your career relationship to Charlie and that Club?" They both sat up in the dark. "I think I'm putting your biography puzzle together. It has similarities to mine, but I don't want to hurt Darlene. Or *be* seriously hurt by an enraged biker."

The sudden ignition of a fireplace lighter cast their prurient shadows onto the walls. "Mah career with the *Knuckledicks?* Ah guess some'd call it the *oldest* career. An' don't go thinkin' like Ah'm a victim. Sometimes Ah think Ah enjoy it more'n them bikers or their friends. Mah, Lord, Walter. Ah was sneezin' nearly ever' day."

EVACUATION ROUTE

661

The lighter expired, leaving only the red glow of a minuscule lump in the pipe. Walt heard Merry inhale, hold, then an exhaling cough. She found him infallibly with her now very warm mouth. The pipe cast a faint rouge stain onto his abdomen. *Please don't spill that on me.* But he didn't have the will, at the moment, to resist the skills, to arrest his alarmingly pleasant engorgement.

"Hey, Walter?" Merry paused, pinching a pubic hair off her tongue. "Wanta try a hit a this?"

Walt reached down to push his skivvies off the rest of the way. "Nah. I need to stay clear of that. I have to be on the road pretty soon soo..."

With no warning, Merry's mouth descended onto his mouth sharing a desert whisper of smoke as from a Hopi oven. "Ah don't think that'll debilitate ya. Much."

Walt held the sun flare in his lungs, hoping to cauterize yet another misstep in his life. Just temporarily, he understood. *Doesn't have to mean anything. Three steps ahead and only a couple back.* His head eased deeper into the pillow.

"It can't," he whispered at the top of Merry's head. "You'll have to drive me."

Antoine leaped up to fit himself in somewhere. The humans were past being startled.

About the author

Chris Dungey is a retired auto worker in Michigan. He rides mountain bikes to maintain some minimal physical conditioning and a Honda Ruckus scooter for the planet. Dungey follows two local soccer clubs, Detroit FC and Flint City Bucks with religious fervor. His stories have been published in more than 75 literary magazines and online. Two collections, *The Pace-Lap Blues,* and *We Won't Be Kissing* are still available at Amazon.

After many aborted attempts, *Evacuation Route* is his first novel. He used to love Florida, but barring seismic political changes, will likely never go there again.

Also by

Also By Chris Dungey:

The Pace-Lap Blues and Other Tales from the Seventies
We Won't Be Kissing

Buy them now on Amazon.

For updates on more publications follow him n Facebook:
https://www.facebook.com/profile.php?id=100008387256371

Made in the USA
Monee, IL
12 August 2025